Blood and Honour

By Lee 'Kostianovich' Gresty

"The best damned book you'll ever read…"

An epic tale of idiotic discovery, featuring a useless would-not-be sorcerer and a b
not simply pissed off Dwarf. This is the first in a planned series of 9 novels, which
centuries of an alternative universe as the hapless Dirk matures and evolves, accor
his conscience-on-legs, Grot.

Dedicated to my dad.
Roy Kelly. RIP

CONTENTS

I) **PROLOGUE**

"You want a drink or what?" barked the rough no-nonsense voice of the doughty barkeeper.

"Ya wanna keep your teeth?" shot back the no-nonsense reply.

The barkeep looked down at the weasely looking man hunched up on the stool in front of him. There was definitely something... *unusual* about the strange looking figure.

Something..., ...a little special perhaps, something; he could not quite put his finger on at any rate. He regarded the outsider with renewed interest.

Sure, the stranger's tattered brown robe was in a far worse state of wear, than anything the most downtrodden beggar would wear. It was full of so many holes, that it was easier to see what he wore underneath than to try to identify the type of garb used for the so-called covering.

The hair of the scruffy chap, (which could only be described as dishwater blonde after two night's worth of dishes), was matted with, well, the barkeeper would not want to venture a guess...

A passer by may have took the stranger to be some vagrant, who had wandered into the open-air establishment in search of food scraps or a job perhaps, though by the looks and smell of the scruffy chap; begging for a bath of some description would likely get him more attention.

A more astute observer *may* have took note of the fact that the stranger always kept his face half hidden within the confines of the slightly less shredded hood that he wore. Perhaps a more scholarly persona may have noticed that the odd misshapen hunch the stranger bore, was also conveniently concealing whatever it was that his hands were doing.

An absolute expert in disguise such as a master trainer of spies; *may* have noticed that the dirt had been applied rather than acquired, and that the strange man's stoop actually hid a good ten inches or so in height.

The Barkeep, who prided himself on observing these things to an extent beyond most master trainers, had noticed all of the design flaws in the strangers disguise and wasn't phased by any of it..., ...No...

The thing that was bothering him was that this strange dishevelled figure had decided to take his best table by the fire for the last half hour or more, sitting there with his dirty, smelly feet resting upon the table; without expression or explanation of his actions and showing a complete disregard to the other patrons and the barkeep, himself.

In all that time, no-one had joined him and though one of his regulars had attempted to engage the stranger in conversation, the miserable bugger had not so much as *smiled*, never mind actually ordering some succour in the form of mead and meat and THIS vexed him gravely.

Considering the following factors, one could understandably concur with the barkeeps right to anger. For not only was mead and meat the only thing that he served in this establishment; it also served as the name of the said premises which incidentally, even had one of those swinging pictograph signs for those patrons that could not read, depicting a jug of said mead and a platter of aforementioned meat.

Moreover, nobody and absolutely *no-one* sat on *his* best couch at *his* best table next to *His* fire, without ordering some of *HIS* Mead and Meat.

"**You!**" he bellowed, tossing an empty gallon keg at the scruffy fellow seated before him.

"Aye let the sod know Morris!" Some unknown shouted as the small barrel bounced painfully off the side of the strangers head in a cringe-inducing thud, causing ripples of barely disguised laughter to spread around the tavern in appreciation.

In slovenly fashion, the injured person rubbed at the unseen lump already forming atop his crown and slowly craned his neck at an angle, all the better to sight his tormentor from beneath his hooded cowl.

Undeterred, the barman brought forth his most sombre tone as he growled out to the stranger in a voice loud enough for all his patrons to hear.

"Ya eider order right now..., ...Or I is gonna thro your scraggly arse in dat der fire you is so fond of ogging!" Morris pronounced loudly: One thing his long deceased father had taught him well, was that one should always be heard in ones own establishment.

"WELL…" He bellowed once again, "ya eider feed yoursel', or ya feed da flames: Eider way I aints gonna ask yas again." The barkeep paused in order to fully impose his presence on those assembled, his stoic pose belaying the threat of harmful intent that was sure to follow.

Furthermore, he managed all this despite the bar counter he still occupied being some several feet away from the man to whom his threats were directed. "Dis town's a long way from any lawmen or Paladin dese days, yer know!"

"Of course I know…" tinkled back the simplistic reply.

A thought, racing through his mind faster than a Wyvern at the Caernthorn races came screaming into his head with such ferocity that all the barkeep could think about was that voice… was that it? Was that the special something that would betray the smelly newcomer's true identity?

Without doubt, it was THE most unusual voice he had ever heard, it sung to him in melodious harmonies, not unlike the voice of an Elf or a bard; the trademark of the master seducer. Was this it; was the stranger before him some amorous caballero in disguise and on the run from one or more dangerous fathers? He mulled the idea over in his head for an instant before rejecting it completely for the voice also carried a most sinister edge, a quality that would cool the most arduous lovers' attentions. The sinister sound came tearing into the scraggy chaps' otherwise sweet sounding sentences with all the fragility of an Orc's cleaver. However, the most disturbing quality of the stranger's voice was the strange low grumble of thunder that seemed to accompany his speech: Carrying the weight of a thousand murderous misdemeanours of barbaric proportions, the strangers sub tones were sinister like those of a common Orc, yet mixed with just enough hint of malice as to make even a Balrog proud. The barkeep struggled to comprehend what he knew of the voice but gave up.

No, the ruffian's identity could not be deduced by the voice then, at least… not just the voice thought Morris who right then caught a glint of purple firelight reflecting off one of the foreigner's eyes…

Gradually, the nightmare of comprehension crept frost-like into the barkeeps rapidly numbing brain. He caught a hold of the tail end of the intuitive contemplation and turned to look behind him at something on the wall, his face crumpling as he did so: The poor fellows growing suspicions were confirmed beyond doubt by the scrappy papyrus dictatorial nailed to the crossbeam section aside the entrance.

Suddenly terrified and momentarily bereft of his already pasty complexion, the barman endeavoured to return his vision the several inches back in the direction of the hooded one. As his body completed the miniscule physical task; dreamt of images clouded the barman's thoughts and they were the most heinous imaginings one could have.

A barkeep hears many stories, and Morris Caitlyn was one of the most renowned innkeepers of one of the most infamous taverns in all of Eyrthe and had heard almost as many tales as he himself had invented. And a lot of them revolved around the legendary figurehead who stood before him at that very moment; a man whose voice he and others had heard quite recently, booming out across the land in fearful proclamation.

He turned back towards the stranger, the barkeeps grubby fingers feeling for the nailed club he kept hidden under the bar for visitors as unwelcome as this one before him now. Though only the Gods knew what help it would be to him now, if this stranger's vague resemblance shared more than a passing familiarity to the face of the person depicted upon the poster on the wall.

He felt the reassuring gnarl of the wooden club under his searching chubby fingers, his eyes never leaving the deep cowl of the stranger. Looking again, the strangers jaw; bathed in shadow though it was, lacked the defining cut of the fellow in the picture and the forehead, though filthy, was lacking the wrinkles depicted. And the mouth was different too; the lips so much fuller than that of the portrait.

Morris relaxed a little, chuckling to himself as he chided himself thrice. *Oh Caitlyn you daft sod; you spend too much time listening to stories...*

As Morris' sweating palm encased the familiar grip of worn leather around his clubs handle, his confidence returned and he allowed himself to draw a breath, but the hiss of his inhalation betrayed him; and his eyes were abruptly locked with those of the stranger whose hood had fallen back a way.

His newfound confidence was shaken a little by the stare. "Now lookee here Mr. I donna wants no trouble; but if yous is bent to't I'll give ya's the smackin of yer life with ol 'last orders' ere!"

No response.

"Now lookee ere, I-I mean it: I wants you out!" The barman

threatened with practiced zeal, as he tapped the named club against the countertop of the bar in self-assuring fashion.

The stranger said nothing but rose and smiled.

Later, many years later, when memory became myth, the moments that followed that statement were readily dismissed as little more than ghost stories best tried out on a susceptible child.

Yet for years before it passed into myth, no one ventured up through Devils Gap anymore, instead taking a much longer fifty-mile hike around where the settlement had once stood.

At one time it had been a bustling little village-come-town and very popular stopover that held several famous stores and eateries such as the Caitlyn's, Mead and Meat or the weapons forge of Yammich. It had been famed too for its cathedral and grand houses; its richly garnished décor and magnificent palisade, or for the military school there that periodically turned out some of the best fighters in all the realms…

Then overnight it was simply gone or so the story goes…, …for there were no survivors left to tell the tale of how it came to be… Everyone and everything within the bustling settlement, down to the last man, dog and bone had been reduced to their ashen composite, leaving a sickening grey waste that spread for three thousand metres in every direction.

The area had suffered decimation to such an effect that even those who had previously visited the bustling environs of Devils Gap found it hard to believe any such thing had ever actually stood there. Not even the deeper dwelling denizens who had previously plagued the town's inhabitants dared venture into the area of death too often; fearful unless they too suffer the same fate as their former victims.

Possibly in acknowledgement to those deceased people. Or mayhap to spare them the indecency or ignorance of uninformed relatives whose disbelieving stares may deny all evidence of the travesty before them; one item had somehow survived total destruction, though no one knew whether it had been by accident or design.

It was a lone segment of wall, standing centrally in the midst of the soul-destroying desolation, around seven feet high and four feet wide, held together by strong oak beams that appeared bereft of all but the merest scorch marks; in stark contrast to the incinerated debris about it…

Attached to the segment of wall, hanging weakly from one side was a decrepit wooden signpost that fluttered alarmingly in the weakest of winds.

Upon it were etched the icons of a jug of mead, and a platter of meat.

Yet more importantly for this epic adventure at least, on the opposite side, posted to one of the walls supporting beams, and scorched way too badly to make out the face depicted thereon, was a poster bearing the declaration, 'Wanted: Dirk Heinemblud; for crimes against life…'

II) **The Twisted Hand of Fate**

"Dirk!" screamed a gruff voice.

"…Dirk yer chicken shite bastard! Quick help me for Keldor's sake" this time the gruffness had lost its edge and obtained that higher pitch that can only be attained when close to death.

Dirk stood facing the two goblins who grinned with evil delight, obviously pleased at outnumbering their opponent by two weapons to none.

"I can't find my sword …" he shouted weakly at no-one in particular, Dirk couldn't see his friend anywhere, but sure as he was about to get his arse kicked by two rather uncompromising Gobbos', he was positive that his friend Grot would beat the living hell out of him too if he did find him…

But that didn't bother him right now, what bothered him were three facts that just would not go away. The Gobbo, his misplaced sword, and the fact that his friend the Dwarven fighter, who absolutely hated all Gobbos' and was so hard you could make a door out of him, was at that moment in time; somewhere out of sight being smacked silly by a Black Orc or two.

He hadn't expected this. Sure, he had expected to run into Goblins, this forest was full of them, but Dirk had thought he would be able to leave the warlike Grot to the nonsense of actually *dealing* with them.

Dirk was a coward: A good coward. In fact he was one of the best to be fair, and his many years of practise had helped hone his yellow-bellied skills to absolute perfection but that had all been spoiled by the cruel hand of fate a mere twenty minutes or so earlier...

The way Dirk had always reasoned it everything held its own place in the grand scheme of things. Trolls hated Dwarfs who in turn hated Elves; who were born with the sun shining out of their arse and Paladins were boring religious fanatics that everyone feared. Between racial boundaries, creatures held varied fearful respect for others deemed more powerful, etc…

From your first breath to your last, Mother Fates hand was there to gently push, shove, and slap you onto the path chosen by her. Father time was there to take it all away; and a whole multitude of gods, both major and minor, lined up to condemn you for betraying their vision of perfection.

It was all an unnecessary hassle and Dirk was resigned to taking whatever shit necessary whilst stealthily avoiding the rest. He held no love for deities and daemons, disrespected most authoritarians and propagated a strong dislike for Law. As for fate, he'd piss her off quick smart if he ever met her and she did really exist: Divorcing her as his mother in no time at all.

He was no rebel however, oh no, Dirk's dislikes were just that. He did not act upon them. Antagonists and Demagogues could be left to their own martyred wishes, more foolhardy them. No Dirk wanted a simple life and though he disliked the law he was one of those citizens who would seek its protective recourse when it suited him, yet seek refuge from justice when he found himself treading the wrong side of the tracks, which was often.

According to Dirk, heroes-to-be were just nice looking babies that Fate had decided would look lovely with big muscles and a nice set of armour. In the same fickle way, those that the heroes punished were probably the ugly babies that simply would not disappear, despite emptying the bathwater several times.

Take himself for example, not exactly ugly, but not quite godlike handsome enough to be deemed one of Fates champions, he was six feet one inches of pure skin and bone; thirty one years of age with everything to lose and nothing he could ever gain. He was a loner and vagrant. A wanderer constantly seeking to get along in life the easy way, inevitably this meant Dirk more-often found himself having to do things the hard way. Take his early chosen career for example, in which he had failed gloriously to attain his dreams…

He was, he considered himself; a fringe wizard… Most people called mere dabblers in magic Hedge wizards but he wasn't good enough to call himself that. Oh no. On the contrary, Dirk reflected, the stinking Goblins that infested these parts of Eyrthe probably had a better magical sense than he did for he found it almost impossible to envisage even the most blatant of paranormal auras and found learning spells the traditional way far too tedious for his personal liking.

Sure, he could cast a flame from the tip of his finger; or make a bird appear out of thin air once a day but lets face it, there were far easier ways to catch a bird, and tinderboxes made a far more reliable light than his piddley-assed little flame thing. Magically he was inept; almost impotent in the conjuration of its base elements an unkind persona may claim. So Dirk had given up on magic; resigned to his lousy lot in life, he was content to merely go on living: Finding danger then avoiding it, being his only fortes.

Of course, Dirk reasoned, it was his own fault that his magic was so dismal. He knew this and was guiltily reconciled to the fact: You see Dirk had once been an apprentice amongst many; given rare auspices under a reputedly awesome master of the arts named Galbor.

Dirk was into his early twenties when he began his tutelage and although he was the oldest (and most reckless) of all his classmates, he did have a hunger to learn. This hunger however, often got him into trouble as it usually involved breaking the strict rules set down by Galbor and he was a somewhat over-keen disciplinarian. He ran a strict punishment regime too, which though not often painfully administered, did involve undertaking long and tiresome duties and it was Dirk who caught his attention the most often.

So while Dirk had skivvied in the Privy, up to his waist in shit, his incompetent, acne-faced colleagues went on to ever more powerful spells, while he had to grab whatever moment he could, in order to learn even basic principles of incantation.

Dirk hadn't minded the humiliation too much; he had had years before that in which to become accustomed to a social status way below that of a one legged blind dog! What did inconvenience him however was that the great Galbor it seemed was an infuriatingly cautious man; much, much too cautious for Dirks liking.

So it had long since came to pass, that when Dirk was dismissed for stealing a look at some magical scrolls, containing spells that Galbor reckoned were far beyond Dirks level of ability. He cast one of those said spells upon Galbor and all his precious little apprentices…

The enchantment in question was a curse hex of some magnitude, and although the casting process was quite complicated, the directions that came with the scroll were simple enough to follow and once Dirk had gotten his tongue around the more intricate syllables of the spell, all he had required to complete it was to burn some personal effect of each person that he wanted to afflict. The notebooks that he had despised labouring over every day, came in very handy for this purpose, thus he had thrown them all onto the small bonfire he had built for the task, along with Galbor's personal register.

The act of revenge had almost gone awry, but Dirk had realized his mistake just in time: Gratefully recovering his own jotter from the bonfire which he'd tossed in along with the others. With his own notebook lent salvation from the eager flames he had completed the spoken part of the ritual pertaining to the intended affliction with which to curse his victims.

Dirk had stricken them all with the full dose; warts, boils, rashes, diahorrea, amongst other things and best of all, or so he had thought at the time, baldness. He had never stuck around long enough to see the effects of the spell in action but he would often chuckle to himself at the thought of a classroom full of bald teenage would be wizards.

It was due to this lapse of judgement, and many more besides in the years fore and after, that he had learned to be afraid of anything and everything. Five years on from his dismissal he had learned, at a personal cost to himself, that those same wizardly apprentices had gone on to become fairly adept in the magical practices, thanks to Galbor's expert tutelage. One of them had even managed to track him down while he was visiting a brothel in Mallmaurg. The youthful, yet bald battle wizard had scorched him with bolts that, were the wizard in question more adept at gleaning the surrounding magical flux, would have killed him without question.

As it was Dirk had managed to survive by wit and luck alone. The magician had burst into the room all vengeful like only to falter in his first casting, due to his sudden embarrassment at the sight of a naked woman, shoving the whore who was currently entertaining him to the side, Dirk had scooped up his pants and made a run for the en-suite bathing room. The wizard uttered a quick cantrip and threw a venomous magical arrow of pulsing green energy at Dirks rapidly darting form but the Whore was not about to let her mark get away without payment and ran after him, yelling for all of three seconds before the magical strike caught her in Dirk's stead.

In the bathroom Dirk expertly donned his trousers at a hopping jog and scanned about quickly for a window, which he spotted and leapt towards, buckling his belt mid flight. The wizard burst in behind him, screaming at the escapee, and blaming him for the death of the Whore. As Dirk made his heroic leap the wizard spewed forth a magical web which missed him by inches. Yet the 'window' into which Dirks flight took him turned out to merely be a reflection and Dirk's forehead smashed into a mirror, badly gashing his eye socket and brow in the process: The bald wizard had taken a few chunks of flying glass to the face and as he staggered away from the piercing shards, he tripped over Dirk's wriggling legs as the escapee scurried away on hands and knees and fell into the web he himself had earlier cast. Dirk was long gone when the Whorehouses madam arrived flanked by two butch female guards and discovered one of her best whores struck dead with what appeared to be a kinky punter, standing over her with glowing eyes and waving arms. The madam had no idea about the workings of magic or its intricacies and neither did her guard but she knew death and how to enact it.

The bald wizard's attempted resurrection spell had been cut short quite literally by the guards' knives and Dirk was therefore relieved of one potential future foe and any knowledge of his irresponsibility.

Several other's from the 'class of 961' had managed to hunt him down and each time, Dirk's none-threatening attempts at escape had resulted in the death or otherwise incapacitation of those who attempted his capture. His luck had held until now but he was constantly on the run from seventeen bald magicians and with no way, hope or means of learning any more magical knowledge with which to counter their paranormal ministrations; not without attracting the attention of the great Galbor that is. So Dirk lived day by paranoid day, honing the skills of survival-by-cowardice to perfection. He had met many people in his time and unbeknownst to Dirk, may have made a decent politician due to his people skills but Dirk was ignorant; not so much in an innocent way but one purposefully courted by him. He forgot most of the people he encountered as easily as he consumed local wines and food without thought to their sublime textures and flavours.

He made many, many enemies in his time, simply by saying the wrong thing, being in the wrong place, or rubbing up the wrong person the wrong way. Dirk had a distinct knack for botching things, no matter how well meaning his intent. Take for example, an attempt he once made to guide a local group of farmers down some small abandoned mine pit, in the hunt for a Goblin refugee. This had led to his being hunted down himself by the farmers' remaining descendants thanks to his magical flame igniting an undiscovered pocket of gas they had found themselves standing in. Dirk himself had been scorched yet survived with minimal burns, while those about him wore smoking grimaces, as their charred husks thudded to the ground in response. He could perhaps have explained the mishap to the various farmers' kin but found himself hopelessly lost in the Dark and when the Goblin turned up, having been alerted by the explosion. Dirk had bartered their meaty corpses in exchange for safe escort out of the mines.

Trouble followed him to every town, mishaps waited around every corner and disaster hijacked him on every road as he struggled to come to grips with a life of desperation and then *'bon-chance'* he had happened across his Dwarven pal Grot. The gruff, stunted individual had served as both mentor and mate. His brawn had far outweighed Dirk's own brainless contributions, and even though his mishaps and misdirected actions continued to warrant unasked for and some times lethal attentions, the Dwarf turned out to be quite the experienced battle veteran and the two unlikely friends had hit it off from the start.

So the two went through life journeying from town to town, damsel to damsel, cell to stinking cell, in search of the next job or adventure; taking on any given mantle in their quest for cash…, …Most recently, Dirk's misadventures had left Grot momentarily bereft of life, due to his incapacity to fight or in any way defend him self or the downed Dwarf, and soon after Grot's subsequent resurrection he had begun to direct Dirk in the art of swordplay.

To be honest, Dirk had applied considerably more time and energy to avoiding training than he had to actually learning the vulgar swipes and strikes of the tiresome Eyrthely practice: Quite content to let the Dwarf battle while he himself bottled; his chicken routine intact…

…And then, that ugly, green little, gimpy git had laughed at him.

Now for those of you who have seen any of the Goblin kind, you will agree they are without doubt the ugliest, smelliest bunch of savages to have ever walked these lands.

You will also be aware, I am sure, of the many different species within the Goblin kin. Dirk was. He had met most and had grown accustomed to contentedly being afraid of all of them. That was until this THING had gone and spoiled everything.

It was a Snurch; so called because of their constantly running noses and mucus textured, green veined skin. The lowest of the low; a Snurch was the unwanted smell and sound that accompanied a relieving fart. A wretched little breed of Gobbo that from meeting one it was easy for even the most scholastically retarded individual to ascertain exactly how this race had acquired such an unattractive name and undesirable reputation.

Great oozes of nasty snot dripped from the huge hooked nose of this, the most downtrodden of all the Eyrthe's underlings and its legs were caked in brown..., ...well let's just say it wasn't mud! Stood fully upright it stood at a little over a foot in height. It had rotten, crooked, pointy teeth; huge pointy ears and a scabby wart covered face that even its own mother would want to thump occasionally. The Snurch's little red eyes had gleamed as it had chased after Dirk, who although he was fast was no match for the speed of this spry little cretin, which galloped along after him with a string of accompanying verbal expletives, each directed at Dirk's impending state of health. The chase had started several feet from his and Grot's camp where Dirk had gone to relieve himself and ended when Dirk had burst into the Goblin camp several hundred metres into the forest, the little red eyed scum trotting up nastily behind.

"Me bringses U'maanses!" It had squealed delightedly to its master upon entering the muddied clearing. The realization settling in Dirk's perplexed brain cells that he hadn't so much as been chased here as guided by the smug little walking bogey.

Fear and doubt had welled up within Dirks mind like a nervous creek and he feared a brief capture and consumption scenario. Then the vicious little tormentor had simply walked up to him, face-to-knees so to speak, and laughed, a cruel mocking laugh that seemed to taunt him down to his soul.

The gathered Orcs, recovering from their state of shock had also burst into laughter and Dirk had felt a familiar urinal flow down his left leg as his worried expression took in his exposed state: The aggressive knowing gestures of the rapidly gathering Orcs, signalling to Dirk that he had lost not only his rights to life but also his place within Eyrthe's origins.

Dirk instinctively knew that this was wrong; everything in him had said so. This..., ...Snurch thing was not acting according to his view of the world. By all that was right, it should have been the *Snurch* that had run screaming; even from an adept coward such as himself! Snurch; as their appearance suggested, were at the very bottom rung on the ladder of life. And as such, a Snurch would *unrelentingly* to a man, woman or grunt; never contemplate entering *even* so-much as a quiet disagreement amongst friends, *unless* they outnumbered their intended disputer by *at least* twenty to one.

And this solo thing was stood LAUGHING at him!

He had felt 'it' welling up inside him. Every sensible thought he had still available to his clouded wits rose in a naked attempt to overcome 'it' but alas, that most basic of instincts was taking over, crying out to be avenged.

He had *heard* the footsteps of the Goblins behind and around him moving confidently closer as he'd stood close to death.

He had *seen* the saving visage of his angered Dwarven friend Grot, come crashing through the undergrowth axe raised, and ready to smite all before him in the familiar rescue of his inept pal. Yet still he could not force himself to turn and run. The unnatural sensation had taken control, goading him on to his own destruction. His Adams apple had bobbed like an apple as he'd attempted to swallow the alien instinct. To divest himself of its responsibility, yet he knew 'it' had a name. The Dwarf had often spoken of 'it', the Elven folk lived by 'its' codes, while even the most evil of wizards or unruly king had 'it' in abundance and now it seemed 'it' was ordaining Dirk himself into 'its' swollen ranks.

His foot had come down with a satisfying squelch, and there was the sound of fragile little bones being crushed and cracked as Dirk ground his boot from side to side. When he had raised his foot, all that had remained was a tiny pair of boots and a puddle of red and green ichors stained underpants; the former Snurch's only garment of clothing in life.

Panic had taken its usual hold on him then; even as Grot made short work of the first few Gobbo. It was totally irrational and completely against his cowardly principles for Dirk himself to become involved in combat in any way, shape or form; excepting his so called 'toughening up' sessions periodically induced by the Dwarf.

A brief wind gathered and whipped at his ears as he dejectedly resigned himself to the truth..., ...For the first time in his life, Dirk had rebelled against a slight to his perceived state of being and felt with virginal intensity the stinging bite of wounded 'Pride.'

Like a cornered rat he had no where to go to and only one way to escape; past or through those doing the cornering. Dirk mentally locked the imaginary barn doors of his mind: No-one was getting out of here without first copping a feel of his pent up anger and frustration.

The melee that ensued after the Snurch's demise had been surprisingly brief and bloody in its own course. Dirk had first whipped out the wooden training sword, which Grot had given to him and whirled it around like a lunatic, striking out wildly at whatever it was that was behind him: The blade was swung with all the grace of a one-legged ballerina, yet as luck would have it, he instantly slew both of the Goblins that had been plodding nonchalantly towards him from the rear, its rough hewn edge taking out both intended combatants.

Dirk pulled and tugged at the wooden swords shaft, from where it had buried itself within the soft belly of the foremost Goblin, as the other clutched at the ropy mass of scratched out entrails seeping from its own belly. The first creature upon being skewered had lashed out in desperation with its own weapon and now its sword had become lodged in the second creature's vertebrae and was stuck fast; such had been the ferocity of its strike. The fear of imminent harm had sent an overdose of adrenalin coursing through Dirks veins and as he'd tugged at the Orcs weapon which he found impossible, he'd turned to his own toy weapon and gave that a mighty yank too; the desperate force employed had sent the pointy stick arcing over his head and plunging eagerly through the eye socket and into the brain of an approaching, rather overconfident; and now very much deceased Orc fighter.

At the same time Dirks friend Grot, covered in bramble and smattered with blackberry and raspberry juice making him appear more ferocious than usual, launched himself axe first into a group of confused Bogey, Owl or Bugbears depending on who you asked for a name. The frightening Dwarf had swung his mighty smoking axe with such vigour, that he was already off chasing down a group of Goblins before any of the obliterated Owlbears' multiple, severed limbs, had even hit the ground where they still stood.

Dirk had turned once again, span and fell on the former Snurch's remains and rose to find himself face to face with a monstrous Black Orc.

These creatures where undoubtedly the tallest, strongest and nastiest of all Goblin kin, but in the grip of pride Dirk didn't even flinch.

"Come to daddy!" He had screamed belligerently, before butting the creature square in the face. The Black Orc fell in a crumpled heap and Dirk was just about to weigh in with a swift boot to the groin when he had noticed another Snurch scurrying away at the edge of the encampment.

Once again he had felt the need to avenge his honour, and this time Dirk welcomed its wrathful intent as with a popping twist he wrestled the weapon from the pierced brain of his previous attacker and with both hands raised behind his head, he'd thrown the wooden training sword with deadly accuracy at the tiny fleeing creatures back.

And hit a tree.

Out of the corner of his eye, Dirk could see the encampment was by this time deserted of any living soul bar himself, the unconscious Black Orc and two rather Evil looking Goblins advancing towards his location.

Dirk had screamed out a string of expressive and undiluted expletives, so vehemently that even a deaf man could hear. He'd cursed the whole Eyrthe over, every event that had brought him to this point and wondered briefly if he would ever make it to the Caernthorn races in time for the 4:30 masters cup? More distressingly as he'd looked down at his bare, evidently weapon-less hands, would he ever make it to Caernthorn at all?

Turning his head to further take in the severity of their intentions, Dirk's heart had sank at their malicious zeal; made clear by the large barbed swords they both wielded and it was then that he'd realized he was actually alone and truly desperate as his Dwarven mates first cries for help had echoed throughout the woods. Rushing over to where he had launched the sword, Dirk had scrabbled about the undergrowth in useless toil. Unfortunately trying to find a brown wooden thing in a brown and green forest is a little awkward to say the least.

Weapon-less and blinking back tears of disappointment he'd turned about and was faced with two sets of malicious red eyes peeping back at his own from out of the shadowed glade, like those of a maddened wild boar...

"Time to die U'maan," spat one of the repugnant creatures as the other licked the length of its own blade in greedy anticipation of the due slaughter.

"U'maan's guts, makes me nice necklaces!" Its mate had snarled with finality, before both began moving in for the kill.

Dirks addled mind, had flittered this way and that. Fear chasing after confidence and cornering it in a dark recess of his consciousness; where his confidence received a swift kicking before quickly running away. He cursed the confident Snurch and cried out in self pity for his unheard of heroics and wished fervently that he could take it all back, wringing his hands in disgust as his eyeballs darted back and forth attempting to espy some weapon...

"Dirk!" the Dwarves voice snapped Dirk out of his reverie.

"Dirk yer thoroughly useless bastard! Will yer get over here and help me for once in your miserable life!" The voice was unmistakably Grot's, yet the shrill edge was most unusual for the surly Dwarf, who was normally as Baritone as a sounding stone.

The Goblins (a lot nearer than Dirk recalled seeing a moment ago,) rushed at him in gleeful enterprise, one of the green protagonists slightly ahead of the other, his swollen appetite chomping for murderous revenge against this stupid scared Human. Dirk cursed his indecisiveness and once again scanned about for his lost offensive device.

The foremost of the two had his sword aimed straight for Dirks midriff, whilst the one slightly to the rear was swinging a repeated feral arc that was clearly intended to separate head and torso past the point of resurrection.

"Cast a spell. Anything, just..., help..." Grots voice trailed off weakly.

'*So that's what a female Dwarf must sound like!*' Dirk thought in his usual piss-taking fashion and then it occurred to him, '*Magic! Of course...*' Dirk realised, he could do magic! Yet what good would his limited talent serve him now..., ...He needed a plan and fast.

Waiting a second or two until the Goblins were nearly upon him, Dirk mumbled a simple cantrip and suddenly a startled white Dove (well, Pigeon actually though the spell warranted otherwise,) appeared from nowhere and flew smack-dab into the first Goblins face. Unaware of what had hit it, the stunned Goblin ceased running and raised its head just in time to connect with the whirling blade of its overeager battle buddy.

There was a sound like that of a tuning fork being struck as the barbed sword first pierced the skull of its unintended victim, then itself broke in two from the force.

Both Goblins fell down in a puzzled tangle of blood and limbs.

Dirk grinned at the botched attack as he sighted his embedded training weapon. He looked down for the first Orcs sword but found it to be cramped beneath the struggling form of the living Orc. Considering his options, Dirk looked to his wooden sword which was stuck in the tree trunk that rose majestically before him. '*Better than nothing!*' he reasoned and ran to the trunks expansive base but after giving his discarded weapon several determined tugs, he realised that it was stuck firm, and decided to leave it there as a memento of the rare fighting occasion.

He turned to the remaining Goblin, who by this time had managed to rise to its feet sword in hand, and met the gruesome creature's fearsome gaze. The battle rage had subsided a little now and Dirk could feel the usual desperate fear once again welling within him. His basic cowardly instincts, developed to a sniper's accuracy; telling him he was no match for this creature before him but now there was another feeling too, one of surety of action, arrogance and complete disregard to the danger posed by the armed Goblin. This was the feeling one gets when some bastard has not only knicked off with the bread but pissed in the butter in passing.

"No more running," Dirk chuffed and he watched with a detached fascination, as the Goblin tentatively reached out and picked up its fallen comrades shield.

"See U'maan is stoopid. Not Gobbos' that stoopid," it boasted, the reassurance of the swords cold hard steel and protective shield lending the creature the confidence it needed.

The Goblin eyed Dirk warily awaiting any sudden movement but found none forthcoming. "Stoopid U'maan shud 'ave kilt Hurak when U'maan could!" It continued confidently. "U'maan dat runs from stoopid Snurchs'…"

It grinned then and stalked forward, undaunted by this stupid human who makes little birds appear and fights with a wooden sword.

Dirk said nothing but simply smiled back at the creature.

He waited until the Goblin began swinging its borrowed sword, then reached out an arm and nonchalantly swatted it to one side before ripping away the scavenged shield, leaving the Goblin defenceless.

Anger surged through the Goblins veins and it leapt at Dirk without ever seeming to take into consideration the fact that this human was almost twice its size in both bulk and height. Neither did it seem to take heed of the crazy surge of newfound confidence this human suddenly possessed. And it most certainly did not seem to take into consideration any vengeful feelings the human may be having, despite the fact that it kept smiling at Hurak in a most alarming manner.

Dirk snatched the lithe Goblin out of the air, one hand wrapped around its scrawny throat. The other bunched into a fist began punching its face repeatedly until the body went limp and only one cheek remained intact. He then lifted the Goblins inert body above his head and thrust it downward, skewering it upon the hilt of the wooden sword that protruded from the tree-trunk still. The hilt pierced through the back of the unfortunate creature with such pain as to wake it from the realms of unconsciousness and Dirk watched with detached amusement as, with pitiful screams filling the air, the mounted Goblin strained its fear-drained muscles, in an unsuccessful feeble attempt to push the sword back through the decimated entrails of its stomach

A grunt alerted Dirk to another danger, the Black Orc he had floored earlier was stirring into consciousness. With a sense of calm he had never before experienced, Dirk ambled over to where the strong beast lay…

…The Black Orc tried to flutter open its eyelids, he was not sure what had happened, all that he knew was that he was Drekk Gallowdodger, so named because the gallows had not been able to break his neck as a baby. Black Orcs are a truly cruel race and have no love for kin and thus Drekk had been hung for a bet between his uncle and his mother. His mother, who had swore during pregnancy he had kicked with the strength of a bull, won the bet when only a few minutes old; his neck had not snapped upon being strung up on a hastily erected gallows of rope and stool. So he had survived that and in later years become the leader of this band of unruly Orcs, with a reputation for him being tougher than a bag of bricks, and then some.

His eyes fluttered weakly again as he felt a bump on his head.

He remembered the white-faced Human being chased into the encampment by Snidt; the Snurch cook. He remembered the Human shouting something too, but *surely*? No pathetic, skinny, *Human* could get the better of *Drekk Gallowdodger*: Leader of the clan of Crimson Cannibals and scourge of all who ventured into these woods…, …His head was muggy, what was it that had happened?

Drekk rubbed at his throbbing face and finally opened his eyes…

The humans face was just above his, smiling down at him.

"Look into my eyes…" the human's voice called to Drekk, "I want you to remember every feature of my face… I want you to scream, when you close your eyes; to dream like I do…" Drekk did as he was bid and fervently wished he never had.

An Orcs eyes can only be described as evil. They are an unnatural, pasty pink through to a vibrant ruby red dependant on actual ethnicity; some had no visible iris while others still had small black pupils that seem to penetrate the soul of those they look at, with their eyeballed daggers.

Dirks eyes on the other hand were a pure crystalline blue, such as you would expect only the most holy of Paladins or purest of Elves to posses, but in this humans beautiful eyes the hate was so much worse to behold than that any mere Gobbo may convey.

In them Drekk saw a thousand humiliations suffered. He felt the countless pangs of regret… He could tell just from looking into those eyes that this… This 'Human' had known what it is to fear and have complete impotence of action; he'd experienced it and hated every second of the familiarity and it seethed from Dirk's gaze in a palpable aura. Yet the thing that horrified him the most was the hate and resentment that spewed out from those eyes. There was no love in them, only wicked, dreamy malice the likes of which Drekk himself would find hard to succumb to. This Human was clearly on the edge, but the question begged; upon the edge of what exactly? He thought he could smell a cooking fire.

"P-please pretty U'maan no kill Drekk?" he stammered desperately and he was now aware of an immense pain in his sleepy lower limbs, almost as if they had gone to sleep and the act of attempting to move had awoken them to an uncomfortable throbbing sensation.

The Humans head hovered above Drekk's own; the radiant misplaced smile grinning back at him idiotically.

Then the smile faded as Dirk held Drekk's gaze, "Fair enough! You can live… I wasn't sure I would kill you anyway, but *as* your asking *so* nicely… *Please*, accept my apologies for all this… *mess*." Dirk said, and without another word, the crazed human sprang to his feet and departed the smouldering encampment.

Drekk looked down to see why he was in such pain, and for several long moments he made no sound as his mind struggled to take in the reality of his own situation and that of his surroundings… For a few moments more, he lay numb still; a wave of desperation blocking out every nerve strained twinge and conscious thought: From his swollen half chewed tongue that lolled about limply to the side of his mouth, all the way down his face, neck and torso, where his skin prickled with sharp needles of pain; the only feeling he could sense throughout his entire body was utter remorse.

All about him lay numerous bodies of slightly differing colour and creed, hacked into pieces so small; they were barely recognisable as the former living, breathing beings Drekk had commanded. Here and there were strewn various fleshy chunks, with only patches of skin on the dismembered parts to confirm the largely green hued identity of those massacred.

To the side of Drekk, the once sturdy huts of his former encampment were now smouldering ruins wherein nothing living dared move nor dart; no singular bird sang nor flew.

And hanging from a tree branch, tauntingly beyond reach but not sight; the grisly hacked flesh of Drekk's own severed calves and feet, badgered to and fro as the tree's branches swayed in the gathering evening wind.

III) **Jin**

Whelp Many humanoids claim to have, met, known or had an Aunt Sally that had been, knew, met or made love to a Dragon slayer at some point in their more often than not; otherwise dull, boring and pointless existence. During these fanciful tales of Draconian butchery, 'Humans' especially, though most other races were also guilty; often conveyed to their idiotic audience that it was *only a whelp*, as if this may somehow give their tall story some credence.

Of course it was absolute rubbish and was particularly derided by Dragon folk themselves. Humanoid races inevitably heard of and came to their own conclusions about Dragons no matter how little or great the extent of their particular races contact with said beasts. *'Beasts!'* that was another casually applied terminology and again the silly short lived humans were chief culprit amongst their humanoid counterparts in its use.

There was nothing a 'true' Dragon hated more than exaggeration, inaccuracy or apparent casual flair... Dragons that dabbled in such nonsense were deemed whelps that needed to grow up, and it was this expression of 'whelp' that inevitably confused the humanoids' that added the noun to their own vocabulary and applied their own meanings to the word... For as much as the loosely applied terminology was deemed the generally correct description for a Dragon of its pre-determined ilk; it failed to convey the reason why a troop of well-trained Elven Ghost-walkers may be killed by a Dragon whelp, whilst a simple Halfling squire may rise to legend by slaying a juvenile beast single-handed.

The reason was quite simple enough, though never fully understood by the mortal races; a *yearling* in Dragon terms was anything from 1-100 years, a *juvenile* may be from 100-350 years old, whilst an *adolescent* would be anything from 350-1000 years old. Where the explanation was lost then; was on those named by other Dragons' as whelps, for whereas humans tended to apply the whelp status freely, the title was truly a Draconian term and within their own society it was only ever applied to a Dragon displaying the frowned upon affections mentioned earlier.

In truth, whelps were never the youngest of their kin as one was aloud a certain amount of time to rid oneself of ones childish urges and factually a great deal of Dragons went from the egg to the grave without ever being awarded the title of whelp, such is the general seriousness of the race. Therefore when one was adjudged to be a whelp by another Dragon their ages ranged between 100 and 3000, after which age, any Dragon still deemed a whelp would be hunted down and executed; their kin reasoning that by three thousand years old, they should know better than to daydream...

There were many reasons that a singular Dragon may be deemed a whelp by his peers, though the easiest way to explain would be to draw a human analogy. Say for instance; that much in the same way as some children are thought docile, others unruly, pedantic or maybe even infantile... Or as adults may be frowned upon as dreamers, should they follow the profession of poets, painters, actors and the like, and yet others still, who may be dubbed merely childish or immature... So too would Dragons frown upon another displaying any of these qualities and more.

All of the above are considered flawed by Dragons; being weighed down by the anchor of free expression was a curse to one of Draconian birth. These mongrels were given one collective title by 'true' Dragons and that was the status of 'Whelp', and, although most other races were unaware of the designations real meaning they felt free to recount the noun in their telling tales of derring-do. Unaware of the difference between a fifty year old sleeping Dragon who has yet to make his first flame and a three thousand year old whelp with a love for levelling villages, the humans especially flower their tales with nest scenes of egg trampling and whelp stabbing and have people take misguided credence from their tales.

Jin found it both amusing and maddeningly infuriating that he was now being told that *some* Dragons had even taken to shape-shifting into human form and spending time with the vermin.

"How many is some?" Jin enquired; his form shimmering as he stood there in the aesthetically lit chamber. He was in bipedal form: He hated the term humanoid and barred those around him from using it except in derision.

In bipedal form a Dragon still retained its races features of clawed large rear legs and short gripping upper claws, whose dexterous movements were remarkably subtle despite the 'hands' being largely made up of the things claws; thanks to thousands of years in which to practice.

"I am unsure oh mighty lord but fifty at least..." The other Dragon drawled. His appearance while not dissimilar to Jin's own was in his very own way unique. For a start his ridge only ran down his back and the spines lay completely flat until angered. His snout was considerably longer too, more crocodilian one might say. His scales were made up of a light shade of brown and he *did* wear a long brown robe that ran so low it skirted the floor as he shifted from foot to nervous foot.

"Lord? I am Jin… Have you forgotten my name already? You may have been a whelp when last we met but I see with my own eyes you have grown into a fine and true adult." Jin spoke softly to curb the twinge of anger, consciously forcing his tail to remain as it was; trailing out long, proud, and straight, some six foot to the rear of his body as was proper.

Most dragons' tails twisted and flicked about as their tempers dictated, just as the one before him did now but Jin knew this to be a sign of ones inability to properly control one's emotions. The brown Dragon attempted to check his tails twitching habits as he corrected himself. "Jin, I am sorry master… it's just-"

"It's? Do you not mean it is? Have you too become, *humanised…*" The brooding prince queried.

"Yes Lo-Jin, I mean no… not humanised but I have definitely picked up a few of their colloquialisms, reflexive pronouns, and such…, …These humans; well their culture is so readily absorbing…" The brown one stated in his hasty defence.

"Careful… Your haste; it betrays you, like the quickening these humans so readily apply to everything they do…! How can it pass that I sleep shortly after the birth of an infant race, only to rise and find it has grown to be my keeper's father?" Jin observed.

"There is more to tell my lord, I apologise; master – I mean Jin. There is more… Forgive me; I *am* nervous it is true. Though it is also true to say; I am the only one who was willing to risk his life with this news… The rest would let you sleep!"

"Then tell it…, …In entirety…," …Drawled the dark majesty of the mighty Jin; his lips curling back into a grin that was as fearsome as it was disarming. He wore his shortened snout well and his teeth held no sign of the rotten flesh one could often see in other less, hygienic members of his race.

"The Giant-kin, Taniara, Dryads, Kraken, Phoenix, Centaur, Unicorns, Whale-Mammoths, Silver Birch trees and Manticores have all had their numbers reduced to the point of extinction, In fact, some eight or so clans of the giant-kin have died out completely; the Magmadon are so few they dare not even meet up to mate and the Dryads only retain high numbers if you take into account their cousins in the sea…"

"Who are…?" Jin prompted as his aide looked away. He wore no clothes and his equally black manhood would hang out for all to see like some basic beast; excepting that Dragon's kept their sexual organs discreetly hidden behind a fold of retractable skin.

Jin had no feelings of shame, and the meaning of modesty was completely lost on him, though neither was he arrogant or lacking in pride, he saw things simply as only Jin could see things. His scaled shadowy flesh pulsed with a multitude of colours, most of which were lost to all but an adult Dragons' eyes. Their throbbing colourful myriad bespoke his great power, he not only knew magic, he breathed it; and his flesh was immune to the effects, for good or ill, of all the known elements; and not merely those found upon Eyrthe and Hell at that. Shadows crept forward as he considered putting to use one of those elements now.

"Oh sorry…! The Merman or maids or whatever; they're still going as strong as ever, well they looked more like fish last time you were awake but anyway the land and fresh water ones; Dryads and such, are very nearly goners!" The brown ones tail flicked about wildly as he spoke. "Dead I mean lo-Jin, I apologise again."

"Remind me Y'shael; these Taniara are the protective creatures of the forests yes?"

The brown one nodded his affirmation and clutched his tail tightly to prevent its further movements as he spoke. "They are tree-folk the Ђ◡ᵔᵉђ, as is proper yes. I remember they were amongst the favoured, but now only a handful of those and the odd rock-herder; I mean Magmadon, exist sorry; only those few still exist: I would add that they are probably *the* most in need of rescue if that is your plan…"

"My plan… A good question…" Jin subtly accused.

"There is one more detail my lord; I mean M-m-m-" the nervous Dragon stammered for several seconds before closing his eyes and calming himself, '*This was the reason they sent me… The cowards…*' he gave up on his uncontrolled speech and communicated his thoughts telepathically.

"Master Jin forgive me please, for a long time now, the elders have demanded to be given proper titles when addressed, it is a habit most of us have grown into as we have aged…, …Yet the worst news is much more concerning great one: Many have taken other races as their consorts lord Jin; Human Lovers, Elven lovers, Dwarven and many more besides. Many, many more and well master, our races future is as bleak as the Magmadon..."

'*Again this variation,*' Jin mutually snapped back; the force of his own will's infiltration bringing with it a slow pulsating ache; '*how many is many? And what other races...?*'

"I am unsure..., ...I have heard of one that was seduced by a Medusa; another that whores amongst Minotaur..."

"Enough! How many...?" Jin's grizzled mental assault bore back.

"A hundred score at least..." the brown regretfully admitted.

A long pause followed then during which the mental link began to fade, but Jin snapped it back with alarming alacrity almost causing a blackout to the Brown.

"Very well, we shall kill them, hunt them, destroy them... rid their worthless souls from our race. All whelps no doubt, but what of their age? Do any of those affected live beyond three?"

The brown one paused in the rapid discourse, his tail snapping out from his grasp before he answered. Again he used his mental skills less the spoken words failed him.

"I am merely the messenger Jin... To discuss numbers and ages-"

"Cease your panicking Y'shael."

"But I-"

"Y'shael..."

"But Master Jin, please..."

"Y'shael... Calm yourself! If you can not even control your own mind..." The Jet black gaze of Jin, trawled over the features of the brown before him, taking into account the flaring nostrils, twitching tail, and several spasmodic convulsions of the ridge along Y'shael's back. The dark ones eyes slanted with concentric shades of black. Aeons of knowledge contained within their soulful orbs looking out with limited sadness upon the Dragon before him in almost hypnotic fashion. He could see the ghost of fear whose mist thin veneer trembled around the spurting globs of bravery that fed off the brown. Jin saw the taint of Human proximity and spoke.

"You know your fate Y'shael?"

The brown was panicked. "I don't understand…"

"Do not. Not, 'don't' and that is why you do not…" Jin paused to once again collect his poise, before forcing his mind past the feeble mental barriers kept in place by the brown. The assault ripped open the mind of Y'shael as easily as one shells an egg. And his secrets were discovered.

"Y'shael you must surely have passed beyond your adolescent period by now… Are you not yet an adult?"

"I am over five thousand years old lord…, …sorry; Jin, can you not see I have aged greatly since last we met?

"I see age in Aeons." The dark attested; "how long then have I slept?"

"Too long great purifier," the brown spoke in reverence. "Far, far too long…"

"How old is your human lover?" Jin asked aloud.

"How did…?" the brown one began but Jin brushed away his protests.

"I told you before; your very nature gives you away, now how old?"

"Mid forties…" Y'shael was intrigued. "Is it true what the Elders say? That you collect others thoughts from the wind…?"

The Dark Prince glowered back, the infinite blackness of his eyes looking straight through the browns own. "If that sycophantic nonsense were true then you would repair to a place wherein the wind is absent would you not? How can you deem an older Dragon an elder when they prevaricate over fanciful tales such as these…? What has become of my children…?"

The brown Dragon fell to the floor without warning in too much agony to make even the slightest sound, his limbs paralyzed with shock.

"I can see why things have degenerated so; I have slept too long while leaderless brats such as your self listen to the ramblings of respected old whelps… NO WHELP SHOULD BE RESPECTED! **NONE!**

Understand me in this Y'shael; we shall spare no fools…"

Jin relaxed his mystical assault and let the lesser Dragon rise while he perused an equally dark, placid pool located nearby. The small oval pools depths grew misty; flashing with light amplified images and the great black paused upon them occasionally as he scanned the revealed contents: Faces, places, towns and villages; dog, woman, Orc, Ogre or Owl. This prize pool of viscous liquid could relay the image of any given article as long as one knew what one was looking for; Jin paused upon one of the images.

"You love her; yet are unsure of her age factor, how human of you. The mortals are not meant to mix with us; that is undeniable but your fascination for study led you upon that which makes whelps of us all; love."

Jin turned slightly as he made his next surprise statement. "Do not be confused Y'shael…, …Love is not merely a human devotion, it is a sickness infecting species both great and small, and you are in its trap. I too once loved an Elf; it was a greatly prized pet of mine for a while until it began making rash requests but you do not hold this one as a pet like I…, …I pity you, now I shall ask anew: Do you know your fate?"

"Yes Jin." The brown acquiesced.

Jin fixed him with a steely stare: "And do you accept it?"

"I do, my lord…" Y'shael humbly replied.

"Good, then I shall kill you last of all, giving you plenty of time to plot my downfall should you require it." Jin said: "In the meantime you shall of course have to **rid** yourself of the source of your infatuation…"

"Rid myself…?" the brown one was astonished to ask.

'*Kill her; the female Human vermin you so adore. What other way can you be sure of being cured.*' Jin's talon circled in the pool as the brown walked over to where his master stood. Jin hovered over a particular point where his nail fractionally pierced the wrinkled waters surface. Lifting his finger-claw with care, he allowed a single droplet of water to drip from the end of his digit.

"Come, observe her Y'shael, she is quite beautiful as humans go…"

"Y'shael looked into the bowl like pools wispy depths to see a picture forming where the droplet had spread on its rippling return. It was Helejja, his Human consort, she was walking near to her home in the village where she lived and the sun was shining. There was no sound but it was evident this watery device was relaying events as they happened. Jin passed his claw through the image, returning the illuminated mists to their random wanderings and ceasing the pictorial transmission.

"You are a shame to your race Y'shael... How could you be such a whelp at your level of maturity? For certain, I expected better of you, I would have made you my guardian but for this... I was certain by now you would be a 'true' dragon, yet strangely enough it is not so. Yet you are such an immense individual, both in bravery, honesty and spirit..."

Jin sighed deeply. "Your death will come sadly, yet your temporary repeal is given only so that you may aid me: In short, afore I terminate your own existence, you shall help me hunt down the others."

"My Thanks to you for your mercy Jin..."

"I seek none. Yet you pause again in your thoughts Y'shael, why?"

"There's a child..."

"...A child you say?" Jin had not detected this. "**Not** your own I presume...?" He said, mentally probing the browns thoughts anew.

Y'shael staggered; taken aback with the gravity of Jin's mental impulse..., '...*No! It is not I. My lover is barren. I made sure of it.'*

'*Good!*' Jin mentally declared. '*At least you have retained some measure of your own senses. Do you know where the child resides?*'

'*We lost track of it aged six: If we ever found her at all?*'

'*...Her?*'

"Well he maybe, we was-were unsure..." Y'shael offered.

"Which parent was the father?" Jin demanded.

Y'shael stood resolute in the pained mental barrage of questioning. '*The male* was responsible lord Jin; we are quite sure of that!*'

*In dragon terms the only 'males' were those of Dragon origin. All other species males were merely regarded as men.

Jin spoke out in his hope, "Dead I presume...?"

"No…, …Though he is an exile in hiding; only occasionally hunted."

"The mother…?" Again Jin hoped to hear good news.

"She's desolate, discarded and suffering dementia. The child may turn out the same…" The brown informed.

"Then we better begin…" Jin surmised.

"Begin doing what; how?" Y'shael was bewildered by the mental abuse and was unsure if he had correctly deduced his masters meaning. "What is it that you would have us do my lord?"

Jin let the annoying title reference pass as he instructed the brown of his plan. "Firstly, see to your own human consort's demise and then attend to me. We shall have to hunt down your conspirators, the cowardly ones who sent you here after you refused to let me sleep… Those same traitors shall pay the blood price for my awakening that they expected **you** would have to forfeit."

"A blood price…?" Y'shael ignorantly asked.

"Do not be concerned. You have been betrayed by those that thought me to be rash. Those 'elders' that should know better; when I am awakened I need to feed upon the heart of one of my own kind. They thought you with your concerned ways would be that one but let us not tarry here; the more haste we make, the greater chance we have of winning the war…"

"We are at war my L-?" Y'shael was doing his best to remember his master's wishes and revert from his last few thousand years of imposed habit. "Who might I ask are we against mighty Jin?"

"Against those I deem my enemy little one," Jin replied, "now go…"

***

A light spreading weakly from a secretive flame shone out in the cellar of the Rancid Racoon. Alan looked away from the candle held by his newly arrived liaison; the small prick of light uncomfortable in the otherwise total darkened chamber.

"Why bring the candle?" Alan asked. It wasn't as if his meeting partner required the visual assistance it offered.

"A good question Mr. Snipes: Many think of the candle as a source of solace; its flame as the essence of virtue. Others believe that the flickering tendrils can measure the life of a man but tell me this; how do you measure the life of a Dragon...?"

Alan looked beguiled, "You wish to know what I know of Dragons eh, okay well my messengers and scouts have been back in touch and I myself have been seeking out a few facts from the deluge of tales told in the tavern above. One of the Luke brothers; Jahn, told me they had just got back from an exploration of Devil's Gap under mountain where he says they witnessed the strangest of things in the vicinity of the L'iezsh'mat citadel. Also young Larky tells me that a brown has taken up residence within forty miles of the Gap..., ...On the west side, quite near the red queen's territory."

The candle swayed a little as if the person holding it was physically deliberating the news. "Tell me of the brown first; I know enough of that fiery bitch Stella already. And of the gap; does the news pertain to the deportment of a certain female princess?"

Alan was taken aback: "Why yes, how did..., ...well no matter she and a troupe of her finest guards headed out on something more than a foraging mission..."

"I said of the brown first; stupid man. The girl is heading to the 'Gap' and her reasons as well as the fate awaiting her are already known to me. So forget her news as you obviously know little of import..., ...who is the brown? Where is he exactly?"

Alan felt a little weak in the others presence and from the thin dripping derision doubted if his limited knowledge would please the person before him. "I know no name sir save he is little more than a whelp sent by Y'shael for some reason to investigate the area."

"Y'shael..., ...he interferes too much that one. Never seems clouded by greed but every male wants for something, do they not? I just wonder what it is Y'shael looks to achieve..." The candle holder spoke, "Is this brown related to Y'shael? Does Stella know he is in her territory uninvited?"

"I don't know boss but..." Alan began.

"Silence Alan, you know too little!" The person seethed, "I gave you simple instruction and quite a large account, not to mention placing you within the walls of the most gossip ridden tavern in all the planes and you come back to report with this? I shall put the Luke twins in charge..."

Alan felt a tremble pass through his being. "I am sorry Mr."

"Sorry? There is no room for sorry in my organisation..."

Alan clutched at his left shoulder; shooting pains were suddenly echoing down the length of his arm though no physical contact had been made. "Boss please; I can find out more, I'm sure just..." He stopped out of breath as the pain shot to its source in hot searing pain and his heart pumped its erratic response. "Remember I said about the flame Alan? Well consider your flame extinguished?" With that two pale white fingers snuffed out the flame as Alan's pounding heart gave out. The figure turned and left the darkened confines: A shot of thinning blonde hair visible on his pale scalp, as he ascended into the light of the tavern above.

IV) **A New Day**

Dirk thought he would have come across the bloodied corpse of his Dwarven compatriot after scouring the undergrowth for fruitless hours, but either his tracking skills were shite or; -oh no, that was right… His tracking skills *were* shite.

He had shouted out of course, but he was not one for raising his voice, especially in a dark, dangerous forest and so he had given up after thirty seconds or so without response. He assumed that Grot must have succumbed to whatever it was that had frightened him so, and felt with growing certainty that he would only find his friend disembowelled and lying face down in some gully

Grot had still been intermittently screaming like a two headed Harpy on a period as Dirk had dissected the bodies of the Gobbo's, but the Dwarves incessant wailing had stopped abruptly at one point mid disembowelment and Dirk had not heard a sound from him since.

'If only I had hurried along sooner' Dirk chided himself, though in truth, once he had managed to ignite the Goblin huts, their crackling timbers had given him a ridiculously cruel idea for revenge: The numerous cadavers he had discovered in Grot's axe-swathing aftermath had been given a little over-engrossed attention by Dirk utilising their own crude swords and cleavers for nigh on two hours…

No sooner had he seemingly expunged himself of his built up frustration, did his gore drenched, charred, blood-splattered visage become a thing to be avoided as he strolled off absently into the unknown, randomly whacking at trees and wildlife alike as he began wandering the forest in a state of empowered hallucination.

Dimly aware of thought during that time; he'd attempted to stay within the perimeter of the Orc encampment as he staggered about in a state of drunken stupor, but as twilight beckoned, the Forest sank into voluminous shadow, and he had traipsed around for several hours in what he thought was vengeful circles only to emerge onto a vast grassy field at the woodlands edge.

"Just Bloody Typical," Dirk cursed to himself with detached amusement as he began to sober up. He swatted at a greedy horsefly.

"What's the bet, if I'd tried going straight, I'd still be going around in circles? I mean forests… What bloody good are they and why is there never an Elf around when you need one?"

Dirk paused to deliver a barrage of blows to a flimsy sapling, which whipped back at him in stinging frustration. Dirk grabbed the reflexive cocky trunk and bent it until it snapped. *'Take that bastard!'* he thought as he victoriously split the offending plant in twain.

'Probably close to midnight…' he reasoned due to the lack of light available even outside the nightmarish forests clutches.

"I need a decent bit of kip!" he bemoaned and gagged himself as his voice echoed into the gathering night's crisp, frozen air. He glanced about for signs of any vengeful Orcish hunting parties who may be lying around, but despite his feverish delusions he could spot none.

He spotted a small stream that ran along the edge of the field before being swallowed by the Forest of Shadows, as he suddenly remembered this place was named. He had seen it on a map back in the Perky Springs general store when he was trying to plot a little more than his route…

Perky Springs was a shitty little mining town with very little prospects located on the other side of the vast wooded area they had been travelling through. Grot had been settling his debts; Dirk's debts that is, and had sent him out of troubles way, instructing him to go and get directions, whilst he settled up with Dirks bloodthirsty creditors.

Figuring they would be eating 'On the Hoof': Killing, cooking and eating whatever wild animal was stupid enough to rear its head on their way to the next settlement. Dirk went to the general store to attempt to steal some herbs; not so much to add flavour to whatever foul beast they would come to eat whilst on the road, but to lessen the stomach cramping after effects of food poisoning they would inevitably suffer from…

The store keeper was a hawk. Or might as well have been and he soon cottoned on to the fact that it was highly unlikely Dirk was in there to spend, being as it was that the storekeeper was one of those creditors Grot was at that very time off in the process of paying. Shortly before he was thrown out and barred for life though, Dirk caught a peek at the map on the wall and decided cutting through the forest would be a nice, quick shortcut to Caernthorn.

Unfortunately for them, Dirk always thought 'as-the-crow-flies' and therefore omitted any mention of the road that ran a short distance around the forest as it would have meant another twenty miles or so in distance.

Neither had Dirk quite accounted for the unrelenting barrage of monsters and beasts that had plagued them ever since getting into the murkier sections of the wood –not that any of those troublesome events jogged his memory of the well travelled road. And of course he most certainly had not deigned it important to mention the whys and wherefores of the legend behind the foreboding name, nor tell of any of the local folklore he had overheard pertaining to the forests inhabitants. All these simmering details had escaped him when, several foot blistering miles along the road later, he had suggested the alternative route.

"Perky Springs… What the cows' bollocks is Perky about it?" Dirk recalled into the ignorant night air. "At least I don't live in that dump! Give me adventuring any day." He half-whispered; recalling the sad little town made all the shit he had endured in his life, seem like a worthwhile sacrifice for not living there. He glanced furtively about and crept to the edge of the stream watching and wary all the while.

The swishing of the wind in the grass gave the impression of hidden movement and Dirk got down on all fours and actually crawled as he covered the last few feet towards the stream, in order to drink and wash away the gore that decorated him like some incredibly macabre war paint.

The evening sky was quite dim now and the moon was temporarily hidden out of sight behind distant thunderclouds; their broiling edges gleaming in the moons pale light. The riverbank sloped gently to the streams edge, which he traversed without incident and while washing himself he noticed spongy patches of lichen that grew along the side of the stream were giving off a weak phosphorous glow.

Uprooting some of the shiny moss, he ventured several yards into the forest reassured by the meagre light source, looking for any sign of a suitably secluded zone. Just deep enough inside the gathering branches to offer seclusion from unseen predators, but not too far that he would end up getting lost –should he quickly have to take flight, he found a suitable refuge. The practiced skills of the coward were honed well in this one.

Setting the still glowing plant before him, he sat down and rested his back against a sturdy willow, whose thicket of dreadlocks hung down in a protective cocoon around him and he settled himself into a comfortably appropriate position as he prepared to meditate in order to regain his meagre amount of spells.

Roughly an hour later, he flickered opened his eyes. The blackness all around him was absolute. The moss light, weak as it was to begin with, had died completely without its roots embedded.

For a moment, Dirk thought he had been swallowed by some gigantic beast and screamed like a choirboy on Sunday, but when he pounded his fist against the imagined creature's ribs, he fell crashing through the flimsy willows branches and headlong into the stream beyond.

The waters icy touch brought Dirk quickly to his senses and he sprang back up from the waterbed only to catch his foot in some unseen submarine depth trap and fall backwards with equal inertia. He was gibbering from both cold and fear as he thrashed about in a panic for some two minutes while he attempted to wrestle his foot free, bruising his ankle painfully.

Having almost rescued his foot, an Owl hooted, causing him to abandon his boot and dive beneath the shallow water. Dirk remained submerged in the freezing stream until his lungs felt as if they were about to burst and he floundered to the surface some six or seven inches above. A repeat of the sound brought with it recognition of the earlier hoot and he calmed a little, managing at last to recover his boot from its aquatic lair, before eventually climbing out onto the riverbank and throwing the doffed item of footwear at the tree he had thought his friend.

"Bugger, damn and blast – you frig… hold on… why do I always start cursing like that divvy Dwiff friend of mine, every time I think he's bloody well dead? Oh, who cares? I'm sick of it… If there's one tiny pothole in life, I'm always the bugger to find it. Why? I mean, the stream is a few bloody inches. *Inches!* 'Life' really must be one big son of a bitch, sat up in the clouds and laughing its heavenly tits off. Is that it? Was I created as a joke, to keep the rest of the whole bloody world amused? Shit!" Dirk mused aloud, "Give me back my bloody boot, tree…"

As he tugged on his water logged footwear he looked out about him into the night, less some nightmare creature should creep up on him unawares. He was starting to shiver and his nipples felt like ice.

The willows soft branches swung around in a gently gathering wind and an eerie fog crept upwards from the ground in an attempt to conceal its hidden foliage from the spying night stars, whose glimmering eyes peeked out here and there from pockets of gathering cloud. The forests treasury of leaved sentinels formed an intrusive crowd about him and their shadowed motives were dark indeed, paranoia began settling in...

Dirk felt very alone and vulnerable and although he could still make out the woods moody perimeter he felt too self conscious to expose his silhouette to the hidden eyes that would surely spot him crossing the vast fields beyond. Besides, he was probably safe within the confines of the willows branches... *'As long as I don't forget where I am this time...'*

Dirk reasoned that to go any further straight away would only lead to his own demise. As the nights chill had already settled on his wet clothes whilst in meditation, compounded by his brief sojourn in the river, he looked at its meandering waters now, creeping ghoulishly through the thickened bodyguards of the forest shadows, lighting up a jagged scar that pushed aside the darkened forces as it led towards its unholy birthing point somewhere within the blighted woods beyond.

Utilising the flame cantrip Dirk had just memorised in order to build a fire from damp wood, he then conjured the bird with the other simple dweomer, which he roasted and ate, bones and all. Lastly, he fished out some of his secret stash of tealeaves, washed out the bird's purposely left over stomach, and stuffed the leave inside. He put this into his tankard along with some water and made himself a lovely cup of Sigwart tea, by holding the tankard gingerly over the spluttering fire.

After his clothes were almost dry, he quenched the fire with some water from the stream and then went back to the waters edge where the phosphorous light gave off small flickering shadows like fairies dancing in the moonlight.

"Of course... The bloody stream!" Dirk whooped with sudden clarity. "The encampment must be near the stream!" He shouted a triumphant war cry of delight, his roar startling several of the night-time's inhabitants, whose fearful cries in turn frightened Dirk, who hugged the protective willow trunk for dear life for nigh on over an hour...

Some seventy or so minutes later and he was still debating with himself; "If I can find the camp, I may find Grot or his body at least." Dirk reasoned when he finally stopped flapping, "In which case, I simply have to drag his stinking carcass all the way back to -hold on! Where does the nearest Cleric live...? Could I really be arsed? I mean even if I could carry him, I-oh..."

Dirk felt a stirring in his stomach which he at first thought may be his intuitive sense of fear, but which actually turned out to be a determined stool of crap, begging for release.

After peering out for ten minutes without noticing any signs of dangerous life-forms, he left the leafy bastion of willow and squatted down on the riverbank, dropping his trousers and grabbing up several tufts of the spongy moss as he set about relieving himself of his previous night's lunch.

He pondered his next course of action as steamy curls of pungent heat rose from the fresh turd beneath him, and he was forced to abandon his position to escape the brown crimper's insulting stench. Several piles and some five hasty manoeuvres later, Dirk came to a decision as he washed his backside with the moss soaked in water from the stream, and vowed never again to eat a bear cooked by either Grot or himself.

As far as Dirk could deduce, he would have no chance of dragging his friend's body all the way to Caernthorn from here and the way back to the nearest village was a complete loss to him, not to mention Perky Springs being right out of the question. So he decided he would set out as far as he dared and bury the poor bastard wherever he may find him.

Looking back at the willow from the well lit sanctuary of the stream, Dirk realised just how flimsy his chosen fortress truly was as its silvery stems splayed and sprayed in a mighty gust of wind whose bitter chill carried with it discarded fumes; Dirk was unsure whether they belonged to his own smelly stool or lingered from the death camp whose fiery glow was nowhere to be seen, though the willow seemed to bask in what little moonlight remained.

Deciding it would be safer in the light than the dark, he resolved himself to bobbing up stream for a while just in case the Dwarf lived, whilst secretly harbouring hopes that *if* his friend Grot was indeed dead, he would also be missing his head or some-such appendage and thus beyond need of rescue.

Reluctant to take any action that may expose his presence, yet more than determined to escape his haunting surroundings, he set off down the middle of the bone-chilling waterway, which was barely more than knee deep, and back into the depths of the blackened woods.

Of course, Dirks theory about Grot's location being relevant to the streams was built on little more than random guesswork, but for Dirk the fact that it was his own idea was often more than enough reason in itself for him to follow a particular course.

He waded through the stream for roughly an hour, stopping occasionally to climb out onto either bank to see if he could sight any burning embers, albeit without success, then the rain started and his slippy, self abusing attempts to ascend the muddy embankments forced him from pursuing the action as he continued down the now not so quaint stream.

The thick woollen robe Dirk wore, while excellent for keeping out the nights chill in summer or winter alike; was a real bugger when it came to staving off the effects of rainfall. It didn't. Instead, his clothing suckled water faster than a hungry piglet at a teat-fest.

To start with, the rain was only a drizzle and although the misty air made it hard to see more than a few feet, it posed no serious risk to health and so, onwards he waded, feeling more and more like a drowned sheep caught in a light buffeting wind on some desolate mountain and in much need of its errant shepherd's attentions.

The rain had been falling quietly for twenty minutes or so when a bolt of lightning and a loud clap of thunder signalled its true intent. The spirited wind gained in confidence as the fine misty droplets from above instantly transformed into hard pellets of bone drenching rainwater, their stinging content slapping against Dirks exposed frozen flesh where it could, and sending a howl of triumphant breeze this way and that as a gale hammered invisibly against impossible targets. Dirk looked about madly for the banks on both sides, and made haste in their imagined direction.

Sloshing towards the telltale glow which now was some several feet away thanks to the stream widening, he floundered up against its slippery borders, and stopped dead in the water.

Somehow, at some point, the banks either side of the stream had began rising and now gave the impression of sheer, glowing walls. They were still covered by the luminescent moss but they now reared above him like an indomitable fortress, Silhouetting thick and thin fingered phantoms above, there bushy embraces swaying about blindly in the blustery weather. At least the sheer riverbank offered him shelter from the worst of the storms affections to some extent, though the water level was rising apace.

"I'll be damned if I'm gonna be drowned in this half-assed excuse for a river" he shouted in defiance to the crooked horticultural figures above.

"Well that's fine by me," a gruff voice rejoined. "Now if ya don't mind helping me out of here we can be on our way at last!"

"Grot...?" Dirk queried

"Of course, it's Grot you maggoty arsed excuse for a paranoid sidekick!" The Dwarf bellowed, in truth he was quite relieved his friend had eventually turned up, though by now his Dwarven eyes could not make out a thing thanks to the rapidity of conflictions betwixt shadow and light thrown up by the tempest blowing about them and the too dull ghoulish light thrown off by the unhelpful moss.

"My Dwarven sight is buggered in this hellish place… What in Keldor's name took you so long?" The Dwarf cried out his embarrassment. He would be damned if he would let his tardy friend off the hook no matter what the bugger replied. "I was shouting for ages…"

"Erm, Grot is that you in the middle of the *stream*? I thought it was a statue at first…" Dirk said straining his eyes in the gloomy downpour. He could barely sight something a little further downstream that stood on a large pedestal; quiet, tall and unmoving against the thrashing sleet and shifting leaves – periodically illuminated against a tormented sky.

"Of course it's me!" *'Had the smarmy bugger mentioned the (S) word on purpose?'* "Now get me off this godforsaken rock before I bloody well drown, yer great-big-good-for-nothing-pleb-of-a-tunnel-troll's foreskin!" Grot shouted; an edge of desperation piggy backing into his voice.

"Do you mean to tell me you've been stood on that big rock, all this time? Why didn't you come looking for me? I've been shitting myself for hours, and I'm sure something's following me downstream –or it might be above us, on the banking maybe…?" Dirk asked incredulous and afraid.

The Dwarf was exasperated beyond meaningful words, he shook his head and was about to answer with explosive rage when he realised he needed the selfish human alive. "Why didn't *YOU* come looking for me!?" was about all Grot could bring himself to shout.

"I did!" Dirk shouted defiantly, he briefly thought of running –well wading away as quickly as he could and returning when the Dwarf was a little calmer but the truth was he would sooner chance his arm with a pissed off ex-tunnel fighter than his imagined hunters that lurked; always just out of his vision. "I went all over for hours, shouting your name – you might be going deaf…"

"I'm not that old…" The Dwarf warned.

"I dunno Grot – I mean how much do you know about old

Dwarves?" Dirk tested, "I know if I was past seventy my ears would be pretty blasted…"

"I'm a Dwarf, you Human gimp and if I was only just seventy I'd probably still be pissing the bed an sucking me mamma's tits dry!

Dirk was hurt by this and stammered in his defence a whole barrage of fanciful theories that he had been planning to tell any authority figures…

"Shut yer bleeding trap!" Grot cried. "Yer a lying yellow bellied bastard is what you are! …I didn't hear ya, and that means you didn't yell at all, but probably pissed off as usual… You never think I might actually be getting to that age where I *need* the odd bit of help in a *battle* as big as that one you just got us into…"

"For your information I tried using that stupid, shitty little stick you gave me and almost ended up dead for my troubles and soon as we're lost in the Forest of Shadows, I doubt either of us would make it to the nearest healer in time to reincarnate- well no… You probably would but I'm not like you Grot, I can't be this bloody person ya want me to be. So I thought you were dead. I still came looking for you-"

"Hold on, you shit. Did you say we're in the Forest of Shadows? And how did you come about this information? Eh? Ask a Goblin? No – you were too busy running from that sad excuse for a Snurch."

"Up yours…"

"What?" Grot growled straight back, "Yer weren't running from a Snurch were ya? You cowardly get! I should just jump in and drown you where you stand. I could piss off with the jewels and find my own way to Caernthorn. You utter, utter bastard! Have you not heard any of the folktales about this place? Keldor give me strength… They not only say it's haunted. It's apparently accursed to all who enter, bewitched against those of pure intent, and filled with *every bad-ass-munching monster you could probably manage to cram into one nighttimes depressive nightmares…!*"

Grot stopped panting for breath, doubling over in his wheezed efforts to regain his composure.

Dirk waited in sullen silence, stone sized pellets of rain smacking of his hung head while the Dwarf fought to compose himself. Dirk knew he was in the wrong, sort of, but didn't really know how to justify himself. He could stand there swearing but the Dwarf cursed much better than he. He could attempt to defend his honour in battle, but knew it would be the last battle he ever fought. Half of what the Dwarf had said was painstakingly true and the rest of it made Dirk squirm in the thought that the Dwarf perhaps knew him better than he did himself. He looked up to the stars in answer but none could be seen through the foliage and clouds blanketing the sky above.

"So why haven't you? Jumped off I mean… Not murder me, which would be daft, 'cause… I'm your mate. But why not…?" Dirk was at a loss.

"You're taking the piss aren't you?"

"Why would I? I'm just wondering why you've been stood on a rock in the middle of the stream all day?" Dirk stated simply.

"Well *If,* you must know, I was chasing after one of those black skinned, red eyed bastards and didn't notice the drop till it was too late to do anything about it, its all right for you sods with legs like beanpoles, but unless you haven't noticed. JUMPING is not us Dwarves stronger points!" He paused to curse several times before continuing. "Now even so, I aint saying I'm a bad jumper, well I'm a damn site more athletic than you at any rate, but all the same you can just about still see how wide it is…"

They both looked up, each evaluating the distance as the Dwarf spoke and Dirk was amazed Grot had managed to leap this far.

"So, I fell into this god forsaken abyss and head first onto this rock as you call it, and maybe it's just me, but I see a bloody **huge *river*** flooding straight past this thing! This gets us back to the point of Dwarves not having legs like beanpoles!"

A long pause followed wherein neither spoke, lost deep in their own deliberations… and in the silence that ensued, the only sounds were those of the rain pattering down on the trees and the constant splashing of water droplets hitting the otherwise sluggish stream and forcing it into rippling resurgence.

"So why didn't you just get off and wade upstream?" Dirk asked and no sooner had he said it he wished he hadn't bothered to open his mouth. The thing about Dwarves is, for reasons best known to themselves they hate water with a passion. Oh sure they will wipe the dirt from their bodies with slightly damp sponges, but ask them to wade through a few puddles along a road and they would sooner see their great Dwarven halls fall to the Goblins they hate so much, than set one foot into its murky shallows…

"Wade!" Grot roared in genuine fear, "You mean bloody swim don't ya! And I don't know if you have been completely dead for these last thirty one years of your short worthless life, but in case you weren't aware; *Dwarves' can't swim!* And you friggin' well **know** we absolutely **hate** that *impure* **deadly shite** that you lot call **water!**"

"But it's only a few feet deep…" Dirk tried, knowing full well that this would be of little comfort towards the terrified Dwarf who stood a little over four feet tall.

'*I suppose I shall have to carry him.*' Dirk thought and conjured a mental picture of his struggling upstream several hundred yards with Grots bulky frame thrown across his shoulders. The thought did little to endear him towards the unenviable task as Dirk splashed over to where his blinded friend stood; frozen like a statue.

Grot waited for what seemed like an age peering out into the hazy night-time torrent, even though he could barely see beyond his own rather large squashed nose.

"Dirk..?"

…, …

Grot wasn't sure which he felt first - the frigid splash of water against his previously chilled bones or the sublime shove that had led to his departure from the sanctity of his rock.

He screamed, splashed, and kicked for all he was worth, all to no avail, then just as he was convinced he was about to die, he heard Dirks irritating chuckle and its arrogant tone drew Grot out of his inane terror.

"If I die >gulp< In these >gulp< damned waters >*gulp*< I'll be taking your skinny bones with >*gulp*< me!" The Dwarfs arms flailed about in useless desperation, seeking to connect with anything solid – namely Dirk.

"Then stand up you daft stump! If you don't want to die that is…" Dirk gloated and splashed over to help the floundering Dwarf to his feet.

A shout came through over the now deafening rainfall, "I expect with your night vision stuffed up ya may wanna stay close… What with all this subliminal light or whatever they call it, so if you don't wanna lose me you'd better stand up and keep up." With which remark he was gone from the Dwarves searching grasp.

Some inner sense that could separate the difference between the very real dangers of being lost and blind, from the imagined peril of drowning, propelled him into action and Grot's stubby legs pumped him along in the direction of Dirks splashing as fast as he could muster.

After a time beyond reason (which to Grot, was anything above a second or two when it came to actually being immersed *IN* water.), he called out to Dirk, who he could now just about vaguely make sight of. The eye of the storm had passed over them and though the rain was still fierce and the wind chillingly competitive, the mists were still, the raindrops smaller and the gale only half maddened, and so he could see a little again.

"How much longer before we exit this watery grave?"

"Oh, err, soon…" came back the vague reply.

This worried Grot, one thing he could say about his friend, was that he never sounded unsure of himself, well not until lately… Ever since leaving the mining town of Perky Springs in fact, and since that time Dirk had been having paranoid delusions that they were being followed. He wondered if his friend might not be hiding something but right now he was more concerned with more important things. Like why they were still in the stream some three hours later with little or no chance of gaining higher ground…

"Dirk, are we lost?" Grot demanded.

"Lost? How can we be lost? A stream only goes two ways." He lied unwittingly. Dirk was worried too, not merely because they were lost, but also due to his realising that the water margin around his upper waist was rising gradually higher.

"Well if we're not lost, why in Keldor's name are we still in the wet stuff?" Grots voice had an edge to it that clearly said he knew he wasn't being told everything.

"Oh, I just think…that…we, well, you know, that we set off in the wrong direction." Dirk finally conceded, unable to think of an appropriate falsehood clever enough to fool the wily Dwarf.

"Huh? WE... What reason in Keldor's name does the word we come into this? As I remember it, *you're* the one who *knows* where he's *going!*" Grots voice held just enough mixture of sarcasm and threat to send a cold shiver down Dirks spine. Or at least, Dirk presumed the sensation to be fear – though it may have easily turned out to be a simple case of deadly pneumonia.

'He's no fool,' thought Dirk, *'A little uneducated perhaps, but definitely no Troll in sages clothing...'* For all the Goblins Dirk may have killed that day, he knew with certainty that a fight with Grot in these circumstances would be most detrimental to his health. Not that the two never fought – they did constantly, but Dirk had long since learnt from the Dwarves tone of voice, when he should feel intimidated and when to be outright fearful, and this occasion most definitely fell into the latter.

"We will be out any minute, I'm sure." Fibbed Dirk with practised ease. *'The water level must be up to the Dwarves beard by now'* Dirk guessed, as it had already risen above his own waist, though it was hard to tell in the enveloping mists that ran above its surface. Dirk found relief in the knowledge that as daft as Grot surely was not, he was obviously stupid enough to have not realized the waters increasing depths.

Sloshing on in dejected fashion, the woods grew ever more deep, here and there a twinkle of emerald green. A stray shaft of moonlight picking out the gleaming eye slits of some curious predator along the banks. The rainfall kept alternating between terrible and horrible and the wind cheerfully whipped at elk, elm and man alike; stinging the skin and depressing the souls of the two misplaced travellers.

"Well, I guess I'm..." The Dwarfs voice trailed off.

"You're what?" Dirk enquired, "Grot? Where are you?" Dirk was alarmed in case the Dwarf may have fallen into some sinkhole and disappeared beneath the rippling tug of the reinvigorated waters surface. "Grot ya stubborn arse, tell me you're all right...?"

"I would be if I could see, and wasn't stuck in a streak of dragon piss!" Grot snapped back but his voice had lost its threatening edge, "There's something shiny up ahead, but I can't tell what!" He added irritably.

Dirk peered ahead and saw nothing at first, turning his gaze away in the manner of one who is accustomed to abject defeat, though as he did so Dirk caught a sight of the glittery apparition and turned back to it in surprise. 'Something' glittered a few yards from where they stood. It was nigh on impossible in the quieting yet still torrential downpour, to make out what the shimmering yellow beacon was exactly, but in any case it was a welcome relief from the eerie light cast by the moss, and perhaps would bear them refuge from the rapidly deepening stream-cum-river.

"Come on!" Grot said, surging past Dirk whilst readying his axe in a single unbroken movement. "Whatever it is, it's gotta be better than this sad excuse for a mermaids grave! Come on..."

They waded forward and the water level began to drop in rapid succession as the river bed rose sharply up at an angle. The Lichen that had bedecked either riverbank was now little more than the odd patch and the Dwarf, regaining the use of his sight, pushed on quickly into what turned out to be the shallowest of caves.

"He-he! Now this is the kind of stream I can cope with!" shouted Grot, triumphantly tapping his drenched boots on the wet stone base in a celebratory jig at having reached the top of the sloping river bed. Here within the shallow depression that served as their proposed sanctuary, the stream bubbled out wretchedly over the rocky floor, its rivulets etched no more than an inch or two deep into the stone.

Dirk clambered up to the rim of the cave, and he was almost as relieved as the Dwarf to be leaving the confines of the stream as his tiring feet sought purchase on the slippery rocky incline. "Here mate, how did you get up this last bit? It's way too bloody slippy for me."

"By wearing these Dwarven hobnailed boots, yer maggot ridden, fish loving carcass of a Sea serpents arsehole!" Grot roared and shambled forward in determined fashion, splodging to the cave mouth. Dirk braced himself for the blow he had been expecting ever since he had pushed his companion into the stream. It didn't help. Grots ham-like fist feeling harder than usual in its frozen state smashed into Dirks jaw, sending him tumbling back down the steep rise and into the waters icy embrace.

"Right, that's settled then!" Grot shouted down having divested himself of a small portion of the anger he felt. "Are you all right?"

"ffhngh..." Dirk tried to respond, but it had been a long tiresome night for the physically challenged Human, and his body decided to take this yearned for opportunity to enter automatic shutdown...

"Bugger, damn and blast... Why could ya not just have fell down where ya stood…" The Dwarf grumbled as he clambered back into the water to recover his pal, fear etched into his features as he did so.

Dirk awoke several hours later sweating and scared; just another nightmare to add to his growing library. His eyelids fluttered against the unwelcome dark-grey, early morning sky at his back, and he closed them again at its too intense light. The rain still pitter-pattered down but not as heavily as before and the wind had died completely, which was nice.

Suddenly remembering he might be drowning, he peered about quickly and was immediately aware of several things. He was alive for one; always a good thing! And he was lying naked on the caves bare stone, with the Dwarves thick fur cape thrown over him –also probably a good thing. Raising his sleepy eyelids a little more he espied Grot, who laid a very short way off to his left and was snoring like a trooper.

It occurred to him that the Dwarf must have lit a fire, as the little grotto was very warm considering it was no more than several feet deep. He rolled over, seeking the fire and quickly clamped shut his eyelids as the full force of the grey morning light bore acidulously into his pupils.

"So we made it then…" Dirk sighed to himself in dozy fashion as sleep beckoned him in once more.

The rain had all-but ceased by the time Grot rose and he immediately set off foraging for food. An Elf hunting for food would be said to 'drift' into the loose foliage at the forest's edge, 'slip' between the clinging brambles, and flit betwixt the tangle of tree roots; pausing here and there to cock an ear or examine a leaf, all the while camouflaging himself against the surrounding fauna. Then when the Elf would finally sight and select its prey, the bowstring would snap back silently and his chosen quarry would fall down, dead within a heartbeat unaware its own life had ended…

A Human Hunter, would probably be deemed second to an Elf, though in truth, both the Centauri and Lizardmen as well as the Goblins to the east belonging to the Red Eye clan and the Pygmy that infest the Huzzalji deserts and jungles, plus one or two other lesser known species were far better than most Humans at hunting. Much, much better, yet still a human hunter would attempt to blend in an Elfish fashion, all the while seeking to bring down the game without disturbing the other denizens of the forest and so on.

The thing is; *every single one* of the species mentioned and many more besides could produce the odd excellent hunters of the wild, but

Dwarves; unless taught for many, many tedious years did not. They were too used to the acoustics of living underground to appreciate the finer delicacies of hunting in the wild and thus would often frighten their quarry into running before they had a chance to near them, let alone release their shot... Even those rare Dwarves, who did learn the arts of the ranger or hunter, would most often find their bulky width inappropriate for navigating between tight thickets and closely entwined branches and thus lose their prey either to a death defying run or an intelligent opportunistic scavenger.

But this was Grot.

Skipping across the streams drier stones Grot spotted an unlucky white rabbit and ran at it screaming, though his greasy soled boots sent him slipping on the early morning mildew that clung romantically to the morning blades of grass beneath his feet.

Stumbling forward, the Dwarf gave an irritated shout that seemed to snap the morning ambience in twain, and amid a sudden explosion of wild and exotic sounds the frozen rabbit swapped its state of near catatonic shock for one of blistering agility as it scampered off quick-smart, with the inelegant Dwarf tear-arsing after it.

Smacking his knees against every prickle possible as he ran, while his shins took repeated torture from every exposed root or trailing bush stem, Grot forged on and still he felt he was making ground on the zigzagging streak of frightened white fur; that is until it zipped down a hole and left him stood facing up against two wild boars in a three way face off.

Grot hated boar, they were stubborn bastards at the best of times, uncomfortably reminding him of natures own answer to Dwarves: Furious sods in a fight, hard as sunken stone and almost impossible to kill without giving the meat a fair deal of damage. He checked for his hunting knife, which was located in a pouch on the back of his belt. Appeased, he left it there crouching down on all fours and stared slowly at each of the boar. The Boar responded by kicking there hind legs in anticipation of charging, imitating Grots own actions.

Sending up clods of dirt from the still damp Eyrthe all three charged towards each other in perfect synchronisation. Grot charged helmet first, into the sooo hard skull of the boar and they both fell, Grot being blasted a little to the side and down like a sack of unwanted shit, while the boar skidded to its knees and rolled over the Dwarf in squealing distress. Monkey flipping to his feet, Grot spun around with a back heel kick to the still downed boars head and followed with a punch to what he guessed to be its kidneys, causing it to squeal again as his left hand reached for his knife only to discover it had fallen loose. He looked to the ground looking for the blade and in his momentary diversion the wild pig scampered away as quickly as it could limp.

Seeing the Boar escaping, Grot made to chase after it but a squeal from behind reminded him of the other beast and he ran back on himself, stopping short of re-entering the tiny pig glade he picked up his trusty hunting knife, whose blade he had seen glinting through a shaft of light that pierced the leafy canopy above... Lifting the blade and readying it for action, Grot went into the dell looking for the wild pig but a roar to his left alerted him to the presence of another; rather more proficient hunter than he: A Pankrideon fiend; most likely an Anzican crossbreed due to the brightly bristling orange stripes running along its otherwise greenish body.

The deadly fiend delicately hung from a high tree branch by a single spindle of its super strong silk. It hissed another cat like snarl as its feline jaws parted exposing an extremely dangerous looking pair of deadly mandibles and closed about the throat of the Boar. A cracking sound followed and the pig hung limp in the grasp of its spindly lower legs. Grot decided to leave it to lunch in peace, backing of out of the small open space and continuing his hunt elsewhere...

After a mere one hour, two minutes and twenty seconds, a battered and bruised Grot returned to the cave; his impromptu scavenger hunt having produced two shiny red apples; three sweet pears and a Mooly bean which; although they tasted like Harpy dung, were one of the best foods available to those in the know. Cooking them was a slightly tricky affair however, for slightly undercooking the ten pound bean would result in severely poisoning the consumer, whilst overcooking the nutritional vegetable would cause the consumer to suffer severe bouts of stomach upset and prolonged dehydration... These two important facts were regularly disregarded by those people that could survive off them for two good reasons: First off, a single bean could keep for over two weeks no matter how ineptly prepared and secondly; they were packed with every nutrient the body possibly needed and then some. Such was the fame of the Mooly bean amongst woodsmen, Elves, adventurers, rangers and the like, that many nick-names had been thought up for the all-in-one feast, though Grots personal favourite was the 'Arse-Twitcher', thanks to the not-so-delayed after effects brought on by his own dubious cooking prowess.

A gentle, steel-toed nudge in the small of his back awoke Dirk from his restorative slumber, and he stretched out his protesting limbs, feeling the summery day's strength coursing through his veins. A foreign sensation throbbed throughout his body and a dull ache took over, as his muscles did their best to repair themselves after the previous evening's uncharacteristic activities.

Dirk giggled; a quiet chuckle that caught him, building into a steady snorting laughter that shook his waking head and strained his facial muscles as he was forced to fight back a flood of sinful tears.

'I'm sorry –I, I didn't mean to… You made me… You made me do it!'

Grot kicked a little harder, "Dirk wake up yer dumb-ass!"

Dirk rolled over reflexively and grabbed at the offending foot biting the Dwarf painfully on the ankle, but the Dwarf responded in equal fashion kicking the half-wake human in the gut.

"Yer crazed bastard!" Grot accused. "Ye were having a nightmare, yer dick!"

"No Grot…" Dirk pleaded in a gush of tearful emotion. "I killed them. I massacred them and ripped up their flesh, I-"

"Calm yourself lad," the Dwarf interrupted, "Who did yer kill eh lad? Nobody that's who, now be calm, you were having a nightmare…"

Dirk clutched at the Dwarfs legs and buried his head in his knees, sobbing, "The Gobbo's Grot, I mutilated them, tortured them and painted the forest with their blood but I didn't mean it, I'm sorry Grot I didn't mean to…"

Grot cradled his friends head in his hands and lifted his face a little towards his own, he was mightily tempted to simply head butt his weepy pal, but resisted the desire, just: "Listen to me now lad. Yer babbling like a baby, ye killed nothing ok? Most of the things were half dead anyways and it was me that killed them, now dry yer tears and ditch yer nightmares from yer mind less a Dream weaver happens by. I've caught us breakfast, well sort of…"

The previous days battling, was probably the first time Dirk had ever willingly stood and fought, not that he had never had to fight for his life before, he had just never done so out of choice -other than scrapping with the Dwarf, and he felt muscles burning that had never before seen use.

The Dwarves dismissal cast doubt in his own mind, had he really dreamt it all? Dirk reflected as he rose from the furs and felt the warm winds refreshing caress. Had he really been so malicious or merely confused real events with vindictive fantasy? He was certain of fighting several Goblins but beyond that his mind was a haze too frazzled by fatigue to be fully aware or maybe it was being dominated by some other unseen force.

"Do Dream weavers venture into these parts?" Dirk soberly asked.

Grot sighed at his pathetic pal's haggard expression, "They have been known to creep into the homes of kings so I would think a place such as this would be fair game to their abilities but… I was just talking… You've had a nightmare and that's that, nothing more – nothing less, now get a hold of yer self while I fix breakfast will yer?"

Dirk thought on as the Dwarf did this and that… He knew he'd fought on when he could have run, but he had not done so out of rational choice. He had felt urged onwards by some alien instinct telling him to appease his besmirched honour, yet…

Dirk had never before felt any sense of pride having been useless at almost every single thing he turned his hand to. So unbearably useless was he; the un-proficient wizard wretchedly resigned himself to surviving at any cost. Pride was simply a luxury one so cursed with ill-luck as he could not afford to bear. To say he held any 'Honour', Dirk thought laughable.

He decided he would leave any future fights to his Dwarven friend and try not to think on too much what he may or may not have done: Until at least he could figure out this alien instinct. Yet even as he resolved to never again become a victim of the possessing urge, his feelings again seized his thoughts with desperate visions of self righteous indignation. He imagined himself atop a pile of bones, made up of those under who he had suffered the pain of humiliation.

The noise of Grot humming tonelessly interrupted his thoughts.

It did happen he thought – half wishing it were true, but then he was not so foolhardy to assume he could easily repeat a similar confrontation and, as he thought on it some more, Grot *had* already taken out most of the 'hard' targets before Dirk had sense to even move. And if he was to be really honest with himself, a rare occasion for Dirk indeed, then he had to admit he had not been so much brave as mentally unhinged and in dire circumstance indeed.

'*Oh Yes, the mocking bird really upped and left the coop last night!*' Dirk considered rather more rationally, last night was absolutely nothing like himself. The Snurch had made him dispute his place in things and Dirk not only rose to the challenge but went way beyond its boundaries with his rampaging massacre and the crippling disfigurement of the Orc war-chief.

Giving it due deliberation as the Dwarf mooched about around the fire, Dirk convinced himself that his horrific act may become the catalyst for some unseen smiting by an angry Goblin cousin or two.

He stretched out once more and put aside fanciful thoughts of empowerment, in favour of a practical urge to satiate his rumbling hunger and smiled at the radiant sun, ready to face the new day despite his self protests; both mentally and bodily. By his side, the Dwarf had laid down a strip of 'beef' jerky and a single pear. He greedily gobbled the pear in three bites and began munching on the jerky as he studied the Dwarf.

Grot, whose battle hardened bod was well used to utilising all available muscle groups, was not only ready for a repeat of the previous days exertions, but fervently hoped for it, so badly wounded was his pride at that moment. Having failed spectacularly in his hunting, he turned his attention to the strange gemstone arrangement that crept about the caves anterior wall. It was gold set in a matrix of seemingly imprecise patches.

A pattern, insignia, or some sort of code was contained within the golden patchwork; he knew it as well as he knew his own name. Thousands of years of Dwarven knowledge pertaining to mineralogical phenomena was contained within the skull of every living, breathing Dwarf and this formation of gold, he was ninety-nine percent certain was not at all natural.

Grot was busily wandering around examining the walls of the cave, when Dirk ceased his own ruminations and walked over to observe him. "You Nobbies and your silly love of rocks… You make me laugh!" He joked, though he meant it. To him, rocks were just that; rocks.

"It's '*Dwarves*' if you don't mind, and your one to speak about making people laugh, wandering about with no clothes on," teased Grot, before gesturing towards Dirks exposed groin and casting his eyes skyward, "And I'd be hurryin' up too if you wanna stay intact, the birds are out and they like a little worm or two for breakfast!"

Grinning at the jibe, Dirk went over to where his dry clothes were neatly laid out on the floor of the cave. "Oh… You must be talking about those '**Giant Eagles**' that eat *snakes*…" He adroitly countered, "Did you strike the fire already?" he added, looking around for any sign of it.

"What fire?" Grot looked about momentarily confused, "Oh you mean the warmth? That was no fire," Grot replied matter-of-fact, to which Dirk simply raised his eyebrows in dumb fascination. "It was the rocks see -you dill-brained Munnakin. Get dressed and then come make fun of me. This rock formation is way too strange to be normal matter."

Dirk finished putting on his attire and sleepily wandered the couple of feet to the back of the warm depression in which they had slept; looking at it in the cold light of day, even the most flowery of Elven minstrels would have trouble describing their shallow shelter as a cave.

"So you're saying this is what's meant by the phrase 'hot rocks'?" Dirk aimlessly quested.

"Hot what?!? I'm sure you're not all there!" Grot blasted back, "I'm trying to show you something interesting, if you've got time enough to drop the 'arse' part from your 'smart-' routine."

Dirk took the insult with accustomed practice, but this time his feeling of victimisation would not relent, and he visibly cringed as he heard the sour retort escaping through his clenched teeth. "There's no need to keep going on all the time, at least I came back for you and besides… If it wasn't for me we would never have found this cosy cave would we…? I think I deserve a little bit of thanks, don't you…?"

"THANKS!"

"Your welcome," Dirk declared at the blared out verb, "See you only had to-"

"**Shut it!**" Grot threatened turning to face his approaching Human accomplice, "I would no sooner thank you than I would shave off my beard or cut off my balls! Keldor control me…" The Dwarf ranted, "First you trick me into these bloody woods, without telling me the full facts! *Then* you get me into yet *another* battle that *you* can't handle… *After me giving you explicit orders to remain within our campsite at all times…* If I'd wanted you wandering off, I would have sent *you* out looking fer kindling."

"Oh really…? Well who died and appointed you the Boss?" Dirk moaned.

Grot's short crossover jab cracked Dirks head back and chipped his lower back tooth, silencing him instantly.

"Don't think I am messing. You more or less admitted you were hoping you wouldn't find me and when you did, what did you do? Drown me - that's what... Not once -but bloody well twice!" And with that he delivered a second blow –this time to Dirk's gut, before weighing in with an elbow and knee for good measure...

Grot returned his seething attentions to the rock-face, pulling out a small ornamental looking hammer, and chipping away at one of the golden chunks set in the rock. Dirk clutched painfully at his jaw, head, and stomach, and fought the strong urge to kick the now crouching Dwarf in the back. *'I deserve it I suppose...'* He thought as he tenderly massaged the fractured tooth. He had to admit, the Dwarf knew him almost too well.

"I only pushed you in *once...*" Dirk whimpered almost too quiet to be heard, a*lmost...* And he peered back to the wall where the Dwarf was conducting his examination in grim anticipation of another retaliatory blow. Dirk blinked, shook his head, and then blinked again before rubbing furiously at his eyes. When next he looked, his eyes positively bulged at what appeared to be numerous chunks of gold of varying hue and size; they would have been on stalks were it at all possible. Dirk forgot all about his petulant defence and jaw numbing pain; gold was gold!

"Bloody Hell Grot...! You genius! How long do you think it would take us to evacuate it?" Dirk ignorantly declared staring in buoyant mood at the fist sized nuggets and their promise of untold wealth.

"You Bog-beast brained son of a gully Dwarf! How you Humans have the cheek to call us Dwarves greedy is beyond me," Grot fumed as he dragged Dirk away from the cave wall and back towards the shallow cave mouth. "I really am trying here and you aint helping... Yeah! You only *'Pushed'* me into that stuff once, but who do you think rescued you from drowning, eh?"

Dirk's attentions were momentarily diverted by the shocking revelation. "Grot you- Jumped in for me? I dunno what to say...?"

"Well, a bit of thanks from *you* wouldn't go amiss. On top of that, I'd say you could shut up for a bit and give me a bit of credit..." The Dwarf declared before continuing to discuss his fascinating find. "...Now I could tell by the varied patterning of the nuggets the buggers were too widely saturated to be a natural subsistence. That, coupled with the missing compound requisites obvious to the structural integrity of say; in this instance Gold, I found that wherein those composite metals such as-"

"Grot..."

"What? Oh sorry, you know me and geology... Well, to cut a long story short; I thought the various ore's complex geodes' were set into a coded pattern of some sort, so I –Well, erm..." Holding Dirk by the shoulders he turned the Human about face from where they stood at the waters edge. "See for your self!" he said and stood to the side, with a hopeful look about his bearded chops.

Dirk did look at the expanse of nuggets, and he saw Gold! And lot's of it at that. "Sooo... we take it all?" Dirk ventured, unsure of what his friend intended him to say.

"No."

"It's stuck in the rock or something?" Dirk probed once again.

"Well, obviously!"

"I mean, is it too...,... *Stuck* or... Something...?" Dirk asked and briefly wondered how long it would be before he was taking another swim. Grot's jaw jarring punch had already formed a nasty looking wheal on his chin.

"No, no and NO!" Grot sighed regretfully. What had he expected, he wasn't completely sure himself, for all the love that he had for his friend, he had to admit, Dirk was useless at just about everything, especially his chosen field of magic. "You just don't get it do you?"

"Get what?" Dirk began getting defensive, "All I can see is great lumps of Gold the likes of which I've never seen, just stuck there... In the rock..." he offered, trying to be helpful in the pointing-out-gold-nuggets-in-the-rock department.

"You have to see past the gold!" Grot implored.

"I...,..." Dirk was deeply shocked. In many ways Grot was not your typical Dwarf, but this was gold! *See past the gold?* That was like asking an Orc not to be Ugly, a Halfling not to be hungry, an Elf not to look pretty, or a Minotaur not to take a twenty pound dump. *'What the shit is he on about?'* he privately wondered. "Grot...? Are you sure you're feeling all right, Dwarves can't see past..."

And then Dirk saw it…

His mouth spoke a soundless "WOW!" His face sparkling with the innocence of a newborn, and his whole demeanour suddenly took on that of a sneaky child on Christmas morning, having just caught a glimpse of the gift fairy.

Grot erupted with pleasure at the change in his friends appearance, '*Well, well the dick has a head after all…*' He beamed happily, his eyes vainly seeking contact with Dirk's, whose saucer-like blue eyes were wider than a great Wyrm's arsehole on race day.

"Dya sees it! Yer see it don't you? The gold's in the shape of a buggering bird!" Grot exclaimed delightedly. "Well, obviously not actually buggering but you know me…" he shook his head in wondrous joy for his friend.

"I'll be betting their might be some magic about this cave! Which of course, we haven't got a hope in hell of finding out thanks to your lack of knowledge in your chosen field of expertise. But magical never-the…" Grot noticed that Dirks face hadn't changed. "Are you listening or have you just gone daft, it's just gold coloured rock! It's-Not-Gold… There's absolutely no need to be gawping like a Halfling at a free lunch!"

Grot waved his hand in front of the inept Wiz's face without even causing him to blink. "Dirk mate snap out of it…" He said, shoving his shoulder, but still there was no response. Grot wondered if Dirk had fallen under some spell, or perhaps was merely overwhelmed by the whole occasion.

In all the time they had travelled together, this was probably the first time Dirk had been able to discern the aura of magic without first utilising some magical artefact. Seeing the magical aura was an innate ability that most of Eyrthe's inhabitants were possessed with upon birth, though few knew how to utilise their second sight well enough to see proficiently.

Illusions for example, though known to exist, required more than a little disbelief in the mindset of an individual in order to counter it, as was commonly believed to be the case. In order to see the magic, one had to 'know' about the magic. And, except in cases of pure luck; its learning involved a tediously extreme amount of study and practice to perfect: Two things which were lost on Dirk.

Even after the magical sight had been garnered a true wizard would begin honing his skills and tempering his visual and mental abilities. This may be no mean feat for any other wizard but it was a miraculous leap forward for Dirk, who had never been given much to practice and who approached study with the nonchalant flare of an ignorant child, told to sit and read in silence. As any clever kiddie would do, Dirk started at page one and then flipped to the end. As he figured it; the middle bit: The working out; was something that came with time. As long as you had an idea of what you wanted, i.e. the beginning. Had at least some idea of how to go about achieving it; the end, one could always worry about the middle bit later.

This approach had inexorably led to failure, but Dirk had one thing in common with Grot at least, in that they both steadfastly held to their beliefs, no matter how ill informed. Of course, now that he had indeed seen the ornithological pattern, even though it was some time after the magically retarded Grot, Dirk could look upon his intended magical persuasion with some small hope of betterment. This was no simple picture of a bird…

"Oh Dirk yer little beauty. Yer see it, don't you?" Grot flattered. "Yer know what this means…? You're just speechless aren't you? Tell me you're just speechless, yer dumb shit? Well…? Will yer bloody well nod your head at least…What the!!!"

Grot fell backwards, though took care to avoid the stream below as a flaming bird, swooped on wings of fire from its place on the pattern in the wall, and landed on Dirks now outstretched arm.

"It's not a pattern Stunty," said Dirk giggling into life like a schoolgirl on steroids, "It's a Phoenix! It…" Dirks voice trailed off, as he fell into uncontrollable fits of chortling delight.

The Phoenix's flames poured over Dirk, but this only served to make him laugh even more so. He was bathed in the flames of the Phoenix and was not burning. His right arm was stretched out like he had seen the falconers do in the castle near to where he was born, and the Phoenix, which weighed very little, yet stood as large as an eagle, was contentedly preening its fiery plumage.

"Oh Grot, what an average day…" he wittily managed to utter before once again collapsing into bursts of prolonged laughter. The laughter was infectious and once Grot had gotten over the shock of it he too was chuckling along with Dirk.

After several minutes of hysterical laughter, his sides hurting so much that he thought they might split, Grot got to his feet and wiped the tears of both joy and pain from his eyes. The Phoenix flames had touched him too, but unlike Dirk he had felt pain. He looked to his right hand as he held it aloft and saw the cause of his painful brush with the bird. His right pinkie had been completely incinerated. '*There's one body part I won't be seeing again.*' Thought the Dwarf as he bandaged his pain numbed wound the best he could while sniggering.

Dirk let fly the hawk, so to speak. Imitating the falconers whom he had so adored watching as a child and the legendary bird flew up, away and back again as Dirks tuneless whistles dictated.

Grot forgot about his lost finger and swollen pride took over once more as he watched his friend playfully frolic with the Phoenix. He felt like a satisfied father on sports day. Gone was the haunted look of paranoia that usually lay heavily upon the lanky human's stooped shoulders. Dirk was stood straight and proud; fearless for the moment and with good reason Grot contemplated as he moved a good twenty metres or so away.

Although taking care to jump the stream where it narrowed, he never *even flinched* as he sloshed into a puddle; all-the-better to wet him self against the heat of the Phoenix's unforgiving flame...

His over-exuberance calming somewhat Dirk smiled at Grot wildly, "tell me the story of the phoenix again Grot, please..."

The dwarf settled himself down on the riverbank opposite and tore into a strip of jerky. "It was many years ago lad, my memory-"

"Your memory is as sharp as those axes ya carry!" Dirk quickly countered, "Please, tell me?" He repeated as he sent the bird soaring anew.

"Some two hundred year back I'd travelled with and fought beside a group of Novula monks and come to know all about the legend of that thing." He said pointing to the golden fire swooping through the sky.

"Back then," he continued, "the Novula were one of those mysterious ancient sects one always heard about yet never encountered. Then again I was well travelled... Well we met up with the monks after tracking an unscrupulous bandit for over seven hundred leagues. The bandit in question had stolen 'Keldor's Gift'; an extremely important ancient Dwarven artefact, and during the chase our posse of over forty hardened Dwarven troupe had dwindled to one; me, always the bloody survivor, never the hero."

"The bandit turned out to be not only an excellent assassin but also had quite a few murderous colleagues only too willing to misinform, entrap, and betray us questing Dwarves. We followed his trail to the reigning Novulan kingdom of Phoenicia, where the monks agreed to help out after one of their own priceless pieces also went missing from a temple along the thief's path. They hailed from the heights of Phoenicia, a remote mountainous region populated by the rare and mighty Phoenix, mind you back then they were a bit bigger, and a hell of a lot more scary.

These monks though, through both racial and clerical edicts claimed the Phoenix to be a holy cleanser of souls and those of their order as well as those converts that dwelt in the high mountain Phoenician settlements had to live their lives good and true, according to Novulan law; less they fail in their official ordainment that all citizens strove towards.

"Huh? What do ya mean ordainment?" Dirk for all he had asked for the tale was only half listening...

Grot laughed out loud, "Well put it this way, you or I wouldn't have wanted to live there... The ordainment was like saying yer at one with the gods and everyone from that society strove to be selected for the ordination, and I do mean everyone, man-woman-and child; in practice it involved holding a Phoenix in much the same way as yer doing now. If the bird deemed the acolyte in question to be virtuous beyond doubt; he would survive and the Phoenix would perform him some great service. If however, the chosen member were deemed to be imperfect in any way; his body would be seared from the Eyrthe's existence; and his blank soul spat back into the abyss.

Dirk choked mid laugh, "Could I...?"

This time it was Grots turn to laugh, "If it had wanted to burn yer, ya wouldn't still be here..."

"Oh right, sorry I just- well what happened then? Did you ever see one of these ceremonies?" Dirk enquired his attention finally caught.

Grot finished his Jerky and continued as the suns rays did their utmost to drive away the previous night's downpour... "Nah! Never actually saw a ceremony but, well, one of them brother Maynard I believe his name was, used to remonstrate long into the night about the decline of his civilization. Ya see, although they were a fairly polite and virtuous bunch, both the amount of novices taking religious vows and the number of believers attending their congregations had understandably dwindled throughout the years…"

Dirk asked the obligatory 'why'.

"Well how many people dya think are pure and virtuous? Not that I actually thought that had anything to do with so many of them being burned alive; methinks that was more a case of a pissed of wild animal getting it's own back for being caged up; revered or bloody well not. Still, the people had to live life in as virtuous way that they could even if they didn't really expect to survive the ordination, so it's understandable that as various kingdoms borders expanded to the limits of their own, the Phoenician populace began mixing more than ever with their social cousins and as with the crossing over of the visiting foreigners' culture, so too did the knowledge of evermore forgiving faiths to follow. So I can appreciate why the sect's number had dwindled and why the Phoenician populace, upon hearing of other less radical theological practices, decided to turn tail en-mass, especially after I'd witnessed an attempted self ordainment first hand…"

"But I thought ya said you never witnessed one?" Dirk pressed.

Grot grinned as he paddled his toes in a murky inch deep puddle left over from the previous night's rain, remembering the happy smiling face of Habukasan, who had been the youngest of the Novulan monks he'd met. "Well, not the ceremony and all that, not a proper one… But there was this one monk; a tiny little fellah but a little more open and amiable than the others. He was an amusing little prick and prone to telling the most awful jokes but I felt a bit sorry for him… The other monks all found his antics to be less than amusing and would often make hurtful jibes as to his suitability or lack thereof to the mantle of Novulan monk."

"Habukasan had ended up being the one still smiling however after they had encountered a beast such as the one upon you now. By this time, I was the only Dwarf left alive and we were getting close to the thieves lair, which was situated right on the highest peak in the district – course I was younger then so I didn't mind the climb but the monks with their frocks well… Anyhow, half way up it's craggy face, one of the monks spots a Phoenix nesting on a rather deadly looking ledge and after a quick vote, they had unanimously agreed to climb the several hundred feet or so up a vertical cliff face in order to gain access to the nest and thereby confront their theological decider of fates, yeah? Oh hold on I gotta take a leak."

Shaking his dick dry Grot continued… "Well I'd decided to leave them to it, figuring that any bird, mystical or otherwise would be more than a little pissed off at having a bunch of strangers come tramping into its nest uninvited. Besides which I knew back then I was definitely no saint so anyway off they went. The climb took a few hours going up and a whole lot shorter time getting down…"

"What happened?" Dirk queried as he examined his own Phoenix's fascinating flight patterns.

Grot snorted in laughter at the memory. "Well I think they must have disturbed a mating pair or something, 'cause those so called pure monks that weren't instantly fried by their bloody revered Phoenix found their lives shortened by the distance it took to reach ground zero. Habukasan survived thanks to his holding onto the beast's talons and letting go as it swept down a mere twenty feet or so above me self.

"Oh so he was pure then…?"

"…As a diamond, annoying, childish and stupid maybe, but pure as…"

"So what did the Phoenix do? Did it attack you?" Dirk panicked.

"Nah I think it had more sense! As soon as he dropped or it dropped him – not completely sure which way around it happened – but once it did, I caught him and it flew up and away to Keldor knows where before swooping back down and landing on Habukasan's shoulders. Course he didn't burn, I figured this bird's interest had been peaked by the cheek of the kid and it sought out Habukasan after the others had been dealt with, coming to play with the bird just as yer doing now yer self! Afterwards, he left behind his monkish habits and went on to become one of the best aniseed sweet salesmen this side of the Phoenician divide. After being vindicated by the Phoenix he had come to the end of his faiths conclusion and felt free to follow his lifelong dream job as a manufacturer and purveyor of fine home made Liquorice and Aniseed based chewable products…"

"Piss off!" Dirk interceded… "Like ya would wanna sell sweets after something like this…"

Grot shook his head, as much at Dirk's comment as at his own selfishness. He wished he had been a little more diligent throughout the years, for although the majestic sight of Dirk playing with the Phoenix made his heart leap about with joy in celebration for his pal, he could not help curtail a jealous pang of sinful proportions. As much as hated to admit it, the fact was that he as himself was a thousand times purer than Dirk yet could never frolic in the same manner as Dirk, because of one small truth, and that was that for all Dirk's faults, he was only being himself and that self *could* have limitless power.

"Oh! I'll be a Goblins footrest. If you haven't gone and made me proud," Grot announced in order to clean his mind, "didn't I always say you weren't *completely* useless? Now If only you had a spell-book..."

"I feel good today Grot." Chirped Dirk confidently, holding his arm out in front of him and examining the Phoenix's strange fluorescent plumage close up.

"Better be putting it back then and we can be off eh?" Grot said sobering up somewhat, he liked the beautiful bird true; but he was not about to forget its threat so easily, his four digited hand would not let him.

"What! How...?" Dirk asked unsure if he even wanted to release it.

"That's up to you I suppose, being a magic user and all." Said Grot and stumped over to where the stream emerged to get some fresh water.

Dirk paused, unsure of what to do, he felt the need to say something or perhaps gesticulate, but he had no idea what. Talk to the Bird! He thought and mumbled a half embarrassed request.

Nothing...

He thought again of the falconers that he had seen out hunting, as they used to practice sending their war-birds into battle. *Maybe...*

Holding his arm out straight and twisting at the waist slightly, Dirk brought his upper torso around in an arc of sorts, and threw his fore-arm forcefully towards the cave wall.

The Phoenix leapt majestically from its perch on his arm and straight at the pattern of gold etched upon the warm caves wall, Dirk was about to shout a warning at the doomed bird when a shower of sparks preceded the walls disappearance and the birds continued flight, itself casting the solely available light in a long dark tunnel of truly epic proportions, where moments before there had been only solid rock.

Grot farted as his arse went slack at the bird's unexpected approach, as usual Dirk had not thought to giving a warning before attempting his latest hair-brained scheme, the Phoenix's wingtips missing the afeared Dwarf by mere inches and singeing his already worn clothes.

Dirk walked over in a daze to stand by his flabbergasted friend, and their exchanged glance explained what Dirk was thinking... *He hadn't wished for that!* Both were too stunned to speak as the Phoenix flew on down the tunnel, rapidly shrinking to a distant speck of flame.

They stood there for a good twenty minutes or more before Grot realised that he wasn't standing in the stream after all, despite his pant legs being quite wet. "You and yer tit-ridden ideas! Look at me bloody finger! Or not! Can you see it? Eh? 'Cause I bloody well can't! I was stood there... *Bloody well right there...!* Keldor's name be done!"

"I... Didn't mean to..." Dirk stammered back, he really did not fancy another pasting from his hot-tempered friend.

Grot was about to punch him, when he noticed the bruising on Dirk's face and he fought to control his rising temper. "Just... Stay away from... Everything... Go and get your stuff!"

Dirk acquiesced and the two went numbly about their business. Grot was not too happy about having to wash the piss out of his pants in the stream and his curses and oaths were the only sound made by the two companions as they went about things. Moreover he had found to his displeasure that the unnatural heat had dissipated from the caves rock and he realised he would have no choice but to hang his flaxen pants on the branch of a tree and wander around bare-arsed naked all day long.

After sorting his clothing, Grot then prepared the Mooly bean in a thick broth, mixing it with the various fruits he had earlier foraged as well as a three legged rabbit, caught by a timely stamp from Grot while he was finding a suitable branch on which to hang his saturated clothes. By the time it took him to overcook the Mooly bean (he always erred on the side of safety) his pants had dried in their spot in the regenerated sun. Donning his flaxen trews, he scooped up the stew, which had by now solidified somewhat, and packed it into bundles of edible Doc leaves, which he then packed away in his satchel.

Dirk meanwhile busied himself with his own soiled underwear, which he had fouled upon the Phoenix's sudden appearance and tried not to do anything else that may appear the least bit stupid in the eyes of his judgemental Dwarven buddy.

When they were finally ready to depart for pastures new, a shared glance was all the communication needed to agree to the next course of action. The mismatched companions; a brave, battle hardened warrior and a confused, rather weakly skilled wizard both held to a common adventurous spirit and the tunnels appearance had aroused their collective curiosity.

Sure it was going to be dark in there and they were both aware of a more than slim chance of encountering danger in some form or other. But given that they were clueless as to their current position on any given map; coupled with a deep desire to avoid any more chance encounters with the denizens of the forest, one could appreciate why they both silently opted to follow the unknown passage before them.

Dirk had thought of little else as he had observed the Dwarf pottering about naked. Perhaps it was the Dwarves bear-assed representation of a dank, scary, unexplored tunnel that made Dirk consider its inviting silence over the squawk's and growl's of the not far enough off forestry about them. Or maybe it was the fact that the trusted Holy Phoenix had shown the way... Then again, it could be the newfound spring in his step. His newfound zest for living... Whatever the reason, Dirk was determined on his course.

As for Grot, he had come to the decision that the only sure way to escape the forest's clutches would be to either follow the river or the yawning chasm of the magically revealed path; and he had no intention of remaining any closer to water than necessary. The tunnel appeared to be dry for at least some hundred yards or so and that was good enough for him. Besides, he would welcome a bit of darkness; it might help take Dirk's eyes off his arse.

Hoisting their gear onto tired shoulders, they set forth into the humungous circular breach; unaware of what troubles, if any; may lie ahead.

Behind them the clinging flora sang to the sun, thankful for its rescuing light. The fell creatures that dwelt within its copious foliage sank into their homes, shunning the light, awaiting the crispness of night once more. A Butterfly fluttered by, chased by a curious Humming bird. Sticklebacks skipped and darted in the stream, hunted by a determined Dragonfly. A proud looking Stag with resplendent horns stopped to drink by the stream where Dirk had washed mere moments ago, before skipping across to sniff at the curious new tunnel opening.

A white spectral figure which seemed to fade in and out of existence as it drifted over the stream continued unerringly towards the tunnel; its monstrous features too vague to fully cipher save to say it was humanoid. The spectres soothing surge showed no change of gait; nor did it speak as it slipped past the male deer in silence, without pausing to touch or interact with it in any way, and on into the tunnel…

Still the inquisitive Stag's knees had buckled and its proud head sank, though it did not fall, for even as it noticed the foul looking cretin; even as its mind began to formulate whether to charge the newcomer or flee, its soul had already began to depart, leaving a deadened shell to formulate the intricacies of survival by itself…, …Behind the mortified deer, the flora peeled back like dead skin revealing blackened earth, the water grew stagnant killing the fish, and all manner of birds and insects dropped from their intended flight.

As the glowing spectre descended into the darkness, the wall that had previously hidden the passage once again rebuilt itself, compressing the death-frozen dear and melding with it in a most peculiar fashion to any who may view it from without.

A Soul Leech had happened by, and in its wake not a living thing remained…

v)   **An Unfriendly Reunion**

Galbor paced the dread looking study in which he spent most of his time. He was vexed and considerably so; the scorch marks that covered the table attested to the fact and the pain-maddened Demon bound thereon the said table, emphasised just a little, the depth of his vexation.

The study was quite large and circular, in keeping with the rest of his tower, yet far more spacious than the cramped rooms above, its own horizons expanded by means both magical and menial alike. He had lived in this tower on and off for several thousand years, and this room, built underneath the actual tower itself was his favourite place in *all* the realms.

Hundreds of Grimoires, bound with the skins of his former victims, lined the embrace of the dark walnut bookshelves that adorned every section of outer wall. The shelves ran in a continuous palisade covering every inch from floor to ceiling with books. So, so many books, of each and every description, but the ones that held magic could easily be told apart from their non-magical counterparts.

Each darkly bound volume was seated in its relevant place amidst the veritable library, held by a connected link of silver chains. Magical energy periodically washed over a tome or two and the power that lay within would then spill out from the pages, sending purple sparks leaping from tome to tome around the room, fluttering random pages before petering out.

Here was without doubt, one of the most impressive collections of mystical incantations and ritualistic summoning collections ever composed, but this was not the reason Galbor loved this chamber above any other place on Eyrthe, Heaven or Hell...

So was it perhaps the varied equipment scattered around the centre of the chamber? Whose monstrous presence, lent the otherwise welcoming living area a ghastly air of suspense. Covering quite a few square-feet of central floor space, lay a fantastic array of torture devices, each specifically designed to inflict incomprehensible amounts of pain upon a subject, whilst keeping the captive alive.

For each piece, Galbor had paid a commission to the most feared and infamous masters of inquisition of their time, going back over several thousand years. Each time he offered the same deal and on each occasion the man accepted without hesitation. It was always a man; for some reason the male of the species always seemed capable of more malicious endeavours than their female counterparts, despite their race of origin.

Each piece was crafted for an extortionate amount of money –cash readily offered without need for barter; on the sole agreement that the torturer put his heart and soul into their preferred apparatus's design. Of course they agreed, without ever considering that the Great Galbor meant it quite literally and thus each rather impressive piece of malicious design, worked with the relentless vengeance of the device's possessing designer, or rather his unwitting soul, whose life fabric was also melded into the piece.

Several of the devices were currently occupied, though many others lay stark, though kept in a state of good repair, their open embrace eagerly awaiting their next captive, irregardless of race, colour, or creed. What was evident of the torture devices presently in use was that they were purpose built for those currently incarcerated within...

There was the Unicorn; its fabled horn now pale and dim, who used to inhabit the glade above; it was locked into a treadmill that rotated continuously causing it to ceaselessly walk in a most monotonous fashion. About the miserable creature, various flogging devices flagged to attention, and struck home with raking blows, should the mystical beasts stride change but the slightest touch.

Next was the Arch Magician Kalamere Majuro, he was a golden wizard from an age some 5000+ years ago, birthed from a union of a human and an Ogre-magi, he was one of the worlds greatest ever ambassadors for light and law and all that is good and true. Thanks to Galbor, none of Eyrthe's history records hold any accounts of neither this man nor the council that he headed. Indeed, most libraries in existence do not even lay down *any* accounts of the eventful era to which the fellow was birthed, again due to Galbor's meddling.

Kalamere's was an era where the fates of entire continents and all those individuals that lived upon them, were decided by thirteen men of magic whose collective power was so extreme; they alone presided over the very elements of existence, in contention with the ancient Dragons themselves. Yet *he* was being held in a state of suspension within what appeared to be a rather large opaque glass ball measuring about seven feet in diameter.

On another largely iron construct sat another incarcerated soul. This device called the 'Porcupine' comprised of a hump of metal spikes that flexed continuously; each time the spikes flexed, ripples of red energy were sent coursing through its occupant. The unlucky inhabitant, who was ghostlike in appearance, went by the name of Shae-Anrra, and though she was one of many souls Galbor had condemned to his keeping, she also remained his greatest treasure… The first daughter of the original king of the Faeries was quite a catch, even for one such as him: Her soul was purer than sunlight and he enjoyed watching it dim day by day, year by year, aeon upon countless aeon. And as her own life force was gradually bleached from her thanks to the entrapping apparatus, its restorative benefits were added to Galbor's own.

The final occupant was tied-up and naked; her open legs and arms spread wide, against a blood stained metallic wall, which seemed to somehow attract the pin like daggers that bedecked the fiend's contorted yet beautiful hairless body. Nothing about this wretched creature was special as far as Galbor was concerned though many of her past consorts would privately disagree…

Her body was flushed with a peculiar pinkness and was nubile to say the least. Human-like in form, she had a fiendishly swishing tail that played about constantly – even in pain. Her long tresses of reddish-brown hair twirled coyly about her exposed torso, erect nipples peeping out from behind silky tresses and cute little horns emerging from her perfectly smooth forehead. Her physical features were sublimely fashioned, but her most impressive feature of all was her sexy, mischievous grin and that at the moment was nowhere to be seen as dagger after dagger pierced her delicate looking flesh.

She was a Daemonic underling that had wished to gain influence by impressing Galbor with a suitably challenging puzzle, though by now she was already regretting it. And it was for this reason that Galbor loved this multi-purpose chamber, which also had room for various summoning circles, several dimensional vortex prisons, a rack of aforementioned souls and various other accoutrements whose actual usage could only be guessed at by all but Galbor himself. *Puzzles* of all types lay within the room. There were various conundrums woven into the curtains that hung from the corners of the ceiling, whose beautifully inlaid surface contained yet more enigmas' hidden within the complex murals and rippling architecture. These puzzles took on many shapes and forms indeed, some intertwined into other purposes.

For instance, if one should follow the eyes of the many painted Adonis's that occupied the space in certain corners of the room; in truth living prisons for those vain creatures whose image they had allowed to be captured in artwork. If one followed their gaze, a formerly invisible book on charms would be revealed.

Even the mosaic floor had various brainteasers hidden within its infrastructure, comprising several levels of deviousness; from the simple positioning of the feet upon its inlaid features, to matching the compound elements to their appropriate counterparts. Yes, everything in this room bore the possibilities of a hidden conundrum, from the positioning of the chairs and other items of furniture, to the placement of key items that literally held the key to numerous hidden dimensional portals weaving throughout the room.

Galbor loved solving puzzles and the more difficult the riddle the better, the more devious and devilish, the more he enjoyed rising to the challenge, yet he himself gained the greatest pleasure in defeating an opponent with something implicitly simple. Take his name for instance; 'Galbor', he hated calling himself Galbor, for it was not his real name, and secretly he hated the self imposed pseudonym.

Oh, how he wished he could sing his real name out aloud in the valleys of men, but such was the curse of his race that their true names could never be spoken, for therein lay secrets that conveyed power and mastery over themselves and associated others. If one knew the true name of a being such as him, one could with sufficient power, commandeer their services and force them into undertakings against their will or control.

Yes, his 'chosen' name did grate on him, but it also delighted him at the same time, for it was an anagram of the name given to his race; the much feared and mighty Balrog.

Balrog was the name given to a Daemon Prince of indefatigable power, and he was a Prince over many such Balrogs and their associated cretins. In all the realms of Hell and Eyrthe only five other beings were higher than him in the chain of Daemonic command, and his eyes were firmly fixed on the number one slot.

'To be number one... Aah! To gain the illustrious title of Dread Lord...' There were many reasons to covet the designation, but none so much as being freed of the power of names. The Dread Lord had no fear of revealing one's name if one so desired.

Some past rulers simply kept with the officially known title while others, such as Loki, Beelzebub and Khan had made sure as many witless fools both knew and regretted knowing it as was possible.

There was good enough reason for revealing ones name as Dread Lord, though there were always associated risks. Being Dread Lord was an easy ride in itself; a diplomatic leader might stay at the top by avoiding confrontation and acceding to certain demands, thus securing nominal power for Aeons.

Other past devils in disguise had gone relatively unnoticed in their secretive reigns, being content to tend to the tasks of running Hell, whilst keeping a low profile and avoiding minimal contact with one's peers. This tactic was eagerly adapted to by many past rulers who merely wished to survive the ordination for as long as it was imaginably possible, before being forcibly removed in some inventive fashion, by a more resourceful and infinitely less forgiving Daemon.

Revealing ones real name held big risks for the reigning Dread Lord, for he could be more readily summoned than any other Daemon, Human or other half-breed out there. The ease with which someone could summon the lord of Demons was laughable in comparison to his subjects, for unlike them even the knowledge of magic was unnecessary provided one knew the true name of the Dread Lord; thus he could be easily summoned by any fool simple enough to mutter his name aloud three times in a row.

This potential summoning left one open to traps both subtle and brutish alike, but the office of Hell belayed the power to hold sway over an audience or to grant wishes in exchange for ones soul. Therefore any future Dread Lord Daemon would have to consider whether or not it felt truly strong or clever enough to avoid being trapped and/or murdered by its enemies, before making the decision to reveal its true name.

'*I would not give it a second thought...*' Thought Galbor, '*If I became Dread Lord, all would know my true name... And fear it!*' He harboured his singeing desire for the role in a most secretive fashion. In fact not many Demons would willingly make public their name, no matter what office they held, but Galbor was no run-of-the-mill Daemon. Galbor was a living leech, absolutely consumed with the concept of power and his megalomania ways led him to entering into many a bargain, in order to capture the souls of others; and his aim if he were to be elected to the throne would be to attract those willing to sign away their souls. For souls contained unique experiences and personal knowledge, and in knowledge lay great power.

Yes the risks were great, but the rewards on offer far outweighed the perceived danger to one's survival. For with enough knowledge, one such as he could challenge those that perceived themselves to be *his* master. Those that deemed themselves so called *Gods!*

A unique example of one such daring individual was Khan: A brutally savage Daemon whose vociferous rise from underling to Dread Lord was one that started out on the path of secrecy and deceit but soon devolved into an explosion of slaughter. His passage to ascension permanently etched itself upon Daemonic histoire in a wholly unsympathetic and homicidal fashion, unsurpassed even to this day. Not surprising then that he went on to become the God of Murderers, Assassins, and Spies the Eyrthe over, as well as the revered demi-god of a whole race of Lizardmen.

With enough amassed power one could challenge for godhood –the right to rule the minds of both men and beast. To become a deity, to be held in fearful reverence, to stand amongst the gods as their equal ...or better, was what Galbor desired above and beyond anything else, but he absolutely adored puzzles. *Perhaps the two were inter-connected somehow*, he deliberated as he picked up a silvery dagger and flipped it end over end in contemplation.

Ever since he had first been born to the twice removed second cousin's sister's brother-in-laws, grandson's wives second daughter's lover of the original Dread Lord, he had believed that he too would one day earn the title. He had murdered, tortured, grassed on, begged, cheated, stolen, manipulated, betrayed, supported, harassed, raped, abused, imprisoned and generally out witted every single creature he had come across in order to gain the illustrious title. This included having to murder his entire family bar *one*, plus any other ill-fated being unlucky enough to know him, or have the potential of knowing his true name. He was not quite ready to rid himself of that last annoyance, for Kalamere's blighted existence brightened his malicious mood.

His conniving nature had led to his genuine love of riddles and he enjoyed the mental stimulation they conveyed. *'But this one is far too annoying. It could be almost anything...'* He reflected.

"Oh Well..." he considered aloud, "You can't make a Draconian omelette without breaking a few Dragon eggs, can you Gweonju?"

Galbor venomously threw another dagger over his shoulder, vaguely in the vicinity of the wall that held the Daemonic underling. Altering course in mid flight, the dagger greedily sped towards its intended target striking her fully in the throat. "Massssssshter!" she hissed, lowering her head as was proper despite the pain rampaging through her body, "Howh mhay this unworthy ssshlave sssherve your mosssht enlightened onne?"

Galbor casually flicked one of the silvery daggers towards Gweonju, striking the creatures left knee and rupturing the cartilage within before 'sticking' to the wall of metallic looking stone on which she was spread out. "You can *start* by speaking in a normal manner." Galbor stated without any sign of sympathy or emotion.

"Butt this isssh …" She began then hastily abandoned her previously suspect impression as Galbor readied yet another dagger, "Pardon my speech, oh great master hunter…" Quickly she groped for an appropriately believable excuse, gulping down her fear past the blade buried deep within her throat.

"The dagger struck my vocal chords my lord; I was struggling to speak… I," she quickly stopped herself mid excuse at Galbor's disapproving stare, "How may this one serve you great master?" The feminine fiend finished in what it thought to be a suitably grovelling tone.

If she had hoped to avoid another dagger, her hopes were quickly dashed, for no sooner had she uttered her reply, than two struck almost at once, the first piercing her eye socket and entering her brain, the other finding her proposed vocal chord like the proverbial Bulls-eye.

Fortunately, or rather unfortunately for her then was that these daggers were not magical – at least not in the manner that she understood, for Daemons may only be 'slain' by a magical weapon, and in death she would at least gain a temporary release from Galbor's painful vexation. Although the pain in her head, throat, and torso was immense, after a few mere seconds she managed to regain her senses, though she played possum for a good while longer.

Galbor walked over to the pretty little Daemoness and withdrew the double slivers from her throat, gently breathing on the ruptured oesophagus in the blades passing. Galbor's breath frosted then regenerated the ruptured flesh of her throat, both soothing her and healing the wound in its entirety.

Next he kissed her shoulder whilst removing the vicious blade lodged there and again she was both calmed and restored. His hand pressed hotly against her breast and he massaged it, gently suckling on her nipple for a moment and rubbing his knee up against her moistening crotch. "I'm afraid that I go too far sometimes. Forgive me…?"

The Daemoness's stiffened poise visibly melted and she pouted seductively, even though she was still held in place, "There is nothing to forgive my most merciful lord..." She pursed her lips forward to nuzzle against the grey wrinkled skin of his neck.

"Good," he responded smiling and nibbled her ear delicately, whispering softly to her and sending a surge of electricity coursing throughout her most sensitive nerve endings.

"Oh beloved master, please let us forget this silly teaser," She shifted her weight and gasped as his free roaming hand groped hungrily at the soft voluptuous folds of flesh, hiding her most precious jewel, "I can pleasure you in ways unimaginable..."

Galbor giggled naughtily into her ear, "I bet you can you naughty Nymph..." She screamed out in painful shock as his nibbling teeth tore away her ear from her skull and his claw-like fingers yanked down on the folds of her vagina without remorse. "...And *I* can torture *you* in ways that are all too conceivable indeed."

"Now listen to me slut. You shall recant this vexing little riddle of yours once more, and I expect every inflection to be identical to your previous telling or you shall feel what it is like to really incur my wrath."

Gweonju choked down her rising sobs of agony and begged him to stop, her powers of charm had failed in most spectacular fashion, and she feared his further ministrations may damage her forever...

Slave mistress of the nine hells she may be, but she was a Jezebel of the highest repute, and had designs on gaining an even better position very soon. Her skills in the art of sexual gratification had satisfied her 'punters' as she liked to consider them, equally well on both Hell and Eyrthe. So it was no surprise her confidence had been somewhat dented by Galbor's rebuttal. With equal suddenness the wizened wizard before her ceased his torturous afflictions and sighed, looking once more the very air of nicety.

As a Daemonic Jezebel, Gweonju's voracious sexual appetite could not be sated and she often visited with and satisfied those beings that exhibited the most debase sexual appetites. And such was her expertise in the sexual arts that she had gained the eye of quite a few Daemon lords of varying differentials of power and repute.

She had first considered whether she might not simply be able to seduce the mighty Galbor as she had so many others, only moments prior to his securing her to this contraption. But that slight back step did not dissuade her and once more she had flexed her charms, only to be littered with the first wave of the annoying 'smart' daggers

'I was a fool to come here... What am I thinking? Nobody has ever got the better of Uncle Galbor, let alone managed to seduce him, if only the gods knew what he was up to...'

"Did you say something my dear?" The once again pleasant Galbor enquired. He held her frightened gaze as he continued to remove the various daggers still plugging holes in her damaged flesh. "Be aware my dear niece, I am not one of your weak willed sops... I have enjoyed the challenge of your riddle, but **do not** take me for some *lusting lord?*"

"Never my lord, never!" she sobbed pathetically. It was due to a meeting with one of these previously seduced lords, that she found herself in her current predicament. The lord in question was in fact one of the Gar'h'ul-Qoua; a Demonic hybrid whose every appendage came in six's, that the snake-people and other cannibalistic societies oft times worship.

During one rather lengthy and somewhat depraved orgy, he had boasted about his designs to rule over three more realms. She listened attentively while he empowered her with his imparted knowledge, told all the more willingly thanks to her arduous attentions. While being flogged by her as was his wont, he had bragged of an ingenious riddle that he'd recently invented. He informed her of his plans to present the challenge to the great Prince Galbor and in doing so, gain assistance in his exploits.

Gweonju had been quick to lash him even harder, pausing to deliver a raking swipe across two of his many faces with her perfectly manicured hands, "A masterful expert such as yourself should have no problem puzzling one so arrogant as Galbor," she had said, gently caressing his vanity with her words, while scraping the skin of his sinful flesh with her purposefully sharpened nails.

"Galbor will find this riddle as difficult to solve as it surely was for every other being you have posed it to. Of this I am sure..." She soothed with calculated disdain, changing her scratches to tantalizing strokes.

Of course the Demon hadn't told any other the riddle, he was too careful for that, but the male ego was as easy to massage in Demons as it was in men. His unsure admittance that he had in fact told no other was all the ammunition she had needed.

"But if the puzzle is so easily solved by just any old creature, what interest will it be to Galbor? He only likes difficult puzzles, the absolute peak of peculiarity. The most convex, complex, distracting confusion of conundrums is every day life to him; his interest can only be gained by a web of truly tantalizing intrigue."

"But this *is*!" The eager Demon had enthused.

"You think so…. And I am sure you are correct, however, I would give it *very* careful consideration before you approach him with it; for all you know it could be so simple that any fool may solve it…" Her large loving eyes flashed concern, "Not that I am saying you are a fool yourself."

The Daemon lord had been riled, so much so, he had even threatened to dislodge her from his lap, but she had soothed his protests with a soft rippling burst of her hips.

"Sweet master of sacrifice, I am not claiming for a single moment that a common slave-wench such as I could possibly overcome your little riddle, I am just concerned that others more devious than I might." she had stated innocently. "Besides, Galbor spends so much time in the world of men, who knows if he still has control over his faculties…? I hear he grows soft these days…"

"Really now, from who, do tell? Who have you been talking to?"

She silenced him by pushing him down and sitting on his most upward face. His nostrils were engulfed by her intoxicating womanly scent and he forgot his cares for a while, being content to lap up her juices with one of his many tongues. After several minutes and just as he was beginning to really enjoy her suffocating aroma, she readjusted her position and planted herself down hard onto several lengths of his thick jagged penis.

She vigorously straddled his manhood even though it caused her much pain to do so, and rode him until he could almost hold out no longer, then withdrew leaving him breathless. "I am sure you are right to be confident. If you conjure riddles with as much skill as you make love, I am sure you will be fine, my little pussy parson.

Contained within the statement lay the seeds of doubt for he knew his love making efforts were probably a good deal below par. Her gentle swipe at the previously confident ego had dissuaded him a little from his self-assured course and she purposely made her body heat drop a few degrees, discreetly furthering her consort's discomfort.

After the insinuation of failure, he had been almost too eager to prove his riddle worthy; repeating it to her so many times over she could remember it off by heart. She took care to notice every inflection he had used, in case that was where the riddles answer lay. After guessing several times, all of which answers were incorrect, he quietened her fuss and she pretended to forget all about it, instead nuzzling him in erotic fashion before performing six mind-blowing oral sex acts. Gweonju, guessed one of her answers must have been pretty close though, for he had said later, when she had tried one more guess, that he was sure the answer lay within her.

Then, three hours later, Eyrthe time, she had come to Galbor with the riddle, claiming it to be her own and challenged him in order to gain his favour for herself. Only now she wished she had not bothered. *'I just hope all the pain was worth it...'*

Gweonju scrutinised Galbor, looking for some sign of his intent, but was unable to fathom this most deviant of her kind. She took a deep breath and fervently hoped he would guess it right this time... *'Whatever happens, I can not take another year of this...'*

"My Lord, forgive my annoyance..." She said, once again addressing Galbor, three years had been a long time to be skewered in this manner.

"The riddle is this:

I am found in men and beasts,

I cover various pockets of the **world**,

You *may* find me in bottles to *drink*,

I am *within* the many planes of hell,

Sometimes residing in *one*,

My *place in the mind* is often possessed,

In churches and temples I'm *never* forgotten.

What am I?"

Galbor snapped his fingers and the Jezebel fell to the cold floor. For the first time in years she was free to move under her own volition and she fastened onto a glimmer of hope that this time, he had indeed solved it.

Galbor moved to speak then stopped and Gweonju pushed herself up onto stiff, forgetful feet, attempting to grasp his attention.

"Hmmm," Galbor conceded after what seemed an eternity, "You've got me. You-really-have-got-me! I can't believe it, but, that is damned good! For that I think I shall turn up the heat on all my guests. You really are marvellous you know. Even for a Jezebel. My, my, that is superb!"

Gweonju was pleased. She physically felt the waves of tension pass from her body as Galbor's praise washed over her. These past three years of torture had been worth it after all. Now, finally, she would receive her reward. "Master, I –don't know what to say. I, well..."

"Well precisely... So what is it?" Galbor ventured. "You know? The answer," Gweonju shot a sudden look of distress. "You must tell me the answer of course or it shall simply drive me insane!"

"I... don'... " she started, her mind racing in panic, Gweonju's tension came racing back through her limbs a thousand-fold and she found that her tongue felt sluggish and heavy. What to say, what to say, she had not catered for this but of course! She should have known he would expect her to tell him the answer or at least confirm his suspicions, it stood to reason, she just hadn't ... expected it.

Considering he had yet to give her an actual guess, it was understandable for her to be caught off guard, but even as she formulated a believable tale, she knew that 'Lies' had the uncanny knack of revealing themselves within Galbor's imposing presence.

Briefly she considered delivering her half-concocted answer, but felt sure Galbor would cross question any answer she may give him, probing away until her fabric of lies unravelled in full. Instead she did that most un-Daemon of practices and opted to offer the truth, or at least a half truth... "I've ... forgotten." She finished rather too weakly.

"Forgotten, FORGOTTEN!" the sudden change in tone was brought about by a similar change of appearance in Galbor's manifestation..., ... Where a rather meek bald headed man had stood moments before, a similarly bald Balrog standing just over thirty feet in height now towered above her.

In his true form, Galbor was a truly petrifying sight, even for a Demon to behold and few saw him in it, less recognition led to knowledge… His entire body was a mixture of beast and fire. Thick streams of red hot magma writhed in unending fashion across the span of the creature's torso and limbs. The limbs themselves sprouted forth sparse patches of wiry hair and (where no magma currently ran), over a dark blue leathery looking, cracked epidermis. Most Balrogs had dark red or blackened skin, but Galbor was an exception to many rules… Wings of flesh and flame, that nevertheless maintained a bat like quality, sprouted from behind the creature sending up thick noxious plumes of black sulphurous smoke every time he flexed his wingspan.

Covering Galbor's face, neck and shoulders were fierce red tufts of hair that seemed to be on fire, as loose tendrils of flame licked and rolled the length of his patchy mane. His face was a terror unto itself, huge misshapen teeth jutted threateningly from his mouth, and piggy little yellow eyes glowed from beneath his huge swollen forehead, which was topped by the most comical of bald spots; spoiling the look somewhat.

"…You vile offspring of an Offal fiend! Slave whore of infidels and mortals! You dare waste my time with an unsolvable mystery…! Do you think I have had nothing better with which to possess my every waking thought these three years last?" Galbor was far from pleased.

"Some of the Tzu say you –never mind, forget it…" She gasped.

"Forget it? As you yourself pretend to. Are you sure you have not been worming your way in amongst the Tzu for too long? Maybe you overheard the riddle and merely conveyed it as your own, yes…? Well whatever your excuse you shall spend your last days in the form that you deserve, slithering through the warrens beneath my glade." Galbor roared.

"Gal-"

No sooner had he finished his short tirade and she was gone, just another hapless soul, transformed into one of the beasts for the Giant held below to feed upon, and he did so often.

Galbor held out a burning hand towards the globe that encircled the ensnared arch-mage. His eyes were pouring with flames of disappointment as he considered his foolish intentions. 'So what…?' With that single thought, Galbor caused the glass like substance of the walls to melt back, exposing the statuesque occupant previously trapped within, yet the mage held there made no movement, not even the slightest twitch.

"Kalamere…" Galbor warmly greeted his captive, his tone was

78

receptive and warm once again. Expertly concealing the boiling anger he felt beneath. "Come spend some time sitting with me, old adversary." His tone was not unfriendly, but any that knew of the treachery of Demons paid little attention to their vocal inflections.

The arch-mage hung still for roughly two hours in the same position. Thereafter his neck creaked slowly vertical, white robed body straightened, and fingers flexed to life as a crackle of magical energy played along the length of the cuffs of the robe that he wore.

Craning his neck around to best see his captor, Kalamere's glowing white orbs stared upon his much maligned foe, bathing Galbor in a faintly judgemental glare.

When the tormenting muscle cramps had eased well enough, Kalamere drifted ethereal-like from out of his magical prison and came to settle upon one of the two identical looking sumptuous armchairs that occupied the area facing the cavernous fireplace.

"My seat, I believe." Kalamere claimed as he sank into the better placed of the two chairs. His voice spoke with a confidence his bones no longer felt. The ancient arch mage Kalamere had long since learned to co-operate with Galbor, saving himself from the same fate as that of the fairy. In fact, Kalamere had often used his own powers to help his gaoler, in vain hope that he may one day find some weakness, and escape this living hell.

Ever since he was first captured by the Balrog, during a summoning that had gone awry, Kalamere had been forced to live within the stasis chamber. Within that ghastly device, none of Kalamere's vast magical powers could be utilised, and it was only when Galbor released him from the glass, that he could bring his saintly wrath to bear.

The trouble was; none of Kalamere's powers had any effect against Galbor though he had never figured out why. Therefore, he was forced to live forever within the circular cell, with nothing but blackness to stare at. Within the glass, the body was kept refreshed and replenished by magic, thus although feelings such as hunger and tiredness remained constant, his body would never actually perish.

Had Kalamere known that a Demon had inserted its vile seed into his mother's already fertilized egg and that by doing so, that Demon had bound him to servitude before he was even born, then he may have figured out, that the Demon responsible was none other than Galbor himself. But the chances of that discovery were remote to say the least, for Galbor took great care in his schemes to remove all traces of his insidious undertakings. Kalamere was the last of his time and there was only one way he would ever know the truth. But Galbor would never allow that to happen.

No. Kalamere had zero comprehension of the chains that bound him so effectively and though he often gave a great deal of thought to his quandary, the likeliness was that he would probably never know until the day he died the whys' and wherefores' of his situation.

Had Kalamere known any of this he would have realised that only by committing suicide would he have been able to lessen Galbor's grip on his tortured soul, thus enabling him to one day take his revenge. For vengeance flowed through the veins of all men; even those as pure as Kalamere... And he hungered for it with a demonic passion.

Kalamere looked up at the towering Demon and coughed in the ashen air. "Methinks the Eyrthe doth do its job most feverishly, without thy own addition", he suggested in a strange manner of common, "May haps thy own flames seek to prove themselves the better?" he finished, a subtle hint that the demons true image did little to impress him.

Galbor had carelessly forgotten to revert to human form before freeing Kalamere, it had been an oversight not to, but he would never reveal a lapse in concentration and so he opted for trickery to win the course, "Silly of me I know, but I grow tired of the constraints of humanity from time to time, preferring to walk around as the gods intended so to speak, does it bother you?"

"What suits thee shall be thy most fitting attire." Kalamere replied evasively, he too wished to hide his true feelings about the creature's hideous current form.

"No matter," Galbor stated and his body began drifting smoke-like into a resumption of his 'normal' human form. "I shall change, and then we can sit together a while, eye to eye. You are hungry no doubt...? ...Municia!!!" The last part reverberated throughout the tower and as its echo died a small, stark red, naked nymph appeared.

Nymphs' are magical beings. A race born from demons, they can often be found in their employ, though a tiny minority have turned their backs on the old ways of treachery and deceit. This one was as treacherous as they come and stood around three feet in height. Its naked body, whose skin radiated a luxurious ruddy glow, resembled that of a perfectly formed human female of twenty one years -or thereabouts, albeit on a smaller scale

80

and while she was attractive –her manner lacked that sexual verve that Gweonju had possessed in abundance. The look was topped off with cute little red horns and a shy twitching tail. The Nymph cowered low as it approached.

"Municia, stop grovelling and go and fetch some lunch for Master Kalamere. Seven courses shall be sufficient, oh and if we have any more virgins left; I shall have six quarts of blood and two fried spleens."

The newly arrived servant made to depart but Galbor's whipping voice snapped her back to attentiveness. "Oh, and call some of your slightly larger sisters, Gweonju has fulfilled her purpose." Galbor ordered distractedly.

This damned puzzle was ruining his concentration. Against his will, he kept repeating it over and over in his head. "I don't know about you Kalamere but my loins definitely need girding!" His flippant comment aimed at attempting to hide the slip in form, he turned back to where Municia still cowered, "Well?!?" he added, "Be-gone!"

The servant Nymph scurried away to attend the various tasks.

They talked about all sorts while she was gone, either laughing at one another's jokes, or pausing to smile upon a shared memory or poignant moment. Galbor poured numerous selections of wines and spirits as they talked, and though both were highly resistant to the effects of alcohol, the ancient Dwarven spirits and fine, age-old Elven wines, were irresistible in their body and flavour and many litres were drunk before Municia had even had time to return with their small banquet...

"...Oh thy do rile me most dearly, doth thee!" Kalamere protested into a 12000 year old port of supernatural quality and taste...

"For being clever, you fool, to be secretive and to have and hold many secrets' is what *IS* clever. The likes of you will always be in chains for as long as demons and men co-exist, and I do mean on both sides for there are many Demons to whom the pursuit of lies and lechery is taken with far more aplomb than that of discovering secrets."

Frost bubbles streamed outwards from Kalamere's eyes, like diamond dust caught in the rain, "Fore-sooth, 'tis a mere morsel of truth; that of mine that I seek after, thou know to be true... Wouldst mine own affliction fair any brook of change?"

Galbor chuckled out loud in response. "Knowing would mean you

81

would know the answer to that question and it is that thing, that most very simplest of things; a secret that is holding your chains and my empowerment! THAT is why I adore puzzles and solving the secrets they share: Your own predicament is testament to my rightfulness on this subject, now we will sit in silence for a while old foe, for I feel the Harpy Masters Finest Port has taken the wind from our bellies and inflated our chests with steam, and betwixt our brows we need to find calm waters."

"I declare, thee doth hearken unto Myllthra herself with thy prattle." Kalamere niggled, in part jesting.

"Really..., ...Maybe she's my half mother? I shall pay her a visit and strangle the wench for her lies, what say thee?" Galbor taunted back in an overly vicious manner. "Now please, let us have silence for a while at least..."

When Municia did return, she brought with her a stream of various demonic servants, each carrying some delicious sweet meat, exotic fruit cocktail, or other mouth watering dish. There was a collection of bowls, each containing soups that varied from the peasant dishes such as gruel and potato stew to the lip-smacking splendours of Birds Nest soup and others far rarer indeed. A veritable menagerie of animals cooked in a variety of ways, took pride of place in the centre of the table and of course, the wine still flowed ...

Kalamere tucked into the feast with gusto, which had been placed upon the hitherto small oak table that stood a little off from the cosy fireside chairs. With a click of his fingers, Kalamere transformed the circular three foot bench into a huge dining-table such as may be found in any palace. This table merely being one of the many magical touches, which Kalamere himself had installed, when he had previously resided in the tower as its master.

Galbor sat and picked at the spleens, his mind intent on the irksome riddle. He paused in his pretence of eating to take a large gulp from the glass that contained fresh human blood. He was observing the mage, wondering whether the great one had picked up on any of his earlier signs of inattentiveness, if he had, he wasn't showing it.

Kalamere practically grazed upon the kingly feast with all the panache of an half starved cow, greedily scoffing his fill for almost an hour with barely a breath nor word so famished was he. A loud belch signalled an end to his continual chomping, and the white mage sat back caressing the egg of his bloated belly and loosening the cord of his robe. After scrutinising his captor a while longer, Kalamere decided to break the silence that had enveloped the two since their meal had arrived. "Hark mine old foe, something vexes thee?" he asked, deciding to do away with the pleasantries that they had both falsely shared up to roughly an hour or two before.

Galbor switched his attention back to the mage, he had been musing over the riddle again. "What? Oh, no, well, no. Not as such for any matter," he thought carefully before continuing. "I am merely trying to correctly recall a fine riddle, knowing how you love a challenge, and why not? I could do with the company... Let you have a little time out of the rat trap so to speak... So what of it? Do you wish to enter into a little intellectual stimulation?" He asked innocently, though in truth it was a bald faced simple lie... The riddles elusive answer was holding a dogfight in the theatre of his brain.

"No..." The unemotional reply caught Galbor off-guard. He had thought to have expelled the last vestiges of resistance from Kalamere, but he could obviously still bite, '*Yes but how hard...?*' the Daemon prince mused.

Galbor was struck cold by the refusal but as sure as he would later torture Kalamere for his insolence, he would for now continue with the charade of kindness. He sat up and leaned conspiratorially towards the cocksure mage. "You don't have to of course; I merely wished a game of you to while away the boredom, but... Damnations be blessed! If you would sooner spend what time I give you in silence then so be it, I will not speak another word!" Galbor said with a pout and went back to picking over his food.

Some time passed, neither knew nor cared how much; to these two Father Time had lost its fretful charm. Galbor approached the fireplace and scooped up several white-hot coals, with which he performed tricks to amuse and distract himself. As he juggled the sprite ridden rocks, the dogfight in his brain gathered momentum as his mind's eye flittered this way and that, attempting to hunt down the riddles elusive answer.

Kalamere meanwhile, sat thinking of ways in which he might escape his captor, all the while thoroughly enjoying every minute of his temporary freedom, and the mental anguish his refusal would no doubt have caused.

Galbor performed his coal routine for several hours in silence, while Kalamere picked at the more delicate dishes set before him.

Finally the silence was too much for the wizard to bear, as Galbor had known it would be, and Kalamere rose to stand directly in front of the fire. Galbor suppressed a satisfied smirk as the white mage spoke.

"What pray tell, wouldst one such as I know of riddles mine tormentor? Hath I not lay trapped within thy prison of blight for countless Aeons...? ...Whilst thy sub-sanctimonious self roams the world most freely, Eyrthe to Eyrthe, homestead to homestead, castle to castle. I know nought of riddles and those that conspire to bring them forth. Mine mind grows weak from lack of labours sway, prithee; yea! I retire from mine former glorification. Yet wetted with time, then 'tis point that, some suitable solace may be found withy's conundrum ye proffer..."

Tendrils of noxious gas flared from Galbor's nostrils, hinting at his displeasure. "You do me a great disservice Kalamere, to solicit me with lies. True you live in a prison of nothingness. Yet it does not crumble the walls of your mind so easily. Oh no. The truth is that you plot and plan, scheme, and scam every living moment, and in all that time you are thinking without any distractions. Do not think I know naught of your plans. *For I see everything my conniving friend...*"

Kalamere drew breath at the insulting truth and countered with one of his own, "If thou doth truly see all, then why wouldst thou seek the answer from a weary soul such as I? Methinks thou eyes are ever dimmer than thee maintain...?"

Galbor shook his head and tossed the coals back into the fire, were they cracker-jacked about upon rejoining their kindred flames, "Maybe I'm wrong. I would have thought you more intelligent than to insult me..."

"I simply mean to express mine concern –did you ever manage to find our friend responsible for your-?"

"Silence!" Galbor growled instantly reasserting his control, and for a moment his illusionary visage faltered, replaced with his terrifying true countenance. *"Your own special bed lies barren, but maybe you seek to rest upon it once more?"* Galbor waved his hand in the direction of a steel bed made up of sharp probes, from which dark purple magic throbs of energy stabbed out.

"Hear me now old fool; until you ever do, **do** me the great courtesy of going completely insane, do not pretend to be so afflicted, or else... ...Well I don't like to threaten and you are a very astute fellow; clever beyond reason in fact, even if a little unwise and dim, but nonetheless if you rile me one more time my dear old adversary; ***thou next torture will be thou last!*** " Galbor mimicked in a dreadful manner, the fires on his flesh incinerating the leathery patches of blue skin and scorching pock marked craters aplenty and yellowing light spilled out from his eyes in a violent stream and yet his loss of control was momentary at best, before quite literally cooling himself down.

Kalamere bowed, he *had* thought of physically attacking Galbor, having already imbued himself with a magically charged strength of unequivocal proportions during dinner. '*Yes but he doth know what 'tis thee plans...*' He thought and a flicker of Galbor's eyelids at the thought made his heart grow cold.

Galbor turned and smiled at Kalamere in disarming fashion, "Enough of this needless quarrelling then, you shall hear my annoyingly difficult riddle and if you guess correctly, I may grant you your freedom… In any event you shall remain in this chamber until I deem otherwise."

This last statement was spoken not so much as a command but as a fact, for Galbor knew his captive well; the deadly challenges that had already awaited him when he first took command of this tower, testified to Kalamere's own insatiable love of conundrums. In spite of Kalamere's taunts Galbor knew he would accept. Besides the true master had shown his colours or so Galbor thought…, …His appearance melted and in moments his metamorphosis into human form was complete…

"Prithee, how long wouldst thou have me figure upon this perchance fruitless task…?" Kalamere asked without ceremony.

"…Until I grow tired of your constant procrastinations!" Galbor replied with annoyance, the wizard was testing him sorely. He then proceeded to repeat the riddle that vexed him so, taking great care to remember each inflection and pronunciation, precisely as Gweonju had orated to him…

"The riddle is this and take heed to remember the exact pronunciation, less its solution lay there, *ahem" he pretended to cough*:

"I am found in men and beasts,

I cover various pockets of the **world**,

You *may* find me in bottles to ***drink***,

I am *within* the many planes of hell,

Sometimes residing in *one*,

My *place in the mind* is often possessed,

In churches and temples I'm **never** forgotten.

What am I?"

VI) **Darkness to Light**

The tunnel wound on for ever it seemed. The two companions had been travelling along for almost five whole days and other than stopping for a quick snooze or bite to eat the journey was quite uneventful.

Neither had said much since entering the tunnel, other than to agree that it seemed to travel roughly in the direction of Caernthorn, which seemed a mute point all things considered. Thus they travelled in almost complete silence, both instinctively knowing when best not to be heard. After the several years the companions had been travelling together, they had become accustomed to one another's ways and often found a shared look to be far more efficient than words; especially when they fell out.

This was the case here, where the tunnel stretched beyond the Dwarves sight, both in front and behind, and every sound seemed to echo to infinity. The tunnel itself was vast and circular and gave the traveller the sense that he was travelling through a rabbit warren - albeit a *giant* rabbit. Smaller tributary tunnels led off at irregular intervals, riddling the whole circumference with the lesser apertures but Grot ignored them and continued down the main stay, less they get lost or worse in endless exploration.

The Phoenix had long since left their sight, and Dirk was forced to rely upon the Dwarves Infra-vision to guide him as he bimbled about from rock to jarring rock.

The one consolation on this tedious journey was that they had not run into anything unpleasant that may want to eat them. That was, they hadn't until about five minutes ago.

The two squatted in silence around one side of a slight bend in the vacuous tunnel. Dirk could see as well as Grot the huge form that sat in the middle of the tunnel, thanks to the massive lantern that splashed light across the area that the creature occupied. A lantern bigger than him and Grot put together

Dirk thought he recognised the creature from stories he had been told as a child, "Is it a Troll?" He supposed as quietly as he could.

They both cringed as his whispered query echoed down the tunnel.

The Dwarf, who had fought a Troll or two in his time, shook his head in reply and shrugged to indicate he had never seen its like before.

The thing was enormous on a scale of fly to horse proportions and Grot wrinkled his nose at the usual stench wafting up from Dirk's trouser regions. Dirk waved his arms in protest at the Dwarf's baleful gaze, "It's just a wet fart this time..." He whispered, "Honest..."

Grot made pretence of buttoning his lips, then pointed in turn to Dirk, then some loose boulders and handed him a wad of Doc-leaves that he hastily fished from his pack. "Go!" He silently instructed despite Dirk's objections.

As Dirk crept off to his impromptu toilet area, Grot poked his head back around the corner and nearly whistled at the sight. The Giant's swollen bulbous head bobbed only 10 feet or so below the roof of the tunnel that reached so, so high above the two companions. Its huge arms as thick as Oak trees, held a huge metallic drum, which it had not yet struck, and for this small mercy Grot was thankful, but it held it all the same.

The globular stomach of the creature hung out like some gigantic water-skin, which indicated to Grot that a fresh supply of food must be nearby. And it absently alternated between scratching its flatulent, spotty bottom and picking its tombstone teeth. Peevish little eyes were set deep within the recess of its eye sockets, indicating the creature was either completely blind *or* completely capable of seeing in the dark.

"So why the light..." Grot mused silently.

Dirk strolled nonchalantly back over, smelling somewhat fresher than when he had left and received a visual bollocking for his carefree approach. Dodging a backhand cuff, Dirk stepped out beyond the bends blind-spot, only to be yanked back into seclusion by his throat.

Grot released Dirk and utilised his body language in an attempt to convey what he would do to Dirk, should any further cock-ups occur...

Again Dirk felt the alien compulsions that had driven him to earlier distractions 6 days earlier, but again he managed to rebuff the emotion, cursing the violent urges spreading throughout his being and singing for redemption. Dirk stared blankly at the Dwarf, wondering why his unwanted instincts were tempting him into so foolish an emotion. Yet the more he attempted to quell the flux of feeling, the more angered in himself he became...

…Grot gave several other less threatening but equally innocuous signals of action leaving Dirk totally clueless as to what his mate required, wanted, or expected him to do. In response Dirk gave an emphatic shrug and associated grimace. Grot reciprocated the hopeless look perfected by Dirk, loosening up his shoulders and strapping his axe to his back, before unhooking a short javelin that looked to Dirk to be completely inappropriate to the task, but was probably very dangerous all-the-same. Dirk stepped back in case he was the Dwarf's intended shish kebob and tried out his friendliest smile.

'The idiotic bugger thinks I'm gonna kill him!' Grot thought and briefly considered living up to Dirk's appraisal or at the very least stabbing him a bit, but a loud sigh from around the bend brought him back on track.

He looked down upon the Emerald weapon which he cradled in his palms and held it aloft in an almost reverential manner. "Süegar Próttegûar!" he spoke the weapons Dwarven name with fondness, carried away on a wave of nostalgia as he mentally recalled how he had come about the useful heirloom which he cherished so…

Grot had spent most of his early life as a tunnel fighter in mount Dammar, fighting the countless denizens of the deep that used to swarm and rise up in hideous fashion in an attempt to overthrow the Dwarven citadel located there: A city-fortress that had been thought indomitable until the night crawling beasts had emerged in their thousands to battle for its control. Ratman and Lizardman had fought side by side with Orcs and Goblins, Dark Wyrms ascended on wings of prophesised doom and the Dwarven citadel fell, though it did so at a price to the armies of darkness.

The Dwarves had emerged victorious after a fashion for the Great Dwarven engineers alone had accounted for such a scenario, by mounting the entire citadel on twenty or so precarious granite stilts. Grot had formed part of a group of ten volunteers, led by one commander Banballardin, Grot's uncle. Their soul purpose on their do-or-die mission was to remove the pegs that kept those numerous stilts in place and by doing so, bury the attacking army beneath the hopefully abandoned cities rubble.

These Javelins had been constructed by the great cleric Ĕdrig, to help fight off the agile Ratmen, who had by that point already overrun the tight warrens below. Uttering several prayers to Keldor, Ĕdrig had blessed the weapons for the duration of the battle, giving them the sharpness of splintered glass and the strength of hardened steel and thus armed, the suicide party departed for the infested lower passages.

The tunnels that led to each peg-hole tended to be so tight that they could only be traversed in single file and the spears proved their worth in those desolate tunnels, holding at bay scores of the fearsome beasts at a time. The mission was a success but came at a price; as one by one the eleven counted down to two, until all save Grot and the commander were slain and consumed by the throng of endless Ratmen. Grot foolishly attempted to rescue the last of the troop to fall and would have been lost to the mob himself, if not for his Uncles once legendary martial prowess.

Though his uncle was one of the oldest Dwarves to ever live, he still had the countenance of man a half his age; unfortunately a man half his age would be on death row in Dwarven terms such was Banbạllaŕdin's longevity. He was also a particularly clever Dwarf however and what he then lacked for in might he made up for in intellect; as each companion had fallen, Banbạllaŕdin had paused to retrieve their spears and slot them into his nap-sack.

When only he and Grot remained, he ordered his nephew to guard his rear and utilised all ten javelins in quick succession, finally performing a whirling dervish of dancing death down the final stretch of the tunnel network when reduced to the final two spears, slicing and dicing almost every protagonist to challenge them.

Meanwhile Grot had attempted to take care of another group approaching from behind, but he had been younger then and his warrior skills were not so attuned. Though he gave it his gallant best to defend his uncle, their attacks were too many and too many blows had penetrated his guard and again his uncle played his part as saviour, though it cost him in both blood and breath.

As the two emerged from the collapsing tunnels, via a secret passage not yet discovered by the forces of darkness, they just about managed to conceal the entrance before dropping to their knees overcome with anguish and regret. Desperate Orcs, Ratmen and others screamed their collective muted cries as the Citadel plummeted down upon them in a roar that deafened the mountains themselves, with Grot and his uncle mere metres away.

In the muted silence that followed the citadels fall, Banbạllaŕdin spotted an approaching crimson rider on the horizon and ordered Grot to run for his life.

Of course Grot had refused, but it was not without being considerably blessed by his own god Keldor, had Banbạllaŕdin survived the many years that he had. Perhaps then it was sensible that it was he whom had first informed Grot of the prophecy and hinted as to his own place in it, without that knowledge Grot would have surely stayed and died that day, as Dwarves for the most-part are a highly honourable bunch and though it broke Grot's heart to do so, he had no choice but to follow his uncles shameful orders.

Banbạllaŕdin had saved Grot's own life in the battle that ensued and though he received a mortal blow for his troubles, he at least bought enough time for his nephew to flee from the Okar general; a foe who was dangerous enough when encountered unarmed and unawares, let alone riding the back of a juvenile Dragon.

Forced to abandon his uncle to his doom, Grot reviled himself and knew his kindred would likely view him with the same discourse. He'd had to travel several leagues across mountainous terrain, in a state close to death in order to report the mission's success to the long departed citizens of the citadel.

When he'd finally made it to their nations temporary home, (a peak they still occupy to this day) Grot's fears were quickly confirmed by the manner with which his fellow Dwarven kin received the news, and for years he had regretted not staying to die on the mountainside by his talismanic uncle's side... Although folk readily expressed their thanks in words their hearts spoke differently, for here was the man who; rightly or wrongly, had abandoned their nations icon in his darkest hour.

Of course being the only survivor also cast an element of doubt on the veracity of his account and some of those less kind had openly questioned his portrayals accuracy: None doubted that the others had perished yet voiced concerns as to Grot's own commitment.

From that day on Grot had felt like an outcast amongst the homeless mountain dwellers. Behind every forced smile, Grot could feel the weight of their unspoken accusations and as they set up their new homeland on the mountainside, he himself found himself moving further apart from his kin both physically and socially. Knowing the threat still posed by their temporarily entombed enemies Grot had pleaded to the notary Jighal; whose trust he still held, to be put in charge of border security and had set about plugging up any exposed fissures into the rock below.

Jighal had concurred and Grot had thrown himself into his new command, yet the men under his charge were no different to other Dwarfs in their attitudes and it was only their dedication to their work that kept the social side of their proximity at least amicable.

Once the exits were sealed however, and a formidable barricade installed against the various land walking enemies, Grot grew more and more distant, leaving the general day to day running of the guard to several of his more capable attendants, he found himself making ever more elaborate excuses to go exploring beyond the borders. Most often these 'scouting' ventures would consist of a handful of Dwarves but after time, that number whittled down to three, then two and eventually just Grot himself, after a time of which, he simply went off never to return, taking with him the possessions on his back.

The Emerald javelin had been one of the items in his possession. In fact it had never left his side since the day he first received it, the spear being more symbolic to him than a thing of militaristic value, representing everything he loved and hated about being a Dwarf. He checked its state of repair, then placing it firmly in his sweating palm; Grot cocked his arm back at the elbow and moved a little around the breadth of the bend.

Dirk breathed a sigh of relief that his own mortality was safe once more, "What are you gonna do?" He whispered a little too hoarsely.

"Take out that big bugger… I just hope I get my aim right… It's been a while." Grot breathed back a little quieter than his friend.

As the Dwarf raised his arm to fling the javelin, Dirk suddenly caught his friend's harmful intent. "No, wait!" He blurted, knocking Grots arm as he let fly the javelin towards its intended target; the lantern.

Dirks nudge sent the Javelin careening off at a slight angle and the trusty spear of so many years service, instead struck home against the huge metallic drum, splintering the weapon with the force of Grots throw as it crashed against the drum's exterior. This caused the acoustic device to reverberate to a most peculiarly deafening, high pitch sound that echoed and multiplied as it travelled the underground network several times over.

Both companions fell clutching their ears in pain, before Grot had the sense to dive back into cover amidst a few large boulders, dragging a similarly dispositional Dirk along with him.

Un-strapping his axe one handed, the unhappy warrior made a vigorous shaking hand signal to Dirk that left him in no doubt as to what Grot thought of him.

Unperturbed, Dirk tore away the arm from his robe and after fiddling around in his pouch for a moment his hand emerged covered in a brown glutinous substance that he wedged into both ear canals. He then wrapped the sleeve around his head like a bandana to keep the stuff in place, before motioning to Grot he should do likewise.

As pissed off as he was, the axe-wielding would-be maniac did so, even though he was unsure of what benefits the vexing wizards plan would reap. To Grot's surprise however, the instant he applied the stuff, the unbearable screaming echoes of the drum were deadened to an acceptable level.

"BEESWAX..!" Dirk screamed leaning in close to his friend's ear.

"NICE! SO WHAT'S YOUR PLAN NOW DICKHEAD...? I SUPPOSE WE'LL HAVE TO TAKE IT ON IN A FIGHT NOW THAT MY JAVELINS GONE! WHY THE FRIGGIN HELL DID YA DO THAT... HUH? HUH? ME FRIGGIN JAV... HAVE I TOLD YA YER A STUPID FRIGGIN DICKHEAD, I, I..., ...THAT JAV'S BEEN WITH ME A LOT LONGER THAN YOU YA KNOW, IT MEANT A FRIGGIN LOT AND NOW, WELL NOW IT'S GONE ISN'T IT, EH? EH!" Grot shouted reciprocating the leaning in process, heedless of whether their shouts could be heard above the Drums din.

"I'M SORRY ABOUT YOUR MOM BUT NOW'S NOT THE TIME!" Dirk yelled back, though not in anger, "I WOULD BE MORE WORRIED ABOUT YA, BREAKING YOUR STICK, WELL I SUPPOSE I DID IN A WAY, SO I'M SORRY ABOUT THAT..."

"WHAT?" Grot questioned.

Dirk shook his head and tried again, "YOUR GREEN STICK..., ...I'M SORRY OKAY?"

"...PRICK? WHAT ABOUT ME JAV YER CHEEKY ARSEHOLE! AT LEAST I HAD A FRIGGIN PLAN..." Grot responded totally missing the point.

"I SAID: I DIDN'T WANT YOU TRYING TO KILL IT AND ATTRACTING ITS ATTENTION..., ...SO MUCH FOR THAT IDEA EH? I SUPPOSE I'VE COCKED IT UP AGAIN..." Dirk struggled to collect his thoughts, "DID YOU HAVE IT LONG, THAT GLASS SPEAR?"

"...ASS SMEAR IS IT!?! I'VE BEEN CALLED SOME NAMES BUT YOU'VE GOT A CHEEK SHITTY PANTS LIL!" Grot spectacularly misheard, "D'YA WANNA KICKING OR WHAT YOU POXIE GIMP? I'M JUST ABOUT *SICK* OF YER BALLSING UP EVERY TIME I TRY SOME SHIT! I DON'T UNDERSTAND HOW A DICKHEAD LIKE YOU CAN EVEN HAVE THE NERVE TO HAVE A GO AT ME?!?"

Dirk shrugged and shook his head in seeming apology, "WELL I'M GLAD IT WASN'T IMPORTANT… LOOK LET'S YOU JUST STICK TO THE GIANT EH…? A PERV WHEN YOU WERE THREE! I'M SURPRISED YOU REMEMBER… WHAT DYA MEAN LIKE; LOOKING UP WOMENS SKIRTS N SHIT?"

Motioning with his hands, Dirk shushed the Dwarf's initial reply and made an expanding notion to indicate the drum's concussive din. The Dwarf nodded in agreement, content to let Dirk's last slur about him being a bender ride for now. Both then scrabbled about picking up what meagre rocks they could, before dashing back to the sanctity of the tunnel's approach. With their backs pressed tightly to the wall the Dwarf counted down with his fingers, and on reaching the count of one, they swung around the bend in unison, rocks in hand ready to assault the drum…

The great Troll like thing looked about in confusion. It couldn't hear the drum, but it could feel the vibration. Something had banged his drum, and it thought for a moment in an attempt to remember whether or not it was he himself who had struck it. Scratching his head and scanning about, his roving eye caught the fractures of light reflecting off the shards of the shattered javelin and, looking warily first one way then the other, he placed the jiggling drum on the ground, and lumbered over to the bend, around which he had just observed the two rummaging midgets dart.

Unsure what to expect from the tiny bipeds, the fantastically proportioned threat crept as tentatively as his great frame would allow, towards the crook in the burrow. The roar of metallic noise hissed teasingly at his ear lobes in a blur of white noise as he neared the curve and, bending down onto his knees he could feel the resulting tremors passing through the thick flesh of his hands. The Giant crawled the last few feet to the blind spot of the bend, and cautiously craned his stumpy neck around to see what lay on the other side. Somewhat predictably, the two friends chose that same moment to launch their renewed attack.

…Arms bristling with assorted sized rockery, Dirk and Grot swept around the bend, and met faces' to face with the humungous brute. Grot went white and Dirk paled whiter and for an infinitesimal moment they hung there, indecisive, before propelling into frantic fleeing motions the opposite way.

The masonry seemed to hang in the air for a moment, unsure of what to do, since just a micro second ago hands had held them aloft with threatening intent. Before the abandoned rocks succumbed to gravity, Grot and Dirk had already ran a good ten feet or so, Dirk screaming all the while, when another sound rejoined with, and completely drowned out both their own racket and that of the drums diminishing echoes.

They could hear, rather vaguely thanks to the beeswax, a deep rumbling roar from behind, that sounded (to Grot who had heard one) like that of a wounded Dragon. They both turned at the consuming sound to see the brutish beast crashing his way back to the light, where he tried, somewhat pathetically for one of his bulk, to hide behind the metal drum.

Dirk and Grot exchanged amazed glances.

"IT'S SCA..." Dirk began, leaning in to his friends ear, but Grot motioned him away and began removing the make shift ear protectors.

"THE SOUNDS DYING DOWN A BIT," the Dwarf calmly explained and motioned Dirk to remove his own wax, which he did.

"I SAY WE GO KILL THE THING NOW, YOU READY...?" Grot added when Dirk had finished undressing his makeshift bandana.

"What I didn't get that, my ears are..." Dirk began to mumble, but Grot cut in sharply. "YOU HEARD ME BOLLOCK BREATH!"

"BUT IT'S SCARED STIFF OF US!" Dirk insisted, "LOOK AT THE SILLY SOD!" He rubbed his ears to help alleviate the ringing noise induced by the drums audio onslaught.

"EXACTLY YOU GREAT DUNGHEAP..." Grot rebuked, "HOW MANY TIMES DO I HAVE TO TELL YA! *THE BEST TIME TO NAIL AN ENEMY, IS WHEN HE'S ON THE RUN!*"

The Dwarves readied axe gleamed greedily in the Lanterns light as the two companions headed over, Grot's determined stride leading the way. Dirk's nagging inner voice drove him to argue further despite the axe, and they were bitterly embroiled in a heated debate as they stalked ever closer.

"LOOK GROT, LETS JUST TALK TO HIM FIRST. HE AIN'T EXACTLY GONNA KILL US IS HE?" Dirk pleaded.

"HOW DO YOU KNOW? HIS GOBS DEFINITELY BIG ENOUGH," then, espying the giant's blatant attempts to fearfully hide itself away the Dwarf changed tack, "I SUPPOSE YOU'RE RIGHT... WE'LL BE ABLE TO TORTURE INFORMATION OUT OF THE BASTARD FIRST!"

"THAT'S NOT QUITE..." Dirk began -then seeing Grots facial expression, he gave up on his crappy attempts at diplomacy and pulled the Dwarf back smartly. "LOOK JUST PUT THE BLOODY AXE AWAY OR YOU'LL FRIGHTEN IT EVEN MORE THAN IT ALREADY IS!"

An enormous head peered out from behind the drum; the giant could see the two menacing midgets still stood there, the taller of which was bending down to its even *shorter* companion, who held an axe in his hand and a vicious glint in his eye. The shorter of the two, motioned with said weapon towards the cowering watcher and made several nasty swiping motions, which the cringing hulk considered bad: Then the other midget snatched the axe from its companion, wagging the weapon several times at the shorter of the two and threw it off to one side, which clearly indicated that it too shared the giant's feelings about the swiping part.

The small bearded one then punched the other clean on the jaw, sending its larger colleague crashing to the floor, before going to retrieve its nasty edged weapon.

Ugg watched on in confused fascination as the scene before it unfolded further. As the smaller creature bent down to retrieve its weapon, the larger one dived on its back and began punching it in the head. This caused them both to fall to the floor and after several rolls, the smaller one sprang to its feet, with the other held above its head.

A well placed back heel, from the figure held aloft, landed squarely on the large nose of the other, causing the tiniest midget to stagger about erratically, the other swaying ominously above the head of its companion.

Then the little one doing the holding tripped on a rock which sent it reeling backwards, its arms flailing in circles, while the larger of the two, now deprived of the arms supporting it, fell bottom first atop of the other.

Ugg laughed.

And laughed...

And laughed...

Its laugh was a deep baritone similar to the rolling thunder of the previous eve, yet nevertheless unmistakeable as anything other than the sound of one most deeply amused. Grot stood up and went to retrieve his axe.

Dirk got up rather more slowly, gently nursing a rather large weal that was forming on his forehead and a twin for the one on his chin. He caught sight of Grot moving towards his axe, "Grot no, I'm sorry…" he murmured, before throwing up all over himself –the stew had begun to work its usual magic.

Grot picked up his axe and flashed a quick look towards his temporarily incapacitated companion, then, hitching the axe onto his back, he went over to where the gigantic creature was lying against the drum, its hands clutched helplessly to its huge jiggling stomach.

"AND WHAT MIGHT YE BE LAUGHING AT, YER GREAT LUMP OF BLUBBER!", a globule of blood splattered down on to Grots boots and his instinct told him to feel his nose, which was bent at an odd angle. Placing his hands either side of the misplaced bridge of his nasal passage Grot pressed down and snapped it back into position, causing more painful whelps of laughter to omit from the huge creature.

Great! Thought Grot, as the echoes of the Drum quietened to a distant echo, "Now we have to put up with your bloody racket instead!" he moaned and kicked the drum in temper.

The drums high pitched echoes reverberated once more, causing the Dwarf to fall to his knees, clutching his ears, which in turn made Ugg laugh more than he ever had in his life.

When everything had returned to normal some twenty minutes later, or rather it should be said, what passed for normal in Dirk and Grot's haphazard lives', the two assembled themselves in front of the gigantic creature that was only now ridding itself of the last few stubborn fits of giggles. The din from the drum too had died considerably.

"Right then you," Grot said pricking the things bare foot with his knife. "As I see it, you'll be telling us your name about now!" he finished with a slightly more forceful jab.

"UGG…?" The creature boomed back, its facial expression as innocent as a newborn child's on tit-less Sunday.

"Right then, Ugg - We wanna know a way out of here, and if you don't be telling us swift like, this here knife will be jabbing at your more delicate bits, if you get my drift." Grot emphasised the point by leaning on the dagger, so that it pierced the skin of the mammoth creature.

"Ugg...?" Ugg ventured, bending over to rub the sole of his pricked foot.

"Yeah I think we got the name part now spill it. We wanna know everything, how many of you are there? Where the exits are? Blah, blah and so on..." Grot demanded, staring eyeballs to eyeball with the immense thing in front of him.

"UGG..." Ugg responded, unsure of what it was the midgets noises were supposed to mean. "Ugg!" he said and gestured annoyingly towards his stinging foot. Ugg would have also pointed out that he was almost stone deaf, had he known how. Regrettably, the many years he had spent trapped down here, had taken their toll.

The Drum that Ugg often banged; to attract the attention of the wormholes inhabitants (which then provided his nourishment), had shot his rather large eardrums to pieces. Unfortunately Ugg wasn't the brightest spark in the thundercloud to begin with, but without a soul to talk to in all that time, the tunnels unbearable echoes had somewhat killed his passion to speak. Thus, his hitherto unsophisticated conversational skills had petered out to mere distant memories.

"Erm, Grot, I think you may find it can't speak!" Dirk offered but knew the Dwarves natural stubborn nature would not accept this.

Grot removed the metal half-helm, that he wore to protect his head, and threw it with some vigour at the creature's forehead. Ugg sat and stared, unable to move quickly enough to avoid being hit, as it slapped him clean in the centre of the forehead.

"Ugg!" he said rubbing his head from the helmets stinging blow and staring at the impetuous midget that now somehow stood on his massive ribcage just below the line of his protruding chin.

No sooner had the helm left his hand, Grot had leapt up onto Ugg's leg, traversed the length of it, scrambled up the hill of its belly, and rolled down the other side springing up from his roll and racing to the foot of Ugg's head.

Dirk was impressed. Having never before seen the techniques the Dwarven folk employed in order to fight Giant sized creatures, he was amazed at how agile his friend moved. Never before had he seen such grace in a Dwarves movement, any Dwarf, never mind his most inelegant friend Grot. *If only an elf where here to see this...* Dirk thought with detached admiration, *they'd soon change their minds about Dwarves...* "Oh shit!" Dirk exclaimed in panic. "He's gonna kill it!"

"Grot...!" Dirk screamed in a 'DON'T YOU DARE!' attitude and the Dwarf stopped mid swing of his faithful axe.

"Do you want another arse whooping? Or are you gonna let me kill this evil git?" Grot demanded.

"Can't you understand, he doesn't want to fight?" Dirk asked incredulously. The gigantic man-thing hadn't made the slightest indication of any vindictive tendencies it may harbour. In fact, this big dope appeared to be more of a coward than Dirk himself! Yet Grot seemed oblivious to the fact.

"He doesn't seem to have a malicious bone in his body Grot. Have you even stopped to wonder why the hell he's down here? I mean, is there even a way out? You do realise that the tunnel mouth closed behind us, don't you?" Dirk drew his breath here and tried to look intelligent while the Dwarf fidgeted indecisively.

"...Oh yeah...!!! Well if it aint some sort of guard, what in Keldor's name does it have a bloody great thing like that for, hmm?" Grot challenged, flinging out a rather tender arm in the direction of the Drum.

The trio's focus switched to the drum.

"Ugg...?" Ugg asked with a shrug of his bushy eyebrows.

"Yes... UGG...!" Grot nodded, climbing down from Ugg's voluminous frame, he went to stand beside the drum, stopping to turn and face Ugg. Grot had the feeling he was getting somewhere. "...Ugg! Ugg! ...Bleeding-well-Ugg!"

"Ugg...?" Dirk chorused, he too was feeling the vibes of the Dwarf and went to stand by his friend's side, arms splayed out towards the drum.

"UGG...!" Ugg roared, and his look changed from innocence, to that of a belligerent child. Dirk quickly backed away from the Drum and was glad to notice Ugg's gaze lay firmly in that direction and not his own.

"Maybe, he thinks were gonna knick his drum... If we just back off and show we mean him or his drum no harm…" Dirk cringed.

"Sod that idea to Keldor's arse! This is getting old, oy you- big ears. Yeah you, yer bloody useless slab of Goblin waste! All we wanna know is what… the… 'Ugg'… this… 'Ugging … drum is for!" Grot shouted back, clearly losing his patience for negotiating.

"Uuuugh!" Ugg bellowed and struck out an accusing finger.

"…Oh yeah…" Grot was purple with rage, "Well Friggin well Ugg you ycr bastard!" Grot screamed back and un-strapped one of his larger axes to illustrate the point. "I told ya we couldn't reason with it! Keldor be buggered!"

"Uhgggggg!" Ugg bellowed and rushed straight towards and straight past the two companions and the drum. Grot managed to deliver a deft blow to the Giants ankle bone as it lumbered by, his axe head biting haft deep into its flesh, and almost getting himself squashed in the process, but Ugg simply lumbered on without pause.

The two miniature mates followed Ugg's movements as he thundered past and physically wilted in concert at the sight of the worm like creature advancing towards them, its mammoth pulsating mass almost managing to dwarf Ugg himself.

It was so big that it not only filled the tunnel for some fair length behind, it also forced the tunnel to expand as it proceeded in its rock constricting advance. Dirk quickly re-evaluated his conception of size. Ugg was gigantic all right, but this thing was mega-ginormous, he thought, noting the word for later inclusion into his dictionary.

Grot too was more than a little frightened, he had often heard of battle fear and once while battling a mere Dragon whelp both he and five hearty Dwarves good and true had all been afflicted to a greater or lesser degree; only his Uncle Banballaŕdin had remained completely unaffected. Back then Grots fear merely served to weaken his blows and cause his knees to chatter uncontrollably and he had managed to help distract the beast while his Uncle and Jarot – a skilled veteran, had felled it with a barrage of precise blows. The others had been completely overcome, two grovelled on the ground, one ran away screaming, and a fourth stood completely froze, just as Grot did now. As for Jarot; his heart had gave out on him shortly after the battle.

"So *this* is *fear*!" Grot thought numbly, "No wonder Dirk keeps on shitting himself. Mind you it aint that bad…, …Is it legs? Hmm, now move!"

Dirk's eyes blinked with all the fury of a trapped moth as he tried to take in the sight before him. The whole tunnel mouth, from which they had both emerged, was filled with a sickly off white blubber that glowed in the same phosphorous white light that the lichen had bestowed on the riverbank. At its centre was a huge gaping maw, festooned with thousands of needle like teeth, even the smallest of which were well over a foot in length. A trickle of warmth down his thigh brought him out of his speech paralysis, though his feet still felt leaden, his mouth stone-wall dry and his heart to scared to beat the drum of the living…

"So, are you going to fight '***THIS***' denizen of evil?" Dirk gasped in the most sarcastic tone he could manage, in truth it was all he could think of to say, but he had to say something.

"No matey!" Grot responded ignoring the irony and yanking on the paralyzed wizard's robes, "I think this is one of them running moments you're so fond of. Come on!" With which sage decisiveness they both began loping off like lumbago stricken zombies in the opposite direction to Ugg and the worm, as fast as their faltering feet would let them.

"Just to think," Grot managed to gasp as they broke into a synchronised shamble, "We only cut through the woods because *you* said it was a friggin shortcut! Yer never said anything about any Gobbo's, rampaging rivers, Phoenix's nor tunnels and I'm mighty sure I never heard ya mention a Giant. And as for worms I'll stick to the small ones I get in me turds thank you, at least I can fit those on a friggin' fishing hook." Taking a deep breath he fixed Dirk with a steely stare, "Next time –we go the long way and I read the map!"

"Yeah well," Dirk huffed and puffed as he waddled hastily alongside his friend, "I reckon we should stop by a village instead…, …of straight on to Caernthorn…, …The races will be a day or two off yet…, …If not more and these gems are hurting my foot… I'm sure we could just… Drop by someplace friendly… You know… Take a breather." He finished rather appropriately.

Grot cocked a querying eyebrow his attention caught by something Dirk said, "They should be tucked in the secret pocket I stitched for ya, not around yer ankles…, …erm hold up a mo, I mean slow down, there's a bend up ahead, come on, hurry up; cautiously that is…"

The two companions slipped towards the next bend in the tunnel, and as they did so saw daylight come creeping around its night-dark edge.

"Bugger me!" Grot exclaimed, "That Ugg thing… he *must* have been the guard." He stated peering back over his shoulder.

"I don't think so," Dirk argued, "He didn't act like any guard I ever saw, and he protected us from that worm, well; I say he did –there could be more of them around the crest of the bend. Are you gonna check?"

Both stopped then, and pulling out an axe in one hand and handing Dirk his knife with the other, Grot nodded imperiously to the bend. "I'm sick of sticking my neck out for you. Plus I'm protecting our rear!"

"Bollocks! Last time I popped my head around a corner Ugg was on the other side –oof!" Dirk's protests were brought to a kidney blow finale and he reluctantly crept to the tunnels edge, as the cavern began to shake loose fist sized lumps of stone.

"Hurry up!" Hissed Grot and he glanced back in time to see the worm spectre peeling its own blubbery skin back to reveal more of its gaping maw as the Giant Ugg charged on.

Peering around the bend took a great effort both mentally and physically and when he turned back to Grot words failed him.

"What's up? Is anything there? Hello…" Grot quizzed, then hearing Dirk's knees stop shaking he smiled. "No guards then? Well come on before Ugg and the worm come after us!" He proclaimed after himself checking to see if the coast truly was clear.

They cantered around the bend and forged towards the blinding light, their eyes looking forward only, whatever came up behind them now would do so without being spotted, thanks to the feisty glow.

Moving fully within the envelope of light, with still no sign of danger, Dirk espied its source; a large jagged scar in the fabric of the rock and he yanked Grot by the sleeve and propelled him towards it. Grot was still reeling a little; as much from the assault to his vision that intense light bestowed, as it was due to his first true taste of fear. He'd been scared before true, but never so much he thought his heart may stop. He tried striking up conversation to distract him as they hip-hopped towards the supposed exit. "Well I suppose you're proud of yourself –talking me out of killing that guard!"

"Oh come on… I'm right and you're just too bloody minded to admit it. He saved our lives from that worm thing. His final '**Ugg**' that he shouted was to warn us to run. He sacrificed himself for us, so that we might live!" Dirk said with certainty, smug in the knowledge that he, Dirk Heinemblud had understood the situation better than his friend.

"And another thing" Dirk continued, a thought suddenly occurring to him as they slowed to a walk some thirty feet off the ragged gap, through which swathes of welcoming golden sunlight poured. "Unless you haven't noticed, the exit is only just wide enough for us to fit through… And the other end was sealed until the Phoenix opened it, so… He must have lived his whole life down here! I bet there's a whole race of them living underground, bravely battling against the deadly worms." He finished with a flourish.

"OK! You've got me on the fitting through, prisoner thing," Grot conceded as his sight struggled back to usefulness and he wriggled through the thick gash of stone ahead of his paranoid pal. It was some several metres thick but a musky scent of flora and fauna wafted from beyond.

Pausing halfway, he waited for Dirk to find the will to clamber up into the exit point before continuing. "You might be right about there being a race of the buggers living here –not that I'd wanna meet them if there were. But maybe, just maybe you're right! But tell me this Mr. Gandalf wannabe, where dya suppose they live, 'cause I can tell ya right now, I…" he paused as Dirk scrambled out into the soulful Glade ahead of him, free of fear once more.

"Blast –I've gotta lose weight. I'm bloody well trapped now!" Grot moaned.

Dirk laughed crashing back in a spongy patch of voluminous grass, "I've been saying your looking fat for a while now!"

"I mean me weapons dickhead" Grot barked, removing the restricting articles and continuing out into the foliage where Dirk lay in fearless expanse. A blood curdling roar spiralled out from the abandoned tunnel to momentarily disturb the peace, causing several unseen birds to flit away. It sounded distinctly 'Uggish' in nature.

Dirk gave Grot a look that said; "See! Sacrifice…"

"Okay, Okay!" Grot blustered. If he's such a sacrificial, friendly unthreatening bastard then, what was the drum for, hmm? The only people

I know who carry drums are military bands and watchmen, so like I said; I should have killed the Bastard!"

"Maybe he's a musician?" Dirk toyed and once again they argued…

***

…Ever since the silly midgets had shown up, Ugg had been wondering when some food would arrive. They normally came a lot quicker, once he had banged his drum. But he had to admit, he had been getting a bit too greedy lately.

It was just so boring in the cave. All on his own with so little to do, his only pleasure was to go and sit by the crack at the end of the tunnel and take in the sweet scents blown in on the gentle breeze, from the harmonious glade just beyond the cleft rock face.

The glade was beautiful beyond compare. He remembered playing there as a child. He couldn't remember his parents' faces, but he remembered his mothers concern whenever she had discovered him playing there. He was of the Ulfdra; a forgotten race of giants cursed by the gods and hunted down by other Giant folk. During the time known as the Rise of the Giants, his uncultured kin had fallen to a man. He could not recall how their decline took place just simply that it had. He was the last.

Nor could Ugg remember why he returned so often to the Glade. All he knew was that it was the only wonder left unto him to behold in his miserable existence. Over time he had seen the things that dwelt within the glade and longed to reach out and touch them, but his confused mind denied him the wherewithal to achieve his ambition and so he had contented himself with the role of silent watcher. He had no ambitions. Harboured no envy, and held no grudge at all, except perhaps against the beast that was currently attempting his consumption.

In fact so simple was Ugg in both life and mind that he was merely content to eat, shit and sleep on a regular basis. So he would bang his drum several times each day, and feast on the silly worms that it attracted, often in the sunny spot by the gap in the rock. Their bulbous flesh fed him well – his vat-like belly was testament enough to that. But the outer skin also held a vital dosage of water and it was perhaps because of the need to drink that he would summon them, but before he knew it; he would often digest the whole carcass in one sitting.

Lately though, the worms had been taking longer to arrive and were getting bigger and harder to kill. This small fact did little to lessen his appetite, on the contrary, the harder the fight the bigger his appetite became, and the bigger the worm was, the better his hunger could be satiated, not to mention that much needed (more plentiful) water.

So it happened that when he had first seen the size of this latest worm-thing, his eyes had bulged and his stomach rumbled in deliciously joyous anticipation. The midgets that had amused him had carried those sharp sticks, which may have helped defeat it, besides –they must have been hungry too the way they kept on pointing at his drum… Or so he had thought at the time, why else would they have set it off?

So with a cry of "**UGG!**" for 'ATTACK!' he had launched himself at his main course-to-be, reassured in the knowledge that his newfound silly little friends were with him, fighting side by side in glorious battle.

After an initial struggle, during which both combatants fought to see who was the strongest, '*mass weight*' and his mates weighed in to finish the argument in emphatic fashion. Ugg managed to punch out two of its twenty thousand plus teeth, as the monstrous worm convulsed its frame sending its massive bulk surging forward. This forward movement negated any possible defence and swatted him to the ground like a drunken fruit-fly, dragging him beneath its crushing ripples of luminous flesh…

Ugg dragged himself backwards on his hands even as his dull senses felt the first prickles of pain: Ugg's feet and ankle bones splitting and splintering beneath the rolling behemoth. He looked around for any signs of forthcoming help from his tiny friends and was left confused when his quick scan revealed no sign of them. He wondered where they had gotten to, and it gradually began to occur to him why they might have done a runner – so to speak.

Foetid breath worse than his own, reminded Ugg of his heavy opponent and he instinctively reached out an arm to ward off his aggressor, the worm responded with several hundred teeth, tearing into and depriving him of his appendage. "Ugg!?!" he enquired helplessly…

He glanced about again for his comrades in arms, and was almost *positive* the midgets had abandoned him now. In *fact* he was almost *sure* of it! What passed for the worm's forehead rammed into Ugg, slamming him into a horizontal posture, and riddling his skull with several major fractures in the process…

...Ugg's brain hurt. It hurt to think at the best of times, but now it was damned hard. His finger scratched in confused fashion at his battered head, where bits of skull-bone protruded as he thought on the midget's whereabouts and he suddenly filled with dread; not -*as one might reasonably expect*- because he was in the process of being eaten alive by his own intended dinner, but rather due to a sudden (and somewhat rare) thought... **The buggers had abandoned him!**

He hoped with all his heart his tiny traitors had enough of the common sense that had so eluded himself centuries before.

Yes the majority of his memories had faded into daydream obscurity, but nothing would ever erase the memory of the Evil wizard whom resided within the elegant tower that rose above the beautiful glade above.

Even as the rampant worm's needled maw tore through his tough, well fed flesh as if it were rice-paper, he thought back to the wizard who had imprisoned him here, all those aeons ago.

He had incurred the mage's wrath for eating some of the pretty flowers that bedecked the towers ivory walls and no matter how much he had proclaimed his innocent intent, the wizard would not be swayed.

He remembered the words the great magician had uttered back then, and mouthed the foreign sounds aloud even as he began to disappear inch by spear stabbing inch, foot by leg by stomach into the great worm's maw and rows of serrated inner teeth chewed into his half swallowed mass.

"No-one crosses the great Galbor and goes unpunished!"

Gweonju felt she could get used to this; life as a worm wasn't so bad, sure she couldn't speak, socialise as such and her looks were far removed from 'beautiful' but all the same, she *could* communicate with her new kind, even initiate sex if she chose to, and for the month or so she had been down here she had already done so many times...

...Old habits die hard maybe, but the truth was far more intriguing, Gweonju had discovered three things from her first communications with the other worms or 'Crawlers' as she had labelled them and those three things helped her formulate a plan. The first fact she had discovered was how numerous these Crawlers were, thanks to a very short birth cycle, conceiving and giving birth to a score of young within days.

So Gweonju had mated at every given opportunity.

Her second discovery was that a Crawler could feed upon and digest *anything*.

So Gweonju began eating anything and everything without stopping, except of course to mate, which she did at every given opportunity.

Her third discovery was that she was large for their breed, larger in fact than any previously known specimen, and because of this the other Crawlers feared and respected her.

So Gweonju began to gather the Crawlers together, stopping only to eat her young in order to increase her bulk and mate at every given opportunity.

She had a plan all right. With her army of Crawlers she would rule the world above and when she did, she would offer the world to her uncle Galbor as a gift and hopefully regain her immortal status as a Jezebel of the seven hells...

When she finished munching down the gigantic meal that used to be Ugg, Gweonju began slithering towards the shaft of daylight as fast as she could manage, sending out scent pheromones calling her brothers and sisters to her, now was the time to strike...

Crawlers are blind in terms of sight but another rather recent discovery is that they could smell pretty much everything; from dung heaps to Dwarfs, including their weapons and emotions and right now she could smell a timid Dwarf and a shit scared Dirk shuffling away for their lives..., ...she set off in slow pursuit.

VII) A Question of Knowledge

"Sod this for a Golems arse! I'm staying here," Grot expanded his arms to take in the full expanse of the exotic glade, "I bet this is what the Elves are always on about and every Dwarven Bugger is supposed to hate, Keldor's beard! Bugger adventuring, I mean what is it? Bumbling about from one place to the next? Always bleeding well hungry and shitting yer self; big bastards and little bastards out to get you at every turn. Damn to the forge the Dwarven halls and their bollocks-full, tens of thousands of *square feet spaces* and **dark** corridors and *non-stop **bloody** invaders*!" Grot cocked a leg to let out a rather squeaky fart before continuing, with a smug self satisfied look, "Oh yeah and be damned too, this stupid get-rich-quick trek to Caernthorn, we could flog the stones to any old Jeweller and still walk away comfortable..." Grot sighed in exaggeration, stretching out his arms and given a good old full on frontal scratch of his nuts.... "...I am here," he supposed "And it is here that my sorry old fat arse intends to stay!" he declared thumping the earth of the grassy glade with his doffed armoury cutting his finger in the process. "Ouch! Keldor be blasted… Well I suppose, when I say stay, I don't mean forever… Just a few months or so..."

Grot pounded the earth by his side as he lay back in the lush green grass, he felt truly alive now, more than ever, fear had been a foreigner until now; he had come close to it, heard of it and even passed by it briefly but until now he had never come to actually meet or know fears true taste.

"Ya know ya went a bit white back there when you had to strip off all your armour and stuff to get through, and when we heard Ugg roar I thought I wouldn't be the only one with packed trousers." Dirk teased.

Grot sat up and stroked his beard in thought before replying, "In honesty I was a bit scared, but I'll have yer know I've shit me pants too in fright on the odd occasion… It's just fright to me its, well it's just like a quick shock and yer get over it, but when the giant ran at me I thought that it was do or die time, yer know, I mean to say I had a friggin fright yeah? But then when I saw that huge bugger of a worm making the giant look like me own kin, well… I very nearly did shit 'em!"

Dirk was shocked, "I was joking matey but if that's you when you are scared then, well, I dunno, I guess what I am trying to say is I get that way when I see my own shadow, ya know you are well brave.."

"Brave eh? Well if yer wanna talk about bravery what about you full on fighting me when you thought I was gonna kill the Ugg thing? Some would say that was stupid but I know you, and that was bravery if ever I saw it-"

"Nah…, …**THAT** was just stupid, I'm still dizzy ya know…" was Dirk cutting quick response.

"Stupid? Nah, well, yeah…, …a bit stupid but brave too, why?"

Dirk shrugged, "I dunno why, just felt I had to save him."

Grot shook his head, "That much is obvious, but why…? We'll never know because your real problem is with the truth, as for me, maybe I just seem brave but believe me if you were me, you'd probably be braver, I sometimes think I go too easy…"

"What on *me*?"

Grot stood up and brushed off a few imagined blades of grass, "Hard to imagine huh? But yeah on you, on myself, on everyone and everything, especially other Dwarfs…"

"Grot you're a bit of a Dwarf hater ya know, they generally seem to like you but ya never hang out with 'em ya know, not properly, not without being drunk and being in a bar full of 'em… That's a bit weird don't ya think…"

The Dwarf gave a grumpy 'humph' in response, gathering up and re-equipping some of his doffed belongings.

"What's that supposed to mean?" Dirk moaned.

"Look Dwarfs are always repressing me all right? They don't like me, they **abide** my presence, ask for my help then blame me for the shit happening in the first place. They think I am a traitor, a murderer, a faggot and a friggin' coward, the bastards why should I like 'em…?"

Dirk shook his head and pulled a silly face, "ERM, **HELLO**… YOU'RE A *DWARF*… And what the hell is a faggot?"

Grot glowered back at Dirk, "Puff rolled pastry best served in a meaty gravy but that isn't important right now, we gotta get moving before it gets dark…"

"Get moving?" Dirk was in disbelief, "I've seen someone avoid a question before but that's just bloody well 'LORDING' it. What about *'and it is here I am going to stay'*? Or have ya forgotten all about how great ya think this place is? Maybe you *are* getting old Grot... Where's ya gold old guy, bet you've forgotten already?"

Grot was suddenly sour, "Yer thinking of Leprechauns yer Dick, and I've told yer before about the old comments, only one person calls me old and that's me got it? As for this place it is pretty gorgeous so I suppose we could stay for a day or two," he added almost apologetically, "after all, we wouldn't want to be getting *too* comfy. Where is me gold by the way? The gems that is..."

"Pretty aint the word for it matey, wish there were a nymph or two around here, need to get me rocks off if ya know what I mean...!" Dirk conceded, skilfully avoiding the question and went off to forage around in the thin thicket of trees that enclosed the glade. "We could stay a day or two definitely!" He shouted back to Grot. "There's a crystal clear pond just under the trees over there and I do mean crystal – It's purer than a gnomes spectacles. After that bloody long trek through the tunnels, I could do with a rest myself."

Grot had not been paying particular attention, rhythmically tapping out a dint in his steel toe capped boot. He looked up at his friends return. "What was that about a Gnomes testacles, I'm not sure I wanna eat *them*? I wonder if this place ever had a Unicorn?" he added aloud to no-one in particular.

"Who's testacles? And what are you on about Unicorns for...?" Dirk remarked removing his own boots and emptying out several gemstones from one of them, which he proceeded to count.

"Well if ever there was a glade with a Unicorn this would be it!" Grot gushed. "Besides they've probably got testacles big enough for both of us..." he added shuffling on his hands and knees a few feet to Dirk and plucking up a brownish-gold gemstone. "Hey this is a Tigers Eye!" Grot declared holding the gemstone aloft, "Brings me good luck this one!"

"It won't if you bet it and lose!" Dirk reasoned.

"Then maybe I won't gamble this one? Maybe I'll keep it and mount it in a medallion when we get there." Grot said holding the stone up to the light and examining its peculiar sparkle.

"Yeah and maybe you'll carry it in your boot or get your imaginary

Unicorn to carry it for you. My foot's chaffing real bad. All around my ankle's swollen *and* I know my feet stink, but not normally *so bad*. It smells just like Old Wendy's boiled mushroom and cheese gruel? And no-one except Wendy ever claimed for that to be a sign of natural goodness."

Grot looked over and wrinkled his nose in disgust, tossing the Tiger-eye back onto the pile. "You've lost a fair few... Try swapping which boot you hide them in – or better still, shove them down your crotch – nobody in their right mind would wanna go anywhere near there."

"Unless some moisten bint happens along you mean? Who knows she might ride up on that Unicorns big bollocks?"

"I'll bollock you in a minute! I'm not saying I believe in Unicorns, I was just trying to point out just how damned beautiful this place was – that is until you had to turn in your own verbal racket!" Grot barked.

"Yeah well if it ever existed, I bet it didn't just spend all day lying around on its back, bitching on about life in general. I bet *it* never said "Bollocks to the world, I'm getting my head down for a bit!" *It* was probably off in the bushes with a virginal wench or however the myths go. Either way, I doubt it hanged around here for days with nothing to do, no matter how peaceful and pretty it looks!"

"For a while it did..." Came back a smooth baritone reply that clearly indicated they were no longer alone. The voice was followed by the clip-clopping of hooves and a hearty if somewhat bestial laugh as, striding out from amongst the bush thicket in which he had been hiding, a very obviously male Beastman now emerged.

"A Unicorn...! Well I'll be-"

Grot clipped Dirk's ear every inch the disappointed headmaster; "You festering boil on the bum of humanity! It's a bloody Centaur! And maybe not a friendly one too – look out for signs of an ambush, if things go pear-shaped I'll whack this one first!" Grot bounded to his feet in an instant, automatically readying his axe and adopting a combative pose.

Dirk cocked his brow and wrinkled his mush in disdain at his ever eager battle buddy, "Hold on a mo Grot, please..."

The beast took another posing stride forward, dragging his cumbersome member tenderly in his elegant wake. "Hold there strangers and strange folk one an all, if I can't smell a whiff of magic on the both of ya! Zen's the name and satires the game. Get it. Satyr - satire, oh well... I suppose not, never mind. But what the hell! If there aint enough magical energy pouring off the both of ya to light up the Eternal Night, I'll be a minstrels daughter." He paused for effect in his salesman like pitch to gain the complete attention of the group, *which*, he noted somewhat disappointedly, consisted largely of a depressing lack of girlish type females.

"Okay Horse-boy stays right where you are or my axe will be removing an inch or two of that cock!"

"Grot please calm down matey and like think of something else to threaten wont ya!!!" Dirk protested.

"I'm sorry it was the first thing I thought of…" Grot moaned.

"That's exactly my point!"

"No not like that!" Grot interrupted, "I was just looking at it and… Look well; -don't look, oh shit of a Banthra. Hey, hold on a bleeding minute – You haven't taken your eyes of it yet either so don't have a go at me!"

"Yeah well, it's just so *big* and… long? Well, actually, long doesn't come into it –It's…" Dirk sought the right word, "Mega-Ginormous! I never knew Centaur were supposed to be so well endowed."

The big black creature before them smiled a pearl white perfect, tombstone smile. "Thanks guys!" He said tipping his grinning noggin at his own cock. "But I aint no poxy Centaur my little monkey-men, I'm a sensuous Satyr and I believe I heard the wizardly looking one mention virginal wenches..? Where would they be hiding?"

A quick note to the unwary; Satyrs are always male, and always on the look out for innocent females. If a person should find themselves within the aforementioned category, then extreme caution should be taken when dealing with these creatures. Especially if travelling without a chaperone, oh and under no circumstances should one ask a Satyr to play a few tunes on its panpipes; especially Zen who might well take the suggestion the wrong way entirely and in an entirely unmusical manner!

Spotting a Satyr is easy enough: They walk around wearing nothing but the fur that protects their legs and hind quarters, which are exclusively those of a goat, complete with a nice tidy set of Billy-goats horns. All of them besides Zen that is! After all Zen was not your atypical Satyr…

Where all other Satyrs skin ranged in colour from flesh-pink, through browns and reds of various hues, Zen's skin was a deep midnight black as found only in races such as the darkest of the men from the south. Atop his head he wore his Goat-horns as proud as any other Satyr though they were more bullish in nature and topped with rings of gold.

Sleek black hair formed on his manly chest and underarms and merged around his crotch with the animal hair so that his scrotum was partially obscured, yet his facial hair was kept trimmed down to a long stylish goatee, that had been braided and intertwined with gold leaf. He also wore what in centuries down the line would become known as shades or sunglasses to you and me. However it was his lower half that commanded the most attention, for it was that of a black stallion, and equipped well enough to satisfy even the most demanding of mares, not that horses were ever his target. His manhood hung so low it would occasionally drape on the ground as he gesticulated!

There was a reason Zen had managed to become the worlds first DIY Satyr. You see, although not necessarily evil in nature; Satyr's are Demonic in nature and thus are created or birthed from the essence of Hell. So when an unborn Zen to be discovered his fate was to be born as a Satyr, his foetal spirit went about making sure the right strings were being pulled for him, even though he was more than a mere soul at the time. Time is perceived differently in Hell, but more about that later.

See Zen had connections. His grand uncles, second brothers mothers, fathers, sisters, sister-in-laws, sisters, brothers uncle was none other than one of the seven great princes of Hell. So when it came down to being created as one of the thousands of lowly Satyr, who were judged solely on the amount of children they sired, Zen thought it would be prudent to stand out ahead of the crowd.

He had heard the stories of the wild spearman to the south and how they would scare their enemies during battles by flapping their well endowed extremities at the enemy, then finishing them off with a quick spear thrust. The intention of the threat was to clearly indicate that they could give to their enemies wives, what the enemy themselves in most cases could not... Unfortunately for the Kikkee-Kuban'ga tribe it wasn't long before they were completely wiped out, care off an alliance of jealous nations of men more adequately endowed in the type of weaponry that kills stuff than the type that thrills.

The Kikkee's story impressed him so much, that when it came to his choice of lower animal half only a horse would do. And not just any horse but that of a strong black stallion! This little alteration was mediated by thickening out his human half with the muscles of an over-peaked Adonis, and the whole visual effect was topped by an over indulgence of Gold trinkets, from bangles to ankle bracelets and back again. Satyrs may be thought of as egotistical, but Zen was so far gone that his ego had an ego of its own.

"Are you sure you're not a Unicorn?" Dirk asked stupidly.

The Satyr looked puzzled for a moment before flashing his teeth in a smiling statement, "Boy you are a weird boy! Do I really look white to you? Do I have four legs, a horn and go neigh…? Save that shit for the Reindeer. Now go on; tell me you aint ever seen no Satyr personified more sexually satisfying than me…?"

Dirk and Grot exchanged knowing looks but Grot came right out and spoke the shared thought. "You're a bit of a loony aren't you?"

"I was going to say show-off but close enough…" Dirk conceded.

Grot snorted imperiously, "Believe me Dirk. Anyone showing off *that* much has definitely let one or two bats out of the cave; I know I used to have a great aunt who went around bare-chested. Are you alone then horse-boy?"

"Satyr, please or better still chimps call me Zen. Whichever you prefer really, though I prefer my friends to call me Zen…"

"And where be your friends like? Hiding in the trees waiting to attack no doubt?" Grot demanded, "Yeah well come and have some big boy. Shit! I mean big boy as in, damn. Come out and show yourselves cowards!"

"Who are ya talking to Stunty?" The Satyr grinned at him.

"Who..? I am shouting your bloody mates. Unless ya wanna die alone, and I'll have less of the Dwarfisms if you please Donkey dick!"

The Satyr looked affronted. "Look my vertically challenged friend, I meant no harm dude. And I aint got nobody with me, and even if I did this place is protected by very strong magic, magic that stops folk killing so chill down my mini amigo and less of the Horse-isms you throwing at me!"

Dirk stood up and went scrabbling about, picking up a few dry twigs as he went. Both Dwarf and Satyr asked what he was doing, to which Dirk replied "Look! Beastman here says were safe from attack, and the trees are so thin you could spot anything nastier or larger than a rat or frog, so if we are still staying here and resting, *although* I would far sooner push on to a town with or without shit in my boots, *I* am going to build a bloody fire."

"You shit in your boots? Whoa man! IS that some sort of trippy human ritual or just you?"

"Just him," Grot answered before Dirk could speak and began scooping up some firewood that was actually useful. Mindless of whether or not his presence was actually wanted, Zen helped out by dusting of a bare patch of soil and building a small stone surround, which both Grot and Dirk thought a little over cautious, but appreciated all the same.

By the time they had started up a fire, and caught a few Bantats to cook, the luxuriant daytime radiance gave way to crimson early evening that was no less seductive. Grot cracked open a bottle of port, produced from the recess of his pack and passed it around as they each chewed their respective burned Bantats and shared a couple of jokes and tales. Such a talkative and amiable fellow was Zen that there were very few uncomfortable silences apart from those times when Grot or Dirk were noticed staring in slack mouthed wonder at his monolithic manhood. Yet even that caveat was ignored after Zen let it be known that he took their disbelieving stares as a great complement, even offering to get it hard so they might see it '...as nature intended', which they respectfully declined.

"What's with the dark glasses Zen, I mean call me stupid but I thought the idea of spectacles was to help you see; not block your sight completely?" Dirk asked fascinated by this Satyr's fashionable accessories.

"Oh! Ya mean these old things? Well the *original* pair was given to me as a gift, and I can still see through them thanks to my super special eyesight. You know, before I was born I asked my Uncle for the hearing skills of a bat and the eyes of a hawk." Zen bragged.

"A Hawk eh? So I take it yer see great distances...?" Grot asked.

"I hadn't finished Grot my miniaturised main man; as I was saying... A Hawk, Demon, Bloodrat, Dwarf, Elf, hell to cut it short Uncsy told the fates to give me everything so as I can see no matter what. See!"

Dirks brow furrowed in thought. "Interesting, so... Who gave you the dark spectacles and why?"

"Well hold on Dirk pal while I finish this feed and I'll tell ya the tale of my greatest conquest ever... Well, actually it's my erm... Oh who cares, listen up you cats, cuz Zen is in 'da' *house!*"

"Whose house..?" Grot innocently enquired?

"I said Zen's house!" Zen chanted, rotating his hips suggestively and threatening to knock off their heads with his lengthy sausage. "That's right Grot –You dig it the most!"

Grot shook his head to Dirk in furious denial – Neither had a clue what Zen was saying half the time and when they did understand it never sounded altogether relishing, but the tale he began to spin had them in alternate bouts of stitches and disbelief as he told it...

The shades; it turned out, had been made especially for Zen by a very understanding Dwarf whom he had heard rumour tell, had a daughter whose beauty was beyond compare. The rumour had actually been spread by the father himself –a Dwarf named Mugwart, who kept his haggard looking daughter hidden in a magically darkened room. His hopes were that some dashing, noble (and rich) looking young Dwarf would approach with a marriage request. But alas, none were so easily fooled except those Dwarves from other regions and even they didn't stay for supper.

Unfortunately for the father and his lies then, that although his wife had since passed away, the mid-wife who had been present at the birth was still very much alive, and she often could be heard in the bars that she frequented, regaling to all who would listen, her own particular tale. She had since quit the office of midwife for the soldiers life of battle and beer, and It was mostly when under the influence of the latter that Aggy the Axe maiden, as she now liked to be called, would often recount the tale of the horrendously ugly baby that had made her give up the midwife profession for good. A baby so ugly she had genuine doubts as to which end to smack and in truth would sooner have touched neither, less she somehow catch its ugliness.

So when Zen had shown up with his flashy smile and his flashy gold, lighting up flashy extremities, Mugwart had accepted that at least his daughter may concede him an heir and help him get rich in the process.

Furthermore; although he was loath to admit it, Mugwart had to accept that it could well be his daughters only ever chance for even so much as a one-time fumble in the dark, for she was so grotesque that were she to be left naked in a field full of wild animals she would only help serve as a scarecrow.

It had taken Zen several months of groping about in the curiously darkened room, a room that even his own remarkable sight could not penetrate the depths of, before he had been finally able to pop both hers and his own respective cherries. Yes. Zen was loath to admit, she was his first.

It was a good thing for him that she d been locked up all that time with little other to do than eat, sleep and masturbate. This meant that when someone actually wanted to spend more than twenty seconds within what amounted to her prison, and when that person was a tall, muscular, Very well hung, hairy guy who found her irresistible, she wasn't the one doing the complaining. It was only seventeen months later when she gave birth to a black half Dwarf-half horse that she ever even expected anything was amiss and even then she wasn't too sure. And at least he had kept his fathers good looks.

So the glass eye shades where made as a present by the girls father whose career was that of an Ocular Technician to many races including that of a family of short sighted Medusa. In thanks for his services, Mugwart presented the spectacles before Zen began his ascent to the Eyrthe above. Of course the sunglasses were meant to protect Zen's eyes against the harsh light in the world above the cavernous tunnels wherein their race resided, though in simple truth, the light that this race of deep Dwarf feared so much was simply sunlight and thus completely harmless to Zen himself.

The shades as he liked to call them, were of little or no real use to a beast such as he who could see equally well in all but magically darkened places such as that in which Mugwart had held his daughter. He was about to throw them away in fact, when he 'caught' his reflection in an underground river and found that he quite liked them, thinking they gave him a mysterious edge. "After all –the chicks dig mystery!" Zen had said, and he intended to give them plenty of it.

Once back above ground he had spent no time at all in getting them magically reinforced and then having several copies made in varying styles. He had his favourite pair on today –a pair constructed from Jet that completely concealed his eyes from view.

"Nah I don't buy it." Dirk declared at the end of his laughter.

Even Zen had been giggling at the details of his own tale but now seemed shocked at the declaration. "What ya trying to say my mystical ape?"

"Ya mentioned a Gruberry Bug and I happen to know that they can see through magic; so you bloody well knew how ugly she was but did the deed anyways..." Dirk challenged.

"Aha..." Zen sighed, "Well she was my first man, and hell yeah! I was a bit desperate so yeah I did her a few times-"

"BULLSHIT ALERT, BULLSHIT ALERT! You are caught out again, you spent 18 month screwing her, so my bet is ya married her but I aint gonna go there..." Dirk continued.

"Don't try bulling a bullshit artist!" Grot cut in with his own chip of advice, "and Dirk you can leave it there or I'll tell of a few of your own past 'conquests'... I seem to recall there was this one brazen little hussy in a town named Syphilis, which I suppose kinda gives you a feel about this little hometown girl Dirk met up with..."

Time passed as they all shared good company and swapped humorous tales of the road, Zen was feeling in good spirits too, thanks in no small part to the alcoholic spirits he, the Human and Dwarf had helped consume. He was vocally thankful he had been passing by the glade in which he would oft-times frolic about in; hopeful of meeting the odd female traveller. Satyr's are creatures of nature –he explained, and were bound to it (nature) in a very emotional way, as such he tended to spend most of his times in the Jungles and Forests of Eyrthe and had to admit that it was not the best place to meet eligible young ladies.

"So how did you know we were here?" Grot enquired, to which Zen replied he had not so much known that they in particular were here as his keen nose had picked up the scent of a human, and he set off to investigate the possibility of running into some desperate females.

"So how do females react to you when you do meet them? I mean – you have met some haven't you?" Dirk puzzled.

"Oh yeah..! Sure have, loads of them..." Zen responded with a little too much zest to be believed, "And I mean loads, hundreds in fact!"

"You have, have you?" Grot asked returning with some orange coloured fruit and passing one to each. "And how many of these females have ye bedded?"

Although the ruddy pink sky had since bled into a voluminous dark crimson, Zen still pushed his shades up to conceal his eyes before answering with a rather vague sounding 'loads and loads man'.

118

"So how do you introduce yourself exactly?" Dirk asked standing with his arm against his stomach, elbow tight to the hip, "Hello Ladies, I'm pleased to meet you!" he mimicked Zen, tensing his forearm and raising it.

All three fell into laughter, Zen later admitting that the way Dirk had let his arm drop down flaccid between his legs on the word "pleased" was definitely a good imitation.

Grot wiped a tear of laughter from his eye and popped the cork on a flask of apple cider. "So go on; how do you really introduce yourself?"

His answer was almost as bad as Dirk's comic imitation, as a Satyr he was prone to appearing out of nowhere in order to astound the ladies, but found the usual puff of smoke too yesterday to be seriously considered.

Instead, Zen had taken to lurking in wait somewhere until a female or two happened along and then springing out from behind a tree trunk or, as in the case today, a large bush.

"You're a flasher!" Dirk roared and both he and Grot rolled about on the floor, pounding their fists and feet in laughter.

Zen was a little miffed at their reaction, he had thought his technique was quite sound. "Well blow me if you aint some supernatural wizard type come to rescue the princess from the tower!" He bitched at Dirk.

Both companions looked upon the newcomer with a mixture of wild bemusement and outright shock. "Did you say ... something about a princess..?" Dirk responded his thoughts trying to take everything in. Despite the laughter and booze he was very much in mind that his own loins very much needed girding.

"I wish man! Princesses are hubba-hubba, swell babes aren't they? Never had one myself but I often wished I could have had a go at the sweet Princess cherry that used to live here! Oh yeah man, yeah baby, yeah!" He added obviously engrossed in the thought. "Say you wouldn't happen to? Oh, yes, no probably not, err..." He let his unspoken thoughts hang temptingly in the air.

"Happen to what?" Dirk managed when it was obvious the man-beast was offering nothing further until asked.

"Oh nothing much ..." Zen began innocently, "I just wondered ... you wouldn't happen to have any nubile young females, you know, with you. Oh I know I can't see any, but you never know, you might have hid

them back down the road –I know I would have! But I'm a cool dude aint I,
If ya got a bitch or two yo may wanna share, well ya know the type:
They've Long straggly skirts that get snared on every bur and rock...,
...Fingernails that break, hair that's never good enough. Ya know the type,
man I gotta get me some coulo... Female booty, womanly hump ya know,
so ya wanna share? Eh? Eh? No...? *Oh well...*" He finished rather less
than hopeful.

"No!" both Dirk and Grot blurted, suddenly comprehending the
creatures intent. "We treat our ladies with respect!" Grot added, "Not that
we've actually got any with us at the moment."

"No? Are you sure, only you're both kinda handsome dudes, well,
you are Dirk. Grot's as ugly as a Troll's backside, and well - you never
know, some may have followed you all doe-eyed like. From whatever hill
you wandered over..." He sighed at the two men's blank expressions.

"Not even a nubile nymphet? A Dwarf with a face full of pigments...
I aint fussy homeys... Well, except about the virginity bit, that's pretty
important I suppose!"

"Why?" Dirk asked.

"Well... You don't get points for taking sloppy seconds were I
come from. I mean what would be the point if some other guys already
been there...? Nah Hoes score zero, nothing, de-nada. Simply can't sire
them."

"Are you mad?" Dirk rebuked Zen, "A female who knows a thing or
two is worth twenty that you gotta teach. I mean how do you even know if
you are any good at it until you've been with a woman that knows?"

"Sorry but we've no women at all, that's one problem we haven't
got!" Grot cut in, he was a bit peeved about the Dwarf in make-up
comment and did not altogether approve of Dirk's philosophy regarding
women, being as Grot was very much a Dwarf-about-town type and
therefore altogether more responsible in the matters of the heart.

"Yeah, no women..." Dirk added with distinctively less enthusiasm.

"Blast, you mean to say I left a cute young Gob- Gullible!" He
quickly corrected himself, "I meant to say: "Cute Young Gullible Girls"",
human ones they were too. Not goblins or Orcs or anything!" He paused
to gauge the reactions of the others but neither were really listening, each
lost in dreams of their own amorous ideals.

"So you mean to say…" He restated in a raised voice; "That I have left the safe confines of a lover's arms and trekked three long miles, over stupid rocky hills, only to find you don't even have any females travelling with you? None at all..? Dwarfs, Humans or whatever, in any way whatsoever? Nubile young pert breasts or droopy swingers, young or old, wench or witch, I don't care man! I mean, all that I ask is that they are chaste and… Well there is none is there?!? I mean it's not much to ask is it, to meet a few virginal maidens? I bet the two of you aren't even virgins!" He finally wheezed, bringing his long stylish whinge to an end.

"Well, err…" Dirk began.

"What? Are you telling me you are?" Zen beamed with misplaced hopefulness, regaining some of his composure.

"Eh? Oh, err, no." Dirk corrected, looking a little worried as a scary thought crossed his mind.

"No?" Zen perked up.

"Damn right it's 'No'" Grot firmly resolved. "And that's final!"

"Oh well…" Zen finished, looking down at his hooves in embarrassment.

Eight hours later and the Satyr, who had long since fully ingratiated himself with the others, was currently dancing around the large campfire that he had constructed, whilst blowing into the legendary pan pipes that these creatures love to play.

Dirk had been the first to take to Zen, who admired any man willing to stand out against the grain, and although Zen's particular lonesomeness was an unsought for one, Dirk had to admit Zen carried it off really well.

Just as Dirk had took to him, so as the spirits flowed the Dwarf too was beginning to warm to his style and would have done so sooner, were it not for the fact that Zen's large appendage kept flapping about all over the place.

As those hours passed, the three had shared stories of one another's adventures, which could not have been more dissimilar in their telling. Whereas Dirk and Grot's almost exclusively mixed a cocktail of surviving near fatal encounters with numerous laundry bills, Zen's revolved around stalking maidens and an insurmountable number of failures to conquer.

In fact, Zen had constantly admitted during several of the quieter moments of the evening, his lack of sexual success was so common-place that if it hadn't been for the strange circumstance with the Dwarves daughter, he would in fact, still be a virgin himself. "Perhaps it's just down to the size of it?" Grot had suggested, but this simply sent Zen into a shocked defence of his prodigious plonker as he proceeded to point out the laws of nature pertaining to the survival of the fittest, fastest, strongest... longest...

The Human and Dwarf had left Zen to his peculiar beliefs, and soon they were all laughing and prancing about around the fire like pixies at a pumpkin piss-up.

Their accelerated state of unreserved interaction was enhanced by two very potent things, the Dwarven spirits that Grot always carried (and which he would now need to replenish at the first stopover), and the magical effect that the pan-pipes had on any mortal that heard its sweet melodies. Thus what would have been a day of grumbling around the camp fire, degenerated into a testosterone charged ego-fest which Zen invariably won hands down, with Dirk and Grot only falling into the occasional scuffle all the while...

They all ran around, dancing naked as the fires glow mingled with that of the starlit sky. They wrestled and chased each other through the small thicket of trees in a childish game of tag appropriately named "Tag the smelly donkey". After that they held a competition for the best huntsman and moved off in different directions, seeking for anything that looked as though it may be edible in the woods surrounding the oasis of tranquillity.

All three had returned one hour later as arranged. Each person's bodies bedecked with the various pelts of the deceased. They made a macabre sight as they entered the glade, the fell animals gore mixing with the sweat from their bodies. Zen re-entered the glade with less haste and more wariness than his newfound friends, but the fire burned as merrily as before and the air of calm remained undisturbed.

They ate well. Yet, while Dirk and Zen's finds where indeed edible, their catch only consisted of a small grass-snake, a mouse, Vulture carcass, a Vole, baby boar and an Owl that hadn't given a hoot. By the time these creatures had suffered cremation at the hands of the inept cooks, there was little meat left that they could actually consume.

Grots find however was made up of one item - an adult deer that had been stupid enough to come sniffing at him while he was answering natures call. It was the deer that was cooking now and the smell that arose from the sizzling meat was an intoxicating aroma totally in contrast to the smell which had served to lure the beast into capture.

"I still don't think it's fair!" Zen moaned, stopping in his gay little dance around the fire. "I mean, just because he got the biggest catch!" he said with a nod towards Grot, "Perhaps the winner should be the one who caught the most? ... I did catch three of the beasts after all..."

"So did I, erm, well –the vulture was dead already but hey it's meat still and only a few pockets of maggots to contend with! Come on Grot admit it; it was nice weren't it!" Dirk whined.

"Aye, and now you're hanging about awaiting a slice of this deer!", the Dwarf challenged and then laughed uproariously as a grumbling sound from the satyrs stomach betrayed Zen's amicable protestations.

"It does smell bitch ass!" Zen conceded rubbing his gut, "Though I'm scared I aint gonna be able to look another Deer in the eye again. Should we do da bitch the honour of naming her?"

"It isn't a doe, it's a stag." Grot said and before Zen could argue, Grot pointed out the creatures charred genitalia that no-one had bothered to remove before roasting it on a spit." It could be said that cooking was not one of this threesomes particular fortes.

"Well, in that case, how long will it be, before Mr. Stags ready to be digested?", Dirk interjected, then reviewing his speech he decided to add, "And I mean ready, that black Bear you cooked on the road between here and Caernthorn has been dribbling through me for weeks!"

Grot laughed at the memory, "Well, I never said I knew how to cook it, just that you could! Anyway if yer do end up smelling like that again, at least it'll keep away the Gobbos' ... not to mention the rank of yer feet, go soak 'em in that pond fer a bit..." He fell into fits of mirth unable to carry on at the thought.

"Yeah, just keep laughing, Nobby, At least my shit doesn't smell so bad, that you could bottle it and sell it to hunters!" Dirk shot back and the three fell into rapturous bouts of jollity.

"You know I half expected you guys to take off during the hunt, but... I don't know – you dudes are different to any other Bubba out there I've met. You don't seem to judge people." Zen became lost in a fit of emotion momentarily. "You are two cool bro's!"

Grot frowned as he tussled with his belt. "Huh? What in Keldor's name are you going on about?"

"He's pissed! Grot judges everyone and kills most of the buggers we meet before they can say so much as how do you do..." Dirk laughed slyly.

"No! I mean it. I love you guys..." Zen protested.

Dirk and Grot looked at each other and shared a knowing smirk. "Yeah well as long as it's kept to a brotherly distance that'll be fine. You my donkey bonking son *are pissed*, so get some sleep!" Grot ordered in mock annoyance.

"I'm not!" Zen protested. Then to prove his point he spread out his arms, tilted his chin upward and walked forward several paces, bumping into a tree as he did so.

Dirk sighed, "Well if ya think Grot don't judge people, you must be pissed. He's one of the most judgemental, Bigotry ridden, self opinionated individuals I know."

Grot looked at Dirk cross-eyed, "What's that about me being big? Are ye trying to be funny beanpole?"

"No way hosez..! I don't believe you two are arguing again. You do that a lot don't you?" Zen questioned.

"It keeps him on his toes – and besides we've hardly disagreed once since meeting up with you. Ya fancy yourself do yer?" Grot leered back.

"Dude you are whack! So what about the cuff when you got here, the push into the brambles earlier, and hey if I aint black but, was that not an outright brain-slapping contest during the game of Tag?"

"I don't mean any harm by it..." Grot seemed deeply perturbed, "I just wanna toughen him up – You aint seen him in battle, he's useless, *no*, *worse* than useless, he's a bleeding liability, if he were in a troop – he'd get everyone killed. He's; well, he's just bad to have around in times of crisis."

"No doubt those Gobbo's would agree, give us a bit of that meat Grot you tight git!" Dirk mulled aloud.

"What Goblins?" Zen asked in a semi alerted tone.

"Oh... They're all mashed up -dead, we left them way back..." Dirk began.

"Yeah, exactly – there's exactly what I'm talking about. Right listen Zen; A few days back, we are lost in some damn woods full of foul cretins, that dippy here had led us into, when he comes across a little Snurch, screams like a pig possessed, and goes running off like a little girl..."

"I weren't screaming!" Dirk objected as he greedily stole away the offered meat, from Grot's hunting knife.

"You were too!" Grot argued then turned to Zen who he also offered a slice of roast venison. "So anyway, he runs off screaming, with this tiny little Gnat's dick of a life-form chasing after him, so I gives up a prayer to Keldor and zooms after him – leaving most of our camping gear behind-"

"No-one asked you to!" Dirk spat between mouthfuls of juicy meat. "I would have packed it away if-"

A crack to the jaw from Grot sent meat flying and temporarily rested Dirk as the Dwarf continued with his tale. "Stop looking at me like that! He was talking shite; if I'd have spent the time waiting to strike our campsite, he'd have already been boiled and garnished."

Zen looked doubtful, "By a little Snurch dude?"

"No!" Grot pulled Dirk back upright and fed him more venison, "The Snurch chased him all the way back to a small Goblin encampment. Hold on! How did you get away anyway? Did you manage to kill the mucus mound at least?"

Dirk's hand automatically reached to touch his boot as he nodded.

"So what happened next my bearded chimp chum? Did you race in and save the day, all heroic like?" Zen stole back in.

"Yeah... That is, I bloody well had to, sort of..." Grot replied.

Taking a moment to slap Dirk into attentiveness the Dwarf offered out more meaty venison before continuing. "See I knew something would happen to him, so I went tear arsing into the camp, took out a couple of the dumbest bastards first off, then spotted a big bunch of bugbears and some right ugly gimps beyond them. So I ran at the smelly bastards first and made like a hatchet at a chopping party, then left them and ripped the shit out of the pig eyed black bastards beyond, no offence."

Zen frowned at the comment but let it pass: "So how did you get separated? Did the Dirk-dude run off again?"

"Nah but one of those evil eyed filth did. I was chasing them down, taking them out one at a time when he jumped across a river and I lost him."

"How exactly...?" Zen prompted.

"He fell in a stream..." Dirk dryly countered.

"Who did?" Zen looked confused.

"Old stumpy here, that's who!" Dirk shouted and managed a full length dive across the dying embers of the fire, feebly clutching the Dwarf by the scruff of his collar upon landing. "Tell him who rescued you old man. Tell him... Tell him. Just... tell him something..." Dirk drifted into slobbering mumbles, sinking to the ground and Grot nonchalantly rolled the human to one side as his robe began to catch afire.

"I think Dirk's a bit pissed too – and we're clearly smashed, well ye are. Let's get some bleeding rest, your welcome to travel with us in the morning, whatever morn it is; though I must admit were a bit lost in time and space." He paused to throw one of the woollen blankets over his inert colleagues form. "Nonetheless we have a plan to stick to; to get to Caernthorn and soon!"

Zen settled down after scraping and stamping the earth where he would sleep, but when it became obvious the Dwarf had become lost in his own rhetoric, the Satyr could not help ask a final question before he too gave in to sleep. "Grot... How did Dirk escape exactly?"

Studying his friends slumbering features, Grot took a moment to collect his thoughts before answering. "I'm not sure he did. Maybe he never will."

In the morning, while Dirk slept, Grot mended a few weapons as Zen struck camp and fastidiously cleared the area of any evidence of the previous night's activities.

"Keldor's beard be bloody well burned..! Are ye gonna replant the grass where we lit the fire too?" Grot exclaimed as Zen brushed the ground with a leafy fallen branch.

"No need to - I used stones to mark it out." Zen replied in all seriousness, oblivious to the gentle dig by the Dwarf.

Dirk awoke an hour or so later and after pausing to replenish water supplies and wash the night's excesses from their bodies, they set off together beyond the glade and towards the fairytale castle that towered high above and beyond the peaceful glade.

"Sure ya don't mind me tagging along Dwiff?" Zen asked Grot.

"Not at all pal." Grot replied with a smile, "You're good for my soul and besides, I'll have someone else to whack if you continue with the Dwarfish comments."

"Do you guys encounter many things ya don't wanna kill…?" Zen hinted suspiciously.

"In what way..? Grot's got a gripe with every single none Dwarven thing out there. But don't worry it's nothing personal against the things and people he kills… In fact the only race he consistently hates is Dwarves…"

"Speak for yourself yer lanky streak of piss, ya know I've got me reasons!" Grot remarked, "Dwarves are bastards and the rest of the shit normally needs killing, whether you friggin well like it or not."

"See!" Dirk ribbed.

The Dwarf turned his face to the wind, grumbling under his breath as he did so, "At least I've got my reasons…"

"How come were going this way?" Zen politely enquired.

"'Cause there's a bloody great castle thing over there that might just belong to someone who knows where the hell we are. Besides –a tower that size is bound to connect to a road." Grot deduced.

"What if there's no dude home?"

"Then we follow the road!" Grot replied with a shrug.

"What if there's no road?"

"Then we do a bit of building reclamation work!" Dirk cried out with a little too much enthusiasm. He treated the two sets of disapproving stares to a quick glimpse of his arse then quipped, "Besides, I wanna check out the view from the top of the tower!" And with that he shot off ahead.

Grot upped his pace to a slow jog and shouted after him to slow down and once again they were off on their trek to Caernthorn. Only now the two amigos had become three.

"I got a bleeding bad feeling about this…" Grot moaned, then turning his eyes to the skies he whispered into the wind "…And you lot up there can suck a spot from my stinking Dwarven ass for every bad experience that comes my bloody way…"

VIII) **The legacy of U'hl-Qoua**

Sf-vil U'hl Qoua, Princess of the imperious U'hl-Qoua…, …holder of the twin swords of K'lsh, and keeper of the ancient scrolls sat awkwardly upon the horse that skittered about beneath her alien presence.

She screeched out almost silent orders to those half-hidden forms that made up her small company of trusted warriors, they were elite, hand picked males, and her trust in them was absolute. Only the Fh'l-Qoua had questioned trusting as many as ten: Indeed, Sf-vil U'hl Qoua had only managed to placate him by promising that she would only take warriors who had personally served by her side in at least three battles and that no other would hold sway over her choices. Even as she had made the promise she had known it to be a lie, for she had already had to promise one of those appointments to Tr'y'al.

She had little choice in the matter, the Tr'y'al (the title given to the royal personal bodyguard), was an arrogant, brutal, untrustworthy male and even though it had been his job to defend her life ever since she was birthed, she had no love for him. Indeed, if it had not been to placate her mothers paranoia she would certainly have picked another in his place.

Yet another four of her suggested troupe had been more or less forced on her by politics and a further male was given preference merely due to their shared bloodline. Nevertheless, she had assembled her males beside her and with her sitting atop the foreign neighing creature they had descended into the valleys where humans lived.

Up until recently, there had been only light skirmishes involving Wolves, Goblins and the occasional Wyvern, but as they descended the mountain from which they had issued forth, the wild beasts became fewer and were replaced by several near misses with Humans.

It was night by the time they had come into actual contact with the first humans and Sf-vil U'hl Qoua had been unsure of how the strange creatures would react when they met a superior race such as her own.

The meeting went terribly awry;: Introducing herself in almost faultless common, the princess had let fall her hood and offered up her dagger blade showing; as was rightful tradition when entering another persons home in peace…

…Yet the gruff balding human who had answered to her call, reacted violently pushing the princess back and swearing piteously for his unseen family to come to arms and the small homestead had erupted into a wailing cacophony of screaming confusion; whose echoes had threatened to betray them to every enemy for miles. She had instructed Tr'y'al to silence them and the blade-butchery that ensued had confirmed his reputation for deadly efficiency. U'hl Qoua was disgusted, ones such as he were needed in all societies… But his enjoyment went beyond a mere love of killing –it was his fix. He had to have at least one murder a day.

He was not a warrior, she reflected looking over to where he now skulked. A warrior would be willing to die at the hands of the enemy. A true warrior shared a mutual respect for his enemy and paid their respects to those that fell to their blade. Not Tr'y'al. He excelled in murder and even in the most clinical of battles he would be capable of no less. Any target that presented them selves on the battlefield he would take, despite the so-called code of battle that those of his caste were meant to live by. His respect for the corpses of those fallen, extended only as far as to what end the corpse could serve him. Be-it as food, furniture or some other unforeseen purpose such as an impromptu shield, Tr'y'al had a way of finding uses for bodies that others would prefer to see buried or burned.

It had only been because she had commanded him by royal order to obey, that Tr'y'al had been dissuaded of utilising two of the young ones as impromptu stools. Instead the corpses of all of the homesteads former occupants had been burned on a pyre, as was befitting to a fallen innocent.

The one thing that had worried her as she had watched the bodies' burn was the thought that they had all been a little too eager to assume their early detection would lead to a threat and although the funeral pyre was proper –its smoke and light had been far too revealing in this open air environment than she had anticipated. Six hours had passed since and they had not seen another human, even though they had moved ever closer to the town which was their target destination.

She paused now as she neared the human settlement, the beast was still skittish and she could only ascertain that this must be due to the equestrian steed being as uncomfortable as she was.

Sf-vil U'hl Qoua's soldiers lay hidden amongst the shadowy trunks of the Elm trees that sprang up magnificently to both sides of the road much like the stalagmites of home. A light near the town gates betrayed the presence of a group of humans and she responded by spurring the horse into a trot. She found it was quite a similar manner of control in which she had been taught to ride brutes rather more exotic than this.

As her horse traversed the 500 or so metres distance to the gates, she noticed that the humans had armed themselves with various pitchforks and such and were making a bad attempt at concealing their presence. She counted around twenty amongst them, and determined two things of importance; firstly she decided this rabble must be the town's local militia and secondly, someone must have discovered the funeral pyre and alerted the town to the presence of danger.

How prepared where they? She wondered. It would have been a short 20 minute trek along the road that led to the town, yet they had taken to the refuge of a goat trail in order to reach the small hamlet unannounced. That journey had taken them well over an hour, so it really was a case of how soon they had heard the news and just how vigilant they were.

"Khan's children fall, Dawn comes already," she hissed as a tinge of treacherous orange light crept along the carpet of the horizon. "I wonder, I wonder indeed…" U'hl Qoua whispered to herself, she was remembering some of the words from the prophecy, but substituted their human equivalent instead as she spoke quietly into the air. "Come into my parlour, ssaid the sspider to the fly!"

She surveyed the hamlet or at least what she could see of it behind its high wooden stockade. She counted several roofs of particularly high buildings and guessed these would be the main fest hall, courthouse, temple, and mayoral residence: Most civilized societies tended to adhere to similar social philosophies in regards to the building of settlements, with the exception of a few.

She had no sure idea of how many homes lay within, but she guessed from the circumference of the walls and the size of the badly hidden militia that the population would be around 200 or so inhabitants.

'Of course!' she thought; the awaiting mob lay in ambush in case the creatures responsible for the carnage showed up, and it seemed obvious that they may wish to question her, but this was not a problem for Sf-vil U'hl-Qoua. She was trained in Disguise as proficiently as she was in battle, and many more skills besides. Hence her plan to ride alone to the gates… Glancing around her surroundings, she wondered briefly how human priests and royalty were reared and found herself thinking of her own…

As a member of the U'hl-Qoua, Sf-vil was accredited with the ultimate respect of her people. The U'hl Qoua were supposedly ruled by a council of ten powerful families, whose eldest presided as statesman. Of course, every now and then one of these family lines would die out in which case the more prominent none member families would petition for the vacant place.

Each and every aspect of the U'hl-Qoua community from slave to queen had to answer to the council. The Queen though had three lethal ingredients at her disposal, loyalty, corruption and power and this mixed with a seat on the council meant that true power had never really diversified from the throne.

The government worked well as its main proponents were fear and intimidation, with the queen leading the way on issues, surrounded by paper politicians, who in truth were little more than scheming lackeys. Every now and then one of the families elder would die and their successor would foolishly challenge the morality of their cultures politics. These leaders never led for long. The last to try it was personally beheaded by the queen; in the middle of the marketplace with a spade no less.

Yes, the government worked but moreover, it worked because the council in its entirety had to answer to their national faiths solitary figurehead. Their were acolytes to the faith, the amount varied from region to region, but these 'faith-finders' were little more than religious tramps or beggars, who had given up 'the life' in order to devote themselves to their murderous god and his biddings, thus their was never a shortage of zealots to call on during times of crisis, but these peoples status was below that of a worthy slave.

A selfish god imbues selfish values and so their religion which was beholden to the virtues of Khan, held but one recognised priest. During *his* lifetime, when the priest in question sees fit, *he* will appoint one of the acolytes as his disciple and that person, upon the priests death (no matter how untimely) becomes the new leader of an entire race and must one day soon pick his own potential successor.

The position of public priest had always been the one and only powerful role within society where males were allowed to undertake a rank of high social status and thus whether one felt particularly close to Khan or not, everybody clamoured for attention when the priest was around, swearing all sorts of shallow oaths to their treacherous god.

To say the appointment was strongly desired would be a vast understatement. Many died every day over events pertaining or related to the title of priest, from arguments to assassination and back again. The elders hated the power of the temple, yet vowed allegiance to their gods chosen one. While the queen consulted daily with the priest and worked with him in concert to govern their joint people; all the while planning his demise and working to suggest an acolyte of her own to his successor. The role merely added another dysfunctional facet to the government; enforced unity.

In the society of U'hl-Qoua murder was permitted by anyone against anyone of the same social status, meaning everyone except the queen and the priest was a potential target for their fellow man or woman. The queen or priest could have anyone killed including one another. Next in line were the other council members who could arrange the assassination of any other councillor and any other member of society they took a disliking too on the downwards social ladder.

Next came lesser nobility, who could war against other nobles and their footmen and then the officers who were almost all female, excepting in the ranks of the royal guard. A notable point not eluded to until now is that only females may kill or have killed other females, so in layman's terms if you were a male religious zealot your life expectancy varied from short to gosh I'm dead already...

In this mighty mix came the devotion law, which meant in simplicity that it was fine to prove your devotion to Khan through murder and deception as long as one did not interfere with the Prophecy; a spoken religious text, foretelling the pre-destined path of the U'hl-Qoua. An oral retelling of a past, present and future to which all were devoted, yet only the ordained priest knew entirely.

What made Sf-vil extra special was that she not only possessed an enormous intellect and aptitude beyond her peers, nor merely was she the only surviving daughter and heir to the current queen but rather because she had been born into the position of acolyte according to the prophecies...

...On the day of her birth, Fh'l-Qoua who had himself only been in the position of priest for a half year, came marching in, snatched up Sf-vil and declared her to be their faiths first female novice in waiting. The Queen was initially amused by the brash young priest's actions, until he went outside and repeated the declaration to the assembled masses and gathered courtesans.

Ten days later on her naming day, he again overstepped the mark when he interrupted her ceremony to announce to all attending that she would be known that day forth as Sf-vil (Saviour of All), U'hl-Qoua (Under God). This upset her mother no end and from here the foundations of a long term feud were sewn. The Queen and church were at constant loggerheads over her tutelage, general upbringing, and more critically her commitments. As her mother grew in age so she gained in mass, and as she grew into her teens, Sf-vil was given command of the empires armies. A nonsensical assignment, the sole purpose of which was to further her involvement in state matters.

At the same time her development as an acolyte meant that she had to undertake several life-threatening trials, not to mention countless studies and endlessly listening to Fh'l-Qoua in his remonstrations of the Prophecy, hence both priesthood and nation began to show the signs of a decline.

By her twenty first naming day it was Sf-vil herself who settled the dispute, she engineered a war between her own nation and that of a race of deep Elf with whom they had shared a border and held amicable relations with for centuries past.

Although their eons old truce ran well on paper, countless acts of espionage had been perpetrated by both sides down the years. Sf-vil had taken the opportunity to enter into a dispute about faith, with a rare occurrence indeed; a young Elf general who had never heard of her. The Princesses own faith required her to be knowledgeable about those of others and she had arranged the conversation so as to draw the elf in question into delivering unknowing insults to her faith amid a host of witnesses.

After alienating everyone save his powerful uncle, the youthful Elven general had begged Sf-vil to forgive his ill words which she had duly done so before nailing him to the roof of the outpost they shared by his tongue. The short war that ensued empowered her with a genuine excuse for missing her theological studies and so she recoiled from the church for a while. After narrowly avoiding a massacre in her first ever large scale battle, she managed to head off several ambitious coup-de-tats; a couple of botched assassination attempts and a small rebellion amongst her own rank and file, funded no doubt by the offended Elven uncle.

Nevertheless, she survived her ordeals through wit an' worth and returned to the site of her enemies' stronghold, where she led a small band through the sewers and up into the enemy keep, slaying their officers in their beds and poisoning the foot-soldiers nightly banquet.

Peace was sued for quite quickly after that, but Sf-vil prevaricated, utilising the time seemingly spent in negotiation to strengthen borders, drive back encroaching enemies and generally restore order among the ranks and generals alike. When she was satisfied with ongoing reparations she accepted terms for a conditional peace and returned to Fh'l-Qoua and his teachings.

"Mistress..!" One of her male guides whispered, interrupting her thoughts, but she silenced him with a gesture and continued her slow gait forward, her thoughts once again returning to the prophecy.

The text of her people was a strange thing -for a start it was no text at all but merely remembered words passed from Priest to Acolyte, and therefore open to possible embellishment and misinterpretation, yet as far as she was aware none had ever changed its telling and in her lifetime she was determined that none will or would. Fh'l-Qoua had told her most of it and though it's telling was varied in focus, the current era was dominated by the prophecy concerning herself. What was stranger than life was that though she disliked or hated most other races, the prophecies deemed her to be the beacon of hope and reconciliation. She was the one to bring her people out of the shadow. Her lot in life was to unite her people with those of the upworlders, and as much as she queried her own role in the great scheme, she believed in its telling blindly, following unquestioningly the path mapped out for her by Khan.

"The Prophethy ith off to a good thtart then!" she mused aloud. She spoke in an imitated human accent this time, renewing her familiarity with the strange vowels that littered the humans' speech. Sf-vil had been instructed in the language by the greatest scholar in her land, Fh'l-Qoua. As well as acting as her mentors for many years, Fh'l-Qoua was her most trusted friend back home. Thanks to his fine academic skills, she could speak the human tongue better than most humans - with the exception of her 'S' sounds. The fault was not in her but due to the shape of her tongue, which was forked at the tip. Fh'l-Qoua had suggested stitches, but to do so, would be a crime against her people, not to mention it preventing her from pronouncing her own tongue and so she had respectfully declined for the time being.

Instead then, he had taught her to disguise the fault in her vocal repertoire as a speech impediment that he assured her many humans shared, even creatively using the 'th' sound to increase the illusions believability.

Her hunched back really was hunched, though not in a way that an observer may be led to believe. Her black gloved hands, and feet swathed in bandages, coupled with a long grey frayed robe with a voluminous hood, completed a particularly clever deception. Even the horse was for show - a flea-bitten old nag that she had found half starved and hopelessly lost in the craggy reaches high above.

"Who goes there?" soared out the voice of the Night watchman, the sudden query matched only by the immediate cessation of noise from the assembled lurking militia. Sf-vil switched off from all thoughts of her homeland in readiness for the task at hand.

"A thtranger on the road," Sf-vil U'hl-Qoua answered back, "I nced the protecthion of a bed for the night. I mutht be away from people however, ath I have a Leprouthy!" She finished and pulled in her horse 10 or so metres from the gate. It would take them a while to sort out what she had said U'hl-Qoua realised and sat quietly awaiting their response.

It came in the form of an ambush as she had half expected, but not in the manner that she had been prepared for.

The militia darted forward just as she had anticipated they would, but not at her. Instead they launched themselves at the gates, throwing them open in quick detail. From out of the gates two Knights of the Faith (or Paladins as some would call them), charged out on huge sparkling, armour plated stallions, giving the impression that some godly twins had descended from upon high. They were dressed in full battle armour, which despite the religious embellishments looked sturdy enough and were followed by several other less impressive but no less threatening Knights on similarly armoured beasts.

"A badly dissguissed trap to massquerade the true ambush!" she said to herself as she steered her horse into a trot back towards the tree lined approach. She was impressed by the plan and made a mental note to add it to her tactical compendium. She also made a note not to fall for the same ploy twice. Sf-vil U'hl-Qoua always made a point to learn from her mistakes, so that she never suffered defeat by the same tactic more than once, if defeat came at all.

Sf-vil U'hl-Qoua had suffered many defeats, more so than any other general of her ilk, yet her trouncing was never complete, her losses little more than short lived setbacks, moreover and what stirred a grudging admiration from all but Tr'y'al, was that she truly did learn to such great effect from any transitory downfall; often revisiting the consequences a thousand times worse upon her former antagonist. It would not be too great a lie to say that most of her racial enemies both knew of her and feared her to a man.

It was said by many in her homeland; both admirers and adversaries alike that unless one was a great tactician *and* confident of an inescapable triumph, the challenger would be a very short lived opponent indeed… She hoped the saying were true here in the up-world as U'hl-Qoua managed to coerce her resisting nag into a full gallop back towards the trees where the assembled males of her small troupe lay in wait. Her flea-bitten charge broke into top stride just in time to keep her ahead of the lesser knights mounts, but not before the Paladins had caught up to ride alongside her.

The Princess whistled a shrill command to the hidden figures of her men, making sure that they stayed hidden until the last of the knights' had entered the leafy causeway, embedded as it were, in the fleetingly moonlit shadows. The Paladin to her right was obviously not as proficient at handling his steed as the one to her left for he clutched at the rains in a manner that suggested he could ride or fight but not both. Leaning her mount towards his own she shoved at his shoulder, propelling the human's heavily armoured bulk crashing to the ground at pace. As bad as his mastery of the beast may have been, the dismounted knight showed he was an absolute expert on the ground by immediately going into a tumble roll, the armours stiff looking plate unfathomably warping to match his movements, and came up onto his feet weapons at the ready.

The still mounted Paladin took advantage of Sf-vil's distraction, drawing a mace from amongst the deadly assortment affixed to his mounts livery. As U'hl-Qoua shifted her weight back into the saddle, the religious combatant swung the round headed mace with unholy malice.

Intense throbs of pain positively pounced through U'hl-Qoua's shoulders as the knights weapon came into contact. Sf-vil squealed as much in anger as from the hurt and she whipped her body around, cold yellow eyes gleaming with annoyance as her hood slipped slightly.

"…Sl'y'nt'dv-eeSH!" She screamed out, and switching back to the human language added. "You will die!" to the one that had struck her.

Her warriors streamed out from their hiding places every ten feet or so along the trees and pounced on the rider nearest to them.

The mounted Paladin swung his mace out towards U'hl-Qoua's face, whilst thrusting a knife towards the outline of her robed back. The deception was a good one, but not clever enough to get the better of U'hl-

Qoua. Flinging her hood back with a toss of her head, she pushed the arm holding the mace upwards upsetting the combatants balance and then shifted her torso to one side as she felt the knives presence tearing through the rear of her cloak.

By this time they had ridden quite a way from the heat of the main battle, with neither attempting to slow their mounts, though the chase proved too much for the dejected beast on which she rode, which was being driven on purely in fear of the situation it had found itself embroiled in. Hers was no war steed after all. She gave its flanks a vicious kick in an attempt to spur on the half dead thing and it did try to respond to the claw ripping footwork, but as it attempted one last gallop the poor things heart simply burst from the strain...

Skidding to its knees on the stone-ridden path, dying eyes fixated upon the ground that would soon serve as its grave, Sf-vil's mount tumbled in flight. U'hl-Qoua fought the reins to gain some amount of control over the monumental skid, whilst eking out every last ounce of her skills in animal mastery to keep the creature from plummeting altogether uncontrollably. The most impressive thing was that she mastered all of this despite having to fight to retain her own balance; whilst also avoiding the thrusts and sweeps of the mighty bastard-sword that her enemy now wielded.

Anyone could have been forgiven for thinking that the Paladin would better her; the crisis warranted it. Yet even before her skills finally failed her and flung her battered body crashing along the bumpy road, U'hl-Qoua was already planning her next move...

...Sf-vil's jaw clenched to suppress the cries of hurt as each jutting rock helped her on her bone crunching way... When at last the erratic tumble had finally come to an end, her body lay twisted at seemingly odd angles, and the only movement was a continuous nervous twitch in the index finger of her left hand.

The Paladin slowed his horse, but instead of dismounting to check the body, he remained seated and pulled in the reins of his mighty beast forcing it to circle the creatures fallen form. The knight's eyes narrowed behind his slatted gaze as he paused for signs of life, but other than the twitch there was nothing. There was a smooth swishing sound as he drew a Steel javelin from the leather scabbard it occupied and nudged his horse towards U'hl-Qoua's prone mass. A yellow eye flickered open, then shut.

Upping his horses canter, the Paladin charged towards the body his

Javelin poised for the kill… Despite the fact she already appeared dead, for Paladins can see through deception with ease. U'hl-Qoua listened as the sound of hooves signalled the sudden switch of pace, and she waited for as long as she dared then sprang upwards leaving the tattered cloak behind. Liberated of the garb that had helped conceal her identity, she was a formidable looking warrior even for a Lizardman, as those of her race were often called.

Her slender supple body uncoiled to over eight feet in height, the dark green hue of her smooth scales being lent a slimy look in the full-moons silvery light. A reddish crest ran from the crown of her squat shaped skull, down the length of her spine and along the ridge of her long twitching tail. The mystical armour that adorned her torso and arms shone with an ethereal blue glow. And sheathed within blue crystalline scabbards, two matt black swords hung by her side, their pommels glittering with jewels of the utmost rarity.

The Paladin, who had thought to plunge the Javelin into an unresisting and somewhat cowardly foe, found himself caught quite unawares. Snapping the reins back, he forced the creature to rear up onto its hind legs; a feat that proved difficult at the best of times was compounded by the problems of having to bear an unnaturally heavy weight.

A great cracking sound gave indication of danger, and the knight leapt backwards out of the saddle as his beast's hind quarters buckled and snapped. Landing on his feet, the knight rushed past the horse that tossed and kicked out in pain, grabbing an axe from its flanks as he did so. Stood some ten feet or so from U'hl-Qoua, the knight whirled the axe around, switching focus; the axe cleaving the head off the horse in an instant, settling its movements almost instantaneously and lending the animal peace.

Freed of the danger presented by the beast's death throes, the impressive fighter switched his stance again, as U'hl-Qoua's tail whipped out towards his face. Spinning and twisting in mid air with an ease that belied his armoured bulk, he came down on all fours beside his deceased former mount, a slight trickle of blood welling upon his cheek and minus his weapon, which he had discarded mid-dodge.

U'hl-Qoua uncoiled her tail and sprang through the air, her well-muscled legs driving her forward. She landed atop the horse carcass and smashed her now bare foot downwards towards her sacred foe. The quick-thinking knight rolled backwards clutching the pommel of a huge two handed sword. The action of grabbing the sword slowed him slightly and a shout of sudden pain escaped his bloodied lips as U'hl-Qoua's extended claws scraped a bloody weal across his brow, ripping through the steel helmet as though butter...

Doffing his helmet in order to clear his obscured vision, The Holy knight just had time to dodge to one side as U'hl-Qoua again pressed her advantage; slashing away with the vigour of a rabid Manticore.

Sf-vil U'hl-Qoua grinned in admiration for her opponent, the needle toothed smile only serving to make her look even more feral than before. She paused a moment to think as the knight tumbled a semi-safe distance away.

Taking advantage of the brief lull in battle, the knight scrutinised the Lizard woman's countenance further still and noticed that her left arm was bloodied and hung limply by her side. The fact she managed to hold a sword in the damaged hand let alone fence off his blows impressed him mightily.

He raised the double handed blade in front of him to salute her, the blade pulsing with white light as he did so. The two combatants then flung themselves at each other with renewed vigour; her two iridescent blades fighting against his solo paragon of justice in even contention.

They fought in a compulsive dance of death, feinting to this side and that, driving each other back and forth, all throughout trying to land a blow of their own, whilst dodging their opponents' unwelcome endeavours. Any other warrior may have fallen at the initial onslaught, but this knight was a veteran of many battles, fought good and true, a true knight of the realm so to speak, and she was the fabled One, who fought to a prophecy, despite her pains both bodily and mental.

As it was, the Paladin managed to last nearly thirty seconds before Sf-vil U'hl-Qoua struck the telling blow..., ...It came as the Knight brought his mighty Claymore swooping around forcing U'hl Qoua to jump into the air, less she lose her legs. As she sprang into the air, the warrior princess again flicked out her tail, this time damaging the facial area of the knight she fought against fair pummelling the left eye socket and cheekbone.

The heavy blade dropped to the ground, as the holy warrior clutched at the tendrils that hung limply from his blood drenched face. A vicious backhand from U'hl-Qoua struck the knight full in the Jaw, dropping him to one knee and breaking several teeth. Yet, even now he attempted to fight on, groping blindly for the knife that no longer occupied the sheath on his leg.

"Tell me your name sso that I may honour your valour!" U'hl-Qoua commanded, dropping the put on speech impediment as she toyed with the knight's confiscated dagger. This was no ordinary fighter that knelt before her and her pains bespoke it in volumes.

"…A-Agrilot." The Paladin replied without expression, his body stiffening as deaths eye passed over him in pain chilling revelry. With that answer, U'hl-Qoua's slicing backhand ended his misery and took his life in an instant, tearing out his throat and leaving him dead on his feet. U'hl-Qoua would bury him later herself she decided, he deserved at least that.

Right now though, Sf-vil began moving cautiously back towards the tree lined avenue that lead back towards the village, yet the silence that pervaded the night air worried her. Either her hand picked elite guard had been more efficient than usual, unlikely, given the fact that they were outnumbered by at least two to one, or there was treachery abroad amongst her own ranks and she knew which option she was going to expect.

'…Agrilot! Agrilot…Agrilot!' She concentrated on the name for a brief moment, but in truth, she had no idea of the man or his undoubted reputation, one thing she knew with certainty was that a fighter of his calibre never just happened to be around. She suddenly had the idea of going back to check out the magical armour that Agrilot wore, but was afraid in case prying eyes may construe her actions as a retreat. Her life depended on her doing nothing to arouse the suspicion of the would-be deadly ambushers, who were no doubt lurking in the shadows beyond…

Sf-vil U'hl-Qoua thought back to the friendly warning she had done her utmost to heed. Her most valued and trusted friend Fh'l-Qoua, had been the one to give her the sage advice. "…Trust No-One!" He had admonished, "Not even your mother, the queen, nor I your mentor and priest, for though I would never lie about the word of Qoua; I too have my own interests to protect. Bear in mind child of Khan, that there are many within our race that would prefer the prophecy did not succeed at all. As you are aware from the teachings I have given thee, remember thy own fate…, …Hardly appetizing yet…, …It doesn't seem to have dissuaded you from your course, strange such devotion…" She reflected on the words and how he had then implored her to take only the most skilled warriors from the elite royal guard from the four remaining recruitment slots. "The deadliest allies will be needed if we are to succeed in our grand plan... For there can be no mistakes."

As she limped towards the death foretold in her own religious prophecy U'hl-Qoua thought upon those words. 'Now I know why, old friend. Your plan was not my own. Nor that staked in the prophecies, I guess or at least HOPE you were simply following the texts that tell of the betrayal by those held dearest. But your minions shall not prevail this day, for whether you truly believe it or not, I AM the daughter of Khan...'

She stumbled then; it was an art she had practised to perfection, playing possum. But the pain in her left side was immense. Her left shoulder, already damaged by the mace early on, had popped out of the socket as she had battled to control her fallen steed earlier; she had further aggravated the problem when tumbling along the road, adding to that several well struck cuts from Agrilot and the left arm was now next to useless. So her intended pretence of stumbling was given weight by the reality of her situation and she thanked the gods for the Injuries obviousness.

Slowly rising to her feet, she looped back the cords that held her twin blades in place once more, and muttered a silent prayer of healing that instantly restored the battered left side to full health. Only she did not alter her stance at all, instead letting the arm hang limply by her side. Regaining her stride, U'hl-Qoua once again pressed on into the very real danger of the ambush she believed lay ahead.

This time it did happen much as she had expected it would; as she picked her way through the various corpses that told of a bitter battle she suspected had never been fought.

Once she was far enough down the approach road, the 'corpses' came to life, rising up to form a circle around her and cutting off any chance of escape. U'hl-Qoua blessed her luck as she counted the opponents that surrounded her. Her 'loyal' troupe stood alongside the knights, mixed in betwixt their ranks, whilst the decoy militia had retreated to within the safety of the town gates, which now were firmly closed. All that remained where six knights, a Paladin and the traitorous males of her troupe.

She could not see Tr'y'al anywhere, which probably meant he would strike her from behind. What did a male like him know of honour? She spat at the feet of the Paladin whom she had dislodged earlier, her spittle deliberately mixed with gum chewed blood.

142

"Thou and thy legacy hath verily run thy course wicked one. Unsheathe thy weapons and bequeath them unto me, and I shall see thy death be swift. There is no honour in following a false prophecy." The Knight of the Faith confidently instructed her.

A whole minute of tension passed without the princess so much as flickering an eye or tail. "Ye have been defeated!" the knight nearest the Paladin laughed incredulously. "Thee are naught but a corpse to be ..." the Holy Knight acquiesced, his disbelief evident as U'hl-Qoua silently stood upright and turned to face him, " 'tis a madness to resist ... ...," the knight was obviously struggling with his conscience and the morals to which he held so dearly... "Might we be forced to fall upon thee where thou stand?" He searched her expression with pleading eyes, but she stood firm.

"So be it..." Ordered the Paladin, pausing to give her one last chance with which to reconsider, yet her resolve showed no change - no gesture - nothing save that cold blank expression of defiance. "Finish her." he instructed the others and began to turn away in pity.

"I AM SF-VIL U'HL-QUA OF THE DJISX U'HL-QUA!" Her tone was eerily commanding in the clawing night air, causing all to be held by the gravity of her words. The Paladin glanced back and began to turn to face her. "Daughter to the queen, child of our godsss, and the Propheciesss chossen bearer and I promisse all thosse that opposse me that It iss not I that sshall die thisss day..., ...but them!" U'hl-Qoua's voice held an Imperial quality that sent a chill down the spine of her would be assassins.

Her blades sang as she whipped them out of her sheathes and crossed them in a scissor like motion in front of her and the once talkative Paladins head neatly popped off doll-like, rolling unceremoniously to the ground, his dismembered torso's arms clutching comically at the previously occupied space.

U'hl-Qoua kicked the body over, without any of the respect afforded to her previous opponent and readied herself as the first wave of shocked combatants rushed forward to meet the cold substance of her blades.

The first group to reach her were two thoughtless knights and one stupid Snake-man. "L'qu'IL...!" Shouting a single word, a cold white light erupted from her blades, causing them to shield their eyes from its piercing intensity. U'hl-Qoua had already closed her eyes before muttering the arcane phrase and using her blind-fighting skills she first disembowelled her own 'guard' member, before hacking into the arm of one of the knights and then severing the tendons of the second mans hamstring.

"...J'hi'ish-L'qu'll!" She spoke again and the light was gone as abruptly as it had appeared. This caused confusion to the second wave of fighters whose eyes had just become accustomed to the lights rays. A Lizardman came stumbling right up to her and she almost felt pity for the fool as her swords flashed upwards and then across, she rolled across his back as the things innards spilled out from the cross shaped cavity etched into his torso.

Two other Lizardman stood nearby, stunned from the light still –or lack thereof. Flipping the sword in her left hand as she moved, she smashed the pommel with all her force into the temple of the first, while its twin blade jutted upwards, cracking the jaw of the second and splitting the creature's maw in two.

She whirled around just in time to avoid being backstabbed by a member of the third wave, whose eager weapon plunged into his treacherous brethren and with a shout in some ancient version of her own tongue, U'hl-Qoua sent a wave of thunderous energy cackling out from the blades, and towards the four knights who stood a little way off.

The knights dived for cover as their brains kicked into gear, but not quickly enough to avoid being damaged by the shocking blast, which would surely have crippled them all had it not been for one unfortunate fellow. The chap had tripped forwards in his confused attempts to escape, sending him instead reeling headfirst into the bolts unforgiving path. There was a fair boom as the magical bolt struck the knights armoured body, the metal layers multiplying its explosive effectiveness and the impact sent his fried corpse flying some fifty feet through the air, where it landed just in front of the town gates, much to the horror of those watching from within as great whoops of smoke belched out from the char-grilled human.

Two of the three knights remaining fled for the protection offered by the towns stockade with desperate pleas for someone to open the gate. But the liveried guards atop the lit tower refused them entry.

Four Lizardmen were upon U'hl-Qoua now and it was all she could do to fend off the thrusts of their blades. Then help arrived from the most unlikely source. Tr'y'al, who had until this point been nowhere in sight, hammered home his own blade, smashing the skull of one of U'hl-Qoua's assailants and covering the melee's participants in pieces of brain and bone. One of the Lizardman, Xs'll-Hs'ish, whose skills with a blade was almost as unrivalled amongst her kind as herself, turned his attention to dealing with Tr'y'al and Sf-vil U'hl-Qoua was thankful for it.

She made space for herself as the remaining two were joined by a third and then screamed out a bone chilling Dweomer, A red sphere of light encased her in its molten glow and her swords left her hands and began revolving around her, making it impossible for anyone to make a clean hit. One of the more foolish combatants made an attempted backstab only to be torn apart by her cyclonic blades. Sf-vil's body arched back and a ghoulish green light spilled from her eyes and open mouth as she was lifted from the ground by an unseen force. A stream of syllables unheard by even herself before that day, spewed forth with a life of their own…

…With a roaring sound to match the intensity of a tumultuous waterfall, the two lights combined and spewed forth a squall so violent, it squeezed the breath out of the two knights who had hoped to escape and sent them tumbling like feathers caught in the wind. The gates and half the escarpment of the stockade came crashing down around them, killing the cowardly pair and no doubt a fair few innocents inside too.

Tr'y'al fought with more ferocity than he had ever mustered and the fight between him and Hs'ish was a bitter no holds barred exercise in barbarity. Both males knew and respected the others blade skills and a swordfight twixt the two would likely never be resolved. A nod from one to the other, traitor to loyal bodyguard, was all the understanding needed and both had dropped their weapons at once and began to doff their protective gear. Once their armoured vestments and weapons had been removed, the two had lunged at one another with a hatred borne from an ancient rivalry. It was a hatred that U'hl-Qoua had certainly never understood, even though she was the cause. For both males were doomed to love her, and though neither had ever spoken to U'hl-Qoua of their feelings, it was undeniably etched into their very souls.

So the two admirers fought, wrestling one another to the ground. Their claws tore eagerly, insanely at the others flesh and their teeth bit deep into anything that bore purchase. The blood drenched both within minutes, their maddened wills driving them to fight through the pain.

U'hl-Qoua came down to Eyrthe with a thump; her swords falling flaccid as her mystical power drained from her, and the three remaining Lizardmen who had cowered away mere moments before, now bore her defenceless figure to the ground, ripping at her flesh as if insane…

Tr'y'al and Hs'ish fought on defiantly neither caring for their own life such was their intent to rip apart the other. And so neither of them noticed the remaining knight's approach…

He did not hesitate for one moment and struck his dagger with such force as to envelop his hand in the spleen of Tr'y'al, eyes bulging with delight at the conclusion of his treacherous deed. Yet In his fury at the intrusion, Hs'ish pounced on his would be saviour and began eating him alive starting with the squealing knights face, gnawing through to the perished knights brain before Hs'ish himself fell to the floor - all his lives regrets and wishes spanning the years he had known flooding into his oxygen starved brain.

U'hl-Qoua, exhausted from the earlier incantation could not find the strength to fight off the three Lizardmen and when it became apparent that she was beaten into submission, their animal instincts took over and they began ripping away her the remnants of her clothing and armour, taking turns to hold Sf-vil's screeching swats down, whilst one of their number attempted to plunge his manhood into her mouth in hateful resolve, laughing maniacally.

Sf-vil U'hl-Qoua screamed out an oath of desperate pleading to her god, knowing even as she did so that even if her prayers were heard Khan would no doubt betray her further merely for showing such weakness. "Why abandon me now my dear father Khan? What has this one done to deserve such a fate…?" Qoua burst into tears as ripping clawed hands pushed unwelcome fingers into her most delicate and private of parts. "Khan I beg you; please…" She plead aloud before adding to those that assaulted her; "I am your princess and future priestess you treacherous scum. Get off me, **I command it**, please…, …*I command you…, …**I beg you; stop!***"

"Cheer up princess…" One of her rapists gloated: "You are about to be pleasured in a way no priestess would ever be allowed to be…" The male leered, slowly licking a trail of saliva across one of her scratched, exposed breasts; pausing to suck deeply on the nipple, while shoving his scratching fingers deeper into the soft folds of her vagina and tearing her hymen without mercy. Another knelt on her arms; her muscles too fatigued to resist whilst the third knelt down and greedily licked at her bloodied genitalia, pausing to nip a little here and there.

The act of being raped pained her more than any battle-wound she had ever received, the unwavering resolve of the sexually frantic Lizardmens' ministrations mixing a sickly-sweet arousal to her painful rejections; and she screamed to herself inside her own mind; slanting all manner of insults towards herself; for being weak, for being helpless, for being aware of her foretold degradation, for being wet…

She scratched and kicked as best she could, but the horror in her heart and the weakness of her limb's, drained the last remnants of fight from her and she fell into a catatonic state of shock. The Lizardmen cried out to one another with whoops of joy, taking her acquiescence and the production of body fluids to be a sign that she was indeed enjoying it despite herself. The one who had been doing the job of holding down the princesses arms abandoned his station and pushed his thick, barbed penis into her glistening pussy even as his companion continued to lick her breasts and neck and forcing the third who had been performing a feral oral sex act, to switch his attentions to her anus, probing with two of his rough fingers while licking and nibbling at the rim of her anal canal.

Still U'hl-Qoua made no great movement and the three took her lack of fight as incentive to be more barbaric in their ministrations, and they bit and pulled at her extremities in lust filled, devilish delight - ramming their penis' into her two and three at a time as if wanting the act to rip her apart. One of their number lifted the flaccid princess in one arm bending her over facing away from him; all the while lining up his penis with her rear, while another began forcing the princess to suck on his cock. When the one doing the holding was satisfied with his position he pushed his penis into her anal passage, forcing his thick length into her inch by pain stabbing inch without slowing then rapidly banging away with his full length.

The third had by this time positioned himself below the princess and he pushed up with his own somewhat smaller but no less invasive prick into her slippery pussies hole, doubling her pain and pleasure in an instant. U'hl-Qoua screamed in her mind, but outwardly could show no emotion as the three laughed, scratched, pummelled and pervaded every one of her senses, plunging their pulsating manhood's into each of her orifices. She hated herself; not only were the pleasures of the body forbade, she genuinely had never felt any sexual impulses and even if she were to she would have wanted any encounter to be far more honourable than this. Sf-vil was desolate; her thoughts shrank to an island in the siege she felt entrapped within for while her body seemed content to indulge, her self respect left her sickened.

When they had finished their most unwholesome deed, the three resumed beating her and when she still did not respond they set about raping her again. Using their arms and teeth to open her further...

Hs'ish felt the pain in his body and his eyes fluttered open, his battle lust subsided; he pushed the knight's half eaten corpse from him. He was covered head to toe in blood and knew not how much of it was his own.

Yet the pain he felt encased in was mind-numbing in its intensity and he knew he did not have long to live. Staggering to his feet, he wiped the blood from his drenched eye sockets only to find that he could still not see out of one eye. Scanning around the battle scene in confusion he espied what his comrades were doing and let out a blood curdling roar.

The others, thinking that Hs'ish wanted his turn stopped what they were doing. One of the more foolhardy of the bunch walked over to where Hs'ish stood struggling just to remain upright and asked him if he would care to share in their perverted past-time. The socially unaware deviant misconstrued IIs'ish's command to move closer as a sign of collusion, and died with a confused expression on his face when Hs'ish ripped the others throat out.

The other two raced to the aide of their fallen companion and in their lusty rage, they tore Hs'ish limb from limb, spending the last of their venomous passion on him rather than the princess, and coming to realise that they now stood alone as the last treasonous members of their own race.

Surveying the panorama of the failed ambush, the two Lizardmen decided against returning home with the body of the princess and so with the help of a few of the town's militia, they hung her from an isolated oak that stood atop the crest of a large hillock, located several hundred yards west of the village. After the hanging, the two Lizardmen returned to the scene of the battle to gather whatever loot they could manage before setting off for their home in the depths beneath the mountain. They left behind the twin black blades of K'lsh, whose substance became as water when they tried to lift them from the ground where they lay, instead settling for the fancy armour that the two Paladins had worn.

Neither knew of the Holy armours powers, and never worked out the draining effect it had on all except those with the purest of souls. The armour was also invested with powerful wards against evil, yet they were equally ignorant of this too and both had decided to don the battle-suits rather than carry them the long distance home.

As they equipped each piece of protective covering it would inexplicably bend, stretch or shrink to whatever shape required in order to best fit its new owner's appendage and reinvigorating the muscles beneath. Renewing damaged tissue and revitalizing tired muscles; or at least that was the armours initial and obvious effect.

Yet the armour somehow 'sensed' the true nature of its newest owner and rapidly began to reverse its own cumulative restorative effects. Even when the armour felt much too heavy to wear and made them huff and puff as they climbed towards the mountains peak, they did not wish to remove the enchanted vestments, so enamoured of them as they were.

Not even after the first had passed away while resting, did the other have the sense to avoid his partner in crimes fate, instead concluding the other had died from exertion, and he climbed upwards for some distance before he himself succumbed to their powerful anti-evil magic.

The scavengers in the area fared better than their prey, feeding well for several weeks until all that remained were too misshapen armoured skeletons, lying some two or three hundred feet apart.

IX) **Unwelcome Guests**

Zen was a worrier Grot had noticed on the so-called short trek to the tower - size can be deceptive, especially to a Dwarf he supposed, but the tower that seemed no more than a stone's throw from their entry point into the glade, was in fact two nights and three days travel away, time that had been spent in a constant mixture of merriment and laughter, interceded by incongruous bouts of violent argument. "Oh sure," Grot surmised, Zen may act confident, but the way he had so meticulously cleared the glade of evidence of each nights encampment made up Grots mind that the Satyr was a bit of a wuss... "You are one troubled little man aren't you?" Grot blurted out his thoughts, tact not being one of his finer points.

"Who me...!?!" Zen looked at the Dwarf as if Grot was something he had just stepped in, "Dude! How can *you* call me little?" he paused to swing his rather cumbersome penis over his shoulder to back up his repeated defence. "Pah! Little! Me? That's just rude man, especially coming from a Dwiff at that!!!"

"Don't call him Dwiff!" Dirk interjected sensing an argument about to start. "Do you two not have anything better to do than argue? I thought it was me you liked moaning at." he finished; accusingly singling out Grot, who for the last few days had spent rather more time berating the man-goat than he.

"What the hell are yer picking on me fer!?" Grot retorted, warming up to the prospective argument as they came over the small hilltop on which the turret like tower sat. The Dwarfs further retort was lost on him however for up close; the structure was a most beautiful sight to behold and did the scenic glade below true justice. Not one to be struck by beauty normally, even Grot had to concede he was blown away by the majesty of the vista before them.

Quite often the structures that humans built would be in clear contrast to the landscape around them but this edifice was made of pure fairytale. Its smooth white, marble like walls rose not indomitable over the area, but rather accentuated the features of the landscape around it, blending effortlessly with the surrounding natural beauty and connecting fertile Eyrthe to azure sky in a lucid transition of natural evidence.

Though given the appearance of marble its actual construct was not dissimilar to that of ivory in truth - though only one still living knew of the definite substance from which it had been constructed - the tooth of a Gargantuan. Its staggering presence eradiated a twisting kaleidoscope of succulent magic to those who had been taught in the arts and this; quite unusually in these situations, included Dirk, who physically staggered back a few feet at the sight of the unaccustomed throbbing glow he envisioned.

The towers central trunk was around eighty feet in circumference, and climbed three hundred feet into the air, where it was topped with an elegant gold minaret of unrivalled beauty. Placed at irregular intervals around its perimeter, jutting out from this central column like the branches of a tree, singular rooms subtly eased outward, complete with delicately arched windows; each of which were topped by steep minarets of pastel pink tiles. What's more, Grot noticed; there was not a drop of bird-shit in sight!

Even more elegantly carved window slots followed a winding spiral staircase hidden within its walls. And the whole effect was completed by a bleached gravel path that criss-crossed the gently sloping knoll on which they now stood, coming to meet in a circle around the tower; forming sigils of mighty power only viewable from the air.

"Gorgeous..." Dirk stammered. "Bloody sweet as a Nymphs backside..." Grot bemoaned. "Dude, that's a mint place to perch!" Zen vowed but such was there wonder that none was aware who had actually spoken what in the overall impression they all shared.

Looking upon the wondrous site with slack jawed amazement, Grot felt a little absurd, if not a little girly. "Right well, as I see it, I am still owed a good kip and this poofy looking place looks like a good place to get one!" He barracked, spoiling the moment.

"Yeah... You, err... Don't wanna go in there..." Zen drawled, "Ya know? There's *far* nicer places than that old place I could show ya, why it looks ready to hit the ditch, topple and roll. Man, catch a load of that evil looking glow..." he finished with a little too much of a sales pitch to be convincing.

"You... What...?" emitted the shrill cry of sheer un-believability from Dirks mouth. "Are you both a pair of pricks!?! THAT is the nicest pad on this bloody Eyrthe! If Grot, by being poofy ya mean it's a thousand times more beautiful than an ancient Elven village, then yeah it's a bit poofy, if not; Shut up! As for the lustrous light..., ...*It* is so bloody holy looking ya would have to be a sightless nipple on the teat of humanity to

miss its benevolent glow…"

"…Yeah, what the hell are you on about? Glow – I don't see no glow, it's just dead pretty you half-assed, donkey brained gimp-boy! Pretty enough for a girly Elf maiden or a really, really, Poofy Bard...!" Grot concurred.

"Grot you great thick bag of shi…, …ah, well I just mean to say that Its glowing hotter than a dragon's arse after seven helpings of Lava broth! So…, …Are you demented!"

"Yo guys, let's not argue, I mean look at it… It's erm, well hey, erm..." He was obviously struggling for the correct convincing conclusion. "Well, you know what they say; erm beauty is in the eyeballs of the owner. No hold on that's not it… What I mean to say is; the book-cover is only skin-deep… Oh man no that aint it too. Damn!" Zen blustered.

"Is this your gaff or something?" Grot accused.

"No man, why you say that? Oh come on don't look at me like that... Take it easy my stunted little pal…" Zen replied forgetting to back off.

"I bet it is! You just don't want us messing the place up do ya? And to think I thought I might like you – ya stuck up, Goat faced…" Grot was visibly angered.

"Whoa Grot man, wait! Just back off dude," Zen cried in pretended alarm, "you know I'm a lover not a fighter!"

Grot clucked his tongue and gazed back at the tower and Dirk who was still stood there drooling. "Oy: dozy bollocks! You gonna listen to this tit?"

Dirk turned to them absent minded, "Maybe he knows something he's not letting on?" he stated immediately returning his attention to the glowing tower as if it was the first sight he had seen in his life.

Zen shrugged as Grot advanced; fingers itching upon axe handles. A palpable statement issued from Grots body language that stated that it knew he was not being told everything, and that if it did not know the said information soon, nobody would..., …Including Zen.

"It's just that… The owners a bit…" Zen searched to find a moderately none insulting word just in case his uncle was listening at some random window slot, "A bit weird..., erm, cheese -unusual, Man, unusual!"

He finished without conviction.

"Weird? Unusual?" Trumped Grot, "I can live with weird... I'm hanging out with Dirk and you aren't I?"

"...No well not weird so much as strange, yes **strange** then!" Grot shook his head and swung his axe in annoyance... "Aah, A bit of a nutter..., ...*mad* even. You know sort of Giants brains for soup and stuff – In a completely non-insulting and none applicable manner of course..." Zen gambled in trying to make the way he flung insults to sound less than insulting.

"You Big **Black**... *Two-Horned*-Tail-*Swishing*-Huge..., ...Ding-a-ling, Piddley-**Assed**, *Pea-Brained* **Donkey**! How dumb do you think we are?" Grot blurted and took a step towards Zen, whose inept sense of survival prompted him to merely smile and blink.

"Well yeah OK, it's a bit pretty outside but inside -man it's a stinking hovel? I mean sure, ok, you've got me. It *is* a nice looking building..." Zen offered and Dirk breathed a sigh of relief that Zen had enough sense to recognise a pissed off battle hardened Dwarf when he saw one.

"...But surely no oil painting." Zen crashed on to Dirks horror. "...No! I know of a castle a *Mere* **league** or *ten thousand* from a stones throw from here, and *that my **short** sighted friend is **Far, far,** far* prettier than this old misshaped mound. *Why,* if we set off **right now**! We could be there in a few **days** this time *next year*..." Zen trailed off and waited hopefully for a response from the Dwarf.

And he nearly got one too.

Grot looked up at Zen, who stood around four feet bigger than he. *Gonna have to jump to head butt the bugger!* thought Grot as he calculated his attack. "I aint never seen no two legged horse kick... and I'll be betting they'll kick even less with one leg? Or maybe losing a few teeth may help loosen up yer tongue!" Grot threatened and unhitched his mighty two handed battle axe, from the selection of those that remained attached to the back of his pack, so that he now held two brutal looking battle blades.

"Grot lay off a mo... I know Zen is an idiot but..." Dirk bartered.

Zen laughed aloud. "Hey little Stunty, you got to learn to chill! Move with the times, barbarism is sooo... yesterday!"

"Yeah well keep on with the insults and we'll change that today!"

Grot added squaring up to the charming yet irritating Satyr.

"He doesn't like Stunty either." Dirk chimed unhelpfully.

"I can see that Dirk man…" Zen considered.

Grots face purpled, "Oh! It's Dirk to him, I see! Keldor's hammer fall! I ought to murder your devilish arse right now you cheeky, good for nothing…"

Dirk pushed Grot to one side as a huge shadow formed overhead completely blocking out the sunlight from above. The darkness became total and it was impossible to see the origin of the mammoth shadow; so sudden was its apparition. Instead of standing there trying to figure out the source of the shadowed veil, Grot and Dirk, who had had much practice at dealing with danger quickly, scrambled for some sort of cover.

Grot peered out from the thorny thicket of Bramble that he seemed to have the uncanny knack of wandering into whenever danger threatened. Darkness exuding from the creature swooping above them was as complete as any eclipse he had ever witnessed and the Dwarf glanced about this way and that as he briefly noted the possibility of an enforced magical darkness.

Within a few seconds his clarity of vision had improved enough to make out the form of Zen still stood upon the short gravely path that ran alongside the tower. *What the hell's he doing? He's completely exposed…* Grot realised and shouted an alert to his green accomplice, "GET IN COVER! YOU ST…"

"…up-id bloody sod…" Grot finished automatically, for his shocked self now appeared to be perched upon the back of a Dragon that was so vast it belittled the landscape streaming past below.

He was actually hanging on with his knees at a point midway down the beast's rotund neck he realised, yet had no idea how he had come to be here. The Dragons scales were a shadowed blackened depth of bony material, which held an iridescent quality that shone oft-times with every colour of the rainbow and then some…

Involuntarily, Grot craned his neck to look behind and was blown away at the creature's vast expanse; from this vantage he couldn't even make out the end of its tail. His eyes caught a sight of the pink fingered tower whose skeletal walls seemed to clutch upwardly vainly.

Seizing upon an unknown thought or instinct, the Dwarf; who had until now been tightly gripping the Dragon's ridged spine, released his hands and produced a small, ornate, silver craft hammer; fashioned in a most similar manner to the icon of his god, Keldor.

Without comprehension or control of his own actions, Grot chipped away a splinter of the bony material that formed the tooth-like ridge and threw the chunk of Dragon-bone tumbling into the void beneath, then pulled back hard on the things rippling scales, forcing the Dragon into a steep climb.

Dirk flinched in his hiding spot as he felt the pinch of a possible flea bite and bellowed out a warning call to Zen. "Zen you bloody crazy nutter..., ...Is that you near the tower...?"

"Yeah why...? And how come you're behind a tree and he's cowering in a bush?" he answered.

"Because... eh? Why? Everything's gone black and stuff and you're asking why– you... You do realise the suns gone don't you?" Dirk quipped incredulously, hunkering down in his chosen place of hiding.

"What..?" Zen shouted vaguely back, "The sun hasn't gone – I can see it quite clearly still, it's just hidden a little by that massive Dragons shadow is all. Ya know ya scare way too easily Dirk... Why if you'd spent any time at all in hell, you'd soon realise that the sun does NOT disappear, tch!" Zen disapproved, Dirk obviously hadn't quite mastered the art of danger recognition.

Grots vision blurred for an indeterminable amount of time and as it snapped into focus he realised he was back in the bush as a persistent thorn or two found its way into his boot and several jostled for the right to stab him in the buttocks. His ears were filled with a whistling sound imparted by the rush of wind from atop the Dragon a moment before.

"Keldor's beard!" he swore. His voice sounded muted to him, due to his impaired hearing and he wiggled his index fingers in both ears, which inevitably only made his predicament worse. He shook his head in doubt and flapped his arms to check that it was indeed himself in control of his body. He was left unsure of what had just occurred and glanced up to the void like depths of the beast's enormous underbelly above...

"W.a. ... ing ... th......t!" was the most he could catch of Dirks screamed warnings to Zen. He could see his friend now, cowering in a tiny bush beside a large tree trunk, and then his thoughts snapped back to Zen, who was shrugging his shoulders whilst still stood out in the open as the shadow above began to slowly dissipate as the dragon began its ascent.

"Will... ...thing ... can... ...ear... a... ...thing... ay... ...rot!" he caught amidst soundless whistles as Dirk gave him a little wave.

"I just had the most amazing... dream!" he answered unaware of what Dirk had said and struggling to gather his thoughts. *Bugger! Zen!*, he suddenly remembered, as both he and Dirk began shouting various cursed warnings in stereo.

Zen's night-vision while not as keen as some few other races; could see well enough in a manner of other unworldly spectrums, yet even so his pupils seemed to discount the evidence of danger before him. With pupils dilated all the better to let in the correct light amplitude needed, he looked about and saw the Dwarf fidgeting about in some thorny bush and the human's legs sticking out from where he now *lay*, in the protection of a huge tree-trunk. Zen shrugged again and swung his cock around as was his wont. *What was their problem? Could it be that they were afraid of the Dark Perhaps? Or maybe they were trying to scare him...*

"I aint gonna fall for that old trick you ugly men. Come on! I can see you both hiding. Stop trying to trip me out..." he said with his usual relaxed confidence.

"Get in cover you great Tit!" Dirk said, his voice trembling as he attempted to swallow a nervous laugh. He admired Zen's ignorance or bravery - he was unsure which it was.

"I'm a 'Tit' huh?" Zen queried, "Tit's not bad I suppose. At least it's a body part that I like!" He grinned at the idea of a perfectly formed breast complete with eyes, ears and mouth.

A Cracking sound indicated danger to all but Zen and they each receded more-so into their receptive areas of cover as the sun's revealing light crept slowly back in its bathing wash of light. Above, some thin black object too small to make out, hit the majestic towers uppermost turret with such velocity, that its thunderclap 'crack' on contact rang out death knoll clear.

A huge slab of white masonry split with menace from its stony confines above and sped hurtling downwards. Dirk could make out very little thanks to the now expanding horizon of sunlight, but his years of cowardice had taught him to pull in his legs and huddle as tightly to the tree as possible, whenever he heard thunder were there was none.

Grot and Zen could see well enough, and they both watched in detached fascination, (Horrific fascination in Grots case), as the chunk of white material raced along its downward trajectory and fair smashed into Zen's fragile forehead, with all the panache of a 20 pound mallet hitting an egg.

Zen's dispensed carcass span through the air as the indiscriminate lump of tower construct skipped, then bounced dangerously along the ground and skidded past the tree where Dirks legs had been sticking out from only moments before, leaving a gash the size of an Ogres armpit in its wake.

The shadow overhead phased away completely as the sun washed everything anew with its rays of forgiving light once more. Grot blinked a few times in order to accustom himself to his sunlit vision. Whereas Dirk just blinked in disbelief as he cowered out from behind his beloved shelter, hugging the tree as if it were his long lost mother.

"Shit!" Dirk spoke dejectedly, "Zen's dead."

"What dya mean; dead?" Grot argued, "You haven't even bothered checking him…" He would have argued further but first he had to extract himself from the biting brambles.

Dirk shrugged in noncommittal fashion and they both walked over to where Zen's blood smattered corpse lay. Each stood in silence for a moment or two, looking in horror on their newly made friends smashed cadaver. Rivulets of blood riddled the gravel footpath, making a mockery of their bleached stone wash. A massive chunk of skull was missing along with the horn which had previously protruded from the missing section, leaving the gouged and bloody brain clearly visible.

"Well go on then…" Dirk enthused with badly timed sarcasm, "See if he's still alive…"

Grot looked down at the crushed wreck that was Zen with the gasp of an unconvinced sigh, "Satyr's are demonic right…?" Grot queried.

Dirk nodded in agreement. He attempted to suppress a smile and wondered why the hell he wanted to smile at a time like this. But the Dwarves refusal to acknowledge the truth was tugging his lips into quivering submission.

"So if he's a Daemon, he can only be killed by magic right? So all;-" Grot stopped as a muffled titter escaped Dirk's mouth, "What in Keldor's name is so funny you ignorant Gollum's arse!" Grot exclaimed.

Dirk shook his head vigorously in defence and felt tears of laughter welling in his eyelids. Again the Dwarf asked for affirmation and again Dirk nodded, not daring to move his lips less the laughter that now caused his torso to shake be given its full head of steam.

Grot fumed at the sight of Dirks rising shoulders and knew the bugger was indeed laughing at him, though only Dirk knew why. "...Yer skinny stupid bastard..., ...SO HE AINT DEAD! He can't be bloody well dead, right? He can't be killed if he's a demon? Not by a shitty piece of rock!"

The bastards actually laughing his cocky tits off! Grot's thoughts screamed, as his hearing returned to normal, though his voice remained at a heightened tone. "Demons can only be killed by MAGIC!" Grot roared in a childlike retort and lunged at Dirk who by this time had erupted into uproarious and uncontrolled bursts of laughter.

The Dwarf beat ineffectually at Dirk who could not be bothered to defend himself such were his fits of merriment. "Stop, stop, please, mercy..., ...ooph! Oh courageous Dwarf. Ouch! Ow, get off. Ha-ha-ha..."

He finally succeeded in throwing Grot off, who didn't resist him to be honest, and came up to his knees, wiping away tears of inappropriate laughter.

"The bleeding castle's magical..." Dirk offered. "You know? The walls... magical." he said with a shrug, as the last few remaining guffaws escaped him.

Shock hits each of us in a different way and Dwarves were no different to men, but years of losing endless loved ones to the enemies of his kin had hardened Grot to the sight of a fallen comrade. "Well what'll we do with him?" Grot enquired with disdainful regard towards Dirk.

"Dunno? Get him to a healer straight away!?" Dirk offered unhelpfully, before unfashionably brightening, "Anyways, you were gonna kill him yourself a minute or two ago so who cares?"

Grot looked at the wide beamed smiling face of his friend and privately wondered if he adhered to the same sense of ethical principles as himself. He was fully aware that he himself took a casual air towards death but Dirk's attitude went beyond simple disassociation –The sod wasn't even connected!

"Dirk, he's bloody dead. I was angry… I would only have butted the bugger in his snout, give him something to think about, ya know…" Grot grasped for the appropriate words, "Scare him. I just wanted to try and get through that thick head of his, some sense of fear…" He finished as the words came to him.

Grot stared at Dirk, who thankfully had stopped grinning like a cat in a mouse-nest. "But really, Dirk… We've got a real dead guy here and there aint a preacher in the land who's gonna restore a Satyr to life -you just don't know what your dealing with. Anything might happen… they just… wouldn't do it."

"Ya right of course, but hey Grot?" Dirk queried, "Have you ever seen a south-man, ya know a southerner from the deserts?"

"What? What's that got to do with anything? Of course I haven't. Who has? You I suppose…"

"No!" Dirk shouted in triumph, "That's my point! You haven't seen one, and I aint seen one and I'm betting there aint many preachers who have seen one either."

Dirk observed his friend, making meaningful eye contact before continuing to ensure the Dwarves narrow mind was keeping track with his own all too colourful one.

"Grot, what do south-men look like?" he asked innocently, yet knew the answer before the Dwarf spoke it.

"…Black?"

"…Black. Thank-you, somebody buy that Nobby a drink… Now as I see it, there's about seven foot of him so he passes for a human near enough…" Dirk began in a businesslike poise, going to stand over their downed comrade.

"Of course – those eyes are a giveaway and his heads a bit beastly with those horns but how about this…" Dirk paused in his patter to position himself on bended knee as he continued his speech, grabbing at the various bodily appendages to emphasise his points as he spoke of the tended parts.

"Now get this for an idea... We cut off his other horn, cover his legs in a blanket; sawing off the hooves of course, and no pillock brained preacher aint gonna know shit different. We just tell him he's a south-man and tada! The priest heals his black ass." Dirk announced with a sales pitch to rival Zen's own best efforts in life.

"Oh but wait! Give us your knife Grot... No not that one, the magic one... cheers," Dirk chattered conversationally as the Dwarf handed him the desired weapon.

Without further discourse, Dirk plunged the knife delicately into the flesh around Zen's eye sockets. Grot felt sick as he watched Dirk's semi-efficient efforts to cut away the flesh, once done, he popped both the eyes from their sockets and then after sawing through the rubbery optical nerve, Dirk lifted his ghastly prize in bloodied hands. "Guess he won't need these little beauties..." He enthused clearly pleased with his own macabre handiwork.

"What in Keldor's name are you doing?" Grot whispered in hoarse disbelief. These last few minutes' events had thrown him somewhat but even so; he was sure his friend *had* in *reality*, just gone and cut the eyeballs from their dead friend's still warm corpse...

"Well, I kinda get pissed off when you can see in the dark and I can't, so the way I figure it; after he's revived by the priest he's gonna regenerate his lost parts anyway so while we're there with the priest, you can cut my eyes out and put these ones in. Then we pay the dumb healer to mend '*my eyes*!!!'"

To emphasise the deception here, Dirk held Zen's eyes aloft in case his mortified friend was a little slow on the uptake. "See, the eyes then attach themselves to the back of my head and hey presto, I can see in the dark like you! Clever little idea eh, what dya think?" Dirk fizzed, positively ecstatic with his deductive reasoning.

"Clever! You twisted stupid useless gimp! All you've done is butchered him! As if he wasn't dead enough already, which for arguments sake, I now think he is... But what in Keldor's name makes you think that I, Grot, would want to cut your bloody eyes out, *even* and I do stress; *even if I have* just watched you desecrate our pal?" Grot turned about and thumped his fist against the tower in rage.

"Have you thought of the pain involved ya great Goblins bollock?" Grot ranted in frustration.

"He's dead, probably… But you aint! What if it didn't work like that, what if your own eyes grew back instead? Would you cut *them* out and try again? Would you kill Zen again or just ask him for his eyeballs? Oh, mind you NO! You wouldn't have to ask him, would you? And you wanna know why…?"

Dirk voiced the obligatory 'why?'

"…Because no respectful priest would bloody well wanna touch him that's why!!! Contrary to your agnostic whims, Fathers of the Faith are no bloody fools and besides…" Grot suddenly took note of a new fact, which he hastily added to the equation; "Besides which, he's only got four fingers! What are you gonna do? Cut off his hands too?" Grot seethed, bringing his tantrum to its wailing completion.

"Well what's wrong with four fingers Grot? I've only got four fingers…"

"…No, yer stupid bony pile of Gnoll excrement!" Grot cursed, "I mean three fingers and a thumb, if you could call it a thumb!"

"Aah, I see!" Dirk sighed as his scheme take on a new turn, "Grot! You're hatchet thing please."

The Dwarf looked confused.

"Pass me an axe please! Your axe, any, yes, that one. Yeah. Thanks." Dirk garbled as he tore the malicious device from the Dwarves resisting fingers and brought it down with some force.

Thwopp, thwopp, thwopp…

The sluicing sound both sickened and surprised Grot as Dirk lopped off one hand and then tugged at the other arm in order to line up a shot at the wrist.

Grot was just about to make some witty retort along the lines of '*why not cut his arms off while you're at it!*', then thought better of it and stopped himself. The crazy idiot would probably do it.

…Thwopp.

Grot grimaced as the other hand was severed; He was so close to murdering Dirk it was unreal, yet at the same time he felt strangely weakened by the whole experience. He closed his eyes and wondered if Dirks sanity had truly been impaired by their recent ordeals, muttering a silent prayer to salvage his idiotic pal's soul.

"And while were at it, we'll lose quite a few inches from this too… Bloody show off should feel what its like not to be so blessed…" Dirk mumbled grabbing an arm full of man meat.

…Thwopp.

Grot threw up quite violently.

When his nausea had finally passed, Dirk; true to his somewhat twisted word, had respectfully wrapped up Zen's body in one of their large camping blankets that Grot always got lumbered with carrying any considerable distance, and had nailed him to a litter that Dirk MUST have constructed during Grot's sickness spell.

"You NAILED him to it?" Grot squeaked. Just when he had thought there were no more shocks to come from Dirk, he would be amazed anew.

"He looks kinda peaceful, don't you think?" Dirk asked, pleased with his own achievement, but seeking the ego boosting praise to match.

The litter was a crude rickety looking thing that Grot knew if they were to try and pull of the stunt, He would have to rebuild. But the most barbaric, Neanderthal aspect of it all was the method that Dirk had used in order to keep the body in place on the sloping bracken basket. Around eight wide wooden stakes were driven into the body at various points and out through the back, where they lodged in the weave of the basket.

Dirk beamed with pride. "Well I gotta say I was never much cop at woodwork, but this is pretty special don't ya think?"

"Dirk, I… You…" Grot gave up. His friend needed professional help he concluded, judging from the innocent schoolboy grin etched upon his friend's pathetic visage.

Dirk looked about him to check he hadn't forgotten anything and started off along the path. "Are we going or not?" he shouted back over his shoulder, a little disconsolate at not receiving a compliment from the sullen Dwarf, who he thoughtfully left to the task of transporting the ghastly litter.

"Not until I've had a look up there." Grot said pointing up to where the piece of stony battlement had toppled. He remembered the dream so vividly even now, and he had a suspicion that it was, or had been in some way, very, very, real.

After a little goading, Grot proceeded to tell Dirk all about the strange vision and his suspicions of what he may find up on the highest point of the tower, even though he felt like life held little point at that time.

"Fair enough," Dirk had chimed, "His body won't turn to dust until the turn of the week. We'll simply enter the tower, kill the mad wizard, rescue the princess and free the land from the clutches of evil. Then we'll find your precious Dragon splint and be home in time for tea." Dirk finished and had no idea how close he was to foretelling the truth, with one big exception. They might not get home in time for tea...

Pausing first to wrap up and then pocket the eyes, Dirk casually swung open the towers single door, "Better put these babies on ice 'til later, don't want them drying up on me... Hya all, anybody home!" He bellowed striding bravely through the vacuous doorjamb. "Hello...? Two unlikely heroes seek the company of...Yow!"

Grot bashed Dirk painfully on the arm, "Will you shush! Ya useless Bollocks-for-brains!" he commanded.

***

Galbor turned his head to one side, "Did you hear something?" he asked of his opponent. Galbor had since settled down to a momentous game of chess, giving both he and his captive Arch-Magus a welcome distraction from the riddle that now vexed them both. They had been playing for hours chattering about this and that, testing each other for signs of mental weakness as well as giving their up-most concentration to winning the game at hand.

The chess battle was hung at an intense stalemate during which neither opponent had spoken for the last twenty minutes and the muted sound had indeed startled Kalamere though he hadn't shown it. "I hear nought Galbor. May haps you seek to distract mine attention from the task in hand..?. Doth the pressure burden thee so? If ye doth seek asylum, then verily wish to concede and I shall accept thy refusal?"

"Fear not then Wizard. I do not seek to end the game until I have your King crushed in my grasp. Check!" Galbor countered as he moved his Bishop in for the suddenly exposed pawn, momentarily forgetting all about the voices he had thought he'd heard mere moments before.

***

Dirk and Grot stood in silence for a few minutes awaiting any

163

possible response, found non forthcoming, then wandered into the spacious welcome hall. The door swung silently closed behind them...

The chamber was an impressive sight to behold, if rather devoid of signs of life. The central sphere of the mosaic floor depicted some arcane symbol the likes of which Dirk had never seen. The circular wall and staircase were made of the same Ivory like substance that covered the towers exterior.

The staircase itself wound around the towers interior at a vertigo inspiring rate, coiled several times over, rising like a crumpled snake, Dirk could just make out an Ebony door on the first landing, of which - neither the landing nor stairs had handrails. Several plain purple tapestries hung straight down from the ceiling at various points against the wall, periodically concealing the stair cased outer wall where ever the two intersected.

The inside of the golden roofed minaret was inlaid with a most beauteous painted mural, depicting an angelic scene involving elements of birth and the harvest and so forth.... However, a disturbing backdrop to the harmonious looking interior was a constant clicking noise, akin to the scurrying of rats' claws upon stone.

Grot's danger sense told him to turn around and he reached for the knife at his belt as he swung around and away from the now closed door.

"What is the matter with you?" Dirk enquired of his friend's oddly amusing behaviour.

"I got a bad feeling is all Dirk mate –so who gives a shite about how silly I may have just looked." Grot replied in quick fashion.

"Well stop being such a worrywart and let's have a look-see behind these curtains." Dirk said and strode towards the nearest of the tapestries.

He stopped half way and instead went over to the magical symbol etched into the central mosaic and started pondering its origin...

"Yo Grot come over here," he mumbled as he concentrated his vision.

The Dwarf came lumbering over with the two smaller of his axe arsenal ready at his disposal should 'trouble' rear its dubiously familiar 'head'.

Dirks eyesight blurred all before him with aneurism inflicting savagery, then as suddenly snapped back into an alien view of full-on mystical clarity of which he never even dreamt of attaining; fragmented throughout the flooring on which he and the Dwarf now stood, Dirk could visualize a strong magical energy flux emanating from numerous, hitherto invisible shallow fissures contained within the mosaic. He looked around frowning as the Dwarves hobnailed boot was about to come down upon one of these glowing depressions, noting his friends intent just in the nick of time. "Grot freeze!" Dirk bellowed and Grot immediately froze in his actions mid stance.

"What?" Grot enquired and Dirk quickly garbled an explanation of the energy sources. Looking about him, Dirk could see that he too had wandered innocently into their midst and although he was unsure of their origin or even whether the Dwarf or himself had actually already stood upon them or not, he WAS pretty sure the Hieroglyphic markings were symbolic of detrimental health wards, albeit in some unfathomed manner.

"Erm...so what do I do? Step backwards, hop about?" Grot murmured while trying to retain his balance. "I guess I'm okay putting my foot down at least..."

"NO!" Dirk turned white in an instant. "Grot, just... Stay still a mo while I try and figure this."

"Figure what?" The Dwarf asked in confusion.

"We seem to have wondered into the middle of some sort of magical trap!" Dirk tried to explain.

"...**WE?** *Yer mean you*, ya dim *witted* lamp-*licker* yer! Why did ye call me over if yer knew you were in a *trap?*"

"I didn't - I mean I didn't know then, I'm sorry, I just thought..."

"**NO!** That's just it... Ye didn't think, did yer. Why I ought to cut yer *bloody* ears off and *piss* into where yer **brain** should be!" The Dwarf said, moving to stride forward.

Dirk's genuinely panicked plea to stay, mingled with the sound of a sudden build up of energy as Grot's heavy boot came within a nail's breadth of settling down convinced the Dwarf and he swung his leg away quickly, leaving him battling for balance.

The Dwarf's tone had changed somewhat when next he spoke, "So,

165

erm, tell me Mr Magic, How do ya know if this trap is harmful or not?"

"I don't...! Shit, Grot, I don't know do I? It just *looks* scary..." Dirk replied with simple sincerity, "But you're welcome to test the theory..."

The Dwarf couldn't help but grin at his friend's cheeky response, but the grin became a grimace an instant later when he asked Dirk if it was possible to retreat away from the symbol.

"I doubt it," Dirk mused, "You would only probably just step on one of those glowing cracks behind you," Dirk scratched his head as he pondered their shared dilemma, "What I know for sure is that somehow we both walked across its surface before it began to glow, right?"

"Okay..." Grot agreed and awaited his friend's further validating instructions as he wrestled to keep himself balanced.

"So... If we stepped on the mosaic, before I noticed the magical energy...?" Dirk figured, "Then we must assume that by one or both of us entering, we have tripped off or served as the catalyst, to activate some magical device or some such..."

"Ok..." mumbled Grot as his hands started to do involuntary little circular motions, "Do I take it by the 'Or Some Such' comment that you mean you don't know what in Keldor's name is going on?"

"I am absolutely bloody clueless me old mate, which is still some seven steps on from your state of awareness, so I suggest you leave this little teaser to me and stop moaning like an old woman. Now... hold on a mo!" Dirk warned and slowly raised his leg at an angle and inspected his own booted sole.

Grot looked about him for the whereabouts of the glowing fissures and saw none. "Are you sure about these glowing cracks? I mean, they *are* magical right?"

Dirk shook his head both at his foot and the Dwarves comment. "I don't know Grot. I simply don't know, before that bird appeared my magical sight had been limited to knowing the difference between a goblin and a tooth fairy and even then I got confused!"

The last statement was followed by an incomprehensible smattering of curses and half thoughts as the Dwarf struggled to keep apace of his friends ramblings. Dirk dried worried tears from his eyes with the help of a grubby sleeve and again lifted his own foot and looked at it as his confused mutterings once more became clearly audible. "No…, …Look, I can handle it myself for shit's sake!" Dirk said looking at the Dwarf as if only just noticing him. "Grot mate it's dangerous all right, but I really don't know anything else. Just assume they are magical and very deadly too in some way or other, OK?"

Finding nothing on his sole to serve his purpose, he carefully put his foot down and repeated the deliberate process with the other. "Aha!" he cried in triumph and placing his foot down with equal care, he threw the tiny fragment of stone he had found lodged there; skittering across the mosaic surface of the floor.

Nothing happened.

"What are ya doing? What was that?" Grot questioned.

"A stone matey-bollocks…, …I wanted to see if it would set them off, but it obviously didn't." Dirk was downcast.

"So I can put my foot down now right?" Grot asked, though he was far from assured, steadily lowering his tiring foot. Grot wasn't even sure if Dirk *was* seeing any strange glowing lights at all, given his current psychological state and even if he were, they would far more likely be the lights from the faeries playing in his attic to coin an old Elven-Dwarven metaphor.

"No!" Dirk reproved, "Rocks are one thing. They're inanimate… Now we need to test a live subject."

Grot paused his foots descent and hovered there, "If ya think ye might be getting on me nerves, I can tell yer you are and save ya the trouble, but if yer think I'm gonna be moving about the place to please you, yer can think again, if ya wanna live test subject or whatever then your bloody well it, not me…"

Dirk finished chanting and then looked disapprovingly at his ranting Dwarven pal as his slender fingers gently stroked the summoned bird now held within his encased palms. "Grot... What sort of sicko do you think I am? You really... Oh tell ya what…, …just shush eh mate? He is definitely losing his marbles Dirk ya know, ya better watch him…, …Take care ya know…"

The Dwarf waited in wobbly legged embarrassment as Dirk continued to caress the pristine pigeon he was chattering to, though why Grot was quite unsure, still he had to interrupt, his question burning up inside him despite his teetering pose: "But Dirk my boots *are* inanimate… That is; if inanimate means what I think it does?" he couldn't help philosophising.

Clutching the clueless bird tightly in one hand, Dirk regarded the Dwarf with an arched eyebrow of disapproval, "You don't quite get magic do you Grot? Even if I were to explain myself for the fortieth time this year you wouldn't get it and I don't really think now's the time…" Dirk held the pigeons head and feet tightly and callously snapped each wing in turn as he continued, "…So if you just want to imagine this little fellows got your boots on I'll just chuck him and demonstrate. OK? Do try to keep your balance in the meantime mate." That said he tossed the awkward thing into the air. The bird attempted to flap, failed and landed with a gentle thump amidst several of the glowing fissures without hitting even a one.

"Well, now what?" asked a somewhat strained Grot.

"Now we wait for it to step on a crack before you do." Dirk responded with a shrug and began making tweeting sounds in order to try and entice the stricken bird into movement.

Grot waited alike a quivering statue, apprehensively watching for five minutes or more as Dirk tweeted and whistled, but understandably, the frightened bird made no attempts to budge, let alone attempt to move towards the uncaring bastard who had just broke his most precious limbs.

"Have you noticed how clean this place is?" Grot asked in an attempt to distract himself from his teetering predicament, he'd grown increasingly aware of the complete absence of any grime or dust and also the connotations this newly noticed fact held. "Come to think of it; the front door didn't creak either did it…?"

Dirk looked about the entrance chamber and had to admit, the places cleanliness, and well-oiled entranceway hadn't occurred to him of any importance before now.

"So something's keeping this place clean right? On a fairly regular basis…" Grot said; turning crane-legged inquisitor.

Dirk, still tweeting ineffectually, nodded his agreement.

"And if the place is that clean, then that skittering noise I thought might be rats' won't be, will it?" Grot probed.

"I suppose not…" Dirk agreed once more. "Actually, now that ya mention it; it kinda sounds like a sweeping brush or something like that anyways, I should know - I spent enough years married to one, metaphorically speaking…"

"…Metaphoric my arse! So why the hell am I stood here on one leg; huffing and puffing for all I am worth, when some buggering cleaner is roaming about the place, probably fully aware of these bloody fissures you say you see?" Grot demanded, though he knew it was an impossible question. Dirk didn't even attempt to respond, instead sucking in his cheeks and calling again to the broken bird.

Grots hamstring began to tremble, sending waves of protest down the length of his supporting leg. "Oh… Sod this for a laugh!" he said "I'm gonna put my bloody foot down even if it kills me!"

Dirk went white. "No Grot, ya daft…"

Grots threatened action was interrupted by a sudden frizzing sound as a crackling column of electricity sprouted up from the floor, instantly frying the innocent bird into burnt chunks as, noticing the humanoids diverted attentions; it had took its chance at freedom and hopped hurriedly away and straight onto one of the broiling fissures.

"SHITE!" yelped Grot and he prevented his own foot from touching down, mere millimetres from the ground.

"You see your boots are imbued with a certain you-ness." Dirk instructed as he continued his earlier explanation. "You've probably heard the old adage about filling a dead man's boots – That's because owned stuff has a memory of sorts… Too hard for me to bother explaining, but your boots 'know' whose feet are in them and the spell does too, so to be simple, if you put your foot down you're a dead Dwiff!"

Dirk wondered if the Dwarf was merely trying to look simple in order to aggravate him, and thought twice about explaining his deductions further, but he did so all the same, "So anyway, I figured how the trap was activated: Being a wizard type I immediately noticed the arcane symbol in the centre and investigated, whereas you would have just 'looked' at it called it 'poofy' and carried on about your business."

Dirk sighed deeply; this was the painful part of the explanation. "See we're in a 'Wizard trap' in layman's terms, the symbol itself is almost meaningless really but the trap is activated whenever anyone attempts to cipher or sense its magic."

Grot wobbled about in a slowly bubbling temper, "So you're telling me you did it are yer? Yer friggin well stuffed me up again..., ...You bastard..."

Dirk felt an unwelcome pang of guilt and worked to rid himself of the emotion as quickly was possible. "Oh come on you can't go blaming me..., ...It isn't my fault I set it off; any inquisitive wizard would have. It's not like I asked you to –oh shit, yeah... Well, look, I didn't build it did I? Come on Grot **–Grot, Your foot!**"

Grot hastily lifted his rapidly faltering foot and regained his balance and a little composure. "Ok fair enough! We're stuck here now anyhow, so it's a waste of time bitching about it I suppose, so what do we do next...? Hold on! What was that noise?"

The magical blast had alerted the skittering sounds owner to the presence of visitors and it came ambling down the treacherous staircase in search of the magical source. Both Grot and Dirk saw the creature at the same time as it noticed them, and it stopped about half way down the steps from the first landing.

The Nymph looked at the two beings, completely oblivious to the birds charcoaled remains and wondered how they had survived the bolts deadly power, or maybe they had erupted from within the bolt itself... The fearsome Maestri perhaps, guardians of the restless light, the keepers of manna themselves... Mind you they didn't *look* very fearsome.

Grot cursed himself, dismissing his fevered imagination when he caught sight of the beautiful little person who appeared, sure enough - sweeping brush in hand. The Dwarf wiped his brow, examining the naked humanoid and relaxing almost to the point of settling his foot down yet again.

"Why hello there little miss; why you are a pretty girl aint ya? Or should I say woman, after all you are, ahem..., ...darn sexy looking!" Dirk managed to splutter in delight, "What's your name...?"

"I am Municia," the naked newcomer announced, though Dirk was too busy studying her to heed her reply. She readily epitomised the expression of woman albeit on a miniscule scale.

The pastel-blue hue of her satin smooth skinned, adulterous thought inspiring body, could well have stimulated any grown male and had she been a few feet taller in height…, …Well; Dirk daydreamed as she spoke…

"Dirk yer dog, pay attention!" Grot seethed.

"…And that means you are both unwelcome trespassers in my masters sanctuary." Municia finished with a confident smugness.

"Ah yes about that…" Dirk began.

A small hand axe whistled past Municia's head narrowly missing its intended target. Shooting one startled look at the Dwarf who had launched it, she scurried rapidly back up the stairwell grumbling about unwelcome guests.

Grots knee began twitching under his own weight, he definitely had not helped his cause throwing his axe, but haste was needed right now less he join the maimed pigeon into barbecued history.

"That wasn't very polite Grot; you've gone and scared her off now…" Dirk's voice trailed off as the rapidly reddening Dwarf took aim with another axe, this time at him! By now Grots knee convulsions had become so wild he was forced to stand on his own foot as painful as that was, lest he stumble onto one of the fissures that his accursed Dwarven sight could not even see. Dirk knew this was the beginnings of Grot in a bad mood and the lusting wizard was far too fearful of his pal to want to see him take it to the next level.

"Shut up all right? Swell work on the clever old wizardly bit, but the way I see it, I'll be dead in a few minutes or less, so unless you wanna go quicker I suggest we'd better act quickly. OK…? So…"

"I heard her murmuring something about sisters," Dirk offered, "So for all we know she might just want to keep us as sex slaves…"

"Dirk…!" Grot cut in, "Will you grow a bloody brain? She's a devil, not a sex maniac, though for all I care she could be both." He paused to wonder if Zen's inane survival instincts had somehow passed to Dirk, whose normally reliable danger sense had taken a beating of late. "You did hear the bit about the master I take it?"

"Oh yes, I suppose…" Dirk sulked.

"Suppose nothing!" The surly Dwarf cut in. "Just listen to me and we might live through this… Ok?"

Grot noticed the hangdog look about Dirk and gave him a confidence building wink in preparation for the responsibility he was about to ask his panicking pal to undertake. He knew Dirk would be resistant to placing Grot's life and thereby his own at Dirk's decision making worst, but Grot had faith in his inept, oft times useless, dolt of a pal. In the several years they had been travelling together, Dirk had never *completely* let him down in times of peril; *I just hope he knows his distances...* Grot wondered of his odd-mannered young friend. The bearded one even managed a last, wry smile as the Nymph appeared back on the steps and pointed them out to some unseen force that lurked just beyond the stairs bend.

"...where? How should I know? But I can't fly, I can't!" Dirk shouted in seemingly meaningless distraction before his attention snapped back to Grot and was suddenly solemn. "What do you want me to do?" he asked of his diminutive comrade in arms.

"Just tell me where the fissures are, that's all, okay? I need to know how many feet behind and to the side. Do you understand? *Behind ME...,* ...meaning *My* right and *left*, ya got it? Oh and yer don't need look so ill all the time, you'll be fine me lanky-legged pal, just..., ...stop arguing with yourself; your worrying me!"

Dirk nodded his response, and focused his attention completely upon the fissures surrounding Grot, completely ignoring the two, double breasted behemoths that came bounding down the staircase. They were crimson skinned beauties that looked almost identical to the Nymph named Municia, yet they were five times her size, had four flabby tits apiece and judging from their carnal expressions, seemed a whole lot more pissed off, and a great deal less talkative!

"OK. Here goes..." Grot said readying himself, "Oh, and Dirk..., ...Not to add any pressure but..., ...Please be precise."

Dirk looked at the mosaic pattern and the criss-crossing fissures and determined (well actually; he guessed) that he would need to land on every fifth square foot of tiles – which for some reason were coloured pink. A speedy check to confirm the bird had indeed not stepped onto one of the pink areas and Dirk gave his first set of instructions; "Two feet left and one foot... ah, no-sorry, eight inches behind. Hold on, how many inches in a foot? Or half – I mean...oh, hold on..."

"...Dirk!!! Ignore the screaming Demons and think about it carefully... Now, as quick as you can, tell me where to jump... No pressure." Grot enthused, his pleadings applying more pressure still.

"They're Demons!?! Right! Ignore the Demons... Why didn't I bloody think of that?" Dirk seethed with undisguised wit, "Ok, well forget about inches, you need to get two feet right and about a half foot back, is that clear enough instructions for you? And hurry, they're getting nearer..."

Grot never asked for a second opinion. Flexing his knees so low his bottom almost touched the floor, the Dwarf pushed upwards for all he was worth, contorting his body into a back-flip and twisting to the side in an attempt to travel the desired distance and no more. He landed with both feet together within a narrow gap between two fissures and not on a pink tile at all.

Grot swayed to and fro correcting his posture and called out to Dirk in frustration, who he now found himself with his back towards. "Well come on, think fast man!"

"Hold on let me figure it out... By my reckoning you should have landed on a pink tile." Dirk answered evasively.

"Figure it out? WHAT DO YA MEAN FIGURE IT OUT? I-" Grot paused in his Preying Mantis positioned rhetoric to duck as an adventurous Demon dived past, attempting to relieve Grot of his newly inspired skull. "Ya great big Mandragore cock! You buggered it up didn't you? Ya meant left didn't ya? I remember you said 'left' first time. Keldor's beard be bloody well burnt if I haven't been patient... And after me telling you to calm down, take your time... I dunno? How many more times will you cock up my life?"

Dirk cowered down in a squat as the soaring Demon landed with a thump directly upon several glowing gaps, and the accumulative frizzle its haphazard landing imposed scorched the cloth of his robes.

"Well...?" Grot baited, "Are you not going to make up some excuse or something? Invent a convincing theory of lies maybe? Or have you finally learned to accept your mistakes as your own...?"

Dirk was unsure quite *how* to react and this bothered him gravely for although he could never be labelled a positive individual; his fear of all things had always lent him an ingrained sense of immediate action. His thoughts and actions; though often weighed down with inappropriate ideas, were for the most part taken with a certain instantaneous flair.

Usually that was; but since that stupid little Snurch had so mischievously grinned up at him with its smart arsed, violence provoking deception Dirk hadn't known whether he was coming or going and his self admired cowardice had mutated into some sterile sort of self preservation mode, which left him feeling confused, disoriented and altogether unsure. Tears began streaming down his face and he began gibbering like a Baboon…

"…Oy dumb-ass!" Grot bellowed, shattering Dirk's reverie.

The day-dreamed Snurch melted to become the visage of a sneering few feet of Grot and he again had the insipid desire to bring down his foot quite hard. Again, the sting of insulted honour arose in Dirk.

A scuffling sound brought Dirk out of his tearful daydream as he saw Grots undulating physique battle both the effects of gravity and the second clawing Demon who had managed to stalk within swiping distance of the said Dwarf. A well placed jump-kick saw the Dwarf land smartly between the unseen cracks both feet apart, and sent the Demon reeling back several feet where it encountered one of the hitherto avoided fissures.

The resultant fiend's trip set off several bolts simultaneously and Grot and Dirk struggled to retain their respective poses. "Are you gonna stand there like a spare Golem at a rock convention or are you gonna bloody well guide me? We'll forget about your little *mistake*…"

Dirk shot a filthy look at the Dwarves exposed back, "Well if you knew I'd said '*left*' you should have gone that way shouldn't you… It's not my fault…"

"…Dirk! Can we argue about this some other time mate? I'm gonna fall over if I have to hold my balance one moment longer." Grot interjected without his usual insulting embellishments.

"Five feet to *YOUR* right and you're clear." Dirk shouted out, un-phased as a third, unnoticed Daemoness erupted in a flash of singed smoke after carelessly stepping onto the mosaic. "If you can make it that is, your in a mesh of cracks right now."

Dirk sniggered with churlish delight at his would be ambusher, as an hitherto concealed fourth Daemoness lunged at Dirk from behind, wrestling him to the floor. '*What a nob! I'm about to have my throat ripped out and I'm giggling like a school girl with a new doll!*' Fortunately for Dirk, his lack of pre-anticipated resistance meant the ambush caused the attacking Demon far greater pain than he, as it took the brunt of the lightning blast that enveloped both itself and its intended victim, blazing the larger portion of its body to ash.

Although spared the deadly pain of the blast itself, Dirk was flung high into the air, and landed face down on the staircase with a sickening snap as he attempted to deaden his fall by instinctively holding out his arms. Blood poured from one of his sleeves and he noted that despite the limb feeling acutely numb, a trickling sensation of pain was rapidly building at the point where the bone of his forearm was protruding through a hole in his tattered garb.

One of the Daemons separated arms still gripped him tightly by the throat, stubbornly flexing in an attempt to strangle him, despite the fact that only *it* remained intact. He pulled his other somewhat damaged arm out from beneath his torso and tossed the frazzled Demonic limb over the ledge. Looking down over the edge of the steps on which he lay; to watch the limbs dwindling fall, he was thankful to note despite his growing pain that the stairs *had* interceded in his fall: The blast had flung him a full five stories in height!

The isolated limb splattered against the mosaic floor and was flung high again on a jet of magical force, disintegrating before it reached two stories in height. If he had not landed on the stairs Dirk realized, he wouldn't have been landing on anything ever again.

A calming thought then as Dirk watched, clutching his fractured left limb, as Grot slowly bent to remove his boots and tossed them one at a time to the safety of the bare floor. *'Oh no!'* thought Dirk, *'The bloody idiot doesn't understand, or does he, hold on...'* He continued watching as, after doffing his pack and weapons also, Grot threw them too to the safety of the mosaics perimeter and then, obviously remembering his friend's earlier instruction; the Dwarf vaulted into the air sideways, tucking his knees in tight as he did so and tumbling down to land expertly besides his discarded gear.

Dirk smiled, then closed his eyes and grimaced as a spasm of pain wracked his damaged limb, and when he opened them again he could see yet more carnal Daemons spilling onto the stairs from where the small Nymph marshalled her troops below.

"There's more!" Dirk yelled to Grot, paying little heed to the fact that he had just revealed his own position by doing so.

Grot gave up on his semi-booted apparel and, kicking each foot he flung the boots with stunning accuracy at the little demon headmistress, Municia collapsed buying him a few desperate seconds as the Daemons milled about in confusion, still awaiting her further orders.

Struggling to pull on his weapon sleeved cuisse and greaves also had to be abandoned and he instead chose to pick up his smoky looking double-headed Battle-axe, "Drundarrin's will be done" he said invoking the arcane power that resided within the ancient axe and its many dull glyphs that thronged the Jet black handle suddenly throbbed into glittering life.

Grot loved his axes, he had one for every conceivable occasion and they ranged in size and versatility, but this one was an awesome weapon of devastation - it was made up of a bluish-black material called Jet and had been forged for him by Drundarrin, a true master of the weapon smith art, whose creative skills had lent it the ability to appear and act as smoke to all but Grot. At four foot in length, its shaft was just a few inches shorter than Grot himself. The broad double headed blades hung down like batwings for some third of the shafts length, where silver and gold runes writhed across its surface. Yet the most astonishing thing of all was that this particular axe was one of his least favoured, due to its complete lack of versatility. I.E. it was good -nay brilliant, for one task and one task alone: Killing. Looking at the pissed off, de-magnified, growling, bare foot Dwarf now, Dirk was pretty sure that as far as Dwarven accessories go; the axe most definitely did suit his current mood.

***

Dirk lay upon his sagging back and sighed a most happy and relieved smile, carefully nursing the mad-pain/numbness of his incapacitated limb. "Smash the shitty things Grot man; cut them up like liver and then get up here and help me before I die." He said quietly and not really to Grot at all.

"Well, my name is not Grot but, perhaps *I* can help you?" enquired a singsong voice from above Dirk.

Dirk looked about in all directions for the voices owner and noticed the semi-concealed face of a Dark Elf hidden in the shallow recess of the 5th floor landing not far above his position.

The injured wizard watched on with a complete lack of trust as the Elves next sardonic statement came out from the shadowy recess, accompanied by the tip of an arrowhead. "You wouldn't want to *fall* from there now would you? Not unless you have had a magical epiphany of majestic proportions and suddenly learned how to fly. Who knows, maybe you have..?"

"Hey there Elf, why don't we just go somewhere quiet and discuss this like adults? You could say; pick me up and take me to a healer for a small share of my loot. What dya say?" Dirk harangued the bow wielding maniac.

The Elf's arched eyebrows and dark eyed gaze lent him a non-compromising look. "I think not my little Shallafey..." He declared, pulling back the bowstring. "I have a far more amusing idea: It involves these arrows thudding into your flesh, until you either resemble a pin cushion or learn the ancient mystery of flight. You seem adept enough at escape I see, so let us discover if you can indeed fly *magic user*!" And with that the Dark elf let fly the first arrow from his bow.

The inept non-hero rolled to the side as the arrow thumped into the ground beside where he had been lay, saving his life, crushing his limb and causing himself untold agony as he rolled off and over the edge of the spiralling staircase, as the Elf had most definitely intended him to do.

Utilising his one working arm in a flapping panic, Dirk managed to grab onto the stairs precipice and wondered what the hell he could do about this situation as his face hinged heavily against the hard white surface of the stairs. Below him, from the corner of his strained left eye, he could see the bitter battle unfolding between Grot and the pack of Daemonesses...

***

Grot shifted his feet in a manner that in our time would probably be deemed break-dancing. First his left foot travelled right, then his right swung forward and pivoted to bring the left foot back across, his right foot came forward to retain balance before stepping back onto, then across his body with his left and into a forward fall on his right foot that not only confused the hell out of his enemy but also lent his full body weight to the axes swooping arc.

Mystical steel met magical bone in much the same way as scorching lava meets warm butter, yet a whole lot messier. Blood spurted freely as the axe carved its way through the Daemonic front rank, leaving behind a trail of diamond like sparks in its gory wake, gristle and bone eschewing out to the sides of the butchered column as the Dwarf steamrollered on.

***

...An arrow thudded into the stairs besides Dirks fingers. He could no longer see his assailant or the troublesome missiles that he fired, but he knew from the localised tremors and detached chippings of the white stony substance that the arrow had only just missed his exposed hand. The next one probably would not. "Look could we not just reason this out?" Dirk tried to scream in a diplomatic tone. "I'm sure deep down you're a lovely chap..." Dirk ventured against reasonable hope.

A zipping, whistling sound, and sudden painful sting made Dirk acutely aware that he had just lost the tip of an ear to yet another wickedly placed arrow, yet the sharp pain merely served to intensify his desperate grip.

"Sorry! You really are out of luck," sang the Dark Elf as he padded down the steps and leaned out carelessly over the edge in order to better obtain Dirk's undivided attention, "I had a bad upbringing..." The sadistic Elf reasoned without any outward conviction. "What can I say? I am the misunderstood protégé of a pseudo-idiosyncratic society. I don't *want* to kill you... *I simply feel **compelled*** with a *consuming* desire to avenge years of abuse and neglect inflicted upon my innocent selves ancestors..., ...And you my unfortunate fellow; merely represent the same codes of narcissistic social depravation from which my much hated and feared oppressors' issue. It is in fact, nothing personal..., ...Just..., ...Hmm well, my calling let's say, which I happen to be damn great at. Thabanek memmissir H'aldonin if you please..."

"You're a what?! Look! If you help me then I'll help you deal with the Dwarf down there eh?" Dirk screamed at the lushly voiced Elf as his grip began to moodily relax in its precipitous hold. "I don't mean to rush you bragging your bollocks off, but come on man, get real. YOU DON'T HAVE TO KILL ME!"

"Well I never!" The Dark Elf seemed genuinely affronted, "You really should have better manners than to butt in when somebody else is speak-"

The third finger slipped, dragging Dirks weak pinkie along with it. "Shut up prick ears and help me. Please!!!" Dirk interrupted once more with even more emotion and urgency.

The Dark Elf fixed him with an odd, quizzical look before bending down within arms reach of Dirk. The long slender points of the Elves ears twitched to a peak as he leered insanely over the edge, then his thin eyebrows arched and the smile was gone, the pricked ears flexed back akin to those of a threatened animal, and the whole look of benign idiot was replaced by disdain and disgust for the common Human scum beneath his gaze. Even when scowling the Elves facial features were far more beautiful than any Human could hope to be: Humans being an ugly, uncivilised race held by most Elven folk in almost equal contempt to their Dwarven counterparts. Both races where oft described by Elves merely as 'Vulgars'.

"I WAS trying to say; although it is nothing personal towards your unworthy hide, it *shall* be…, …Most **highly enjoyable.**" The cruel Elf placed his soft soled leather boot on Dirks two remaining fingers and thumb; pressing down hard in a swivelling motion cracking and grinding the bones within.

"…Aiee! Hook, ya barbaric needle dick bastard!" Dirk cried in agony.

Dirk was in decision making heaven. Now, if the easily offended Elf would just apply a little more pressure. "Wait. Please. Let me at least know the name of my worthy conqueror…" Dirk panted, dabbling in flattery as his fingers reluctantly lost all grip.

The Elves foot shot down with renewed force, pinning Dirk's rapidly travelling hand in place beneath the sprightly Elves surprisingly heavy sole. Dirk's shoulder felt ready to depart the socket, such was the fiery pain that burned down the length of his right arm. Yet he needed to buy time and this Elf was exactly the right type of proud fool to fall for his simple ploy. He'd taken the bait…

"Ha-ha! …Line!" Dirk grimaced in a needle stabbing pain of delight.

"Certainly you may know my name so that you may fear it in your next short life also… Some call me DhÆÏÐ-Uœffor. Grand A'hal'll and scourge of the living light, other less eloquent factions, such as the dirty little existence from which you yourself probably hail, know me quite simply as Adin; which is a mere two syllables of my full first name, but I doubt your limited vocal comprehension would be able to afford you understanding of that intellectual property so I shall press on. Now, others…" The Elf continued to recount, as the first echoes of painfully enjoined battle rippled upwards from below…

***

Grot swung his enchanted weapon again, this time falling into a roll as the axe-head met with thin air. He followed the vain action through with the arch of his body and came up at speed, perched atop the immense axe as if it were a pogo stick, its blade stood upright on the floor. Tumbling forward whilst maintaining his hold on the lengthy shaft, Grot landed on his feet and whipped his vertebrae forward, lending the axe a greater force in its forward momentum. The spry Dwarf let go at the last minute with optimal timing, and the axe went thwacking through the Demons' decimated ranks end over tail, spreading redemption as it rotated onwards.

Rushing through the temporary gap his huge axe throwing trick had un-mustered, Grot flicked out two matching curved blades from the belt he still wore at his waist and span them viciously side to side, kneecapping several more of the creatures as they stabbed, bit and scratched at his much craved for flesh. By the time he cleared the infuriated group of demons, only one of the curved blades remained in his grasp, the other having become lodged in a shin somewhere amidst his gauntlet run. A quick glance about him as he ran revealed no sign of the large trusty axe of Drundarrin.

Grots momentum took him up the short first flight of steps and onto the landing occupied by Municia, who was screaming orders to yet more troops emerging from within the door to the left. Municia looked up as the Dwarf arrived, harried by the remaining Daemon pack. She gulped, thought of speaking and then ducked as the enraged Dwarf struck for her throat. Grot reversed the arc of the blade to cut a path across the space occupied by Municia's legs.

It seemed though the tiny figure seemed doomed to be amputated, yet Municia's reflexes were too quick - even for Grot! Flopping to her back with an almost boneless suppleness, the nymph easily evaded the Dwarfs cut then, uncoiling her arched back, she flipped cat like to her feet —over the intended low blow and cart-wheeled to the side as the Dwarf despatched with four more eager Demons who had foolishly thought to catch him off guard. Turning to face three more particularly brutish beasts, he span the blade in propeller like fashion, driving it into two of the trio's faces before eagerly renewing his pursuit of the troublesome order giving Nymph, closely followed by two injured Daemons.

Municia looked back in time to see the Dwarf lining up the first of a volley of swipes and thrusts and In rapid succession her evasive form darted into several continuous cartwheels with the Dwarfs blade a hairs breadth behind all the way, on her fifth cartwheel she sank down into a backward roll, then sprang forward kicking up into the dwarfs throat and springing backwards of his forehead.

***

'...Oh boy...!' Thought Dirk, almost wishing he had never asked for the Elf's name, *'does this guy like to talk!'* Acting on his chance while the Elf launched into his lengthy liturgy, Dirk took the only option that was left to him, or at least the only one his scatter-brained mind could think up.

Dirk was pretty sure if he were to die here there most probably wouldn't be any resurrection in the offering. So quite literally using his head for once, he began to rock back and forth utilising his forehead for leverage, pushing against the butt of the stairway, starting a gentle swing that threatened to yank Dirk's deadened fingers' loose before he was even ready to bring his plan to fruition.

Luckily for Dirk then that Adin; sensing that his victim may fall before he had finished informing him of his name, rank, titles, and proclamations; pressed down hard on the three digits beneath his boot with enough force to pin them there indefinitely...

***

"Sounds like Municia's sisters have arrived." Galbor noted as he heard the muted screams echoing from the tower above.

Kalamere looked up from his study of the chess pieces, "I fear the company of Daemons as wenches doth douse my appetite for the carnal pleasures," he said before picking up and placing his Queen down in front of his opponents King, removing the Bishop from the square it had previously occupied. "Check...mate, methinks -oh no...!"

Galbor grinned at Kalamere's oversight and wasted no time in taking the exposed Queen with an aptly placed Rook.

***

...Slowly Dirks small rocking motion gained momentum, sending creases of pain driving through Dirks skull each time his swinging torso caused his forehead to press into the marble. Knuckles cracked and popped as the flesh of his hand began to peel away, causing Dirk to sob despite him self. After several severely painful moments further, during which the Elf rattled off his numerous supply of designations, the Elves foot lessened its weight on the tortured digits and Dirk swung for all he was worth towards the wall, at the same time yanking all but one of his somewhat semi-detached fingers out from under the Dark Elves kid-leather boot.

For a moment Adin the Dark Elf thought Dirk had slipped to his doom on the mosaic floor far beneath, yet leaning over the edge he clearly saw this was not the case. Confused, Adin's eyes roamed about in vain until a slight movement caught his eye and his vision was drawn to a strip of clothing material hanging as limply as the body it encased, off the steps of the floor directly beneath. Cat-like and deathly quiet, Adin started down the flight of steps, in search of his injured prey.

The remaining Daemon pack launched at Grot howling insane whoops of malicious joy like the maddeningly possessed creatures that they were. At the same time, Adin's footsteps brought him around the curve of the steps and into the angle of Dirks sight. He was conscious, though the fall had left him in worse shape than before. "And what the hell for..., ...I mean did I actually achieve anything but a slower death...?" He asked himself. What was he fighting against; why did he not just accept that he was going to die and get it over with quickly?

Had he really thought the Elf would simply assume him to be dead after all his ordeals? No - Adin may be a proud fool, but he was a professionally deadly one too. His heart sank at the sight of the Elf pulling back on his bowstring, a glinting arrowhead aimed towards his unprotected heart. Dirk had pulled out of a lot of similar brushes with death, but in his lame state, with no weapons or spells at his disposal, he realised that this was probably the end.

"...The way I see it," the Elf gloated in anticipation, "You have two chances remaining..."

"I have...?" Dirk asked incredulously, He no longer felt any pain – except at the base of his skull –thanks to probably breaking his neck on landing... "These chances... Do you mind me asking what are they?"

"No, no, no, not at all... They're really quite simple really!" The Elves eyes twinkled with mischievous delight as the human took the bait... "No chance and not a chance in Hell!" The arrow flew from its holding...

***

Grot leaned back enough to avoid taking any real pressure from her kicks and stabbed his curved weapon straight for where he expected her midriff to be upon landing, but again Municia reacted the smarter, transforming her intended somersault into multiple back flips as she sprang backwards off the steps one and a half storeys high, her lithe form sailing effortlessly through the air.

The Dwarf lovingly swept after Municia in full on battle lust and only just stopped in time to teeter on the rim of the staircase for a moment as his momentous pursuit almost took him over the edge: Then laughed as he realised the nymphs lateral movement out into midair began to take on a definite vertical trajectory, straight down towards the lightning trap. A growl from behind however alerted him to yet more Daemons, and he turned to discover that her last yells had alerted yet more recruits, leaving Grot alone with his little curved blade, trapped in the middle of around twenty of her lesser-Demon kin. The Dwarves rumbling groans transformed into a happy growl as behind him a certain Blue Nymph went 'pop'!

***

...The arrow came whistling through the air, its course set to make contact with Dirk but instead it struck into the small blue charcoaled body of Municia, as she suddenly came spinning through the air along with the magical charge that had caused her to do so, this caused Dirk to chortle uncontrollably, bringing up great gulps of blood as he laughed.

Adin proved so startled by the surge of electricity and screeching frazzled Nymph that he completely lost his footing on the steps edge and toppled over the side dropping his bow in the process. "Oh my, my, my...!" He managed to gasp before tumbling forward into open space.

As he plummeted past the lower section of stairs on which Dirk's giggling form lay, Adin's melodramatically flailing hands connected with the outer ledge of a step in a wondrously fluky manoeuvre. A loud crack was followed by a girlish scream as the Elves weaker right hand ripped clear of its fleshy confines, popping champagne cork-like into the air and leaving battered tendons and veins protruding from his stumped wrist. His left hand managed to survive the breakneck rate of the fall however and he clung perilously to the stairs edge, shocked and fearful of the fate awaiting him below. Dirk and Adin were separated by a mere four steps and Dirk, coughing up blood all the while though he was; could not help but laugh through bloodstained teeth at the situations turn around.

The painful throb in his neck sent another stab through his brain and he instinctively reached his hand up to the affected area. *Huh? I can move...* Dirk thought in surprise. He tenderly shifted his weight and discovered that he was no more paralyzed than a prancing tiger –well; maybe a little more... However, the numbness in his body did not completely restrict him and though both his arms were truly knackered

183

beyond usefulness, his right leg was just about capable of producing a bodily shove.

After adjusting his ascending trajectory to make certain he was not about to propel himself over the edge, Dirk started shoving his broken bones slowly upwards, seeking out the Elf on whom he would avenge his own impending death…

***

As Dirk ascended the grudgingly slow few feet upwards; far below Grot descended a whole flight, but no sooner had he charged his aggressors Grot fell under the barrage of the vengeful horde, losing the curved blade in the process. In their frenzy for blood the Demons and Daemonesses tore painfully at Grot's buried torso, but such was the compression of bodies atop him, their claws served as more of a danger to each other.

Several of the more wily Daemonesses pulled back from the tangled mass of blood splattered limbs and waited, while their brethren swiped inefficiently at Grot, notching nasty chunks in each others hides.

By this time, the Dwarf was bleeding quite badly from a wound on his shoulder along with a terrible bite to his side, yet it was still the Demons themselves hurting most in the turbulent melee; gifting the Dwarf a brief amount of time in which to collect his scattered thoughts. Grot had entered into this battle as little more than a confused and disoriented fighter, but within those few moments of calm, Grot - the warrior of legend had taken control.

One by one the demons that could still rise did so; leaving Grots static bloodied remains prone to their next move. His eyes were fixed and watery, his bearded jaw sagged onto his chest which rose once then remained like his other organs; static. Devoid of any and all signs of life!

***

…Pushing himself along on his back, Dirk paused for breath as he finally made the short but no-less exhausting distance between himself and the helpless Elf who still clung on dearly though his knuckles were beginning to purple and the tips of his fingers had gone white.

"Hello!" Dirk panted popping his head over the ledge and affecting a muffled puppeteer voice as he waved the Elves own unattached hand in his clenched teeth.

Words escaped the Elf and Adin found he could not respond to the taunt, not just due to the pain wracking his body, but rather the more annoying fact of his predicament, the Elf was not familiar with playing the role of the Inferior being.

"I am Mr. Handy hand, will you be my friend?" Dirk slurred in a high pitch, wiggling the severed limb for effect.

"Please be my friend?" He again prompted, then paused to wait for any possible reply, found none forthcoming and so continued the morose charade unassisted. "Wanna shake on it?"

"I know! Let's play piggy!" Dirk shouted, spitting the puppet hand out over the middle chamber. With that he brought his chin down hard on Adin's thumb causing it to lose its hold and chipping Dirks back tooth in the process.

"This little piggy went to market…" Dirk sang amidst painful whelps from himself and Adin continuing by biting through each digit in turn. When only Adin's third and fourth finger remained, his grip gave way entirely and the Elves flailing form went tumbling downwards to land in a semi-folded heap, on the mosaic pattern below.

Adin's crippled body had not finished crumpling up when his flailing hand triggered one of the magical glyphs, the blast spinning him back roof-wards carried by an electrical column of light and accompanied by several of the unfortunate Daemonesses who had backed off from Grot a little too much and thus found themselves stood in the wrong place at the wrong time when Adin fell.

Satisfied of the Elves skyward demise, Dirk allowed him self a grin-come-grimace before he lay back and awaited Death's cold welcoming embrace. *Maybe the light's just blinded me?* Dirk thought, and rested his sightless eyes for a while. His breathing became laboured, and apart from an annoyingly uncontrollable twitch in his left arm, his breathing carcass began cycling through a systematic shutdown of his body parts, until everything ceased to function and his mind closed to the distant numbing lights and sounds…

***

…Grot too lay close to death, but the Dwarves indomitable, stubborn will, refused to let a bunch of Demonic servants get the better of him. Most fighters the Eyrthe over would think twice before entering into a fight with

185

even the basest of Daemons; which these last few opponents were most assuredly not. Grot though was no ordinary fighter, he was the last of his line and would rather be half-eaten alive than give up his lineage to something that did not even belong to this world. Moreover he was more than a mere living being, more than a Dwarf. He concentrated his remaining strength while awaiting the fiends' next move lying still as the first morning mists.

It came in the form of one of the twin breasted Daemonesses. She leered down at him, a foul gunk dripping from her open jaw and onto the cheek of Grot, where its acidic touch burned through his rough skin. The Daemoness brought its head forward at speed, butting poor Grot full in the mouth, before crouching on all fours over the unmoving Dwarf, its hot fetid breath stinging his bruised and bloodshot eyeballs.

Grot awaited a single heartbeat before putting his plan into action with admirable warrior instinct. His rough stubby fingers gripped vice-like onto the foul cretins uppermost breasts and he swung himself out through its legs and down the stairs to where four other deadly denizens awaited.

The Dwarves equilibrium served two purposes, bringing the stunned Daemoness crashing to the ground headfirst, whilst swinging Grots own body down the steps with enough velocity to topple the demons below; like so many Gobbos' in a game of 'Toss the Goblin' (A favourite Dwarven pastime).

Grot bounced down the steps with many a grunt and groan, cracking his helmet in two in the process and losing his two hidden daggers, which he reached for as he hit bottom. Quick wits and battle instinct was what was important now however, and he wasted not a moment in getting to his feet and racing around the lower hall to retrieve some weapon from his abandoned kit, which lay some way around the mosaic perimeter.

The remaining seven Demons collected themselves and following the chief Daemonesses lead; they raced around the perimeter in opposite directions, hoping to entrap the scurrying form of the Dwarf, whilst one of the remaining smaller daemons leapt upon his exposed back. Grot ran on all the same, he was weapon-less and a daemon could only be defeated by weapons of magical origin, so he had no choice; as the lesser demon reached it's yellow gnarly claws around his neck, Grot took a hold of those same magical claws and dug them into the beasts own thighs, forcing it to leap clear in pain. "Zen's dead!" He shouted suddenly remembering and punched the pained Daemoness hard in the face, following up by smashing its head repeatedly against the outer wall, whilst holding the screaming Daemoness in a headlock as he raced for his abandoned weaponry and gear.

Reaching his kit, he let go off the now permanently silenced Daemon and hunched down for a quick rummage…, …From the two axes he chose to retrieve, only one had enough magic in it to permanently harm the beasts' still bounding towards him, but this was not his only need. He rushed over to one of the velvety purple drapes that intermittently swathed the walls and waited. When the two packs were almost upon him, he threw the non-magic axe at the cord tieback that held the vast curtain in place and hung onto its sumptuous material.

The axe struck the cord, severing it and after shooting several feet up in the air, Grot released the cord and leapt to safety as the tapestry came crashing down atop of his surprised opponents, covering them in its silky confines. "Keldor's work be done, and done well!" Grot shouted proudly and set about hacking at the random bits of confused and temporarily blinded demons, that periodically tore their way free of the fabrics clutches. It was an easy lesson in mass murder; Grot's eager axe severed a limb here or a head there with the rhythm of a happy lumberjack.

Soon only one struggling form remained intact in the bloodbath of material and gore. He swung his axe down with all the force he could muster and breathed a satisfied sigh as its wicked edge caught purchase in the things rising skull.

***

"Hark! Again I do think it cometh. Truly, I do hear something?" The voice that spoke was Kalamere's this time. Losing his queen had cost him dearly, though he still had two Rooks, a Bishop and a Knight as well as his unprotected king.

Galbor cocked his head to one side, his mind pre-occupied with too many things to pay proper attention to the clamour coming from above. *His remaining Rook was in danger of being taken and if that fell, then his counter attack would fail… Why hadn't he chosen white? He needed a not so clever diversion…*

"Knight to Rook: E4." Galbor declared then added somewhat belatedly, "You may take my Rook for all I care!"

With a snort of derision, Kalamere did indeed take the proffered piece as the game charged closer to its climax, interrupted by a hellish

187

shriek that pierced the air, and momentarily, the thoughts of the contestants were invaded.

"Sounds like they are having *too much fun...*, ...The bloody whelps! I'll get Municia to quieten them. Municia...!" Galbor shouted, but only half-heartedly. *'Damn!'* he thought privately, *'I really needed that Rook.'*

***

Grot wrenched his axe free from its bony confines and struck down with vehemence as the remaining Demon continued to rise ghostlike, enshrouded in the purple material.

The axe struck home once again as it came into contact with bone, but this time it was Grot's trusty axe that splintered, much to his dismay.

The same Daemoness that had led the earlier charge erupted from the materials depths. Her skull was split down the centre and the two upper breasts were purpled and bruised. This did little to add to the allure of its naturally life-frightening appeal. Two of its four arms ended in long needle pointed pincers and its head was a horrible fusion of human and bull.

Looking as ghastly as it could manage under the circumstances, the Daemonic thing's mooing voice hissed out at Grot in hatred, "YOU! WILL!! Perish!!! Kneel and I shall kill you quickly!"

But Grot wasn't in the mood for exchanging pleasantries. Instead he barged forward, ramming the stunted remains of his weapons handle into the creatures open mouth and out through the back of her throat.

"Try not to talk with yer mouthful!" Grot quirked as the thing sank to its knees, clutching at the pulpy mass of its larynx.

"You are only making things worse for yourself." It managed to gargle in defiance swiping angrily at his legs...

Looking about him for some weapon with which to bring an end to the murderous debacle, Grot spotted a huge lantern hanging by the side of a door, previously concealed by the tapestry. Quick-smart, he ran over to retrieve the lantern, but the stubborn Daemoness lurched after him on all fours. Grabbing the huge lamp and arching his back just in time to avoid a last desperate pounce from the Demon as it smashed into the door instead. Grot pivoted 360 degrees bringing the lantern arcing into full contact with what remained of the things garbled face and knocking its head clean off its shoulders as its torso forcefully cracked back into the door splitting the holding beams…

…The detached skull was sent spinning back through the air and hammered against the door with such force that the meagre latch gave way, and lent the decapitated daemon-head passage as it went soaring through the open portal beyond. Here it bobbled wetly down the short flight of steps and rolled with a dramatic inevitability towards the chess set, where two open mouthed participants were sat.

Galbor leapt up from his seat as the decapitated head smashed its way through the chess set scattering the remaining pieces far and wide across the study floor, before coming to rest in front of the voluminous fireplace, vacant eyes staring up at the two men who had followed its path of destruction in slack-jawed amazement.

"SHIT!!! Erm… … Sorry about that. One of you must be the owner of this tower I take it?" Grot said with all the aplomb of a ballet dancing rhino. When no immediate response came, he attempted to feign innocence pointedly averting his eyes in shame and whistling as distractedly as was possible.

Still, nothing but an indignant expression on the face of the foremost fellow and a slightly bemused expression on the other answered his own shocking introduction. This was going to be hard work, Grot could tell.

"Erm, nice place…"

X)   **The Master and the Student**

The two men before Grot vacantly stared at the chess pieces rolling and skittering across the floor. A larger piece went rolling towards the open fire and the robed man bent down and interrupted its roll into the fires inferno. The human picked up and rolled the King about in his fingers, a smile itching its way across his lips. The other man to the right seemed less pleased. This one was staring cold and hard at Grot who still stood in the open doorway, unsure of what to do next.

"So, err… Do you get visitors often?" he ventured through a hazy pain.

The robed chap seemed to Grot to be about to say something, but instead he swallowed what words he had had in mind and instead turned to face the fire. So, thought Grot, I guess the happy one aint the Master.

The Dwarf stood there still, awaiting some movement or gesture from the glowering human, but even clearing his throat several times in a polite manner was not enough to spur the man into action. His adrenaline rush had all but subsided and he was now feeling the after affects. The pain in his side caused him a fair deal of agony too. Grot glanced about the room to distract him from his pain and whistled again as he took in its splendour. '*NOW THIS…! This was a proper wizards study!*' Grot thought nodding his approval. "Dirk would love this gaff." He said without thinking.

"Who's Dirk?" The moody man responded sharply - his attention immediately caught by the name.

"OH! Who? What, me, well, my mate is Dirk? He's a, erm, well, a mate of mine. Bit of a wizard like yourselves… I take it you are a wizard? And the master of the tower to boot, I'd guess…, …It's down to that all powerful commanding aura yer giving off!"

"Ye-e-e-s…" came back the long drawl, "I guess you could say that… and you have come to defeat me and plunder my loot no doubt? With this Dirk character in tow to combat the mad wizards spells no doubt? No? Your face suggests this is not truth though the thought has obviously crossed your mind at some point… Perhaps you are not the leader…, …maybe Dirk hired you to navigate the traps. Is that it? Are you some sort of scouting lackey for this Dirk character…?"

Grot shook his head as vigorously as he could manage. He could barely stand, much less fight, and even if these two gents were the very incarnation of evil, which he much doubted they were (Demon infested tower aside), he needed to get the wound in his side seen to before he bled to death.

"No. We joked about killing you, of course! But I promise yer, that'll be all yer sensing at least for my part and considering Dirk's more of a cowardly type than me my-self not to forget to mention most probably dead..." Grot spoke in panting bursts. "But we wouldn't really do a thing like that... No... We were just looking for a bit of help to be honest. See, one of our friends is dead outside and well we need to get him to a healer as soon as possible, so we just..." Grots mind swam from the dizziness that accompanied the distressing memory of Zen's butchered body staked to the litter outside.

The slightly taller and altogether more benign looking of the two seemed a little distracted; stood a little behind and to the left of the towers master and thus out of his eye line, the white dressed one constantly flickered his eyes stair ward. Was he signalling? Grot couldn't tell for sure and hadn't the strength or feeling left to care. The sterner of the two glowered in the manner of an overly strict schoolmaster.

"Where was I?" Grot said shaking the dreadful visage of Zen from his mind, "Oh, yeah. So we came in and well, we got attacked by some erm..." he searched for the right word, thinking demons might be a little insensitive, especially if one of the wizards had summoned them. "Erm... Minions... Right nasty bitches from hell to be precise, one of them did this!" he painfully stated awaiting some response as he stood clutching his half eaten ribcage.

Galbor stood up slowly and began walking to the back of the room. "So you came across Demons?" he asked nonchalantly, "And what pray tell happened to my intended company, brave Dwarf?"

"Grot!" replied the Dwarf, "My name's Grot and you are...?" He asked of the fellows before him, purposefully avoiding the question.

Neither of them indicated a response, but the nastier looking of the two did stop and turn in his tracks, glowering at the Dwarf in answer.

"Oh yeah: the demons! Well I was sure they must have come to the tower uninvited like, and thought I'd do you a favour if..." Grot again felt queasy, this whole place reeked of death and he would shortly join their number. "If we, erm; you know, killed them all!"

"We...?"

"Well yeah you're right, we? Oh erm... Well no! I mean **I,** *I killed them all* to be precise. I mean Dirk's a nice guy but a bit of a useless pillock in a fight to be honest. Those Daemonic bitches were bloody vicious buggers they were, especially that last big bastard with four tits - that's her head there!" Grot finished, pointing helpfully in case either man should have somehow missed its intrusive presence.

"Galbor is my name..." The nasty one unexpectedly announced, once again turning his back as he did so. This time he strode over to a strange circle of red light that seemed to emanate from the symbols embedded in the floor there. Upon his entrance the circle sprang to life, irradiating a multi-coloured semi-sphere from around its perimeter.

Kalamere almost reacted. He knew that while within that sphere, Galbor could be trapped. If Kalamere were to react quickly enough he would be able to seal the thing from this side, forcing Galbor to remain within the sphere, less he unleash every denizen in hell. Yet why would he go in knowing that Kalamere had the power to do this... unless... it was a trick of some sort? *'Mayhap thou wish for it or some assimilation.'* He thought, quickly changing both his plan and thoughts...

Kalamere went back to his seat and decided to let the chance go by. If the Dwarf had been able to help, but no, this Grot person was in no position to fight..., ...indeed, Kalamere had never seen a Dwarf look so white. *'His needs must be dire, I shall tend him forthwith,'* thought Kalamere.

Half heard, mumbled words bounced around the room as Galbor completed several complex incantations. *'Why had the old fool Kalamere not attacked?'* he thought desperately. He had expected the Wizard to do something at least. Yet he hadn't and Galbor was glad for it. He had work to do, work with his own kind, and he needed to start by getting some beasts to come and clean up the mess above. Galbor cursed himself again for his tardiness, he was becoming sloppy and sloppiness led to an unfortunate demise or worse -servitude. He nearly spat at the thought, but stopped lest he summon some vile greb-monster.

Focusing his concentration, Galbor summoned up the eleven un-dead spirits he had employed as Guardians for centuries past. They were the vengeful souls of former heroes, and he had trapped them into servitude for all eternity. When a soul was captured in this way, the summoner could raise them in a variety of forms - the most powerful being the deadly Wraith-form and it was in this state that Galbor now summoned them.

Wraiths were powerful creatures indeed. Able to turn invisible at will. Their fearsome touch would sap the life from a man and although some Wraiths still used weapons and armour, they were quintessentially, Ghosts' with attitude.

With a thought, Galbor ordered them to remain invisible and impassive unless any of the rooms other occupants attempted to disturb him in any way.

The ebony door creaked heavily as it seemed to slam shut of its own volition, almost bowling the Dwarf over in the process, as Galbor began the first of the complex summoning rites involved in raising demons, his moment of weakness passed.

Kalamere rose from his chair and bowed graciously to the Dwarf, "Kalamere be mine moniker. Haps sake, I may be of assistance?" his hand gestured towards the Dwarfs wounded abdomen.

"Oh, yeah…, …Got a bandage or two spare…?" The reply was vague, Grots head was swimming faster than a tuna-fish in a shark pool, and his queasiness had nothing to do with spike ridden bodies. Well, not much. Grot took a step forward, his axe slipped unceremoniously from his weakened grasp and he fell headlong down the steps…

…And awoke upright in front of the fire. "How…?" Grot began to say or think; he wasn't sure which. He tried to stand and realised he was floating, being held aloft in some magical fashion: The terrible pains that invaded every synaptic response and sheared through every sinew of his being were drawing back: Fading even; drying the sting of warm tears from his eyes. He watched in detached fascination as the Wizard with eerie white glowing eyes, began placing his palm points at carefully considered points on Grots body even touching some bits of his anatomy that he would sooner be left untouched. Grot was thankful however for *all* the regenerative caresses: Each time the wizard touched his hands to a spot, it healed the flesh anew, rolling back the years on each wounded section, rebuffing the limitations imposed by injuries both past and present; even his arthritic pain felt better.

The pain Grot felt intensified immensely as each lesion first flared up, expelling blood and dirt from the wound in an altogether far too gruelling ordeal and Grot instinctively reached down for his last remaining hip flask of Gnomish whisky but the wizard was quick to snatch it away. "Alcoholic beverages thin ye blood!"

Grot squirmed in mid air as his blood vessels seemed to erupt, yet instead of splurging out in any old fashion as one would expect blood to do, each globule followed its brethrens droplets into the fires heart in a fixed orderly line dancing through the air, much akin to a floating exodus of army ants hell bent on their own fiery destruction. As a gob-smacked Grot continued staring at his own extremities and the gory queue trailing out from each wound; each drip of blood firstly entered the fire where they were bathed in a golden sheen then marched straight back into one of his many sores. As each golden drop reunited with Grot's body, a doping sensation would help dull the pain in that spot, whilst flesh would instantly mend.

After a quick glance to check on the status of the other wizard Kalamere shifted his ministrations to the dwarfs lesser injuries, rotating Grots body so that he lay horizontal in mid-air. Kalamere then proceeded to gently kneed specific points on the Dwarfs body, which produced a calming and rejuvenating effect in the placid Dwarf. The whole process took barely more than ten minutes, during which time Grot was struck dumb in awe of the kindly wizard's powerful magical art. Once finished, Kalamere mentally guided the Dwarfs levitated and much refreshed form back to Eyrthe in an upright position.

"A fair deal better, I should wager, 'tis it nay?", the 'nice' wizard said in his funny manner.

"Yeah it is nay." Grot said happily, "I mean, ye, or yes, whatever..., ...Thanks." The affable gents jabbering reminded him of an affable old Great Uncle from his childhood days.

The wizard smiled at Grots uncertainty, "My name is Kalamere. Pleased to meet your acquaintance at last old Dwarf of yore. Grot, hmmm..." The wizard paused in his thoughtfulness. "Might you not be descended from the line of Alfrik the Damned?"

Grot nodded and could not hide the surprise spilling out from his countenance. "How did...?"

"I know? The question most prominent should be; what is one so important to his races survival doing so far from the bosom of his ancestral home..? The prophecy of which ye are most assuredly aware foretells of

194

thy own fate too and how the death of the line of kings brings about a new beginning for your people…, …That battle is foretold to take place within the confines of the Dwarven keep of Ghour L'mash Dhoom in the mount of Keldor's Fask, or keep of the dead in the mount of Keldor's Fist to give its human name, not that I believe any human doth live that would know it."

"Karanza lives no more; she fell a hundred and twenty years past…" Grot kissed his knuckle and swore an oath to Keldor.

"Then I am saddened, know I was a friend of Alfrik's. Thy bear the marks of the battle still. It tells in thy eyes. Pray tell, was thee of an age to enjoin the battle itself?" Kalamere probed with massaging hands as smooth as the questions he posed.

Grot laughed despite the situation. "Do not be fooled by my youthful looking arse. Put it this way: This body is old but I am older still; aged as the mountains I sometimes think, well old enough to have grasped palms with my bleeding ancient uncle anyhow…" Grot collected himself from his emotional reverie. "…And you can forget all your bollocks before yer start. Fer right now I'm Grot, plain and simple. Anything else I leave to the poets and doomsayers alike. Oh and I don't give a single turd about other peoples interpretations of the prophecy and I hate the finality of mortal destiny so bugger all that; my own part will be revealed when apt and no sooner…"

It was the white wizards turn to laugh, attracting Galbor's attention too, such was the rarity of the sound of Kalamere's mirth; "If that were true Grot of the Damned," the mage whispered, "thee would be advised to a better choice of travelling companion as well ye know!"

Kalamere proffered his hand to Grot who reciprocated by reaching out his own hand. Yet before their hands clasped, Grot was suddenly flung by some invisible force towards the back of the room. He landed on a wooden table with four strange wheels and some rope on it.

Temporarily shocked and winded, Grot was unable to even struggle as the coils of rope began mystically wrapping themselves around his arms and feet. Footsteps, far too heavy for the dark wizards small frame, signalled a determined approach as Galbor came to stand at the foot of the rack to which he was now tied, his summoning rituals obviously complete.

The various demonic servants that Galbor had summoned had already been issued their orders and scurried off to attend the duties of their newly appointed offices. With a thought and a gesture, Galbor dismissed the wraiths to the upper floors to guard against further intruders and then turned a malevolent eye to the helpless Dwarf.

"Really Kalamere, you seem so eager to waste your time healing he who cannot be helped…, …*Now* my fat, bearded little troll fettler - perhaps we shall discuss your problem with the word *we*." Galbor sneered.

"…My what? Is this some sort of piss take or something, because if it is, I've already got one of those called Dirk!" the Dwarf grumbled, perturbed at being treated like a rag doll. His reinvigorated body tensed against some unseen force. "Hold on. This thing's a wrack - a mate of mine got stretched a full foot taller by one of these things for stealing another Dwarfs hammer. Poor bugger could never walk again, never mind hammer anything…, …Here! You aint gonna stretch my bleeding bones are ya?"

"Your bones are no longer '*bleeding*' I see, though I doubt that is what one so crude as you would have meant by that statement…, … **I NEARLY WON THAT GAME! Nicodemus be damned!** And I still can't stop thinking of that stupid bloody riddle, but see, all that is going to change now that I have you…… Kalamere…!" The last was a barked order that said '*heel boy!*', and Kalamere instantly teleported to Galbor's side at the head of the wrack on which Grot lay.

"Kalamere what do you see?" the nasty one said.

"Why 'tis a simple Dwarf nay Galbor?"

"A dead Dwarf Kalamere, a dead Dwarf called no name…, …that is what Grot means is it not, or no one-no place, no something; some stupid gibberish anyhow of which you will inform me, as well as everything else I need to know whilst also ridding myself of you in this plane at least! I too know of the prophecy…" The foul mage corrected in detail.

"Oh and if you do not work out that blasted riddle soon, you shall join him whilst I feast upon your soul. *Understood? Good!* Oh and as the subject of one said prophecy is being talked about can I take this opportunity to clarify two things; firstly you are like a *son* to me dear Kalamere and as much as it would pain me to do so; I am foretold to bring about your ultimate demise so don't *tempt* me before your ready to face death." He smiled unpleasantly.

"Secondly and hopefully the last word we shall all share on the prophecy is that it also foretells the violent doom of all who should ever

speak of its machinations; by the great Emperor of Destiny no less...,
....Now I don't know about you but I don't fancy falling to *him*! So you
will forgive my further discussion." The nasty one continued without
waiting for a response. "Now leave my sight. Though do not attempt to
leave the tower, my minions are in place?"

The one called Kalamere nodded and began turning away, "Oh and
Kalamere..." Galbor supplemented, "I would have won sooner or later."

"Yeah verily..." Kalamere conceded, unwilling to bite at the
challenge as he made to leave.

"So tubby," the remaining figure saluted, "Let's play..."

"My name's Grot, not tubby you bas-aah!" His words were ripped
from him with a few quick wheel-spins by the nasty mage.

"Yes, yes, and I am the great Galbor" he said spinning the wheel
with another deft flick of his wrist. Grot cried out in agony as he did so.
He hadn't meant to; didn't want to, not even when the demons had bitten
chunks out of his flesh he had not cried out. But now he did; right now he
whaled like a newborn babe as each cord tightened to its full extent, and
then stretched him further still.

"Please. Stop! You sick, Shitting bastard, there's no need..." Grots
pleas were cut short as the wracks wheel tightened on his left leg, popping
the knee joint and shredding the tendons that held his various muscle
groups in place. He was sweating profusely, and the beads of sweat were
taking on a ruddy sheen, as various blood vessels burst like dragon-fire all
over his body, covering his skin in small pricks of red.

Leaning over to intimidate his victim Galbor sneered at the helpless
Dwarf, "What's this Dirk's full name? Hmmm?" and span a single wheel,
stretching the damaged tissue of the left leg disproportionately at odds with
his other appendages.

"Yer a bloody bum licking Basilisk! Pl-plea-se..." Grot sobbed
uncontrollably, "Why are you d-d-d-do-do..."

"D-d, d-d, -d-d -does it hurt much my squealing midget? Either shut
up or tell me his name!" Galbor spat in disgust, impetuously spinning
another wheel and causing the tortured Dwarf untold writhing agony.

"Dirk's last name, come on Grot, say it. What is it hmmm? Or
would you like me to guess?" He said as he flicked a switch and a huge

half moon pendulum came slicing down towards Grots stomach. Grot stiffened awaiting the killing blow that would easily snip his body in two, but a laugh from Galbor, made him open his eyes and when he did, he saw that the blade was a full foot above him and swinging in a tick-tocking motion much like the little pendulums in the Dwarven water clocks back home, only a hell of a lot sharper...

"Dirks name fool! What is it?" Galbor enraged, doffing the gold and silver fop cap that he wore and throwing it to the ground.

"Dirk H-Aiee..." Grot trailed off, the sight of the wizard's bald bonce had kicked his recollections into gear and he suddenly remembered Dirks tale of how he was once a sorcerers apprentice to a mighty wizard named Galbor. The details were sketchy to his garbled mindset. To be honest he had never actually believed the story fully, but he remembered something about Dirk turning people bald and them wanting revenge and this mans shiny dome had 'slap-head of the year' written all over it.

"Does it have a 'B' perhaps, or a 'D' come now I do enjoy a conundrum..." Galbor taunted

"Go screw yerself!" Grot spat, but the sorcerer laughed out loud at his retort, simply waving his hand over the Dwarves stomach and shouting out a shrill syllable, suddenly Grot felt a burning throughout his body and little pocks of flesh began to explode upon his rapidly heating skin. "Hein..." The Dwarf battled against his weakness but screamed out all the same...

The wicked sorcerers maddened features lit up in bestial joy as he played the sweet and sour syllables across his tongue, "Dirk Heinemblud, how I missed you..." Galbor turned back to the Dwarf and Grot was certain that for an instant he had the face of some horrific beast.

The intense burning subsided and he quickly fought to recant his admission: "No, no, not Heinemblud!" Grot managed between sobs of pain. "I aint ever heard of a Dwarf with that name..." Grot tried, hoping he might fib his way to freedom.

"Liar...! You know quite well he's as much a Dwarf as I am human. Do not think to deceive me with half-truths for I am far better at that game than you." Galbor hissed victoriously, releasing a little irritation by playfully grinding Grot's dislodged kneecap. "Besides which I already know his name!"

'Wake up and smell the Goblins!' Grot thought, 'This guy would probably love nothing better than playing catch with your head,' "I was just clearing my throat..." Grot gulped up a cough for added effect, "See?"

Galbor looked down on the impudent little fool and briefly contemplated letting him know just how powerful he really was but settled instead for gouging out his left eye and squeezing it ever so slightly, causing Grot to pass out, but not before popping it back into the vacant slot.

The Dwarf screamed in absolute agony once more, but the pain passed quickly and was merely a distraction in comparison to the wracks terrible afflictions, nevertheless he passed out all the same.

'At least the bugger isn't turning those damn wheels!' Grot thought as he awoke afresh, but just then as if reading his mind, Galbor span all four devices and left them tuning for a full 30 seconds until every bone had popped its socket and cracked, all surrounding blood vessels had burst; skin had stretched and shred and every sinew had severed, along with most of his major tendons. His heart was racing and the sweat that bathed his body was more like blood. He fainted again after soundlessly sobbing his resistance for twenty or more seconds; then his body snapped into jelly-like submission. Thankfully for Grot he passed out from the pain long before the last ligament had torn from the relevant bone.

'So much for the nice Wiz's nifty bit of healing,' Grot thought from a delusional wonderland somewhere deep in the realms of his conscious; a place where his brains chemicals did a good job of separating his fevered mind from the pain. *Was this heaven?* He wondered from the sanctuary near death awarded.

A surge of warm red light swept against him, dragging him back from the gates of heaven. Grot's eyes snapped open as Galbor wandered off out of the Dwarves line of sight, tending to some other matter in hand. He was on a hallucinogenic high he was sure for he felt healed. Completely! And in far less time than the white wizard had taken it seemed; that is if Galbor were responsible for the healing. Or perhaps, the white wizard's magic was working still? Preserving him for some reason...

Kalamere had already closed the door behind him as the unfortunate Dwarf left behind screamed out upon the rack before sobbing once again. He cast a spell of silence upon the area of the door to prevent what sound he could from echoing out from the room and went off for a seemingly random wander through the tower. The Dwarves screams were muffled yet still uncomfortably audible so he wasted no time in moving away as fast as he could. He tried his best to put Grots undoubted suffering to the back of his mind, somewhat comforted in the knowledge that Galbor was far too cruel a being to let his captive die within a single day. As long as the legendary warrior lived there was hope for freedom and the prophecies peaceful conclusion. It had been 176 years since Kalamere had last been allowed to roam the tower and as he strode across the charred, limb strewn mosaic flooring his initial thought was to rush out to the glade where his fellow the Unicorn had once lived.

Kalamere checked himself, sensing an evil presence that filled the vacuous chamber around him. He cast a simple Dweomer that allowed him to see the presence of invisible or hidden creatures. They were everywhere, and he could tell from the signatures of the Wraiths present that they were each a formidable opponent even for one such as he. Who or what they had been in their former life he could not be sure of, but he would hazard a guess that at least ten of them were old comrades of his. Comrades who would no longer blink at the prospect of destroying the friend they had once loved as their own brother. The mage checked him self, he sensed a familiarity with the Eleventh spectral figure stood guarding the door.

His gaze flashed upwards; his eyes drawn to the summit and the vast mural implanted at the towers peak as he made his way across the chamber. Again that familiarity came to him and he knew then what he must do in order to avoid the fate of his eleven ghostly friends, so instead of attempting to leave the tower, Kalamere headed to the stairs and the rooftop gallery.

Of course he could have teleported there within the drawing of a single breath, but he loved and longed for the exercise. So he turned and started to ascend the greasy blood drenched staircase, picking his way past the various minions who were attending to the task of body-part and bloodstain removals. He had a plan to escape the tower. It was going to take an enormous risk and a great deal of sacrifice but then if this was not meant to be, why had he carried the title Kalamere all his life? And why had that life spread so far beyond that of any other being? No, he knew his destiny and accepted it: the prophecies were pretty convincing and exact and he formulated his plan to account for their telling: Born into Hell on Eyrthe, destined to live through un-death: Kalamere was derived from the old tongue; it's meaning: Son of Khan..., ...Liberator of Gods!

...Galbor wandered off out of the Dwarves line of sight, tending to some other matter in hand, while Grot valiantly fought against the urge to cry out once more, albeit to no avail. His mind began swimming with memories from the present day, all the way back to early childhood. Then suddenly he was free of the mortal coils and drifting towards some other mysterious destination. Briefly, Grot wondered if telling the truth would help him and decided against it, he would rather die than betray a friend, besides which he felt like he was an angel; flying towards a reunification with his god... "Pah! ...Keldor's arse!"

Searing heat waves awoke Grot from his happy slumber and he found himself to now be in a huge metal basket that hung invitingly over a larger vat of feverishly bubbling oil was where he found himself unceremoniously plopped. Trussed up like a chicken, there was little Grot could do save wriggle, wait or pray.

"Where is he?" came the polite, almost casual question from Galbor as the Dwarf slipped in and out of consciousness due to the heat radiating from the boiling black oil below.

Grot tried to stammer a cursed reply but before any possible answer could leave the great Galbor's latest captives lips, Grot was lowered into the bubbling vat for the very first time and if Grot had imagined his body to be burning before then he would soon be frying.

He tried to stammer a cursed reply but his words faltered as Grot was briefly dipped into the bubbling vat for the very first time. The veritable forest of hairs that encased the dwarfs body in their downy protection, singed to their core, bubbling the skin at the roots as his body neared the boiling inferno, then just before his sizzling torso sank into the fetid smelling brew rotund belly first Grot swore an oath not to but rather from Keldor.

His epidermis crackled and fizzed like so much freshly cooked Pork scratching as his skin came into contact with the murky liquid and his Beard and hair erupted into flame..., ...All the while Galbor watched with malevolent delight. His look of wonderment was sickening to behold as the dark mage whooped like a schoolboy watching a halved worm struggle for survival. Grot's screams would hurt a mortal man's ears such was their pitch as the basket plunged him vat-wards, but Galbor merely looked on laughing. The immersion itself merely pitched the Dwarf into an instant black-out as his skin came into contact with the broiling stew, instantly silencing his screeching and lending Galbor unhidden delight...

***

...Dirk awoke to the sound of tormented screams erupting up

through the vast central chamber of the tower… He was also minded by the constant thumping of his head as something dragged him down the steps by his feet.

Dirk craned his neck just in time to prevent another headache inducing knock from the steps and peered down towards his feet. A creature no bigger than a few feet tall (in high heels,) was holding his left foot and dragging him along behind, as it walked with its back towards him, down the spiralling stairway. He waited for the next descending clunk then booted the creature in the small of the back, sending it tumbling down the steps; slimy head over squiggly tail.

No sooner had he kicked the creature away, Dirk rolled to his side, (making sure that he rolled towards the wall) and sat half crouched on his haunches as he surveyed the towers central hub. The chamber below was dotted with various creatures of multiple shapes, sizes and features. The varied beasts were in the process of cleaning up the tower, though it seemed to Dirk that no more of the clean up squad had seemed to make it quite this high yet.

'*Grot's made quite a mess*!' Dirk thought though in truth he had no way of knowing for sure, that the blood splattered walls were mostly his friends handiwork, he had a gut feeling that the Dwarf was indubitably responsible for the carnage spread out in the gory manner below.

When he was safely assured no other monsters had ventured this far, he caught sight of some movement near the roofs peak, some one hundred feet above. Dirk could make out something with flapping leathery wings, flitting betwixt the supporting beams as it vigorously scrubbed at the scorch marks left by the lightening bolts earlier. He realised he would probably be spotted any moment if he didn't find some form of cover. The creature that had served as 'Corpse Removal Expert' had probably assumed he were dead, yet Dirk knew sure enough that the unhelpful shove he had delivered, would soon alleviate the being of that assumption.

Sticking as tight to the wall as he could whilst crouching, Dirk crawled up the steps as quickly as he dared to go. He had no idea how far up he should go and decided that he would simply keep ascending until he was either seen or he discovered an open door.

It was only after he had climbed four or five flights of stairs that he thought to remember how badly injured he had been last time he had knowingly drawn breath…, … "HOLD ON! I was nearly dead!" Dirk thought and he paused to regain his breath and shush him self; perching on a step as he did so.

'Or am I dead...!' The panicky revelation suddenly occurred to him that he may very well be a ghost and he peered back down the steps for any sight of his own body. "Dirk ya silly shit!" He admonished himself, "how can you be dead when you just kicked that sludge-ball down the steps, unless it was taking me to hell!!!" He slapped himself and felt the cold sting in his cheek. "Ouch that hurt..., ...Well how the f..."

Dirk could remember each stab of pain with alarming clarity. Sure enough Dirk was no Cleric or Surgeon, but before he lost consciousness, he remembered being a broken man. His arms had been a mangled mess of decimated flesh. Both his legs had been snapped badly - his left knee had hung loose from ligament and socket alike and he wasn't completely sure on this one; but his back had seemed unnaturally twisted, though the numbness down its length had left him unclear as to the severity. Now here he was bounding up stairs, sometimes two at a time, with not a painful bone in his body, something most definitely did not add up. "Shit! Do not tell me I just kicked my rescuer down the steps!" He hissed as loudly as he dared.

He patted himself and examined his body parts with disbelief. His off-white robe was smattered - nay - drenched with blood, but his actual body was completely clear of even scarred tissue where before it: *He*; had been so much ruined flesh.

"So How the..." Dirks rhetorical self question had to wait as he flattened himself against the stair. The winged cleaner above had descended and its growing shadow had alerted Dirk to its presence, only moments before the creature had actually appeared.

He waited for what seemed a minute or so, but what was in fact a mere few seconds, as the sound of the huge Gargoyle things beating wings signalled both its approach and passing as it fluttered down clutching a body in its arms; thankfully facing away from Dirk.

When he was certain the Gargoyle had sank at least another few flights Dirk rose and began moving steadily upwards again. None of the creatures; the departed winged beast excused, had reached the upper floors yet, and so Dirk continued with less caution and a hell of a lot more haste.

Thirty seven flights of stairs later and Dirk was still no nearer the top, "This place goes on forever..." he mused aloud to himself and turned to sit down for the twentieth time or so. Then he noticed something on the step below. It was a plain brown pouch such as is used by many practitioners of various arts for carrying small essentials, but in this case, what made it stand out was that he knew without doubt that it was his. He reached down to retrieve the pouch and wondered when and how he had come to drop it.

'The bloody steps must be an illusion!' Dirk thought and he strained his mental reserves in an attempt to see through the mirage before him. He had heard that if you suspected a mirage was being used to mask the reality of something, you simply needed to concentrate on seeing the truth and you would. Of course Illusions were oft times a lot more ingeniously devised than that simple prognosis, but Dirk was completely clueless as to anything beyond the basic.

Dirk let the pouch fall to the floor and once again set off up the steep steps, and after climbing up to yet another ebony ensconced landing, Dirk stopped, looked down and sure enough, there was his pouch. "Bugger!" he exclaimed as another scream, similar to the one which had awakened him, erupted from below - he heard it more clearly on this occasion and it was undeniably Grot who was in trouble, but if Grot were in trouble, so was he. Dirks first thought was to run up the flight of steps once again, but he checked himself. *'Grot's your friend you sod!'* Dirk chided himself and began descending the steps, much against his body and minds own will to turn and flee. He walked several steps down and then stopped dead.

Something was coming up the stairs...

Not daring to turn lest the ascending beast pounce upon his unguarded back, Dirk slowly inched up the stairs backwards as the creatures footsteps followed...

He had travelled about 30 steps or so when his foot touched on a landing, panic caught up with him for a moment as Dirk realised he would be back to the spurious beginning upstairs hallway that marked the start of the illusion. He checked about the floor for the pouch he had left behind, but there was no sign of it... Had the creature below pocketed it? Or had...

Dirk turned around and saw an open portal where he had expected to see a firmly closed door. The unseen creatures shambling footsteps had come to a sudden stop to be replaced by a scrubbing sound, accompanied by the grunt of effort that manual labour unwillingly produced. So he hadn't been noticed then and somehow he had beaten the illusion. One glance at the daylight pouring in through the open archway convinced him what he *should* do, and as yet another shriek of unspeakable pain rang throughout the tower Dirk crept quietly through the portal...

Whatever Dirk had expected to find, he was damn well sure that this was not it. He had emerged onto a spacious balcony that ran around the perimeter of the towers uppermost reaches and offered views far and wide of the land sprawled out below. Dirk followed the balcony around in search of other doors while scouring the flowing vista beneath.

Roughly fifty feet from the tower itself, pleasant forestry forbade an all out assault for some five miles or so, thinning almost tree by tree as it did so before submitting to vast rolling plains and grasslands. In one direction, to his right these plains stretched for several miles more from the last stubborn remnants of foliage, beyond those plains; just about visible edging onto the horizon, massive leaping dunes of wind whipped sand, bristled their sword-grass wigs at the surging waves of the mysterious eastern ocean.

He paused there enthralled by the sight of the ocean - he had never seen the sea and even from this distance; wherein its majestic proportions had been reduced to a grey streak, Dirk was impressed. He continued to traverse the battlements as he now understood this area to be, and saw the hills peter off into ever more rising clumps, bejewelled with various small pockets of woods, before dipping into a valley from which a smoky haze rose, and coming up into a mountainous range on the other side from which all manner of foul beasts regularly emerged. "Devils Gap..." Dirk spoke the name of the small hamlet that sat in the valleys centre.

Dirk braced himself against the gusty breeze that just about took the edge off the warmth of the sun, thinking about the famous small town below.

Devils Gap was a former mining colony that had sprang up when some settlers chanced upon the area. The band of some forty families - refugees from some long forgotten war, first settled in the valley before exploring the mountainous peaks above.

The valley were as lush as any race could desire, an abundance of wood from the small patches of mighty oaks that littered the valley, provided centuries of needed accommodations and utilities. Several clear freshwater streams ran from deep within the bellies of the mountains that rose thousands of feet to the west and partly to the north and south. In the westernmost mountain range lay a narrow cleft, that later served as a mountain pass for those that passed through the village. The positioning and height of the mountains meant that the valley enjoyed warm temperatures all the year round; thus sheltered from the cold northern rain and bitter western winds and all but the occasional squall from the south.

The fertile grassland that lay about the valleys centre for some fifteen or so miles offered prime soil for farming, while the hilly sides of the valley offered excellent grazing for cattle. So it was that the village occupants settled in Devils gap and lived there for some five generations without disturbance and in complete bliss. The families that now numbered around seventy or so, had found their beloved Eden.

Even Eden had its snakes however and Devil's Gap's came in the form of greed. A prospector showed up in the area one day, saying that he was on his way into the mountains to pan for gold. Ten or so of the men of the village were intrigued. Until this time the villagers had shared all their crops and lived in a co-operative society; living as one large family. Over the generations, the lack of need, led to a lack of desire for riches and so they no longer traded with one another, making Gold obsolete. However, in any given place there are always a few bad apples and so it was, that these ten or so men had become disenchanted with the whole communal network and sought to branch out and discover their own Eden, make their own homes and their own fortunes. Moreover they wished for adventure like those questing vagrants that passed through would tell off, others wished the life of a travelling merchant or bard and others still hungered for a military life or at the very least to merely have the monetary means to travel.

Several days after the prospector had left for the rocky peaks above before the band of enchanted eager men set out for themselves on a quest for riches, there were many tears shared as the peace loving people bid their loved ones a safe journey, and so they went to claim their fortunes..., ...They returned soon enough; the day after in fact, with maddened stares and wild whoops of delight. In their possession, they each held clumps of sparkling jewels that they claimed protruded from all over the rock face itself a mere several hundred feet up, in fascias of unbelievable proportions.

The village's inhabitants had buzzed about the find, each citizen, young and old alike fascinated by the various stones physical proportions, while incredibly aware of the untold promise of wealth awaiting them all above.

A single fist of such gems would suffice to bring about a fortune beyond ones wildest dreams. So the very next day every man, woman and child that was able; ascended the lofty peaks where they did indeed find the ten men's hitherto estimated exaggerations to be not only true; rather extremely understated.

The whole rock face, for about several hundred metres in every direction was bedecked by clumps of finger like crystals and silicone of various textures, colours and hues, with more than a few fist sized jewels of various hues and mineral composition, not to forget the occasional boulder. For the next fifty years the villagers mined the precious stones from the rocky crags above, joined by a wave of ever increasing prospectors and miners alike, to whom tales of the find began to filter through to.

Under the influx of strangers the village grew in size comparable to that of a small town, complete with a fest-hall, huge marble plaza and masterful place of worship. In time the goodly needs of the small church expanded to that of a small cathedral, and Knights Templar took up residence in the rapidly embellishing Cathedral to keep order in the now thriving settlement.

Then one fateful day the town's relative peace was shattered. A group of Dwarven miners had been dislodging a monstrous slab from a Jewel encrusted overhang, when the progenitor to disaster struck. At the hub of the overhang stood a glowing stone of pure crystalline blue whose epicentre flickered with a ghostly flame; easily the size of an Ogre's fist or a Dragon's frozen heart. The slab came away according to plan and no-one was hurt, yet as the Dwarves abseiled down from their treacherous perches they found that the slabs removal had opened up a cavernous black gap in the rocky crags eastern face.

The Dwarves investigated and found that the tunnel descended deep into the mountains ominously cavernous interior. They reported back to the village just as soon as they could and told the village elders and Paladins that although they had found no traces of any creatures living within, the murky mountains heart could well contain such, and like as may, whatever did live down there would almost invariably be of a malevolent disposition towards the towns then numerous inhabitants.

The leader of the Dwarven band, one Bokkal Banballaŕdin, suggested that he and his men; along with the help of some of the other towns miners, seal the gap by collapsing the rock above. This idea was met with instant approval and seconded by the towns vigilant Knights Templar.

The town elders in their ill-placed wisdom declined. Their reason for refusal was none other than greed, they believed the Dwarves had really discovered yet more gemstones in the uncovered depths and sought to seal off the entrance in order to keep the goods for themselves. Bokkal argued furiously with the council, but his attempts to convince them of his sincerity, merely led one member to label him a secretive scoundrel. Bokkal came close to fully throttling the councillor before a group of guards managed to separate them, and he and his entourage were immediately banished from the town.

One of the Templar residing in Devil's Gap had argued the Dwarven solution for hours after they had left; this knight had formerly stood besides Dwarves in battle and had always found them to be honourable at worst. Yet again the council refused and once more due to commercial reasons for in order to collapse enough rock it would be duly necessary to collapse a great ledge that ran the length of the mountain. This ledge was located above the mining area and ran the full length of its enticing bejewelled majesty.

Collapsing the ledge would only mean a week or two's delay in mining but the council of elders would have none of it. And so the gap was left open and the Dwarves responsible for the original opening left with nothing, or so the story goes. That night several people went missing, thought to be scared off by the eerie gap that now dominated everyone's thoughts. Over the following weeks more people went missing and then one of the outlying farms was found to have been ransacked, the family's maimed cadavers located inside. Cringing villagers sought nightly shelter in and around the town, others still fled in droves for calmer lands. The Knight Commander ordered an investigation and when one young squire; a boy aged eight known simply as Agrilot conducted his own probe and after some applied logical thinking the militia arrested and beheaded a middle aged man who had used the thoughtful fear of monsters as cover for his monstrous crimes in an attempt to gain the horde of gems for himself...

The boy had been found to cry wolf and so the sheep had returned. The town celebrated the ending of an unfounded paranoia and people partied long into the night and following day, before returning home to sanctuary.

The night after the murderers execution, 96 families were wiped out, their homes raised and livestock eaten or slaughtered, the only houses that remained relatively unscathed, where those built by the original towns families, and of these only ten remained completely intact. These houses were ensconced behind a wall of wooden stakes and so apart from the odd isolated fire, they were largely protected, as untold monsters poured down from the mountain slaughtering all in their wake. Exactly how many creatures came and what type are unknown, save mention of the inevitable Goblins; the only other identifiable species of mention in the church's historical archives were those of giant beetles and snake like devils who wrought savage destruction that night. What collection of structures survived beyond that night formed the village sized settlement that still stood now. From that terrible time onward the village drew its current name, because of the narrow canyon or 'gap' that ran through the mountains westward, and due to the creatures referred to as Devils that periodically had plagued their village ever since.

Those days were ancient history and forgotten knowledge to all but the most knowledgeable, but Dirk knew the story better than even that. This knowledge had been obtained from one of the many campfire chats he had evoked from his friend the Dwarf. Grot had told him the story of how his great uncle Bokkal Banbạllaŕdin, who had visited the town and mined its wealthy exterior. Grot told how his uncle had mined the slab and told the elders of the danger, only to be shamed and turned away. In fact he had told him everything the scholars knew and more: Such as Grot also telling Dirk of the magnificent blue jewel that shone with a myriad of reflected light, so that its heart seemed to flicker with a cold blue eternal flame.

Grot had further elaborated his uncle had secreted the gem, fearful of its sickly sweet allure affecting the minds of his men. Upon his reaching a Dwarven stronghold he turned it over to the safe keeping of the mountains king until his return. Unfortunately when he returned the king had grown evil in his ways and refused to part with the gem that Bokkal deemed the cause of his moral deterioration. Just as had been the case in Devil's Gap again Bokkal had his name sundered and barely escaped with his life. The king grew malevolent, and over time his people suffered under his sick whims, until his entire family line fell into disgrace when the Jewel's proximity was linked with the disease that almost destroyed the population of their Dwarven city. The people revolted, overthrowing their king and his corrupt kin, banishing some and executing others. The Gem was never to be found.

Grot had elaborated further; telling how the gem had in fact been stolen away by his uncle's few loyal men and carried off to be buried deep within the Eyrthe. Banbạllaŕdin's own aide had been slaughtered by a sickened mob, when it was discovered that he had tentacles growing from his left eye and no explanation of where the stone lay.

Such knowledge was trivial, of no use to anyone but bards, but Dirk smiled broadly at the thought of the fabled rock face, if it did indeed exist;

his boot felt in great need of jewellery restock.

These days anyhow, Devil's Gap was more widely known now for the short passage through the mountain, the beasts that regularly roamed the area were far more famously mentioned than any idea of untold wealth, oh and a pub called the Mead and Meat or Meat and Mead: Dirk could never remember which way round; that served meats supposedly never tasted elsewhere, and meads of apparently similar distinction. So although he didn't doubt the area was once mined he believed the fabulous rock face was little more than a myth.

"I'll have to visit that gaff some day!" Dirk grunted to himself and continued his stroll, which took him back around to the doorway through which he had entered, with no other exits visible save the ledge and he wasn't feeling particularly suicidal today. He rested his elbows on the battlements ledge and cupped his chin in his hands as he thought about his own uncompromising situation; scooping up a few small fragments of chipped masonry and tossing them over the edge in absent minded fashion.

Dirk had two choices, well three if he were going to be sarcastic: Choice number one - Learn to fly really quickly. Two - Jump off and hope to land in an invisible lake. Three - Go back down the steps and be torn limb from wretched limb and it was this last choice he regarded as sarcastic. Sure he had been lucky with the Goblins, but he didn't think that mother fate would be so kind twice in one week and besides, Grot had been telling him for years that anyone can beat up a Gobbo! *"No!!!* No..., ...more likely," his pessimistic self but in, *"you* would encounter the *bloody* Snurch that had escaped the Goblin camp and get *your* arse kicked. So what *are you going to do against demons?"* He wondered aloud?

Dirk's gaze wondered downwards as his mind thrashed itself in search of solutions, and his eyes fell upon the Corpse of Zen on his litter and then to the glade beyond. It looked even more beautiful from up here if that were possible, and his mind thought back to the huge shadow that had quietened even the chirpiest birds in mid song. He pondered its foliage and the animal life contained within even as he tossed more shards mindlessly over the side. "Poor daft bugger Zen bought it before we even got in here..." He mused.

He suddenly thought of the huge chunk of masonry that had fell from the tower, killing Zen beyond Dirks then blinded vision. Looking now, he could see just how close he himself had been to getting mangled by the errant stone slab; where a huge gouge in the Eyrthe ran within what he could only guess where inches to the side of the tree at which he had huddled. He looked for the thorny patch where Grot had cowered and the thought made him recall Grots tale and his reason for wanting to enter the tower. He glanced about as the thought hit him and instantly his eyes were drawn to the gap left behind by the detached masonry block.

No dark splinter though, Dirk thought as he began retracing his steps around the towers balcony and then he saw it - he had missed it the first time because it rested against the inside wall where he had stopped to gaze at the sea…

…He couldn't believe it, the Dwarf was right! But if Grot had thrown it from the back of what he had said was a Dragon then how could Grot have been able to shout a warning? Had he been teleported to and from the creatures back? Impossible! Given that hard fact, what person or thing would want to and why? Or was it possible to have two Grots…?

Dirk glanced at the Heavens and shook his head. One Grot was enough thank you very much.

Dirk twirled the dagger like splinter in his hand; it was the most fascinating substance he had seen. So black that it seemed to suck at the shadows cast by the battlement walls, yet played all over with a liquefying iridescent quality that seemed to pulse with all the colours of the rainbow. '*Wondrous!*' Dirk sighed to himself. He waved it about a few times, just in case something mystical should happen; nothing. He clutched it with all his might and wished he could grow wings, but even though his shoulder plates quivered in anticipation nothing seemed to happen and he was about to give up when he felt its light solid mass pulsate beneath his palm.

Excellent! Thought Dirk as he patted his back for evidence of the prayed for wings. *I wonder …?* Dirk jumped up and down to no effect. *Bastard!!!*

He mulled over several variations of the wing wish but each time his leaping and patting produced no evidence of accomplishment, as somewhat disappointed at the lack of wings he sat astride the dark sliver and considered its ability to levitate. *Maybe it will stop my fall if I jump off…*

Before jumping clear of solid ground, he first lifted both his feet off the ground in front of himself and promptly fell to ground with a thump, the curious object unharmed but his buttocks sore and in need of several minutes' restorative massage.

Interesting... He twirled the stick around above his head in a circular motion then pointed it forward at the crest of the wall but no explosion or wished for fireball was evident.

Unusual I suppose... Dirk mused with less passion, rubbing his body with the black splint of Dragon-bone and awaiting some feeling of empowerment that never surfaced.

Dirk could feel the sense of magic that radiated from the dragon splint, and was in no doubt that it was magical, but was the magical effect merely limited to its mesmerizing appearance? He tried several times to exude some response from the splint, *anything* that might hint at some hidden power, but nothing at all happened; for ill or good.

Briefly, Dirk considered tossing the black spike over the side, then thought of explaining it to Grot; should he still be alive and instead slid the thing inside his trouser leg, tightening the cord that held them up as he did so and carefully descending back into the tower and down its perilous steps...

***

"He's in the tower!" Grot screamed unable to bear the pain any longer, he was now on a contraption that stretched chicken wire over his skin, exposing small humps of his smoking, grubby flesh in small square patches, which Galbor was in the process of slicing off at random, when Grot emitted his pitiful admission.

Galbor paused to meet the Dwarf's crazed stare, "Where... exactly? Do pray tell?"

"I don't know - on the stairs somewhere. He's probably charcoal. ...Was blasted... by that magic trap." The Dwarf panted his sobbing reply.

Galbor turned to face the other way and as he did so Grot again noticed the bestial face hidden beneath the humanly visage. Kalamere re-entered the room at that moment and walked straight over to Galbor without a second glance at Grot.

Years of enduring his own tortures and witnessing that of countless others had dimmed his distaste and by now he was accustomed to; if not even a little excited by the sight. Though he did his best to stay ignorant to Grots pitiful pleas, he could not suppress the sickening feeling of despair wrenching at the pit of his own stomach, as Grot repeatedly begged for his own death.

"Galbor...! Methinks I may hap stumbled upon some key to discover the riddles lock, wilt thou permit me the study of thy Grimoires?" he asked without emotion.

Galbor nodded his reply and went once more to the centre of the summoning circle, this time he did not bother with any protection as he only needed a single syllable to awake this Demon. "Qu'iahal come!" he ordered and within moments a demonic hellhound erupted from a cloud of smoke, bathed in blood and ash.

Qu'iahal was the name of his treasured pet and also one of the most dangerous beasts you could come across, but he greeted its master with slavering licks and thumping, scraping claws like the most attentive of adoring pups.

"Sit down Qu'iahal!" The hellhound instantly obeyed, ceasing its affectionate welcome. Galbor instructed the dog-thing to find and return with the unharmed body of Dirk Heinemblud and then returned to torturing Grot. The blood soaked scalpel was snatched up by Galbor in a matter of fact way and his fingers twitched methodically as he worked the torturing scissors in vicious splits and slices; the riddle that vexed him so once again took prominence in his thinking.

***

Dirk had descended two flights of steps when he came across the first monstrous goon, that wasn't actually that monstrous and more of a gimp than a goon. He snapped the things neck like a twig and flung it behind him on the stairs and continued his descent, sticking to the wall as he moved, so as not to be seen on the open staircase by those below. 10 steps more and he came across a small fire imp sat on the edge of the step, its feet dangling into the void below. "BOO!" Dirk hissed and the creatures surprise carried it over the edge in the direction of its smoking legs. Dirk chuckled to himself and started to creep forward once more and came face to face with a huge dog like beast beyond any further need for description, save evil blood and ash smattered Hellhound. The creature emitted a low growl and Dirk stood stock still, a nervous tick developing in his cheek.

A moment or two later and then the things jaws where upon him. Dirk was amazed (and rather relieved) to find that instead of the gruesome death he had expected, the thing merely snatched him up and carried him off in its maw like it probably would its own newborn.

***

Cold water splashed in Grots face arousing the Dwarf from the dullness of the unconsciousness he had slipped into and back into the reality of his pain filled world... "Please don't sleep..." Galbor jeered, "I don't want you to miss your friend's imminent arrival..." A scratch at the now refashioned door indicated Qu'iahal's arrival. Galbor nodded and the door swung open to reveal the hellhound had indeed returned with its commanded prize and it trotted down the steps, clearly happy with itself.

Released from the grip of the creatures slobbering maw, Dirk dropped unceremoniously to the floor in front of the chairs that faced the fireplace, which the beast now went to curl up in front of, licking at its paws and maximizing the amount of fiery glow received.

Dirk lay too stunned to react for a moment and offered a jumbled prayer of curses to the entire pantheon of gods that he had heard of. Subsequently he sat up, saw Galbor..., ...And fainted.

Grot watched, between loss of blood and consciousness as Dirk was raggedly hoisted up by the throat, and effortlessly tossed onto one of those chairs by the slight framed Galbor. When Grot again awoke, he saw that the snoozing Dirk had been covered with a blanket and turned to face the fire, in short; made to look as comfortable as can be, while Grot himself was in the process of being dissected.

Galbor waited with the patience of a father while Dirk slept, even tolerating two hours of snoring before getting fed up and slapping him. Even Kalamere was taken aback amidst his studies by the amount of affection shown. *'He seems to care for him like a father would a sickly son..., ...or is it merely the pride of one in possession of a most **valuable** prize?'*

Galbor smiled and then groaned as Dirk came-to, only to lapse back into darkness at the sight of his old nemesis. The Dark Wizard stood and sent a curling green mist spraying out from his fingers towards an unsuspecting minion, throttling the thing with the green misty vines before turning back to Dirk. Unfortunately for Grot, it was he, that Galbor's eye settled on however, so this time instead of waiting by Dirks side as before; Galbor decided to amuse himself by carrying out several other methods of torment on the helpless Grot, who had just been caught thinking that he would have by now, passed beyond the sensations of pain.

It was quite late that night when Dirk finally managed to remain conscious for more than several seconds, though he simply huddled in a prone position clutching his knee's to his chest and staring with a fixed daze at the bald dome of Galbor as he went about his distressing activities on the inactive Grot.

The Dwarf grimaced in disgust, Galbor was being way too kind and understanding to Dirk, if whose own exploits were to be believed in the tales that he told, deserved a heck of a lot more than just a slap. Yet, HE was the one being persecuted; he was the one who now found his half-dead self lying on the wrack once more, not Dirk. In his delirium Grot grew convinced that this man with the changing face was a vicious devil from the planes of hell and that Dirk was his most revered son. The dog thing and the white wizard lay beyond his damaged vision, but he knew they were all in on it. "Daddy what's a geode?" he wept, his mind bowing considerably...

Grots painfully slow death was temporarily abated when; with a sudden snarl of bone shaking proportions, Galbor pounded away from the wrack with thudding footsteps far too heavy for his stature, he then hoisted Dirk's much large albeit bony frame one handed, and hurled him ten feet into a bookcase. "Speak you lousy piece of excrement...!" Galbor roared: "Scream or something you miserable excuse for an adversary!"

The shelves splintered on impact, and the large tomes they had supported fell down on top of Dirk who huddled tighter still for further protection against the crushing avalanche of dismounted books. The immense bookcase itself teetered to and fro, before lending its own weight to the downpour, and slammed down upon Dirk, only missing crushing the life from him by the timely intervention of one of the chairs by the fire - which took the brunt of the force before collapsing. The time for illusion was over; the pretence of consideration had run its course. Galbor was angry and he could hide it no more.

The dark mage snarled. It wasn't a human snarl, nor even like that of a rabid dog, but belonged to something far more unwholesome. He was irritated and when he got irritable he could no longer hold his human form. Grot watched in muted terror as Galbor's full Daemonic majesty came writhing through his limbs, bones popping, snapping and quadrupling, his jaw twisting to hang limp and the head pulsating with bulbous infections of flesh and bone.

Within seconds Galbor's human form vanished along with his polite veneer of humanity to be replaced by a gruesome towering beast of pure evil, whose completely terrifying, impotence inducing effect was only slightly dulled by the large pink bald patch atop his otherwise hairy body and face.

Grot laughed aloud at the sight. Fear and pain had seen his mind dance the tango though his will was strong; still Grot thought him self a little insane for allowing the laugh to escape. His body began healing a little and the sensation brought on by nerve endings reforming made him giggle further..., ...True the spectacle of a beast so frightening as to freeze a mans heart on sight would probably have done just that but Grot was in full on giggle fit now and simply could not stop himself tittering at the idiotic monk like dome that graced its otherwise fearsome black head. Dwarves seldom laugh long and hardy though when they do they are hard to shut up. Grot was positively pissing himself accompanied by the most baritone laughter possible; like smooth granite boulders tumbling down a mountain of marble.

Even so, Grot hadn't meant to laugh - it had simply been a nervous response but now Galbor whirled on him. "You..., ...Scum!" Galbor seethed as he strode forward, "**You dare mock *me*?**"

Grot was unsure of what to say or how to answer, he simply stared at death cometh with a stupid smile, desperately attempting to hold back the mighty guffaws desperate to escape his lungs; but another answered instead.

"You dick...! Of course he dares to laugh at you, I do too," Dirks chuckling voice mumbled out from beneath the fell bookcases confines. He had been left a small air pocket, thanks to several of the tomes acting as support beams for the wooden shelving above him. "I do dare to laugh at you, I mean. In case you didn't understand..."

Dirk's statement was cut short, to be replaced by wailing screams as Galbor spewed forth huge gusts of murderously hot flame from his huge tusk ridden jaws. The entire bookcase and all but the most magical of books within Dirks confines were reduced to smouldering ash within seconds.

Tears ran uncontrollably down Grots cheeks, as he stared at the silent smouldering mound of ash where his friend had roughly lay.

"You Bastard...! Now you're gonna pay son..." Grot screamed through tears of sorrow, "You Utterly stupid, bald headed; big ugly bastard of a stinking maggot infested, lice ridden devil dog! Let me out of this Bleeding thing and I will slap your sorry fat shit-hole all the way back to hell!" With that he tried to bite at the ropes still holding him down and kick his legs as best he could. "I'll kill yer fer killing him, I will!!! You didn't even give him a chance to defend himself, he's a useless harmless bastard is all, not the monster you think he is, was: *Was yer bastard!!*"

The dust shifted and a cloud of it pouted upwards as a wheeze erupted from Dirks lungs. Getting to his knees amidst the ash, Dirk's ghostlike face gave a little grin. "Actually I'm completely fine Grot. Not a scratch mate. Hey, but thanks for the concern... I bet you would kick his arse too... if you could walk, by the look of your legs matey, you won't be running anywhere in a hurry, never mind all that jumpy twirly-stuff you did earlier. Oh that reminds me, I meant to ask... Where did you learn to do that...?" Dirks tone was conversational, as if he was passing the time of day with a friendly neighbour across the garden fence.

"Erm... a ... circus," Grot answered a little disorientated, had he finally gone mad with the pain or was he talking to Dirks ghost? "It was way before I met up with you..." he continued despite his confused pondering.

"ENOUGH!" Galbor roared, and lashed out his arm towards Dirk mumbling the jumbled sentence of some spell...

Grot felt two hands upon his legs and, raising his neck the few inches he could manage, he saw the other kind looking wizard who had healed him earlier.

"Shhh...!" The kindly fellow admonished and putting a finger to his lips, he muttered a short incantation that sent new strength coursing through the Dwarfs veins as bones knitted and flesh scabbed over.

Kalamere continued to hold the Dwarfs legs for a few moments more: Each minute of contact lending his considerable regenerative benefits to the receptive body of Grot. Then just before Galbor finished his own incantation, Kalamere slipped away with a wink of his eye. Grot pulled on the straps on his wrist, mustering every ounce of strength from the cable like sinew that muscled every inch of his well toned body. The straps resisted for a few seconds and then gave out with a snap.

The temperature dropped alarmingly as a white mist enveloped the room, eradiating outwards from Galbor's outstretched palm. The mist expanded then imploded, sending a continuous stream of freezing liquid spilling out with venomous accuracy encasing Dirk, and everything within 10 feet of him, in a deadly icy veneer.

Grot leaned up and began un-strapping his legs with all the haste he could muster. Galbor flexed his fingers and spoke in some arcane language and black and brown rocky shards lanced outwards from his clawed hand and into the ice covered area. Everything that they hit shattered into a thousand fragments or more; so low was the temperature of the objects trapped within the icy confines. Yet even though the rocky shards fair smashed the frosty coating around him Dirk him self remained completely unscathed.

"Well thank you for that impressive display master. Might we be going now or is this some magical lesson you wish to teach, should I copy it down to learn later maybe?" Dirk inquired with feigned child-like innocence. "Oh shit! I forgot my grimoire and stencil sir!"

Grot leapt to his feet noting he felt somewhat sprightlier than usual and ran to grab a whip from a nearby rack to use as a weapon. The truth is he had never used a whip before and was just as likely to strangle himself with it, as he was to draw any small weal upon Galbor's tough looking magical hide, but holding something; anything rather more hurtful than words alone made him feel further re-assured all the same.

"Why will you not die?" Galbor quizzed Dirk furiously.

"I dunno Master Bates…, …Stubborn I guess? Did you word it right? You always taught me that you have to be careful with the phrasing…" Dirk said, knowing full well his former master would never make such a mistake. "Hey nice going on the Demon form thing too - never knew you had it in you. Looking so mean…, …Grrr tiger! Another illusion is it? Like the one on the stairs? It *is* my often distracted old mentor Galbor aint it? Well assuming it is you and I aint completely mad, then I would have to guess that I somehow simply am not affected by illusions: Or at least I'm not phased by them, besides; I got past that staircase one easily enough…" Dirk lied.

"…Simpleton! **THIS** is my *true form*…, …Though I must say your lack of enlightenment causes little surprise." Galbor paused to scrutinize Dirk, flinging Grot back with bone jarring force as he attempted to sneak up behind: The whip clutched ever so tightly like a strangling chord.

"So… You finally became a wizard eh? And of quite some power too to survive my spells magical wrath…, …So this is the foretold showdown, no? I dare say you hardly look ready for this, which means my own version will surely attest to be the one to which the scholars shall award a greater degree of accuracy, and all the while I shall manipulate further…" Galbor jeered.

Dirk let out a short snort of derisive laughter at the thought, "No master Galbor, I am the same pathetic wretch that turned your hairy head bald. The only thing that I have been learning these years past is to constantly shit myself in fear. I don't mind too much though because I can never stay in one place long enough to take care for other peoples opinions; and I don't mind adding that right now I've badly soiled my undergarments such is my fear, but my gob blabs on regardless all the same; fear does *that* to me too, I get ever so talkative…, …In fact the only reason that I am talking to you now is so t-"

"Shut UP!" Galbor stopped him. "You lie - I can see you glow with a magic stronger than that sewn into the very fabric of these walls. Do not lie. I can see it, taste it, touch it… The magic emanates from both within and without. The truth is; having mastered the mystical arts and yoked your bodies last vestiges of potential for power, you have returned in an attempt to destroy your former master in a tumultuous showdown of unparalleled magical aplomb. Is it not so…?"

"Not." Dirk said, plumping down on the one remaining armchair. He knew it was silly to push his luck, but as he reasoned it, he should have been dead several times over already and so whether his former master was indeed a horrible Demon or not mattered little to him at this moment in time. All that he could do was enjoy the rest of his life while it lasted; however short a time that may be. He slumped back in the armchair, his knees falling apart, ensuring a good crotch scratch would follow and asked, "Any chance of some refreshments? - I would kill for some Dwarven ale…"

Outside on the gravel path leading to the tower; all manner of species of previously fully fit creatures fell still, stopped dead in the prime of their lives'. Trees' withered instantly and the flowering fauna and grass by the wayside shrivelled as the Soul Leech travelled ever more eagerly onward towards the Gargantuan tower.

"There…, …Power…" It whispered in un-Eyrthely sighs.

XI) **A Desperate Act**

Grot struggled to his feet and rubbed at what he hoped was only a bruise developing on his still damaged right shoulder. Everything was at a momentary standstill, war-wise that is. From his position to the rear of the action Grot surveyed the room, weighing up his next possibly futile move.

Galbor was stood in the rooms centre with his back to Grot, hands on hips and little wisps of smoke actually rising out from his ears. Dirk faced him nonchalantly in the armchair, or at least he tried to. Grot easily took in the wild-eyed stare and small tremors of cowardly emotion convulsing through his friends body and thanked the gods his friend still retained enough sense to be scared.

"Fear is to be embraced," he had often told Dirk. "It protects yer from over-confidence and tells the brain to keep your legs alive. There's a time for fighting and a time for running, but yer will always make time for that clever old bastard, *FEAR.*'

Sometimes Grot thought that Dirk took that most particular sermon rather too much to heart, but something about him was different lately. They had not talked much about what happened in the woods, but Grot sensed that Dirk had done more than merely survive the Orc attack.

Dirk noticed Grot; in his bloody and burnt state looking every inch as much a monster as Galbor did. "Are you trying to tell me, *you're* a demon? Piss off... What were you doing teaching a bunch of crappy kids candy spells for then? And besides, if that really were my mate Grot, there's no way he could be so badly burned and live, never mind looking as if he's about to launch a counterattack. I bet you aint even Galbor are you? In fact I wouldn't be surprised if you're just some little fat Gnome illusionist trying to mess with my head. In which case I'll have some whisky instead; Grot's tight with his."

Galbor's snorted laughter rang around the chamber in a brief interlude of ignorance on his part and he stamped on a flagstone at his feet, shattering it as if it were a milk jug and sending stinging splinters flying out around him. "Foolish Dirk... As ever you remain blinded to the fates..."

Grot meanwhile was searching for an effective accomplice when his eyes alighted upon the Unicorn trapped in a bizarre wheel shaped torture device, before he spotted Kalamere stood off to the side of a huge library-like bookshelf. The mage was wiggling his hands, digits, ears and nose in a wriggling frenzy of dweomers, causing little lights and explosions to leap from the pages of the open tome in front of him. *'The Bastard's trying to figure out how to beat the Demon!'* Grot deduced and then silently launched into his next plan of attack.

Dirk Grinned up at Galbor, attempting to calm the growing sensation churning at the pit of his stomach. Galbor smiled; or was it a snarl? Dirk wasn't sure which but he now knew this was no mirage or illusion before him: The horror of his stupidity forced his teeth to part as copious amounts of puke came spraying out all over the carpet. "I'm sorry, please..." Dirk yelped mid-vomit. "I thought... Oh, I'm sorry. Please don't hurt me..."

Galbor roared some spell ending with the word syllaelabub whatever that meant, and Dirk was encased in a shaft of brilliant yellow light that instantly eroded everything it touched including the armchair on which Dirk was sat. The armchair degenerated in a brief sunlit aurora; its particles whipped away by an invisible wind, and Dirk found himself seated upon the bare floor as even that slowly deteriorated.. As the rays particles started to dissipate, it became obvious that Dirk, despite the desolation surrounding his ten metre perimeter, was fully unharmed and alert.

"Grrrrrrrrrrraaaaahhhh!!! Good for nothing useless, foul … dah! **Kill Me Then!** You cannot though can you? Because you are **weak!** Much, much too weak for Hell and **nothing** on **Eyrthe**; I think **obtaining Heaven** is going to be quite simply beyond you. **I** intend to make **sure** it is so. **But why will you not die, grrrrr!!! You are mightily irritating...**" Galbor raged and with a motion of his left hand he sent the entire contents of the western wall flying through the air in tantrum.

A rather large book entitled: "How to ensnare Demons within a Pentagram," fair slapped at Dirks forehead, sending him sprawling across the floor with pathetic yelps of pain. "Shit, shit, shit my head, you wan-aah shit my head, aah!"

Galbor froze; the various books and ornaments falling limply to the floor. He glared at Dirk who was still rolling around holding onto his skull where a huge bloody weal had developed.

"So… you are only protected against magic..." Galbor paused to let out a truly demonic howl of laughter that caused even Qu'iahal to pause in his dogged self gratification and look to his master.

…Somewhere below the laboratory Gweonju rumbled along with her slithery cohorts, she stopped for a moment all the better to hone her senses and realised the Dwarf and Dirk were nearby; somewhere above them in fact. With silent screams she ordered her chubby worm brood upwards towards her prey and hopefully the forgiveness of Galbor…

…Meanwhile Grot had been busily going about the business of freeing the unicorn from its wheel of torture. The lock was a simple teasing latch and bolt set into a barred enclosure. Grot wondered briefly if the Unicorn would be of any help, and could not help smirk at the thought that such a magnificent beast could be trapped by such a simple device.

Opening the gate he reached forward and pushed a large lever that was pitched fully downwards, hoping it would cease the circular drums perpetual turning. Instead the wheel began turning faster, forcing the plodding beast trapped within, into a rapidly spurred on full gallop, if ever a horse could look less than amused it was right there and then.

"Shit!" Grot cursed and cast an eye towards Galbor who was currently shredding the entire contents of the room around Dirk, whisking their disassembled fragments into oblivion. He turned back to the Unicorn and wondered aloud: "Now what in Keldor's name, am I supposed to do?"

"Pull the other lever" gasped the unicorn, mid gallop.

Grot jumped at the remark, "Bloody hell! Yer can talk!?!"

"*Well... I am... a Unicorn...*" The tone was dripping with a sarcastic disgruntlement that only a speaking horse could achieve.

"Well, yes, but... a Horse that talks… that-"

"Get the… lever…" came back the curt interruption.

"Aah yes…" Grot said fumbling about the machines confines, he found the lever was set into the floor and rose about 3 feet upwards, and he felt a little foolish for not noticing it straight away - especially as the thing was labelled 'On' and 'Off'. He pushed it and it moved with ease bringing the rolling of the circular drum and the clattering of desperate hooves to a satisfying halt.

Galbor turned around.

Blue lights sprang up in the ever more terrifying Galbor's eyes as he stalked towards the Dwarf and the Unicorn. A rippling surge of blue and red energy coursing down the length of his arms and causing combustive sparks to play along Galbor's deadly sharp blackened fingernails. No spell incantation prayed upon his lips. No arcane patterns of any Dweomer needed be traced by eye. Galbor's intent was glaringly obvious and simple. He intended to tear the two interlopers' limb from limb.

Kalamere strode out from behind the bookcase where he had previously taken refuge and called to Galbor, "I do believe one may verily have solved thy riddle, or at leastways have conjured the possibility of gaining its evasive conclusion."

"**WHAT?**" Galbor ceased in his menacing advance to take stock of the mage. "What are you on about now? Do I have time for riddles? Do I look stupid? Speak!" The growling narrative was accompanied by noxious black clouds of sulphuric ash as fiery spires of flame danced jaggedly from the tips of his flexing black bat-like wings.

"Why I do believe the answer that vexes thee so, resides within the one known as Dirk..." Kalamere answered.

Galbor turned back to Dirk his anger personified in the cracklings of various energies and convulsive spouts of flame that now erupted from his being at every given gesture. "You... Know the answer... Pah!" A fiery spurt accompanied the speech, "What would you know... How could you know it...? What trickery is this Kalamere?" Galbor ranted.

Dirk had staggered to his feet and regained the dark mages faltering interest with a disheartened whimper of: "...shit!" He shrugged his shoulders and shit his pants anew as Galbor sensing he had been tricked in the most simplest of fashions, returned his attention to Kalamere in time to see the treacherous arch-mage enclosing both Grot and the Unicorn within a magical sphere of resilience as they charged towards Galbor's previously turned back.

Springing with the suddenness of a cat, Galbor dived headfirst into Kalamere. His outstretched claws made contact with the mages abdomen an infinitesimal moment after Kalamere had completed his spell and the two rolled across the floor and into a bookcase that began teetering dangerously back and forth.

Kalamere rose to his feet first, but his immediate task was to hold in his guts that began squelching their way out from the huge open gash that Galbor's claws had cleft. It was a blow capable of killing any man, but Kalamere was not simply any man, his healing powers were an innate gift, rather than magical in the way that priests or wizards might heal themselves. As his hands worked to keep the various offal inside his body while his mind worked to heal the divided flesh.

Alas it was all for nought. Galbor rose too a moment later and smashed Kalamere's clamped hands apart. The demon then leapt into the air with a mighty shove of his quads, his steel clawed slices shredding viciously into Kalamere's throat. Kalamere had several seconds of life blood left but instead of panicking he merely locked his own blue eyes with the constantly changing hues of the Balrog's and gurgled a short phrase: "Tu mil ensa mil bei…"

A blue streaming photon light sparked out from his pupils connecting in a steady stream with Galbor's and sucking blood from the demons orifices to make up for Kalamere's own shortfall. The pain inflicted by the holy blue light must have been immense for Galbor's screaming roars attested to it as he shook his head in his hands.

Moments later and Galbor's screaming had ceased, yet Kalamere pulled out his own parlour tricks to buy a few seconds more; a sharp breath precipitated the emission of a black seeking wind which enveloped the air around Galbor. "Excumitis parlance Litiari, advance!" Kalamere implored and suddenly almost the entire room was filled with birdlike flapping books as several hundred tomes leapt into life and swarmed around the white wizard in his defence, forcing the mighty Balrog back for a time.

Several of the books slapped their solid hides into anything that their artificial intelligence perceived to be a threat and this included the Dwarf who, amidst fending off their advances, managed to temporarily take cover beneath a table. The pure and noble Unicorn was left alone by the tomes and other than being buffeted by their initial explosion of life, wherein they had whacked into everyone and thing, it was pretty much at liberty to attack Galbor at it's pleasure. Galbor was still a little disorientated and the Unicorn marked out a path of destruction with its hooves.

Kalamere's hands slapped together forming a rippling crack in the mosaic marble flooring; shaking the very foundations of the tower as it sped towards Galbor and he continued the assault with the blue light still emanating from his own eyes, locking them with his adversaries and sending the needle like pain stabbing into Galbor's brain, driving him to the floor.

The crack caused the Unicorn who had been about to attack, to once again change the trajectory of its charge, this time looping around in a long circle and charging towards a bookcase guarding Galbor's back.

Grot sensed it was now or never and did a neat little forward roll out from under the table, snatching one of the manic books out of the air mid swan-dive and using it to whack away its brethren as he sped towards Galbor and the growing crack.

But Galbor had ideas himself, and one did not survive as long as he without great strength and even greater instincts. Calling on a truly iron resolve, Galbor ceased his attempts at blocking out the agonising lights, instead welcoming them into his warped brain. One huge parboiled hand grasped Kalamere by the head and pulled him in closer. Then blue turned red, as the light was driven back into the white wizard's skull with the speed of a runaway horse. The negative energy bounced back into Kalamere's lamp-lit orbs and he instinctively screamed, slapping ineffectively at the palm holding his head in place, but the pain was so overwhelming he began to gibber and drool as he did so.

A massive crashing sound from behind lent Galbor just enough time to stand firm and no more..., ...The Unicorn had enjoined the melee; care of the bookcase it had just rammed into. It came down towards Galbor, but he merely snarled in derision as he sent huge gouts of flame unfurling from the length of his body and up into the air to meet it. As the bookcase met with the wall of flame it disintegrated upon impact and the Unicorn too was forced to back up, lest it become so much charred magical horsemeat.

Kalamere's constant slapping enraged Galbor and returning his attention thus, he carefully slipped two long blackened fingers into the newly knit flesh of the white mages stomach where only a small hole remained and then snarled a singsong sound as he leant his weight to that arm. "Like it God-watcher?" he said slowly popping the scar wide open, "Did I not warn you of the consequences for speaking of the prophecy, did I not state I had no wish to kill you, you were more of a son to me than you could realise."

Something small, dirty and unwelcome came bounding across the crack towards Galbor and whacked him in the side of the head with a tome that set alight on contact. Without looking up he slapped out with his free hand and sent Grot sprawling through the air semi-concious.

"Time to end this...!" Galbor declared and with a face of wicked emotion he first yanked the white mage closer, despite the defensive books, cruelly shoving his own fist not only into the mages freshly opened abdomen, but driving it deep inside, then bursting out through the shattered remnants of his backbone, splitting his Cox down the middle and sending gory chunks of bone eschewing into the air. As he did so, Galbor rose upwards, disengaging the eye to eye light barrage between him and the mage and pushing off the floor with his mighty bovine legs and flinging his gruff, bullish neck around; his Jaws tearing viciously into Kalamere's side and throat anew.

Whilst in the air, the demon unfurled his ominous wingspan, shaking Kalamere's decimated corpse to the floor and circling about amid the torrent of swirling books, which schooled together for one last orchestrated attack. Wave after wave battered Galbor back earthward and it took all his effort and composure to repel the text bound tide with flame. The books burrowed into him still, smacking at his flesh with their magical pages, several of the holier texts evaporating his flesh upon contact, but Galbor was winning albeit at a cost to his health. His back slammed down upon a solid surface as the remaining fifty or so tomes drove him towards the floor, and he lay there engulfed in his own purple flame, totally annihilating the table under which Grot had sheltered a few moments before.

The Unicorn dashed at full tilt towards Galbor across the fire pocked marble deck; prancing this way and that to avoid the more fearsome of the flames as the semi-stunned Daemon staggered to his feet, the books finally dealt with as a force.

As the Unicorn bounded towards Galbor, Grot ran over to the side of the door where a pole-axe lay in the grip of a suit of armour. He grabbed the pole and wrenched at the gauntleted fingers holding it, noticing Dirk staggering to his feet as he did so, his hand held to his temple in order to stem the blood and pain. "Hey Dirk!" he yelled, even though his friend was only feet from him.

Dirk turned and moaned, catching sight of the Dwarf in his blurred vision, tugging at a suit of dark, rune engraved armour whose eye-slits were glowing with two pinpoints of red light. "Groff..." He managed to mutter before falling flat on his face.

Grot pulled even more fiercely as he witnessed the draw and counter-feign of the Unicorn and Balrog locked in a battle of tactical strikes and evasions.

"Come bleeding loose!" Grot shouted at the stubborn statue and it did. The poleaxe came free with such immediacy as to send him tumbling down the short flight of steps that led from the door. He retained his grip on the poleaxe though and came up into a defensive stance, weapon at the ready as his sixth-sense warned him of danger. Grot turned around more than a little suspicious in time to witness the suit of armour marching down the steps towards him. It drew a sword from a scabbard upon its back and, those misty red eyes flaring with hatred of the living, the armoured Wight clattered forward with alarming pace.

Galbor, now able to fly again, swooped down on the Unicorn for a third time, but a blast of holy energy came rippling from the beast's illuminated spectral horn and scorched his midriff sorely. The thing was using its magic with an amazing show of mastery that had until now, managed to keep Galbor's marauding form at bay. The ceiling of this room, though high enough to fly, was not of a sufficient height to avoid the painful burst of energy that the Unicorns horn emitted. He twisted to his side as a purple bow of light lanced across his quarters; still finding time to slap out with a hand as he passed Kalamere, who was resolute in his struggle to stand; despite the mortal blows Galbor was sure he had already dealt the white mage.

Galbor knew he was in danger - he had not the power left to summon any more minions and although things were evenly matched at the moment it would only take one of the mages - Dirk or Kalamere to regain his senses to tip the battle against him. Galbor briefly considered escaping upstairs and ordering the Wraiths' above to finish his business, but he hated to run from anything and his stubbornness and confidence of his own abilities kept him there.

Dodging yet another magical blast, Galbor landed next to Dirk and noticed that Kalamere had been trying to reach him. He only had a moment to do what he must, but he had time to take note of his situation and the others around him. Kalamere crawled on the floor a few feet from Dirk, who lay quite devoid of movement, blood seeping from his exposed skull.

Grot was embroiled in a bitter battle against the guardian Wight and the Unicorn was still circling around behind him. He reached a wickedly clawed hand down to Dirks scrawny waist and lifted his inert form like a rag doll. "So the answer is in Dirk is it dear Kalamere?" Galbor sneered, stepping on the mages creeping hand. "Then I guess we better pull him apart and see…"

Then Qu'iahal leapt. Qu'iahal, Galbor's faithful beast servant for countless Daemonic generations, was joining the fight, yet it leapt not at

Grot or the Unicorn but rather towards his master. The once faithful beast turning from lifelong companion to foe in the one moment it had sensed a weakness. Its Jaws clamped down painfully on Galbor's lower extremities causing the Demon to adopt a most comical pose!

The Daemon Prince squealed in a most unbecoming fashion and he discarded Dirk in an instant, all the better to clasp the beasts head in his hands and crack its fearsome jaws apart. The hell-hounds desperate yelps were cut short as Galbor split his previously beloved beasts head in two and tossed the remains towards the fireplace.

Clutching his damaged groin, Galbor turned to look for Dirk but instead met the gaze of the Unicorn, as it came crashing towards him its horn glowing white-hot.

With a toss of its mane, the mythical stallion sent its horn searing upwards, slewing a bloody trough along the length of Galbor's inner arm, before burying itself within the pulpy mass of his armpit. Galbor screeched in a mixture of pain and angered indignation as flashes of white light erupted from various points in his body; its elements eradiating a holy flare from deep within Galbor's fleshy enfolds.

Elsewhere, Grot dodged a swipe to his legs as the Wight swung its sword with frightening efficiency and ease of movement and planted the tip of his borrowed pole-axe into the armoured ghost's eye-slits. It faltered in its movements as it reached out to remove the axe-head from the skewered helm giving Grot all the time and opportunity needed to run away and in doing so - he stumbled upon a pack and weapons neatly piled up under the torture wrack. As his eager hands rifled amongst the newly found plunder, he was elated to discover they were his own. As fast as he could manage, Grot tied on the belt and weapon girdle, and hastily attached all but two of his axes by the time the Wight reached him. Ignoring the throwing axe still left behind, he hoisted the huge smoky axe that had served him so well before and muttered a promise to Keldor.

There was a whir of spinning metal and the sound of clashing blades as the two danced and parried. Neither retreating from the others deadly blows, lest they lose the momentum. Grot spun off to the side and felt a sting as the tip of his ear plopped to the ground, then countered by revolving onto one knee; whilst scraping his trailing leg around and transferred the spinning motion onto that foot, his fully outstretched arms, guiding the blade through a rising path of circular devastation.

Chunks of sheared metal peeled from the rapidly diminishing

Spectral Knight as Grot's slicing ballet showered the ground with sparks; bereft of many rivets, the leather straps separated as the repeated clangs resounded with each connection of the deadly rising pirouette. As his spinning stretch neared its zenith, Grot slammed his free foot down hard, stopping his self solid. The eyes came at him then yet the Dwarven veteran was prepared for this and reacted by merely dropping his axe and raising the symbol of his god. Unprotected and weakened, the Wight backed away from the holy talisman, before dissipating into the floor.

The Unicorn pulled away from Galbor, raking its singular horn out of his bloody cavity, causing the demon to collapse to one knee from the monumental amount of pain this action delivered. The Unicorn backed away to what it thought was a safe distance in order to regain the strength needed for another attack while Grot strapped his huge double-handed axe to his back and picked up the throwing axe, readying it to throw.

Dirk stirred somewhere of to the side of Galbor as Kalamere, who's own immense wounds were almost mended, kneeled over Dirk, tending to his wounds.

Grot cocked his arm back and then threw his arm forward, releasing the rune etched throwing axe at the optimal moment. The Unicorn, closing its eyes to focus, began summoning a degree of magical strength once more and Dirk cried out in pain as Kalamere applied curative hands to the exposed skull.

Galbor turned to the side as the axe wound its way towards him, and it ripped through his beating defensive wingspan before burying itself in one of the bony protrusions atop his nefarious bald head.

A flash of the holy light again pierced Galbor's body, completely evaporating his right arm in a point around the elbow vicinity. The pain was almost unbearable and his retaliation was both swift and decisive.

Galbor's arms parted and a vermillion light formed from his chest: "*Ja'hz'eehriezt Kaduo'che!*" The Daemonic Prince shouted and the stone ceiling above the Unicorn began to collapse, entombing the stricken beast among the rubble and opening the view to the tower above.

With a mighty shove, Galbor sprang high up through the gaping masonry, spreading his wings to limit the rate of his descent while he planned his next attack. Grot had already launched himself forward without knowing quite what to do; other than get away from the rubble and flame, and stood a little off from the two wizards and entrapped Unicorn, weapon at the ready.

Galbor turned to the two wizards crouched together side by side. The venerable arch-mage and the appalling apprentice, co-joined in the process of healing and vulnerable to the whims of the Daemon slowly descending from above. His huge barrel-chested frame expanded as he swallowed huge gulps of air, and then contracted as he spurted out a huge roar of flame that once more incinerated the very air and everything else around Dirk.

Kalamere had no time to muster a defence against the vicious infernal heat wave that engulfed both he and his ward; as the flesh melted away from his bones, he simply whispered into Dirks seemingly inflammable ear…, "…*Sorry!*"

Dirk felt a weird tingling like when a lover gently blows on the nape of the neck, and then the Wizard was gone; incinerated along with everything else bar Dirk and the safety zone lurking Galbor and Grot.

Grot vaulted a full six feet clear of the ground, using the bed of the wrack to propel his body forward and crashed into Galbor's back, sending him crashing into his own imparted flames. At that exact moment the floor of the tower erupted in shards of discarded stone and furniture. The ground rumbled and rolled as a tremendous earthquake shook the very foundations… The ceiling, already weakened began caving in, as pulpy white giant maws' rose up from the rapidly deteriorating floor tiles. Galbor crashed about, amongst the debris of the formerly grand study room and Grot being of a somewhat squat well balanced build, not to mention rather more used to encountering earthquakes; picked up a large tome that lay near by and whacked repeatedly at Galbor's bonce, sending the Demon rolling to the floor.

Losing sight of Galbor midst the rubble, flames and worms Grot span this way and that for a few seconds more in the inferno of the former study, but no attack came nor seemed forthcoming, so without wasting a backward glance, Grot hefted Dirk across one shoulder and flew up the steps two and three at a time nimbly dodging the thrashing trunk's of the giant worms they had previously witnessed in the caves below the current landscape. Behind him the chamber began a landslide into the cavernous maw of Gweonju.

Out in the upper hall, he paid no attention to the minions and various nefarious forces milling around impotently and crashed out towards the single collapsed entrance that now led into the glaring sunshine of the great outdoors. Grot wiped a gash of soot from his face and breathed deeply of the fresh forest air wafting in from the open portal. The various (often putrid) odours of magic were enough to send anyone reeling, let alone a Dwarf with little tolerance of magic and he appreciated the smells anew. Settling Dirk down on his feet, he shoved him in his back, propelling the stunned wizard tumbling through the door. Grot then clutched the book defensively in case of pursuit and called over to his stunned pal without shifting his gaze from the portal before him. "Are you well enough to run...?"

Dirk looked about in a daze; then focusing on his Dwarven friend he managed a bemused smile. "We'll need to take Zen too..." His head bobbed to and fro as he looked about for their deceased accomplice's carcass, and the way Dirk swayed almost defied gravity it seemed, but hey! No sign of Zen's carcass bearing litter anywhere.

"Bugger can't have walked could he?" Grot puzzled, "Check around the other side will ya...?"

Dirk dutifully trotted off in a dizzy jog around the towers perimeter, his legs steadying with the fresh air. It was some trek around the base, especially when the person traversing said perimeter not only kept bumping off the circular wall but continually tripped over his-own two feet also. Not surprising then that he also failed to notice the wolf pack until it had already taken note of him. Dirk rubbed diligently at his eyeballs to free up his terrified sight some more, but unfortunately he still saw wolves and began to run like the proverbial clappers; straight into the tower's stunning perimeter.

"Oy...! ...DICKHEAD!!!" Grot had been waiting almost five minutes inside the towers rapidly crumbling interior. "Hey Gobbo-todger, have yer found him yet or not? It doesn't take that bleeding long to get lost does it, eh Nobhead?" A shadow fell across Grot's own and he turned to greet Dirk, "About f..."

Galbor's remaining intact arm clutched Grot by the throat and yanked him closer, animalistic head charging for the kill. Yet the only evidence of Grot's surprise was the slight arch of his eyebrows as he butted his daemonic nemesis full on in the snout. Daemonic blood soaked Grot's face from the forceful collision but the daemon lord merely threw Grot down in disgust. "You are no ordinary Dwarf, but you will die..." Galbor taunted.

The Dwarf was badly winded from the fall but knew he had to move and fast. Galbor's hoofed foot came stamping down towards Grot's midriff and caught him fully, cracking several ribs, but the fight wasn't over yet. "*Dirk...*" Grot wheezed pathetically as the daemonic magician booted him; vaulting the dwarf backwards and into the remnants of the shattered doorway.

"Minions do my bidding!" Galbor barked, and immediately Grot was set upon by unseen spirits. Their invisible hands were colder than the deepest ocean, their grip as encompassing as the darkest night, and they tore eagerly at his living flesh, stealing away the life in parts and sucking all the while like some gluttonous leech upon the fabric of his erstwhile soul... The first to feast upon his most precious lifeblood faltered at its unusual taste. The second and thirds fingers bit equally deeply in the same instant and both recoiled at his soul's distinctive age. The fourth sank toothless teeth, through Eyrthely flesh and bone and sought out his heart. The fifth grabbed at ankles; ageing the bones therein. Grot screamed as his soul sought to protect itself by separating from his body. Death loomed large and the spirits still coming towards him came shrieking into sudden clarity as his mortality wavered... Bloodless face's, drained of both liquid and life, reaching out, their taut stretched skin over emancipated bodies, whose bones seemed all but withered and all the while enveloped by a darkness which seemed to emanate from beyond the confines of the world.

The sixth...

"*Not, friggin well, yet, me matey...*" Grot shouted from this world to the next and pushed sodden bones upward through the mists of death. Evil hearts guided evil hands as they attempted to push him back towards death, but Grot forged forward, regardless of the pain he felt with each successful step. Smiling ruefully through the pain, he reflected back to the torture he had already endured at the hands of Galbor and spat in contempt of his forthcoming demise; "*I'm coming for yer Galbor, yer bastard. Yer minions can rip away me health, but I don't feel a thing..., ...I suppose I should thank yer, because nothing compares to the amount of shit you put me through!*" Another spirit passed right through him, or rather he passed through it and as he did so the cold almost froze his limbs, but he inched forward still, "I mean it... You bastard... It can't end... Here!"

"The prophecy...?" Galbor teased, "Whatever makes you think I have any interest in ancient rumours and old wives tales...?" He continued, making sure to stay clear of the towers doorway and the mightily stubborn Dwarf. "You are almost dead Dwarf; your features almost match those of your attackers, who I am sure you can by now make out... One of them is an ancestor of yours, though I doubt you would recognise him, for he is from a time before men and Halfling's populated this Eyrthe of ours: From a time before history was readily recorded by all but the most fastidious Elven scholar. He is from a time when Gods ruled from earth as well as heaven and those that would be gods lay silent..."

Sensing the Dwarfs final breath would come swiftly; Galbor strode over to the doorway and paused... Grot appeared dead on his feet, though the resolute fighter had made it all the way to the doorjamb before his footsteps finally faltered, though even now the Dwarfs depleted muscles strained to move. Grot's eyes were wide and vacant yet etched within their pupils was a steely determination to survive no matter what the costs. No matter, he was moments from death... Galbor leaned in close. "And you know something...? Once you're soul is consumed, their will be none left from that time... Bar myself of course..."

"*And Kalamere...*" Grot croaked against the odds, proving he had not only heard the dark mages boast but could also respond...

"Kalamere...?" Galbor protested despite his shock at the Dwarves reply: "Why, I am sure I sent his bones straight to the fires of hell. Or did you forget in your pain my soon to be depleted nemesis?"

Grot raised his chin with a painstaking slowness of movement. It was meant as a defiant gesture, no more, but the words that followed caused Galbor a great deal of consternation, NOT merely because of the message the words contained, but also in a large part because of the manner in which the Dwarf spoke. "*...aye, yer* may *have sent his* bones *there... But I don't see no twelfth ghost: Which means **he** aint here. And if he aint here, then that means he aint really dead is he? So I asked my Uncle if he's dead, and you can have a guess at what he said...*"

"Your uncle always was a liar..." Galbor hesitated as he spoke.

"Really...? See you think he told me something important don't ya? Whether he's a liar or not don't really matter but its what you thought, well it don't matter cause he didn't tell me nothing. How is **he** supposed to tell me...? **He can't bloody well SPEAK! Thanks to your gnarly arse he can't blink, breathe, fart or do anything but feed on me, so I tell him; chew on my face if Kalamere aint dead, and guess where he munched on next...?**"

Because of one of the powerful screening Dweomers cast upon the tower, one had to step within the portal's radius in order to see inside its portly five metre arch, yet Galbor had to be certain of Kalamere's status. His crushing step faltered as he pondered ever so briefly why and how the Dwarf knew of Kalamere's intended fate; he was almost positive that he had never discussed his plans for Kalamere's demise or after-death with anyone, let alone the Dwarf. Had he bragged of it during torture he wondered. Was Kalamere's ruse with Dirk something to do with it; maybe the clever conundrum so marvellously construed by Gweonju was in fact of far more import than its hitherto hinted at severity and still its elusive answer escaped him. "Bah!" He growled shaking his head and stepping forward.

Grot's tone had become considerably less laboured Galbor noticed as he did indeed step inside the invisible aura to look around: No sooner had he done so however, and he felt a fatal stab of regret. **IN FACT!** He felt a fatal stab from a small circular pin thrust hard into his solar plexus by a leering, jeering half dead Dwarf...

"That pain yer feeling would be Keldor's sister; well Myuriin's charm to be precise." Grot brightened: "Hope you don't mind it being her. I don't follow her much myself; just a bit of lip service on holy days yer know... But me great Uncle, see... The one ghost in here you thought I wouldn't recognise: The lying bastard as yer should have put it; I know him well yer bollock brained git!"

"Yer think I won't recognise me own kin... Yer think his soul wouldn't recognise me own? Well yer don't know Dwarves do ya?" Grot shouted into Galbor's rippling forehead. "See there's a lot more to me than meets the eye yer daft bastard; just like there was to me dear old uncle... Hurts don't it yer big demonic shit-bag? Well he gave me that charm a long time ago, me uncle; had it pinned to me vest ever since just like I've pinned you. Back when he gave it me I was young, very young, and at that time I knew little about myself an less about me future; funny thing was when I asked him why he just laughed and said I should keep it until I know myself better and he couldn't talk no more! Well times have changed and I know who I am now and I know what I gotta do about this bloody prophecy, but I never did figure out what me scheming old uncle meant by him not talking no more; but then yer point out me uncle and I see his warped features on his warty old face, so I say hello... And guess what? Go on guess? He couldn't speak could he..."

Grot paused, his bottom lip aquiver, it was taking every last ounce of strength to hold onto Galbor's unstable form; the Daemon lord was breaking apart before his eyes, unable to speak or move: Paralyzed in the growing realisation of his impending extinction. Fragments of torso and limbs began disappearing at random, fingers crumbling to a smoky ash. Dry tears stung in Grots dying sockets and he screamed as he yanked the Demon back to eye level to finish his tirade through gritted teeth.

"He knew... Knew you were an arrogant bastard. He drank deep from my soul; his soul. I asked him to stop, but he couldn't answer – couldn't stop himself from eating me either: Well, I could swear I was gonna die, but I sees you there: All bleeding high an' mighty and deadly looking, and I thinks to myself; isn't it right that Daemons can only be killed in their natural form? And doesn't it have to be with a holy relic of some sort, and then I thought of me uncle again and yer know what? It looks like I've won this battle... Aargh, Bastard!!!"

Grot fell to the floor; all eleven spirits now feasted greedily upon him, restoring a little of their own mortality in the process. He forced his eyes to snap open again and saw that he still held one side of the Daemon lords crumbling face complete with an intact eardrum, which he screamed into it for all he was worth. "SEE YOU IN HELL BASTARD!"

Dirk awoke in a muddy ditch, a wolf cub licking at his face, startling him enough to elicit a quick punch to the snout before his legs screamed run ya bastard: Which he did, promptly! He checked himself visually whilst patting himself as he ran and was pleased to find everything intact, his legs churned through mud and grassy earth like a rabbit on steroids, and his arms could certainly be described as 'pumping' when he entered a sheltered glade containing a hungry, pissed off looking bear and Zen's emaciated corpse. Without pause he ran screaming dementedly past the bear and out the other side of the glade, spotting the ruined towers crumbling mass ahead, he ran as fast as he could towards it and hopefully Grot: Mighty slayer of Wolf and Bear; hopefully!

Grot's lungs froze mid-breath, he was almost there now; more dead than alive. His body ceased to function, and his mind was slowly ebbing away. The long dead men commanded to guard the place, ten of them being members of the legendary council to which Kalamere once belonged: Men of unequalled honesty, righteousness and virtue; now full of hate for the living and double their previous potency in life. Immortal to an extent beyond even Demons thanks to Galbor; they existed purely as a collection of souls, and troublingly vengeful ones at that...

A growing hiss filled Grot's aural perceptions, a white light stung his eyesight blinding him momentarily, then suddenly he was seeing them without the use of his eyes; hearing them without listening…

"We wish for the blood of the living." Spat one.

"We drink to death in honour of the undead…" Sang another…

"We hunger for the souls of legends…" A third prowled.

As each spoke they sucked away at his soul. Causing his frozen extremities further emaciated torment.

"We herald the death of heroes…" A fourth scoffed greedily.

Another deadly caress by the now visible shades and Grot's chest ceased to heave… "We supplement our strength on that of kings…"

"We salivate at the thought of a god…" Another enthused.

The seventh was no man at all he could now see, but a sharp featured woman who kissed him forcefully: "We long for the kiss of life…"

Grot's frozen face; etched with a look of determination, wrinkle by scar slowly uncoiled into a relieved grin as the eighth did not even gain the chance to speak, let alone snog him…! A burning whiter than white light blurred his intellect, and out of it floated an angelic being of tiny proportions. One of the blinded foraging worms caught her scent and streamed up towards the floating mini angel, but it plopped back to the Eyrthe as fast; shrank to the size of a common Eyrthe-worm. Denizens from hell stopped in their shrieking chaos and the painful depreciation of Grot's tortured soul temporarily abated. The Dwarf's mind swam in a whirl of colours and emotion and through it a voice spoke to him forming a placid lake around the turbulent well of his tormented body and soul, then she withdrew with almost the same suddenness with which she had appeared taking a good portion of the demonic denizens and worms along with her into the vanished light.

Grot's eyes functioned in the normal world once more, his breathing began slowly, his senses gradually recovering as he took in his situation anew; the spectres looked equally as shocked and some looked away from him as if in fear of something.

The revived Dwarf followed the errant gazes of those few phantoms even as some of their spirited number forged forward to renew their feasting on his decimated soul; he didn't resist; he accepted their feeding, content to let himself be consumed: His gaze remained affixed to the cause of the few worried Wraith's consternation, for the Soul Leech had arrived.

True these undead souls were immune to anything of Eyrthely origin but right now a Soul Leech born from a plane of anywhere but Eyrthe was stood on the other side of the doorway, eagerly breathing in their doomed and all too readily edible souls.

The souls wailed in collective distress as (due to Galbor's orders) they were unable to flee, despite having no defence against this predator of any given soul; living or dead. Normally a Soul Leech must first dominate its victims will in order to consume its spiritual essence; instructing the body to firstly let go in much the same way that these Wraith's had been decimating Grot's own sense of self; yet unlike him, these severed spectres had no bodily vessel to cling onto, no emotional attachment to mortal coils and as such they were presented like so much unwrapped candy before a greedy child.

As the remaining spectres perished, so Grot's own strength returned, yet even as the last one was consumed by the Soul Leech he dared not take a step. "What now? Me? Is it me or my mate yer come here for... Or maybe ya fancy chewing on Galbor; well he's dead fer now, gone! Mind you, if it's me or Dirk yer want, then I ask ya take me and let him go, he's got a destiny, me I aint so sure of now..., ...What dya say? I won't resist; not that I could much anyway, just leave Dirk and take me..."

"Take you where Grot?" Dirk sparkled, his face suddenly appearing through a gap in the diminishing tower wall. "Hey I can't step through this hole and I don't wanna, there's a worm behind ya and wolves and shit behind me. So should I come to you or will ya come to me: Oh sod it, I'll meet ya there!" He added without awaiting a response.

'...*Shit!*' Grot thought; '*Talk about bloody bad timing as usual!*' He wracked his brain trying to think of any mortal way to defeat one of these, knowing full well there was none, then his heart almost froze anew, about the same time as Dirk, rounding the tower and sighting the Leech, typically soiled his pants at the spectacle of the grotesque life taking fiend...

Dirk's legs began to tremble and he hoped to hell it hadn't noticed him as it seemed it was about to munch on Grot's frail looking form. The hungry wolf-pack, paused to howl for a moment before fleeing as one.

The terrifying thing looming over the Dwarf looked down from the infinite grotesque darkness it emanated and dipped the void of a ghoulish long fanged snout leeringly towards Grot's pallid features; regarding him for some time, before passing through his sagging body as if he wasn't even there. With great effort, Grot whipped around in case of a possible feint by the foul thing reaching for a large nearby book as means of an impromptu weapon, but it merely turned to face him and..., ...belched!

"Appetite..., ...Satiated!" It gasped quietly. "May..., ...Leave..."

Grot couldn't believe his luck and he belted it for the former entrance, swiping at a rising white worm as did so and hoisted Dirk up, whose knees had given way, roaring excitedly in his friend's deafened eardrum such was his delirium. "Did you hear that? It said it's full... Bloody well full up, nice one! Now are you well enough to run like the clappers, cause as much as I'm getting stronger, my will is all but spent... them worms are coming thick and fast, and cracked ribs or not, I'd sooner flee than fight...?"

Dirk looked about in a daze as his pal placed him down and focusing on his friend he managed a bemused smile. "We'll need to take Zen too..."

The companions heads' bobbed to and fro for several moments as they looked about for their friends carcass, but he was nowhere in sight.

"Bugger can't have walked could he?" Grot asked, "Check around the other side."

Dirk trotted off around the towers perimeter, his legs steadying with the fresh air and headed straight over to the bear glade. "Found him!" he yelled back to Grot, who came rushing around the tower after him.

"Where is he?" Grot queried as he glanced about.

"Over there!" Dirk pointed to a woody copse fifty metres or so to their right. Grot followed his gaze and let out a bellowed oath, as he witnessed a Great Bear ambling towards the trees, dragging Zen's dismembered, stinking carcass after it.

"Grot; you *sure* you're okay? I've seen you looking ill mate, but... Shit me boy! You look *dead*!" Dirk cheered.

Grot grew a little angry, his cheeks weakly flushing, nose barely red: "Yeah well, so would you if some bastards had just bit away half yer friggin soul!! While you were out here looking for that dead dip shit mate over there, *I* had business to attend to back inside."

"Are you crazy? You went back in there? What for, tell me you didn't try killing Galbor?" Dirk seemed genuinely concerned, understandable given Grots deathly pall. "He's a master illusionist you know... He even had me believing he was a Demon for a while."

"I didn't *try* **anything**... And I didn't exactly go in there willingly, but don't yer worry all the same; we won't see his ugly mug again for a while. He really is the kinda bad bugger yer made him out to be and then some. Mind you; he needed his minions help to try finishing me off!"

"Whoa Grot how long were we in there?" Dirk asked, amazed at the depreciation of Zen's corpse. Besides Dirk's butchery delivered earlier, there had accumulated huge chunks of missing mass, where muscle was missing from his torso and the maggot-ridden skin had turned a pasty bluish-white.

"I dunno but shut up and let's get after that Bear, eh? I'm feeling somewhere between life and death right now and any fighting is gonna be hard I can tell yer!" The Dwarf grumbled.

The Bear and Zen had moved on a ways and the two trudged after it at a safe distance for a while. "So you are dead then? I take it your some sort of zombie now. Well its cool by me mate, I always thought you were a bit of a stiff when you were alive, so I guess you wont really change much... Do you have to lie in a grave at night or something? I gotta know this shit if were gonna stay pals?"

"...Yer Great Wyverns Tit! For starters: I aint dead, an' I certainly aint no bumbling buggering zombie. *If I bleeding well was...*, ...Yer would do well to slay my rotting arse as quick as you bloody well could or at least stick to bloody running away. You're pretty good at that don't I know!" Grot seethed. "Ya know; I really could have done with a **bit** of help at least..."

Dirk looked affronted by the verbal assault his compadre delivered. "...Well you obviously managed without me..."

Grot pushed Dirk away and pointed to a spot, indicating he should walk there as the Dwarf brought the point of conversation to a temporary lull. "Remember the little Faerie trapped in the cage? She turned up and rescued my ass. Like you should have done...!"

Dirk's interest peaked... "Wow! I didn't notice any Faeries. Was she dead pretty like in the fairytales?"

"...Dirk! She was too small for even your maggoty endowed self to deflower." The Dwarf reproached, "She turned up and the Demons an' those spectres just bowed down before her. Then one by one, they all nodded for some reason and walked into the light. Or at least they appeared to…"

"What light?" Dirk shouted hoarsely across the bushy divide that now separated them as they circled the hungry bear.

"The light around her…, …Didn't I say? It was like an angel had suddenly appeared the moment Galbor split into so many atoms. I thought it was his soul finally at rest or something at first, but them wraith things knew, they settled down straight off: The howling demons in the background; even the worms stopped pissing about for a bit. Then she looked at them and-"

"**You killed Galbor?**" Dirk declared too loudly, causing the bear to regard him for a moment.

"Course I did! What type of a naff fighter do yer take me for?" Grot replied indignantly… "So like I was saying; all these things went into her in my minds eye so to speak, and she grew brighter each time, and then she turned to me and said… Well, it's kinda hard to explain… She didn't really speak; it was more like singing -or humming! But I knew what she meant anyway, weird…!"

Dirk was crouched down in the same manner as Grot on the opposite side of the glade, but his act was more out of cowardice in case the bear should decide to investigate his voice. Still, he couldn't help but whisper across, "So what did she say?"

The hairy carnivore peered over Dirk's bush and was just about to take a swipe at him when Grot stung its backside with a well aimed stone. Shocked and confused, the bear retreated to its previously intended dinner and picked some more at Zen's rotten carcass, before dragging it off again for a hasty takeaway snack.

"She said thanks…," Grot shouted back over, "…then told me to be still in the coming moments; to be ready for death, so I did! Then that Soul Leech turned up and sucked up their souls like soup before getting to mine and hey;" Grot interrupted him self, "that bastards taking our mate to lunch, without his permission…"

The rambling Bear paused in its loping gait to tear off a chunk of Zen's flesh whose snacked upon corpse was still attached to the litter;

attesting to the usefulness of the ghastly spikes keeping him in place. Then, turning its massive bulk the beast paused to gnaw on the putrid mass of his bulbous forehead, snarling when Grot got too close, before setting off again, dragging its dinner behind.

One thing for certain, despite Grots unlikely story, was that Zen at least, had definitely not risen from the dead: Least not yet... "Well at least he looks a bit more convincing now." The human enthused.

Grot crept out of the bushes. "Right, let's go get the bastard. And if any worms come tearing out of the Eyrthe, forget Zen and run like that lame ass, bowel churning, bear stew that we made a while back..., ...Oh and yer might wanna be ready to make some more depending..."

The two ran screaming at the fluffy predator, which sat back on its ample haunches and stared at the two eagerly approaching snacks with interest and Bear brained confusion; food didn't normally run over all enthusiastic like.

"You grab the litter, while I deal with big old hairy nuts here!" Grot told Dirk and whacked the Bear in the snout with the book he still held. The injured animal whimpered and backed up, then showed its ferocious wild side biting at the swiping book; lifting itself up to its full height in the process.

"Bleeding Keldor be burned!" Grot swore as Dirk gingerly pulled at the litter supporting Zen's savaged corpse and he again whacked the beast on its muzzle with the hefty literature.

"What's up?" Dirk asked, only glancing back over his shoulder as the hitherto sat upon litter came easily away; the Great Bear launching forwards on all fours attempting to barrel the Dwarven snout smacker to the ground.

Grot was trading swipes from the Great Bear's claws for swipes of the heavy tome in return. It was difficult to adjudge who was winning. "Have you seen the size of its piles?" he sounded in disbelief while turning away a massive thump of a paw with the lofted book but Dirk had already turned away and was busily ensconced in his favoured endeavour; escaping.

Grot let the book follow the momentum given by the bears assault, and then levered his arms around to bring the voluminous grimoire crashing into the Bear's testacles and trailing cannonball haemorrhoids. The book flew open and Grot grabbed at the flailing pages with one hand while holding the precious cover with the other and brought the two separated book halves together with a sickening pop.

The bear up tailed and ran away whimpering faster and louder than Dirk; its lower legs wobbling in an odd looking manner as it fair scampered off through bushes too deep for the Dwarf to be bothered giving chase into.

Grot folded the book with satisfaction; happily slapping closed its helpful pages of gibberish, then re-fastening the simple hooked clasp that held the books leaves in place. Appreciatively patting the massive impromptu weapon of choice, Grot stuffed the mammoth volume into his belt, so that the books top rested under his chin and ran after Dirk who was already some distance off and showed no chance of stopping any time soon.

Dragging the litter behind them, the two ran long into the night until Dirk's fear driven adrenalin evaporated and he collapsed in exhaustion. Grot simply picked his friend up and dumped him onto the litter too, splayed across Zen's stinking carcass and continued jogging on, until exhaustion caught up with him also and he fell unresisting into a long, much needed sleep…

…An indeterminable amount of time passed before Dirk was the first to awake from a lengthy slumber. He had slept for a long time and it was now a full moonlit sky above him; when last he had looked up, the moon had not been as full as it was now that it had reached its zenith. All he could deduce was that he must have slept for at least a day, if not several. Lo! After ridding his shirt of maggots, Dirk went over to a muddy pool of water to wash the stench of death from his clothes, then went back to where Grot lay, snoring, beneath the litter.

Dirk's muscles ached from the moment he had first awoke and so he struggled as he pushed and pulled at the litter, his muscles deprived of the chemical surge previously inherited, and they merely now burned and ached with the least strenuous activity as lactic acids built up in his system. Eventually though, he managed to free the Dwarf of Zen's dead weight, sleeping throughout the entire process. Heaving the litter to one side, Dirk looked about for a more concealing place in which to rest.

No shelter was apparently forthcoming and he couldn't discern any caves, leafy corpse or so forth. What he could make out in the moons silvery glow was that they lay amidst a depression of hills, whose silvery green sloping mounds rose in an appreciatively protective cocoon all around them.

Dirk tried nudging Grot gently with his boot, but the Dwarf didn't respond in the slightest, so he shook his mate some more gently calling his name all the while...

Dirk scratched his head to rid some maggots and install some sense into his sleepy skull. "...Grot? Grot are you awake matey?" He paused before whispering with added venom. "Stumpy..., ...? Grot you wanker, wake up!"

The inept wizard waited and a snoring falsetto answered his patient vigil. "Grot, you lazy bastard wake up...!" He coaxed more forcefully.

He shook him by the legs but their was still no response, so after around a minute or two whispering and prodding the sleepy bearded one, threatening to burn what was left of said beard and generally insulting in all manner of ways, he then cocked back his leg and booted the Dwarf in his mid-riff. This time the Dwarf did respond startling Dirk but despite a brief spluttering cough, the only other response was to alter the pitch and rhythm of his snoring.

"...Ouch: ya sturdy *Bastard*!" Dirk screamed clutching his foot.

Dirk reasoned that he had better stop before he really did himself some damage or the Dwarf woke up and did for him; then did a double take. He hadn't hurt the Dwarf because something hard lay half hidden under his soft leather jack. He parted his friend's jacket, to reveal the book the Dwarf had so barbarically utilised earlier. Pulling the volume from his friend's waist to lend his mate a little more comfort, he put it to one side and went off to fetch what meagre firewood these hills had to offer.

Although a fire could attract unwanted attention, Dirk reasoned that the cold when it came, would be a bigger killer and anyway, he had paper now..., ...So lighting a fire would not be the usual labour of unwanted love he hated so much.

Once he had collected all the wood he could muster, Dirk rifled his sleeping buddy's pockets for his tinderbox but to his vexation discovered it was missing. That meant that he would have to meditate for an hour or two, in order to gain the flame ability he knew so well it hurt. However given their location and current state of affairs, coupled with the fact that Grot and Zen where of no use what-so-ever, Dirk had no desire to go into the trance-like meditative state for the sake of attaining his piddley assed flame spell.

"So what the hell do I do now?" Dirk asked of the night air in general.

He looked at the book again and sighed at the corruption of his plans for a fuss free fire. The books title was wrote along its spine and the metallic letters shone weakly in the pale moonlight. "*Magical Compendium Memorandum...*" Dirk read the spiny writing.

Promptly he jerked bolt upright. "***BLOODY HELL!***" Dirk wheezed with sublime joy and half fell as he scrambled over to where the book lay.

Dirk's fingers shook as he reverently traced a delicate finger across the surface of each of the letters, before smoothing his palm ever so lightly across the hide bound reddish-black surface. He lay there on his stomach; his cheek pressed to the books cover, as if listening to the heartbeat of an unborn child. After ten minutes or so of this affectionate ridiculousness had passed Dirk sat back and giggled. The giggle was infectious and demanded a whole platoon of giggles to come along for the ride and Dirk spent over an hour sat staring at the tome and kissing it; chuckling like a man possessed.

When he had at last calmed down, he inspected the book in a more scientific fashion. Gone was the hallowed joy of the discovery. In its place was a seriousness that brushed aside such menial concerns. Dirk checked its cover for any hidden traps or glyphs that may protect the book, spending several hours more doing so...

...Of course had Dirk turned around in his haste to escape the Great Bear, and witnessed Grot's use of unenviable force, and the ease with which he'd adapted the book's usage into that of a castration device, he would have already known that no such enchantments lay upon the spell-book that now lay within his grasp, but he hadn't he'd run away and was glad for it.

Once he was satisfied, no dweomers protected its exterior, Dirk slipped open the latch and peeked at the pages within. The words inside were written in the basic code of magic and as such were easy enough to decipher for even the least middling of apprentices. He had expected as much, and hugged the book tightly to his chest as the wondrous joy of discovery returned.

The tome was one that Galbor had written with the pupils use in mind. It was a simplistic method of casting that Galbor had developed. Applied to any given spell taught in the school of apprentices that Dirk had attended in his youth: A spells inflections, intonations and flow must be exact for it to work as I am sure most of you are aware. They range from simple cantrips that mostly involve some hand or facial gesture to be performed either independent of, or inclusive with speech, to the more powerful dweomers cast by learned necromancers and mages alike. The more powerful the spell, the more demanding the incantation becomes and the hand gestures ever more complex. Thus the practices of certain spells are grouped into what is commonly referred to as levels; meaning levels of wizardly adeptness.

In addition, the more powerful magical practices often require a physical sacrifice, be it a gem, a drop of blood, or some other physical element and the most complex of dweomers most often require all three elements in order to complete them successfully.

The Tome that Dirk now read had been written slightly different to the spells normal casting however, the text crawling with purposely laid errors. This had two effects; the first was to make the casting process simpler and easier for a pupil to comprehend. Secondly, its purposely ill-written format would dampen the spells magical effect, in order to protect the inept apprentice from his perceived lack of ability, should the spell casting go awry; as it often did with inept pupils. So much like a cannon loaded with cotton wool, the wizard to be could practice the rudiments of a spell without getting hurt by or injuring others while learning its intricacies.

Dirk however, had a 'gift', as he liked to think of it. He was good at jigsaws and these texts were written like that, so he felt it was quite easy to fill in or guess at the blanks. True: He had an unscientific approach that relied on instinct and appraisal. As for organization and methodology well let's just say Dirk viewed mistakes as part of the learning process but he had an undeniable knack for deciphering the meaning of things and could do so with such competence that he had used those creative skills to fill in the blanks and correct the mistakes on the curse scroll which he had utilised so mischievously in his youth.

He slammed the book closed and then opened it again at the first page, he scanned through the writers notes with little interest and flicked absently through the books numerous sheaves of vellum pages until he alighted upon one that interested him slightly; it was a camping spell that supposedly provided both a large tent and fire, should one cast it successfully. Dirk smiled at his friend Grot, who snored on still oblivious to reality.

Dirk put aside the book and removed his robe to better cover the sleeping Dwarf with; besides which he was sweating despite the slight breeze. "I think I really do like you Grot. Its hard for me to explain how I feel much, I can't really figure shit half the time..., ...I just, well, I dunno, I aint saying too much in case ya just being ignorant and pretending to be asleep, but I really do think I like you..., ...as a mate of course..."

"I guess only the gods know why, but you have saved my life so many times... Why pal, what have I done to make you like me? I mean..., ...why do you even stay with me, ya could have buggered off a thousand times!"

Dirk shook his head: "What have I done to deserve a pal like you?" Dirk stopped to wipe a tear from his cheek and brushed back the hair from Grots closed eyelids, smiling once more saying: "Sleep now little buddy and let me protect your ass for a change..., ...I'm gonna learn me some magic!"

Dirk wiped at but didn't attempt to stem the flow of tears as he stood, still smiling stupidly down at his friend. He gazed at him still; even as he walked back over to where the mystical tome lay, all the while sniffing like an Elephant. "You've done so much for me already; I don't think I could ever repay you as it is..." His words were pure emotion despite the Dwarfs snores echoing out louder than a roaring tiger, caught with its dick in a tree.

"...And now you've given me this mother!" He shouted to the unconscious Dwarf, who still didn't respond other than to alter pitch slightly, but Dirk hadn't expected him to and didn't care for his company at the current time even if the Dwarf had stood up and done the Ghour Mashj Jig.

Dirk sat down in the tall grass, crossed his legs and rested the mighty spell book upon them, the evening was warm and the balmy wind meant that he could still espy Grot and Zen through the gently waving grass without being sat too close. Satisfied that all was well, he turned his attention to the tome on his lap. Tenderly unhooking the clasp and once more peeling open the binding cover he eagerly scrubbed out the unintelligible name there and scratched in his own, then once more began to leaf through the pages within to see what treasures he might find.

Dirk had a bit of revising to do and for this shit he'd meditate like a maddened monk if he had to.

XII) **A Getaway to Disaster**

Grot awoke two days later in the mid-afternoon of a bright, warm, sunny day. The warmth of the suns rays warmed the chill of death from his bones and he simply lay there, smiling, enjoying the moment. Dirk caught his eye and nodded to a fire out of Grot's line of sight. "Cup of warm bean stew?" he asked.

Grot didn't answer immediately and found his answer of little consequence, for as he sat upright he saw that a bowl of the foul smelling broth had already been placed by his side. Resting on one elbow, Grot gobbled the stew greedily - the taste was of no importance, when Dirk cooked something you simply ate first and tasted later; the quicker the better.

Pulling his knees up, he huddled there for a moment, studying his sunny surroundings, grassy hills and four or five small bushes, nothing to shout home about, although from the scorched patches of grass and small craters, it was obvious there had once been a huge battle fought here and judging from the smouldering peat in places, not too long ago. Grot was amazed they had not been set up on in the night. He looked to Dirk then whose nose was pressed into the big book Grot had earlier nicked.

Dirk felt someone watching him, and looked to Grot, who was in the process of un-hitching his weapons and readying his whetting leathers in order to sharpen and clean his remaining axes. "What?" Dirk challenged.

Grot gave him a look as if to say 'why are you asking me?' and carried on staring at Dirk. Dirk reciprocated by ignoring the Dwarf and turning his back on him. He attempted to read the spell-book for several minutes, but couldn't concentrate. Grot was getting on his nerves now. "WHAT?"

Grot sighed and picking up a small crafting axe, he began scraping its edge up and down the strip of wet leather in long practised, evenly measured strokes. "I see you found my book," he said conversationally, eyes still firmly set on Dirk. "...I was also wondering how the shite we managed to survive the night..."

"You're a poet and you didn't know it. Oh and it's been closer to five nights I have had to protect your sorry, smelly, snoring Dwarven arses; both of em!" Dirk riled. "So, I thought... soon as Dwiffs' can't read magic, I would take, well not take, you know what I mean..."

"Steal. You mean; 'you thought you would steal my book'. Is that what yer meant? Yer did, didn't you?" Grot grumbled back, "...and stop calling me Dwiff, or I will severely kick your arse and feed you to whatever passes for a monster in this neck of the woods."

They glowered at each other, each daring the other to say something offensive, simply by the way they looked at each other. Dirk broke eye contact first but not gob tennis. "Unless you've took one bang on the head too many; we are in the middle of bloody grasslands, with no forestry whatsoever for some two or three miles back that way..., ...Tit! If you are gonna use a euphemism at least use one that's appropriate!"

Grot slurped down the piss stinking bean juice and ran his grubby sleeve over his mouth and chin. "I can see we aint in no woods dickhead, but I don't see much 'grass' here either. Now I'm guessing you haven't been battling hordes of monsters or you'd have been quick to bloody wake me or sod off; so I'm wondering about shit at the moment, okay? And if you want to get it going on, then maybe I will drag your ass all the way back to Galbor's gaff, through the glade, into the tunnel, and back to the bloody woods we left them Gobbos' behind in. Maybe, I'll take you back there and let the short arsed Snurch give you a kicking, what about that?"

"I would dearly love to see you try..." Dirk said testily.

"You wanna see me try, Wizard Boy?" Grot challenged stopping mid bowl licking.

"NO! Not you: Well; I meant, I would like to see you try and feed me to that Snurch, seeing as I killed him..."

"Bugger off. You! ...*Killed* something. What? Did you give it a heart attack chasing yer?" Grot let out a deep laugh.

"I did too!" Dirk objected but the Dwarf merely laughed again and returned to his whetting stones and leathers.

Dirk ambled over, determined to drive his point home. "It's about time that you realised that I do not need a wet-nurse any more." Grot looked up but said nothing. "I protected you these days past, and what do you do but insult me?" Dirk moaned. "You never even thanked me for the bean stew!"

"I'll thank thee, if it don't come rushing out my arse in the next half hour!" Grot countered, "And, if your so brave-"

"I am, I bloody well am!" Dirk interceded.

"Well then, you can kill that there Troll all on your own can't you?" Grot said, gesturing at a point just past Dirk's shoulder.

Dirk blanched, the colour draining from his features.

"There's a Troll behind me!?!" Dirk tried to disguise the nervous edge to his voice, but a small growing piss stain in his pants gave him away anyway and he once again cursed his bladder weakness to no avail.

"No there isn't. But that's my point see…"

"You humungous gaping arsehole ya!" Dirk protested. "I nearly shit myself too then…, …Anyway, that's not the point!" He argued turning defensive in an attempt to hide his embarrassment.

"No? Well, brave mage. What is the point?" Grot goaded. "Have you slain a load of monsters here, protecting me? Huh? Is that why there are burnt out potholes all over the gaff?"

Dirk looked about himself as if seeing the potholes for the very first time. "I… tried to learn a camping spell… Anyway, listen-"

"Camping? Well I am just glad it was camping and not a bloody meteor storm or the heavens help us…" Grot responded.

"Look. I am not bothered about that right now. You're going of the subject."

"Am I? Bloody big potholes, scorched grass… I'll kiss Keldor's arse if you've just been learning a camping spell. I take it that *was* a spell-book that I nabbed from *your* old master?" Grot challenged, resuming his scraping motions with a different axe.

"Look. Will you listen! I am trying to discuss something here and all you wanna talk about is the sodding state of the local plant-life!" Dirk waited for the expected interruption that didn't come before continuing with a little less aggression. "OK. So I got bored with the camping spell; it was too difficult anyway. So I started…, …Experimenting with a few other spells and yes it is a spell-book and no - I have not slain loads of monsters protecting you but that isn't my point, my point is you saying or thinking whatever it is ya think of me. Yet ya just won't listen…"

"I listened to yer then, didn't I? What do you mean I don't listen? When do you ever listen?" Grot started.

"I always listen! It's just you - you never listen. If I've got a story to tell, you just close your eyes and-"

"Horseshit!" Grot roared, "I have listened and am sick of listening to all your half assed, no brained, schemes and stories. I close my eyes and mouth to better concentrate with the ears is all; yer should try it some time!"

"Well why will ya not listen now dip-shit? I killed those Orcish scum! Every single one of them left living anyways. I gutted them like pigs while the rest watched. Half of them you'd attacked were still alive, but I dealt with the green bastards. **Me!** *I skewered* them to their huts still breathing and set the bleeding things on fire and then, I, *ME*... I dealt with that gluttonous, bullying bastard of a boss. And you know what...? When I'd finished, I scratched my name into that stupid wooden stick you had given me for a sword, so that everyone will know who bloody well did it! ME. **Do you understand? It was *ME*, DIRK-*bloody*-HEINEMBLUD and don't you or anyone else forget it!!!**" Dirk ranted uncontrollably, actually coming to stand over the Dwarf in his wrathful admission.

It was now Grot's turn to look shocked. But he delivered a solid punch to Dirks gut all the same, dropping the wheezing wizard to his backside; who clutched at his stomach and raised the ridged sole of his right foot towards Grot in defensive gesture.

"Look!" He cried fearful of the Dwarf misreading his actions, "ya can still see a bit of that Snurch's eyeball wedged between my front toes!" Grot leaned forward and inspected the raised boot carefully, then sat back nodding his head in appreciation. "That looks like an eyeball all right. May Keldor's warriors fight the eternal battle: If you haven't at last shown yer self to be a man..., ...Sorry about the thump too, I just don't like nay bugger standing over me. Puts me on edge a bit..."

"It's okay, apology accepted!" Dirk huffed back, "But that's not all. I managed to kill a Dark Elf up in that tower too. And I don't know how because I had a broken back... Or at least it felt like it at the time." He said reaching a hand to the imagined sore spot.

"What I mean is I'm better; my body is in better shape than ever, I don't know how though because I was nearly dead..." Dirk prattled on.

"That would have been Kalamere; he left the basement while that bugger tortured me. I wondered why you took so long coming to my rescue. To be honest, I am surprised that you did..." Grot stated truthfully.

"The dog b- never mind, bollocks to it... We got out didn't we? And besides, we're both pretty well healed up too, ya splattered nose aside! That Kalamere eh..." Dirk thought it best not to mention that he had indeed wanted to run away and save his own life.

"What was it that he said to you? I saw him leaning over whispering something just before he got fried..." Grot queried.

Dirks remaining anger fell from him at the memory, he felt deeply saddened as well as bitterly confused and doubtful over his actions. Then felt even more foolish to be touched by the mages memory in this way, "I dunno?" He offered, unsure as to why he felt so personally touched, "It's like..., well he said something, but I don't know what the hell he meant. Thing is, when I think of him, you know -dead! It's like well; I feel something different, I dunno, I really can't explain it..."

Dirk looked at Grot and the two exchanged puzzled glances, "What did he actually say...?" Grot asked.

"Strange bugger..., ...said: ''Thou and I art in unicorn or something... the next thing I know he's turned to ash; and that's another weird thing, how or why was I not affected by any of Galbor's spells?" Dirk shook his head, hoping for some inspirational discovery to tinkle down from the voluminous cavity that he passed for a brain-box. He had so much knowledge contained therein and yet his brain was positively throbbing for more, he felt empty headed yet sage like too in an indefinable manner.

Grot went to speak then thought better of it; as Dirk continued on. "Grot there's more..., ...When I woke up - or should I say when you woke up, you felt cold didn't you? ...Even though you were covered with my cloak."

"Of course I was you Orc lover, I was asleep on the ground for how many days...?" Grot asked suspiciously.

Dirk ignored Grots crass taunt, "Yes well I wasn't! I even washed my shirt in the middle of the night and I didn't feel cold, I felt a bit knackered occasionally... But I didn't feel cold at all," Dirk glanced up at the beating sun. "How warm is it now?" He said changing tack.

Grot who was in the middle of removing his shirt looked about embarrassed, "Why? Yer not going to moan about me showing my abdominals off is yer?"

"No," Dirk said eagerly, "You haven't got any anyway. No, my point is; I don't feel particularly warm or cold or anything, just… cool. It pissed down for an hour the second night. But I kept you dry with: Well let's just say I kept you dry."

"You've always wanted to be cool…" Grot could not resist the jibe.

"Look really Grot, you've gotta consider these things, something weird is going on and I dunno what it is. It's freaking me out…" Dirk waited, but Grot merely went on tending to his weapon craft. "See that's what I mean about ya never listen…!"

Dirk went back to reading the book he had spent the last several nights and days poring over and tried not to think about the disturbing missing details. Grot meanwhile finished tending to his weapons, then after cleaning his clothing the best he could in the various muddy puddles that were embedded around the grassy floor, he lay sunbathing stark naked.

Grot donned his clothing and various accoutrements several hours later as the sun beat down still. It was midsummer and this little valley they were in the middle of, was most certainly making the most of it. A grumble in Grot's stomach reminded him of the hunger left unsatisfied by Dirk's meagre offering. "Tea-time I reckon!" he said standing.

Dirk nodded in agreement; no matter what the strange feelings his hunger was still a definite priority. He closed the spell-book with a thump. "I checked out our surroundings - we are about a half days walk from Devil's Gap. Zen's getting worse all the time; if we don't get him healed soon, no priest will go near him." They both looked over at the foul looking corpse.

"Right, let's go then,", Grot fished about in his pack and tossed an empty sack to Dirk, "You might wanna put that book away - Some people don't trust magic, and others just might wanna nick it."

Dirk put the book in the sack and tied it onto his belt. This had the effect of dragging him and his clothing to one side and as the two walked on, pulling Zen and his litter in tow. The heavy tome slapped constantly at Dirk's soon bruised thigh, and though they talked as they travelled, the idle chatter did little to relieve the painful connections of book to leg.

They discussed all that had happened to them since leaving Felbric's Tavern, the baby Wyvern that they had slew in Brightmoor, whether to travel to Lorellien or Caernthorn and how to trick whatever priest they found into raising their fallen friend. The journey however was all-together uneventful and they travelled past nightfall in the warm summer night, laughing and joking and only once stopping to argue when the litter eventually fell apart...

Grot spent over an hour rebuilding Zen's broken transport and so it was around midnight when they reached the large protected town gates of Devil's Gap. The smell of death hung pervasively in the silenced grove leading to the town and Grot was pretty sure he could make out signs of a recent battle thanks to his night vision and military know-how. A voice rang out at their final approach.

"Hold. Who goes there?" called out the voice of the night watchman.

"...Us!" Dirk quipped cheekily back at the guard's silhouette and received a jab to his ribs for his troubles.

"Friends," Grot countered, jabbing Dirk with a stubby finger. "We have travelled from afar and seek refuge for the night, not to mention a good meal from the fabled Mead and Meat."

"How many of you are there? Speak!" The watchman commanded.

"Look will you just let us in?" Dirk shouted up to the figure above.

"We are three," Grot said, again giving Dirk a gentle shove. "We were ambushed by monsters further back along the trail and one of our mates is in dire need of healing. My forefathers name is Banballardin..." He added with an air of expectancy.

"OPEN THE GATES!" The night watchman belted out. Immediately, the machinery holding the gates closed could be heard grinding back on its metal cogs. There was a little activity on the battlements too as several guards mustered around the Night watchman on the battlements above, hoping to catch a glimpse of the shadowed party outside of their town gates.

"The name carries weight," Grot smugly informed his companion. "They must have had some trouble of their own; the walls are quite heavily manned for some reason..."

With his infra-vision, Grot could make out the heat patterns of those assembled on the battlements above. He counted at least twenty, including the night watchmen and reckoned they must have some reason to be so alert.

The gates swung open a few feet and the watch commander came out to meet them. Grot noted the men assembled above readying bows or moving a hand to their weapons at least and he gave Dirk another quick elbow, "Let me do the talking okay or we are pin cushions?"

"But I thought we had agreed an equal say; -oof!" Dirks reply was interrupted by a more forceful jab, winding him in the process.

The watch commander was a well kept fellow in his early forties, his slick backed hair and well trimmed beard was in keeping with the style of nobility of the time, yet Grot doubted if he was truly of Noble birth: A hanger on then no doubt, and by the looks of his hawk-like features; a sly bugger to boot..., ...Grot patted Dirk's back as the wizard doubled over in pain from his hastily administered blow.

"Hail and well met kin of Banballardin! I am Karl Zeffer, commander of the night-watch." The commander smiled a carnivorous smile, leaving Grot with the impression of a hungry lizard. He wore a black leather Jacket that was interwoven with silver thread, Cuisses and Greaves of Silver and black, kid leather gloves and Knee length boots completed the slithery look.

"No doubt you have come to finish what your ancestors could not?" the question was derivative and delivered with an arrogant sneer.

"Begging yer pardon, but it was more a question of them not being allowed to, thanks to the council of the time. Mind you, I'm sure we live in more enlightened times, and I would be honoured to appraise the current situation should the council wish me too. In the meantime, ye might wanna try a few history lessons..." Grot was in no mood to listen to insults about his ancestry.

The man smiled, "Forgive me -my mistake I am sure. So you are here to meet the council - what happened to your companion!" he said stepping back. He had just noticed the state of decomposition Zen's body had undergone. By now his half maggot eaten corpse was only just recognisable as humanoid and stank terribly.

"Flies got to him - yeah err, he's our labourer - a black man from the south. We bought him as a slave." Grot hopelessly lied.

Dirk made a waving motion, placing a grubby hand on the shoulder of the commander as he tried to rise, but the man rudely slapped his hand away. "If he is a slave; why not leave him where he fell?" Karl held his nose in disgust of both Zen *and* Dirk; his eyes betraying the suspicion he felt as he studied Grot's expression.

"Why not leave him? ...Because he's a bloody good worker!" Grot said without missing a beat, he and Dirk had rehearsed the story several times before, but now he was having to adapt it slightly, "He's strong as an Ox - the bugger can lift a wagon all by himself and can man the forge better than any other," Grot urged, "Good help like that is hard to find."

The commander fixed Grot with a stare of sheer scorn, "Why would you travel all the way to the south, and then all the way back to the north again for one such as he; if you have truly come to collapse the ridge. It makes no sense. And why does the other not speak?"

"A touch winded from the journey commander Zeffer. Now are you gonna let us in or should we stand here freezing all night, discussing our business?" Grot disliked the man already and had little time for wannabe politicians.

"You are welcome of course. But let me tell you this. I am watching you. We know why you are here, so you had best not deviate from what is expected. Cover your friend before you go through, you can take him straight to the mortuary if you would like. The priest will see to him in the morning." Karl turned on his heel and strode back towards the gates but was stopped by a shout from Dirk, who had regained his breath at last.

"We wanna go now, Zeffer. Not in the bloody morning -my eyes are goosed!" Dirk shouted, and he winked at Grot before covering his eyes with one hand and placing his other on Grot's shoulder.

"What the hell are you up to?" Grot whispered fiercely, to which Dirk merely patted the small pouch hanging from his belt in answer.

"Very well, I shall have the priest woken. Please hurry gentlemen, tonight is not a night for visitors." Zeffer said as he re-entered the gates. Grot tugged a small camping blanket from the confines of his rucksack and threw it over Zen's cadaverous remains. Dirk chuckled at the thought of what he was about to do, a sudden wave of fear induced adrenalin pumping through his veins as the two entered the fortress type town, pulling the reconstructed litter in tow.

Once inside the gates, a small trip through the well maintained courtyard led to the main town square; inside the town proper was similar to any other small settlement with small wooden houses scattered loosely about the muddy Eyrthen floor of the outer part. Further in and most of the fancy stone paving and gardens of yore were omitted in favour of more practical improvements such as a Barracks and training facility, storage houses for food and weapon lock-ups abound. The marked difference in this town was the strong multi story houses belonging to the original settlers. There were ten of these, and they rose majestically above their simple wooden cousins akin to the stately homes typically found only in the wealthiest inner cities.

These grand houses were built from stone and could easily house whole generations within their walls, though most had now converted their lower floors to the various banks, eateries and stores that drove the town's economy. Each head of the ten families that resided within their walls made up a town council of ten governors, who governed all law matters that arose within their settlements borders. The title of governor was attached to the house owner, rather than the family patriarch as per norm, and though most of the houses were still run by the original families, one of them had been sold several generations ago, and so *that* council seat had passed to an '**outsider**'; a name afforded to any who could not trace their ancestry back to the villages humble beginnings.

An immense monolithic, grey stoned cathedral loomed up amidst the houses seeming completely out of place to those that did not know of the towns past, and it was to this building that the two companions now dragged their cumbersome load. As they made their way over, they did see a well lit marble/granite plaza in front of the town's largest building; the fest-hall. This large patterned area of various hued stone served as both the marketplace (on Sundays) and the Drill square for the towns numerous not to say much needed militia.

Since the time of its construction, the cathedrals gates had remained permanently open to welcome all those in need. Once they were inside Dirk's need was to close them. He managed to shut one, but the others hinge had rusted completely so instead Dirk ran into the small chapel behind the massive central altar, calling out for Grot to follow him. This cathedral was unlike any other either had come across, though neither companion had the time to contemplate their surroundings as they sprinted across the bare rock floor. The design of the place was simplistic elegance.

A massive central altar made up from various precious stone slabs;

256

rose up to within a few feet of the roof. Various facial and writhing twisting bodies had been masterly crafted into the surface on all four sides of its structure. The rest of the cathedral was plain. The floor was cold grey slate, slightly uneven from the scores of previous pedestrians to have walked within these walls. The side walls of the slightly rectangular building housed some twelve cells: Each with a wooden cot and a small slit that served as a window; in place of glass various panes of gemstone from emerald to diamond let in a kaleidoscope of colour through each of these chambers and out through their bare portals and into the main hall. Atop the cathedrals central point a huge bell tower fitted with a semi-opaque collection of gemstones let in a myriad of light shades.

To the back of the church was the private chapel. This cramped room, which also doubled as the bishop's quarter was the only room with any of the idols and religious accoutrements normally associated with churches. Yet the idols and various vestments were not those of this faith, but a motley collection of some forty other different faiths icons, collected for the purpose of theological studies.

Once inside the confined room, Dirk looked around for other exits and, finding there was none, he turned around to Grot with a satisfied smirk, "Shut the door quick!" he said, indicating the small aperture that led into the inner chapel.

Grot closed the door and tried to get some sense out of Dirk, but was quietened by him with a dismissive shooing gesture. Dirk opened the small pouch and was momentarily overwhelmed by the noxious stench that wafted out. "Not exactly fresh are they?" Dirk said, spilling the two rotten orbs onto the room's fanciful, gold inlaid table of some unknown god. "Right, cut my eyes out!" he said and lay his-self out on the table, brushing the small idols and candles that littered its surface to the floor.

"…What?" Grot cried incredulously, "Yer not still serious about shoving them things in, in place of your own are yer?" Dirk nodded the affirmative. "You're a barmy bastard and I'll have no part in it." Grot spat.

Dirk leapt up and gripped his companion's shoulders, "Look the priest will be here any minute; we haven't got time to argue…"

"I'm not bloody arguing pal!" Grot countered. "And I aint gonna cut your bleeding eyes out either!"

Dirk harrumphed at this, somewhat put out, then his puzzled look of concern twisted into a wicked grin, "OK. Keep nicks for anyone coming…" Dirk said hurriedly and placed his head on the table after grabbing some sacrificial dagger from a nearby bench.

"Have you got any idea how much it's gonna hurt?" Grot began to protest, but he was too late to alter his friends intended course of action.

Dirk held the gold weapons silver braided handle just above his left pupil and then drove the tip in and flicked his wrist back, popping the eye from his own socket and delivering the forewarned pain.

Dirk screamed so loud that Grot thought the whole town guard would come surging in to investigate the reason for the feral sound. "*You Bloody Idiot!*" Grot half shouted, half whispered and he raced over to insert a candlestick in Dirk's mouth in order to muffle his screams. "You want a bloody job doing, your better doing it yourself," He grumbled aloud and reaching for his own dagger, he sliced at the optical nerve still connecting the dislodged eyeball. "That Galbor plucked one of mine out, so I know what you're going through matey *but for Keldor's sake*, **SHUT UP!** If you think you're in pain now yer should try being dipped in boiling oil for a second or two… Now hold still while I get the other one out." Grot remonstrated as he fished about to squeeze the nerve and one of Zen's degraded eyeballs into the empty eye socket.

Dirk thumped and kicked at Grot uselessly, in a feeble attempt to somehow redistribute the pain but as Grot attempted to gouge out the other eye, Dirk rolled off the table and scrambled for the safety of a shallow alcove, trembling in knee clutching cowardice.

"No -no more! Leave me alone." Dirk managed, as at that very moment the door swung open and in stepped the priest flanked by two rough looking guards.

Grot turned around with a stupid grimace etched upon his features, as he attempted a disarming smile. His hand padded about behind his back and he gratefully enclosed his palm around Zen's spare eyeball, whilst casually flicking Dirk's own decapitated eyeball into an upended chalice with his toe. "Hi there…" Grot greeted the priest as if there was nothing untoward.

"Permit me to introduce myself, I am brother Grim, these guards are here because we heard screaming?" The priest questioned imperiously.

"Oh yeah, well… Ye see, we came in for water, and my friend tripped and cut his-self on yer dagger he's holding." Grot looked about the seemingly ransacked room and added, "He fell backwards onto yer table, and then wriggled about like a silly bastard. Sorry about the mess. You're the priest, I take it?" Grot said quietly sheathing his own blade.

The priest nodded his affirmation and dismissed the two guards, not exactly convinced by the story, but not guessing at any small truth of the situation. "Are you all right my son?" He asked of Dirk who still clutched at the pulpy mass of his left eye socket, tears streaming down from his right.

"He's fine aren't yer Dirk?" Grot answered for his friend, who made the slightest of perceptible nods. "And he's in the right place to be healed aint he? So why don't *you* do the goodly thing and heal his eye up, while I tidy up this mess. I can see yer follow a just god; not too bothered with all the gimmicks, idols and shit: A god after me own heart no doubt; I follow Keldor myself! So anyway if yer wanna heal him up…"

The priest did as he was asked and took Dirk outside into the church proper, whilst Grot cleaned up the inner sanctum and hid the gruesome looking eyeballs inside a hollow idol of fearsome design. Outside in the main hall, Dirk was ordered to lie on a square slab at the foot of the church altar, while the priest delivered his ministrations. Healing the eye was a simple task and after delivering a soothing incantation; the priest only briefly questioned Dirk as to how the injury had occurred, "Got infected with Demon spit!" Dirk had answered with simplistic, yet effective deceitfulness. The priest finished by applying a clean bandage across the eye and instructed Dirk to keep it on for three days, lest it become re-infected.

Grot came through from the chapel looking rather distraught and shook his head at Dirk's self satisfied grin. "What about the dead un? Can you do anything for him? Is it possible to raise him from the dead?" he asked hopefully. "He's our best slave and we really need him to help out with the-"

"We paid a lot of dough for him, can ya revive his black ass or not?" Dirk interrupted Grot's blabbering tale.

"It all depends on how many days have flown since he passed away." The priest replied, confident of his own abilities.

"About eight," Grot conceded. The absolute longest time anyone had ever spent as a corpse, before they could successfully be reincarnated was about seven days, and unless this priest was a veritable version of the god that he worshipped, the Dwarf doubted very much if the priest could

259

do anything for his fallen friend.

The priest stopped short of removing the cloth covering on Zen's corpse and turned to face Grots troubled visage. "Then there is nothing I can do for him. Would you like to arrange a funeral service?"

"Actually, it's only about four or five days," Dirk said ignoring Grot's confused look before continuing: "So what? I lied about how many days you slept, Grot. Everyone lies, isn't that true father? So, you can still heal him right? If it's only been four days or so…"

"I can revive him, yes." The priest confirmed and pulled away the sheet from Zen…

Whatever reaction the two had expected, this wasn't it. The priest chuckled then smiled at the two friends saying with kindness, "Yes I can heal him, you may go now. The ceremony will take the rest of the night. Please make yourself comfortable at the Mead and Meat 'till the morn."

The two companions left him to his ceremony and got some much needed sleep in the barn located next to the Mead and Meat, that the innkeeper informed them was the only room he had available. The spiky straw and mewing cattle hardly disturbed the two companions who felt like they had been to hell and back over the last two weeks and they slept quite soundly for most of the night.

***

Dawn was beginning to pierce the slatted wooden wall with its golden seeking rays as Dirk arose with a start. He was stood in the epicentre of some vacuous whirlpool that spiralled out to infinity. Numerous rotting body parts periodically pierced the watery surface of the whirlpool, crying out to him or reaching out to entice him to follow. He stood frozen, terrified beyond compare, unsure of his part to be played. Then the priest called Brother Grim rose from the pool, drenched in blood and called out an indecipherable name: In response a massive severed head wreathed with purple flames, came searing towards him from above and engulfed him whole. Then an answering blue shaft of light erupted from within his body and repelled the demonic blood smeared skull.

Dirk screamed in agony as the monstrous head continued to pull away from him, yanking his essence along with it, but the blue light wrestled for his soul's protection. A gradual tearing sound echoed all around him, then gave out with a sudden snap. The skull had won and it span back through the tunnel of the whirlpool, rising up and Dragging Dirks flailing body along with it. The assorted appendages emerging from the tubular sides bit, clawed and kicked at him as he passed and suddenly everything was fire and brimstone: Galbor appeared; Zen stood smiling by his side.

Dirk awoke with a scream. Grot was stood over him, a medium sized axe in his hand. "Are you all right? You were having a nightmare…" Dirk looked up at Grot's dangerous presence, and though he was still muggy with sleep, he could see the Dwarf knew there was something amiss. "I never have nightmares." Grot said, "Especially not the same one as you I'm betting; something to do with Galbor and Zen?" He finished, giving voice to the unspoken thought they both shared.

"Zen's…, …Something's wrong, come on…" Dirk said with urgency and they both made for the small wooden door set within the huge barn doors. Grot flung the door open and they both raced out into the early morning sun, which was already bright enough to force the two to shield their eyes as they ran the short distance to the cathedral.

"Halt!" A voice cried out behind the two, but still they ran, paying no heed to the mounting shouts arising all around them. They turned the corner of one of the larger houses and stopped short of a troop of guards and several townsfolk, who were milling around in front of the cathedral.

"There they are!" A voice warned and some thirty of the town militia ran to block off their retreat as they neared the crowd gathered outside the cathedral. A guttural roar resounded out from the cathedrals confines and the crowd retreated a little; though still strained to see the manner of beast responsible for emitting the sound.

The guards reeled back to allow someone passage and a sneering hawk-like individual came stalking through, resplendent in a long flowing gown of black silk, complete with fop cap and slippers; though he had took the precaution of bringing along his sword.

"Karl Zeffer…" Grot groaned, wary of the slimy individual.

"Imprison them," ordered the newly arrived commander.

"What the bloody hell for?" Dirk rebuked. "We haven't done anything…"

"You have brought a Demon among us - that is what you have done. The prophecy foretold as much. They are the predicted enemy within…,

…Traitors! Arrest them. …NOW!" Karl roared excitedly, waving his sword in the companions' direction.

"…You Dick!" Dirk stepped forward, pushing down the rising fear in his mind. "Whatever has happened, it's your priest who is responsible - I saw him in my dreams."

"Liars - take them or kill them where they stand." He called to the growing numbers of militia now present. Grot noted that a few of those present bore bandaged wounds, likely gained in some recent battle fought outside the gates.

The men inched forward, unwilling to be the first to succumb to the mighty axe the Dwarf had readied in defence. Karl flew into a rage, threatening to kill the men himself if they continued to dither, even going as far as hitting one of his own men with the hilt of his sword. He probably would have killed the man too, were it not for the ghoulish apparition of the priest suddenly emerging from the cathedral.

Floating ten feet or so above the ground, the priest drifted forward, his arms outstretched to the side and his head flung back at an unnaturally extended angle. A red fiery glow shrouded him within a magical firestorm of blood and when he spoke, his voice boomed out with the clarity of a death knell and seemed completely detached from the body to which the words belonged.

"HEAR me NOW." The tone of the words pitched and lilted as they tolled out in the crisp morning air. "I BalthiZARR, BrinGER OF peaceful DESOlatiON. ComMAND All worthy MORtals to LAY DOWN their Lives in SUPPLicatiON."

The detached words sent panic through the milling crowd that now began fleeing in terror.

"Bugger that!" Grot exclaimed, throwing his most favoured throwing axe at the priest's eerily floating form. The axe scythed through the air with deadly accuracy, striking the priest fully in the chest and knocking his frail corpse back to the ground it had ascended from.

"I think you better explain your dream sometime soon, because mine never had the bloody brother in it." Grot said as he pumped his legs as fast as he could to make up the twenty feet or so that separated himself from the slowly rising form of the un-dead preacher. Several guards, some exceedingly brave, others unwittingly dumb, attempted to stop Grot from reaching his intended course. The Dwarf left his dwindling supply of axes strapped in their place and opted for a less lethal form of reproach in the form of two small cudgels.

The first guard Grot encountered was overeager indeed as he met the Dwarf before he'd even took the time to draw his own sword-blade from its scabbard. "Halt!" was the only word he managed before the Dwarf smacked one of the small iron-hard cudgels into his jaw. Leaving behind the man with mangled teeth, Grot ran on to face the next two willing combatants.

One of the two was armed with a pike, the other a short sword. Grot went into a forward roll, throwing one of the cudgels at the pike man's forehead, and came up running without breaking his momentum. A heavy Dwarven boot crashed down on the pikes long wooden haft as the guard ducked to avoid Grots improvised missile, and the wood splintered along its length, leaving the man defenceless..., ...Grot then span around; knocking the hand still holding the splintered shaft away, whilst grabbing the mans nether regions with his other hand. A forceful tug brought the poor bloke racing down to his knees just in time for Grot's knee to connect with his face, sending the defeated guard reeling backwards.

Grot ducked as he heard the swish of the others blade, but he misjudged the petitioners intent. The sharp edge of the well kept blade ran some six inches along the length of the Dwarves back and he fell forward at the sudden stab of pain. "Bastard," Grot berated himself, "I must be getting old..."

"Kill him!" shouted the voice of Karl Zeffer, and the burly guard in possession of the short sword first kicked Grot in his balls before spinning the blade around in his palm and striking its pointed edge down towards his back. Grot was momentarily incapacitated as he clutched at his privates, but the human's blade struck one of the many accoutrements strapped there and with a brief thanks to Keldor, Grot wasted no time at all in regaining the advantage...

...Rolling onto his back, Grot clasped the guard's blade with both palms and manoeuvred it to the side, where it planted itself into the safe confines of the Eyrthen floor. The guard released the short sword and drove his clenched ham-fist down into Grot's unprotected face, breaking the Dwarves nose anew. The Dwarf's response was to kick repeatedly at his opponent's kneecap until it gave way and the guard fell to one knee. Grot flipped to his feet then and struck the man fully in the face with two mighty blows of his own, felling the oxen fellow.

An arrow sunk eagerly into Grot's invitingly well muscled deltoid, toppling the stout Dwarf and as he fell two more brave chaps waded in with kicks and punches of their own. He fell onto his stomach; huddled against the pummelling onslaught, completely incapable of any action other than to watch the scene unfold and protect him self as best he could. As Grot lay there he could see the priest was carelessly floating around sending small blue energy bolts into the innocent people caught up in the act of running or bowing as commanded: The maddened laughing throughout, reminded the Dwarf of someone else and then it hit him; the ethereal voice with which the priest boomed out his threatened malice belonged to none other than Galbor. '*He's after Dirk then,*' Grot thought, '*but where is the bugger?*'

The guards' blows rained down heavier and some others approached a little more cautiously, though most of their attentions were now focused on defending against the unscrupulous brother Grim, whose sole intent seemed to bring death to everyone and everything present. Zeffer paid the monk no heed however and continually harassed his troops to divert their attentions to Grot and Dirk. Then up stepped 'Golden.'

***

...Dirk in the meantime had attempted to seek refuge by hiding behind a rather large, overflowing hay cart. It was parked in the alley section betwixt the cathedral and one of the larger townhouses, and had served his purposes most efficiently as the chaos had ensued. He was safely hidden within its concealing confines and nobody had so much as spared a glance towards his preferred hiding space: Nobody that is until temptation got the better of the skulking Dirk and upon seeing a solo guard running his way with his dagger drawn, he had been unable to resist sticking a leg out for the unfortunate fellow to at least trip over... It had worked perfectly and the ignorant fighter had tumbled over, impaling himself on his own dagger in the process. Unfortunately for Dirk; a troupe of some twenty guards who were rushing to the scene from the other direction, witnessed Dirk's cowardly act and set about unveiling the villain to whom the deadly leg belonged.

Dirk heard their angered cries and made haste in climbing to the top of the cart; rolling to its centre so as to avoid the swiping of swords and poking of spears and kicked viciously at the faces of those that dared attempt to clamber up to his lofty position. This kept the guard troop at bay for several moments, before they decided to give up on their unsuccessful approach. Dirk breathed a sigh of relief, and he lay back for a moment to gather his wits then smelt a few wispy stings of smoke rise from the smouldering haystack.

Dirk tumbled forward and over the rear of the crackling hay, landed on a clueless troupe member and rolled underneath its spacious protective undercarriage; hoping nobody apart from the downed guard had noticed his switch. Someone barked out a command in that stupid military voice that civvies can never quite understand, and Dirk scanned about in panic at the numerous legged pairs that now lined the cart to both sides.

"...Hut! Hut! Li-f-t!!! Two-three-four..., ...H-up!" The strained voice shouted and the cart was lifted completely off the ground and carried away, leaving Dirk's apologetic countenance open to the skies and the ten or so surrounding men. Dirk rose to his feet somewhat unsteadily as his knees knocked with fear and the cart lifters returned to fill in their comrade's ranks; hungrily readying their weapons. *'Cast a spell...'* Dirk whispered to himself, but he argued back *'What bleeding spell? I can't cast any crappy spells.'*

'The camping spell..., ...Try to cast it.' He told himself reproachfully. Unsure of exactly why he was arguing with himself and without any conviction that the camping spell would provide any useful purpose, Dirk intertwined his fingers and incanted the magical words to the dweomer he had previously attempted to master.

A huge fiery globe erupted several feet above Dirk's head and exploded outwards sending globs of fire out all around him, the fire caught on the clothing of those not clever enough to run, duck or cower and the troops sudden panic was further embroiled by the attention of the floating priests blue magical bolts that flashed indiscriminately into their ranks.

Dirk stumbled as he attempted to run, his body feeling as though the life had been sapped right out of it, and he instead had to settle for staggering his way across to where Grot lay under a barrage of kicks, blood seeping out from the arrow wound in his side..., ...Then 'Golden' entered.

***

'Golden,' was the self appointed moniker given to a handsome lad of some twenty two years or so of age, so self named because of his beautiful golden hair and radiant tanned skin. He was a freelance warrior who fought for the sake of glory. His glamorous looking mythril armour was inlaid with golden rivulets and his sword also glowed with a golden sheen. His was the lot of the knights of fairy tales, always showing up in the nick of time to rescue some fair princess, defeat some newborn dragon or courageously turn back the Goblin raiders. *His* courageous deeds had earned him respect in these parts and beyond; and the plucky lad; who was rather more versed in bravery than brains, had now appeared on his own..: Did you guess? ...Very golden haired, gold inlaid liveried steed, in order to save the day. Dirk hated his flashy type with an envious passion.

Wasting no time in dismounting, the golden saviour strode confidently over to where the priest bobbed up and down in the air, just above the cathedrals steps. The blue bolts sang out all around him as he made his way forward, his steps never faltering as he issued his bold challenge to the deathly member of the priesthood ahead.

"Foul worshipper of devils and demons. Give up this deadly charade, or join those you really worship, in hell." He stopped then and called out to those stupid enough to still be in the deadly area, "Let it be known that I, Golden, have uncovered a terribly evil plot," he announced, bolts flying past his ears... "This priest has turned to darker gods than those known by most, and intends to destroy this village, but I, Golden will put an end to his tyrannical ways and those that serve to assail us from within." He finished as he climbed the short flight of steps up to where the priest hovered.

Streaks of the indiscriminate bolts flew off all over the place, severely incapacitating, maiming or outright incinerating people left, right and centre but Golden remained unscathed and completely un-phased by the surrounding carnage being wrought.

"Drop ya sword dickhead please!" Dirk devilishly thought aloud.

By the time Dirk reached Grot, only one assailant remained to harass the stubborn Dwarven veteran, who was now attempting to kick back at him albeit unsuccessfully, the other few soldiers having had their torso and face respectively melted away by an erroneous blue bolt. Dirk picked up a large stone with which he wasted little ceremony in whacking Grots oblivious attacker over the head: He fell instantly, blacking out from the shocking rap to his skull, and would in years to come, lament to his children of the great battle that he had took part in, and how bravely he had fought, knowing full well yet failing to add that were it not for being knocked unconscious he probably would never have survived.

Dirk helped Grot to his feet and they both limped over to the shelter offered by a nearby stinking outhouse. Golden was hacking away viciously and Grot noted; with not a great deal of skill. However, the wild slashing of his golden sword served to ward off the blue bolts that weaved their way through the air, seeking to inflict death upon their chosen target. The priest swayed this way and that in the air, his body bobbing about in an attempt to dodge the righteous strikes of Golden's blade, then Golden reversed his motion, sending man and sword spiralling upwards in a gravity defying arc that severed the priest into several parts, his hacked up pieces plopping unceremoniously to the steps below. Blood ran down the steps and as it did the ground beneath them began to tremble, shaking slates from rooftops, and sending chimneys toppling as people lurched this way and that attempting to retain their balance.

Grot snapped the arrow still protruding from his side as he looked on in horror, "That bloody priest wanted to be slain; there's no way that poncey fighter would have caught him so severely, something is happening, and I can tell you it is gonna be bloody well bad!"

"We could run for it," Dirk suggested, "I bet the gates are unguarded right now."

"We could, aye!" Grot agreed, but Dirk knew this wasn't going to be the case: "We could, but I'm thinking we better sort this shit out first. The honour of me ancestors call's for it."

Dirk studied his mate as he made his next notion clear: "So dya mind if I run? Having no poxy ancestors to worry about offending an all…"

Grot returned the gaze with a set jaw and cocked brow that said it all. Still he could see his friend was worried.

"Zeffer mentioned a prophecy…" Dirk harried changing tack.

The Dwarf managed a grim smile. "There's a lot of prophecies out there lanky lad; not all of em are connected. Still I aint so sure about this or that; I just feel we've fell into a trap of sorts, Zen was a decent bloke I'm sure of that…"

"Was…" Dirk questioned, "…didn't we just have him revived?"

"That depends on yer maths matey bollocks! I was lying when I said 8 or 9 days…" The Dwarf admitted amongst an explosion of nearby rubble.

"Me too…" Dirk enjoined as he dodged a falling slate.

The Dwarf was studying the ongoing disorder but still had the wits about him to hear his friend's needless admittance: "No shit yer lied..."

Dirk thumped Grot's arm in frustration at his mates determined plight: "Grot! You can barely stand let alone fight, and I am knackered; did you see that spell I cast? Man it was awesome! I never knew..., ...Oh my giddy goblin..., ...The rumbling's stopped!" Dirk finished and indeed it had.

Golden picked up the priests severed head and climbed to the top of the cathedrals steps, stopping in front of the fully re-opened doorway. He turned to the wary spectators, slowly gathering and held the head aloft claiming to all, "The villain is dead, I, Golden have saved you all!"

The scattered people, guards and commoners alike; crept forward and here and there was a little patter of polite applause for the hero of the day, as the remnants slowly gathered together. Karl Zeffer, who had survived at the cost of many of his guards, began climbing the steps to greet their saviour, unmindful of the clanking footsteps echoing out from the cathedrals gloomy interior.

"Do not be afraid, fair people of Devil's Gap; I have thwarted your oppressor!" The golden warrior cried somewhat elated. Grot got to his feet, feeling a little strength restored and ordered Dirk to be ready for trouble as Zeffer came within a few feet of Golden. "I have smote the un-smitten, brought my own golden virtue into the dark recesses of evil intent. I proclaim from this day forth this town and all its inhabitants shall live in peace under my fair protective hand; and should any more rise to threaten the tranquillity of this town..." He droned on.

The crowd, who were now joined by others who had fled the scene earlier, began applauding in earnest as if their joyous shouts of victory could somehow lessen the horror of the events unveiled mere moments before; the dead momentarily forgotten as they gave thanks for their collective survival.

Grot walked out from hiding, wincing at the pain in his side -the arrow had not embedded itself too deep, but was nonetheless a pain that could not be ignored completely.

Dirk was about to come out of hiding to join his companion, when he caught sight of the figure that caused the clanking footsteps of which only he seemed aware; as Zen loomed out from the doorway, looking resplendent in a matt black suit of armour, a sinister looking claymore clutched in both hands.

"Hey Zen…, …it's Zen, Grot look!" Dirk jabbered excitedly but stopped when he noticed the burning red pits of his former camping partner's eyes… "I got a bad feeling about this Grot: If my dream matches this reality, he's not such a nice guy anymore is he?" No sooner had he spoke, Zen brought Golden's vast proclamation to an abrupt closure: The claymore slashed down wickedly, cracking through bone, screaming through armour and separating sinew in one vicious stroke; sloughing through Golden's head and back and split him in two from gut to gullet; armour and all, slaying him mid-prattle without so much as putting up a hand and saying 'excuse me'.

"Should call himself 'butter' from now on," Dirk muttered before shouting; "Zeffer, look out, he's not normal!" Yet the commander simply continued his advance, only stopping when face to face with Zen, who was present now in body alone. The black gowned Zeffer said something out of earshot to the black giant that was Zen and the people gathered around moved closer in order to hear.

"Run you bloody pricks!" Grot blasted the gathering crowd as he ran forward. "Can't you see he's bloody well evil, get out of here -piss off! Run for your miserable lives!" He raged; kicking, punching and pushing people in an attempt to dislodge them from their ignorant revelry. Dirk had a better plan - he meandered over to the wooden ladder that led up to the cathedrals bell-tower and began to ascend unnoticed.

Grot meanwhile gave up on the onlookers and headed up the steps to confront the two beings there, but Zeffer moved inside the cathedral before the Dwarf could reach him and Zen stood barring Grot's way. Grot readied his axe, which although mighty in itself; was tiny compared to Zen's newly acquired blade and the two prepared to do battle. "Look Zen! I don't want to hurt you but…" Grot cut short his dialogue instead swinging a measured stroke towards Zen's black armour bound frame. There was a clash of metal upon metal as his axe dug deep into Zen's armour encased calve, sending out a relentless spurt of blood that covered the steps in its nauseous ichors.

Zen reacted by smashing the pommel of his own weapon into the side of Grot's un-helmeted head, a cracking sensation ran through the Dwarves skull causing him to drop his own weapon and clutch at his ears. Grot staggered to the side then ducked; his survival instincts helping him avoid a nasty haymaker of a slice that would have cut him in two had it connected.

Moving towards the Dwarf, Zen pivoted 180 degrees and swung a mighty booted leg at Grot, landing with full force in the Dwarf's stomach and sending him reeling backwards down the steps. Grot wheeled his arms frantically in an attempt to regain his balance on the treacherous bloodied staircase as Zen wound up for the killing blow. "Keldor stop my fat arse!" Grot huffed as Zen's deadly swipes neared his faltering self: An arrow from some unseen source found its way unerringly to its target, where it sank a full six inches into Zen's weirdly discoloured right orb. Grot was hopeful the arrow would at least slow his former friend's advance as he slipped and turned over; spraining his ankle and losing his balance altogether.

The monolithic tyrant didn't even flinch, almost as if Zen was not even aware of the axe and the arrow that were greedily depriving his body of his lifeblood. Grot reached out and grabbed the end of his embedded axe's shaft in order to steady himself, but he was already out of time as the huge blackened Claymore arched down towards his unprotected bonce. "Keldor; yer a dumb assed..." Grot muttered closing his eyes in readiness for a swift demise but the death-blow never came. Gingerly he opened first one eye, then the other to find that the black armoured giant had been pinned to the doorpost by an impressive volley of arrows, most of which had managed to find their way through the solid looking breastplate.

"Run away!" A voice shouted in warning, as another volley of some thirty arrows sought purchase in the Zen knight, one stray arrow took a deflection off the cathedral wall and bounced back at a most unfortunate angle, punching its way though Grot's outstretched arm. The pain caused him to lose his grip on the axe and he spun away clutching at his skewered wrist, turning so fast, that he again lost his footing and slipped upon the gory steps, tumbling his way to the bottom, an errant stone bouncing off his raised posterior to add insult to injury.

Several of the hitherto unseen rescuers, ran over to Grot and dragged him out of harms way, while the formidable bowmen, let loose yet another deadly payload of arrows. Grot was propped against a wall, on the opposite side of the square, and he watched with concern as Zen began to pull free of the doorpost, despite the barrage of missiles. "Zen... What have they done to you?" He thought of his former campfire pal.

The cathedral bell began to chime.

***

Dirk was knackered, he had thought that by now he may be able to rest up, have a good, well cooked meal and perhaps do a little womanising with a farmer's daughter or two. Instead, he found himself swinging on a bell rope, while trying his best to cast a flame spell, suspended some 100 to 500 feet up in the air; numerically, the difference might have been great, but maths was not his great concern at the moment, especially when a fall from either height would mean crumpled bones. The flame appeared and he held it with reverence towards the lower half of the bell rope from which he dangled, whose loftier end was attached to the bell itself. Of course someone with more knowledge of how church bells actually work may have thought to grab hold of a rope other than the one to which the bell is attached.

Dirk didn't know about bells however, all he knew was that some poor sod had to go and ring them at all sorts of ungodly hours, and as the flame caught a hold of the rope, he briefly wondered what all the other ropes were for, and how exactly they were attached...

The mighty cathedral bell - which was a good twenty feet or more in circumference, gave out one more peal of disgruntlement, before the rope carrying it first frayed, then began parting strand by strand. Putting out the flame, that had now served its purpose, Dirk placed both hands on the rope and pushed with all the force he could muster, his feet planted firmly upon the bells rim, swaying back and forth. The rope rapidly unravelled.

***

Grot looked up as Dirk swung to and fro like some demented ape, and realised his friends somewhat suicidal plan. "Hold your fire!" He yelled to the archers to his right, who were readying their bows for the last time. Zen strained forward against the arrows that pinned him all over. In fact the archers had spent enough arrows to bring down a brace of dragons, their multi-coloured flights protruded from various hooks, nooks, pocks and crannies on the cathedral wall, making the whole façade resemble some garish, gigantic pin cushion. Still, Zen appeared to feel no pain and Grot knew that he needed to entice his former friend away from the wall if Dirk's plan had even the remotest chance of working.

"Dwarf, why do you ask that we stop?" One of the assembled archers asked him of his plan, but he had no time to explain, instead he merely shouted for them to take cover, which they dutifully did, leaving the square deserted except for Grot, Zen and a persistent Halfling named Boris, who continued to whip his ineffective sling back and forth, sending small stone bullets cracking into everything but Zen.

Grot limped forward as Zen strained against the arrows holding him in place. The wooden shafts popped free one by one, in an achingly slow procession and Grot was a-feared that the bell may come free before Zen did.

"Come on ya big fat bastard! Come on, you great black, wimpy piece of- OUCH!!", Grot's taunting was cut short as one of the Halfling's many wayward shots, sent a sting of pain rippling through Grot's backside. He turned and glared at the resolute Halfling who had not seemed to notice how bad his aim actually was. Another stone struck the Dwarf on the hand. "Ooh!!! You stupid little bugger! Aim at him not me! Or are you actually on his side?" Grot exclaimed with indignity.

The Halfling looked at the Dwarf and fired another stone off that whizzed past Grot's head, merely raising his huge bushy eyebrows in reply before doing so. "You hairy little arsehole…, …If you hit me with another, I'll kick your arse before his…" To which Boris simply raised his ample eyebrows again and made nodding motions with his head, as he released another stone, whose flight saw it smash a nearby window.

"Oy…, …Half-pint! Stop with the bloody stones already; or at least fire them at him!" The Dwarf turned to follow the line of his finger, and came face to face with Zen, another stone flew by inaccurately. "How did… bugger it…" he mumbled, diving to the side as Zen punched his sword forward, it's deadly thrust cracking the flag on which Grot had just stood.

Grot came up to his feet, pulling a seemingly insufficient dagger from his belt and sprang forward: Slicing at the length of Zen's torso; the peppered breastplate offering less protection than a paper colander, and spilling his former friend's guts out onto the floor. Grot had then intended to spin off to the side, but his painful ankle gave way with a snap and he instead went sprawling uncontrollably to ground besides his gutted accomplice.

Grot lay there severely winded from the force of landing on his still cracked ribs; compounding his painful fall with yet another rebuking sting as again the Halfling's unhelpful arsenal of bullets slapped excruciatingly into the Dwarves upturned buttocks. Grot instinctively rolled onto his back as the bell's timely chimes became a cacophony of clangs and Zen stood over him; the sword arm stretched behind his back began trailing downwards, Grot's own well fed stomach its doubtless target.

Then an odd thing happened, one of Boris the Halflings bullets actually found its intended target so to speak. The small stone projectile connected with Zen's hand and the huge claymore span out from his grasp, planting itself firmly into the ground at Grot's side.

The Dwarf let out a sigh of relief which turned into a desperate scream as the cathedral's bell came tumbling down towards him through the air…

***

From his lofty vantage Dirk could see why the bell had not dismounted: One thick ropey mass had coiled together, trapping the frayed knot of the main strand. He left the bell swinging back and forth and clambered down tugging on various ropes as he did until he sat atop the source of the problem. "Now what…?" He asked of him self.

The bell rope snapped and Dirk suddenly found himself zooming upwards towards a rolling beam around which various lengths of rope were coiled. It had not occurred to him that the rope's tension was due to the bell's now very much missed weight, though it rapidly dawned on him as he rose. His speedy ascent almost saw him connect with the bell's former mounting beam, even though he released his grip on the rope almost half way up the bell tower; screaming gibberish as his body's projection slowly altered, narrowly missing the sturdy beam, yet continued his wild ascent.

In an almost comical fashion - he later had the good fortune to reflect - his trajectory slowed and pitched as he rose, so that just before he began to fall back to ground; he seemed to hang precariously in the air for a second as his head collided ever so softly with the bejewelled ceiling above.

***

The bell slammed down with a deafening series of thuds and clangs and Grot was still screaming; eyes screwed tightly shut, some twenty or thirty seconds later when the Halfling nudged him with his boot and coughed politely to gain the stricken Dwarfs attention. Grot ceased his screams and looked about him as people began to emerge from their places of hiding, hoping that this time the squashed pulpy mass that was once Zen would bloody well stay dead.

"What happened..?" Grot asked of the Halfling, who let out a childish giggle of delight before answering.

Boris, who epitomised every exaggeration of his races features, relayed to the still panic stricken Dwarf the short story of how Grot had cheated death and how he; Boris the Demon slayer, was the hero of the day.

He began the tale on the way to the barbers: Who incidentally doubled as a part time surgeon, when fathers of the faith were in short supply, and continued with the finer details while Grot was being bandaged.

Once proper healing poultices were applied to his more serious wounds; his ankles ligaments were inspected and found to be damaged though the bone was intact so he was also loaned the use of a cane. The barber-cum-surgeon was a kindly man and asked for nothing in payment for the costly medicines used and even gave the Dwarves frazzled beard a stately trim free of charge, all the while questioning various portions of the Halflings varying account of the battle.

Boris proceeded to ramble on incessantly, reliving the glorious details over and over as they awaited a very frosty meeting with the guard commander who appeared beyond reproach and the town's mayor; a gentle if somewhat naïve man Grot ascertained from their brief conference. The rushed meeting gave the Dwarf little chance to speak, while Zeffer stole the show. Grot wanted to air his own opinions but felt he needed a somewhat more public audience in which to air his suspicions..., ...besides which the commander wanted to have them confined to a cell and it took all of Grot's gruff persuasiveness to keep him self out of jail: The meeting was adjourned and the Dwarf was aloud to leave only after agreeing with the mayor to attend a meeting with the council proper on the morrow to further discuss the matter. This vexed the commander greatly and Grot was glad for Boris's interruptive presence as it was due to his prattling that the mayor brought the confab to its early conclusion, though Zeffer successfully solicited for Dirk and Grot to be unauthorised to leave the town's interior...

...All the way through Dirk and Grot's thank-you lunch in the fabled Mead and Meat, the Halfling constantly interceded with ever expanding embellishments that were bound to pass into legend somewhere along the line, due to the sheer emphatic nature of the Halfling's delivery. Even Dirk who prided himself on his ability to lie was taken aback by the Halfling's ease of truthful liberation, despite the fact that most of those he addressed had actually witnessed for themselves the events as they had truly happened.

Grot, who if truth in truth be told, did not have time for idiotic Halflings one bit, listened with an admirable pretence of interest. But after the ninth telling, he was thoroughly fed up with Boris and decided to try and get the little fellow so drunk that he may slip into a coma. The owner of the establishment; a well-liked though rather gruff individual named Neville Caitlyn, offered them his best table by the fire and they were soon surrounded by others who utilised empty barrels as impromptu stools, all the better to hear of their heroic deeds.

Grot's plan turned out to be a disaster.

Instead of collapsing into his beer, the rotund Halfling; who seemed to sprout hairs from places that even a bugbear would be ashamed, drank both companion's and crowd alike under the table, and still continued to regale them with his heroic deeds of that same day.

Grots head wrecked, and not just from the drink. The Halfling just didn't seem to know when to shut up. The most irritating thing for Grot however, was that he knew Dirk would want the irritating fellow to accompany them on their trip to Caernthorn and it was most likely Grot that would end up acting as chaperone to the little gimp, as Dirks initial bemusement faded.

It was glaringly obvious why he wanted him too, for Dirk had already made several veiled enquiries of the Halfling's favoured food. Putting his heroic tales on hold, the Halfling rejoined with infectious enthusiasm, and after a handful of culinary accounts, it became apparent that Boris was no less a cook than any other of his stereotypical race -for everyone knew Halflings with their innate love of food, made the best chefs of all; quite the opposite to Dirk and he, un-coincidentally.

What made it worse was that once you had the basic gist of Boris's expanding tale, the blanks were easily filled. The bell had come down atop of Grot, encasing him inside its spacious hollow, and continued to tumble onwards into Zen who had been knocked off balance by a fluky sling-shot to the head by Boris. The bells weight and trajectory had made short work of the already severely weakened armour and splattered Zen's reanimated corpse into so many pools of goo and bone.

Dirk himself told his own tale of how he had released the bell and fell into a tangle of pulley's and so forth, leading to his being suspended some forty or so feet from the floor. Yet given Dirk's truly cowardly nature - the story largely revolved around how many times he had soiled himself during the feat and how stupid he had been to attempt it: "It's as if I didn't know my own mind. I knew what I had to try and do, but I couldn't stop myself from doing it, I just did the opposite - and kept thinking; '*Sod this, run away*', but part of me was saying: '*No we must stay and fight this evil incarnation! Let's save everybody…*' I tell you I shit myself…" and so on.

It had taken two hours to free Dirk from his perilous entanglement half way up the bell tower and in all that time, Grot had been privy to the company of Boris, the mayor and the scheming Zeffer and now here Dirk was; unhurt and enjoying the good times; mashed out of his brains on copious amounts of mead, while the Halfling still twittered on unwittingly.

Grot sprang from his stool with amazing agility despite his drunken state, and slammed the Halfling against the wall, smashed his fat little body on the counter that served as a bar, snapping his neck in the procedure, and tossed Boris's remains casually into the flames of the fire.

That is at least, what he imagined himself doing as he sat there, covering his ears, in a vain attempt to block out the Halfling's incessant chatter. His mind wandering back over various events of the last few days, whilst all around him, men clamoured out for more of the Halflings tales and imagined accounts. They were celebrating the slaying of Zen, while all Grot could do was mourn him.

By midnight Grot was almost ready to commit murder, for although he was pissed as a newt; his strong constitution prevented him from drifting into the drooling state of pathetic-ness that men of most races enjoyed. Dirk had already attained this notorious state, slumped on the chair opposite after a meagre amount of the barkeeps best mead; his head lolled to one side, mucus and saliva mingling as it drooled down his chin. And still the Halfling warbled on in an irritating unrelenting fashion.

A minstrel had been playing for his supper that evening, the song's he sang offering some respite, despite being somewhat morose in the aftermath of the day's events, but now that beer flowed readily through the assembled patrons veins, the minstrel began a jaunty little number entitled "A Maidens wish for a kiss", though in the song she got a hell of a lot more.

Grot knew the number from his years back in the military and wasted not a single moment in abandoning the Halfling and joined with the jovial group gathered about the minstrel.

Most of the men there belonged to the town's militia, and although Dirk and Grot were still to be officially cleared by those in charge, the men gathered appreciated that it had been Grot who was the real hero of the day, and welcomed him heartily.

Inevitably, Boris noticed Grot's absence and followed him over in smart fashion, closely followed by several hangers-on. The cheerful guards welcomed the Halfling and his entourage with almost equal vigour, much to Grot's personal dismay and the minstrel played on with encouragement from those guards who joined in with the locally well known song.

The minstrels tune finished and another was requested by one of the battle scarred veterans from the company of militia. It was a song entitled "Lost Soldiers Lament" and tears of frustration and regret flowed down Grot's cheeks as he sang along with the company.

Most of those men gathered about him were also affected by the song to varying degrees having themselves experienced battle firsthand and so no-one commented on the Dwarves emotional display. Yet Grot was wracked with guilt over what he had done to Zen.

Yes, Grot knew that Zen was a Satyr, and Satyr's were demons and thus bound to the servitude of evilness - but in the too short time that Grot had known Zen, he had seemed to be one of the nicest, honest and open persons you could ever meet, with an infectious zest for life. One day he would like to hear the story of his friend's life in full.

It was not as if Grot was not used to seeing friends and companions slain in battle; he had served his youth in the deadly warrens of his former mountain home and in that time, many people had died; some closer to him than others.

Even he himself had died and been reincarnated several times past, and although it was a thoroughly unpleasant experience; as long as there was a knowledgeable high priest at hand one could always be brought back from the dead.

Of course some times reanimation wasn't an option, if someone's head were missing, or they were half eaten, for example, then reincarnation would not be attempted, less they bring back a tortured soul. For the eclectic theory that ran concurrent throughout most Eyrthely religions was that the body existed on two planes of existence and if the two did not match, it spelt trouble. Yet he and Dirk, well, Dirk.... Had made the decision to bring Zen back, despite the prosthetic injuries, which had indeed regenerated as Dirk had repeatedly predicted they would.

Grot had known what Dirk had done was inherently wrong, he knew that he should have done something to interfere. Instead, he had first let him cut Zen up; a thoroughly shocking act and one he would never have thought Dirk capable of; then concurred to bring him to this village to be raised from the dead and that was were his main glut of guilt lay. Grot was a god-fearing man at heart and the teachings he both preached and followed warned of events; which while differing, were not too dissimilar to their explicit act.

It hadn't bothered Dirk of course, for Dirk was a wolf in sheep's clothing when it came to gods, conveniently taking the mantle of one, only to supplicate it for another as situations dictated.

Grot remembered the time, some three or four years ago when Grot had first encountered Dirk; who had been placed in the dinner pot of some hungry Ogre's lair. Dirk had pathetically appealed to the Ogre to reconsider the stewing process, proclaiming himself to be an acolyte of G'leszh the one eyed deity of Ogres and Cyclops the Eyrthe over.

Around ten minutes earlier as Grot had come crashing to his rescue, flanked by two Paladins of Perdius; the most stoically virtuous of Gods, Dirk had sang out their gods name proudly, claiming to be one of 'The chosen of Perdius'. Grot had been knocked unconscious and the two accompanying Paladins had fought bravely until jumped from behind by two more Ogres. And believe me; you *do* **not** want to be jumped on by an Ogre, whose bones weigh far more than the heaviest stone. Grot wasn't so bitter about the cowardly fashion in which Dirk changed his allegiances, but more by the way Dirk seemed able to shrug off the death of another human being or discount the importance of Gods, time or fate.

Moreover what bothered Grot was the fact that Dirks lies inevitably worked. The mentioned Ogres far from eating them; had ended up feeding both he and Dirk and treating them like Gods for several months. Plying them with 'pretty stuff' made of gems and gold galore. Indeed, if it had not been for a search party of Perdian knights showing up and slaying the Ogres, Grot and Dirk would probably still reside there now being fed strips of Paladin and adored by one eyed monstrosities. Oh and yes, he had once again changed his godly affiliation back to Perdius. *Priests must bloody hate Dirk!* Grot surmised, *No wonder that minister went postal.* Dirk was a proverbial easy lay as far as those of a clerical persuasion were concerned. *They tell him to repent – he does so. They accuse him of being ungodly – he admits it. They order him to convert and he readily agrees; until the next time he's in trouble...*

He had often admonished Dirk for his Holy disregard and warned beyond reproach that his heretical ways would one day bring about some irreparable harm. He had not exactly envisaged the situation as it had arrived, yet he knew this was the first indications of those warnings coming true. He could forgive Dirk these weaknesses for he knew they were merely a cover for his inherent disorder, but he had not foreseen how warmly he would come to regard his pan-pipe playing pal in such a short time; furthermore how wretchedly his newly acquired friend would come to be parted. Demons were demonic true, but that merely meant they were devilish or fiendish, much like one could accuse a child of being and Zen had certainly been the most childish demon Grot had ever encountered.

Yet Zen for all his inexplicable niceties *was* a fiend from hell, and Demons were never really alive in the manner that other races lived. Attempting to raise one from the dead would in essence, rip the creature's soul from the very same hell that humans feared being consigned to upon death. Because fiends were not only born but lived out most of their unnatural lives in Hell, the resulting ritual would understandably, bring about the reversal of the desired result. Thus, the summoning had not brought him back to life, but rather it had brought him to un-life - terminating the spirit or soul of Zen and leaving behind a hollow carcass that had no more control over its own actions than a reanimated skeleton.

"I am a sick bastard yer know!" Grot spewed into a nearby soldier's ear. "I knew what would happen. I tried lying but, erm; what? Oh, oh, sorry matey I loved her you know..., ...I killed me mate, well, my mate killed him... I should know this shit! Dya know? Oh I love this song..."

Long before he had appeared on the steps, before the bell had tolled its death knell as it struck into his decimated form, Grot and Dirks well meant, yet misdirected actions had murdered him. Whether or not, the two had realised the possibilities was mute. The hard facts were that the priest most certainly had known. The priest ordained in the cloth of Goodness who had been anything but Godly...

The song brought back the memories of Zen's amusing anecdotes and escapades, as he himself had told them. As well as the good times shared with several other deceased companions; no matter how short lived their company. So it came to pass, that by the time the minstrel had finished the sixth verse, and nobody else knew; yet everyone wanted to hear the other four, Grot himself stood upon a stool and sang the remaining verses, accompanied by the minstrel's beautifully crafted, well struck lyre. The verses forming an appropriate anecdote to a Demon that broke the mould, and a conformational lament to Grot's guilty conscience...

279

...From where these troubles lay down to bray, I know I must find the true way. Through deep ranks of confusion, I reach the conclusion of this last fight afore I return... For their will come a wanting, from which I am jaunting away from... Eyrthe's ancestral voices from home...

"SO I... Follow in fashion as the hordes come a crashing against the great shields of my home, I stand fast and factual with a weapon that's true, and the dream I cling to in my heart: And it starts a racing and my girl comes a-pacing down the dirty old streets of my home, and I find redemption, from the hell I've been sent to, and the only life that I know..."

With Demon to drink and a girlfriend to think of, I look on ye man o'er there... Though my enemies scoffing I shall make him a coffin of bones. And I'll kill off his kin and bury them with him as my teeth set firm in my jaw... For they threaten my kin and although it is grim, I shall help conquer all in this war.

"SO I... Follow in fashion as the hordes come a crashing against the great shields of my home, I stand fast and factual with a weapon that's true, and the dream I cling to in my heart: And it starts a racing and my girl comes a-pacing down the dirty old streets of my home, and I find redemption from the hell I've been sent to and the only life that I know..."

For young eyes shall hate me and my deeds disgrace me as I follow the creeds set in war. How shall I ever leave these nightmarish troubles behind...? My hands show blood cold and raw, and I think of holding the one who awaits me, but the things I've done in this war just cannot be ignored...

"SO I... Follow in fashion as the hordes come a crashing against the great shields of my home, I stand fast and factual with a weapon that's true, and the dream I cling to in my heart: And it starts a racing and my girl comes a-pacing down the dirty old streets of my home, and I find redemption from the hell I've been sent to and the only life that I know..."

I shall sleep in a fit of a-feared fallen foes', take applause and excitement from those who don't know. But those who knew war as an old bedfellow will often seek to redeem themselves in her sweet thighs. For it's only her and drink; that could ever truly make me think! – of my sweet innocent girl back at home...

"SO I... Follow in fashion as the hordes come a crashing against the great shields of my home, I stand fast and factual with a weapon that's true, and the dream I cling to in my heart: And it starts a racing and my girl comes a-pacing down the dirty old streets of my home, and I find redemption from the hell I've been sent to and the only life that I know..."

By the time the birds came out singing their own cheerful notes, the nights revellers lay about the bar in an unsightly fashion, clutching at beer jugs for pillows, noxious fumes of stale mead and sick filling their lungs as they slept.

And relatively out of sight in a corner by the fire, the blathered man mountain of Dwarven strength; Grot, cried quietly into the morn..., ...A lone and desolate figure.

XIII) **Running on the Wings of Prophecy**

Grot awoke to the smell of boiled milk and melted cheese, he could not remember drifting off to sleep and felt all the usual pains associated with a heavy nights drinking followed by sleeping for a few hours in an impossible position - in his case slumped over the back of a broken chair. Boris was stood there, offering a cup from which a smell like dragon dung issued forth, a big stupid smile etched onto his childlike, yet hairy features.

Grot grunted at the Halfling in an attempt to speak, and motioned the food and drink away. "Now, now, it will make you feel better, I made it with my own special spices - and it is the best cure for hangover in all the lands," Boris said placing the food and drink beside Grot. "Trust me."

The sullen Dwarf glowered back at the Halfling and snatched up the cheese, biting a huge chunk out of it, in the hope that it may stop this Halfling from talking. The cheese was delicious, but very dry, so he sipped at the milk, which was …unusual. Within seconds there was nothing left. "Got any more?" Grot couldn't help asking despite the sour taste residing in the roof of his mouth.

"Oh you don't need any more… That much will make you sick enough." Boris said meaningfully.

"Sick? What do you mean sick, that was delicious- well, not delicious but definitely different; besides which us Dwarves don't get sick easily- oh no. By the gods…"

Grot turned to the dying embers of the fire, just before the stomach churning contents were ejected, and managed to contain the nauseous fluids within the confines of the fires dying embers. He was only thankful that the bar was now empty of all but a few of last night's patrons. Boris stood patiently to the side, as bright as can be.

"I thought, you said it was the best cure for-" Grot paused as more vomit erupted from the pit of his rapidly emptying stomach.

"Oh it is," said Boris interrupting the incapacitated Dwarf, "It cleans out your whole system, gets rid of you headache - why, Granny said it even gets rid of spots, though to be honest I'm not sure about that one…"

"…Why not?" Grot moaned betwixt bursts of yellowy-brown fluid.

"Oh because, I never had any, so I dunno about it. Mind you she did make some cream once that took a boil clean off a Trolls bum! Mind you she made Uncle Hammond apply it. Poor sausage..."

After several minutes of sweat lashed vomiting fits Grot plopped back against the wall for a moment to catch his breath. He inspected the Halfling, who studied him back. "You sure you aint some mad ass wizards experiment? Galbor's apprentice maybe sent to drive me mad?"

Boris raised his seemingly sentient eyebrows in surprise at the statement. "Whatever do you mean?" He replied; hairy ears wiggling up and down as he spoke.

Grot shook his head and moved away from the fire, he was suddenly feeling very hot and the pitiful tendrils of flame that licked the dying fire could not possibly be responsible for the sudden infusion of heat.

"Go on then..." the Dwarf demanded, "Explain to me why I'm feeling so bloody hot of a sudden...?"

"Oh!" Boris looked surprised at having been asked to explain, "Well, that will be the after effects of the pimientos; they'll help flush the alcohol's poison out of your spores or something, least that's what granny used to say... Fire-plums she always called them."

"I take it you had some yourself earlier?" Grot asked in a somewhat stroppy manner as he removed his shirt. The Halfling was far too chirpy for his liking.

Boris laughed at the thought, "Me? Noooooo! I never touch the stuff! Not that there is anything wrong with it mind... I've just never had the need..."

"Never... I need some water..." Grot began to protest but thought better of it as any attempt at anger was skull blindingly dizzying... His unusually pasty complexion was pinking like that of a newlywed fairy.

Grot's abdominal muscles tensed in anger and he clutched at a stab of pain that began in his stomach then spread throughout his entire torso, before letting out a lengthy trump that echoed out around the rapidly emptying tavern like some warped battle trumpet.

"Oh yeah, you may wish to find a latrine quite quickly too!" Boris added.

Grot wasted no time in asking for an explanation, instead rushing out into the street and down a shadowed alley where he squatted for some time. When he later returned, the barkeeper was busily tidying the place, righting tables and so forth, whilst Boris was the only other person that remained.

"Feeling better?" Boris asked and Grot had to admit that he did indeed feel much better, despite the brews methodology. "So now you can go see the council and collect your reward, I've already got mine." The Halfling went on, patting his stuffed pack in response to Grot's questioning look. "They gave me some jewels; sparkly big ones too!"

"I don't want any bloody reward," Grot sulked, "Where's Dirk?" he asked looking about in case he had missed sight of his friend.

"Gone, but I doubt he'll be happy. Fancy just bobbing off without so much as a parade, not to mention his reward, when I got mine; I asked that snooty commander Zeffer if you two would get what you deserve and he just said 'oh yes..., ...they'll get what's coming to them all right' like its some big secret, I mean everyone knows you two helped me out a bit, well a lot actually..." Boris replied simply.

"Boris..., ...Hello, Dirk's gone for shit's sake..."

Boris looked confused, "I know; I just told *you* that!"

"So forget Zeffer and rewards..., ...Gone where?" Grot asked; he had been expecting Boris to respond by saying that he too had gone to collect his reward. But to simply leave..., ...'*The uncaring bastard*', he mentally added.

"Dunno!" Boris replied smartly. "No-one does, several of the guards went looking for him; they were quite concerned. So much so, that they left me here to wake you up and deliver you to the council..."

"Deliver me..? And how does-oh forget it. Dirk wouldn't have just gone and left me to face the music alone!" Grot snarled, secretly perturbed by the fact that Dirk probably had done just that.

Neville the barman had his own ideas, "The tall, gangly one? I saw him chatting to one of the farmers' wives last night..."

"That'll be it – he's probably had his arsed kicked... Where does this farmer live?" Grot asked the barman.

Boris looked at the Dwarf, with one bushy eyebrow cocked at such an angle that it was impossible to tell where his eyebrow ended and his hair began - if indeed they ever did end. "If you keep looking at me like that - I'll rip those eyebrows off. What's up now?" Grot demanded of the Halfling.

"What music?" came back the Halfling's puzzled response.

"What -what do you mean music, you barmy bastard...? Ah Right! Erm it's just an expression, now put your eyebrows away, they're making me warm up again." Grot explained crossly.

"The woman; her names Sarah, and she seemed quite friendly with yer geeky friend; though only Helaena knows why..." The barman stated, invoking the name of the God of hospitality.

The Dwarf shook his head in abject agreement. "I know what you mean, all that bone and no meat and women still love him... I can't understand it either. Was her husband around?"

"Her husband's dead... Sarah lives alone with her daughter, and she's not so much as talked to a man for the last few years; save me self of course..." The barman replied, his voice betraying the emotion he hid.

"Have you got a thing for this Sarah by any chance?" Grot was still a little unsteady but he could easily stand his own in a fight if need be...

"If thee means do I care for her? The answer's yes, but I aint got no trouble with you good Dwarf. Yer uncle knew me well enough to take me along as guide on his fool quest when I were but a nipper and I be nearing my eightieth now. That fool quest left me family with enough diamonds to start up this place..., ...Though we've carried our establishments name back down the centuries, we ne'er had a place as fitting as this one..., ...No I aint got no brook with yer Dwarf, but others have..." The barman Neville stated.

Grot relaxed at the statement, his uncle had been a good enough judge of men. "Okay Caitlyn I hear yer, me uncle spoke about yer but he never mentioned yer by your name... Let alone yer age; to be honest I thought it was but men that accompanied him: It is Caitlyn is it not?"

"Aye Caitlyn will do. Nev or Neville to my friends, of which I'd like to name yer self were it not for yer mate's seedy actions... How come ya knows of me name then if yer uncle ne'er said it?" the barman queried, "Or has the fame o this place spread as far as the Dwarven mountains?"

"No such luck, though the gods know why not? Your mead is some of the best I've ever tasted, what's the secret?" Grot harried. "As for your name I heard one of the militia call you last night..."

"Aah! The militia, they're a good bunch; petty so few are left to defend the town..." Caitlyn sighed, "Sarah's husband; my brother, was killed defending it. That's why I care for her. I'm wanting to marry her to take proper custody of her and her daughter, not that she admits she needs help with the farm, I just can't see me and her together; or rather I can and it scares me sorely... and then yer bloody friend goes and..."

Grot considered the barkeep's words before inserting his own thoughts. "How come you say there are only a few militias left? Their seemed more than enough yesterday, though to be honest most were pretty useless... Half of them just stood there doing nothing, especially the buggers in silver and black-"

"Those aren't militia yer be speaking of but Zeffer's personal guard. Tell me true Dwarf; should yer blindly follow orders without thinking first? Most his warriors seem to think so but you... The way you sang that lament suggests you might be ready to give it up, or might that be me own."

Grot was unsure if he had caught Neville's sly intent. "So why did most of them stand off? Did Zeffer command it...? But that would mean-"

"The priest was Zeffer's twin. The church has always been the true power round here... All the councillors know it too. But now..." Caitlyn slowly shook his head, unwilling to reveal too much of what he knew less he himself became embroiled in its tumultuous web of deceit. "Zeffer got away with some fair goings on when his brother was head of the church, meant he didn't have a minute to spare for the governors. Mind now the church has got nay paladins nor preacher they'll be wanting answers..., ...So 'tis a pity to hear that John; the commander of the day watch got stabbed in last nights battle... Means Zeffer will be too busy to mourn his brother, never mind answer the council's questions in full. The militia needs a master and as yer may be aware Dwarf, we're kept quite busy around here."

"So what has that got to do with Grot or Dill?" The Halfling asked.

"He'll be looking for someone to blame right...?" Grot snapped, clicking his fingers in conclusion. And that someone will be us, I get you now Caitlyn... He'll tell them we brought the Demon into town and probably say we possessed his brother and whatever other shit. That droopy-hawk-nosed bastard will pin stuff on us we never even knew was possible! All that bollocks I heard about a prophecy last night; what of it?"

The barman looked perplexed, "I aint sure I hear its telling rightly, but from what I gather the town is doomed to fall to an enemy from within."

"Which is why that bastard Zeffer wants us kept here," Grot proclaimed. "...I get it now; if ever there was an enemy it's that bugger! Dirk was right to piss off, though I regret his manner Caitlyn..."

Boris frowned at this, the two ginormous caterpillars on his brow that served to ward off would be admirers connecting like a bushy tree line. "What are you trying to say? Are you not going to see the Elders?"

"Look I'm just tired is all Boris... I've hardly slept a wink for days and now that I'm up I've gotta get going again; and all you can tell me is that I've gotta go see some bloody council who most probably will want me dead by the end of the meeting..." Grot grabbed his gear continuing.

"Not to mention that Dirk's missing with Caitlyn's would-be lover. If that greedy bastard hears of a possible reward, Keldor knows what'll happen," Grot attempted a fake smile, "I just hope he aint in trouble already. Caitlyn, look I'm sorry about Dirk and if he's dishonoured your future missus in any way, I promise you I will personally kick his arse, but right now I gotta get going... Where does she live again? I've gotta get to him before Zeffer's guards do..."

"Oh I doubt he'll be with any woman!" Boris beamed, "He most probably went off with that Dark Elf he was chatting to..."

"Dark what?!?" Grot said redressing himself and searching around for his belongings. The statement caused even the barkeep to raise a disbelieving eyebrow.

"A Dark Elf I said..., ...Dirk was chatting to him last night while you were off singing. What are you looking for?" Boris queried.

Grot glanced back at the annoying Halfling, "My stuff. You know - axes, pack, that type of thing; all I've turned up is my jacket so far -and what are you on about at all? A Dark Elf, I never saw any Dark Elf... Did you see a Dark Elf?" He asked Neville who responded in the negative.

"Oh yeah, well you wouldn't have noticed him, being so bent on

singing those last sixty-odd verses… As if the song didn't go on long
enough already… I went off to get a few more pints down me, cause
Granny always said you should never travel on an empty stomach; and
besides, you were off key once or twice too often for my ears liking, so you
know, I wanted a bit of space between us, Granny always said bad music
can never be listened to from too far away; actually if you wanted, I could
give you some singing lessons. I was-"

"Shut up!" Grot butted in, "I asked about the Dark Elf..?"

"Oh yeah well, he turned up about the same time as them fellows
took your stuff. I thought that him and erm… Dick is it, your mate? Well
whoever… I thought they might be friends cause they both started
laughing when they saw each other and then when the human sat down
they both kept teasing each other, name calling and making pretend threats,
but then I thought they were gonna start fighting the way the Elf waved that
silver dagger under his chin, but no they-"

Again Grot interrupted, "Someone took my stuff?"

"Yes -two blokes they were human. Friends of yours are they?"
Boris asked, eyebrow cocked quizzically, "I only ask because they didn't
appear to be local… Kinda brown skinned like your self. We're a bit
whiter up here in the north…"

"Friends -I don't have any friends - other than Dirk!!!" Grot roared
at the Halfling - a fast forming suspicion that he had been robbed gaining
momentum in his rapidly sobering mind.

"Well, It's a bit careless off you, I must say, letting two strangers
walk off with your stuff, they could be thieves or anything!" Boris lectured,
"Why granny always said, you can always trust a stranger never to be
trusted-"

Boris was this time cut short as a rough hand gripped him by the
throat and lifted him into the air. Caitlyn took the opportunity to slip away.
"Look, you hair infested little weevil. I do not want to hear another word
about your buggering granny! I don't know anything about your bloody
family and neither do I want to. It seems to me very much like my stuff
has been nicked, AND YOU STOOD THERE AND WATCHED THEM
TAKE IT!!!" Grot bellowed; swinging the Halfling in so close that his
eyebrows tickled Grot's face, which in turn caused Grot to drop Boris
unceremoniously to the floor as a powerful sneeze racked his torso.

Boris attempted a quick getaway from the maddened Dwarf, but Grot stood on the hem of the Halfling's robe -choking him for an instant before the nimble Halfling undid the clasp about his neck. Boris bolted forward towards the door, but was brought down when the quicker thinking Grot; thanks to Boris's hangover cure, grabbed a chair and sent it spinning into the hapless Halfling; taking his legs out from under him in the process.

Before Boris could rise Grot's hands were upon his shoulders and lifting him upright to his feet. The Dwarves grip while firm was not painful and he spoke in a much calmer manner than before. "OK. So, I'm upset at losing my stuff; I didn't mean to scare you. Well I did. But you know what I mean. I just wanna know about this Dark Elf, because me an me mate Dirk have built up quite a list of enemies in our time, and not long back Dirk bumped off a Dark Elf or so he says..." Grot paused to hold the Halfling's gaze and forced himself to calm his actions further.

"Now I aint saying that this particular Dark Elf wanted to kill Dirk, but when you say he had his knife out; that kinda bothers me... Did you not even think to come and tell me?"

"But you were busy singing..." Boris pleaded helplessly. His granny had always taught him that you should get on with your own business and let others get on with theirs; though he thought better of informing Grot of the fact.

Grot released his grip and turned away dejectedly, finding a semi-clean table to sit at, and buried his head in his hands. It was hopeless: Dirk was probably lying in a ditch right now with his throat cut and if he were not already he probably would be when Caitlyn or the town guard caught up with him. And NOW, the only person left to offer any sort of companionship was an irritating little sod whose throat was temptingly close to being throttled. Life was shit.

A scraping sound upon the table made Grot lift his head and he saw that the Halfling had placed a small silver axe upon the table. "I found this... I suppose it's really yours... I'm sorry...about everything..?"

It was his favoured magical throwing axe. It had been given him by a high priestess, in return for saving the lives of several children and was etched with her God's symbolic design. He looked at that symbol now - a stylised hammer encircled by a wreath of Dwarven runes and crested by two Gadrach's; proud honourable beasts that dwelt solely within the mountains. The symbol seemed to shine brighter than the rest of the solid silver piece, in this hour of need, so close to his own crest; that of Keldor.

"Where did you get it?" Grot asked without much feeling, his finger delicately trailing the symbols path.

Boris bunched his face up so that hair, sideburns and eyebrows fused momentarily, "Well, to be honest, I was a little worried about Dyke, so I followed him and the Elf outside when they left the pub. I spotted the axe when I was crouching behind that hay-cart you honoured before. I figured it must have been dropped by those friends of y-oh! I mean the thieves. Sorry - I forgot then. If I'd have thought they were thieves last night I could have followed them… Sorry about that. I was gonna give you the axe later, but I just thought, soon as you'll not be going to the council-"

"Stuff the bloody council," Grot said standing. He paused to look down at his hairy helper and made a decision he would most probably come to later regret.

The poor sods throat was beginning to purple from Grots earlier ministrations… "We've got work to do, we gotta find Dirk."

"…We?" Boris wasn't sure there was or that he wanted a 'we' to be involved.

"Well of course, you owe me one for letting the thieves get off with my stuff, and besides you're an excellent shot with a slingshot." He lied.

"You think so?" the Halfling said brightening despite the soreness of his throat, "Granny always said; "The only practice you need is more practice…""

"That's because your Granny was a wise woman. You can never have too much practice!" Grot said, hoping his remarks would indeed provoke the fellow into more practice, for Keldor knew, he needed it.

"She used to say that too!" Boris beamed incredulous, "And she used to say; "Better is better - but there's always better than you." I bet you would have got on with my granny."

"I don't doubt it." Grot lied again, "Well let's go, he's probably left the village no matter what. Lorellieña is only a few days west. Quite a few unfriendly Elves live there I'll bet."

Boris frowned at the thought. "I think you might have a problem leaving. I mean, I didn't think anything of it, but I'm pretty sure with the mayor saying you're confined to the town, that the guards wont let you just leave. Then again, Granny always said don't stay we're you aren't wanted!"

Grot deliberated on what one of the guardsmen had told him last night about the town's recently increased security measures, and gave the bushy Halfling an appreciative nod. "Your dear old granny wouldn't have given any advice about escaping by any chance?"

Boris shook his head, tittering. "I'm afraid not…, but I can still leave can't I?" Grot sulkily nodded his reply; he supposed it was too much to expect anything else of the Halfling, than for the hirsute little fellow to scarper while he still could.

"Fair enough… I don't blame ya. This town's no place for a decent bloke like you. Besides, it's only a matter of time before Zeffer turns his attentions towards you. Maybe we'll meet again someday, no hard feelings, eh?" The Dwarf conceded offering his hand in apology.

Boris however was looking about in confusion, quite ignorant of the Dwarves apology. "Old Nev has disappeared! Very strange that… Right in the middle of cleaning too! I wanted to ask if I could borrow his cloak but never mind. I'll just lend it anyway –I'd leave him a note but Neville can't read so let's just nip around to the stables, Oh and nick that beeswax polish too, it'll come in very handy…"

Minutes later a bushy faced Boris left the town gates, cloak wrapped loosely about him, one guard waved as he left the town confines, but Boris didn't bother to wave back.

At the changing of the guard some thirty minutes later, Boris was followed out by Boris; this time sporting a bulging pack, with a pan, spoon, knife and sling hanging from his belt. Again a guard waved and this time Boris did stop to wave back, even shouting out a friendly hello and quick goodbye to the guard he had known so long. "I forgot my stuff Edward - see ya again soon I hope!" And with that he walked onwards to liberty.

Grot waited behind a grassy knoll, the poor but effective disguise of horse hair, beeswax and robe having done its duty; lay discarded by a small leafless tree. "No-one suspected anything?" Grot asked in disbelief.

"Not a dickey bird as my granny used to say." Boris beamed.

"Good, now let's move, we'll follow a path around that next big hill there and climb to the top from the other side, that'll give us a good view of the valley without being spotted." Grot said setting off silently. Boris simply shrugged and followed him, clanking all the way. "And stay beneath the horizon or the guards will come running bloody quick sharp!"

As they neared the highest hill's summit some ten minutes later, climbing up the blind side of the nearby town, Grot caught sight of a lone figure ambling down a path from a farmhouse some half a mile distance away; strolling towards the town. "It can't be…" Grot gasped.

"Can't be what, high? Cause I'll tell you it is high, my legs are tired and my heads swimming from the climb." Boris countered.

Grot grinned at his tubby little companion, "That's the effects of the beer. Maybe you should have had some of you granny's concoction after all? How's your eyesight?"

"Good why?" Boris wondered.

"Can you see that farm over there?" Grot asked, pointing it out.

"The one what Dinks just left? Oh, is that your mate Dink!" The Halfling exclaimed, relieved to see the fellow alive.

"His name's Dirk! And yes it's him. So he's alive after all, been with that Sarah no doubt; well I've gotta hear about this one. Hold on…! The daft sod's gonna walk right back into town." Grot flustered.

Boris was fishing about in a pouch and removed a small round stone, which he fitted into the readied sling, then began whirling above his head.

"What are you doing!?" Grot asked in amazement.

"Warning him…! If I can get him to look up here…" Boris's voice trailed off as he released the stone and followed its imagined trajectory while besides him, Grot let out a strange sounding string of Dwarven syllables, consisting mainly of grunts and curses.

"YER TINY LITTLE TIT YER!" Grot declared punching the Halfling painfully in the arm as he readied another shot. "Leave the sling alone." The Dwarf added, gently nursing the slow weal developing from the Halflings miss-skewed shot.

"Oh I'm sorry - maybe you were stood too close!" The Halfling panicked in realisation of his offence.

"I'm not stood too close! It's just your bloody aim, why do you insist on using that thing –you're frigging useless at it!" Grot moaned, now that he almost had Dirk back in his grasp he was less inclined to humour the clumsy Halfling.

"But you said I was good before-" Boris appealed.

"I lied," Grot said interrupting, "Let *me* get his attention eh? I've got a lot better chance than you have with that thing." Releasing the leather strap around his wrist, Grot untied the axe that Boris had returned to him.

"What are you going to do? Kill him?" Boris cried, his eyebrows undulating in concern.

"Just watch and learn!" Grot said as he aimed and then unleashed the axe with fury. "Sheekash Mallarrdictum!" He invoked as he released the deadly weapon.

"What were those words? Do you know magic?" Boris probed.

The Dwarf laughed and briefly glanced down to the Halfling by his side before returning his gaze to the axes passage. "I'm a Dwarf bushy boy! How would I know magic...?" He teased, "It was Dwarven."

"What did it mean?" The Halfling puzzled.

"A literal translation would be; 'Seek out mine enemy' but for my purpose that tree he's approaching will do. Now shut up and watch..." And they did... The axe's silvery form glinted in the strong sunlight as it wended its way for what seemed an age down the steep hillside. Some several hundred metres away at the bottom where the hill met the main road, it flashed past Dirk some ten feet away, knocked a nest from its perch and began spinning back up the hill towards them.

"Now here comes the tricky bit; catching the bloody thing! Watch were your standing." The Dwarf spoke ominously.

The whole attention gaining process took some thirty seconds. From the axe leaving Grot's hand, to its remarkably precise return, which Grot caught effortlessly amidst the frantic waves the Dwarf directed at Dirk's now ascending figure.

"How..." Boris was almost speechless.

"A bit of *Keldor's* magic..." Grot said winking; delighted at showing off the weapons abilities. He felt good, the Halflings presence wasn't nearly so unbearable now. Dirk had notably seen the axe or the nest falling - or both, and was now coming this way and what's more there was not even a suggestion of any imminent danger for once.

"Keldor must be some magician!" Boris said biting down on a cake.

Boris decided to wait for Dirk being as knackered and hungry as he was, leaving Grot to clamber up the several metres distance to the hillocks crest alone. When he got to the top, the ancient Dwarf had to look twice to believe his eyes, for there in the centre of the hills crest, hanging from the leafless branch of a small copse of lifeless trees was a Snakeman or Lizardman - he was never sure which you were supposed to call them...

The truth of the matter; as I'm sure you're already aware is that the species of Snakemen derives from the jungles of the east and the deserts to the south. They are very territorial creatures and extremely dangerous barbarians, and although bands of five or more of the creatures had been reported, by and large these Beastmen tended to live alone, treating other Snakemen with the same contempt they seemed to hold for all the other creatures that were unfortunate enough to meet with one.

Lizardmen on the other hand, whom many thought were a distant cousin of Troglodytes, were both infinitely more sociable and considerably more dangerous. Their organised and evil race had been inexhaustibly responsible for some incursion here or there as the centuries went by, and when they attacked they left nothing standing in their wake. Their race hailed from all pockets of the world, and they were easily adaptable to life in almost any environment, though most clans preferred to spend their life in damp environs such as those underground.

The reason for the confusion over the two races was simply down to exaggerations, misinformation and the general rarity of living and reliable sightings, but there was *one* very easy way to tell the races apart. There was no trick to it, no knowledge of species needed; in fact it required no more than ones eyes or sense of touch: For Lizardmen had a short tail of between two and four feet in length and powerful humanoid legs, whereas Snakemen didn't. Have any legs' that is... Instead their entire lower torso was comprised of a snake-like stomach and tail. A petty then that Grot was; like most others to come across one, completely oblivious of the fact.

"Wow!" cooed Boris's irritating voice as he finally reached the summit; half-eaten sausage sandwich in hand. "What's a dead Snakeman doing way up here I wonder...?"

Grot stood staring at the creature which was hanging from the tree by its tightly noose-choked neck. It was hard to tell the things exact height being strung up so, but Grot guessed head to tail, it was probably about eight or nine feet long. The dark green body was covered in scales which lacked the lustre they had probably held in life.

The tail was ridged similar to an alligator's and the thing's legs were double jointed much like those of a dog albeit on a larger scale -with massive quads and an extra join above the ankle which led to the beasts feet. These feet looked particularly vicious, ending in three curving, yellow and black coloured, wicked looking claws. Its arms were slender yet muscular and the hands led to three long slender fingers and a thumb, tipped with similar claws as to the things feet. A yellowing, deadly looking horn like protrusion, extended from each of the creatures elbows. And Grot touched them to discover they were as he suspected; retractable.

The things head was covered with a hard carapace that formed about its scaly flat crown and ran from the things brow, but the reddish colouring was too faint to be noticeable. Its teeth…

Grot and Boris climbed onto the trees stumpy base to get a closer look at the thing, as Dirk appeared at the knolls summit off to the side of Grot's scope of vision. The Dwarf then inspected the things teeth and found them to be white, very pointy and flecked with small bits of captured meat. "Well! It aint a vegetarian I'll be betting…"

Dirk glanced at the Halfling in shared surprise and walked over to join them at the base of the hangman's tree. "…No. I've met Troglodytes before; they're worse than Gobbo's and bloody well stink worse than Dirk's cooking! Mind you this one smells quite good considering…" Grot was rambling as Dirk approached.

"Look at that bit there; it looks like something's been trying to eat it!" Boris said pointing to an area of exposed pink flesh.

"Who'd wanna eat a smelly Troglodyte? Not me that's for sure." Dirk chimed.

"Welcome back Dirk matey but it aint a bloody Troglodyte, yer great demons tit! It's a Snakeman. And that gash was caused by a dagger or I'm stupid." Grot said jumping in and reasserting his authority.

"Oh! You think so? Well - I think I should know - I mean. I'VE met one before. How many have you ever met? Huh…?" Dirk was a little miffed that no-one had yet asked him of his previous whereabouts and was therefore determined to pick an argument about something.

"What dya mean: Troglodytes or Snakemen? Cause I aint never seen a Snakeman," Grot paused turning around to give Dirk the full benefit of his attention before continuing.

The Dwarf was pissed off, and Dirk was the main reason for him being so as he intended to show in no uncertain terms… "However *if* you mean *Troglodytes*, I've met and killed about seven hundred, which I am sure is nothing like the number of the very same beasts you've probably whored with. So if you're done with your sodding whinging, you can just stop right now before I throw you back down this bloody great hill… And end your miserable life once and for all."

"I'd just like-" Dirk began to retort.

"I mean it. Shut up and look pretty; that's what your good at." Grot's tone brooked no argument. Stopping Dirk's excuses dead.

Dirk studied his friend in silence. Grot returned his knowing stare and for several seconds Dirk received a well serious dose of the old eyeball, yet having received no thump inviting retort Grot returned his attentions to the Snakeman's corpse. Dirk waited for the surly Dwarf to turn away before making several obscene gestures behind his back.

Boris decided this was an astute moment to chime in with his own ten pennies worth. "It is a Lizardman *-or Snakeman*," he quickly corrected as he felt the full force of Grot's stare, "What I mean to say is; I was in the Gap when they attacked. The militia were ready for them though. Mind you - all our best fighters died… but we won! She was the only survivor, so they hung her from this tree the night before last."

"She..?" Dirk and Grot both found themselves asking the Halfling.

"Well -that is unless they've cut her a new bottom in the front of her lower abdomen." Boris tried tactfully.

"The-who: did what?" Grot said making as little sense as was possible.

"Oh I see." said Dirk.

Grot then saw what the other two had now noticed and corrected what he had been about to say before the Halfling's interruption. "OK. So what I want to know is… Are they edible? I mean… Can we eat her?"

"hlllllllp mmm… plssss" A voice said as if in response.

"What?" Grot asked in shock, spinning on Dirk, who began trying to explain his innocence in turn; meanwhile Boris gave the things legs a little shove sending it into a gentle swing.

He waited for it to slow and then, as the other two continued to argue, he gave another gentle push, but this time he received a slap in the face from the things vengeful tail.

"Hey! I swear it did that on purpose. I wonder if this is still a-" one of the beast's beady yellow eyes opened, sending Boris into senseless panic: "Aaaaaarghhhhh!"

Grot and Dirk; who were already involved in fisticuffs, turned to the panic stricken Halfling, "What's up with you?" Grot asked, momentarily releasing his head lock on Dirk.

"Whoooohwwwoo..." was about the most that Boris could manage under the circumstances and he pointed a circling finger at the Lizardman. From Dirk and Grot's angle it seemed that nothing had changed and so they resumed their fistfight. Boris in the meantime, having recovered his wits and courage a little, loaded up a fumbling stone into his trusty slingshot and flung it limply at the beast.

"Aargh! My shittin' arse!" Grot screamed out, leaping up into the air, clutching the cheeks of his backside as he did so. Dirk let go of the Dwarf as he jumped and stepped back, waving his hands to protest his own innocence, just as a second stone struck Dirk sharply on the knee. Both former combatants turned to the demented Halfling who was already whipping his sling into another misdirected frenzy.

"plssssss..." The voice seemed to drift down to them from the miserable creature hung above them.

"Well I'll be buggered. It aint dead... Here Dirk get your knife out and kill the thing will you –Half-pint! Stop whizzing them stones about like they're out of fashion. You'll end up killing yourself..."

Dirk climbed the tree knife at the ready, but when he got into a position to slit its throat he stopped and shouted down to Grot, while staring at an open yellow eye-slit. "Why kill it? I mean it hasn't done anything to hurt us has it? I say we just cut it down... It keeps trying to say something that sounds like please..."

Grot looked at Boris and then back at Dirk and briefly wondered if he were the only sane one. Boris's pleading hairy stare seemed to be saying something along the lines of "my granny always said you should help those in need, because one day you may be needy yourself!"

"What you looking at; haven't yer just been whizzing stones at it!" Grot moaned looking away from the Halfling. Dirk's smirking idealism shot back at the Dwarves hardened countenance and he knew instinctively what the human would be thinking; it was just like the stupid son of a bitch that he *was* and would most likely be thinking it cool to have a Snakeman - or should that be Snake-woman or Lizard, who cares what?- along as a companion. Grot considered arguing reason, of attempting to talk some sense into their empty heads… "…Nah! Forget it; give us one of them pies Boris I'm off for a scout about." He said more to himself than the others and turned to walk off down the hill.

"What exactly does that mean? Can we help her or not?" Boris asked of Dirk, somewhat confused by Grot's reaction.

"Of course we can, we just do what the hell we want anyway don't we? Now move out of the way…" Dirk instructed the Halfling as he began sawing through the thick ropes braiding.

"Yes well of course we do what we want, but… will he be okay with it? Grot I mean?" Boris asked stepping back a few paces. "Well to be exact… I mean, what if she kills us and eats us..? Will Grot…"

"Oh yeah…, …now I get ya, well right, look, don't worry. He'll just sulk for a bit. Unless it attacks us; then he'll come storming up here, kill it and tell us he told us so… Grot loves being right. If that happens just ignore him. I do!" Dirk responded kindly as he cut through the remainder of the ropes width. After cutting half way into its heavy coils the rope suddenly split and the Lizardman crashed to the ground, where it lay still, unmoving.

"Water!" exclaimed Boris and he wasted no time in rushing over to the creature and tipping the contents of his flask into the things mouth. For a moment she didn't respond, then, slowly, the creatures tongue began lolling about in its mouth, searching for more of the elusive life giving juice.

Its tail started twitching back and forth for some unknown reason, and Dirk went and cradled the things head without a thought for his own safety; holding the water-skin to the things mouth as it drank sparingly.

Several minutes passed before it once again opened its eyes, which were a golden yellow hue with a large oval iris dominating the centre, causing Dirk to drop its head and scarper backwards on his backside. Something that could pass for a smile played across its lips.

298

The Halfling remained by her side though and the beast made no move to harm him and Dirks confidence slowly returned though he made sure to keep a safe distance just in case. Dirk himself had been in enough close scrapes with death that he could readily appreciate the creature's unenviable situation... When you're up to your neck in Dragon turds, even a hatchet wielding Goblin was a pretty welcoming sight he reminisced and then instantly scolded himself as he was reminded of the devastation he had wrought on the Goblin encampment.

Dirk's brow furrowed as he spoke to block out the haunting mental pictures, "Don't worry lady, I never judge someone on appearance; if you need help my snaky friend- you've got it!" The thing nodded in acquiescence, its eyes locked with those of Dirks as an understanding passed between them. Boris came to his feet and helped as Dirk aided the Lizardman to struggle into an upright sitting position.

Grot ran dashing back up the hill announcing the unwelcome news of; "We've got company!" then bounded back over the crest.

"Can you walk?" Dirk asked of the strange being, more hopeful than anything. The creature slowly shook its head in response as it polished off a second full water-skin without pause, other than to choke occasionally.

"...Dirk! There are at least twenty of them and you saw what tough little bleeders some of them can be yesterday..., ...I know why they didn't all wade in... I think their commander told 'em not to... The buggers must have scouted us somehow." Grot warned as the wizard approached.

Dirk digested the information while Boris; having run out of water, offered his hip flask of brandy to the Lizardman, who greedily lapped up the juices offered.

"Do you recognise any of them?" Dirk questioned Grot.

"None...! Well it aint any one of them from last night; in the pub I mean... I think these wear Zeffer's personal seal but I couldn't make it out for sure from this far. They'll be here in a minute tops." Grot shrugged in the direction of the other two as if to add that rescuing the Lizardman would not be considered a prudent option. "Yep they're wearing black and silver all right. I'll bet any money that they are Zeffer's personal thugs. Didn't trust that bastard from the moment I lay eyes on him."

Dirk looked down the hill at the ascending soldiers; he could plainly make out the silver eagles emblazoned upon most of their breastplates.

"You'd better get cracking with that axe again then if ya can see them old man... I guess I'm lucky that tree was so big, eh? Soon as you can't make out a few poxy eagles..."

Grot ignored Dirk's jibe and returned his attention to the Halfling and his charge. "Boris there will be a bit of trouble; they're not after you and it isn't your fight so yer welcome to bugger off if you want..."

"What about her?" Boris asked of the staggering Lizardman, the Halfling was feeding her strips of cured chicken as he walked around in a backwards circle, forcing her to follow unsteadily. Dirk looked at one then the other and was about to express some witty *'til we meet again* statement, when he realised the brave little Halfling had already given his answer in a polite, non-controversial way.

"So are we taking them out? Or ditching her! You know me, but it's your choice -they could be innocent... and we could be dead o' course, but as I say it's your choice." Grot demanded not unkindly; fingering his axe.

Dirk loped over to the hills crest where he could see the men ascending roughly only five hundred yards below, one of them saw him and pointed him out to the others, before continuing their now hurried ascent.

"What makes you think we'll have to fight them? If you really thought they'd want to kill us you'd have been whizzing your axe about by now..." Dirk responded.

Grot's face purpled as he came to join Dirk at the crest. "Are you bloody stupid? Surely you can't be asking me seriously..." Grot's retort petered off as he studied Dirk's blank expression. "They tied her up to that tree, didn't they? And we cut her down, and if you ask me that's reason enough to start with. Add to that the fact that I think Zeffer's in league with... hold on, we'd better duck!" Grot said pausing to pull Dirk to the ground as a lightning bolt came streaking over their heads.

"They got themselves a mage with them too. Can you match that? Funny sending a mage up on a regular scouting trip don't you think?" Grot enthused, cursing himself for choosing to ally with someone so blinded to glaring reality. "If they aren't involved in some immoral nonsense, then I'm an Elves brother... That bastard is trying to blame us for yesterday's fiasco, which I admit we are responsible for in a way..." Grot paused to throw his axe in what Dirk thought to be a one off warning throw. "...And I'm also sure that your plan to get Zen resurrected was somehow a part of some much bigger plan in which we we're just bloody well pawns; well I'm buggered if I know what it is but I bet it's something to do with her too, how else would Zeffer know were here? What yer decide now can seal many a fate."

Dirk sneered pure scepticism, "Grot your way too suspicious for your own good, there's probably a normal explanation for all of this. But oh no! You have to bring in some dark meaning, pawn of the gods and all that shit. I think your torture spell in the tower has addled your brain a bit, me old stumpy mate..., ...As for fate I had her mother..."

Grot thumped Dirk painfully in the side of the head swelling his purpling earlobe instantly.

"Ouch! Ya shit, that hurt!" Dirk protested, and received a brisk procession of several more beatings for his mouthy troubles.

"Listen to me *you* arrogant dung heap! That Galbor was an old friend of yours -*Not mine!* And yet *I* took all the **shit,** while yer self ponced about completely untouchable. That was the worst bleeding pain I have ever been through in my mortal life and yer know what? I, Grot Banballardin told him where you were... I, me; I gave in... For the first time in my *old* life I couldn't take it any more... The bastard was just such a good friggin' torturer; I'll probably have nightmares about it until the day I die. But fair's fair... That was that mess and this mess is my mess, I think, and we are both up to our necks in it. So I guess it's a case of what goes around comes around. But I will tell you this much Dirk Heinemblud... You are an uncaring bastard trolls-spawn son of a bitch and as much as I like yer, if I had my way, it would be you who got turned into some evil monster and not Zen... You haven't so much as shed a tear for him you... Oh I give up! Why do I bother! Just piss off down the hill and say hello to your friends if that's what you want, I've heard they're gonna give us our just rewards!" Grot finished his tirade by administering a final thump to his pals already thick ear.

After pausing a few moments for his head to stop ringing Dirk gradually got to his feet, still defiant. "I don't get you sometimes, I liked Zen too but... he **is dead!** And why is it your fault that these guys want us so bad? I'm just a bit confused... You've not exactly explained much-"

A second lightning bolt slammed into Dirks chest with bone jarring alacrity and sent him reeling back twenty feet through the air. Grot and Boris rushed to his side leaving the Lizardman to totter after them and found him fairly winded but otherwise completely unhurt.

"I have no idea how the sod yer managed to survive that bloody hit, never mind get away without so much as an item of charred clothing but yer did. So like I was saying before yer got hit, you'd better decide what it is yer wanna do? I'm all for running if yer want to…" Grot demanded.

Dirk felt silly, like a child not quite grasping a certain lesson and being scolded for it: He knew roughly what he meant though; he could either run or stop running, but he had to decide now. "Okay we kill them. But give them another warning first!" He instructed.

Grot lobbed his axe down the hill narrowly missing one of the soldiers, while Dirk shouted out for the men to go back, but they simply continued to climb with slightly more conservatism.

The two friends looked at each other in condemning agreement and Grot's axe flew down again, only this time it cracked an unwary fellow's skull in two before returning expertly to Grots hand.

Grot was at battle stations now and Dirk left his Dwarven friend to attend to the gruesome act of clinically picking off as many of the 'soft' targets as he could: Their helmeted heads cracking like so many boiled eggs.

Seeing that Boris had rejoined the Lizardman, Dirk walked over to the pair, mentally noting the various incantations required to cast the spells he had memorized that morning and not one of them involved bloody pigeons, though a large part of his growing repertoire *were* most assuredly concerned with flame.

"They'll be here soon…" Dirk began, "You two may want to try and hide or something." Boris's eyebrows knitted in puzzlement and Dirk permitted himself a wry smile as he thought of the permutations involved in trying to hide such a huge creature as the woman before him.

"Okay well… Just keep a look out for…, …Shit too late," he corrected as two men came over the steeper eastern crest on the town's side. "Grot they're coming up on this side too…" He shouted as he stepped forward and sent a small rock spinning into one of the two men's faces, knocking the man back over the crest. The other grasped a small resilient plant to aid his purchase and attempted to vault up over the precipitous brow, yet he hadn't reckoned on the Halfling who appeared out of nowhere to stamp on his clutching fingers and then as the climber wound his arms in balance seeking fashion, a light shove on his forehead sent him too to join his fallen companion at the back crippling base of the hill.

302

"Well done Boris!" Dirk said in admiration as Grot joined by his side. Everything was silent for a moment except for the rustle of grass blades swaying in the gathering wind and the odd scream from a pained survivor of the initial assault.

"Ok. Let's get her picked up and climb down the northern slope." Dirk nodded indicating the Lizardman. The three amigos went over and helped the drunken woman as she struggled to her feet from a recent fall. Dirk's eyes locked with those of hers though and for a moment blurred visions invaded his mind.

"…Dirk!" She said huskily, "Dirk of the Blood, I've found you."

Dirk didn't know what to say; about the vision or the creature's mental reference to him. Instead he simply grabbed her arm and swung it around his own shoulders and began walking to the northern edge. "You'll get down quicker if you roll, both of you. Don't walk down just roll…"

"Dirk -move it!" Grot shouted as he moved back to the hills summit, and the small party turned their heads to find themselves staring back at a small army. All with the strange silver on black insignia that could only mean that these men were indeed Zeffer's own elite group and Grot noted they were no eagles upon their breasts but the insignia of a Dragon.

"Why are you here? What do you want of us?" Grot said attempting to stall for time.

The answering response was quite different to the one he had hoped to elicit and was delivered with an appallingly large amount of pain. A black arrow flew from one of the many archers' bows and bit deep as it sought purchase in Grot's left arm, narrowly missing the bone and piercing through the skin on the other side.

"…Aargh! *You Bleeding Arsehole!* Dirk, Boris…, …Lady-thing: Run!" He shouted as he sent his axe spinning into the ranks lining both the southern and eastern crest.

Dirk turned to run as fast as he could manage given his weighty burden, but again Dirk's vision swam and he saw his friend Grot stood nailed to the very tree from which the Lizardman had earlier hung. "Not if I can help it!" he mused aloud, and slipped from under the Lizardman's grasp causing her to momentarily stagger as she adjusted her weight under the bowed figure of the tiny Halfling. "Sorry Boris, but Grot's right I get it; it's not a case of wanting to fight but being willing to. I thought; well, I hope I know what I think anyways…" Dirk sighed. "Just Go for it, and whatever you do, don't stop and don't look back!" Dirk said and he turned to walk calmly back towards Grot and the pressing mass of soldiers. There were around forty all together, all armed with various daggers, swords, automatic crossbows, and bows built from ironwood.

Most of the men had scattered for cover as Grot's axe had swept along in a malicious sojourn around the hills perimeter. Some however had simply risked their lives in order to stay on their feet and thus retain their advantage and these now fired their bows at the multiple fleeing fugitives, before feeling the axes deathly passing; across their own exposed throats.

An arrow struck the tail of the Lizardman who let out a roar of affronted agony. Another glanced along Dirk's cheek, slicing through the thin flesh. A third arrow struck Boris full in the centre of his back, sending him tumbling over the hills edge without a sound. Several had been directed at Grot, but all of them missed as he rolled forwards into their ranks. His small axe had returned to his hand once again but was pretty useless as a melee weapon, so Grot slipped it into his belt and instead concentrated on using his much ignored unarmed combat skills.

His wasn't the pretty, deadly, martial arts that may be used by ninja's, samurai, or the odd late night reveller who had downed just a little too much to drink and suddenly thought himself an heroic crusader, but his style was, unlike the last of those mentioned; effective. Grot had honed his skills in the tough bars and mining colonies he had habitually frequented in his youth; brawling or street-fighting as some would call it and the thick muscled Dwarf was one its finest ambassadors.

He began his assault by launching himself feet first into two of the men, connecting with some force; he planted a foot in one of the unfortunate's groins, then as his motion carried him past, he reached out a hand and grabbed the hair of the second guard who had deigned it unnecessary to wear a helmet.

Yanking himself around in a motion that tore a huge wad of hair and skin from the poor chap's scalp, Grot altered his trajectory to send him self travelling head first into a group of three nearby men, who hurriedly dropped their bows and attempted to free their swords.

Grot delivered his diving head butt into the belly of the first man, winding him severely in the process. Rolling to his knees he bit the second ones balls, who screamed in astonished pain as the Dwarf flicked out his right leg and booted the third in the elbow; causing him to lose a grip on his hastily clasped sword. Deprived of his weapon the third man swung a vicious kick at Grot's head, which connected numbingly but the Dwarf had had his fair share of cauliflower ears in the past and the mans well placed blow only served to enrage Grot who slammed first one, then the other fist into the offending blokes stomach and bashed his way to his feet with a succession of left/right combo's…, …Several seconds later and the huge hitting Dwarf connected with a blow to the temple that slew the fellow instantly; killing him before Grot had stood up to full height. Then, swooping up the beaten chap in his arms like a baby, he hoisted the battered cadaver above his head.

Two men further away managed to let loose their arrows as he charged towards them with his limp victim still held aloft, but they panicked at the rampaging threat of the enraged Dwarf and their shots went wild, one of the bowmen's arrows lodging itself in the throat of a companion of his across the way.

Dirk noticed that the soldier struck in the throat was not a soldier at all, for as his blood spewing body fell to the ground, it dissipated to nothingness as though no-one had ever even been there. *They're bloody Illusions!* Thought Dirk and he quickly re-evaluated his options, but upon noticing several bodies still littering the battlefield he had to rethink again.

Grot pumped his arms forward propelling the human missile above, directly at the two panicking archers, who had just enough time to dive out of the way before Grot was upon them. A solid punch to the jaw of the first of the two sent that combatant crashing unconscious to the floor. The other man however, who was at least 6 feet tall and built like a bear, took the initiative and jumped on to the back of Grot's much smaller frame, thumping the Dwarf repeatedly in the head.

Grot managed to stay on his feet, despite the pummelling and span his self around to disorientate his piggy-backed attacker… It failed as the brutal giant of a man stopped his thumping for a second while the Dwarves spinning action threatened to throw him off, and Grot reacted by smashing his head backwards into the face of the clinging chap whose weight he bore. This hurt the giant fellow for a moment and the nimble Dwarf used that time to roll forward, thus shedding his stunned heavy load, just as two others ran to their larger companions rescue.

Grot whirled on the two and saw Dirk, casually ambling along in his usual cocky fashion excepting: "No Bollocks!!! It can't be can it? Well Keldor be praised!" Grot swore…, …Dirk was actually heading in the direction of the fight for once, though given their numerical disadvantage and lack of deadly weaponry (Grot's fists aside) his choice of fight was unwise to say the least…

"Oy Pratt…! Pull your bleeding finger out will ya? You *should* be going in that direction" He managed jabbing a finger in the direction of the Lizardman who teetered uncertainly on the crest of the steep hillside. Before Dirk could begin to answer, the two reinforcements were already upon the Dwarf. Yet Grot's unreceptive mind couldn't yet mentally grasp that several of those he had felled had simply disappeared once incapacitated.

Of the two now facing Grot, one had a sword, the other a dagger. Grot calculated their position and stepped back a few paces, ready for either one of them to strike. The dagger man reacted first, lunging forward in an attempt to gut the Dwarf, but Grot had different ideas.

Dodging to one side, he grabbed the mans outstretched arm with both hands and brought his knee up on the straightened elbow joint with some force.

Grot felt the bones shatter beneath his palms as he reversed the arms thrust and jammed the dagger up to its hilt into the poor soul's forehead, killing him instantly. This gave the second man with the sword the opportunity to strike freely at Grot, but the canny Dwarf had been expecting this. As the sword sluiced towards his body, Grot fell to the ground, narrowly missing the blades arc and it instead connected with the dead mans body, hacking him into two before he had even had time to fall to the floor.

The swordsman stared in dismay at what he had unintentionally done, but Grot was giving the horror stricken fellow no quarter, booting the chap in the balls, full force. And with hobnail boots on that hurts!

Thinking he was safe for a moment, Grot bent down to retrieve the dead mans fallen dagger and was more than a little disgruntled to feel a heavy blow to the back of his head. Stars flashed before his eyes as he whirled to find himself face to face with the newly risen bear of a man he had fought a moment ago.

"You dirty bastard of a Goblin shagger!" Grot screamed and dived at the man. The two rolled to the floor and as they reversed and countered each others wrestling submissions, another brace of arrows was fired indiscriminately at the both of them. Yet the bear got lucky while the luckless Dwarf received a hit to the right shoulder, which luckily passed straight through and one to the left hand that did not; pinning it momentarily: Long enough for the giant he wrestled with to apply a double wrist lock.

Standing on Grot's upturned back the giant fellow planted one foot on the ground and roared like a bastard as his own ample muscles strained cable like in an attempt to break the Dwarves wrists or at least pull his arms from their sockets at the shoulder.

It seemed that the human's strength would win out when suddenly he arched back in pain; the Dwarf had managed despite his pain, to back-heel his aggressor in the Cox. Instinctively the big fellah reached one hand to the pained spot and as he did Grot took advantage of his smaller size, swivelling and spinning around on the shoulder of the arm the giant still held; unlocking and reversing the wrist-lock, then flipped up onto his feet and drove upwards with his free hand: Grot's bloody fingers protruded from the man's nostrils. The Dwarf then used the lodged fingers, to give him purchase while he swung his legs around the mans shoulders, before removing his digits from the brutes bloodied nose, releasing the locked arm and instead grabbing hold of the large mans handlebar moustache, which he tore this way and that.

"Yer like that do yer bastard? Yer smelly overgrown Jabberwocky shit-mound! I'll rip your bleeding bum-fluff off for that!" Grot screamed, clearly dismayed at the hidden assault he had suffered. Six more men came running over now and behind them the rest followed suit. Grot was about to get off, when he yelped out in pain, the big man proving himself to also be adept at street fighting by nipping the inside of Grot's thigh very hard. One thing for sure was that this man was no illusion! Grot rolled off the mans back as he rose and the two faced each other on level terms once more with the rest of the small army closing fast.

Grot turned as if to run, forcing the big man to react, then he swivelled his movement and kicked at the Eyrthe sending up a spray of sod and stone as the big man charged forward covering his eyes: Sinking to one knee and pivoting on it as Grot span around, he delivered a jarring back elbow to the chasing giants kneecap. The big guy fell and Grot: By now thoroughly pissed off and angry *and* serious; lifted the menacing fellow's head by his lank, greasy hair and began systematically kicking his teeth out.

"You fat, ugly, wanna-be bastard!" Grot raged at the bloodied fellow as he continued his assault on the dazed chap's dentistry, "You ever heard the bigger they come the harder they fall? Well I've shit better than you matey…, ….Dirk! What in Keldor's name are you doing?" Grot added, noticing Dirk's odd behaviour, despite his earlier warning.

Dirk stood in the exact centre of the hill, where funnily enough nobody had bothered to attempt to apprehend him, completely ignored his presence in fact: '*The fools must think I'm surrendering,*' he thought to himself smugly, a wry smile playing upon his lips. "Well that suits me fine, because Dirk's in town; no that aint it…, …too lame, what would Zen have said? Oh I know. Something like…, …Back off people cuz Dirk is in da house!" He imitated, donning a pair of familiar looking shades.

"**Hear me now!**" Dirk bellowed out in an inhuman voice, the sound effect delivered by means of an extremely simple cantrip he had picked up from the spellbook. However: Due to the spell's effects and Dirks natural affinity to tamper with everything he shouldn't, his unnatural voice could be heard not simply for several hundred metres as he intended, but for several hundred leagues unbeknownst to him.

"**I am Dirk Heinemblud, and I order all those who wish to live to leave for their homes now! I don't wanna kill nobody but; you've been warned…, …Anyone still in my face in the next three seconds will suffer my wrath, and I aint shitting ya, you should see what I can do…, …I will murder yo pathetic asses with one simple click of my fingers, dya want me to…, …huh? *Do ya?***" The effect was quite dramatic, so much so that even Grot was stirred from the relentless bashing he was dishing out.

"**Kill him!**" One of the men shouted and several groups stopped in their pursuit of the Dwarf and began charging towards their unarmed prey!

Dirk let out a long, thoroughly evil sounding laugh before cancelling the dweomer in order to concentrate his magical energies…, "…Grot run after the others." He ordered, then added, "Oh and do it quick numb nuts!" as the Dwarf stared at him with a blank expression.

A huge wall of flame was suddenly birthed from the Eyrthe around Dirk and expanded outwards slowly. Grot gathered his senses and began legging it as fast as he could in the direction the Lizardman and Boris had taken. The Lizardman had stopped at the crest of the hill, and without warning Grot launched himself at her, toppling her and sending the two into an uncontrollable barrel roll as they plummeted down the hillside.

The growing wall of flame suddenly snapped back to a tiny fiery globe sat serenely in Dirks outstretched left palm and the remaining soldiers charged at him. "...Ky-ilkli-deevash!" Dirk cried as he flung his arm forward and the small circular ball of flame erupted into a towering inferno as it left his hand, crackling the skin and smelting the bones of all those in the vicinity. The Illusionary men had made up two thirds of the army, Dirk noted as they evaporated.

Dirk himself remained completely unscathed despite being engulfed by his own flame and as the survivors, who had been at the blasts edge ran hurtling down the hill as fast as their legs would carry them, Dirk strolled away calmly to the northern ridge.

Screams ripped the night air in two, as the moon dripped blood.

Dirk jumped in panic as his mind again swam..., '...*Another bloody vision!*' He wondered briefly if he had been slipped some drug in the night; then stopped in his tracks as some fearsome apparition appeared in front of him. "Are you real?" He wondered aloud and reached forward a hand to touch the gruesome looking fellow draped in black. It looked human, though its flaky, grey skin was stretched tightly over its skull and long carnivorous fangs protruded from the mouth. The eye sockets, though empty at first, suddenly flared with a silvery light as it spoke.

"Dirk of the blood..., ...Your demise shall sweeten the hatred that dwells in your heart. A dark future awaits your presence in the halls below. Know this - if you do enter the catacombs, you will not leave alive. I have foreseen your doom, for I am death cometh. Do not venture downwards lest you lose your precious life ahead of time." The apparition's words echoed as if being spoken in some vast cavernous space.

Dirk blinked and rubbed at his eyes, he had tugged the things sleeve, so it had definitely been real, but as the echoed words faded, so too did the apparition. He stood there for several moments, more than a little afraid as he digested the things words and appearance. The birds had stopped singing and dark clouds were gathering overhead. A distant rumble of thunder foretold of troubled times. Another person may have interpreted this turn of events as a bad omen of things to come. Yet to Dirk, who had just won the day in style so it seemed and was therefore far from unhappy; thought it was probably just down to the unpredictable climate of the region. Even when a thunderbolt arched down from the heavens to scorch the Eyrthe where he had just been stood and a foul smelling wind assaulted the Hilltop, dragging with it scorched body parts and dead plants, Dirk wasn't phased and continued ambling over to the hills northern edge with

309

something of a spring in his step. "Shit to it!" Dirk laughed aloud: "Who says I'm going down any smelly cave anyways?" He challenged as he sprang over the edge without any thought of looking to check for land on the other side.

Another lightning bolt; this time rather more lateral than the one that had struck the ground just managed to frizz a few hairs on Dirk's head as he did indeed discover terra firma beyond the hills ridge; though some six feet down. The fall hurt him a little and normally he would have at least sulked if not cried for a few minutes, but now didn't seem the right time; someone was hurling lightning at him. '*That'll be the spell caster from before of course! The bugger responsible for the illusions...*' He could see the others untangling themselves and waving up at him from their position at the base of the hill but as he plodded towards them a sound from behind stopped him.

Dirk's single arched eyebrow and quivering lip stated he was ready for a showdown as he turned to face the stave wielding magician; a man whose robes were a filthy mixture of fell colorants, his hair long, frizzled and matted and a face that bore more than a passing resemblance to something Dirk ate last night...

"I will have my revenge Dirk Heinemblud..." The wizard snarled.

"Oh!" Dirk was genuinely surprised: "Don't ya mean Dirk of the blood or something silly like that, a few people have been calling me that lately..."

"I know nothing of the whims of others fool..., ...can you not see the foulness that haunts me...? That vexes my soul?"

"Well yeah, ya could do with a bath and an all over shave for sure." Dirk conceded.

"Bah!" The indeed foul mage cried, "I am this way because of you!" He stated throwing back his hood to reveal a bald pink dome atop his head. "I was paid to aid the commander and his soldiers; no more. But when I heard your mighty proclamation; still cocky as ever: yet still the impotent Heinemblud. Well, say your last words because I am here to end your life!"

Dirk lay in the pit of fear once more, but again his newfound confidence urged him on; 'Get up, stand up tall, proud, that's right; think! If you reduced this man to the shallow figure he is now when you were as bad as you were then, well, let him try…'

"Okay mate listen…" Dirk began but the wizard unleashed a lightning bolt straight for him. Dirk deftly stepped to the side and caught the electrical blue bolt between two fingers, chopstick style, then sat back and began to imitate smoking the rapidly dissolving bolt. "Illusion's don't really cut it with me mate, ya may wanted to try something a little more subs- aah ya sod, that hurt!"

The wizard hit him with his staff again. "Stop it or else!" Dirk threatened but the smelly chap was having none of it bashing him again. "Right that's it!" Dirk said jumping backwards and blowing a little dust towards his target shouting…, "…Ky-ilkli dee mor vash-obbre!"

As Dirk landed, his trajectory spiralled him head over heels down the hillside and he didn't even get to see his resulting spell go off, but his friends already at the bottom did, as an orb of fire first surrounded the odorous mage then imploded; incinerating both him *and* his smelly clothing.

By the time Dirk had tumbled to the hill's base, a little bruised but otherwise unhurt, he was pleased to see both Grot and Boris alive and well. Grot was helping the Snake-woman remove the arrow from her tail, while Boris was playfully swinging on the limb of a long dead tree.

Dirk did a double take; the Halfling had been hit right between the shoulder blades, yet was swinging with the enthusiasm of a nipper. "The arrow stuck in my sandwich box." The appreciative Halfling offered as way of an explanation for the massive arrow protruding from his back.

"What was that?" Grot asked of Dirk pointing to the hills summit and referring to the spell he had just witnessed.

"Oh! That's a fireball of course. It's what I practised the other day, when I got bored with the camping spell; which kept making an even worse fire anyways…" Dirk flashed a smile from ear to ear, "Of course, you normally wouldn't be able to cast it so close, see it expands to quite some size when cast outdoors, but as I don't seem to be affected by heat any more I just thought: What the heck?"

Grot seemed less than impressed with Dirk's timing as usual. "So yer didn't think of using it against Zen or the priest did ya not? Nor when those buggers back there were charging up the hill?"

Dirk could tell the Dwarves temper would not hold for much longer, so he quickly jotted out a hopefully comprehensible reason for his actions… "Well I didn't know I knew it at first; I knew I could botch up the camping spell, but didn't know how, and besides I sort of did use it in the town. But the fireball spell just came to me when I was stood there thinking about it. I used a bit of illusionary magic see, to combine with the missing bits of: Well; to *make* the fireball, I can't really explain it, I can just do it!"

Grot scrutinised his growing number of companions for a moment, as he and the female Lizardman bandaged each others wounds, then nodded his approval to Dirk. "Fair enough; we'll talk about things later no doubt. Right now, I wanna get as much space between us and them buggers in that town as soon as possible. Let's head for 'the gap'." The 'gap' Grot referred to was the canyon that wound its rocky path between the mountains and on to the fabled City of Lorellien and it was towards these craggy heights that the companions pushed towards, as they made haste away from the town of Devils Gap. A few hours after nightfall, the four made camp, keeping their fire small, yet staying out in the open, less they get trapped in the recess of one of the many caves that pocked the walls of the canyon below to the west.

Grot sat keeping watch some thirty feet from the campfire, less the firelight interfere with his infra-vision and it was he that first broke the silence that had fallen; shortly after they had consumed a splendid mutton soup specially prepared by Boris.

"So, what happened to you last night then? The little guy says you went off with a Dark Elf…" Grot called over from his perch on an eastern overhang.

Dirk coughed down his last piece of cinnamon bread before he could make his scornful reply. "Yeah right…! …I copped off. This sweet little farmer's daughter, whose old man had gone away somewhere, didn't catch where. She was quite something I'll tell you. After a few hours, it was her swinging me around the bedroom. Women! They just can't resist me…"

The Dwarf grunted in derision; "And her mother…?"

Dirk shot back a cheeky smile, "A bit *too* fat! Even for me… Put it this way her tits hung lower than a Dragon's bollocks!"

A polite hiss brought Dirk to his senses and he blushed as he not only remembered but could also physically see that the Lizard-cum-Snakeman was actually a woman.

"Here!" he said, after removing the shirt he wore beneath his flimsy robe. "It smells a bit, but it's silk!" he added, tossing the shirt to the woman who gratefully donned the newly acquired sweaty garment. It fit her torso quite well considering, '*so body wise she's about the same size as lanky legs there...*' Grot pondered for he liked to know where he stood with people; height wise that is.

"Well I don't know whether to slap yer or not now; I promised master Caitlyn I would give yer arse a good hiding if you'd deflowered his missus, but soon as it were his missus' daughter. Well I can't moan at yer for bedding another woman now can I?" Grot calculated then grabbing a thought added, "*She* weren't married was she?"

Dirk laughed at the thought..., "...I doubt it matey; for starters she was tight like a virgin and barely fourteen or fifteen years at that!"

"Yer big long streak of... Yer know yer must be sick. You'll turn down a woman who's got enough weight to keep yer both warm in winters grip, but you'll gladly bed her no doubt skinny assed daughter who's little more than a child..." The Dwarf chided.

"Hey hold on a minute!" Dirk objected. "She may have been tight like a virgin but she was definitely no child. She rode me like a thoroughbred, up and down quicker than a bunny and her rack, well let's say momma weren't the only one with huge tit's, besides which she rode me that hard all night I only am now realising I have got a terrific itch along me man-meat; she may have been fourteen or less for all I care but she knew exactly how to please a man and how she wanted a man to pleasure her-" He stopped embarrassed at realising yet again what he was discussing and in front of what company..., "...Sorry Miss..." He added.

The Dwarf shook his head and spat at the ground in front of Dirk. "So what's this about the Elf then?" Grot persisted.

"Huh? What Elf are you going on about? I don't know any Elf, Dark or otherwise!" Dirk retorted a little too defensively.

An explanation ensued, wherein Boris acted out the actions of the Elf in his telling of the story which was constantly challenged by both Dirk and Grot and changed more often than the wind as numerous embellishments were both added and retracted at an alarming rate. Grot argued that the Halfling had probably had one too many beers, whereas Dirk simply denied all knowledge of the incident.

313

"I think I would know what I *did* and *didn't* do better than some halfwit Halfling!" Dirk blurted; finally unable to control his rising anger at what he now took to be an affront to his honesty and integrity, even if he normally had none.

Grot reacted in defence of Boris: "Well I remember Perky Springs, in fact if I remember; you had a brush with a Dark Elven type as far back as Felbric's gaff, so what's going on Dirk-boy, what are yer not telling us?"

The scaled newcomer; who had sat in silence all the while, brought the rising argument's crescendo to a crumpling close by picking up a small stick and weaving it around in front of Dirk's face.

"That's it! It was just like that!" Boris enthused as the Lizardman played the stick along her fingers and twirled the pretend dagger end upon imagined end repeatedly. "That's it! That is it I tell you!!! How did you know?" Boris asked in wonder gulping down some Fennel stew.

"It iss an old underworld craft, ssimilar to hypnossiss; your friend here will remember nothing! It iss taught to a very sselect few." She said, and the companions were momentarily stunned into silence by the revelation.

"So how come you know it?" Boris asked brightly.

"The Fein-Lueish were amongsst my mentorss as a child." She said simply, not realising that further explanation was needed.

Dirk looked at the strange woman with a stare that clearly indicated to all but the blind, that he had no idea who or what the Fein-Lueish were or did, let alone what they had to do with dagger tricks...

"The Fein are a rasce of Dark Elf, the Lueish are highly trained asssassinss hand picked from amongsst their elite. One of them wass a mentor of mine; for a time..." She paused, unwilling to reveal too much of her past so soon.

Each of them spoke at once, wanting answers to their own particular questions, but the scaled woman fended them off with a gesture. "All that I am willing to tell you iss that I wass once an esstablisshed member of my clan. Now I have no-one, I am an outcasst, you would ssay. I wass taught in sseveral artss, including the common tongue ussed by humanss and other land dwelling racess. I pose no threat to any of you. Thiss I can asssure you."

314

"*How*: I mean how can we be sure?" Grot questioned from his perch.

"What do you eat where you come from?" piped up the Halfling.

"Why did you address me as Dirk of the Blood up on the hill?" Dirk probed immediately silencing the other two out of curiosity.

"When...?" Grot asked.

"When we found her matey, but not out loud; she was in my head; someone else also called me by the title, a few people..., ...I just wondered why...?"

The Lizardman looked a little bemused herself and studied Dirk carefully before answering. "I admit to knowing you by that name, though in truth, this iss the firsst time that I have sspoken to you. You musst... be misstaken. I have no mental powers ass ssuch!"

Now it was Dirks turn to look bewildered: "You lying bitch! I heard you clear as day; when we were cutting ya down ya said, 'I have found you Dirk of the Blood': Deny it if ya bloody dare!!!"

The Lizardman hissed an angry curse, while she struggled to keep her temper. "Do Not! *Ever* pressume to *quesstion* my integrity *Dirk of the Blood*, for thiss onsce I sshall let it passs. But know now I do not give my wordss lightly;" here she paused to collect her thoughts and calm herself: "I think I did think thosse wordss when firsst I ssaw you, but I did not – could not, utter them aloud!"

Dirk digested the explanation, as well as the threat and decided that her word was probably worth ten of his own. "Okay, I apologise, things have just been a little freaky around me lately: Anyway sod it!"

"So you can read thoughts, eh buddy?" Grot jeered, "Well what am I thinking right now? And I'll give you a clue, it aint pleasant!"

Dirk stood and walked a few feet towards his Dwarven friend, "Grot, I never said I could read minds, I just..." Dirk stopped himself, he had a funny feeling the Dwarf was imagining drowning him in a huge bowl of Giants piss, he changed tack..., "...Grot I *am* sorry about –I mean *for* Zen; *and* for leaving you back there in the town, to be honest I don't even remember most of the night, because I was piss-eyed from the fumes alone. So okay I went off and dipped my wick without telling you... Fair enough, I shouldn't have, and yes, I apologise for *all* the *really bad shit* that happened *to you* in the tower, and right now I admit; I'm *more* than a little screwed up *myself*: Hearing voices of people who aren't talking and having strange visions of ugly dead dudes who aint even there, and the old wizard that died in the tower keeps making me feel bad; like I gotta be a better person and I cannot begin to tell ya how much *that* is stressing me out... Back up on the hill, I had some guy fresh from the grave telling me I'm gonna die and now this..., ...Snake-Lizard woman thing, knows my name and some nutter of a hairy Halfling is telling me I've been kidnapped by some knife wielding Elf, that no-one else can seem to remember. I tell ya, when shit falls on me– It's a Behemoth doing the crapping!"

Everyone was momentarily silent, each lost in their own thoughts and opinions over Dirk's unsolicited outburst, then Grot blurted out a simple, "How did you know that?" stunning everyone back from their reverie.

"What?" Dirk said, utterly confused.

"Well while yer were yapping on I was thinking..." Grot began: "Not that I was ignoring yer or not gonna listen or anything but I just started thinking it and then you said it..., ...When shit falls... Yer did it to me! *You* read *my* mind!"

Dirk span back on his heel, turning his back on the Dwarf and addressing Boris: "Next thing *you'll* be telling me ya were *just wondering* if they grew their own *carrots* **underground**..." His tone dripped with seething sarcasm and yet Boris could only blink his bushy lidded eyes in amazement several seconds more...

"That's amazing..., ...How did: Do they?" Boris trailed off in amazement.

"How the hell should I know?" Dirk objected. "This is too weird! I am gonna have a kip!"

Grot scrambled over to join the others, hastily stamping out the fire as he did so: "I'm afraid there's no time for that Dirk me mind reading mate."

"A bloody big Gobbo patrol's heading this way I know..."

"Stop it will yer!" Grot moaned then put a hand out in reconciliation: "Are yer really sorry about Zen?"

"I've got one of his eyes haven't I? Do you really think I'll ever forget him?" Dirk said with a quick handshake and a wink from his working orb.

"Good enough for me!" Grot enthused and hugged his friend proudly, "You're a bloody nutter but you're also the best friend I ever had on this bloody Eyrthe. I don't suppose yer can read them Gobbo's thoughts too eh?"

Dirk shrugged his denial, "I guess they're probably just patrolling like you say. We could probably lay low here and hope they pass us by!"

Grot shook his head, dismissing the possibility, "They're heading this way, and there's quite a few bugbears amongst them. I don't know about you, but I'm in no shape to fight, and I doubt the Lizardman can help much in her state. That leaves yer self and the Halfling to save our necks and no offence, but I'd sooner be guarded by a batch of headless chickens than trust my life to your two's fighting skills: Unless you've got another fireball up your sleeve; have yer?"

Again Dirk shrugged in non-committal fashion. "Sorry, I've been trying my best to learn that single one for the last few days..., ...Mind you I *do have* a *camping spell*..., ...So what's ya plan - or maybe the Lizardman has got something in mind?"

All three cast their eyes towards their latest companion in hope. She studied them in return, not sure what they expected of her.

"Hey!" Boris suddenly piped up, "I been meaning to ask, what's your name? I mean, everyone has a name right?"

"Boris, this isn't the time to be exchanging pleasantries and titles..." Grot berated the inquisitive Halfling.

The Lizardman looked from one to the other, whilst an internal debate raged within her; if she was to fulfil the prophecy then she would have to entrust her life to this Dirk of the Blood sometime, and though she had not foreseen the need to entrust anyone other than he, these people were obviously friends of his and so must be taken into consideration. People of her race had a problem with trust, almost every meal would be poisoned in some way, every secret shared, embellished and re-whispered a thousand times, and those that one allowed to come close, almost invariably ended up betraying you for their own ends as circumstances dictate.

However, she calculated, the Dwarf was a proud if somewhat belligerent being, whose core values seemed to be more in line with her own than most 'friends' she had known; and the Halflings meal had been unlike anything she had ever tasted, moreover was unmarked with even the slightest traces of poison. In fact, the one of these three she trusted least was the person whom she needed to trust the most. Getting to her feet she came to a decision.

"My name iss Sf-vil U'hl Qoua, former Princesss of the U'hl-Qoua, one time holder of the twin swordss of K'lsh, and both sslave and masster to the ancient sscrollss, I am charged with fullfilling my peopless prophecy pertaining to a nation to which I no longer belong. I onsse sstood for Honour, but now my own Honour hass been taken in a mosst vile and hurtful manner and sso I must work to find a new honour and purposse: For now, I sstand before you, a lowly Qoua and wissh to be addresssed ass the miserable being that I have become. If you will allow me, thiss one humbly asskss your acceptance and pledge to sshow loyalty while in your company..." She stated sinking to one knee; head bowed awaiting their collective answer.

"...Qoua?" Dirk chuckled, "What the Hell's a: Qoua..., ...A duck with a speech-"

"...Dirk!" Grot barked, "Know when not to be heard, by all the gods!" Grot went over and placed his hand on the shoulder of the bowing female. "We accept yer fer now U'hl-Qoua, but be warned, I'll brook no treachery from no bugger; be it from a Halfling, Gnome or Lizardman!"

Sf-vil slowly rose; her head still bowed as was proper in her own culture, so as not to look in the eyes of ones better..., ...However the Dwarves diminutive height made a mockery of the gesture. "I apologisse Grot, but would you pleasse addresss this one ass Qoua?"

She gave up diverting her gaze then, having noticed that the others attempted to maintain eye contact during their own conversations so far: Instead she looked the Dwarf directly in the eye when next she spoke. "I mean no challenge to your authority but my former name; no longer hass meaning: I am dishonoured and in my own ssociety one iss nothing without honour..., ...Less than nothing, therefore I am now Qoua; in your tongue you would call me Lizardman without anything or *of nothing*..., Oh and pleasse do not keep confussing thiss one with the treacherouss Ssnakemen of the ssouthern regionss or thosse that live in the easst - mine iss the original clan of the race of L-iezsh'mat or in your tongue - Lizardman. You call uss this I pressume becausse men in your own racess tend to hold the possitionss of power no? Unlike my own: We have no sseparate word for our maless and femaless all are ssimply Qoua of different denominationss; such as U'hl-Qoua or Ng'iujl-Qoua."

"Okay no probs - you wanna just be Qoua, that's fine by me; an I doubt Stunty bollocks over there won't because his name means something similar funnily enough," Dirk enthused, "Now what about finding some friggin cover? That is, unless the patrol has decided to stop patrolling and go back home instead..." he added with more than a touch of sarcasm.

Grot scowled back at his irksome pal while running back over to his belongings; adding to Qoua; "Yeah well, let's just say Honour is the same were *I* come from at least, so we'll get moving like skinny boy here says!"

Qoua pointed off to the shadowy recess of some rocks. "I ssuggesst, we find refuge in one of the deeper cavess over there..., ...If we find an Ambull warren any passsing patrol will not dare follow, whether they have picked up our sscent or not?"

"Good enough for me!" Grot said, hoisting up what was left of his belongings, "it's been a while since I've gone up against one of those buggers; and I'll be hoping it's a while longer all the same but I like yer plan! Like something I myself would come up with..." he said setting off with Qoua in tow, leaving Dirk and Boris to play catch up.

"Yeah..., ...okay let's go into the damp, dark, bloody mysterious cave, I mean why not: What the hell is an Ambull anyway? Oh and why bushy little Boris do you suppose the Gobbos' wouldn't dare follow us pray tell? Let's see, erm..., ...Ooh, ooh I think I've got it: Could it be because they're bloody well dangerous maybe?" No one replied; instead trudging silently over to the collection of caves with as much haste as they dared. Dirk briefly contemplated taking his chances out here despite the others.

"Maybe the patrol will pass me by?" He wondered aloud..., "...in fact I would say hiding in the shadow of these rocks would be very possible for my skinny arse," he paused then as he caught sight of a multitude of flickering torches moving in procession and reluctantly found himself gravitating towards the safety of the caves and his companions.

He was about to shout out to Grot: "Okay but we come out as soon as they're gone!" Then thought of Grots earlier spoken advice; "Know when not to be heard...," ...and decided not to bother. Instead he scrabbled amongst the rocks, moving as fast as he could, all the while thinking of a certain grey faced visions warning...

"Do not venture downwards lest you lose your precious life ahead of time…"

XIV) **Gloom to Doom**

The four exhausted companions may have formed a distressing sight to anyone who cared for their welfare. The haggard expressions that haunted each of their faces and the way they walked in a melange of stilted, shambling motions, may have shown the fatigue that was now clearly taking its toll on the four, as they meandered down a gently sloping tunnel so tight that they were forced to walk single file. Grot had took the lead, his keen infra-vision absorbing what meagre light the gloomy tunnels interior lent; filtering an octal-toned mirage over his normally colour filled sight; still this limited viewing version served him well enough for him to see comfortably. Behind him came Qoua, hunched over in order to fit within the tunnels confines, her steps were laboured and she more so than the others looked to be moving by will alone, despite being able to see best of all four of them. Boris the Halfling came next, blindly stumbling over the various rocky outcrops that decked the tunnel floor. The Halfling had a somewhat limited night-vision, but down here, without much natural light source; he could see no further than the end of his hand. Last in line was the jumpy form of Dirk, continually looking back over his shoulder, lest some unknown creature may come sneaking up behind him and smite him from behind; though he wouldn't have been able to see any given monster, smiting or otherwise, even if it had kissed and fondled him first.

As the tunnel deepened and narrowed further Grot stopped to fish a thin rope from his pack, Qoua noticed and stopped short and even Boris's outstretched hand stopped just short of fondling the Lizard ones buttocks. Dirk however came bumbling over looking the opposite way, tripped over Boris and fell headlong towards Qua who wheeled away, tripping over the bent over Dwarf in turn. With many an 'oops' and 'sorry' the companions rose one by one to be greeted by a pissed off noose holding Grot, "time to tie you bastard's up I reckon…"

All four had then tied themselves together for both safety and to avoid those with limited sight; namely Boris and Dirk, from getting lost. The latter however had discovered a smug little secret…, …Down here, in a rocky tunnel whose clammy walls suggested a nearby water source, this gently sloping, winding passage that in all probability, led to the very bowels of hell, in this hellhole that neither sun nor moon had ever visited, Dirk discovered that he could actually see, well *sort* of…

As Dirk had been dragged along by his bound companions, bumping off the walls of the tunnel and tripping every few feet, the dressing covering his newly acquired two day old eye had become loose and with it his new gift of sight was unveiled in glorious Technicolor: It happened while leaping a small blind fissure, Grot had instructed him to jump forward while the others pulled but the Dwarf had not figured on weight to strength ratio and Dirk had been fair flung down the passage much to his bitter annoyance…

…Dragging himself back to his feet, Dirk had fumbled about for the bandage that had fell to some innocuous spot on the tunnels floor, when the companions began moving again without waiting; the rope going taught and dragging him onward against his will. He lurched forward, arms outstretched in fear of falling, but when his hands came into contact with another creature his eyes opened wide in shock. It was then that he realised that he could see, and the creature before him was none other than Boris, who jumped himself at the unexpected touch.

Dirk stared incredulously at Boris's strange appearance, then realised what was wrong. He closed his 'good' eye, and the eye he had 'borrowed' from Zen suddenly flared into life. A whole new world of vision opened up to Dirk, and a stupid grin played across his face as he took stock of what the new eye could see. The Halfling before him appeared in a pastel green shade, yet Boris's backpack and several other accoutrements appeared as a ghostly white, yet better than this, Dirk could also make out each bead of sweat on the Halfling's exposed neck - each droplet encased in a halo of luminescent violet light. He looked about at the cave and again found that he could see every detail perfectly stretched out in a multitude of coloured veins. Yet as the scope of his gaze lengthened, Dirk's eye produced some sort of oil and his vision was flooded with red. He blinked away the bloody substance and though some of the red drained away, his vision remained primarily filled by that colour enabling him to see well into the distance as his lens zoomed along the detailed caves interior: His eye wandering in this fashion for some time as he picked out the various colours and features of the normally unremarkable cave tunnel: That is until alighting upon some fractures running at intervals but gaining in regularity the deeper they progressed.

"What are those claw marks in the walls Qoua? Please tell me they aint an Ambull's?" Dirk said in reference to the long gouge marks that criss-crossed the tunnels circumference for what seemed its entire length.

"The what?" growled Grot, a little too loud for comfort, "how can you possibly know there are claw marks –you're just being paranoid- as usual, and besides, if there were claw marks here, don't you think I'd have seen em and warned yer about them?"

Dirk shook his head, "not necessarily…"

Qoua cleared her throat, "I concur to both of you, I too can ssee no ssignss of any markss, though I would not be ssurprissed. Thiss tunnel hass been carved from the rock by such a creature after all."

"See this is what I was on about - I tried asking out there, what these bloody Ambull's were but did I get a reply; oh no! Instead, I come trudging in here, blind as a bat, without any idea what might wanna to eat us when we get down here!" Dirk protested, a slight panic creeping into his voice.

"Will you stop your bleeding whimpering?" Grot's barked suggestion echoed out around the cave walls, "For Keldor's sake, this tunnel is small aint it? So whatever made it is also gonna be small - and if we meet *it*, we'll kill *it*!"

"And eat it?" ventured Boris, whose stomach was beginning to rumble.

Dirk grumbled in half tones about so-called 'cocky' dwarves, getting their possible come-uppance if they do come across the tremendous beast that dug out this bottomless cess pit…, …Unfortunately for Dirk his newfound vision didn't bring with it newfound sense and his half mumbled words echoed down to the Dwarf at the front.

"Right you backstabbing lanky streak of Dragon piss!" Grot raged and turned back down the tunnel towards Dirk.

Luckily, the tunnel was too narrow for the Dwarf to pass by Qoua, who in any case stood firm, her arms outstretched to placate the fuming Dwarf. "Forgive hiss unwisse wordss, proud Grot. He sspeakss out of fear of the unknown, I am possitive he meanss you no harm. Bessidess, the Ambullss are indeed much larger than you give them credit. Do you know how they excavate their warrens?"

Grot nodded: "Course I do; Ambull's huddle into a tight ball to use their back legs better. Dirk on the other hand tends to huddle into a tight ball for many other reasons. Got taught that shit in school so what of it?"

"Becausse in their lairss, they are much freer to manoeuvre than we and if I had to guesss at the height of the oness ressponssible for thesse caves, I would ssay they are around twelve feet or more in height."

"Yeah, but?" Grot started then switched to Dirk who was pulling faces, "I'll rip yer ears off an nail em to yer testicles, yer big anaemic pile of shite!"

"...Ya reckon fatso-Stunty-man? Bring it on!" Dirk taunted.

Boris decided to throw in his own two penny's worth: "Look; will everyone please just calm down a moment. Granny always said; it's not worth talking to a panicked head..., ...Now I know one thing: *I* can't see a thing, and **I** do not want to be stuck down here arguing when we're trapped between a stinking Goblin patrol and this nasty sounding Ambull thing; does it eat Halflings by the way Qoua?"

"Goblinss eat Halfling yet you need not fear little one, the Goblinss would not dare follow into an Ambull warren..." The Lizard placated.

"Ha! See, *she admitted it again*! Those so-called *stupid* Orcs' and Gobbos' are *far too* intelligent to walk into a death trap, scum sucking pit like this...," ...Dirk moaned belligerently.

"They are not intelligent merely afraid..." Qoua responded.

Boris sounded way too chirpy as he piped up with: "Wow I never realised Orcs were afraid of anything; why my dear granny used to say..."

"Hold on! If bony bollocks here is right to have a whinge then why for all that's holy, have you led us in here? Some sort of trap is it? I warned you..." Grot growled, turning his angered attention to Qoua.

Qoua pleaded for quiet before she spoke again; eager to end the argument that now embroiled them all.

"Pleasse, all of you, be calm and lissten to thiss one. The reasson the Goblinss will not follow iss becausse they are indeed sscared of thiss beasst, but they do not know how to read the signss. The lack of debris within the tunnel indicatess that *thiss* warren hass been exscavated a long time ssince. Although I cannot guarantee that we will not meet with one of the beaststss, I do inssisst that it *iss* mosst unlikely. I gave you all my pledge and in doing sso I gave you the lasst of my honour; my word: I sspeak in truth!"

"So the tunnel is safe?" Boris inquired.

"Yess. I believe sso." Qoua replied.

"Fine!" Grot retorted. "I will take yer at yer word for now lady but as for *you*, yer friggin beanpole, any more comments about me getting chewed up an' I'll be cutting *YOU* down to size the first chance I get!"

Dirk, rather wisely, remained silent. So downwards they trudged into the deepening gloom..., ...and a possible appointment with death...

***

Captain Haggryd bent down to one knee, in order to light the decorative pipe he had plundered from an inauspicious group of Halflings, whom he and his band had happened across earlier that week. The embers of the small campfire had all but diminished and so he coaxed a small flame with the gentleness a father would show for his newborn son. When his pipe was lit, he stood and took a long pull of the pipe while gauging the surrounding rocks.

"Stoke that fire! We'll camp here!" He barked, then despatched the obligatory cuff that was called for when dealing with Goblin underlings.

"...Corag!" The commander's voice snapped again. A large, well armoured Black Orc came rushing to attention at the mention of his name.

"...Ready sir!" The summoned Corag nodded his head in an informal salute that betrayed his close friendship for the officer before him.

"Put a couple of your best beaky-eyed troops on that outcrop, tell the cooks to get busy, then come and join me by the fire for a jar." Haggryd said dismissively, before dropping to his backside by the fire that was hastily being rebuilt.

Humans had been here, he could tell - or at least one human, it was hard to tell given the size of prints and weight of the impression but he knew it was most likely a Dwarf and a Human, though he did not discount the possibility of an Elf presence either. From the tracks he *had* discovered, he could tell some other creature was also with them - although of what nature he could not discern excepting to say it had a tail. However the fourth race present was known only too well to Haggryd; down to three facts that other less enlightened beings may not be aware..., ...Firstly, the foot size of the fourth party member was noticeably softer and smaller, secondly the rockery encircling and crossing the fire had been 'tidied' into a multi-hob design favoured almost exclusively by Halflings, and thirdly the cooking aromas still hung clammily in the air hinting at Rosemary, Cinnamon and most importantly of all: Fennel; a herb cultivated for

325

culinary use solely by the race of little folk. Even while they were down below the ridge and he had first spotted the fire that led them to this spot, his nose had picked out the subtle aromas of a Halfling stew of some sort and his nose had led him here.

Corag dropped down beside Haggryd; his rotten tusked jaw forming a grotesque smirk as he uncorked a rather potent bottle of liquid. "So what's crack? Corag not see nothing: No Halfling for Haggryd belly-pot here..!" He roared with laughter at the last comment, only stopping when his Captain snatched the bottle of spirits from his arms and swigged at the contents.

"Corag not mean no bother! Plenty meat here Golly gosh. You eat Snurch. Or maybe Corag chop-shop Buggy-Bear. Who care? Not Corag, me; you? We start war. Eat all things; Half or full! Me swig now, you get fatty fat, drink too much; talk too much." Corag finished by snatching back the bottle from his commanding officer and friend.

One of the Orc troopers tripped over the outstretched legs of Haggryd as he passed by. The Orc cursed and began to walk off but Haggryd was stood upright in a second, he put his hand on the Orcs shoulder, spinning him around and snarled at him. The Orc snarled back and then turned to leave once again. This time there was no restraining hand from Haggryd. Instead, he delivered a shocking blow to the back of the departing Orcs head, shattering the bottle with which he struck. The Orc turned, its eyes glaring with contempt as it considered responding with its own attack. Haggryd though was in no mood to give the insolent trooper a chance. His free hand flew out and gripped the offending Orc by its thick neck pulling it closer towards him, while the hand still clutching the bottle shards drove his mitt forwards, cutting tight circles in the trooper's soon shredded facial aperture.

Two minutes after the mangled Orc had ceased in its struggle for life, Haggryd finally dropped what was left of the worn down bottle and with it, the quite literally defaced Orc's carcass. "Fry his remains; feed him to the bugbears!" Haggryd bellowed and plumped back down to Eyrthe.

Corag went to order some grunts to supply more spirits, leaving Haggryd time alone as he washed away some of the blood drenching him in its whiffy tackiness. Haggryd hated himself for what he had just done. It wasn't really his way: It was the *Orcish* way, and he was technically thought of as half-Orc, though strictly speaking he wasn't half anything. His mother was a half-Ogre mixed with Human: His father; a cross between a Hobgoblin and a Black Orc with some part Elven ancestry. So how his Human side remained so prominent and why he still clung to it confused him no end. A lot of the time one military life served as well as another, without much difference as to day to day running, camaraderie, etc..., ...It was merely a case of Goblin kin rules of conduct being rather more belligerent than that of most other races.

Haggryd thought back to his days as a foot scout as he removed his vest and leggings and handed them to a scurrying Snurch with orders to be quick about it..., ...In the human army of the glorious empire an officer would be court-martialled for acting as he had just: Yet here in this largely Goblin force, the absence of such an act would see him dead the next night at the very latest and by any means thinkable.

Those days had been the best in his life. As a boy; growing up with distinctly Humanoid features in the midst of a Goblin stronghold, he had been picked on and bullied by everyone who cared to do so, be they child or adult; which meant the majority of the strongholds inhabitants. By the age of six he was so weakened from the constant beatings, that his life was held by an inch of fates thread. His mother, who dearly loved him, stole him away one night and took him off into the wilderness, leaving behind his brutal father and all the other members of Orc-kind who shunned him and her for looking so alike their enemy.

His mother carried the sickly young Haggryd for many leagues, before finally collapsing in a shallow hedge on the fringes of a great forest. That night, wolves came and devoured his weakened mother while he slept, yet they showed no interest in him; so much was he enshrouded in the stench of death. In the morning he had awoke to the horrible discovery of his own mother's mutilated half-devoured corpse but was too weak to move under his own volition. He had lay there for days, a scared witless child, lost and alone, yet hoping that some creature may happen along and put him out of his misery: He had not even the strength to bury his mothers ravaged body parts..., ...The days did pass though and after almost two weeks with neither food nor water, hunger took over and he was forced to eat what was left of his mother's rotting flesh in order to survive. More days passed, during which he was haunted by nightmares both during sleep and whilst awake, until eventually a human tinker happened across him in his depreciated state, and took pity on the boy Haggryd, enthusing him from the thicket and offering him the succour of his wagons tiny interior.

The tinker it turned out; was a seemingly kindly old man who travelled the empire in his solitary wagon, never stopping in one place too long: Mending this and that and entertaining children wherever the road led. Unaware of Haggryd's origins the tinker he came to know simply as Nick, nursed him back to health, and as the years passed, Haggryd learned to speak the common tongue better thanks to the man he came to know as his Human father - though he never forgot the beatings, his mother's liberating demise, and his *true* heritage.

They passed throughout the land, mending pots, pans, shoes and all sorts of broken things, wherever their travel took them. Most often, they would visit small Halfling hamlets, and it was while visiting Hamlets such as these; Haggryd came to know the race, and gain a liking for their pot-bellied flesh: Though that is another story in itself. As mentioned Nick had seemed a kindly old tinker, but the truth was the solitary life was not self imposed.

Nick was also a small time crook, a scam artist and worst of all a paedophile who took great pleasure in abusing the children he 'cared' for on a mental, physical and sexual basis in equal measure…, …Haggryd being alone with the pervert for longer periods than others was systematically abused night after day, yet Haggryd who had only ever known hate to this point, took the old man's admonishments to be truth and thus when gently chided with whispers of: "Don't cry: It only hurts because we love each other so much…" He had took it to be truth, then one rare day spent alone with another child; he was ten at the time, led to disaster from which he came to know his 'father' for what he was and which similarly led to said fathers downfall. Haggryd had attempted to instigate anal intercourse with the other; a teenager, when apprehended by the father of the offended party. A severe scolding and brief investigation into the child Haggryd's reasoning in the matter and it became obvious who the true culprit was.

Haggryd however, still hurt and confused escaped his warden and went to warn the tinker before the others reached him. Nick was no fool and he beat a hasty retreat, dragging along poor Haggryd, who went on to abuse him with far more revile, thanks to his refugee state. By the time Haggryd had reached his thirteenth birthday, the tinker he had come to know as father passed away, thanks to contracting the pox from Haggryd, who had himself been afflicted with the disease at age twelve: Nick had loaned the boy out to some whorehouse madam as a manservant in exchange for several nights respite. Free of the beatings and sexual abuse Haggryd had proved himself an excellent worker in the eyes of the madam and she had rewarded him with a visit with one of her consorts, who in turn had rewarded Haggryd with the venereal disease, who in turn again had reciprocated with Nick.

So the tinker; not made of as stern stuff as Haggryd passed away, and as there were no known family or will left behind, all his possessions fell to Haggryd..., ...Knowing no other life he continued the business, albeit in a far less sleazy manner for a further four years. As time passed by though and those plump innocent looks gave way to brawn, complete with jutting forehead and a strong thrusting jaw and due to his slightly animalistic looks, villagers were slow to trust him until business became almost none existent.

The final blow came while drinking in a roadside tavern, he was cheated of both his money and wagon and all the goods it had held were stolen during the night. He had nowhere to go and no means of living, but the barkeep if not rich; was an understanding sort and hired him as a stable-boy, in return for his arduous labours, he had been rewarded with gruel and a place in the hayloft above the stables.

Haggryd lived this life for some six weeks further, until an army came passing by. They had a need of more men and the pay was good, besides which they seemed to know where they were going, unlike Haggryd, who had wasted no time in joining up, where he soon made an impression both amongst his peers and superiors. One of his commanding officers, a man named Hammond; recommended he be given a try out amongst the scouting core, due to his reported keen sense of smell and the natural ease with which he had picked up the art of tracking and sniping.

Haggryd excelled in the role; often being assigned the more daring roles on solo missions, other times leading small foraging parties, one of the generals; a fussy old brigadier took quite a shine to him and whenever vital data was desperately needed from deep within enemy territory, Haggryd had become the scouting cores 'go to man': The core adopting a phrase of their own; ya need something doing see the scouts, ya need something done see Haggryd. Often Haggryd would be scolded all the same for overstepping his boundaries, even though that inevitably meant he had merely brought back additional data: That data being some souvenir, war eagle, fugitive, POW or reporting how an enemy brigade had met with a mishap crossing a bridge... He was relentless in his application; eagerly hunting out the Emperors enemies and although he was promoted to the position of mounted scout, he continued to work mostly on foot, where he soon earned the moniker of 'Animal', due both to his looks and his unrivalled tracking skills.

Haggryd really did love his time in *that* army; a much more ordered and disciplined bunch than these rabble rousers he currently commanded, but his time in that military had come to a head when they had captured an Orc patrol deep in enemy territory. Haggryd and two others called Zeffer and Lipstick (so called due to his oversized lips) had been on a recon mission when they came across the patrol. Haggryd or 'Animal' had been in command and had ordered the other two to lie low, but half the core had bets on with one another worth up to five silver per Goblin ear and Zeffer had fired off his bow at them anyway. The ensuing battle had been fierce but brief, but they did capture a Goblin soothsayer who had been mortally wounded and agreed to divulge much information in exchange for the healing intervention of a priest, so Haggryd and the others had rushed back. The gods of misfortune smiled upon Haggryd that day when far from attempting to flee once healed as everyone had expected; the Goblin marched into the brigadier and informed him of a half dozen truthful plots and plans, starting with his recognition of Haggryd. Brigadier Hammond felt a great pity for the man he had seen rise from a lowly Squires Helper to indispensable Chief Scout.

His remaining within the army became untenable over the coming weeks however as others came to know half truth's then in turn think they knew more than they did. Someone was giving out the information but apart from the General who had no cause to, Haggryd had no idea and even less care. Several week and many scuffles later and he was summoned to the Generals office anew, the brigadier gave him more sympathy but less hope as he ordered he leave before his life become bitterly endangered. Haggryd was not sent empty handed however; Hammond giving him one of his own finest steed (which he ate) and a considerable amount of money (which he squandered), then told him to leave, never to return. Thus he left for home, his hated Orcish home in the lands of the green skins. But in place of the sickly beaten boy who had been spirited away in the night stood a strapping twenty two year old who towered over all but the very tallest Orc and was twice as sturdy than most! Furthermore, this man returned with one thing on his mind; vengeance! For every illness and abuse he had encountered: For every fear driven annex of sweat filled sleep; vengeance for every hour of regret and neglect…, …For the beatings attributed him for being of another *colour* and *creed*. ***For the death of his mother!***

It took some several years of scouring the lands before he once again discovered the small citadel which held the stronghold in which he had been born. Years of expert military training and years more of living alone in strange lands had taught him to be far more cunning and wise than most of his compatriots, so he wore a cowl to disguise the full true nature of his humanesque features and obtained work in one of the many seedy taverns situated in one of the roughest districts of his kindred city. Not just any tavern for he though, no…, …The tavern he chose to gain employ in, was the one most frequented by those that had abused him and owned by none other than his childhood nemesis; an oversized Orc with a waist as thick as a bull and arms like steel named Klurk; non-coincidentally an Orcish word describing something as 'stupidly effective.'

For months he worked as an underling without the slightest scare of recognition, then on a terribly hot midsummer's day when the intense heat was making many of the Goblin kin sick, he poisoned the landlord Klurk, before informing his employer of his immediate predicament and demanding that he sign over the inn to Haggryd in exchange for the antidote. The landlord was furious with the deceit shown by his underling, but fear of dying forced his hand. After making sure the papers were all present, Haggryd duly handed over the antidote as promised but tainted with acid; he had watched the relieved Klurk gobble down the healing elixir only to scream in silence as his jaw dropped to the floor and his mouth melted away.

Haggryd continued to work the inn for a further six years as its sole proprietor though he kept on Klurk as a general dogsbody and someone for himself and the customers to kick when frustrated, as he often was. In that time he managed to poison nearly all of those whose faces he could remember, or who repeated tales of their victorious racial abuse. His Inn being largely comprised of Orcs and Hobgoblins who were by and large not known for their intuition, innovation *or* intelligence meant he could walk around quite openly, though he chose to cover his face still by means of a turban and scarf.

Most of his former tormentors had already passed away in some battle; or to disease and so no-one ever suspected Haggryd of any crime as week by week, another old companion passed away until the day that a Black Orc commander and his patrol; returning from some inconsequential battle, decided to visit his Inn. Haggryd had several Goblin servants rushing around serving drinks but when one of the soldiers complained about the price and quality of the ale, the commander himself came to complain to Haggryd.

Haggryd was in shock, for as the two locked eyes with one another; both the commander and he instantly recognised each other as father and son. Haggryd's emotions were in turmoil for here was the man whom he both despised and loved, but the love was not reciprocated. The commander had dragged him across the bar, removing the flimsy hood that had served to suppress Haggryd's full identity all the while and proceeded to humiliate him. Haggryd let the insults pass, still unsure of his feelings for his long absent father, yet when the commander turned his degrading comments towards his long dead mother, Haggryd could stand no more.

In front of the assembled patrons Haggryd fought with his father, but it was very much a one sided fight. Haggryd's father, somewhat old for an Orc, battle weary and a little the worse for wear from the ale, thrashed about with his sword in an almost inept manner. Haggryd, however, with his years of military training behind him and youth on his side, simply sidestepped the blows of the huge claymore his father attacked with, belittling his father's feeble attempted death blows. As the crowds favour began to turn Haggryd's way, their taunts of derision spurred Haggryd's father into more wild slices of his sword -each stroke becoming more desperate, even accidentally hacking into the thigh bone of one of his own men, and Haggryd took to cruelly slapping at his father as he sidestepped the inaccurate strikes and lunges; evoking yet more derisive sneers and whelps of laughter from the enthralled fickle audience.

Some minutes later Haggryd's father had sunk to one knee, exhausted.

Haggryd himself had stood a few feet away, awaiting the next ineffective onslaught when one of his father's own foot soldiers; a grunt some seven feet tall, took his bread knife and plunged it into his downed commanders back. The grunt roared with delight as Haggryd's father slumped to the floor, proclaiming him self the new commander, but a few of this grunts peers had similar aspirations. As two of the grunts came forward and attacked the newly proclaimed commander, the whole bar erupted in melee. Haggryd himself was also embroiled in the fighting, as the bloodshed speedily degenerated into an all out slaughter that quickly escalated into a battle which only one would survive.

Haggryd was that one. For his troubles he was summoned before the chief council, where he was sure he would be put to the sword. He decided to confess all, and told of his return and how he had selectively murdered all those who had once tormented him, and how the fight had started because his father had recognised him. He asked that his sentence be swift and was left in a cell to contemplate his death, while those above deliberated over his life.

When the council reconvened the next day Haggryd was both amazed and relieved at their decision. Speaking for the council, a battle scarred war-chief named Tarkkat proclaimed that while there was no proof to back up Haggryd's 'boasts', the council had to admit that he had displayed all the qualities admired by those who wished for advancement within Orcish society, and duly awarded him the title of Border Security Chief, together with a platoon of one hundred men under Haggryd's command. Haggryd accepted the role, though in truth he did not relish the opportunity.

He had been in charge of this troop for five years now and although his numbers had dwindled to around sixty, they were still a formidable force, being mainly made up of veteran skirmishers. Occasionally he would ask for more troops, but would inevitably be turned down, for he now understood Orcish society. They were a race that depended on only the strongest surviving. Treachery, deceit, distrust and unmerciful behaviour were attributes that were applauded, as he himself had been, but the post given to him was one that no-one expected him to survive in for long. It was thought amongst his superiors, that it was best to keep this human looking 'animal' at the proverbial arm's length, in the hope that he may die in some frontier battle or maybe even be assassinated by one of his own men.

Haggryd was no Mr. Average however and although he had advanced by showing the brutish side of his nature, he also made full use of his Elven/Human traits too, showing diplomacy and tact when needed and carefully considering the probabilities before committing his troops to battle.

Slowly, ever so slowly it seemed to him: The men under his command; or at least those veterans who had survived long enough under his charge, were gradually adopting an ever increasingly professional attitude; their outlook changing to align more closely with Haggryd's own ideals…, …Of course there were still certain taboos that could not be overlooked; such as the faceless Orc who by his own provocation had sealed his fate. If the soldier had begged forgiveness, Haggryd could have, and would have let it go at that, perhaps making a harmless joke of it in order to ease the trooper's conscience. Yet the trooper's actions had not allowed him to take that path for, when the Orc had cursed at him, Haggryd had been forced to save face…, …For if he had not acted as he did, others amongst his command would have taken it as a sign of weakness by their commander, and within no time, the entire troop would have suffered problems of dissent, mutiny or worse…, …The Snurch bearing his now clean vestments returned and he started dressing as he studied his gathering force…

Haggryd loved the military life beyond any other and it was for this reason and none other that he stayed within the Goblin civilization. Haggryd wanted to change the views held by practically all Goblin kin and this posting helped him to achieve those goals, by first changing the outlook of those under his command. He treated his men with respect, he kept beatings to a minimum and trained all of his troops in the manner he had been taught whilst serving in the human army. Slowly but surely, those under his command were becoming more civilised, choosing to shun some of the more barbaric tendencies still enjoyed by most of their respective races. True, he was still expected to cuff Goblin underlings when despatching orders, but the blow he delivered was less painful and more playful than most could dare hope. In truth, without realising it, Haggryd was slowly turning his men into outcasts amongst their own kind.

As Haggryd's border patrols numbers dwindled due to the many skirmishes they encountered, Haggryd had began to offer captured prisoners a choice -to be taken back to the citadel where they would be cooked, enslaved or made into playthings, or to serve under his command, to swear allegiance to him and fealty to each other. The idea had not been his, but Corag's; a largely uncouth individual, who had most readily of all, taken to Haggryd's human persuasions and nuances. Corag may look and sound like a barbarian, yet he was in truth the one who had most eagerly learned from Haggryd's teachings and to who both owed each other their lives several times over. Corag was the one person Haggryd trusted implicitly, the only one he would stand back to back with in the midst of the most intense battles and Corag returned the sentiment.

So the idea of recruiting from those captured had been a success and apart from a few deserters, who were invariably hunted down and executed, the various races had bonded together as only those who truly rely on one another do. Six dwarves, an Elf, A half Ogre, eight Bugbears, fourteen Goblins, eighteen Orcs, three Hobgoblins, eight Black Orcs, a scurrying mass of Snurch's and a fallen Human Paladin made up his troop and of those one of the Goblins and two of the Orcs were magic users; Shamans to be precise. In fact, the only race Haggryd never gave the same choice of redemption to, were those of the Halfling persuasion.

The reason for this was simple, many years ago Haggryd had discovered a taste for the plump Halflings flesh, a taste that never left him and so whenever their race was encountered, survivors would be quarantined for Haggryd's pleasure and just a handful kept on as chefs.

Haggryd looked about, his perfect night-vision; helped by the moonlight, meant he could see all around him even though midnight was rapidly closing in. He wished he had not had to deal with the Orc as he had, and silently cursed his men for steadfastly hanging on to the notion of 'might is right.' His thoughts were disrupted when Corag sat down beside him, two bottles held in his arms; he offered one to Haggryd and greedily uncorked the other and took a long pull on its contents.

"...Good thing no poison, eh? Haggryd do good. Keep men happy. Happy Orcs say stupid Orc, not be so stupid in next life. They drink for you." Corag happily informed Haggryd.

"They drink *to* you!" Haggryd corrected, "Where's Adin at? I've got a little job for him."

"Me see Elf at cooking fire: **G'ib'hlash!**" Corag roared over his shoulder to an attendant Pygmy, "Tell silly Adin, Haggryd want him *now*."

The unseen attendant rushed off to fetch the Elf while the two friends sat, joked and drank for thirty minutes more until the Elf called Adin turned up, his tunic covered in evidence of a feast.

"Where you be, silly Elf? Haggryd want then, not now Golly gosh!" Corag admonished.

Haggryd, simply stood and smiled at the Elf who reciprocated, "Take no notice of blabber mouth Adin, would you care for some, ahem, *Dwarven* spirits?" The leader said, offering the bottle from which he drank.

"He take notice of Blabber Size 14's!" Corag threatened.

"My apologies Commander, the suckling pig was just too much to tear myself away from: I meant no disrespect!" The Elf eloquently replied.

"None taken; now drink!" Haggryd jokingly ordered and again he took his seat on the rocks by the fire.

"Perhaps you mistake me for someone without taste buds good Captain Haggryd, have we run out of the wines?" Adin asked.

"You know Elf! You be *only* one drinking them!" Corag said accusingly.

At this all three fell into laughter, Adin took the proffered bottle, and the three carried on trading mock insults and drinking for twenty minutes more until Haggryd became serious once more. He informed them both of his suspicions, and asked the elf to investigate the tunnel to which he had discovered Dirks parties' tracks. Adin complied, but asked to take one of the Dwarves, an expert subterranean tracker, with him. Haggryd agreed to his request and so Adin and the Dwarf left to investigate. They returned some several hours later. Haggryd was sleeping alone, in a small tent stationed some 50 feet from the rest of the camp, and it was here that the Elf came to report.

Adin was adept at moving almost silently, yet no sooner had he got within ten feet of Haggryd's tent, than the flap flew open and out came Captain Haggryd, wickedly barbed sword at the ready.

"I am alone Captain, and unarmed as is right. I have come to report my findings sir." Adin said, unable to suppress the lump rising in his throat. He had taken care to make no noise; and was sure he had not, yet even so the commander had somehow been aware of his presence. He briefly thought that it might be magical, yet discounted the notion almost immediately. Adin had a way of knowing about magic.

Haggryd sheathed his sword, but took care to conceal the dagger attached to his wrist and hidden by his shirt sleeve: The dagger was coated with a poison to which he himself was totally immune and had come in handy more than once during his command.

In fact Haggryd was immune to almost every poison known of, but this was a fact he kept firmly to himself, lessening his chance of being assassinated due to the portion of his enemies who attempted to poison him occasionally. He trusted this Elf before him so-so, but his near thirty years of harsh survival had not come about through tardiness.

"Speak, Adin. But make it quick, I was resting." Haggryd never referred to sleep itself; for that was something that did not come easy to him.

"Captain, there are four of them - they spotted our patrol from what I can gather, and made haste into the deepest cave so as not to be spotted. They are led by a Dwarf from what I can gather, an ugly brute of a thing he is too; with short prickly stubble rather than a beard, his hair is patchy too for some reason, which is very strange; it is most unbecoming for a Dwarf not to maintain his beard." He paused to let the information digest, though the scheming Elf had already made up his own mind as to the cause.

"Another among them is L'iezsh'mat or Lizardman as *you* may have heard of them; though the irony of the situation is that the Lizardman is a she. Very rare to let a prize such as her wander far from home…" The Elf considered explaining about the females' dominance of the Lizardman culture, and thus her possible importance; but decided against endowing more knowledge than necessary.

"A bedraggled looking human brings up the rear of the group, though he is very nervous and continually looked behind him, though the Gods only know why, when everyone knows a Human eye cannot see without light. In their *midst* is a *Halfling…*" Adin hung on the last words, delivering them teasingly, and thereby diverting Haggryd's attention.

Haggryd digested the information, fixing the elf with a stare in case any information may have gone unsaid. "A plump Halfling: That is to say nice and fat?"

The Elf permitted himself a sly smile; "Oh *perfectly rotund*, with just enough hint of muscle as to be satisfying to the pallet; mind it will require some shaving…"

Haggryd licked his Lips as he spoke: "Is he fatter than the Human?"

The Elf nodded a little too eagerly, "Of course he is fatter than the Human; he's a Halfling, stout and true; most delicious I am sure…"

Haggryd smiled back: "Sounds like a veritable feast my posh speaking friend but I am afraid I am full to brimming, so how about you tell me about the Human. Who is he?"

"I beg your pardon…" The Elf seemed lost for words then a mischievous grin playing across Haggryd's face sparked his intellect and he realised he had been found out…, …somehow. "He is a wizard type, not much power…, …I am sworn to kill him."

Haggryd seemed surprised at the information, "sworn?"

"Well paid then if you permit; I am a little more than I say and perhaps less than you would think, yet the fact remains that I am a solver of problems, an expert in the removal of dilemmas and general righter of perceived wrongs…, …And this Dirk is my latest assignment." Adin would have said more, but felt the information offered adequate enough.

"So you are a hired killer; an assassin. People don't like being around assassins you know; it puts them on edge…" Haggryd provoked.

"I realise of course but that is why I seldom tell others my profession if you will…"

"People don't always like being around a half-cast either most of the time so forget it: Besides which, Corag said he felt their was more about you than you let on…, …How far down are they now?"

"When I left them, they had entered large cave filled with stalactites and a radiant silvery pool. They intend to sleep there for the night. To be honest, they all looked like they were desperate for sleep, and they all show signs of injury, I would not expect them to wake for a good twelve hours, unless disturbed of course. Oh yes, for some reason, they do not believe that we will follow them…" The Elf bowed then, to indicate this was all that he knew or was at least; willing to divulge.

Haggryd dismissed Adin, and when the Elf had retreated back to the confines of the camp, Haggryd returned to his blanket inside the tent, and got back to dealing with his nightmares. In a few hours it would be morning and they would strike camp; he would send two Goblin runners back to inform the council of his location and intention, then they would leave most of their excess baggage, including the baggage train and Snurch's of course and follow the four suspicious intruders and discover exactly what they were up to and why they were heading towards the back door of their Citadel. With a little luck he may even get to eat some Roast Halfling stew...

***

…A cave-bat fluttered away as Dirk awoke, seeped in sweat. More visions, more nightmares and now some bloody bat and been biting his ear. How he wished for Caernthorn and the excitement of the races: The wonderful aromas of freshly baked waffles and other sweetbreads: The company of sensuous women; the hustle and bustle of civilization.

'*Instead I'm in a cave full of bat shit!*' Dirk thought. Inspired by the curse, he quickly sprang to his feet and searched around for some of the stuff remembering its use in several spells. Although he didn't generally need to use spell ingredients, unlike most other mages, it did make casting them that little bit easier and everyone knew that guano; or bat shit as Dirk rather uncouthly put it, was an excellent supplement for creating fireballs!

Dirks scurrying and scratching briefly roused a sleepy Grot, who somewhat numbly asked what in Keldor's name he was doing. Dirk flippantly replied that he was taking a dump and the Dwarf nodded off back to sleep, assured of any worries. Hurrying, and scratching about the cave disturbed yet more of the caves winged inhabitants and as one rather large swarm swooped away from their roost situated near the stony ceiling, Dirk noticed some sort of crystalline formation some fifty feet overhead.

His view was partially obscured by bat droppings, but Dirk was pretty much excited by the discovery none-the-less. With renewed vigour, Dirk ran back to his kip bag and sitting down, he leafed through the spellbook, an idea forming in his head all the while. His fingers flicked steadily through the books pages until he caught sight of the spell that currently intrigued him; its name was self descriptive and the casting process looked simple enough, so he set about ingratiating himself in the knowledge of the spell: 'Flight'.

xv) **The Death of an Alliance**

Grot awoke to a cacophony of noise erupting all around him. His mind was filled with colourful confusion and his vision blurred as explosions of intermittent light sent his sight into a dizzying switch from infra red and back to normal every millisecond or so.

"Fireballs…" he grumbled to himself, having fought in many a battle where the deadly magic had been used. He felt blindly about for a weapon and his wandering hand brushed against his one remaining axe from his once proud arsenal. His grip tightened as he peered around the cave that rattled with the sound of explosive contact.

"What in Keldor's name is buggering well happening? Are we under attack?" He shouted in no particular direction.

He stood there waiting patiently for some unseen attack or answering clarity but nothing came. Instead Grot decided to take refuge beneath a pile of unstable rockery he could just about make out, some twenty feet from where he stood.

A zipping, popping blast of flexing light caught his attention somewhere off to his left as he wended his way across the rocky terrain beneath his feet, his half turned face catching the blast of heat early enough for his honed reflexes to take over. Without conscious thought, his Dwarven muscles issued their almighty response to the infernos danger, by catapulting him beneath the sanctity of the rocky shelter he had spotted earlier.

The Dwarf scrunched his eyes for a full thirty seconds during which he endured three more booming resonations as yet more of the deadly fireballs crashed into some undetermined target.

When the booming stopped, Grot awaited a full ten seconds before opening his eyes and so his sight was clear, for the moment at least. Popping his head above his simple shelter, Grot scanned about the cave for any sight of a dragon or some almighty sorcerer perhaps, all the while hoping his friends had the sense to hide themselves. Imagine Grots vexation then, when he suddenly espied his stubby companion Boris, bounding about on some rocks a fully 100 foot or so away with all the excitement of a child.

"Boris; get down you tiny cows tit!" He yelled but just then another throb of sound signalled a forthcoming explosion and he ducked his head.

When again he looked up some forty seconds and four blasts later, the Halfling halfwit was still prancing about like some over-exited school kid. Grot again yelled a warning and as he did so he noticed the origin of the continual blasts; originating from a dark spot some sixty feet or so above the Halfling. As Grot watched a tiny fiery ball began forming up in the air.

"Bloody Dragon…" The Dwarf said not without fear, "Boris will be roasted fer sure!"

He watched with detached fascination, a tear forming, welling, and then beginning its gravity-defying roll down his cheek as the small globe of fire in the distance gradually began to expand, popping and fizzing with intentional rage. Even from this distance, he could already feel its bleeding warmth.

He glanced to the Halfling who seemed unaware of his forthcoming fate, still dancing and bumping about happily. This fireball was growing beyond any size he himself had witnessed before and he looked for signs of the dragon behind it, but could see nothing.

For assurance; Grot looked back to the Halfling and as did so he caught a sight of Qoua sprinting towards the Halflings position. He glanced back to where he presumed the Dragon to be and observed the fireball now forming some fifty yard in perimeter to be floating towards the cave wall. Then, as his vision again began to blur he espied the source from which the almighty fireball spewed and was both shocked and awed to discover it was none other than his scholastically retarded friend Dirk.

"How the bugger has that Hags acne…" Was all the stunned Dwarf could utter before the next blast pounded into the now hot white rocky outcrop directly above the Halfling, slamming the Halfling and Qoua down in compacting protest, and even catching Grot who had forgotten to duck for cover; so awestruck was he of the flaring blast that followed, carrying his unhidden arse along the jagged rocks for some twelve or so feet.

Again, the preceding blast was closely followed by some three or four others, and all the resulting cacophony of sound that ensued. Each blast, buffeted the now half-conscious Dwarf up against some cropping or other, yet each time he struggled to crawl whatever small distance he could manage towards his seemingly suicidal friends. Some forty five seconds each lot of blasts tended to last, before the following ten to fifteen seconds gap of holy acquiescence, wherein all would be calm. At least the blasting infernos had cleared the underground warren of bat-life for some distance.

Some two minutes later Grot managed to stumble within earshot of Boris and yelled for all he was worth even as his hairy body and beard were singed down to size. Boris, who had managed to stumble to his feet; looked to the Dwarf in puzzled fashion as his swaying hips threatened to teeter too far to one side. The buffeted Halfling was clearly stunned senseless: Boris's head began swaying too as he smiled at his Dwarven friend.

Another volley of blasts erupted as Grot flattened himself against a jut of stone, some fifty metres from where the fiery storm connected with the near molten rockery above the no longer dancing Halfling.

The last few blasts had exceeded seventy metre and been accompanied by a groaning sound quite peculiar to and out of place with the rest of the audible noises. Grot, judging to perfection the sound of an underground cave in, screamed at Boris to run. But the downed Halfling merely raised his head to better look at the cataclysmic sluice of rock that was now rapidly crumbling above him and fainted.

Grot cursed himself for his inability to reach the hairy idiot when he noticed a spiralling rocky fracture slam into the hitherto floating figure of Dirk. The bear-sized rock caught him full across his back and sent him throttling Eyrthe-ward. Grot's bloody fingertips scrabbled at the stony flooring as he scuttled forward on hands and knees in desperation. There was little chance of him reaching either of the fallen in time but he launched himself with the strength of a dying bull, undeterred as he was.

Smaller rocks, up to the size of a hay cart were crashing down all around as Grot forged onward and the main dislodged outcropping of rock, which spanned some fifty to sixty yards, cracked and creaked in imagined agony as it detached itself in slow motion fashion from the rest of the cave.

The Dwarf screamed out as a fist sized rock roughly struck the back of his hand, fracturing several of the bones contained within its meaty confines: Forced to try to stand; Grot just about managed to rise to his feet in time to narrowly avoid being flattened by a monstrous rocky fragment. Rolling to the side as the boulder shaped piece steam-rolled towards his position, Grot again glimpsed Qoua.

Grots eyes sparkled as he realised the burden she bore upon her back was none other than the unconscious Halfling. He followed the path that her fleeing form was taking as her loping gait took her from spot to spot as she attempted to outrun certain death. He could see Dirk some thirty feet or so away from where she was heading and felt positive that she too must have noticed him as her leaping course wound his way...

Yet as the Dwarf observed Qoua come within a few feet of his downed friend she stopped and, Grot watched with disbelieving rage, turned sharply on her heel and ran to safety, abandoning Dirk to a fate not too hard to discern. The glowing gigantean of tortured rock came crashing down with vehemence, narrowly missing Qoua slamming down upon the body of the person responsible for its and his own collapse.

"...No-o-o!" Grot screamed and sprang forward with murderous intent, oblivious to the random debris still showering the area with deadly shards.

Qoua had barely had time to throw down the still unconscious Boris when the comet sized stone section bore into the stone floor where Dirk lay still. The resulting vigour of contact was enough to precipitate a small Eyrthe-quake and as rock battled with gravity against its floored brethren, the resulting contest forced up huge thick clouds of white, chalk-like dust.

Qoua fought to retain her balance when a cloud of such dust enveloped her, sending her into wheezing fits. She stumbled and staggered, coughing all the while as she sought any form of shelter available, yet before she could react to anything, a ferocious chunk of crystal some forty or so feet in length; drove toward her, sending up nasty chunks of forgotten rock as it gouged a splintering trench along Qoua's seemingly doomed path but she flung herself to the side in time to avoid becoming one with the trench, yet not without cost as the eschewed stone thumped into her scaly hide.

She glanced to the Halfling who had just rolled onto his stomach indicating he was alive at least, when she caught the scent of another close by. Painfully turning around and crouching down she shipped out her strong tail in case of a back attack and attempted to sight the possible protagonist.

Nobody was in sight but she knew someone was there thanks to her keen nose. Unfortunately for Qoua, the dust clouds that colonised the area had somewhat depreciated her senses however and thus it was possible that Grot managed to attack her before she could react to his presence.

Grot's thrown axe bit deeply into her thigh as he emerged from the boundaries of a nearby thick white cloud. Her instinctive response was to turn away and whip her opponent's feet from under him with her tail; but the Dwarf was an astute warrior and anticipated the move with practised expertise. Waiting an instant after his initial attack, the Dwarf leapt before Qoua had even began her move, and the resulting whip of her tail caught naught but clear air.

Utilising his diminutive presence the Dwarf launched himself into a flying lariat, catching the lizard woman around her slim waist and pulling her face down to the ground, upon contact with which, the Dwarf drove his elbow down into the base of Qoua's spine with a crack.

Qoua hissed in searing pain as she felt a break in her tailbone but the Dwarf span her over with one arm regardless, grabbing hold of and raking his axe from Qoua's wounded thigh as he did so. As he rolled Qoua onto her back, Grot rose up and flung his small thighs across her body and arms, pinning her, and raised his arms with both hands clasping the throwing axes short haft in readiness to strike the telling blow.

"Grot…, …No!" a pipsqueak voice pleaded from the precincts of some nearby shady billow of stone dust.

All about them the confusion mellowed as the devastating effects of the separated rock died away, leaving only the hazy pockets of smoke-like white and the intermittent separation of some small fragment or other, longing to be with its cast off brethren that cooled below.

Grot stumbled to speak, his attention momentarily diverted. Qoua took her opportunity to try and dismount the Dwarf that straddled her, but his misdirected attention was brief and he quickly exerted enough pressure with his thighs to still her momentary struggles. His mind focused on the Halfling and what he would have to witness. His jaw clenched and his shoulders went taught as he tried to assemble the words to explain him self. He knew what it must look like to Boris, but he had made no secret of his mistrust from the start…, …Snakemen-women, Lizardmen, whatever you dressed them up as they were all voraciously evil bastards. Grot had known all along it would only be a matter of time before she began killing them all off.

He had seen Dirk. He'd seen Qoua. There was no doubt in his mind that she had easily enough time to rescue him. As for strength, he could tell by the way she continually tested his restricting grip that she had plenty left in reserve. No, she had to die for her betrayal but he had not anticipated Boris witnessing it. Grot's well muscled arms flexed in anticipation as he targeted the skull of the green scaled, evil eyed foe beneath him.

"Grot... please..." again the Halfling pleaded, emerging fully from the clouds perimeter.

'THE EVIL BITCH IS GETTING IT!!!' Grot imagined himself screaming. 'Maybe I'll even hack you to bit's too, you ball of Daemons puss!' The truth was the Dwarf was upset.

"That's not like you Grot... *I like it*... but it really isn't you at all..."

"...Dirk? Is it... No, hold on a moment... Who said that?" Grot demanded of the disembodied voice. In reply he heard a chuckle that sounded eerily akin to Dirks; while somehow completely different.

"What? Are you asking me? It was me? I said it and I'll say it again. **Grot Please Stop**, she saved my life!" The Halfling babbled approaching to within a few feet.

"She..., ... Dirk" Grot mumbled in confusion.

Boris's brows did a little dance of apprehension... "What do you mean? Grot, are you ok? Please don't go crazy. Listen to me. Grot; we all regret what's happened to Dirk but it will be okay, we can just dig him up and get him to a-well..., ...Actually, I think he might be a bit splattered but listen: My old granny used to say-"

Grot snapped into a livid retort: "*A thousand Goblins be buggered*! Who gives a Giant's *turd* about what *your* granny *used* to say. I'm gonna kill this scaly bitch, and if *you* object... I'll-"

"Careful Grot; wouldn't want to lose your manners in front of a lady..." Again the disembodied voice taunted.

"Did you hear that?" Grot shouted to Boris though he had no need to.

"Hear what?" Boris replied with a shrug of his tiny shoulders.

Grot's eyes held an infuriated glaze as he spoke and he gripped the axe with yet more fervour. "Dirk spoke. I heard him speak; although I dunno if it was him but I did. Did you hear him speak I mean, and what in Keldor's name was the bugger doing anyway??"

"I don't know properly, well, I mean I do not know quite how he discovered it but, well; he saw all these diamonds hanging above us and so he learned to fly and..." Boris struggled to get his explanation out.

"Learned to fly? Yer saying that like its nothing special..." Grot stammered, "well that explains him floating but what by Keldor's beard was he casting fireballs for; how was he casting them...? The useless tit could only cast em one at a time a few hours ago..."

"I-"

"And why in all the sevens did you get involved?" Grot ploughed on.

Qoua's voice rang clear as she interrupted the Dwarf's maddened rant. "It wass foretold Dirk would risse again from an imposssible demisse!"

His grip relaxed for a moment as he looked down in shock at the statement and this time he was not so agile to regain his poise. Lightning quick Qoua bucked her hips sending the Dwarf toppling forward into the nearby trench. Gingerly she rose to her feet, her lips pulling back in pain as the wound in her thigh compressed.

Grots hand appeared on the crest of the trench and both Qoua and Boris spurred themselves forward to assist in his exhumation but the murderous Dwarf pushed Boris away and grabbed Qoua by the side attempting to force her down to her knees.

Qoua lost patience and hissed in the Dwarves face; jets of blinding venom stinging Grot's eyes and kneed him soundly in the bollocks before pushing the wheezing Dwarf away, who rubbed at his eyes and looked about for his axe. The Lizardman approached him again all the same, this time holding out her hands in a non-threatening manner.

"Grot you are dillussional. Dirk will live again, desspite what you think you ssaw." To this Grot started to protest, but Qoua quietened him with a warning hiss! "You are in no fit sstate to battle Dwarf and will not catch me unawaress again in any short matter of time, sso lissten to what I have to tell you and you may learn something..."

She paused here to take a breath and study the desolation around her before continuing. "I never imagined it would be sso desstructive but then again I am ssure of it. It iss for thiss reasson that I left him... I *know* for certain he will live again ass shall we..."

Grot looked at her and was about to protest anew when again his thoughts were invaded by that irritating bodiless chuckle.

"She speaks so-o-o eloquently for a reptile don't you think Stumpy?"

That concluded any doubts Grot may have still harboured, as the statement was definitely Dirks. *'Yer Bastard'* Grot thought. *'If your alive, come out where I can see you; yer bad excuse for a-'*

Again the chuckle…, "…*Oh Grot…*"

"You hear him don't you? Even now…?" Qoua questioned Grot.

"He's alive; I can hear him!" Grot confirmed.

Qoua put her hand on Grots shoulder in pity. "He iss not alive Grot; but he shall return. You musst be hearing the echo of hiss ssoul…"

"Hear who?" asked the uncomprehending Boris.

"Yes… Hear who exactly, because I would dearly like to know about anyone thinking of a return?" a grating newcomers voice rejoined.

All three turned around where they stood and as they did so, their movements were in concert with the clicking of a hundred or so crossbows.

All around them a small army had amassed themselves in more or less a circle and their leader; a barbaric looking Human/Orcish crossbreed came forward a few feet as he again spoke, this time with a more threatening demeanour. "I said: Who can you hear? Because I'll tell you this; you won't be hearing anything in about twenty seconds!" He signalled his men into action.

"Who the shite are you and your lot, turning up here all quiet like…, …A bit well organised for a bunch of; oh, my mistake, I was gonna say a bunch of Gobbos but I suppose I should have said; Gobbo lovers." Grot seethed back, rapidly coming to his senses, though still irritable. "What are Dwarves doing with the likes of green-skins, black-skins and half-casts?"

"Look around stupid…, …Haggryd ask question, not you!" Corag chimed out.

"See if I was stupid I'd give out my own name but as I don't intend to get to know you it would be a waste of my bloody precious time," Grot snarled, "How about me and you right now Gob-shite?"

"My name is Haggryd or Captain if you prefer. You seem quite weakened and yet you offer to fight my best? Who really is stupid

Dwarf?" The company commander studied the Dwarf adding, "Oh and do not even think of it, you really couldn't survive a challenge against myself. How about one of our own Dwarves? Think you could handle one of them…, …That could be a fun match lads eh? What do you reckon, should we watch two Dwarves kick each others heads in."

"I will not fight my own kin unless I absolutely have to…" Grot warned but Haggryd merely made a mock applause throughout his objection, signalling one of the mentioned Dwarves into action. Grot and the others watched as the wiry one eyed veteran ambled over, shrugging of all his weaponry bar a spiked knuckleduster which he bore with purpose.

Qoua whispered to the Dwarf, hoping he would listen to sense; "Grot you are in no position to fight, let him take you quickly…"

"Do you ever shut up?" Grot argued, "ya seem real eager for me to die don't ya, well listen to me…" He continued as the fighter approached.

"I," Grot began to speak as he ducked beneath a straight jab, "can bloody;" the Dwarven fighter jabbed again and this time Grot caught his outstretched arm and delivered a solid counter to the armpit of his aggressor, and slammed upwards with his flexed palm, shattering and displacing the Dwarven opponents jaw and knocking him down in an instant. "Where was I? Oh yeah: I can bloody well take care of myself…, …Now what about a fight with yer self captain numb nuts…"

"Oh well said ya dickhead…, …Now you've done it!" Dirk teased.

"Okay…" Haggryd replied and let loose an arrow that struck through the Dwarves hobnailed boot and into the rock; temporarily holding his left foot in place. Another quickly followed pinning the Dwarves reaching right arm to his left leg and a third pierced his right shoulder. "You still wish to fight me Dwarf?" But Grot was in too much pain and suffering too much from embarrassment to answer.

"Nope…, …Okay I will give you all the chance to join with us and swear fealty to this band of brothers, do you accept?"

Boris went to say something but Qoua quickly clasped her mouth over the struggling Halfling.

Haggryd sighed at the thought of wasting their lives…, "…I could have used a reptile, oh well: Kill them but don't damage the Halfling too much; archers…, …Fire!"

As the first hail of wooden bolts came tearing through the companions' flesh, Grot again heard the voice, chuckling all the while.

"…Oh I am dead Grot. I have been for some time, I think mate, and you're my last hope! I've really screwed it up down here. As usual…" It spoke to him in the singsong cheery fashion of a madman as a second wave of deadly missiles consumed the three where they stood.

"Dirk…" Grot managed before an arrow struck home, forcing its way through the back of his neck and up through his wagging tongue.

"*Come get me…*" Dirks voice chuckled in devious response…

The voice emitted a sigh then, as the troops came wading in, a multitude of personalised weapons littering the veteran armies arsenal. Qoua fought bravely, killing three or four before being sliced down the back by a Black Orc's rusty plough-like blade. Even the Halflings wild slingshots managed to break the jaw of one attacker before he was swept up by a bugbear. All Grot could manage however, was to clutch at his victors knees as it smashed his head in with a simple wooden club. His eyes popped out of his skull before he ever got the chance to see what it was that actually attacked him.

"I'll see you in hell…" The disembodied voice jeered again before Grots brain finally ceased to function, when a totality of darkness consumed his very being…

xvi) **To Hell and Back**

Darkness…

Nothing…

No wait there is something: A thoughtful touch upon his unfeeling skin. A velvety texture beneath…,

…Beneath?

A sharp intake of breath and an infinitesimally short fall precipitated Dirk's entrance to Hell and suddenly he could see a foggy grey waste spreading out all around him. Bright fiery globes were burning lazily in the sky here and there, as if reluctant to part with their helpful light.

Distantly and close by figures could be seen shambling in a seemingly random, erratic manner; very interesting, quite peculiar creatures for the most part, yet here and there stood or walked a Human or humanoid.

Dirk made a conscious decision to avoid as many of them as possible and looked about the some forty mile expanse his daemonic eye was capable of seeing. Everything was Grey and intolerably muggy he looked to see any signs of shelter and it suddenly occurred to him that not only was there no shelter, there also appeared to be no other type of features whatsoever bar the infinite shades, shapes and patterns of creatures dressing the monotonous landscape. Dirk screamed; a trick that usually woke him from seeming disaster only to discover he had soiled himself in his sleep but nothing changed. He knew in his heart he was dead but he had died so called once or twice before and usually you were transported to Limbo, not here…, …If here was where Dirk believed himself to be. "Friggin typical aint it…" Dirk quipped to himself, "I have hardly sinned according to most beliefs; beliefs which *I* don't even *believe* and yet here I am in Hell: How? I mean what have I, oh wait; there was that Orc camp incident, and the lies…, …Infidelity, disloyalty, cowardice, oh shut up Dirk…"

'*No wonder them sods are walking about looking lost,*' Dirk thought, 'they are bloody lost!' He glanced behind him as best he could; for some reason his feet wouldn't work, "So this is Hell is it, or one of the seven or nine depending which god ya believe in, which I bloody don't if ya listening? Can't say I'm impressed or particularly surprised to end up here.

Just my luck really, just when I start thinking I'm getting somewhere in life…"

Dirk sighed, "Well I can't say the bugger didn't warn me; I thought he'd come along himself but instead a bloody stone decides to splat the idea right out of me. Well one thing's for sure I'm not going to turn into one of those blank looking gits; if I'm gonna interact it's gonna be on my terms…"

"Oy hunted; wants bee lunches or wanting bee slave?" an irritating voice chirruped from behind him.

"How the bugger, how did you get there so quick?" Dirk questioned disbelieving. When he had just looked the nearest creature had been some 1000 yards away at least.

"Aah teleportation; sees hunted. Now slave or lunches will bee…" The creature retorted.

Dirk struggled to turn and spat at his body in thought; *'move you dickhead, turn around and look at whatever the hell is talking to ya!'* and with that he turned and looked down at the squat brown creature beside him. It was more or less a mouth on legs. The legs; which were so skinny they looked in need of a scaffold to operate to any great effectiveness, made up most of the creatures two foot in height. The rest was taken up by a devilishly flat stomach followed by a conical head around which ran a huge mouth at its fattest part, and topped off by a single eye.

"Hmmm…" Dirk mused aloud, "How quickly can you teleport? Is it faster than say… this?" Dirk followed by stamping down his foot quite sharply.

The creatures eyeball lifted up on a stalk and looked down at where his foot had stopped just above it and blinked twice, "not think so… Why?" It asked at length.

"'Why?' is a good question I suppose: One that a little green fellow around your height probably asks himself every day in whatever part of hell I've been sent to…, …I am dead aren't eye… I mean I- oh forget it…" Dirks foot came down again and as he lifted it he was somewhat stunned and amused to hear the thing still speaking from its smashed in skull, through which its lips now quivered.

"Did needs to? Not need, not need do? Hurts it does much, too hurt bad. Hurts must do? Eats will, when hunted hold still." The beast spat in protesting outrage. Dirk frowned down at the nasty mouthed beast and delivered ten or fifteen further stamps until it eventually ceased its threats and began whingeing instead, coercing Dirk into yet further violence.

Dirk wasn't completely sure whether it was dead, nor was he sure if death as he knew it even existed on this plane of existence, but it seemed to no longer be a viable threat and so he left it alone and turned from it as he began his journey through hell. Once again he found his feet refused to budge. '*Walk dickhead walk...*' he self threatened, '*before stalk eye there gets up!*' His physical self strained every muscle as he thought and suddenly he was ploughing off through the grey waste before him.

Some twenty years passed after that first day of arrival though Dirk had no way of telling as he made his way from random point to random point across the featureless plain of hell. No Cerberus was here, no Khan or Nicodemus to bargain for his soul. Nothing that claimed any interest in him whatsoever except the hungry and occasionally violent. Not that he felt hunger; but some did he found, and most often these would be the humanoids he met whose ghostly flesh would be shrunk onto emaciated bones. Of those afflicted with hunger in these dread planes, Dirk soon learned to avoid as theirs was an insatiable appetite and they would attempt to eat anyone or anything; even themselves. Other hungry denizens were merely browsers, those who could eat so did so out of distraction; most often these were the misshapen devils that spotted the vista, though sometimes they belonged to a completely different being altogether.

In that time he managed to come into constant conflict with some several thousand of hells lesser denizens, as well as one or two of varying degrees greater repute. It was not as if he did not attempt to avoid contact on a daily basis and a score of days in all that time he did indeed manage to, thanks to his perfect sight. But the place seemed to have a habit of sending its occupants; both devilish denizen and condemned citizen alike on a gravitational pull to one another. Space and distance had no defined parameters here; therefore the imagined forty miles that Dirk could see, would equally be an imagined 4000 miles as some far-seeing creatures that dwelt here could envisage.

Just like that first creature Dirk had met, many (way, way too many), of the denizens of hell used teleportation as a means of getting around. Dirk wished he could teleport right at this moment in time, but he couldn't so he instead opted to attack…, …Using the tried and tested technique of a swiftly delivered head-butt to the toe may not have had much effect on the vast stone giant, but it did have the desired effect Dirk had intended;

knocking him into a half conscious daze. This helped a great deal: For a start, it meant that all but the most miniscule pain wouldn't get through to his brain; and secondly it prevented him from having to witness his own demise.

In all his twenty something years in hell, Dirk had discovered hundreds of time to his detriment that whilst nothing could actually die down here… One could go through an excruciating amount of pain during the actual process of 'dying'. In many of Dirks encounters with other inhabitants Dirk always had the uncanny knack of being 'killed' in some manner or other; normally concluding with his being consumed by whatever creature it was he had encountered as was the case with the gargantuan beast present. With one huge spade like hand the living mountain of rock scooped up Dirk's stunned body and tossed him into its spacious mouth, not even gulping as it swallowed him whole.

Boulder like bits chewed up his bones a little en route to the stomach, snapping his body here and there and ripping apart various sized chunks of his ethereal body. The pain was excruciating and one couldn't simply pass out like in the mortal realms, here one had to endure. He started singing a chirpy little number instead of the normally associated panic; that is until his lips split apart…

"A man called Dirk was such a berk,

He fought a lump of rock,

And he never had a chance,

To get so much as a dance,

Cuz he weighed even less than its co-mph!"

Without being fully aware of the how, Dirk had managed to acquire a hidden skill known to a very rare few throughout the entire known realms. As accustomed as he had become to receiving limitless amounts of pain on an almost daily basis, Dirks pessimistic self had learnt to accept it, and just as the old adage goes; once you learn to accept a given thing, it becomes so much easier to bear, so it was with Dirk. Well, Dirk had certainly accepted the fact, but to be totally truthful, simply accepting that one is going to receive pain does not necessarily lessen the sensation. After roughly six years of simply 'accepting' the pain however, Dirks self-pitying stubbornness kicked in and one day, whilst involved in a particularly gruesome death, Dirk simply refused to be ruled by the agony instead choosing to languish in the sensation, laughing then; as his parted lips did now. Dirk's reasoning was simple at the time: "If I'm sad I don't always cry. I'm happy sometimes but hardly ever laugh, so why should I always suffer when I feel pain. If suffering is an emotion then I'm just gonna friggin enjoy it, so bring on the pain dudes, bring it on, cuz I'm gonna bloody well love it.'

Thus Dirk had managed to conquer his pain, though he in truth merely became hooked on self abuse; his body growing excited when in the presence of suffering. In Dirk's mind he had tapped into his emotion in much the same way as an actor 'taps' into his or her mental emotions, and Dirk had learned how to turn that tap off. In reality his tap was stuck on full flow and there would be many times like now when Dirk would purposely start uneven contests in which there could only be one outcome.

A wry smile played across each of his lip halves and he let out a contented, disjointed sigh, as they were sent splashing into the creature's stomach ahead of his other bits and pieces. '*Aah! Quiet time...*' Dirk reflected, settling into a relaxed state of mind even as his main torso sloshed into the massive bowl like tomb and began to be digested in the gargantuan thing's powerful stomach acids.

Quiet time as Dirk labelled it, was that period of time that one spent dying and reassembling oneself. The time period could take hours or days but no matter how long or short; the time elapsed was always one of solitude, wherein Dirk would not be bothered by a single living (or un-living) thing.

His head tumbled down relatively intact into what he assumed to be the pit of the stomach, though his lips torso and one of his ears were ahead of him, he scanned a rolling eye over the creatures ruby veined interior with the air of one impressed by the design..., ...Somewhere off to the side one of his lips wet-whistled. Dirk waited in humming meditation for a few hours until all the parts of his essence had entered the things stomach then undertook the task of consciously fitting them together again; before he was shit out of the thing. Dirk hated that part and there was nothing worse than having to pull yourself back together covered in and comprising of shit.

This was another skill acquired through his time in hell, though it was a skill that almost every denizen eventually became aware of, though getting ones appearance exact was an art form in itself..., ...While Dirk was most definitely not an artist, he did have a strong sense of his own vanity and this simple force of will was enough to force his bodily elements into their correct anatomical position. To start with, however, one had to go through the mundane task of gathering up the various body parts. His half-chewed left arm swam around and picked up a semi-digested leg…, …Dirk was busily assembling himself in the said fashion. Having reattached both legs to their correct feet and stuck them onto their previously disconnected pelvis. Next to arrive was his own melted stomach, closely followed by his backside complete with dissolved bum-cheeks. On this he mounted his chewed up torso to which was still attached his right arm.

Utilising his right arm, Dirk managed to connect both his mangled left shoulder and arm. Dirk took a breather. He had been doing this for several hours now and the resulting search had proved very productive. Not that he was in any particular rush, but now that he had started he was lost in the cycle, in a strange sort of way he found it quite fun to reconnect his pieces – it was therapeutic, almost akin to building a jigsaw. What he was even more proud of was that he had managed all of this while blind, for he had still not recovered his eyes or head.

His body waded about erratically as he fought both the pain and the escalating desire to fall apart. His foot tapped something solid and he reached down into the burning viscous liquid to retrieve a scorched and largely de-fleshed skull that he took to be his own and his other hand gripped onto something small and oval shaped, resting at the bottom of his face. Dirk plucked it up and jammed it into one of his vacant sockets then began searching around for the other eye.

Another several hours passed and Dirk grew quite concerned that he still could not see...

Dirk removed the 'eye' from his socket and reattached it elsewhere.

Thirty minutes or so later Dirk came across a badly deteriorated eye. He planted it in his socket and it supplied an extremely limited line of sight, which he utilised to help his renewed search for both the other eye, which was the one stolen from Zen's corpse and his other testacle; whose brother he had thought to be an eye for some time, and which he construed to be in grave danger of complete erosion should he not find it or be shit out soon. He was beginning to panic a little, that eye was his prize possession.

Once in the past, Dirk had been burnt down to ash, forcing him to spend many months re-establishing him-self, many long, boring months during which he could not completely recover his right hand. He had resorted to nicking another dwellers body part's to make up his own shortcoming and now had a reddish scaly little digit where his right index finger should be.

"Oh Bollocks to it...!" Dirk cried, not without irony. The truth was he didn't care about his bollock, either he would find it – or knick one. No... It was Zen's eye that was worrying him, that eye had special abilities that you just cannot get in most humanoids. Of course, he had not been aware of that when he had first desecrated his friends fallen corpse, but he damn well was now and he wanted it back...

"Zen, Zen where are you my eye?" Dirk sung out. "My pie for an eye, oh piddley die, oh where for art are you, me wonderful I?"

A faint slash of light across his shattered vision alerted Dirk that 'something' had just happened.

"...Eyeball-sky-ball, diddle-eye-do..., ...Don't go getting melted, I'm coming for you!" Dirk sang again, choosing to ignore the singeing pain he felt in his missing eye.

"Aargh now you are just pissing me off Zen! Where are you?" He threatened as he thrashed about half blind. Again, he caught a glimmer of light and paused, turning to face it.

"Hello?" he meekly asked, feverishly wishing beyond hope to receive no reply.

"Hello..." A girlish voice answered back.

"Do I detect a bit of Horsiness about your voice there?" Dirk recklessly jibed the newcomer. Most of Dirks deaths had been induced in such manner...

"Not horse, no..., ...Do you want my help?" It demanded. The things voice was indeed feminine yet she wheezed as she spoke in a similar sounding manner to that of a horses neigh.

"Neigh..." Dirk responded, "I mean, no. Not unless you can grow magical eyes out of your anus. That is – if ya have one! It wouldn't surprise me either way. If you want to eat me get in line, we're in a stomach already see..."

Dirk ignored the vague creature and continued in his desperate search, finally securing his missing testacle, yet still no sign of the eye.

"I am here to help you, not hinder or 'eat' you. I'm afraid I much prefer my food prepared for me and served in a relaxed environment. Not that I am saying you do not taste nice. Its just I'm a bit of a pub grub girl myself." The female voice entreated.

Dirk was about to tell her to go away in a most graphic fashion when he suddenly realised what she had just said. "Ya mentioned a pub? Ya don't mean like a tavern, do ya?"

The thing nodded its acquiescence unknown to Dirk.

"Naff to it then. If you don't know what a tavern is what good are you? Watch if you want, kill me if ya can, I really don't care. Either way unless you can help me find my eye, I don't want to talk to you." Dirk snapped, before resuming his search.

The beast; a Daemoness of the Khill-vaar stood around twelve feet tall on cloven hooves leading to slender (in proportion) sensual thighs, an uncovered, large, hairless crotch and slender waist. Her upper torso and arms were bare also; revealing her gloriously large proportioned breasts of which she had three.

Her principally muscled shoulders led to a thickened hair covered neck that was chief to her cow like head. Her right arms; which alternated between three and two, ended in slight fingered humanesque hands, the upper of which gripped a thin metallic staff and her lower right mutated in to a large crab like claw. Her body was completely covered in a sensual pinkish skin such as may be found betwixt the thighs of a plump lover. The cow-hair covering her neck and head was made up of black and white patches.

Dirk became privy to this information when the faint light from the Daemons staff suddenly flared with life.

"Oh shit, you're a Daemon," Dirk blurted, "Sorry; I mean your one of those killer things…"

"I am Khill-vaar to be precise; yes. And as I stated before; I am here to help you. That is if you want it?" The Daemon offered.

Dirk considered this, knowing the Daemon could very well be a probable saviour for his eye, but at what cost? He asked her without further recourse. "What could you offer help with and what do you want in return?"

"Whatever makes you think I would want anything in return for this?" The Daemoness innocently asked. Unexpectedly she produced Dirk's missing eye from a pouch attached to her waist and began twirling it about in the fingers of her lower right arm.

"You Bitch!" Dirk growled, "Give it back or I'll rip you to-"

Dirks barrage was cut short as the Daemoness' claw shot out and snipped off Dirks head at the neck.

"Do not deem to threaten me Dirk, not yet..." She threatened, momentarily revealing the true side of her races somewhat barbaric nature.

Dirk thrashed about thumping the wall of the stomach as his severed head screamed out every curse that he knew, most of which he had learned from his dear friend Grot, as he struggled to bring his senses under control.

Slamming his head back into place, Dirk let slip away the last vestiges of resisting pain and turned to face the Daemoness with such speed his head lolled weakly to the side on the ravished neckline.

"That was bleeding uncalled for ya bitch! There was-" his derogatory remarks were cut short as the Daemoness threateningly snipped her claws over his prized eyeball in anticipation.

"Don!" He gulped, momentarily unable to gain proper command of his speech.

"Why did dad hurd me? You shouldnay be abedo hurd me. Budder! Ode on – me darynx az libbed!" Dirk garbled, then paused to fish around in his throat and pulled his innards into their correct positions.

"Testing, testing..., ...Aha! Right, that's better. I'm sorry about that. It's just been a long time since I... Well erm, how dya do?" Dirk apologetically enquired.

"Do you want the eye or not hunted?" The Daemoness demanded referring back to Dirk's given title. In these realms one was always referred to as either a hunter or the hunted and just like on Eyrthe, Dirk had been one of the hunted from more or less day one.

"Sorry but do ya mind not calling me that, it gets on my tits. No offence intended," the misshaped Human added taking in the three breasts, "my name's Dirk and I'd appreciate you addressing me as such!"

"And I suppose you tell this to everyone you come across do you hunted?" The Daemoness knowingly enquired, a wide hungry smile playing across her lips.

"Yeah what of it; I always ask but they never do, then we fall out and I normally end up coming much the worse of, as I invariably expect will happen with you. Now please don't get me wrong and whatever you do, don't destroy the eye but see, normally I get some quiet time to myself after a fight or whatever but today you've gone and spoiled that by teleporting into a Gargantuan's stomach to get me! So if ya wanna kill me that bad, why don't you just give me the eye back, cut me up or whatever and quit wasting my time blabbering…, …Don't get me wrong, I know you're powerful. But I will be damned if you won't use my given name when addressing me!"

The Daemoness smiled and then laughed aloud, tossing the eye to Dirk who caught it in surprised fashion. "Have you ever stopped to consider that the reason you may keep coming off worse is because you continually insist on revealing your name? Knowledge IS power here, and your name is a vital source of knowledge best kept hidden."

She paused here and looked with wonderment as Dirks head suddenly righted itself and the gaps in his body started the process of knitting skin and reassembling missing fragments of bones. He still looked a mess of course but his body was replenishing and rebuilding at an astonishing rate – a rate far faster than she herself could even hope to achieve. And he was doing this whilst stood almost waist deep in the most powerful acids in all existence.

"Look I do want something, but I am here to offer you a way out…" She briefly stated flinching at the burning sensation rising up her legs.

"…A way out? Are you kidding? I don't want to get out? Not out there. Nothing bothers me in here; well apart from you, nothing has ever bothered me when I'm lying in the stomach of some beast or whatever. THIS Is the ONLY QUIET TIME I GET! Why? Would I ever want to get OUT?"

The Daemoness was taken aback by this slightly. It was not quite the response she had expected and she was more than a little disconcerted. In fact, so distressed was she that she wondered if she had not made some mistake in her planning, yet she tried again despite herself.

"Because hunted, if you and I do not leave here soon, then we never shall… This is no mere gigantic-rock-beast you have found yourself inside of but a Magmadon. A beast far more powerful than you and I: A race of Giants that helped form the multitude of stars that surround us and the Eyrthe above. And my dear hunted Dirk if you were hoping to become an associated number any time soon; you are sadly mistaken for Magmadon do not *do* number two's."

She paused here for effect; then proceeded with the cutting culmination. "If however you do not want to be digested out of existence, I would be willing to pop you out of here at a small price…"

"I'd rather die." Dirk stated and he meant it.

The Daemon considered this. "What if I were to sweeten the offer?"

Dirk spat at her as his mouth shot back into shape, his teeth pinging back into position like so many whitened fence posts.

"And what would you want from me, I wonder? Oh, oh, I've got it, my soul maybe? My eye..? Ya can't have my eye, diddle I…, …Perhaps my servitude? Ah but what point is there living life as a slave?" Dirk prattled.

"Would it really be any worse than the existence you lead now? What If I was to tell you that you have never moved from the same spot in the last twenty years…?" The cow faced Daemoness accused.

"Twenty years…" this was the first time that Dirk had ever had confirmation of the amount of time he had spent down here and hearing the affirmation made him fill with dread at the thought of spending eternity in this place. He wondered if he should simply stop fighting, like so many others had done before him. He did not doubt the veracity of her statement, for even now he was struggling to keep his left foot intact as the powerful digestive juices surrounding him ate away at his fragile flesh.

"Ya said I have never moved? Surely I've moved now. I mean – I'm in the stomach of this… Magmadon, surely '*It*' has moved." He queried distractedly.

The Daemoness smiled that he had seen past the testing rouse: "Of course *it* has moved, just as most of us can and do. But you, my unwary hunted, do not! I can teach you how. I can take you to other places, realms if you will, of hell and all I ask is a little servitude and love in return."

Dirk abandoned his suicidal ideals as her offer grew on him. "Other places you say? But there's nothing for miles: I've been here twenty years ya say and in all that time I have never come across *anything* like a tavern. Are ya saying I've missed some detail cuz I doubt it. I can see far more things, for a greater distance than most with this eye: The living and dead, both Illusion and reality, I see everything and I have never caught sight of anything except monsters like this bastard and those humanoids that I try so desperately to avoid becoming like. Dya really think I am so stupid?"

"Yes... But let's not call it stupidity, rather I would refer to it as naivety or stubbornness; if you ever stopped your own mouth long enough to listen, you may begin to learn. As I said, YOU have never actually moved anywhere!" The Daemoness said at length.

"So what do ya want? What service or servitude do you require me to agree to and didn't ya mention sex?" Dirk reluctantly asked. It was a very delicious carrot being proffered and he was the kind of Donkey to bite..., "...I suppose it's only understandable that women down here have heard about me too..., ...So what now? Do I sign something or what?"

The Daemoness laughed a genuine laugh of wicked delight, cut short while she clutched at her sizzling thigh in pain. "That's not the way it works dear Dirk of the blood, you must offer me something on your word..."

"...My word?" Dirk blurted out hysterically, "Okay, if you want my word, get me out of here and I will serve you in whatever manner you choose for a whole month of Eyrthe time..." Dirk blurted laughing manically at the thought of someone actually taking him on his word alone: A feat he never had achieved back on Eyrthe. Maybe this Daemoness was not quite the cunning mind he had taken her to be...

An instant later he was stood in the middle of a busy Bazaar, thronged by a multitude of creatures bearing out a variety of words and actions such as one would expect on Eyrthe. Tents and low buildings spread out in every direction all around them, Interceded by larger buildings of indescribable dimensions, defying gravity and other Eyrthely laws.

Town Guards could be seen here and there, not simply because of their militaristic, uniform dress code, but also because their appearance was also uniform. They were invariably snake-like demons of some forty feet in length, their upper half supporting six long tentacles to either side, each in turn gripping a fiery javelin. Their flattish heads were surrounded by a crest of eyes – giving each a 300-degree peripheral vision. Their uniforms were a simple ice-like tabard that covered most of their upper torso and neck.

"Pay them no attention…" The Daemoness gestured in the direction of the guards suddenly appearing besides him: "Leave them alone and they will leave you alone, unless you get involved in trouble of course… Anyhow, if you should ever be unfortunate enough to have to converse with one always address them as Guardian for that is what they are; Hells Guardian. Note I say 'Guardian' not 'Guardians…' Names have power here remember and theirs instils terror. As for my self, you will need something by which to address me and I you for as much as I adore your simplistic nature you really must stop using your real name before someone steals your soul."

Dirk looked at the Daemoness as if she were stupid.

She continued, "I shall call you slave and you shall address me as mistress. Now first thing is first you need to know how to move. It's easy watch and study…" Here she pulled him in close and bending down to his height she touched her forehead to his. "If I need to tell you something that I do not wish others to hear, I shall communicate with you mentally but always be aware; for there are some that are practised in the art of reading others thoughts."

She pulled apart from him and continued the conversation mentally, having formed a link of some description. *'If you ever wish to address me for any reason, you shall beg to be granted a private audience. Now heed my words; to move you simply must be there. It is a little tricky to master at first as you must not consciously want to be there, yet subconsciously know- or believe you **are** there."*

This said she drifted away from him and Dirk shook his head to clear it from a momentary bout of dizziness. Some transitory urchin shone a toothless grin at Dirk's obvious discomfort before passing by on its way.

"Now go and get me an apple from that stall over there." His mistress commanded pointing out a nearby fruit-stall.

Again Dirk looked bemused and he cocked a newly reformed eyebrow in her direction, clucking his tongue at her own innocence. "Did you really think I had any intention of keeping my word? I am nobodies slave my foolish," he paused to snigger: "Mistress…" Dirk broke into laughter and looked around, spotting a nearer stall and moved towards it but found his legs would not walk or rather they did but he was travelling nowhere fast. "Well, I was gonna get you an apple at least but as you've obviously lied about moving; I can't so let's just leave it eh?"

"Slave you use lies so often you would make the Dread lord himself blush. But your lies will do you no good here; most can see through them to some extent and even if you could fool their senses that doesn't apply to the Word of Law." The Daemoness continued undeterred.

"So the Dread lord is real? I mean, like – as in the master of hell?" Dirk asked his face beaming with delight at discovering what he thought to be a childhood tale to be an accepted fact.

"Yes it is real: It is the title given to the supreme Demon; the lord of the lower realms. He is master over all our tortured souls..., ...Believe me now if I speak no other truth: He is one bad occupant you do not want to come across; though I have never met anyone who claims to have met him since his ascension and lived but WE all fear him all the same. I'm afraid Dread lord is a Human term I have picked up, whether or not I would dare address him as such should I ever meet him well, that is another thing... Now! Enough with the questions Slave: Go and get me an apple!" She enthused.

"But I have no intention of doing anything for ya. Don't ya get it? I lied... My word means nothing to me..." Dirk retorted.

A Slug like passer by with no apparent eyes, ears or mouth burst out laughing at somehow hearing Dirks remark and tipped what Dirk took to be its head in his direction. "Well if that's true you are in BIG trouble!" It somehow taunted before sloping off.

The Daemoness paid little attention to the creature though it tipped its head once again as it passed her by in apparent respect. "That is a Mub and they are one such race that communicates telepathically; as I said, be careful what you state in public. Knowledge-"

"I know; I know damn it! Knowledge is power." Dirk interrupted.

"Then if you have learned from it. Why have you still not retrieved an apple from the fruit-stall? You know you can..., ...So why have you not yet done so?"

Dirk considered her words, he realised she was not lecturing him – rather hinting at something. As much as he hated her and everything in this place he had to concede that she did appear to be at least trying to help him. "I guess it's because deep down I don't want to..., ...If I do then I've given up haven't I? I just wish I were dead; I mean..."

Her gentle hand pressed an index finger almost lovingly against his lips. "You have a destiny and this moment of weakness will be forgotten. For now you may hate me. I know you may never change but…"

At this a tear, unheard of for a Daemon, rolled slowly down her furred cheek. She touched her head to his as she blinked away the tear and again her voice pervaded his mind. "Do not worry about that now. Right now, you are my slave no matter what you think and you must learn to listen to me or our time together shall be very tedious indeed!"

Dirk pushed back from her; his hands planting accidentally on two of her boobs as he pushed off and his embarrassment got the better of him for a moment before he himself spoke.

"You don't rule me! NO-ONE, NOTHING, **NOT EVER**-SHALL RULE DIRK HEIN-"

What the?

Dirk no longer had form or substance; he was conscious of being conscious and that was about it. There was no black or white: No sense of light or dark; time, nothing: So this was what oblivion felt like…, …What a bastard, what an idiot, all he'd had to do was serve for a while.

Why am I such a Dick? Why didn't I just move…, …she told me how, what was it she said again? Just see yourself there; I can't see myself anywhere now. An indeterminable amount of time passed as Dirk remonstrated himself thus. It was scary to be this dead and the former human screamed for seemingly hours on end mid taunts and self administered mental abuse.

Suddenly sound exploded around him and he was back in the bazaar. He fell to his knees as a thousand and one senses came to him anew. The ability to see, to smell, touch, hear…

"Should I do it again?" His mistress leered.

Dirk grovelled in genuine fear, "m-no… Mistress, mistress, mistress…, …Please forgive me; I'll be good slave, please…Mistress, please…" Dirk had no idea how long he had spent in oblivion but had no wish to return there ever again for it comprised of the heart of his fears.

"Good slave," she said not unkindly; she had not meant to hurt him so, but he was as stubborn as her unborn daughter had told him to be. "Now listen and heed what I say…"

Again, she touched her head to his, blocking their shared thoughts from outsiders as she continued…, "…*Word of Law is Hells one law that all must abide by. If you agree to give your word; you are bound by it, upon pain of losing your soul to the hood winked party: Permitting that the aforementioned duped party did indeed fulfil their side of the bargain which I did. In short, while I have your soul you have the option of servitude or the existence you witnessed a moment ago, your essence cast into oblivion until I deem fit to restore you. I am trying to rescue you Dirk Heinemblud, for I know you, and you are in dire need of succour…*"

"*Bullshit! What can you rescue me from? Hell? I doubt it? Myself? I…*" Dirk paused unsure of his own mind as a crack in his mental armour appeared. "*Even I can't rescue me from me.*" He eventually conceded.

They shared a moment of fragility that ended the moment that the Daemoness pulled away. "I just hope you remember my kindness through the dark times that lie ahead. Do not ask how I know; for time itself is manipulated differently here to on Eyrthe and so I know many things you simply could not comprehend at the moment. But you will learn…, …Let me begin by explaining how everything constantly expands and contracts here in Hell, that includes time *and* space, so you need to *know* where you are, not simply *think* or *imagine* it…"

XVII) **A Lifetime of Lessons Learned**

Dirk learned to his own displeasure that his 'mistress' was no brainless wonder. If anything in fact, he learned that it was he who had been a fool. For when he had agreed to serve her every whim for one month of Eyrthe time he had no idea that time down here was so capricious and to be truthful, even if he had known that sad fact, he would still have given his word for he and others that knew him held no value over any of Dirk's given statements; sworn or otherwise. Thus by his very own words he had condemned himself to an entire existence of servitude, for in real time mere fractions of seconds had passed; his mistress so enjoyed taunting him still, some one hundred and thirty two years on.

During his travels Dirk had learned many things about a multitude of matters. He had mastered movement and as mistress had told him many years before; that discovery was the most important skill of all. Yet its importance was not as readily discernible as it seemed, or for the basic principle it implied of which around eighty percent of Hells denizens seemed to be unaware: Most of the under-realms dwellers eventually managed to move in some fashion or other without fully realising what that essentially meant. See, Hell is a place of chaos true but even the state of 'chaos' is defined by certain rules. Once one learned those rules which could be bent, a being could begin to grow in power and movement was the first simple step along the path of discovery. The process was no picnic however. Each life, or should that be 'death' skill involved a period of harsh reflection often becoming aware of ones own true strengths and weaknesses, tastes and distastes, pleasures and perversions…

"I am most definitely bored!" Dirk's mistress cried out, languishing upon a plush oval bed bedecked with sumptuous silks.

They were staying at an inn located on the outer edges of the Nargath region on the thirty-second lower plane of Asmoth: One of the many divisions of Hell. The Inn itself was situated within the Hellsphere; a desperately treacherous region of no-man's land which occupied all spaces betwixt realms. They were safe here however from most of the hellish creatures occupying the busy tavern two floors below. Safe too from hidden eyes and ears, for *this* tavern was owned by Dirk's mistress herself.

"Oh slave, come here and look at me…" The Daemoness ordered, stretching out on the bed. She was her usual almost naked self.

Dirk approached her and as he did so he struggled not to notice the exposed crotch glistening moistly up to the stiff, almost thumb sized clitoris. "Yes mistress? What dya want me for?"

Again, she shifted about on the bed, stretching out her lengthy supple form as she tensed this way and that. Again Dirk caught a flicker of her crotch and forced his eyes upwards where they caught upon the peaks of her breast, where her nipples, all three of them stood erect and swollen. He snapped his gaze of to the side then back again. This time his eyes settled on her head with its Bulls horns and cows features and immediately his threatening erection died. '*Man it's been way too long...*' he thought.

"Mistress what dya want? I was reading a good book..." Dirk stretched his arm out behind him, pointing to the said reading material.

Her claw flexed as she tweaked first one; then the other nipples. Both her other hands wandering down; the upper right tenderly flicking out over her inner thigh and the lower arm grabbing Dirk's belt buckle and pulling him onto his knees on the bed.

"Do you want me Dirk Heinemblud, sexually? I wonder. Have you ever wanted me? Perhaps you are gay..." she emphasised her words bringing her hand slowly up between her thighs, playing with her exposed, throbbing clitoris as she did so.

"Another of your stupid games..., ...Or a lesson perhaps, if ya want to take me ya need but command it? You're becoming obvious now ya know: If I admit to having fantasised about ya, you'll exploit it as a weakness and if I deny it you'll twist what I say in some bloody manner, probing away, questioning my morale fibre and values or some shit..."

He paused as her claw reached out and pinched his right nipple. "Ouch! That hurt..."

"I know..., ...but you liked it really didn't you? I can see you want me Dirk, you always have... Would you like to take me now?" she teased.

"See! That's the type of shit I mean: I've been waiting for this; well not waiting..., ...Damn! I mean *wondering* when or **if** it would happen. Now if I say yes you'll probably go and tease me like this for weeks, months or whatever. If I say no well forget it: I aint falling for that shit; so I'll just say no comment."

Her free hand snaked up his slim thigh, gently cupped his scrotum and brushing against his swollen member.

She giggled as she pulled him closer, that rasping naughty laugh. "It's a good job your body is not as good a liar as you are Dirk Heinemblud: I just want to have sex..., ...with you; no strings and I want it now!"

Dirk pushed her back onto the bed, causing her eyes to fill red with blood in anger. A surge of painful separation washed over him and he immediately sank to his knees begging for supplication.

"Do you want me or not, get down and lick my body, hoof to horn slave..." She ordered, and though it half sickened him to do so. He heeded her command. Only half sickened though, for as much as the sight of her animal features repelled him, the rest of her was in absolutely perfectly female proportions; even her extra breast and Dirk was sorely desperate!

He paused at her gleaming vagina, drawn in by her sweet odours and she slapped him sharply across the face. "I said *all over* my weak little slave!" Dirk continued his oral Olympics up and over her lengthy body, making sure to cover every part of her form in his moist trace, but as his tongue reached her hair-covered neck, he balked. "I'm sorry mistress..."

"Take me!" she ordered, "Take me now." Dirk reacted instantaneously; almost as eager to divest him self of one hundred plus years sexual frustration as he was to distance his gaze from her bullish features.

And he did indeed ravish her. He threw her long slender legs up over his shoulders, ignoring the hooves, as he took her with force, pounding away like a man possessed, which, given his present company he might very well have been...

He achieved orgasm several times before she took control of him, by which time he rejoined willingly. Mounting him, she straddled his face and sucked long and hard on his genitals in reciprocation. Her particular oral practices were new to Dirk who had only ever known (in a physical way), innocent farm-girls and filthy whores: Both of which had been more than content with a simple roll in the proverbial hay and a quick lick of the pussy at best, they hardly ever licked, sucked and nibbled on his penis in such manner and definitely not all three together with such practised art: Moreover they most certainly did not scream at him to return the favour with haste. Dragging his head around by his hair and telling him to go harder, softer; to bite more..., ...Several times they both came in this manner until his mistress was almost at the point of orgasm and she pulled his head up a little thrusting her hips and commanding him to suck her clit like protrusion which Dirk actually discovered to be an undeveloped penis.

All the while she licked at his anus and sucked on his balls pulling at his manhood.

When he next came, It was simply a glorious coming together, as she reached climax; all three erect nipples pinking as she came in his mouth, then reached multiple orgasms as his tongue lapped at her vaginal excretions and made her come even more due to both her carnal sexual appetite and his lengthy enforced abstinence.

They thrashed about wildly pleasuring each other in various positions, utilising various practices all of which Dirk proved to be more inept at than she. This Dirk thought a little strange at first then discounted the notion; assuming she had probably obtained her current powers by playing succubus to some evil demi-god or other shadowy character. Yet here he was; a shadow of a mortal, teaching her a few things too, or at least giving her almost as much pleasure as he himself received, though it must be noted: Some of her suggestions tested even *his* boundaries of what was acceptable.

Three long 'weekly' periods passed as they made love throughout what passed for day and night, Dirk tirelessly divesting himself of the urges he had felt magnified a thousand fold ever since he had been condemned to this infernal hell. They were entwined in one such position when she did something she had never done before. She entered him by a most unusual and wholly demonic fashion… As they lay there, making love a small wispy tentacle snaked delicately out from its hiding place within her dimpled belly button and in through Dirks own – forcing a small hole as it snaked about within him in search of its elusive prey. The sensation was immaculately spectacular, overwhelming any pain he could possibly suffer from as he his senses were inundated with explosive natural highs. The probing tentacle caught a hold of that which it pursued and wrapped itself around the shadowy essence. Strangling and cutting off a small segment which it greedily devoured before retracing its path back into its dimpled abode.

Dirk, who was experiencing utopia, gasped at a pinch of pain as she stole a tiny fragment of his soul. "Forgive me, my love but I must have your seed." She said, bending down to kiss his forehead as she rose from their shared bed. "Sleep now, lover. I have tasks to attend to…"

That night she returned to him and immediately he was upon her, amorously nuzzling her underarm as his fingers crept over her sultry figure. The passion was returned with redoubled enthusiasm and they made love long and hard, yet all the while Dirk avoided looking at her facial features.

After a few hours his mistress decided to bring up the subject. "Why will you not look at me? Are you ashamed to be making love to a Demon perhaps? Or is it because I remind you of an animal?"

"What does it matter? Just don't spoil the moment." He said slapping her backside as he expertly flipped her onto her stomach and took her from behind without breaking his stroke. He took her in this fashion for nigh on thirty minutes before, groaning with pleasure; she withdrew his stiffened phallus and inserted it into her anus.

This was no new thing to Dirk as many of the fore mentioned farmers daughters would often use this method as a means of having contraceptive sex without losing their imagined virtue before their wedding day. She still insisted on speaking however as he slid in and out with impassioned yet gentle strokes. "It's my head isn't it? You'll kiss any other part. And I notice you grip my legs with excessive force…"

"Look ya face is bloody ugly to me as a human; ya look like a bloody cow; I mean, you've not even got a nice looking animals head, why couldn't you have chose a cat or some other fluffy pet that– oh you know what I mean. What do you expect?" Dirk argued and pulled away from her.

She nudged her arse back onto him and pushed back, filling her sodden hole with his hardened staff. Dirk acquiesced, the truth was he found her impossible to resist, despite her facial looks.

"You should learn to look past that which you see and take for granted," she stated as she increased the tempo. Dirk followed her impetus and the two were nearing orgasm when her physical appearance suddenly changed to resemble that of a large panther like cat/human hybrid. "Is this a more acceptable animal?" she yelled out in half maddened ecstasy. "Or are you going to pull away again?"

Dirks response was to lift her by the waist and drive into her with renewed ardour, they each rose to their orgasmic peaks and collapsed onto the bed side by side. "I will take ya in any way, shape or form ya desire… just don't tell be lecturing me all the time okay…, …Besides I've already given ya everything I've got." Dirk lied.

"Not yet you haven't!" she said changing her form as she did so to that of a Dog, complete with lengthy tongue and begin licking at his buttocks and balls: "Come now, what really turns you on? What's your ideal of the perfect woman? Is she tall or short? Fat, slender or skinny or perhaps you prefer them hairless…, …Or hairy?"

"Hairy right…, …Well if ya gonna insist. She would be about five feet tall. Dark hair, green eyes, and her body would be slightly daintier than yours but without the head, neck and feet of course…"

Dirk's words suddenly tailed off as he realised she was adopting her form according to his description and he turned and sat in fascination as her physical form responded to his words. Her legs became slightly more elegant; the hooves replaced by the tiniest feet: Two of her arms disappeared while the others took on a slender feebleness with a slight sloping of the shoulders: Her neck stretched while contracting and losing the hairy cowhide as it did. Her face changed to resemble that of a vaguely beautiful woman somewhere between her late teens and twenties. Dirk was inspired. "Fuller lips and an ever so slight shadow around the eyes; make them slightly slanted, almond shaped like an Elf. Dimpled cheeks…" He went on to describe her in every detail and she responded knowledgably to his every preference, until at last he was fully satisfied with her looks, at which point they made love yet again and with the passion of one incapable of holding back. When, several short minutes later Dirk lay down momentarily expended she turned to him and smiled a wicked smile. Unnecessarily asking "Would you like me to remain in this form?"

He readily gave his approval but her new look came at a price, so she informed him. "You say you have given me everything, but you have held something back from me all this time… If you were willing to give that up to me I might be convinced to keep this form forever…"

Dirk leapt at the opportunity, his genitals were already stirring again as he stared at her feverish body. "Whatever it takes; it's yours. I like how ya kept the third tit too; ya must have caught me thinking it: You never can have too many nipples…" Dirk cooed, delicately nuzzling each perfectly rounded breast.

"Maybe I should become a dog then?" she toyed: "If you want me like this; you have to give me your sexuality in return so we may become one…"

"…**My WHAT**?" Dirk spluttered, his hand dashing to cover his crotch instinctively.

"Not that!" She cried in laughter, "I meant your masculinity: If you want my feminine side to remain, I ask for your masculine side in return. I want to please you like you please me as one."

Dirk's eyebrows rose in understanding, "Ya wanna shag *me?*"

She vigorously nodded her delicately featured head and rose to her knees next to where Dirk lay and he stared with a mixture of curiosity and suspicion by the sight of a lengthy hard penis manifesting in place of her penis shaped clitoris.

"Okay but make it a little bit smaller…, …That bitch is way bigger than my nob and *I've* never done this shit before…" no sooner had he finished the sentence and she pushed him onto his stomach and gently slid her newly formed cock inside his anal tract. He felt a brief moment of pain and then a build up of sinful pleasure as sweet as anything his senses had tasted before, yet indescribably different. At the same time, he instinctively felt ashamed and humiliated…, …Like he had somehow cheated himself.

"You like this…?" His mistress queried, adjusting her stroke to push in an inch or two further. "It's only in a few inches; just wait until I am giving you all fourteen inches…"

"You better be joking" Dirk moaned; "I don't think I could take much more than what your giving me now…, …It bloody hurts ya know."

She slid a few inch deeper then pulled out almost completely, the nub of her penis catching on his anal rim, before pushing in four or five inch deep in long, smooth, rhythmic motions, to which Dirk was reduced to panting and moaning in response; partially through pain but primarily due to pleasure. "See if you are willing to enjoy something it can be much more enjoyable; you will want me to do this every night soon my little slave…"

Dirk winced at the bittersweet sensation, groaning with pleasure all the same and managed through clenched teeth to cry out a response. "Oh yeah baby; I don't mind ya screwing me if that's what it takes…"

"But it's what you want is it not?" she asked, toying with her phallic size and girth; making it shrink and expand as she gauged his reaction.

"Oh yeah baby yeah…" he moaned, truthfully in more than a little discomfort, yet thought he should play the game; "I want to feel your big – ah, yeah bigger baby; oh push deeper; yes slow, long and hard that's it baby, oh I think I'm gonna come. Give it to me; yeah baby, bigger, harder..., ...aah that's too big, aargh!" He cried out in pain as she plummeted into his depths relentlessly, her penis was now swollen to quite gifted proportions.

"Stop!" he yelled in discomfort. But she hammered away ignorant to his pleadings. "Get the shite off me, you're hurting; Aah, I can't take it: Okay I can," he changed tack as his nipples exploded with prickling sensations of pleasure and his cock began pumping out spunk like it was out of fashion, "Oh keep going baby don't stop, aw yeah; aah baby, no... stop; aargh my arse, stop..., ...get off!" he screamed and forcefully attempted to pull away as she filled his rectal canal with her own come for minutes without relent. "You Bitch!" he spat when she at last pulled out.

"I think you'll find it's you that is the bitch dear," she joked. "What's up? Not woman enough?" Dirk looked down at her delivered taunt as his groin changed in feel and he saw to his distress that he had been denuded of his penis and had the correct women's bits instead of his own sexual organs.

"What's the matter with ya? Why dya do this shit to me: So we can swap roles properly or so that you can reassert your dominance over me? Or has these past few weeks simply been yet another test; to show me how sick and twisted I have become? Because if that's it; you've wasted your time. I lick the arse of depravity and eat sick and twisted for breakfast. Making love to ya as a goat, donkey or shrub wouldn't matter as long as I get sex."

"But you don't make love do you?" she seethed in retaliation, "You screw me, but you don't love me, do you? I never wanted this penis. Your mind grew that; it was what you wanted..."

"I never..." Dirk faltered, he had thought that was what she had meant and he had looked to see if her body had changed, which of course it duly had done. "Well okay I did but I didn't want ya to shag me..."

The Daemoness shot him a derogatory glance, "I'm afraid you very much did. I can read your mind remember..."

Dirk revised his protest as his anus contracted painfully, "Ok look, I did want you to... Because I thought that's what you wanted and I didn't wanna get shit wrong; besides which I get a kick outta pain; so I thought..., ...Well you said if I wanted you to stay like that..."

"...I wanted your whole being in return... Your *love* you dolt! I gave you my all; my very being; I took your seed. I let you treat me like some common succubus, I lead you through tests and the like with all the thoughtfulness an attentive mother gives to her wayward child and still... You are such a selfish being Dirk of the Blood..." She seemed at a lost for words. "I even let you make love to me..."

"What does that mean?" Dirk riled, "moreover what the shit dya think it's gotta do with me? So you're no different to every second woman in my mortal life... Besides which, I always figured you were a succubus..."

"That was my first time you pig! My family runs back generations: *We* Khill-vaar demons are not merely moulded from the essence like some common succubus; we are born. You never change: I wish I'd never met you..." She turned away, tears forming in her big beautiful eyes and Dirk felt himself melting at the sight of his designer maiden in distress.

"Then why did you seek me out? It was you who found me remember...?" He said edging forward and gently massaging her perfectly sloping shoulders, breezily passing his lips over her neckline.

"To protect you from yourself: To help you to learn and understand about knowledge. To help you gain a respect for anything, something; everything. Dirk, have you never loved me?" She cried.

"...Of course I haven't!" Dirk shot flippantly back at her and suddenly realised why it was he had led such a charmed existence by her side. He knew now that she really did love him. And he knew, she knew, he knew.

She gave him a lasting look and then rose from the bed. Her tone hardening as she spoke, "We must never let this happen again..., ...I am going away for a while slave; a day or two perhaps. Do not leave the tavern until my return."

Here she paused to deliver a long lingering kiss to his forehead, a sadness etched upon her brow as she did so, and dirks suspicions were confirmed beyond doubt by the affectionate caress that followed. "That is my final order." She whispered and drifted out of the room.

When she was gone Dirk lay back down on the bed, clutching at the throbbing sensation in his swollen prostrate. *'I'm a right thick shit some times...'* he mused and began to wonder how he could turn the newfound knowledge to his advantage. *'We all have weaknesses...'*

"I shall miss you my love…" He mulled aloud.

Dirk slept then and his dreams were wrought by tormented visions the likes of which he had never known… Many of those beings who had died by his hand came rushing in from the edges of his mind's eye, some merely contented themselves with taunts and accusing screams, whilst others still held numerous one way conversations of appropriated guilt. Dirk turned away but as he did so his faceless parents came striding forward hand in hand. He reached out a diseased hand in desperation which his mother took hold off. But instead of holding it affectionately and lifting him to sanctity, she held him down whilst his father began beating him. He screamed for help and the ruddy pink form of his mistress came striding out of the dark and swooped down onto his fragile physique. Her lower half was that of a horse whilst her upper was replaced by the revolting torso and head of Snurch; the one he had previously slain. She drove her huge phallus into him and with each stroke he felt his body dissolving inch by inch, piece by piece, part by body part. All the while the screaming, the beating and arguing continued.

Dirk cried out and rose sharply from the bed. He was floating in the air and for a moment panic rose like a peeping tom as he thought himself under attack. No attack came however and as his senses returned he realised he was still very much alone, in the dimly lit light of the bedroom.

"*I'm doing it!*" Dirk realised and slowly drifted to the floor as he calmed his fluttering heart. "Well, I never knew I could do that!" he cheered. His slackened jaw raised into a smile as he considered the implications of his newfound skill and he thought back to the event that had triggered his unbound levitation.

The dream came flooding back and he blanched at its recall, but instantly he deciphered its meaning. "The bitch took our soul… or at least, a part of it…, …The bitch took our ***Frigging SOUL***!"

'*So that was her plan was it: The sexual test of our morality. Well we have none. Or at least none we intend to let her see just yet. What should we do though? Is she trying to play with us? Why take our soul now when she could have taken it any time before. And why the hell do I keep saying ours and we…?*'

'*Or is she doing it,*' Dirk thought on, '*maybe this is it, she's merged our souls or…Hold on a minute… our? Who the hell are you? You're not me, I can feel me – or a lack of me but that's why; my head is so battered it feels like a Gollum's arse! Has the bitch been lying all the time? What should we do? I don't feel right. This isn't us; which is weird: I remember when I was alive; before I 'died', I felt like I was more than me. Someone knows something that can help us and we have got bollocks knows how long before she gets back. What if we're trapped here forever though? No you're right, let's go downstairs; just get outta here! What can she do that she hasn't already? We-no, I have got to think.'* Dirk checked himself in the mirror but he was or still appeared to be Dirk. He rinsed himself under several large jugs of water then dressed without bothering to first dry himself, and half stepped half floated out of his Mistress's master bedroom and down the short hallway leading to the staircase. At the top of the staircase, Dirk paused to calm his feverish mind and cease his intermittent levitation, before proceeding down the stairs and into the tavern below. Dirk had thought to leave immediately, but his attention was diverted by the presence of so many various members of the damned and the clear, lilting voice of some minstrel. The fellow was dressed in fine shades of silk, coloured in a variety of shades of pink that bedecked every part of his body and rose snakelike around his neck where his garb tied off in a turban, concealing all but his hands and humanesque face...

The barman flagged him over and Dirk approached as bid. "Do I know ya?" Dirk asked. He had never spent more than a few seconds in the actual tavern vault before. It was a cavernous structure with thick beams of writhing twisted souls, and walls built from the skins of the damned. The tables and chairs were –in the main, a collection of slaves –whose souls had long since been sucked from their corporeal forms; and were chained into place so that they may be used as furniture by the inns patrons who did so with little regard as to the comfort of the 'furniture' being sat on.

"I know ya, favoured slave. The mistress told me you'd show. She said; erm… Do ya mind not doing that?" The hairless, slug-like barman yelped.

"I don't get ya?" Dirk puzzled leaning harder on the bar, "What did she mean…, …Do what?"

The barman's fat pulpy arms lifted Dirks own from the countertop before responding, "Not her; me. She said to '*take care of ya.*' I said to gets your elbows of me back!" The point was emphasized by the barman's wild shining eyes and the rippling of the counter as he stretched out his back.

"Oh! You're furniture too? I didn't take any notice sorry." Dirk smirked apologetically.

"Less of the 'furniture' comments," remarked the offended bartender. "We don't take kindly to it round here and lets me tell ya; the absolutes worst thing you can says about us, is that ya don'ts notice us!" the barman growled back. "Lastly my back is for serving drinks on only; I am not a P.L.P."

"Huh…" Dirk ventured, "What's a bloody P.L.P?"

"Public Leaning Post," the barman scowled back.

Dirk felt a little guilty at the meaningless comments but then as he considered his own multiple list of humiliating, downtrodden life experiences, Dirk wondered how hard life could be as a stool or whatever.

"**Sod you!**" Dirk argued: "Who gives a shit if ya get leaned on? So bloody what!" Dirk was incensed and his rhetoric grew in volume as he berated the barman, intentionally jamming his elbows down hard on the spine of the bar as he did so. "Do ya think just because nobody else calls *you it, you aren't all* **just** bloody stuff for all of **us** to sit on? I mean who is it that ya think cares so much about *you* or your feelings? Look at that bugger over there in the corner; he's bent over double and got his arms raised behind him; despite him being way too old; if he were my chair I'd chuck him out!"

"Oh and if ya think that's bad; how about being beaten senseless in a pub brawl you had hardly anything to do with; then blamed for the whole thing, beaten some more and thrown outside in the gutter only for some buggers tethered horse to piss on ya…, …Then when ya go to wash the mess off ya get savaged by a pack of dogs, only to be rescued by a girl; who ya then shit ya self in front of…" Dirk was clearly quite incensed and working him self into quite a rage…, "Oh and ya know what? That was one of the less embarrassing experiences I had in life but in my time by that nasty bitch of a mistresses side: I've had almost every nasty bugger thing done to me that you can think of and probably a hell of a lot of things that *your* dumb-ass brain can't even comprehend…, …Ya know; just before she left telling you to take care of me; she buggered me and ate a good part of my sodding well soul, so if you think you've got it bad spending your eternal un-life as a bloody P.L.P, believe me; *you aint*. Now shut your whingeing and get me a pint of mead and the rest of ya dicks can stop gawping and listening to me and my confessions and pay attention to this bloody sweet sounding poet chap instead; I'm sure he's far more interesting…"

Those patrons and stools that had cocked their heads to listen in, diverted their attention to the suggested poetry of the garishly dressed minstrel, who stood atop a table, placed more-or-less in the centre of the inns taproom. The barman dutifully brought forth a jug of strangely red coloured liquid and a glass, whilst Dirk too listened in on the minstrel's sonnet...

"...Through twisting mounds of snow, interspaced by eternal trunks rising, rising..., ...Stretching twilight tinged finger tips towards a brightening vast panorama of moonlit sky: Rising again and yet, as the green petals flow; down upon the tender breach, the rabbit sighs-"

"Rabbits don't sigh!" A Cyclops shouted from a table in the vicinity of the impromptu stage.

"They squeal!" bellowed a sloth, mimicking the actions of a frightened rabbit.

"...the hunters bow of hardwood pure; lengthy and featured with rivulets of willow; tenses with the breath of a thousand artisans, each ones practised art unique. A flicker of movement, amongst green and white; then sudden brown-" the minstrel melodiously continued.

"Did the hunter shit himself?" again another individual barracked.

Continuing unperturbed the minstrel sang on, "...Drawing sight; his amber eye aligning with the eye's of the determined quarry, he let loose the taut chord, accompanied by the singing of a harp's soul..., ...The arrows flight true runs towards its predetermined prey; the rabbit's back arches in a crest of excellence, hind quarters thumping out a beat; 'let me flee, let me flee' but arrow sight finds right taking those very legs through thigh muscle and bone; the hunter's prey comes down. As eve draws in with the folding of a curtain of clouds; the hunter feasts on soulless meat. Yet the small fire of hunter becomes hunted one's doom as a beast of great fortitude approaches from above; the bow unwinds in hands gripping as steel; an arrow finds purchase on his string and sing, sing, sing arrows ping. Yet the beast is mighty and the arrows of alacrity serve merely as nuisance to the newly crowned hunter as its stretching talon treacherously scratches across the symphony; ending its motioning and carrying death to the heart of its owner as the Griffon of yore feeds on his fallen flesh, and on and on events revolve and turn, hunter hunting hunter..., ...Until no other could fall: Though this one remained to sing his song and lament the souls of all."

With a final exorbitant bow, the minstrel brought his act to a close and awaited the absent applause. Dirks solitary clap of hands rang out like a signal to the other patrons and they responded, though not in the intended manner. The Cyclops was first to deliver a blow as the minstrels table reared up, unexpectedly tossing him into the suddenly angered crowd.

"You call that entertainment!" accused the Cyclops, kicking out as the mob thronged about taunting and pummelling the slight humanoid minstrel.

"Lamenting a stupid little rabbit…, …What sort of sick beast art ye?" A hideous looking Demon said stepping forward: It had the obligatory claws in abundance; even possessing wickedly clawed feet: Wings too although these were formed from an unsubstantial smoky texture. The eyes were bleeding inferno's that seemed to hold untold depths if not realms; two gnarled, spiralling, goat-like horns topped of a feral face but the humanoid being's innards were turned outwards for the most part, even displaying a prominent stomach and the whole mess of sinew and bone was finished off with an excess of purple, red, green and white veins. If Dirk had been alive he would have puked and shit himself for sure.

"I will not hear such disgusting lyrics here in the holiest of the infinite hells planes: You poison my presence with that crap!" The richly veined Demons voice resonated, as he lifted the beaten chap from the midst of the excited throng and threw him against the man-bar; much to the barman's discomfort, who scowled at the discarded minstrel. The upended Minstrel crumpled into an upright sitting position and his turban slipped in shocking revelation.

"An Elf?" the Demon exclaimed sighting the minstrels exposed ears, which were irrefutably those of an Elf. The whole pub erupted in jeers.

Dirk too glanced in surprise at the chap; his skins shade and texture suggested another fact – here was no Dark Elf, one of those who had *'strayed from the lightened path'* as the Elves themselves put it. No, here before them was to all intents and purposes an Elf of *'the forest'*. A soul thought *'Good and true'*.

"Might you have caught the wrong afterlife?" A nasty puss-ball of a creature taunted as it threw a mug at the downed Elf.

Dirk thought quickly – there was going to be trouble and he wanted as much distance between him and *it*, he hopped off his stool and chugged towards the door but found himself stopping in front of the Elf, whose pleading eyes locked with his own. *'Move yourself you dick!'* Dirk enthused in his mind.

'We need to help him!' Dirk shook his head, "Like balls we do..." he said aloud and turned to find himself facing a semi encircling throng of deadly onlookers, not appreciative of the seemingly defensive interloper. *'We shall fight them – concentrate on a thunderstorm –visualise it...'* He thought to himself: "Hold on –I've got a better idea!" Dirk again argued aloud.

"And what, pray tell is that...?" The large and by far deadliest looking Demon enquired.

"What? Oh-no, I was... I'm sorry what did you say your name was again...?" Dirk blathered as he gambled for time whilst desperately attempting to formulate a hopefully non-violent plan of action.

Dirk waved his arm in a non-threatening manner as the assembled masses poured forward, gulping from his mug of red ale as they did so. The throng slowed then stopped when it became apparent that Dirk had no intention of moving from his imposed, if relaxed position. Only the Cyclops and deeply veined Daemon approached to within fist-fighting distance of Dirk, behind who the Elf attempted to rise, before clutching painfully at his demolished rib cage and slumping back to the deck.

"Who are you that would stand in our way hunted?" the approaching Daemon disparaged.

"Yeah... yer fink yer can stop dis?" the Cyclops blurted, swinging a single mighty fist in Dirks direction.

The crudely thrown punch failed to connect however, as Dirk momentarily blinked in and out of existence; a skill long since taught to him by his departed mistress, and he sighed before dumping the stunned Cyclops onto his bruised backside with a simple flick of the wrist; in reality he had simply given the hellish matter beneath the Cyclops feet a gentle tug, much like one might pull a rug from beneath the feet of another: A trick he had taught himself along the way.

"Impressive..." the Daemon said with admiration, "I shall enjoy battling with ye both..."

Dirk may have picked up considerably more knowledge about the realms than the dim-witted Cyclops before him but he new beyond doubt he was no match for the inside-out Daemon so he tried a different tact.

"We desire no conflict with *you* oh great and masterful hunter; simply to entertain your good selves, besides which; do ya really want to get involved in a bar-room brawl that could end your very existence? For all ya know him or I could be none other than the Dread lord himself..." Dirk loudly declared bowing to the floor as he did so.

"A bold statement from one so weak looking as ye are..." The Daemon countered, "Only a madman bent on destruction or the Dread lord him self would declare such a thing..."

Dirk rose slightly though still kept his gaze low: "Then I leave it to your selves to decide which; like I say; we are just here to entertain..."

The Daemon regarded the Human and Elf quizzically, "We...?"

Dirk grinned at the floor as he spoke, "Of course we, master hunter... For we are a pair him and I; one the master the other the student and we act, sing and dance for other peoples enjoyment, in exchange for no more than their fair treatment and..."

"Ye want fair treatment? If ye truly are the Dread lord then you're the most polite one I ever came across: That sounds like the statement of a do-gooder. We don't get many of *those* down here and *when we do*..." The Daemon thrust its upper torso and face toward Dirk's own in the blink of an eye; its slavering jaws mere inches from Dirk's bowed head.

"You misunderstand; I mean, I didn't explain, oh lord Vaar Ghourm send forth a million wraith's to rip away my soul if I aint the most unholy son of a bitch down here!" Dirk exclaimed worriedly raising his head to a hot blast of fetid breath but thankfully no Wraith's.

The demon's jaws quivered with blood fused spittle as he spoke: "If ye worship that man hating bitch ye must be both be desperately twisted *and* a fair bit demented..."

"We are mighty lord; and I didn't mean to sound girly;"

"...But ye are a girl are ya not?" The Daemon asked confused.

"Ah yes, well no..., ...See when I said we wanted 'fair treatment' what I meant was that we are two weak souls who simply entertain to avoid incurring the wrath of beings such as your great self: Thus we get fair treatment. I am *sure* ya dealt fairly with my friend here for that soppy tale; I was just coming over to kick him myself in fact when ya stopped me, of a sort..." Dirk paused to deliver a hoofed kick to the Elves already ruptured torso, "…but it aint his fault, see; he forgets himself sometimes, ever since I got turned into a girl and him into an Elf, in fact…"

"Turned into an Elf? And ye into a girl, what will you tell us next; that ye were a ferocious Balrog before this untimely incident? By what power were you changed so, hmm Mr. Liar?" The Daemon accused as its sinewy claws wrapped around his jaw and lifted him, unresisting, from the ground.

"Galghow!" Dirk shouted the first name that came into his head as the pressure on his clamped jaw increased.

The Daemon dropped him to the ground without care: "Who?"

"Galbor oh ferocious hunter," Dirk whispered, "He was a wizard called Galbor… Might you have heard of this devilish fiend?" Dirk grovelled, cleverly slipping in the reference to Galbor's true identity.

"…Galbor? Ye say Galbor do ye not? Tell me how this came about?" the Daemon demanded; as both its own and the gathered patrons' interest grew increasingly intense.

"Galbor…!" Dirk piped up, hoping the abused barman would stay schtum: "Yes! Well, we came across him some 100 or so years back and he cursed my companion here with the appearance and manners of an Elf; since then, everywhere he goes he gets battered, hence the reason for the shitty disguise. But that's not something we should be discussing great one; surely you wish to be entertained," Dirk pleaded: "If you could just see your way to healing my wounded friend he would gladly sing to you of war and wenches…"

The Elf sighed in some sort of confirmation.

"Your *friend* will be fine enough for now. But something concerns me about your *story*… Ye said that ye both entertain; yet I have yet to hear anything but whimpering supplication from ye…, …I suggest: *You* should be the one who entertains for now, that is; if you and he wish to retain your soulful existence here in Hell…"

Dirk looked to the Elf who shook his head to indicate he was in no position to offer him any help, let alone speak. Dirk cleared his throat and rose to his feet. A song often sang by his old friend Grot coming back to him. *'At least you'll not end up down here ya bastard! A hundred years ago I asked for your bloody help. If ya heard me; he heard you, yeah well if he bleeding well did he ignored me or ya found ya self a nice spot in friggin heaven to bed down on…, …Oh Grot I bloody miss ya…, …Shit man think, how did that song go; help us out me old amigo.'* Dirk thought to himself.

"My lord Daemon, I shall sing to you an old Dwarven song of battle…" Dirk said blagging for time by rumbling his vocal tones

"By all the hells ye will ***not***! We want amusement not the dour mourning atonement of Dwarves. Come now, deliver us something jaunty. War and wenches ye promised…"

***

A vast chamber whose exact dimensions were too mind numbing to fathom and filled with copious gradients of pure white light; at the eastern 'end' a small arch of some thirty foot span, lay open to the dark void lurking beyond. Barring the exit to Hell however, was a snarling white-knight type chap called Dave. And Dave was hard as nails so to speak. No-one, not even the gods messed with Dave.

His job was not only simple enough but was his sole ambition in life (and death), furthermore, nobody bothered to try and change things; the exit needed guarding by some omnipresent power and Dave's dream job was to guard the gates of heaven. Okay, so some other power had the job at the gates so to speak, but at the time of his demise no-one had been around to guard the portal to the abyss; a back door route so to speak, that warranted wanton passage to all those who bothered to find it.

Dave had found it though, for he had known it had to exist for everywhere he had been in life had always had a front and back door; an entry and exit so to speak and considering the front gates seemed to be very limited for the most part to the act of '*entering*', Dave had gone searching in earnest for the planes exit: Once he had found it, he had wasted no time at all in staking a claim as its guardian and after being confronted by an angry travelling demi-god; who deemed Dave to have no right to refuse him access and attempted to exercise the point by force, Dave's reputation as one to avoid arguing with had travelled far and wide.

After he had been in charge a few Aeons without any major delegate from either side forming any major dispute to his self imposed authority, Dave discovered the back door to be a truly neutral zone, wherein no force; no matter its strength or size could be more powerful than its opposition no matter its own size and strength, additionally those of true neutrality lay no claim to it *because* of their very neutrality; whilst those of a firm allegiance to either side were outright banned from claiming ownership. Dave himself was rather more chaotic in his own view of neutrality and thus had no qualms about taking on the self appointed post. He had ground rules, fair and simple as they were; nobody could leave without his or some other higher beings permission and those souls that did apply for release Dave thought of as weird and simply placated them by force: Those that argued got pummelled and those that truly belonged to Hell invariably received a beating followed by a sermon on ethical attitude and the accoutrements of sin.

In Dave's life, he had been the most right royal, pain in the tit, puritan Paladin one could ever have the misfortune to meet. His ideals of right had obviously never quite made the simple computation of violent enforcement itself being a sin but hey; nobody's perfect. On his final living day he found himself stripped of his knighthood and excluded from the order at around about the same instant he died..., ...An Elven male who had served alongside the order in a number of missions and battles for a score of years had applied to become a knight and had been turned down flat because of his ethnicity. Dave had gone away and studied the books regarding such matters and found no reference to racial exclusions. Armed with such knowledge he publicly challenged the Seers of the Illuminari, bishop and Supreme Guardian Templar, an act that inevitably led to his typical violent challenge, a great bloodshed and a public dismissal for his own pains by means of decapitation.

He bent down and offered his hand in assistance as the Dwarf lifted himself unsteadily to his feet. "Have ye given thought to thou heretical desires or doth thou require yet another kicking my surly friend?"

Grot stood and thought of punching the guy while he wasn't ready, but the glowing Paladin dumped him back down to the floor as he thought it; stamping his foot down hard on Grot's throat.

"Silly Dwarf will ye not learn... I am invincible and thou shall not leave. Go ask at the front gates if you desire, for I shall offer no short access to Hell." He pushed back on the foot, leaving the Dwarf momentarily incapacitated as Dave shuffled back a little. "Thou simply need receive a letter of refusal for thy pains, from the holy gates of heaven and I shall oblige in sending thee where thou belong."

Grot rubbed his throat and for a mere second his usually pragmatic demeanour wondered if this being could really be invincible. *'Everything's got a weakness'* he mulled, *'What would Dirk do?'*

Grot swallowed a sickening lump in his throat at what he was about to contemplate and wondered if there were any ramifications for lying in Heaven. It wasn't as if it was a bad place, in fact many of his relatives resided within Keldor's heavenly halls but he had a job to do. *'Yes but the place stinks of sweat, sick and ale and anyhow I've a job to do on Eyrthe first.'* Besides Dirk needed rescuing and that was that. There would be plenty of time for socialising later...

He wondered briefly about the Phoenix, whose flames had left Dirk unscathed and wondered for the millionth time why his friend had then been transported to hell. The truth was he felt the bird had been mistaken, but that could not be the end of it. A Phoenix's touch burned whether by chance or intent and only the purest could survive its touch. He himself had gone to heaven upon death even though he had sinned enough for the Phoenix to hurt him so –even in death he was missing the disintegrated pinkie. And he even doubted whether the puritan brute before him would stand up to its fiery wrath. Yet Dirk was a sinner of monumental proportions and that was from the little Grot knew of Dirk's many endeavours and yet *he'd been untouched*! Grot spat on his hands; Dirk told lies quite simply, simply, *simply*; of course!

He decided to risk it: "Can I visit my Granny then?"

Dave seemed a little surprise at the question, "I suppose so..., ...As long as she is deceased of course?"

"...Oh yes!" Grot responded, "She's dead all right..."

"Very well go and see her. I shall not stand in the way of thee contacting thou loved ones... Where doth she reside pray tell?" Dave supplemented.

"Erm, Hell!" Grot responded a little too quickly for his own liking.

A reddish glow surrounded Grot as he spoke and remained thereafter and the Paladin instantly knew he was lying. His huge double-handed sword came sluicing out of its scabbard in a perfectly controlled arc and back around his body where he swapped hands and delivered the blade bloodlessly back to its scabbard. "Liar!" he screamed as he did so.

Grot blanched as he noticed the fire type glow surrounding him and then felt his body to begin to slip from his hips with the sweet moment of numbness before a searing pain accompanied his torso's separation. Grot had never encountered an after-life 'death' before, Heaven being the place it was and screamed in anguished pain as he felt he was descending to his death.

The pain was as intense if not more-so, than that final act of torture inflicted upon him by Galbor, but the Dwarves death took rather longer to come to him than Grot had expected, through clenched teeth he decided to make the best use of his time. "You utter, Utter, Bastard! How the bollocks yer get to go chopping people up here in heaven is beyond me. So I lied... Aargh, yer shit, aah! So I bleeding well lied... Is it really that bloody bad that yer had to friggin well go and kill me in me afterlife? I only wanted to get to bleeding Hell yer great Mountain Gorilla of metal..., ...Now why the shit am I taking so long to die... Aargh, my bloody legs, Oh shite me stomach.... Aah, Aargh!"

"Grot ssilensce your criess and pull yourself together pleasse..." A newcomer ordered.

Grot raised his head enough to see a scaly foot and calf, before falling back in agony...

"You – gatekeeper..." Qoua ordered, "He doess not know the lawss of thesse planes. Pleasse fixss him for hiss ssquealing iss dissrupting the harmony of thiss plasce."

Dave strode forward and scooped up the Dwarf by the shoulders and planted him firmly upon his detached hips. The Paladin's eyes shone white and pure ripples of lightning crackled over his armoured form as he spoke a single word of magic.

The unbearable pain was gone and not only did Grot's body work fine as he stood, it worked even better than before. "Erm... Thanks?"

"Thou need but ask..." Dave responded graciously.

"Ask!" Grot roared, "Yer shouldn't even go around chopping people up here anyway..."

"Really..." Dave said, fidgeting the bastard-swords pommel.

"...Grot! Be graciouss, you forget yoursself..." Qoua demanded and her words had an instant sobering effect on the stubborn Dwarf who at any rate, did not want to go through that pain again.

"We wissh to leave..." She stated turning her attention to Dave.

"...On what grounds?" Dave asked with more than an air of

suspicion.

"Why to vissit my relative of coursse…" Qoua smirked back slyly.

"And where I wonder do they live?" Dave asked with an outright gust of doubt.

"Hell." Qoua said with simplistic elegance. There were no flames of suspicion much to Dave's annoyance.

"I'm afraid it would not be a good idea to visit one tainted by the depravities of hell, permission denied. Sorry…" He apologetically added.

"That iss not jusst and fair… You offered to let my friend through."

"That is because I knew he would be lying. He's been coming here for twenty years now and every day it is the same thing, he asks to leave, I refuse, we fight; he leaves. I mean give me a break; It aint as if I can really kill him. I just want to *really* discourage him. 'Sides which; what do you know of the values of justice and fairness?"

"I know enough to sspot a fake when I ssee one… What happened to 'thou' acsscent?" Qoua taunted.

"Well I shall- Oh… Fiddlesticks!" Dave looked genuinely perturbed to have been caught out. "Look it goes with the job okay? People see a Paladin, they expect certain aspects and mannerisms and well; you know… They're a little disappointed when they don't get it. So just keep quiet about it okay?"

Qoua raised a scaly arched brow, "My own culture iss not too dissssimilar to your own, though *we* live by honour; most of uss, and our ssocial sstructure dependss upon a very harsh ssysstem of justice. But we alsso know when to deceive and I suggesst to you that your very demeanour is a lie. How may we keep this fact to ourselves while ssocialissing with other heavenly beingss… We merely wish to depart and I gave you a truthful reasson sso what iss the harm in letting uss leave? Bessidess which you are no Paladin, I met and killed one mosst worthy of your pretended rank by the name of Agrilot, a fine man whom I had the pleassure of meeting up with in heaven, mayhapss I sshall return and talk anew with him; thingss to disscuss yess?"

Dave considered this situation and its implications should his little secret get out and he decided upon a compromise. "Very well, thou doth indeed speak truthfully," he said once more affecting his dubious manner,

"Thou can leave, but as the Dwarf hath no reason to leave, he shall stay…"

"Aaah but he doess have a reasson, dear knight: For wc are bound together by fate." Qoua countered and again Dave was disconcerted at the absence of the flames of deception. *'Maybe she's mastered this Dirk characters art too!'* The mind reading guardian wondered and shrugged his shoulders. He was quite stumped.

"Okay, go through…" He conceded and stood aside as the two strolled smugly past. Grot couldn't resist the instinctive thought of a sly attack as he passed the Paladin by and once again he got a thumping as Dave delivered a final pre-emptive kick and punch combo.

"Okay smart arse; how the bollocks did ya do that?" Grot coughed and wheezed. Qoua paused while Grot caught his breath and helped the Dwarf to his feet once more before he reluctantly continued down the short passage that separated the lower and upper planes…, …Dave called down after them: "A long time ago; I gained the gift of one single wish which I put to goodly use. I asked that I be able and at will to read the full intent of others with regards to myself, be it on a physical or mental scale, in a way that I intercept, decipher and calculate their thought patterns a single second before they themselves know: From this day forth and all eternity; they say be careful with wishes or ya might get what you asked for. Well I did!"

"I see, handy that gift, very handy: see yer; bloody nutter: As for you," Grot chided turning to Qoua, "how did you get away with lying to the righteous bastard?"

"I did not *'Lie'*; we *are* going to vissit my relative." Qoua smiled knowingly as she regarded the determined fellow beside her. "Ass a cleric of my god, I become her daughter, and if anybody knows where Dirk iss it shall be her!"

"Or him!" Grot countered showing off his skills honed deep in the practise of male chauvinism.

Qoua chuckled as they paused at the end of the short tunnel, a black void before them devoid of any light or sound.

"…After you good Dwarf…" Qoua suggested.

"…Oh no;" Grot theatrically reacted with frantic waves of his arms, "I wouldn't dream of it… Ladies always go first."

A shove from the Paladin who had appeared behind them unnoticed settled the matter flat. And their time within the void seemed endless...

***

Dirks mind raced back to his many times spent in taverns and Inns all over Eyrthe as well as a fair number frequented in his time spent in the depths of hell; his memories were little more than a blank haze of womanising and half-remembered snatches of song. It was useless to even try recalling bar-room events; Whenever Dirk spent any considerable time in a taproom it inevitably led to his being as drunk as a Dwarven distillery owner. He fervently wished he had paid a little more attention to those around him and a little less to his own former paranoid existence.

The truth was Dirk had become very insular in life; sure he had laughed ever so occasionally on the proverbial outside and often he had shared a jibe, or fought with friends but his inner feelings were kept to himself, for though he would often hint at his own insecurities, he would never reveal them in full. In truth, Dirk trusted no-one but Dirk, not even Dirk half the time in truth; or Grot, though the Dwarf was without doubt the nearest and dearest of Dirks lifelong companions. *'Not now he aint'*... Dirk thought to himself bitterly. *'Not now that we're dead, and even if the Dwarf is too: There's only one way his god-fearing arse is going; up! Why did I not bother whispering my fears to some high and mighty god when I had the bloody chance? Cuz they're a bunch of vain wankers that's why Dirk!'* He answered in self critique mode: *'Why must ye always do thy self injustice?'*

"Hunted... We are awaiting your bawdy communiqué...?" The Daemon vocally prowled interrupting Dirk's thoughts: His words spiriting the onlookers into rapturous shouts; each clamouring for a song. Dirk had become the focus of an awful assemblage of vile creatures; amidst many belches, farts and small contained fights all were now demanding a tune.

'I have been a proper ignorant tit all my life!' Dirk mentally rebuked. All of his companions the last several months before he died had been prone to song of some sort. Barring his current mistress, there was Grot with his battle odes of Dwarven contemplation, Boris with his casually spirited ditty he sang while cooking; inevitably *about* cooking. Zen had sang them a few saucy folk songs, an Elf of a somewhat darker nature whom Dirk knew; often sang baritone salutations of death and even the Lizard woman had intermittently hissed what he personally considered a monotonous whistling dirge.

A Lifetime of Lessons Learned

"Last chance hunted…" The Demon spat as he effortlessly flicked Dirk's form tumbling through the gathered crowd and onto the table previously occupied by the still downed Elf.

'*What a bunch of bastards Demons really are,*' Dirk thought, '*except Zen of course, that poor sod was bob-on!*'

A thought occurred to him as he floated up from the table gracefully righting his body as he did so. "*We kill them now…?*" Dirk shook his head and mentally laughed, '*Whoever or whatever you are; you've got the balls I only wished I had, but no… Just…, …Listen.*'

"Ladies and Gents, Daemons and Devils alike, I give you Zen's song; a tale about a maiden who had less virtue than a stimulated succubus or as he called her: "My old aunt Agg."

***

"My old aunt Agg"

Well give me a bag and a spout and a rag and that's me old aunt Agg…

They remind me of her with her terrible glare for she was such a slag…

I remember the first time; must have been around nine, when I first went round for tea…

But as I ate my supper, she went through nine lovers and then came down to me…

'One thing' she told me, 'Possibly, one and only, thing a nice young man should do…'

'Is to put aside their fears, as the woman grips their ears and lick her womanly stew…'

Oh my old aunt Agg was such a slag, she shagged all night and day… And she always smelt like haddock, left hanging in a hammock; swinging by her blubbery sea…

Well the months went by, from that virginal time; that I first smelled her thighs…

390

And I licked her creamy bunions; though her buttocks felt like onions and come dripped in my eyes...

One year later when I was ten and she came to call again:

Told me to shut me gob and whipping out me nob; she swivelled up an arse that was scored with many a scar ...

'You must slide it up and down, between the arse cheeks and her pubic mound, if you wanna earn your half a crown again...'

'For you'll send her all a quiver, so she'll want what you deliver, if you just tease her first...'

Oh my old aunt Agg was such a slag, she shagged all night and day... And she always smelt like haddock, left hanging in a hammock; swinging by her blubbery sea...

'Fore I got to age eleven I was always wanting heaven, but only found frustrated hell...

Though her mouth would often bleat, as I licked her toe to teat, she would only say I had done well...

I would pluck her woolly crack as she lay there on her back and nibble her belly button...

But she would simply sigh as another bloke dropped by and use my back to put his foot on...

She would wink back down at me, as I crouched down gingerly; some big bloke or other pumping her...

'You must always be ready to let her have her bevy; if you want to have the lions share...'

Oh my old aunt Agg was such a slag, she shagged all night and day... And she always smelt like haddock, left hanging in a hammock; swinging by her blubbery sea...

It was upon my twelfth birthday when I finally did get dirty as she sat upon my proverbial 'cake...' But as I stood up cock-ready, she urged me to be steady and; 'Not to make a premature mistake....

And she rubbed her sweaty pussy in my tiny birthday prize; right before my smiling eyes... Then she crouched down off her feet with her arse cocked up to eat and told me to devour her pies...

So I gobbled down on her buttocks, licked her body free of clutter and rammed my cock in her anus…

And she told me to go slow and then faster, then yo-ho, as she guided me into her dark disaster… From which I'd never wander.

Oh my old aunt Agg was such a slag, she shagged all night and day… And she always smelt like haddock, left hanging in a hammock; swinging by her blubbery sea…

When I turned thirteen things became so obscene my mother ordered me out of home…

So I called to my aunt Agg, who was sucking off some lag and promised to do me too…

But before I had my kit off, she had told me not to strip off; unbuttoning my fly as she was tipped by the guy…

And before he'd even departed my aunt Agg already started; wrapping her lips round my genitals…

As her swollen tongue swirled around, her head bobbed up and down and I only heard her mumble…

'If a guy pleases a girl, she shall be glad to return… Mph –mm-mph- mm mm-m-mph…'

Oh my old aunt Agg was such a slag, she shagged all night and day… And she always smelt like haddock, left hanging in a hammock; swinging by her blubbery sea…

Well I lived with her for years; enduring many drunken leers from the 'odd' sod who also liked men…

Yet she never left her bed and it was left upon my head to clear away their sticky veneer…

With a… wire-wool or cloth, or my tongue I'd lick the sloth, and clear up crusty bed and berth…

And when a punter pounced upon me to fondle and besmirch, my aunt Agg would just laugh with mirth…

And by the time that I reached fourteen she pronounced 'Darling, you're a Queen!' and had me given a buggering cock's worth…

So with her thighs she pulled me over, forcing me to lick her clover as the 'odd' fellow continued fondling me…

Oh my old aunt Agg was such a slag, she shagged all night and day… And she always smelt like haddock, left hanging in a hammock; swinging by her blubbery sea…

By the time I hit fifteen I felt like such a man, I pronounced that I would take her by force…

But she stopped me short with a witty retort about my size being oh so short, and fitting only for her rear…

And so I felt rebuked, though her charms were a little obtuse as she massaged my adolescent fear…

So she knelt down there beside me and with huge hips she derided 'you're most probably queer…'

Robbed of my honour and bustling with pride; I ripped open her legs and shoved my cock inside…, …Hoping to cause her pleasure and pain…

But my rampant quick disaster; only brought forth tears of laughter as I spilled my load after ten seconds strain…

Oh my old aunt Agg was such a slag, she shagged all night and day… And she always smelt like haddock, left hanging in a hammock; swinging by her blubbery sea…

By the time I was sixteen I needed a job, so I went back home to aunty…

Where she'd have some mug licking on her jugs, while another one pounded her fanny…

When they'd had their fill they'd pay at the till and tip their hats to me in passing…

…For I was the man who'd clean up when he can; and shag her though she looked like me granny…

And now that I'm almost seventeen I finally know the reason,

Why the men come around with their crown or their pound to commit their carnal treason…

Oh my old aunt Agg was such a slag, she shagged all night and day... And she always smelt like haddock, left hanging in a hammock; swinging by her blubbery sea...

***

By the songs final chorus even the ferocious looking Daemon was swinging back on his man-stool and chanting along and Dirk thanked the gods that *someone* had made an impact on his otherwise ignorant existence.

"Well done human; I shall heal your 'friend' and he can sing while we speak," the Daemon commanded and with a snap of his fingers the Elf was fully healed and standing. Dirk paused wondering what the Elves reaction would be, but to his vast relief the Elf wasted no time in righting his turban and taking to the impromptu stage once more.

The Elf took his hand in both of his own as he leapt onto the table.

"We shall speak later young one..." The Elf said admirably, "But for now you must speak with the infernal one..." Dirk smiled dumbly as he left the tables confines and moved between the crowds in a half wonder; he had heard elves speak before but felt privileged to have witnessed the dulcet tones this one managed. *'I will see the organ grinder again beyond doubt, but right now its time to deal with the monkey...'*

The crowd reached out to slap his back or hit Dirk in some other rough, but non-threatening manner as he wended his way through the rabble but as he reached the Daemons table something thumped heavily into his chest; knocking the wind from him as he was hoisted off his feet.

The Cyclops had him in his grasp and was looking to even things up, his vengeance carried over from their earlier encounter but as he hoisted Dirk's body up above his head, in a clear precursor to the back breaking drop to its proffered knee, the veined Daemon roared its own dissatisfaction at being interrupted in such a manner. The veined ones disgusting roar brought with it a plague of flying insects that began devouring the screeching Cyclops where he stood. Dirk however, drifted gently to the floor completely untouched by the swarm and laughed at the diminishing Cyclops.

"Sit!" The Daemon commanded and ordered another float of pulverized urchins and a churn of bull's blood wine for Dirk. The canny wizard seated himself and studied his gruesome companion, seeking any indications of a possible advantage to be had and wondering desperately how he was going to get out of this tavern alive. He was pretty much out of songs…, and well, he was unsure of this for certain but something about how the Daemon had belched forth a plague of insects told Dirk he may have gained the interest of someone you do not generally want to meet.

XVIII) **Soulfully Aware**

Five years of continually falling later and Grot and Qoua had long since abandoned their shocked screaming for polite conversation as they tumbled downwards. "…Not even sure I saw him dead yer know. I looked around for him in Heaven in case but their aint even a proper God of Halfling's so who dya speak to? I mean, it's gotta be a bit shitty that. Your own people not even having a god to look up to; little wonder so many of the buggers look towards Coulin the god of chefs or any one of the number of gods like Lycos, Max or Brandy…" Grot was discussing Boris's absence.

"I am ssorry," Qoua responded, "I am quite knowledgeable about theology though I have not heard of those three; are they well known?"

"Who: Lycos, Max and Brandy? Hell yeah, I mean, Lycos is god of fortune and discovery. Max is god of mischief and mayhem and Brandy deals a little with luck but is mainly known as the mostly Human god of adventure; Halflings love him mind." Grot added: "No, believe me, if they are gonna survive as a race they need a brave god of their own."

"Sso no ssign of Borisss then, maybe he livess sstill; I hope sso, for no offencsse but he chief amongst the three of you sshowed me the most compassssion…, …Our own brief misssunderssstanding assside of courssse!" Qoua conceded: "You have ssstill to explain how it isss you are ssso different here…"

"Different..?" The Dwarf seemed suddenly edgy in his psycho spin.

Qoua reached out and grabbed at the Dwarf by his shoulder and pants, steadying his inertia. "You sswear far lesss, have a great deal more intelligent conversssation to impart and ssseem a great deal more…, …Undersstanding."

"Aah!" Grot declared. "Well that's best explained in little detail. See yer gotta understand that I got a lot of enemies in a lot of different planes of existence. I got me mate Dirk to take care of too, so I best explain it most truthfully like this…, …On Eyrthe I'm something of an enigma; I epitomise Dwarves yer could say, I'm like everything a Dwarf could hope to be and most things he's ashamed to be all rolled into one, whereas now that I'm dead I can be more me old self, which is to say I'm mostly a nice bugger!"

"I ssee, sso you are more in control of your emotionss here;" Qoua dissected. When she next spoke it was with rather more concentration and no small mental effort as she formulated her thoughts into vocally correct syllables... "I see this place readily allows for change; strange as both Heaven and Hell are ruled more or less by the same entities... at least to my own small comprehension..."

Grot gasped as a tiny demonic thing hurtled past them and audibly thudded into the ground yet he and Qoua continued to fall: "Strange...! I'll tell you strange... Did yer see that then? How come we haven't hit ground yet? It must be near..."

"I'm unsure but we will one day." Qoua informed.

Grot almost cursed then caught himself: "Yer seem awful confident of a lot in life..., ...and death: Why the certainty?"

Qoua regarded the Dwarf for a while before answering: "To that question I must be as elusive as yourself I am afraid, if not for my own future health then most defiantly your own: I follow the prophecy of my people; a text who's knowledge is imparted by the spoken word alone; most cruel considering that all those that speak of it are doomed to die a premature and somewhat nasty death. As I say, I will not speak of it more than to say that my own involvement concerns Dirk and his survival, therefore I know certain things are destined to happen and therefore firmly believe they will take place and I am yet to save Dirk's life..."

"Aha, I thought as much!" Grot declared slapping Qoua's hand. "I too know of the prophecy yer speak and I too have talked about it far too much for me own liking, as yer must know then I am 'he to whom Dirk holds dearest' and if yer like, I took a big chance Dying for his sake but I too believe in this prophecy. Well, I follow it to a point anyways, see there are a few slightly different versions and I think that's why whoever started it forbid its being spoke of..., ...knowledge is power and even the wrong belief or interpretation if held to by enough people that matter, can win out over the truth or intended purpose."

"So you know of my own fate too I take it?" Qoua inquired.

"I do now!" Grot declared. "Though in truth I hadn't put the dots together in life..., ...Dwarves are rather bigoted people and well, I am sorry I attacked yer back on Eyrthe. I know yer better than yer self I don't doubt. Yer may wanna keep the speech thing when we get back; yer can be bloody difficult to understand sometimes yer know and Dirk aint that patient a person, not yet anyhow..."

"I find it pleasant too I must admit but in life I would have had to sew my tongue in order to correct the impediment; an act of disgrace I refused, whereas here I found I merely had to wish to sound like a human in order to gain the desired effect. Hell in some ways is most refreshing!" Qoua joked. "You remember; two years, one month and forty five days, thirty seven minutes and twenty two seconds ago..."

"Well I didn't remember it quite so well but yeah, you're gonna say how yer started talking normal for a change..." Grot interrupted.

"Yes, I was quite perplexed that you could not understand my words and I wished I could have spoken more clearly; then when I next spoke, or rather before I began to speak I concentrated on delivering my words in a manner that a human would..."

"I've got it!" Grot shouted in triumph. "Prepare for impact; we've just gotta think we're hitting the ground!"

"Clever Grot: Oh of course we must, silly..." Qoua's answering rhetoric was shortened by the intervention of solid matter; the resulting splattering impact, ejecting her entrails no mean distance apart.

***

"So tell me," the Daemon before Dirk seemed at ease but was no less threatening than before, "What is your name Hunted?"

"Dirk," he answered with a complete disregard to all the rules of survival he had been taught, "Dirk Heinemblud, pleased to meet ya and you are?"

"I am Khill-vaar, why? Do not be so stupid with me human, ye would no sooner give ye own name as I would mine own and besides, I have heard of Dirk of the Blood and ye are not he..." The Daemon paused to chew a chunk out of a still living yet somewhat gory urchin.

"Not Dirk of the Blood; Heinemblud. Dirk Friggin' Heinemblud; It's my name whether you choose to believe it or not, the last person to call me Dirk of the Blood was a semi-delirious Snake-woman, not that I've anything against this other Dirk plonker-"

"Silence hunted, there is only one of the Blood and it is *he*. I wish to know other things for I know ye are no more a friend of the Elves, than ye are who ye claim to be but I *would* hear what ye know of **Galbor** unless that name too was picked up in hearsay…?" The Daemon's tone brooked no argument.

"Okay; I will truthfully tell you what I know of Galbor in exchange for some information I require of you." Dirk offered in his best take it or leave it manner.

"Ye dare barter for knowledge with me…?" The Daemon reasoned and rubbed its spiky chin as it thought, "Very well, impudent human, I shall grant ye the knowledge ye require to one question on two counts; firstly, I must know of the subject already and secondly; its telling shall bring me no ill harm."

"Good enough." Dirk confirmed and proceeded to recount to him everything that he knew of his former master, with the exception of certain details about him self of course, which the Daemon customarily expected him to do anyhow. When he had finished his de-embellished tale Dirk observed the fiend before him for any signs of delight or disgust but the Daemons gestures gave nothing away, instead he merely fixed Dirk's gaze with his own and asked what information he himself required.

"My mistress the Daemoness that resides here, what do you know of her?" Dirk queried, fervently hoping his question was not in vain.

"She's here?" The Daemon entreated.

"Erm, yes… Well, not here but somewhere. She told me she would be back in a day or two. Do you know her…?" Dirk was astonished by the Daemon's infectious response.

"Know her; yes I know of her and if I'd known ye did too I would gladly have given the information for free…, …So my cousin **is** to return here, ye may need haste hunted for time in Hell is ever contracting and expanding; what may be days where she's headed may be but seconds here!"

"In that case, soon as you're a friend of hers perhaps you can inform her that I'm leaving this stinking hellhole and if the slut ever sees me again it will be with a dagger between those three tits of hers…" Dirk stood and strode for the exit, but as he swung open the door and tried to step outwards, a jarring force threw him back inside, much to the amusement of the nearby patrons who made no shame of pointing and laughing at Dirk's expense…

Dirk leapt to his feet, lashing out with his mind in embarrassment and sent a bolt of mental force surging through the hitherto amused ranks. In response several stood and threw their own glasses, fists and bottles at Dirk which ducked to avoid and an indiscriminate scrap immediately started up in retort against those whose blows had miss-hit their target with Dirk smack dab in the middle. Thanks to the Elves quick thinking, Dirk avoided the ensuing bare fisted melee however, as he was yanked to the side by the amazingly strong yet agile Elf.

Leading Dirk by the hand, the minstrel darted this way and that nimbly evading all challengers, until their pursuers were too busily embroiled in fighting yet more patrons, whose drinks had been spilled in their passing. The two refugees came against the slugs long bodied bar and the Elf huddled down at its side, dragging the distracted human with him as the fight raged about overhead.

"My thanks for the intuitive rescue, friend," the Elf said hunkering by his side, "I am Farwen Melearden of the order of Shaelwood, sonnet master and performer of fantastical tales, bringer of merriment and mirth; aiming to bring serenity to these planes: Are you a walker too?"

Dirk grinned. "Something tells me ya don't mean someone who travels on foot so I'll say no Farwen. What the heck *is* a bloody walker?"

"Someone who is flesh and blood like my errant self, who walks amongst the planes of existence; although I must admit I tend to 'walk' less than ever. It is so overrated don't you think? When I get back to Eyrthe I really must invest in a mount of some sort. Do you ride?" The Elf asked in a singsong barrage of information.

"Bugger riding; can *you* get me out of here? Hell I mean?" Dirk could not suppress his mounting excitement.

"Why yes of course, but where is it that you wish to depart to?"

"…To Eyrthe!" Dirk croaked with longing, "I just want to get back to Eyrthe, Caernthorn preferably…"

"No problem…" The Elf smiled disarmingly, "You wish to leave forthwith or shall we witness the splendid spectacle of a daemonic bar fight unfold, look the veined Daemon has entered into the fray…, …There is a song to be had from this episode I am sure…" The Elf paused as he noticed Dirk tugging on his sleeve. "Ah you wish to depart right away?"

Dirk looked at the Elf with a derisive sneer. "Well, Dah! Of course I wanna go now, or would ya rather wait a few hundred years…?"

The Elf sprang to his feet and prepared to move, "Well come on… We need to get out of here first…!"

"We need to…?" Dirk paused and pulled the Elf back down as he gauged his inept possibilities. "I can't bloody leave. It's impossible."

"Why?" The Elf asked unaware.

"Because I am a slave and because my mistress commanded it. I have no choice but to obey." Dirk almost sobbed as he spoke. How could he be so close yet so far?

"In that case, it sounds as though you need a new master, how did this mistress come to own you?"

"She tricked me into giving my word." Dirk moaned.

"Then if she tricked you why not rescind your pledge?" The Elf stated simply.

"Because that isn't the way Hell works: Word is law here… Look, Its too complicated to go explaining right now but once ya give your word on something that's it; ya can't go back…"

"Then why not give someone else your word?" queried the Elf.

"That's it; *you* little minx ya! Wait here!" And with that Dirk floated up over most of the still raging melee and sought out his intended future conquistador, the Daemon from earlier. When he sighted him tearing two combatants limb from limb he drifted over and made his presence known.

"Excuse me…, …Might I bother ya for a moment of your time oh great one?" Dirk grovelled from a safe distance.

The Daemon slung the two shredded torsos' to one side, "Why of course silly hunted. Let me guess now. Your mistress has commanded ye stay and ye wish for my assistance in leaving, yes?"

"You're too shrewd by far oh mighty lord and stuff…" Dirk hastily supplicated: "…sorry about starting up a fight but I gotta go and quick!"

"And what do ye offer in return? I see no value in any deal ye may be able to offer me…" The devilish figure snorted pushing aside the driving metallic horns of some determined creature.

"We never finished up on part of our earlier bargain. I asked what you knew of my mistress and you did not tell me much…"

"You're wrong Hunted; I gave my word and honoured it, to tell you any more would be to endanger my own being." The Daemon gloated at its successful completion of the deal. But the human before him seemed resolute, shaking his head and tapping his foot in annoyance while building a protective sphere around himself.

"Might ye await something else? I have already spoken; I see nothing ye have to offer…, …and I warn; do *not* to provoke my true anger."

"Nah it aint that see: You are just too ignorant for your own good; or bad I suppose depending on your outlook." Dirk paused as a nagging voice arose within his psyche. *'Do we really wish to test* **this** *one?'*

"If ya remember; I gave ya *my* name but like a typical Demon ya didn't look for the truths of my bullshit, ya were too bent on fleshing out the lies; well I know Dirk don't have long blonde hair, tits and ass and I know the real Dirk H is a bit of a wanker, a right bastard and a thoroughly selfish, ignorant prick of a weakling. I know this shit, because **I** am frigging well him and I don't care if ya believe me or not because…"

The Khill-Vaar demon thrust its grating claws through the purple veneer of Dirk's formidable protective force clutching at the wizard as the hands clasped together; each one growing to twice his height. Dirk had endured enough experiences where size had indeed won out to know well enough he was in danger of being crushed. *'May I?'* Dirk asked himself and within a heartbeat he had formulated the correct combination of low and mid chlorean elements to cast an explosive spell: "Eppa mai D' partais…"

The shorn sanctuary still encasing Dirk and the engorged palms split asunder in a blast that threw back most of the taverns occupants and furniture as far back as the hidden Elf, including the veined Daemon who roared in discontent as his body flew back against the wall of the tavern; his hands returning to normal size once more. No sooner had the Daemon lord put the finishing touches to the accompanying growl, than with the briefest flutter of his wings, he had transported himself within touching distance of Dirk. "**Enduree Felch**-shit, stop it… I mean no wait, we don't need to fight this bugger, listen…" Dirk argued, interrupting the beginning of some ominous spell and instead flung his own arm out *towards* the Daemon and shook the astonished Khill-Vaar by the hand. When next Dirk spoke it was in full on voice effects mode, which here in hell echoed even further than the several hundred mile distance it was capable of on the Eyrthe above.

"Listen to this one ya hasty arsed prince of Khill-Vaar: My name *IS* Dirk *Theodore* Heinemblud. *The* Dirk of the Blood if ya frigging well want to call me it; mind ya, I warn ya now I am just about sick and tired of this shit…, …From now on, people I hear talking about this prophecy and me are gonna meet with a nasty end. I aint saying I forbid it or anything either cuz it occurs or rather; it did occur to me that ya self might be a bit more of a bastard than ya letting on…, …See ya said ya knew I weren't the Dread Lord but ya screwed up when ya said I wasn't me, because if ya definitely knew one thing and not the other. Well let's just try something shall we; something I heard about I dunno if it's true but some monks reckon if ya chant Dread Lord six times in a row he appears…"

Dirk sneered at the expressions of the patrons around him; some were of middling to vast intellect and picked up on Dirk's meaning almost instantly thanks to being almost deafened by the declaration; other's less gifted individuals were merely deafened into considering something or someone very bad was very near and their faces showed it…, …He permitted the sneer to become a grin and returned his features to the Daemon prince who had paused himself to digest the information and how far Dirk was willing to take it… '*What the shit…*' Dirk decided.

"Dread Lord one, Dread Lord two, Dread Lord three, Dread Lord four, Dread Lord five, Dread-"

The veined one shook his head announcing; "that's all wrong ye naïve…, …Ye have to say; 'he of the sixes cometh, take me oh Dread Lord that's mine' and ye have to say it six times in six seconds without faltering or your soul will be consumed, the fact that I often consume the souls of those that summon me should be evident; repeat the mantra; it's obvious, ha-ha-ha…, …mostly Human's that fall for it obviously!"

"Very well; if ya the lord of Hell himself as I thought, I: Dirk Heinemblud offer *you* and only *you* the *current* Dread Lord; this deal: I willingly give ya my name to use in whatever manner ya desire as long as it is of no harm to my own being and offer complete and humble servitude for but one day in my naturally living life, if you in return, will only help me leave this bloody tavern, so that I may go about my business. Do we have a deal or do I have to let my psycho self have a go at killing ya? Decide now cuz if that's the case I wanna

change my shoes if I'm gonna be dancing with the Devil in Hell."

The Daemon greedily snapped up the offer with a nod, "We have a deal foolish slave..., ...Now please speak normally before ye say something else..., ...Oh and tell me if ye may how do ye propose to do this: A slave can only have one master."

Dirk smiled. "Yes but you're no friend of my mistress are ya? Otherwise you would have known she was here; she told me how none can spy on her here and how this is her solemn sanctuary."

"She also told me how the current Dread Lord was a distant cousin of hers, though she said she knew little more than that thanks to the Dread Lord being a bit of a bastard and killing off his close family, though ya don't need worry she told me others have been far worse..."

"Like Galbor..., ...yet he's not even me!" The Dread Lord sighed.

"Yeah well anyways," Dirk continued, "This was the one place she could be undisturbed and *you* bloody well knew it was a matter of time." The Daemons mouth hung open ever so slightly as Dirk spoke and he noted the zealous glint in the fiend's eyes. "You're here to kill her aren't ya?"

Dirk received no direct answer but instead found himself suddenly floating outside the doors of the Inn: "How..." hurriedly he descended to the ground and popped his head over the swing doors whistling to the Elf who still crouched by the bar. Elves have excellent hearing as a rule and this one was no exception. He caught the human's intention and headed out of the bar as Dirk moved off out of sight, away from the saloon door and any inquisitive patrons.

The Elf came sauntering out of the saloon doors with a practised casual air and noticed Dirk's head popping out from beneath the mass of Eyrthe-matter he had gathered about himself. *'Is it safe?'* Dirk's eyes seemed to plead, and the Elf chuckled, as he walked over to the uselessly disguised refugee.

"For one who stood up so bravely to help one such as myself, you display a remarkable flair for cowardly behaviour..." The Elf remarked.

Dirk looked truly crestfallen at the Elves admonishment. Here outside the tavern, all around them the epidermis of life was as putty and could be freely moulded to whatever way, shape or form that a traveller required. Of course this was true all over hell but here in the void; the source was so malleable that a one legged swamp Gart would have no problems changing its humble stinking nest into a glorious castle fit for a human king. And they were the only beings for miles.

"Perhaps you are being a *tad* overcautious?" the Elf sang in amusement.

"I aint afraid of stuff out here, well, I am; but not as much as the things in there… Plus my bitch of a mistress might be getting back anytime and I don't wanna be around here when she does, considering I just backstabbed the bitch and disobeyed her direct orders. When are we off?"

"Off?"

"You know buggering off! Getting outta here… Skid-addling…?" Dirk responded in animated fashion.

"Aah! I apologise it struck me as a little odd," Farwen explained, "In Elvish, I am sure you are aware our vocabulary is way beyond that of your own…"

Dirk shrugged noncommittally as he mentally pushed the hitherto surrounding mud shelter away from his body.

"Well if you permit me the explanation…" The Elf recanted, "Our consonants and vowels roughly equal your own in number, yet each has up to seven different inflections in addition to some words also being accented as a whole to give the meaning a different translation entirely though I admit that the changes apply in the most to the written rather than the spoken-"

Dirk had finally freed himself off his self-imposed disposition and turned to Farwen *who,* he had only just noticed, was still rambling on. "Excuse me for being rude but, shut up. I mean, have you got a point? Besides, I wanted to ask you a favour…, …Something a lot more about me than you, well actually it's-oh bollocks to it…"

The Elf cast sulky eyelids Dirk's way in response and wobbled his head in some unknown meaning. "Look!" Dirk bantered, "I'm just messing with ya…, …I'm dead interested really; go on, you were saying…?"

"You don't even know where I was up to…?" Farwen whimpered.

"I do…!" Dirk thought back feverishly… "You were on about

words being spoken…"

"Or the written!"

"Oh yes! You can't forget the written. I mean; where *would we be* without *that*. Now, about this favour…" Dirk yammered.

"You have no idea of the words I had previously spoken, do you?" The Elf accused through pursed lips.

"Not exactly…" Dirk conceded, "But I know you got something against written words, now I just wondered-"

"Something A*gainst* The W*ritten Word*? I assure you sire, that **I** *am Poet Laureate* to no less than *three* kingdoms; so I can attest to you, *most strongly* and without *any* contextual conjugal tardiness, that **I** positively *adore* the written and spoken word, if not am verily *smitten* by its *conception*, **structuring** *and* delivery…, …*As* for having *any* **problems** congenial *or* veracious; *pre-conceived* or otherwise…, …It is *you* I accuse; for so *conscientious* a misuse of the *vocalised phrase* "**OFF**". *That* was what **I** was about to *attempt* to explain but you have the equal patience off an ass. Now if you would-"

Dirk lost his rag. "Look, scrub it. Enough of the blabber pointy ears or ya not gonna stay as one of the living for long…, …**I** *do not* **wish** to *bleeding* well know. **I** just *want you* to bloody well teach me, *how* to talk like yourself. Not all poncey I mean; just…, …Friggin well interesting. Ya know, attention grabbing."

"You would be wiser to ask for the blessing of hearing as even though you seem far from deafness you never seem to listen to others…" Farwen objected, somewhat insulted by Dirk's abrupt manner.

"Yeah well, whatever. Can you do it; the talking, you can grant wishes can't ya, if someone saves ya life?" Dirk harassed.

"How did you *know* such *privileged* information I wonder, and besides I am unsure as to whether thy own earlier *interference*, could actually be construed as saving this ones life…" The Elf shook his head in matter of fact pity for the simple human. "I *can* bless you with a somewhat more beguiling tone, yes. But I would rather offer you help with your other multitude of problems, for a start you seem to suffer from schizophrenia…"

"Don't talk to us about problems…" Dirk mumbled. "…Can you fix us? I mean we – no I don't I mean **I**; me, Dirk Heinemblud! Can you grant us my wish or friggin not?"

Shaking his head and tooting on his flute all the while, the Elf set about spreading small herbs and flowers in a seemingly random fashion about the ground after which, he placed a single leaf of mandrake to either of Dirk's shoulders commanding him to remain stationery. After several minutes that passed far too slowly for Dirk's liking, Farwen turned to him announcing: "I am ready to perform thy most arduous wish..., ...So what is it you long for; the dulcet tones of a demonic debonair: The striking verse of a Satyr perhaps or the larynx of a harmonious Angel?"

"I dunno, it depends," Dirk said, "What's a larynx?"

"I assume it is the part of your throat we wish changed..."

"Dunno, probably; at least it sounds important," Dirk stated.

"It is, so please state your dubious desire and let us be done with it..." The perturbed Elf was less than happy with his belligerent ward.

"Okay..." Dirk ventured, "I wish to sound like you; ya know real charming with the ladies but a bit sinister or deadly sounding too. I want my voice to sound important, or at least make a lasting impression but I want to be able to sound intimidating, not girly like an Elf; no offence intended."

The Elf sighed as he thrust his forefinger into Dirk's open gob, caressing his tonsils and speaking a strange mantra needed to grant the wish.

Dirk spat the Elves fingers out and spat and briefly considered thumping Farwen, who did not look like much of a fighter, but decided against it as he still needed the pointy eared one's help. "I didn't wish to chew on ya bleeding fingers did I?"

Dirk's ears pricked up to momentarily contest those of the Elf's as his wide-mouthed grin spread from ear to burning ear. "Whoa! I sound..., ...Friggin Cool Man..."

"As you imagined yourself wanting to sound..., ...Now as for your other concerns, why do I not start by removing or at least diluting your endless paranoia..." Farwen offered.

Dirk span on his miraculous companion, drawing up a bolt of dark energy from the matter about them and bringing it within inches of the

Elves face. "Don't you dare mess with my mind Elf; paranoia is what keeps me alive!" Dirk threatened; his tone silkier than an eastern kings underpants.

Dirk was deadly serious but once again he remembered his need of the Elf and he retracted his stance, harmlessly dispersing the threatening bolt into the ground. "I'm sorry," he lied. "I just wanted to test out if I could sound intimidating..., ...Now come one, let's get going somewhere. Hell isn't the kinda place you go to for the summer ya know and I really need to piss off quick if you get my uncouth Human meaning."

"Very well, we must first separate our souls from our ethereal selves whilst maintaining a link; I shall illuminate my meaning by way of example..." The Elf sidestepped to his left whilst pitching his weight to the right and suddenly there were two of him stood side by side with a small link of blue force surging between the two; one bathed in a luminous glare.

"Ah shit!" Dirk bemoaned. "I didn't realise I had to be alive; I just thought ya could take my soul along with ya!"

"Oh I do apologise if I gave off the wrong impression but I do believe I mentioned my being of the living still..., ...Of course I could redeem your soul of sorts; take it with me through the eternal flight; which is far shorter than you would imagine and in my own opinion badly named at best. Yet even if I did transport your soul in such a manner; you do realise I hope that once we return to the world above; when travelling by my methods, that you will be as before? If you have only died recently I may then be able to restore you to life but there is a strong chance you may only be able to experience un-life. If *that* is the case, I shall have to kill you as the doctrine of my own faith warrants... In any case as I began, you will lose-"

"Whoa! For shit's sake you Elves are so-o-o gabby!" Dirk was fast loosing his tolerance for the long winded individual. In truth he was also feeling increasingly desperate due to the Elves confounding harmony of logic and Dirk hated feeling unsure of him self. "Look if ya saying what I think ya saying then ya can't really help me can ya? I suppose I gotta do this and do it alone somehow; its not that I hate Hell that much funnily enough but I got too many enemies down here and not enough friends!"

"Does that include us?" A gruff voice jumped into the argument.

"...Grot!" Dirk cried spinning on his heel, "Qoua! How...? Hold on; how do I know it's really you? What am I saying? Of course it aint you, you'd never be sent to Hell… What are you? A mimic: Daemon? What? You better tell me cause I tell ya it aint funny and I aint in the mood for games!" Dirk pulled slightly at the distant fiery glows that bedecked the grey skies; stretching their essence and bringing them into closer molten proximity; searing those gathered with their intense heat.

"Dirk…" All three started at once.

"Dirk, listen to me yer great suspicious son of a Foetal-Fungus. We came here to get yer; and the Halfling if he's about. Nobody in Heaven had heard of the blathering little sod! And before yer go asking us to prove we are who we say we are don't. All yer really need to know is why *I'm* even down here and me answer is this; I'm here because you asked me to come, so bollocks to yer: Now do ya want us along or not?" The Dwarf blasted back.

"So how did ya get here? Don't tell me that cave led here? I wouldn't put it past it or maybe that army ya tangled with actually manage to cut ya down to size? I sent that message friggin years ago, so if ya did die then, ya could have at least responded but no-one did. I've been down here a hundred years or more, why didn't ya answer me then…?" Dirk was troubled; this looked and sounded like Grot but he severely doubted the figures veracity.

Qoua hissed as she strode closer, "Dirk must you always be the fool? We died shortly after your own demise, though our own deaths were… Shall we say more painstakingly executed than your own…?"

"So I should believe you should I?" Dirk questioned. "Qoua used to sound like she was sucking through a reed at the best of times."

"Believe in your self then Dirk. You know that I am truthfully an Elf do you not. Personally I know not who these beings are but they are indeed your friends; I see their aura quite clearly defined and now yours too a little though the constant flux makes it hard to cipher…"

Dirk whirled on the Elf, briefly wondering if the fellow was in fact merely another demon in disguise. Nothing down here could be taken for granted; not normally that was, again the wizard felt confused relaxing his tension on the lava like suns a little and trying to take in the chances of such an occurrence happening in Hell. He needed to steady his thoughts, control them; quell them…, …He needed to see what the others were thinking.

"Are you in truth Dirk of the Blood?" The Elf chimed in breaking Dirk's concentration. He was studying Dirk in a fashion that reminded Grot of him self when studying geological rarities.

"He is that!" Qoua answered in Dirk's stead who responded vehemently in the opposite. "I apologise Dirk, I meant to indicate that is a term others also know you by: The translation is almost identical regardless of whichever title is applied."

Farwen addressed Qoua directly, speaking across Dirk; "I had not realised he was speaking the truth earlier in the tavern, though in honesty I was trying my utmost to defend my delicate Elven ears from his verbal onslaught."

"Don't worry we heard him too!" Grot interjected, "that's how we found him in fact; we'd only been in hell a few years…, …Took us that long to pull ourselves together after landing, when we heard matey bollocks voice here ringing out loud and clear…"

"So Dirk of the Blood…" Farwen began.

"Dirk Heinemblud sunshine or else…" Dirk corrected.

The Elf visibly recanted what he was about to say and instead tried to explain himself. "While I am sure your own given name is a more descriptive analysis of hereditary title, the translation favoured by the L'iezsh'mat and Khill-Vaar is far more acute in its meaning."

Dirk sent a mental convulsion rippling through the ground beneath the Elf forcing a pause in his chatter: "What are ya going on about meaning and titles; translations…, …What exactly and in a single, solitary freaking sentence are ya on about at all?"

Grot spoke before the Elf even drew breath: "Exactly matey, we aint got time to be standing around here discussing our different cultures, when we can spend that time getting out of Hell. Besides if I know yer self at all; yer name would translate into Elvish as 'numb nuts on a stick'…"

"Then it is well that I meet you now, when you have sinned relatively little, for otherwise I would surely have divested you of your spiritual core. And the translation actually means far more than that *simple* Dwarven rhetoric. Dirk to begin with means 'weapon within or inside' in Elvish: In many other cultures a Dirk is a weapon of concealment similar in design to a dagger…, …in the Khill-Vaar it is translated as a 'concealed weapon' and-"

"Shut up!" Dirk hissed through clenched teeth. "The Dwarves right as it happens; I much prefer his explanation, far less blabbing and much more descriptive of the Dirk **I** actually know!" The others where stunned into a thoughtful silence by the news, all except Dirk who continued. "Besides what bleeding legend are you on about? I'm Dirk so what. Not of any given blood. All this must be an illusion; I-I'm confused…"

The Elf seemed surprised, "oh no…, …Blood in L'iezsh'mat means or rather it refers to the brood; as in their term for their collective people, so a Lizardman would refer to you as that, if for instance you was the saviour of your race, but then note as you connect with the word brood in the L'iezsh'mat sense with or alongside that of the words 'Of The' meaning belonging to, and Dirk meaning what Its true reference, then It is obvious why people continually refer to you as that instead of Heinemblud…"

Dirk blew a storm: "I am just about sick of it, did ya not hear what I said in the pub…, …I mean it, while I've got the power I am gonna stop everyone I can from spreading shit about me…"

"Fear not, Dirk of the Blood!" Qoua said, placing a meaningfully reassuring hand upon his sagging shoulders.

Dirk's response was guttural instinct and without much rational thought. "Everyone keeps saying that name! Why?" His arm came up in an exaggerated Arc, sending ripples shuddering across the landscape in an outward direction. Distorting everything in its path and hammering the gathered protagonists with waves of undiluted pain. NO bones cracked or crumbled, no joints were twisted in pain but the nerve endings which acknowledged the distribution of pain, bloated with agony from the feeding kinetic force weaving out from Dirk's limbs. Dirks eyes were shot with streaks of black and purple as he uttered Daemonic commands to the landscape around him and gathering arms shot up from the ground and wrestled down the bewildered associates.

"You'll reveal the truth, feeble Daemons or I will thoroughly fry your arses!" Dirk threatened in elegant tones of dark promise. "You're not really an Elf are ya and you weren't going to let me escape from here were ya? See that's just too good to be true. So what I wanna know is where you were gonna take me and what were these two gonna do about it?"

"Dirk yer great smelly arse of a Shit-Demon!" Grot shouted, entering full on Grot mode. "We really did come here to save yer: I personally have had my bollocks kicked in more times than a mule's barn door just to get into the void and even then I only got in cause of Qoua here showing up!" The Dwarf contemplated his current status for a moment before continuing. "How did you get so powerful anyhow and how come you say you've been down here so long...? You only died a few minutes before us and I've only been dead a few years..."

"I dunno time is different here; it stretches. A minute can take forever, or an hour; a day or vice-versa. Why am I even talking to you? You're a Daemon, I can't-" Dirk began.

"It is Hell: Your Hell Dirk! Look around and tell me do you feel and see colour? Whatever would be the least amiable scenario for yourself is what your Hell is made of. In effect, its essence is made up of your nightmares and your nightmares are being passed onto the rest of us..." The Elves commanding voice sang out. "Please Dirk think; you need to trust yourself; your own emotions and not those projected by others. See what you truly feel and you shall reveal the seen truth of your soul."

"Then ya really are an Elf?" Dirk asked, already assured of the answer. "Then you cannot really lead me back to life, for that I need..."

"You know it to be true. Look in your heart. What is it that your senses tell you, how do you define your instinctive feel? You must;" Farwen continued to advise Dirk before being rudely interrupted.

"All right...!" Dirk screamed, "I believe you."

Dirk lessened the painful waves, gradually rescinding them until they formed a black pool of emotion around him self: "...But if you're all real and speaking the truth then my nightmare would end with me cocking up so what can I do...? I'm going to be caught by either my mistress or the Dread Lord and no doubt have my soul devoured and for what? What the shit have I done to deserve it eh? I'm a thirty something with less going for me than a five year old orphan. All I ever craved was to find my own little niche in life and get old and die in relative peace shagging as many birds along the way as I could manage. Do you think I wanted a life on the run? Even the women I have bedded all have husbands, lovers or fathers that want me dead. The first woman I meet who hasn't got anyone happens to be a sick and twisted Demon..., ...I was so popular in school that my ex-fellow students all took major's in 'How to kill a Heinemblud' and my master turns out to be some well known Daemon whose soul intent seems to be to see me dead..., ...So I was immature for a while longer than most; it happens. Maybe I'm a bit ignorant sometimes but I've come to realise that, I can't help it but I realise it. Other times I have problems controlling my bladder but at least it works: Worked rather; here in Hell ya don't even need take a piss…, …I miss life that's all. I'm sorry I turned out to be a miserable excuse for a conceited Human but I always felt like life wasn't being fair to me; like life owed me more ya know: Some exalted existence where I didn't have to shit myself every five minutes and clean my own laundry…" The companions though shaken, had risen and Qoua was visibly upset by Dirk's speech, whereas the Dwarf seemed to be glaring at the Elf who had a quizzical look about him as Dirk continued…" I sometimes wish I had a god I felt close too, or at least believed in at least a little…, …I know I wish I'd had a Father growing up; I can't say I ever really knew my mother. In fact Grot's the one I hold dearest out of anyone I've ever met and yet I'm sure I never wanted to hitch up with a sulky bastard of a Dwarf and go through endless jobs like some erratic mercenary; barely surviving and endlessly hunting for that elusive pot of gold only to encounter death and bloody disaster; yet I had never even killed anything before that-that, bleeding shite of a Snurch…!"

The Dwarf, Elf and Lizardman, try as they might through strength, skill and cunning could not free them selves from the grey grasping matter.

"I never even wanted to learn magic really. I just wanted respect…" Dirk broke down and sobbed uncontrollably; his ears deafened to the pleas of his constrained companions. When sometime later he wiped the tears from his eyes, he raised red blubbery cheeks to face a gathering dark cloud of apprehension made physically factual by Dirk's fertile imagination.

"Dirk Free Us!" Qoua entreated but as Dirk thought to do so, bang on cue the Daemon from the bar came blasting out of the Tavern in an expected maelstrom of attention seeking majesty; his presence seem-fully expanding to merge with that of the vast expanse of cloud; dominating the landscape.

"Shit…, …Now I've done it!" Dirk gasped.

Clouds of black thunder pealed in around them, as the Daemon burst into vibrant crimson flame, again rather more due to Dirk's own imaginings than any desire to further impress the entrapped and soon to be dead 'wayward' souls.

Dirk awaited the imagined tirade, but it was rather shorter a rant thanks to him being the producer of said rumblings… "Dirk of the Blood, the legend is only just being written and yet here I stand, a humble king of the planes…, …One in the most desirable position I might add of gaining the undying respect of Galbor and others, by doing what: Killing ye?"

Dirk wondered whether it was his turn to say something but decided to await the continuance of the precocious tirade. It didn't come. The next time the infernal beast opened its mouth a plague of large, voracious and particularly carnivorous locusts spread out their dark humming wings and descended upon those entwined with rapacious delight.

Meanwhile the Daemon itself surged forward, trailing an emaciated scar across the tortured landscape in its wake: Its target of intent none other than Dirk himself. "Why me…" Dirk gibbered, "I'm nothing; less than nothing, why does every bastard want me dead…?"

"Oh but ye are so much more," the Daemon responded to the pathetic plea by pausing to gloat. "Ye are like everything contained within the Eyrthe above, unobtainable. But unlike us Daemons who are content to abide by certain unspoken rules, ye are not. Like the Elven walker over there, ye are not content to live by the guidelines set by others. Yes, ye want your own little niche in life but at what cost and at what point will ye be content?"

"You were listening?" Dirk asked incredulous.

"It is only the Inn's interior that is protected by your witch-mistresses simple dweomers. But of course a slave could never see beyond his masters wishes. The simple truth is ye could have left any time ye wished to, because only a sick mind like yourself would think up a world in which ye are your own jailor. Ye are a strange being Dirk of the Blood but a thoroughly mistaken one if ye think I wish ye dead."

"Then why attack me?" Dirk railed: This made less sense than his own fevered imagination.

"No Dirk I do not seek your death. Yet my own doom is closely linked with your own. Another came to Hell with ye and this person and I have unfinished business: We were both of the original Men, he and eleven others formed a council to deal with those others thought to be misusing their powers, I am sure ye can guess where I stood on the matter. I am like the walker…" The Dread Lord referred to the Locust ridden Elf. "Flesh and blood, still living in un-life but I have been like this for far longer than he and will survive a great deal longer if I but rid myself of *his* existence, an existence to which ye self and he are tied; sharing the same thread of fate…, …Feed my ravenous insects, feed."

"I don't get it, how can he be; I don't believe in fate…" Dirk said and the flicker of energy across the globes of his eyes died as suddenly did his will to fight. "My own jailor… My mistress-"

"Was real…" The Daemon interrupted. "But she is as misguided as ye are yourself. I would not expect her help anytime soon. Her misguided affections have brought about an unhealthy interest from our side. In short her extended family wants her dead, and her immediate, even more so. I know. I'm not so much her cousin as her sole surviving brother."

The Daemon flung its essence forward engulfing Dirk in consuming flame as it grappled him to the floor. The searing pain inflicted by the Daemon's grip froze Dirk for a moment but he refused its paralytic suggestion and fought back through an alien force of iron resolve.

"Why attempt to resist, Hunted? Ye must surely know I can continue a fight of a thousand times this magnitude *and* maintain it for decades… Whilst ye!" The Daemon spat, "Ye are a simple trickster who knows how to bend the rules slightly…"

"And what are '*Ye*' then?" Dirk shot back as his eyeball's blazed anew with the crackling pulses of magical energy, "Don't you too have to live by the rules..?" Dirk's eyes verily swamped with colliding atoms of energy and blasts of dark matter seeming to hold within them the same voids of space like desolation as the Dread Lord's own. The Devil blinked; launching a concentrated supernova straight at Dirk just as the star collapsed. The supernova's intense heat: Though aimed in the opposite direction and some way off from, still scorched the collar, neck and face of the entwined Elf; bubbling the flesh on his nearer left arm though Dirk, despite taking the brunt of its expanding force full on, didn't even flinch.

In fact he merely remarked on its brightness before birthing a black hole into which the star spiralled as Dirk's force battled the Dread Lord's. Then as the Daemonic overlord forced the black hole to collapse in on itself; Dirk let out tears of frustration; whose ionic forms swept small holes through the Daemon's figure as Dirk fought back with the desperation of a cornered were-rat.

"Impudent one…" The fiend growled, "*I am Dread Lord. I make* the rules of Hell."

Dirk's fear magnified; this really was his worst nightmare but somehow it wasn't as bad as he'd imagined. Summoning all the energy his panic stricken soul could muster Dirk struck the Daemon with a ghostly giant backhand, which sent the Dread Lord hurtling back into the horizon; the dark cloud of his extended torso peeling back to reveal a glorious azure sky in response. Dirk breathed a sigh of relief at the temporary lull in fighting and instantly began weaving an opaque dome of steely texture around him self, sucking up the life essence from the ether; which itself was formed with the psyche of those whose souls had been destroyed or contained within its sphere...

The Daemon teleported back within the blink of an eyelid, but Dirk had already half formed his cocoon like structure as the Daemon hurtled himself forward in another determined charge. The formerly inept wizard had already consumed as much he could absorb of the surrounding landscape and he let a good portion of its power out in another defensive charge which crackled with scorching pride, unleashing its furious assault on everything in the fifty mile vicinity of Dirk: Further tormenting the captured forms of the Elf, Grot and Qoua in the process, as well as ending the magically infused lives of the ravishing locusts.

Grot flipped up from his prone position as the grasping arms, depleted of their energy, flopped simply to the ground. "...Kh'a'Yag-MaR'Ihd...!" The Dwarf bellowed spreading his arms out palms flipped towards the bright blue sky above. White light shone protectively around himself, Qoua, and Farwen who staggered a little more sluggishly to his own feet. "He's... Draining us..." He managed before falling back to one knee.

Dread Lord came at Dirk in a hail of brimstone but it was a ruse. He had expected the human to throw up another defence, and so had sent an illusionary combatant to mimic himself, but for some reason Dirk did not react in the slightest. His eyes were closed and his brow furrowed in fevered concentration as he wove the dome around himself but nothing, it was as if... *'He's reading my thoughts!'* The Dread lord contemplated.

'Like yeah Dickhead!' Dirk shot mentally back in the affirmative. His shield was almost complete and the Daemon was screwed, he just needed a little more life force, he concentrated on his three compadre: *'Well they said they're here to help!'* He thought to himself then cursed as he realised he had just let mentally slip a vital piece of knowledge.

A blurred force slammed against and shook the almost complete structure around Dirk as the Dwarves rather large nose squashed against its exterior and he mumbled something into its glass-like confines. "Shtopp bwainin ower fuffan eneggy ya felfif vastad!"

The broiling mass of clouds encroached again on the companion's sky-lit territory, their prowling blackened edges fraying as they unfurled themselves into long gaunt shadows. At a thought or command issued by either Dirk's paranoia or the Daemons bidding; these shadows leapt into sudden life. Separating themselves from the silhouetted surrounding force and leaping upon the grouped allies, their vague forms transforming into a scowling horde of Demonic minions, whose hides were formed from such a deeply rich vein of magma as could only be seen in the belly of the most tumultuous volcano, where ash meet's fire and neither is willing to surrender supremacy. The rushing hordes scream's pierced out in maddening cackles of insane delight, in anticipation of the forthcoming decimation of those that dared offend their master.

The Elf finding himself without an escape route opted to swap his harp for his less used bow, though his arms were almost too weak to pull the string even the slightest degree. Grot and Qoua meanwhile, rose to their knees as best they could, to at least die with honour by facing their oncoming assassins. Dirk sneered at his companions shaded reactions of their own life-led ways. They were already dead and yet still they felt a need to maintain their honour. Dirk had always assumed that the point of keeping ones honour and virtue intact was to get in to heaven but to those two it was already in their hearts, it was the only way they had ever known and the only manner in which they would ever wish to conduct themselves no matter what their physical *or* ethereal state. That was the difference, the real one. The one that actually mattered; when it came to putting the clothes through the wash, the shit like himself always got left in the bottom of the proverbial bathtub. He'd never known honour to bring him anything but pain. Dirk didn't care how his death came as long as he himself had endeavoured in his own best efforts to avoid whatever manner it came in. Grot, Qoua and many, many others like them were bound by constraints of honour Dirk realised.

Grot and Qoua felt a tingling resurgence of life surge through their ethereal forms as Dirk released his grip on their collective spirits. The dome around Dirk began to fade and puncture as a carpet of the minions swept forward on his position and engulfed him. The Daemonic Dread Lord entwined upward upon a massive plume spiralling off from the assembled smoky mass of Eyrthe matter and cloud below.

"I never realised you knew magic Dwarf! I'm impressed..." Qoua cited.

"Well, don't be," Grot countered, "The glow is due to the oath to me god. I just thank Keldor the bugger was listening. It should protect us against everything but the odd bite and the big fella. Seems like Dirk's give us our rightful strength back so what do yer say to us returning the favour by whacking some of them dark looking red bastards off him?"

Qoua approved and the two loped over and began ripping the carnal beasts away one by one. Which beasts, completely oblivious to the two antagonists, would then pounce back upon Dirk's rapidly diminishing shelter and tear or puncture another portion of the magical bubble.

Dread Lord's chest huffed with pride. He was not an impatient being, becoming head Daemon had been no overnight triumph of sheer audacity but had rather more involved complex intricacies in Yarns, tales of disillusionment, rumours, counter rumours, lies, deception and general subterfuge on every level. His climb had been more a meander around rather than a direct assault on the mountainous throne but he would throw it all away tomorrow but for this…, …Dirk's destruction would not only carry with it the blessings and fear of thousands if not millions of disloyal subjects but also the death of his predicted nemesis Kalamere. Yet before Dirk could be dealt with Dread Lord had the small matter of the Dwarf and L'iezsh'mat to deal with. Firstly, the Daemon decided, he would have to take care of the annoying gnats that were Dirk's two lifetime companions.

A prickling heat warned the two intended victims of Dread Lord's restricting approach as they dragged themselves and their latest victims to one side. The resulting gigantic hammer-punch thudded into Dirk's dilapidated structure, smashing the remaining shards and squashing the daemons gathered there, while setting fire to others, but Dirk himself and the other two were nowhere to be seen.

Suddenly two charred corpses were thrown up in the air and Qoua and Grot bounded towards the momentarily off guard Daemon; its eyes blazing with feral light as it scanned the landscape for Dirk's manifestation.

He bid his remaining impish drones to attack the Dwarf and Lizard woman, before swimming about the air in search of his own prey. His borrowed physique still attached to the landscape around them by means of the coiling plume of smoky cloud.

Qoua and Grot battled hard against the minions for some several minutes when Qoua slipped and suddenly felt fire freezing claws pass deeply through her right shoulder. "I thought you claimed your god would protect us?" She complained to the Dwarf fighting at her back.

"I did and he has" Grot berated "but he's got a lot of us Dwarves to protect and his help is temporary at best! Be thankful for what ye receive!

Or have ya never heard that one?"

"Tell me…" Qoua asked in a manner one might affect whilst casually sipping morning tea, "Have you ever realised how much alike you and Dirk are?"

"…oh yeah sure I have! Apart from he's a dreamy tit with impossible ideals. I suppose you could say I'm a strong influence if anything…" Grot paused to punch a hole in the gluey ribcage of the nearest clawing Daemon before continuing, "Or at least I try to be. The lad needs it, dear Keldor, the lad needs it."

Qoua stood and removed her pained arm at the shoulder, utilising it as a club… "Stand close now the Daemon king approaches and he looks… What is the human word you and Dirk often use: Pissed? Watch how my own god's blessing deals with Pissers…"

As Dread Lord did indeed bend his head low in their direction, though not intentionally seeking them out, so did Qoua utter a fantastically confusing array of words in her own native tongue…, …Grot knew Dwarven was hard enough to fathom and he even knew a little Elven he had picked up from a druid in years gone by but what he had just heard was beyond his comprehension and he wondered how hard it must have been for her to learn such a perfect pronunciation of the common human vocabulary; though her definitions needed a little work in the swear word department.

The effects of her whistle-spoken words was to bring forth a blasting chill of death that instantly drove the life from their attackers whilst leaving themselves relatively unharmed… The Daemon above glowered down at them and snorted his disgust at the Lizard woman's handiwork. "Wench of Khan; I know his handiwork when I see it. He's a has-been. His magic is wasted upon me. Your prayers are to a doomed god."

Qoua turned a brave and unflinching face towards Dread Lord's approaching fiery presence and spoke out in strong defiance even as he struck her. "I know well my gods limitations, and his prophesised fall but it shall not be by your hand he is prophesised meet his demise; do your worst!" With that his blow landed knocking out most of her teeth, severely dislocating her jaw and fracturing the right side of her skull and cheekbone; which although it was all in her mind in this place, it hurt like pure Hell.

Still she pulled her self to her feet and faced her aggressor and the Daemon gripped her by the throat in disgust, boiling the scales there and blistering her face, shoulders and chest. Still she looked on in defiance though gasps of pain involuntarily escaped her constricted throat.

Her pain and suffering did not come to no avail as the Dwarf dropped the mighty Daemon with a perfectly executed sacrifice slam, wrapping both arms around Dread Lord's natural sized neck and throwing the surprised Demon into the bubbling ether beneath their feet. Grot dived onto Qoua and quickly dabbed out the resisting flames on her flesh before getting to work on his own sticky patches of sulphurous adhesive.

Behind them, Dread Lord rose in a storm of Dark purple more velvety in texture than that perpetrated by Dirk's own earlier efforts. This was the colour assumed by the powerful magic of darkness, to most humanoids eyes at least. Though to Dirk and others from other planes, there was a vast variation of light and dark textures within its consuming purple depths.

Grot rose to fling a fist at the smaller sized apparition of Dread Lord who now occupied a size and demeanour no more or less threatening than that which he had assumed in the tavern earlier. He was rather more threatening than his countenance hinted at however and his response to the Dwarves attack was to send a searing point of light slicing across the Dwarf, cutting his midriff badly and severing the threatening arm straight off.

"No more games..." Their Daemonic nemesis spat and swung his arm out straight smashing the bones of Qoua's raised defensive forearms and ripping away her jaw completely. She staggered and swayed, but did not fall, all the while fixing the Daemon with that same defiant gaze. A stinging backhand rapped across her knees and a long barbarous spike extending from Dread Lord's elbow ripped out her knee socket; dropping her onto her chest in the pose of a supplicant. Dread Lord slammed his foot down on her back; his three clutching claws, elongated, puncturing her ribs through her back. Still she raised her numbing head in defiance and the Lord of Hell slammed his fist down hard towards her bobbing bonce.

A shaft of light broke up not only the attack but also, Dread Lord's body parts as the Elf appeared from nowhere to enter into an attacking whirlwind of frenzy induced slice and dice. Having healed himself, he had put aside the bow and brought out two short swords which he now utilised with an inspiring show of skill. The Daemon countered as defensively and cohesively as he could manage but after disconnecting one arm at the elbow, in defence against one strike, the so called 'Lord' proceeded to lose digit after appendage after limb until there was little more than scraps left from the Elves tornado of butchery: Thoroughly attesting to the survival skills of a Plane-Walker or Wind-Walker as some were called though he himself was of the Ghost rank; the elites, in short he was a Wish-maker and though Dirk knew that, neither he nor any of the others present had ever witnessed one such Elf in battle. The Elf dashed back some five seconds later to an astonished Qoua who recovered her senses enough to go and help repair the Dwarf, who was still struggling to come to terms with his illusionary pain.

"What force are you? How can you produce such an effortless display of battle prowess against the Lord of Hell himself? Are you a god? Come to our rescue?" Qoua fervently questioned then caught sight of an assembling shadowy form and the silhouette it cast chilled her so utterly it caused her to grow faint: Dread lord was back; goat-like and deadly. The Elf turned his face to his enemy and charged. This time it only took the walker Farwen slightly less than four seconds not to return victorious but rather, after which time, he had been shredded where he stood and devoured. His soul stood uncomprehending its predicament a moment longer than he should have and as a rippling bright light broke the stormy sky above, once more revealing blue sky in its wake and streamed down towards the Elven soul; the Demons pitch fork proved faster and in the course of a millisecond he was gone; his righteous soul cast into deep recess of Hell where Heaven dared not fare.

From his hiding place Dirk decided they all needed a miracle if they were to make it out of this alive, and he achieved one of sorts, when his mistress suddenly turned up without warning. "What happened to you? Why is your skin shredded so badly? Have you been fighting downstairs or something?" She paused but he made no response. "Hello, Dirk... I am back you know... Why are you cowering at the window?" She teased bouncing forward; her earlier dry departure seemingly forgotten.

Dirk turned from the bedroom window and pushed her back towards the bed which now disgusted him. Once more he was struck by how beautiful she looked thanks to his design, and even though he was mid-crisis he could not dismiss the burning urge emanating from his nipples.

"Look, ya don't need to look out there... I realise ya love me; I mean, really love me, because only an idiot like me could imagine that the one person to truly accept me is one I thoroughly despise and well:" Dirk noticed the path honesty was taking him down and changed tack. "I mean, I don't despise ya exactly; more your race and how they hunger for power. To be honest, I find *you* damned attractive actually babe but the simple truth is we're in deep shit!"

"Dirk your voice… How sweet, how did you change it; it sounds more sinister than a Balrog in a bad mood, yet…, …sweet and sensual. It is *most* beguiling…" His mistress said with the wide eyed smile of one in love.

"It doesn't matter…"

"Oh but it does… It's so beautiful; is that how you got the scars; here let me heal you straight away…" And she did so, even though Dirk moaned at her to stop fussing and listen.

"Outside," he said at length, "My friends are dying and it's because of me. They don't even belong in hell apparently and to be honest I'm not surprised but they did come back for me…"

"Dirk what's the matter; you can't have been outside, I forbade it…" She began.

"Yeah and I know the way the rules around here work and you're wrong; though ya wont believe me anyways. They're just like rules anywhere; ya don't have to choose to live by them, so I have been tweaking with stuff over the centuries or however long has passed and found shit out; then something someone said in the bar made me think of something and well; ya can't condemn my friggin soul no more for a start. Go on, try it; ya won't hurt me I promise; just say it. See I may be able to handle life here if shit inside this tavern can't affect me…, …So try it; condemn me. I break my pledge to ya; I refuse to honour my word. Condemn me bitch!" Dirk provoked her, even going so far as to fling her onto the bed but she met his taunt with a repeat of the earlier un-demonic tears. "Ya can't condemn me can ya? Ya won't in case ya hurt me; all because of some bloody rule…"

"…Because of my love!" She cried, "I thought you would have realised by now. I love you, not your imagination or fears, *ME*…"

"Then why did ya knick some of my soul bitch?" Dirk cursed.

"To have a child…, …our child as spoken of in the prophecy…"

Dirk slapped her. The connection it made was audible and Dirk felt the reddening sting on the back of his palm. "Wake up ya silly cow. That bastard is out there busily dissecting my friends and he's here because of me. Ya know why he's here because of me? Do ya? Well I'll tell ya should I? It's because some dumb bitch got me mixed up with someone important: Some tit called hidden dagger or something who is just probably way more important than me and therefore twice as deadly but all the same; if the wanker turned up right now I would slug him on the chin for the amount of crap I've had to go through on his behalf. So now ya pissed off sibling is coming to kill us all..., ...at least I now know why thanks to ya friggin quick pregnancy; no time for your lover to bugger off proper that's for sure, though I honestly don't know why he let you live so long when ya say he butchered his own siblings and trapped his parents in a void. Unless ya lied about your brother too..."

"Which brother...?" The words shocked her more than the offending slap.

"Oh I don't know which could it be, Drongor the invincible bog cleaner? Meghmarr the mighty pen pusher..., ...? Oh-oh! Oh no-no-no! That's it erm, bed sword, dreadlocks, Fred lord something or other..." Dirk dramatised going through his entire repertoire of histrionics.

"...Dread Lord?" She panted, her breathing convulsively restricted.

"Well give that woman a fairy cake and call her Mary!" Dirk whooped in a pathetic over the top piss take. "Oh yeah that's it! *You* thought he was your distant cousin for some reason..., wonder how that came about then; forgetting he was your brother..., ...so why did he keep ya around, because believe me; his plans along those lines have changed a fair deal."

The Daemonic princess scowled in thought and painful admittance; "I was to become his bride..."

"Kept his sister to be his bride eh? Talk about keeping it in the family; no wonder half of you demon lot are demented..." Dirk harangued.

"But how could he know I was to return here?" She wondered aloud.

"Perhaps because some shit betrayed ya, it wouldn't be unlikely considering we are in Hell..." Dirk reasoned, tactfully omitting the perpetrators identity and thus extending his own existence for now.

"Why are you thinking of daisies?" His mistress queried having attempted to read Dirk's thoughts.

"Oh am I?" He said switching to mentally describing daffodils, "I dunno, they're pretty aint they? So are we off? Before big bro knocks: He pretty much wants to kill me too but I guess ya already knew that...?"

"Dirk, why are you attempting to shield your thoughts from me and with mental pictures of flowers of all things? You have *never* mentally described flowers before and you once told me that gardeners were simply a breed of crass old dictator wannabes intent on dominating at some level and taking it out on weeds. Dirk is he even really-" The Daemoness froze and quickly withdrew upon sighting her wayward brother as he dealt with the elf in short course. Real blood and gore spat out from his split and separated flesh, shocking her with the thought that one so full of life would wish to willingly come here... She read Dirk's thoughts her eyes transfixed on the windowsill. He was thinking of fishes...

"Dirk, what have you done...?" His mistress collapsed to her knees and sobbed and Dirk wrapped a comforting arm around the poor maiden before him.

"There, there... Don't cry now..." He coaxed, lovingly nuzzling her damp cheek, "Just whisk us off to another plane of existence and we'll forget all about him..." Dirk lifted his chin to nibble on her delicate ear, but the sudden expansion of her girth made him aware of a change in her, and he found himself chewing on the ear of a cow.

"Eugh that's just nasty! Turn back into the sweet thing I designed..." Dirk derided, pulling away. "Turn back I said! Come on babe..."

"What have you done...? Dirk you have betrayed me..."

"Well yes," Dirk said and dropped the imagined picture of an Elephant that looked more like a fat dog anyway. "For a while but I was being rash; it was your brother that told me that ya loved me; in his own little way and he'd come to kill ya anyways; its not like I got ya pregnant: Well actually it is just like that aint it..., ...Bugger I've been down this road before in life. Look, come on, all I'm saying is; I know I was a bastard and I'll change. Forgive me all ready. I promise I'll stay by your side for the rest of our days together..., ... Just let's do the plane hopping thing and quick."

"That sounds ever more like a statement a Daemon would give. Dirk I will never trust you again. Tell me, did you promise him your soul in any way? You sick Faljar..." That last comment being delivered through lips quivering with rage. "Weak Humanoids often strike deals for their souls..."

"Look just calm down and let's get out of here. I know ya won't hurt me. You've never really tried to. Ya love me too much see;" Dirk's rhetoric was cut short by a stinging backhand of her own.

"Do not be too sure slave..." The Daemoness threatened, "I may have lost my powers but-"

"You've lost your powers, why?" Dirk didn't know whether to be extremely delighted or morbidly glum at the prospect. "How...?"

The Daemoness regarded Dirk with a quizzical air: "You mean to say you did not know?"

Dirk shrugged his upraised palms to indicate he was baffled by the admission then cocked his hip to one side in order to let out a long wet fart.

His mistress wrinkled her nose in disgust – she doubted the cleanliness of his underwear from the smell. "Humans..., ...I do not even wish to ask how you came about the means to break wind..."

"I just wanted to..., ...ya know let of a little steam as the Dwarves and Gnomes say." Dirk grinned.

"You know very well what I mean," the Daemoness remarked, "I am unsure how you managed the feat, let alone how you discovered it."

"I figured shit out like I said..." Dirk scoffed.

"Obviously..." His mistress dryly added. "Yet the Dread Lord's presence automatically nulls the controlling powers of all others in attendance. I could no more teleport us to another plane as I could issue a *flower* or *fish* from thin air... Your stupid and senseless betrayal has doomed us all. Well done, Dirk my love."

"I'm not your friggin' love ok? Lover; yes, I admit it maybe but love: Most definitely not. If that's true about your powers, how come you can still try to read my mind and you healed me no problem at all?" He accused.

"I'm a Daemon princess. Those are borne of an inherent ability," the Daemoness vouched, "*controlling powers* are the ability to manipulate Hell."

Dirk paused at the news and was suddenly mindful of times in the past when she had mentioned her true nature; now things made more sense. "Dread lord could read my mind all along couldn't he?" He asked as he moved brazenly into the windows revealing light.

"...Indubitably." She conceded.

"I'll take it that means yes," Dirk said continuing his outspoken reasoning, "But he couldn't for some reason and I wasn't thinking of fish or flowers, yet I could read his. And you, you're concerned all right but ya aint panicking too much and I can guess why. It probably works something like a vampire right? He can't come in here unless invited upstairs by *you...*" He caught her stiffened poise and knew he spoke the truth. "So we're safe until we try to leave, which will be never. And so this gorgeous little pad is going to be our prison for oh... I don't know; the next few millennia perhaps...?"

"It's my friends I feel sorry for. They've just turned up from heaven to rescue me from Hell and well, to be honest; I've witnessed better salvation attempts in my time..., ...mind you, I shouldn't be too hard on them, because that paranoid edge we seem to have cultivated saw me pulverise them with a sonic boom, drain them of life and then pin them down ready to be attacked by hungry locusts, courtesy of your brother... Oh yeah:" Dirk added his words fascinating her; "did I mention building a sonic shelter?"

For the first time in many an aeon, the Daemoness was lost for words, unsure of any possible solution, yet infinitely aware of the prophesised outcome, although the exact nature of her ending she was unsure of. She studied Dirk's apparition.

"Funny thing is..." Dirk tittered turning to face his mistress, "I didn't know he drained everyone of their powers, because he never bothered to; or rather couldn't drain me of mine..."

She opened her mouth to speak, but no words could come to her quickly enough. "Don't waste your time. Bitch! Your brother has got something I want out there and guess what I have got going on here? Ya get the meaning don't ya?" His face was a grimacing mask as he grabbed her roughly by the horn and threw her; not through the window as could probably be expected, but through the outer wall instead. She landed with a humiliating thud and Dirk jumped out and drifted down silently behind her.

Dread Lord was all around them now formed from the very ether; he no longer was represented by some humanoid form but rather blended with and epitomised Hell; terrifying Grot and Qoua huddled in fear. Rather he was the stuff of ground and air, all of which was now no more than a smoky black amalgamation, blocking the Inn from sight even though it lay only five or six feet away. Red slit's pierced the cloud at heaven-height casting their solitary luminance down upon those gathered in its judgemental spotlight.

Dirk casually plucked at a bit of the blackness and attempted to fashion it into a bunch of carnations, but as he had suspected his powers too had now been invalidated. "Ya know; that's why Hell is so shit..., ...Not a single bloody flower!"

"What happened to *your* fear Hunted?" Dread Lord demanded in his natural infinite voice, its sound washing across the furthest reaches of Hell's planes like a tortured wind being forced onto a confined subterranean path.

"Listen to me ya bastard, I'll do the speaking and that body will only listen to me from now on understood Dickhead!" Dirk mumbled and bubbled. "...An enlightened rightful heir, my hairy arse!"

His mistress rose and turned her head at Dirk's antics but as she locked eyes with him he shook his head slightly side to side and screamed back at her with the unruliness of a child, his large maddened pupils boring into hers without recognition.

"You Bastard Heinemblud..." The discarded Daemoness cursed. "By word of law I condemn your soul to the realms of the b-r-o-g-hl..." but Qoua's wickedly sharp claw across her throat, temporarily disabled her voice box and prevented her from completing the damning sentence. It also did a whole lot more. Robbed of her powers, as well as her voice, she was at a loss to explain why she was suddenly bleeding profusely; she commanded it to stop but the pain caused her to topple over in crippling agony. She had known suffering before and like Dirk though to a lesser extent than he, she had learned to become its master but its painful coldness was spreading and her healing powers had unfathomably ceased to function...

'...*How come my brother?*' She asked in her mind as her eyes closed and she drifted towards true death.

Dread Lord as wicked and unmerciful as he was, was also her brother and loved her dearly though he hated her more out of jealousy. '*Relax now Khillvar Uatroq Jaierimanyi. She is the daughter of Khan: Your slayer. Remember the prophecy for its telling is twisted; it is not Dirk nor I but she, and that one shall bring down three demi-gods if the prophecy runs true, let us hope that I am not one of those three as are now ye?'*

She struggled to retain clarity within her speedily fragmenting mind, *'Please... Remind me beloved brother...'*

Dread Lord felt a strong pang of regret, she had been the closest thing he had ever known and now she was passing to a plane he would never be able to access unless invited and he severely doubted that. *'Sister, listen to me, do not be afraid. Your actions these past hundred years have brought about your souls salvation, ye shall travel to heaven to be reborn true.'*

'But I don't want it. I'm scared brother. I feel cold. What was the prophecy, why do I have to die...?'

'Because sweet sister it is prophesised that 'his' time in triumph over Hell, begins with the end of your own. But I swear I will avenge ye, for I have a part to play in his downfall at least once before my own fate becomes unclear; I already had my time amongst the living: I doubt heaven holds out any signs of my own redemption..., ...I know ye will not remember any of your former life as a Demon but heed my words: Do not waste the life given to ye, no matter how seemingly insignificant it may be...' He paused then to hear his sisters reply but she was gone; a large bloody pool the only evidence of her ever having existed at all.

*"**What do ye want!?**"* Dread Lord's eerie voice whispered from a thousand points of origin.

"...To go home?" Grot gasped as his stomach began the painfully slow process of stitching together again.

"Home: Where pray tell is that?" The lord of Hell cried.

"Well anywhere but Hell." The smarting Dwarf moaned.

"L'iezsh'mat ye will answer me!" The screaming voices came roaring into the Lizardman's ears and as her body was whipped into the air by some invisible force she gained the use of a mouth again; though it did not feel familiar. The truth was Dread Lord was determined to hear her speak and he had gifted her a new oral cavity for the purpose, but like many of the ignorant races occupying the Eyrthe above, he too got mixed up between the race of Lizard and Snakeman and instead of the proud, jutting, crocodilian jaw she had once owned, complete with rows of razor sharp teeth, she was now left with a rather more alluring skull complete with long green flowing tresses of hair and large almond eyes; full red, luscious lips that concealed a long, slender, flickering tongue that would dart out occasionally from between two cute but no less feral looking Snake-woman's fangs, whose smooth jaw and facial features she now adopted.

"Do you know why your god dies in the prophecies?" The Daemons voice sang through hers and everyone else's senses. "Tell me; I want your friends to hear..."

She raised a hand to her face and tried to form a few sounds in her own ancient tongue but found their intricate pronunciation too difficult for the alien maw. "I onssse sthought I hknew..."

"He will die because of ye!" The all pervading voice interjected. "My father will die because of ye..., ...Sf-vil U'hl-Qoua, daughter of the faith..., ...For ye have killed our sister in his name." The Daemon bent his rotten will to warp her own, "Our sister... Yours and mine..."

"Ssss-I- I'm sssorry hsss, hi sssneffer hrealisssed..."

"So bleeding what?" Grot said from a renewed standing position, his bravery returned: "So another Daemon bites the dust, who cares...?"

Dread Lord mentally sat Grot back down and forced the Dwarves own limbs to slap himself twice smartly, across the head and face. "Quiet Dwarf, this is her doing not yours. Scream for your god wench!" And with that the Daemon compressed his invisible grip on her torso, forcing her body to quiver in jelly-like fashion.

Qoua screamed. Her oaths too intelligible and diverse to pick out, but none of which were directed at her god. Dread Lord dropped Qoua's stinging self to the floor and snatched up Dirk; whose simple, lunatic expressions did not change to one of fright but rather induced a fit of exaggerated giggles from the maddened wizard.

"No!" Both Grot and Qoua shouted in unison. The disembodied red eyes focused their unholy corona on the two then back to Dirk as it began to suck out his life matter with an audible hiss. Qoua struggled upright and Grot rolled back to his feet but Dread Lord paid them no heed whatsoever. As they watched helpless, the King of Hellish domains sucked every living cell from Dirk and spat them out in a random spray across the empty space...

"**I** can put him back together, call your god." He said, pointedly illuminating Qoua in the searching red light of his eyes.

Qoua considered her options; If Dirk was to be destroyed now her life would probably end too. Beyond that the prophecy would fail and her people would be destroyed. Dread Lord wanted her to deliver Khan; no doubt so that he could destroy him somehow but that made no sense if her father; her god was also the lord of Hell's father. In the end Dread Lord *was* only a Daemon and she doubted very much his ability to bring down a god. Besides which: The prophecy as laid down in the book of Qoua, by which she lived her life, made no mention of Dread Lord being involved in her beloved Gods demise. That was the fate of another. She made the decision.

"sfery weldss. hto shssomesching ahbout mhai voiceess" She requested. "Fhor I chan nort..., ...speak his name in–ah done I see, my thanks!"

"Snake people are infinitely more primitive than my own kind and their jaw lacks the proper–ah, I can see you do not wish for a lesson; no matter; heal my friends and return us all to mortality and I swear I shall summon my God Khan!" Qoua declared to shouts of 'Qoua no!' from Grot.

No sooner had she made the declaration and the three of them were stood together in true flesh and blood; each was instantly aware of the fact thanks to the various ways in which Hell assaulted the senses of the living here. The stench of pestilence around them was absolute and thick as broth. Screams of unenviable magnitude rang out continuously, clashing against each other in mingling contrition. The body felt cold on the inside, like when one has a violent flu, yet their naked flesh tanned alarmingly at the heat thrown up all around them. What was worse still however was that they were not just surrounded by; but also standing upon the souls of the damned whose collective mass made up the ether from which reached out pathetic fingers clutching their skeletal selves in desperation at being so close to the living. The ground, the sky, everything but what passed for air was made of a living, tortured soul.

Qoua wondered how the Elf had managed to cope down here and resolved to find out more about these 'Walkers' should the opportunity ever arise. She attempted to summon Khan but the required syllables were too complex to wrap her tongue around. "Oh sorry to be an awful bother Lord of Dread but when you fixed my speech you seem to have given me a human tongue! I only say as I sound human, yet am unable to sound

L'iezsh'mat –s-s-s-s-sound; I *sound* human!" Qoua almost physically leapt such was her excitement at the strange new sound of her voice and almost forgot the magnitude of the occasion.

"I bestow the power to speak as ye must!" Dread Lord rumbled, "Use your voice in whatever manner ye desire, just please do get on with summoning Khan before my patience wanes..."

Qoua was still rolling 'R's and sounding S's when the Daemon's words filtered through to her. "Oh but if I say L'iezsh'mat or something simple like Qoua; oh, you've fixed me again. How nice..."

"I apologise brother..." She tried her new tongue out-slithering it around her mouth and was surprised to discover it still felt as though it were forked. Never the most digitally agile of creatures, the Lizardman gripped her tongue roughly between her fingers and felt its familiar/unfamiliar dimensions. It truly was still forked, only ever so slightly and was now much more slender than her old tongue. She felt again at her feminine face and Jaw; so he had brought her back to life as she stood, Qoua wondered...

*"**Summon Him!**"* Dread Lord commanded, interrupting her probing.

"Oh of course..., ...I am in shock brother that is all; the prophecy claimed I would undergo a transformation but I had assumed it had been meant in a meta-physical sense, to find out otherwise is..., ...pardon your Lordship I will tarry no longer in completing my own side of the bargain: Sh'y'souy'll Quy'yy'lleu Khan Amshaa!" Qoua cleverly recited; her niggling narration precise in every way.

"You will transport us to Eyrthe now yes-s?" Qoua questioned, over-inflecting the last 'S' through habit, rather than inability.

"I'm sorry; do I see any sign of dear old father? Besides, *and,* correct me if I'm wrong but, when did ye ever ask to be transported back to Eyrthe?" Dread Lord laughed.

Qoua thought to protest, but Grot stopped her; "Listen now a minute, yer cocked up the deal; no harm in that, yer just cocked up is all but don't argue with him cause yer never mentioned us leaving for Eyrthe." Qoua seemed unsure and asked Dirk for his opinion but he responded by spewing back a stream of gibberish and trying to chew on his clenched fist.

"Do I have 'the Devil Supreme is an idiot' tattooed somewhere my word breaking L'iezsh'mat: Or are ye merely testing my patience?" Dread

Lord interrupted pointing her out with an oversized spectral finger. "Why has my father still not come? Do ye seek to trick the Lord of Trickery himself?" That is not advisable here in Hell; I fulfilled my own part of the bargain and ye are expected to complete your own too or your soul shall be damned to the brink of existence: A most unpleasant experience your demented friend knows about only too well."

"Yer saying you've sent his soul to the brink?" Grot asked testily…

"Not I; my sister, she finds or rather *used* to find it much simpler to invoke than *I*, being the former Goddess of echoes and spaces. No…, …For my own part I am reduced to awaiting some slip such as one not honouring their deal, in order to deliver a soul unto the brink."

Qoua seemed puzzled "What is this brink you speak off: A void or…"

"Yes, yes like a void…" Dread Lord cut in, "yet so much worse; it is a place where the only thing that exists is the mental knowledge that ye alone exist. Some who have witnessed it claim it's worse than true death or the long sleep as we gods like to think of things…, …no matter! If ye do not call Khan, your lives will be very unpleasant to say the least: I alone control events here in Hell and nothing here happens without my say so, okay?"

Right on cue it began to rain though no indications pre-empted the stormy arrival; neither associated breeze nor temperature change, no drop in humidity; not even a single storm-cloud (besides those already generated) blew in on agitated turbulence.

"So why ya making it rain then? Proving to us all that Gods can get pissed on too?" Grot yammered. "We all ready know that…"

"…Foolish Dwarf…!" Dread Lord roared, "It is not of my doing…"

"Are you sure because I'm certain yer just said-"

Qoua stood and standing upright on her remarkably strong tail, stretched her arms out wide, tilting her head back and opening up her Jaw to accommodate the refreshing droplets. "It is Khan!" She said.

Grot too threw his head back only to receive a large dollop of the falling liquid directly in his eyeball. "Bugger," he said wiping back the watery teardrop of rain as the newly birthed deluge took on new potency; "It's blood!" Grot yelped in surprise, "It's raining blood!"

Qoua turned at an instinctive thought to see what she assumed to be the human form of Dread Lord approaching, his layered robes fluttering in the swelling gusts of gathering wind. But as he reached their vicinity the wind dropped to a low whistle and so too did his flapping garments. His visage was revealed to be that of a mean looking old man; the type that never tipped bar-staff and moaned at anything less than a relieving long wet fart. Qoua felt immediately disarmed by the feeble looking father figure, but the Dwarves gasp of fright and Dirk's sudden fainting spell told her she should feel otherwise. At least Dirk had had a reaction at last, though obviously not the one hoped for, under their current circumstance.

"…Hello again old friend." The old man cried, cheerfully wrapping his arms around the Dwarf affectionately. Qoua relaxed again and strode forward her hand outstretched in friendship but as she neared the old fellow, his visage turned suddenly into that of a truly terrifying Demon. Its dark red sulphurous body tapered off to blackened appendages, a tail swished about in buccaneer fashion and the stiff brush of hair that decorated every inch of its body gave off a feral accent to further accentuate the huge rotten tusks jutting from the lower corners of his mouth and the beady black eyes at the base of the beings integrity. Demon fear is as strong almost as that induced by a Dragons appearance and though this was Hell and therefore a place where one wherein one might reasonably expect to meet a Demon in its natural state.

However, with Hell being largely governed by the mental aspects of ones soul, rather than physicality of Eyrthe; the effects of any fears were magnified so strongly that even the Dwarf stood stock still, unable to respond for several long moments. Qoua though couldn't help herself despite her trepidation and started sniggering; which in turn led to a heartily felt and much too loud burst of laughter. Qoua was delightedly surprised at the cultured sound articulating from within her own throat, for atop the otherwise ferocious Daemon's head was a shiny patch of bald pinking scalp. "Galbor…" Grot managed in deference to the Balrog before him and the glowing red eyes still set in the cloudy patch way up high, twinkled with mischievous delight.

"Paul my dear little Dread Lord you may go. I do not need your prying here…"

Dread Lord's current manifestation did not dissolve away however; rather the smoky texture appeared more omnipresent than ever. "Why should I leave my Uncle? I rule these realms remember."

"Impudent little Gremlin!" Galbor span around and the cloud shrank back a little and faded to a slightly grey shade, though the eyes remained fixed in their positions.

"Uncle I am just stating that it's me who rules supreme here. I don't mind helping out but let me ask; why have ye come here? Could it be ye seek out your errant charge here in the afterlife? Rather than spending the time needed to trick some unfortunate into summoning your good self back to life?" The Dread Lord's disembodied voice had lost its volume and the associated gusting authoritativeness earlier demonstrated.

"Maybe I have come to take what is mine: If everything went as I have planned which it always does when *I* plot and scheme; you will have killed your sister already," Galbor gloated, "thus negating your undisputed right to sit upon the throne of Hell. There were three Balrog at that meeting and every wretch and urchin knows it, the only reason I kept my own part in it hidden was because of your interfering sister and her uncanny knack of deciphering the location of others..."

The eyes belonging to Paul's voice grew in size; burning with the brightness of a thousand suns... "Ye are most truly an evil, malicious, conniving Bastard! I'll kill both ye and the L'iezsh'mat for her demise; my sister had nothing to do with me or my staying in power; ye think she would have come to my rescue? The poor wench avoided my presence like the plague *and...*"

"She loved another, yes, yes I know; Dirk has an indefinable 'knack' with the ladies..." Galbor scoffed.

The eye's glare diminished a little; "I was going to say I loved her but whatever; ye know nothing of that..., ...What does the god of Terror know of anything but fearful emotion?"

Galbor laughed a single derisive snort. "Is that why you were going to force her to marry you? You truly are a knave. You spent too long as a human and it shows. Adopting the emotion of love... Pah! Pathetic being you are; you should have stayed as a human Paul the Wanderer for you have strayed back to a place you never even belonged."

With those words Galbor released his full fury; his powers seeming undiminished in the slightest. And his grotesque ashen figure expanded to fill the horizon with molten rock and noxious gulfs of black and grey sulphurous smoke. The companions could only huddle at the sight; Qoua clutching at the knees of Grot like a frightened child: While Dirk stopped picking at the Soul packed ether and merely gawped listlessly at the turn of events, his head periodically cocking to one side as if to say 'what?'

Dread Lord's eyes disappeared in response; his essence becoming the embodiment of Hell in itself and a sleet of icy hail and drenching rain spewed forth from everywhere; up, down and all around. A mighty typhoon whipped at the rapidly gathering water as a hurricane blew in from behind the huddled mortals; drenching them to the core and striking Grot with as much fear as Qoua held, grabbing her for dear life in return.

"We're all gonna die...!" Grot screamed in a girly pitch as the battle above and around them raged on. Wherever the two opposing elements of fire and ice connected, huge gulps of corrosive steam exploded, resulting in a fearful roar or several from either and often both combatants. Whenever the water dampened down the billowing ash of Galbor that one would suffer, yet where the smoke gathered thickest Paul would choke on its depreciating fumes. All the while, throughout the temper flared tirade; through gale force winds and boiling flame, small droplets of blood pitter-pattered here and there in a steady downpour.

Several drops of blood fell several feet from Dirk, connecting with a forming puddle and drip-dropping a steady beat which grabbed his otherwise vacant attention: Though after a minute or two of the soft steady blood rain, it began to hammer down with a passion; much like a sudden summer hail; the small pellets of blood, splattered down passionately about the landscape, decorating everything with its fast congealing ichors.

From one of the many small pools of blood dotting the landscape, one quite close to the action in fact, which bubbled, spat and foamed with an abundance of verve; appeared a fat red Daemon with many skinny arms, each of which were clutching long wicked daggers. It snarled and padded about to slowly turn and sight those behind him; his pin like head, complete with crocodilian snout, also rotated its view and his body stopped turning as his head sighted Galbor and Dread Lord above and behind him.

"Son of an infidel whore-hound; which of you dogs dared summon me? My death summoning I presume dear siblings?" Khan's voice dripped with despicable hate as he spat every unwelcome vowel from his mouth; splitting through the tumultuous battle like a death knell. The cowering companions looked up from their solace as the two Daemonic combatants instantly ceased in their endeavours; both resuming a somewhat less frightening, man sized form; albeit a tall veined man with his insides popping out.

Again the huge feet slip-slop padded about and again the head got there first commanding Qoua's whole attention with his singular great eye. "You there foolish L'iezsh'mat child: You and your idiotic actions are evidence enough why I put men in charge of your people's faith. What have you done? Followed the legacy to the letter, blindly following the path mapped out in your oracle? Imbecile…, …You have betrayed me because you believe you were meant to? Stupid Girl I am trapped in a worse state than yourself. I am without my controlling powers in the presence of Paul, even though the weakling excuse for a Dread Lord is my bastard son. And that dark horror there is the guardian to the gates of heaven…, …My treacherous brother Galbor: The darkest, most ruthless, horrible bastard this side of Eyrthe. So is this a trap of some sort?" Khan's tiny head span about independently of its massive blood drenched bulk. He regarded Galbor, ignoring the Dread Lord hovering in dimly lit shame. "Why call me from the void if not to finish me? Or do you really think she…, …a mortal, could kill me? Whatever your plans; I plan to put an end to her role in this now. Just let me cut them up first. I need vengeance for my summoning…"

Galbor smiled broadly, "Cut away…" He said, backing off a little.

The skinny arms whirred into motion and the sluggish body began chugging forward towards the three companions. Grot had roused Dirk who was now running away and hopping simultaneously whilst pointing back and jabbering like a gibbon. While Qoua merely stood stock-still within a short distance of the advancing minor god. Grot wasted no time in arguing and snatched up her tail as he ran, dragging the scrabbling Lizardman after him. Khan's eight blades came chopping, stabbing and slicing after her in quick succession as the Dwarf's sudden surge caught the knife wielding god off guard and managed to put a good twenty feet between them and the slow moving Demon.

"Oy Idiot! This is no time to be sacrificing yourself and don't try to tell me you wasn't going to 'cause I'd have done the same me self. But right now Dirk's gone all whacko so we need to protect him and *US*… Watch out!" The Dwarf cried, ducking from a dagger swipe by the near-most long spindly arms of Khan.

They both turned and ran over the ground that suddenly became very unstable thanks to the Dread Lord's meddling. "If we go any further we shall sink Dwarf. Let us bravely fight…" Qoua ventured.

"Sink? Sinky stuff is good! We can't drown can we!?" Grot said vigorously nodding and pulling Dirk down into the quagmire along with him. Qoua staggered and leapt back for several feet avoiding more murderous thrusts and then she too leapt into the unknown depths of the abyss thudding into Dirk and Grot rapidly rising from some several feet down. "Swim back up or something!" The Dwarf blurted in a panic.

"Why?" Qoua wondered.

"Because I've just remembered we *can* bloody die. He made us mortal again didn't the bastard; thanks to your own ill thought out wish? In Keldor's name, I; hey: Just hurry! I can hardly breathe." The Dwarf panicked, shoving upwards frantically and dislodging Qoua like a cork bobbing in the ocean; only on this ocean one could obviously build a house on it. Qoua reached down her hand and between her pulling from above and Grot shoving up from below, they managed to yank out Dirk.

"Firm up the ground nephew, we have a straggler..." Galbor ordered.

The devil incarnate laughed as he took up the challenge, constricting the Dwarf still trapped within and slowly crushing him to death: Another effect of the hardening ground gave credence to a new attack by Khan as he pursed forward over the newly hardened sodden souls, blades a-twitching.

"You are supposed to be my God and I your daughter why strive to kill me? It will end the prophecy... I don't understand Lord. Why?" Qoua cried, crouching to the ground and turning to face her advancing aggressor.

"Because stupid child once I am summoned I must take a soul and unfortunately my brethrens powers are beyond my own; thanks to you!" Khan spoke as he continued his trawling advance.

"Yes and I've got a budgie called Bill..." Dirk sang back from some way off.

Qoua shot him an irritated glance and returned her attentions to the god she had lived her life to serve. "That can not be true, if it were so, you would just take the Dwarves life force. You know I would help you so why? Why would you want to kill me? ...To end the prophecy? Why? I do not believe I can kill a god, any god, let alone my own..."

The Daemonic God was now dangerously close to herself and the cumbersome Dirk, who had wondered off picking imaginary flowers. Khan's blades switched about in preparation as he came within feet of striking. "Because *you* and *that* fool are what perpetuate the prophecy and I am not dead yet…, …No fool Mortal *can* kill a god and if you are prophesised to prevail or fall then I am afraid it is you that shall fall!"

Qoua digested this, she had suspected as much from their earlier meeting: When she had sought an audience only to be referred to one of his minions in his stead. One other thing bothered her and that was why, when dead, she had found herself in Heaven, when her deity was the divine embodiment of murder and deceit… "So you're willing to murder us in order to save yourself…, …To sacrifice the prophecy for the sake of your own survival…? Why should it come to this: I believe that no god can die at the hands of a mortal so what am I: Something more? I have already killed one of *your kindred* today, and many others that thought themselves better than I…, …It *was* cruel growing up in a culture where honour and power were the two most important factors by which you were judged. It was hard to judge men as weaker when you witness or sense greater nobility in a lowly slave, than you do in your own sisters…" She paused to run to the side, diving over two of the blades as she did. "To lose your place in that society, to be cast down from your place of adoration, to lose your people, your *way* and then to lose faith in your god…"

"You would be surprised how easy a god can die down here but heed the prophecy it says I shall fall because of you; which my summoning here would indicate but it does not mention who brings about my death other than to mention myself…" He charged her again, whisking six of the blades out in spiralling arcs to the side and jabbing forward intently with the other two…, …Qoua turned and ran as fast as the uncooperative ether would allow.

"What does an honourless whore like you know of the ways of Khan; you are without virtue, admiration or integrity, as you admitted yourself! Luckily for you there is no sign of pregnancy or your shameful waste of your chastity would soon be noticeable too; how could you let yourself be raped; by a supposed inferior too?" Khan spat and lurched forward another foot to make sure of keeping his range. His blades whirred down as he collected his strength for another charging blender. "You cannot run forever dear daughter, a downside to being mortal I suppose; which you will not be for much longer…"

"And atop my head is a big, fat, hairy cock…!" Dirk sang again.

"Enough…" Qoua screamed as a blade bit deeply into her buttocks drastically reducing her movement; she rolled forward then twisted back towards the temporarily slowed Khan, then from her crouching position she sprang up to land atop the mountainous god's torso; gashing at Khan's exposed eye from her vantage. The sword arms stirred into a whirring confusion of life, eagerly swiping at her and closing in as she had expected and she dared not move from her position lest the blades change in their reflexive arc.

"I remember the prophecy now Khan; it said…, '…Khan will be smitten by his mortal rival, struck down of his own doing!' Thank you for the tip…" She whispered before falling from her god a fraction before the blades struck. Several of them nicked and gouged bits from her gored flesh as she fell and one of the blades followed her procession with unerring accuracy; skewering the base of her tail upon its jagged metallic length.

At least five of Khan's blades stabbed home however, finding Qoua's intended mark, and as they did so, the other arms not involved in skewering, ceased their flailing and the plodding feet ground to a halt. The arm Qoua was impaled upon fell limply to the side, narrowly missing piercing her fallen self on two of the many clutched daggers already held there by other unresponsive arms…, …The embedded quintet of barbed daggers responsible for the slain god's sudden demise, were stuck fast in Khan's own skull, criss-crossing one another in their deadly embrace.

Qoua rose from the ground, having severed her own tail near its base to escape, and snatched up Dirk who stared back at her blankly. Then she ran over to where the Dwarves beard and arms could be seen poking out of the constricting ether and scrabbled at the cloudy mud to help extricate the busily scrabbling Dwarf who had witnessed first hand his fair share of underground cave-ins albeit not of souls and was not for being buried without a fight. The Daemon calling himself Dread Lord laughed loudly at his father's demise and the clouds about dissipated as, blood-black as night; the veined Demon approached them from behind. From the front Galbor stalked forward in vengeful strides looking his terrifying self.

"That is another of our kin you have sacrificed to the void. Well done. You've killed another god…" Dread Lord applauded in mock appreciation.

Grot got to his feet and brushed the dark lumps of Ether from his body, "Well I aint killed one yet… But I see two hanging around who might serve my own purposes…!" The Dwarf tested with a nerve he did not feel. "To be honest yer both look a bit knackered after that right godly display yer put on…, …dunno about yer self Qoua but I'm feeling a bit tasty…"

"I do not know why you feel suddenly full of flavour but yes I agree; come fight us on physical terms if you will." Qoua rejoined.

"…So if you come back fine, but go and help us or not if ya will…" Dirk chorused dementedly.

Hells master streaked forward, a mere blur before their eyes as he pummelled them into submission with lightning quick jabs and stabs of knuckle stabbing, rib cracking, badness. Galbor meanwhile uncoiled a lengthy whip of fire from his hand and sent those fiery coils looping about the waists of Grot and Qoua, entwining the two in its restraining blistering coils; scorching the two's flesh and draining them of movement. Only Dirk remained free of the battle. Mumbling to him self and attempting to eat lumps of the Hellish Eyrthe from beneath his backside.

Qoua rocked back and fell atop the Dwarf, apologising all the way. Her balance was shot to pieces and she didn't have a moment to think from the torrent of pain. Fortunately she didn't have to.

Dirk all this time had been stuck in conversation with his self, while he had left the task of his running his body to its own devices. To say he had been conversing is a little incorrect. It was more like a verbal version of the battle that had earlier raged. Dirk had joined some other dots as he had leapt from the window, dots that had fully joined and spelt out the name Kalamere…, …Dirk was unsure how the wizard had come to be with him but he was! Here in this body and mind, there was and had been for some time a being other than he, something that had leeched onto him somehow.

Dirk was really pissed by the time he had hit the dirt so to speak and had already left his body; dragging this other entity along with him and began arguing things out Dirk style. By the time Qoua had killed her god Khan, things had gone from bad to worse then round the block again. The resulting eviction notice had been served and though Kalamere's enforced connection remained his soul had been sent packing during a moment of truce: In which Dirk had suggested a 'cooling off' period…

…A streak of lightning like liquid silver came soaring through the murky sky and atop it a bright white figure blasted streaks of pure holy light down in a parade of thumping strokes, sending the two previously delighted Daemons scurrying for cover. The streaky silvered thing being ridden suddenly reared up, spreading its vast wingspan in order to induce freefall, during which it sparked a trail of white lightning from its mouth, which caught Dread Lord's fleeing black form fully across the back.

Galbor never missed an opportunity and he smashed his cloven hoof down hard towards Dread Lord's mercifully exposed skull. But the master of Daemons called Paul was also a clever trickster and the hapless Galbor only succeeded in painfully striking his foot against what turned out to be a near indestructible dummy, causing the Demon the temporary discomfort of imagined pain. Having witnessed the expected double cross, Paul came from out of his place of hiding, directly behind Galbor and wrapped his shadowy arms around the gory red and black form of his uncle's neck. Galbor burst into searing flame and so reciprocated his nephew; as they fell sizzling through the ground, wrestling and goring each other while their various applied enchantments fizzled about them.

Another simultaneous blast; the Dragon's lightning attack plus a strike from one of its mighty claws, at once put out the two combatants flaming auras and sent both reeling apart, as the riotous energy rippled through each of them in devastating shock. Next mercury spilled from weeping Dragon eyes and engulfed the two demons head to toe, poisoning and weakening them.

Both Paul and Galbor sent a simultaneous concussive blast at the other and attempted to make for the shelter of the tavern. Spotting their actions and intent, Kalamere struck the ground with his staff sending a shockwave outwards that rippled the soulful ground, gathering like a tidal wave as it washed over the tavern. Paul hammered against the souls and commanded them to part as the Dragon leapt up majestically into the air, before coming plunging down, its talons making short work of Galbor's digestive system as it plucked him from the ground and tossed him up into the air, drawing a mighty breath. Galbor responded by unfurling his own wings, the furry roughage on his necks and face bristling as he let out a blast of magma from his own Jaws, straight towards the Dragon, surplus lava spilling out from his decimated torso.

Meanwhile, of the two figures that had dismounted the Sylva Dragon, the small, hairy one jumped up and down waving madly towards Grot and the others, whilst the second; who was vaguely familiar to the Dwarf, shot bolts of tearing light from his staff, which pounded into Dread Lord's dark form with fracturing delight. Paul screamed in recognition as he turned towards the wizard and his hole-shot body dissipated before any more of the holy blasts could take their wrathful toll.

"Look Grot! It's Boris!" Qoua enthused, finally noticing the scampering, arm waving Halfling.

"Yeah… I noticed." The Dwarfs expression didn't brighten any.

"Thou shall not deviate from this place Galbor. We have unfinished matters that are in dire need of resolving. Advance him unto me if thou wilt dear Guinevere, for I wish to finish this feud now." The White wizard cocked his head to deliver a reassuring smile to the gathered companions, then vaulted forward as the Dragon found itself being pulled to the ground by the remarkably strong Daemon that was Galbor.

"Guinevere leave him be; his fight shall not be with thee this day but with I." He regarded and the Daemon let fly his captured quarry and turned his snarling tusked maw to regard the wizard before him.

"Kalamere… You've changed…,… Your body…" Grot's bottom lip jutted out in nodding appreciation: "Nice touch…"

"Unlike the Great Galbor here I had no need to steal from another. The body thee hath tortured were naught more than a living mannequin, I laid mine original self, placed in safe keeping a long time hence you came along Galbor. Know that I know my place in this prophecy and know further that I know this Dirk Heinemblud better than most…" Kalamere paused to change his resolve slightly, "Galbor it was a mistake of thee and mine own great one, to place thee at the heavenly gates. Thou know it to be true and should thy self be willing to stand down…"

"You'd leave me be, because that's all you want is it not Kalamere? You want my Job? Well, you can't have it! Furthermore you will not get what you came for…" Galbor rankled.

"But 'tis my right." Kalamere bleated out in anger. Upon my conscience I desire to place mine self into its unenviable employ and to manage the roll as best I find possible, but thee! Thee hath all but divested thou self of the role. I have heard tell in my time down here, that you have nay so much turned up at the post in nigh on a thousand year. Instead thy time is spent chasing dreams of Satan-hood and thy true duties left to sad ministrations of corrupt flunkies who care even less so than ye!"

"And what of the prophecy: For what side do *you* heckle?" Galbor philosophised, biding for his time.

"Heckle. Ha!" Kalamere quipped, "Mine dear old ancient adversary, I shall make thee privy to some extremely limited knowledge if that is thy wish..." The wizard paused to smile belittlingly at his weakened Daemonic opponent before him, leaning in close to spell out each word. "I... Follow... Order..."

"You unholy bastard, little wonder you both came here!" The oath surprisingly leapt from Galbor's lips not Kalamere's. "Dirk's soul *should* have gone to Purgatory, that's where I waited..., ...yet you had already weaved your magic hadn't you? Back in our tower in the mortal realms you knew you had to die to flee." Galbor paused considering something then sprang forward at the wizard who dropped his staff (which incidentally held the most enormous diamond one could imagine.) and reciprocated by locking his arms with those of the Daemon Galbor. "But you had not died, quite clearly you were not co-joined in fate with your peers; investigating cost me my own mortal existence but I had to know, just to be sure. So you had somehow escaped death and the tower I knew, yet it wasn't until I discovered Dirk had been transported here that I knew the full scope of your plan. You knew where *you* were destined to travel to upon death and by attaching yourself to him you bade him that same fate. Furthermore you have him close to you, very close; now I know friends like to hang out and I am all for the goodly and dim getting together but sharing a body is that not a bit uncomfortable?" Galbor flew upwards in a rage as Kalamere divested himself of the robes he wore and swam upwards in a stream of heavenly light, sprouting the translucent wings of an angel from his glowing denuded form.

"I'd liken it to being sat at yer mates house when his missus is around, ya wanna fart or belch but yer gotta squeeze those cheeks and hold the bastard in or else..." Grot decided to comment but nobody paid any attention. "Typical that is yer know..., ...The one time Gobby arse over there's quiet and no bugger hears me: What yer all listening to; the wind?"

The Dragon came down softly beside them. The Halfling had not stopped jabbering throughout the fight and the magnificent beast's descent; being one of those awful people who like to give an explanatory commentary to every clearly witness-able event.

"Go on Kalamere, smack his backside! Woohoo! Did you see that? Wow! He hit him with an excellent head-butt. Oh hya Sylva- I mean, erm, err, I mean erm, err –oh I – I know it, I just can't think, erm-Gwyneth; no Gwen. Damn! I mean Guinevere. Sorry. I'm sorry, I just forgot in the excitement. Sorry. Oh he bit him, should that be allowed You did notice Gwen drop in on us didn't you? He or she is a silver, I know because she's silver..." The Halfling yammered.

Qoua immediately found Boris's irrational prattling unsettling but many were affected by Dragon fear in different fashion and even she, the perfectly detached warrior that she thought herself to be, was right now dripping sweat herself and not just from the heat of Hell.

Dirk noticed nothing and ate a few tufts of grass he had managed to grow from the ether.

Grot heard more than the fear; he heard the stressful curse of 'damn' issue from the small hairball's lips and this from someone who regarded saying the word 'fart' as a sanctimonious dereliction of duty. Without drawing undue attention to himself the Dwarf went and answered the forced call of nature for the first time in many, many years.

Just as she was about to begin exchanging pleasantries with the Dragon, Grot's quick toilet trot passed by Qoua and they exchanged knowing glances as she too scooted off to the side to answer the call of nature, her years of bladder dereliction lent weighty need, due to fear.

Boris ran off to get nearer the daemonic action on which he was still commentating and to distance himself from the frightful Dragon. Dirk was left temporarily alone with the beast as Galbor and Kalamere raged a riveting battle some safe distance away. "You're a Dragon. Whoa man, that's shit hot!" Dirk said affecting the docile tones of an infant. "I have like wanted to meet a Dragon for like, ever…, …You're frigging cool…"

"Ye-e-e-s…" The majestic silver beast drawled back disinterested.

"Silvers are good!" Dirk cried excitedly hopping up and down on his bottom and clapping shaky palms. "I like Gold ones too; can I meet one? DO ya have dark ones too, or like see through ones?"

The Dragon sniggered in rasping gulps of laughter as it snaked its smiling head down to the little human's height. "There was only ever *one* Gilder Dirk…, …Heinemblud…?"

The serpentine neck snaked up and about as it first checked that the battle was going well for Kalamere then looked for signs of the other two who were defecating to the Dragon's left and right. A stirring in her abdomen, reminded the Sylva of her own need to divest her body of manure and she settled down to it right there and then as she spoke. "Heinemblud – I find that an interesting name…" She quavered, her head winding closer.

Dirk giggled at some imaginary sight beyond her shoulder as she spoke bringing her enormous jaws to within whispering distance of Dirk. "A very interesting name in Draconian that is; for if you were to inflect the paragraph it would spell deep shit…" The Dragon caused to cock a leg and let out a long blast of wind to the accompaniment of another shit-load. "Well actually it would spell: Ðĺяж ҤЄĩŇŋ€шßlʹϸϭϭ. But you are too 'Human' in your outlook to comprehend the full meaning of it just yet, even if I could be bothered to explain; which I can't." The Dragon sighed with a smug sniff.

The Sylva then took a quick peek in Kalamere's direction, only to decide that the battle would likely rage on far too long for its own comfort. "Why wait for lunch when you can snack anytime?" It sighed and opened its meat strewn fangs around Dirk's stable position.

Qoua and Grot acted on cue. Grot rescuing Dirk from the snapping fangs with all the stuffiness of a taxidermist, while Qoua leapt magnificently around the Dragon's tremendous snout; jamming her left elbow hook into the beast's nostril and plunging her right arm deep into its open ear canal, lacerating the delicate eardrum within with her claws. The Dragon responded by leaping into the air and Qoua did well to let go only some thirty feet high; severely winding and bruising herself but no more, as the dragon swept first upward, then away until it was less than a speck on the horizon.

They turned their attentions to the two combatants but saw that the fight had already been determined during their own brief pitch. Galbor had called on the help of some of those drinking in the tavern: No doubt a few souls who owed him their favour or wished for his in return. These tavern revellers now revelled in bashing the sense from poor Kalamere. Galbor was walking over to the three amigos in the form of an old man, smiling once again, though the effort was obviously a strain, while his ten men team of homeys went to work on Kalamere good and proper, intent on tearing him piece from piece. Galbor stood some hundred metres or so away, yet after only a few short strides, he was in their company.

"Give me a reason not to eliminate each and every one of you: Is there any one reason any of you can think of that I shouldn't just kill you all right now?" He asked in a brisk business tone.

Qoua and Grot looked at each other then to Boris and shook their heads at which Galbor chuckled most alarmingly; a dark unholy light growing within his encased right palm which he held aloft like one ready to pitch may do. The three braced themselves but Dirk started giggling and stood to face his nemesis. "Don't mind him Galbor; he's gone a bit mad!" Grot stated in Dirk's pre-emptive defence.

Dirk turned to Grot and grinned, then turned back to Galbor: "Ignore the Stunty will ya Galbor? He's a bit of a nob. Oh and ya might wanna save that energy of yours for other enemies like Kalamere who is winning those dicks from the pub as I speak..., ...besides what do you think a little unholy light would do against us unholy bastards, oops; he's here matey..."

"Ha!" Galbor scoffed, "like I am going to fall for the old 'he's behind ya ruse,' surely you can do better than that!"

Kalamere flew from his attackers, jetting horizontally across the landscape and thudding straight into the Dark wizard Galbor, bearing him the short distance to the encased tavern wall and slamming the Demon into, through and out the other side of the Inn. Dirk cheered loud and far from genuine: "So ya decided to come and help!" Dirk stated as the white wizard flew back towards them.

Kalamere landed in front of them with a soft thud and strode the last few feet to where Dirk stood grinning. "I apologise most profusely to thee if mayhap mine actions have struck thee odd. However it is ye that are struck verily in apprehension. Nay; methinks ye shall die this day all the same..."

Kalamere then struck Dirk in the stomach, causing him to double over from the winding blow and proceeded to slap him with first a forehand, then a stinging back hand across Dirk's puffing cheeks. Grot was caught quite by surprise by the action as were the others and quickly checked for an hitherto unseen bald patch, less the mage may somehow be one of those whom Dirk had previously offended.

Dirk rose to his feet, hands still clutching his stomach as he wheezed: "Okay dickhead if that's how it's gonna be..." Dirk's sentence was cut short as Kalamere delivered a stinging uppercut, vaulting the wizard backwards ten feet in the air and leaving him a crumpled wreck on the floor.

"Right yer bastard!" Grot threatened and went to strike the mage as Qoua too leapt to Dirk's defence.

"Jull Diss-para..." Kalamere declared and the others were blasted back from their speedy assault and sent spinning across the ground some distance away. "Rise Dirk of the Blood, so ye may be the first to fall..."

Dirk stumbled to his feet mumbling something the white mage

couldn't quite discern but as Kalamere awaited Dirk's standing attention his ears picked up on the distinct syllables of the repeated mantra.

"He of the sixes cometh, take me oh Dread Lord that's mine…"

Dirk rose and turned to face Kalamere as he recanted the last quick verse and smiled. If what Dread Lord himself had told Dirk were true, to miss-pronounce the tongue twisting mantra would have led to his souls swift departure but Dirk was desperate. "I dunno why you've decided to start attacking *me* now but you're gonna be sorry as a bastard ya did!"

A cacophony of thunder and the gathering of Dark clouds from the ether signalled the arrival of the black, red and purple/blue veined one as Dread Lord came strolling up from nowhere. "Aah Dirk! Oh and my arch-nemesis Kalamere, what a pleasant chance meeting this is…, …Might our final battle be enjoined today?"

Kalamere's bottom lip quivered sulkily as he attested: "Yea mine staff hath been misplaced and mine beloved Guinevere gone but I surely still hold enough pure light in reserve to smite thee even if that should cost me mine own life."

Dirk smiled again, that big broad smile he only ever divulged when he felt he held all the aces. "Kalamere, ya know its funny but ya should really look behind ya. What is it with you guys sneaking up on each other?"

Kalamere did indeed look behind him as Dirk winked at Dread Lord; the Daemon instantly sent a searing riff of molten metal that sluiced through Kalamere's thigh almost severing his left leg at the hip. The white mage fell forward as with a black beat of his smoky wings Dread Lord transported himself in front of the downed mage and rammed his fist through the hitherto holy ones skull. Kalamere had only an instant to respond and within a millisecond he had abandoned his doomed vessel to return to the sanctuary of Dirk's body, just as Dirk had been expecting.

Paul snarled victoriously, howling into Hell's copious spaces in accomplishment then suddenly ceased and turned on Dirk. "What trickery is this? He is not dead; I know for I would have felt his soul entering into my realms…, …He is back with ye is he not? No matter; I was going to kill ye for my summoning all the same, I simply destroy you and I destroy him…"

Dread Lord's powers had been sorely tested all ready this day and though his strength was waning he still sent an avalanche of icy vapour gasping through the air as he considered his next move. Boris, Qoua and Grot, making sure to stay clear of the vapour ran as close as they dared, to better espy Dirk but as they did the master of Hell sent a column of thundering wave straight down upon the misty area, followed by a deadly blast of chain lightning, then capped off the overkill assault by causing a tremor of meteors to come crashing down around them. The racing companions turned on their heels and ran as quickly as they dared away from the bombardment, their attempts to rescue Dirk second to lung bursting sprints for survival…

Yet as the mists vapours evaporated and the water all but washed away and the last of the electrical charges had died, with meteors still raining down, Qoua could be seen vaulting towards Dirk's guessed position, nimbly dashing between the falling rocks… She almost made it too if not for a small fragment of stone from a nearby grounded rock deflecting off at an unfortunate angle and knocking her senseless. The meteors crashed down still and from his safe distance Grot considered re-entering the firing range so to speak when he noticed Dirk; dry as a bone and totally unmarked go over towards Qoua and bend down over her; receiving a direct hit from a ten foot boulder without so much as flinching. Dread Lord noticed it too and at once the pounding racket came to an immediate halt.

"Dirk of the Blood how ye have power over the elements here in Hell is beyond me? Never-the-less ye shall die; merely in a far more physical manner…" Dread Lord announced and stalked towards Dirk in teasing bursts of winged movement as the ground around the human rose to become the bars of an impromptu cage.

"What about a deal then?" Dirk bartered: He hoped the Demon was not taking any of this personally. "A deal for my soul…"

"Speak on…" the veined one permitted.

"Ya said before you had no specific desire to kill me but ya know or rather think ya know something about me because of this prophecy so what if I could give you my soul; or at least part of it in exchange for one wish…?"

The Daemon rubbed his chin thoughtfully; calculating: "Go on…" He said at length, "What is it ye offer; speak it and I'll tell ye yes or no!"

"Okay…" Dirk stalled formulating his words correctly in his mind before speaking them aloud.

"I offer you half my soul in exchange for granting me the power I had before I last left the Inn of my mistress, in addition to ninety percent of the power of the current Dread Lord from this day and any future Dread Lord title holders, for any time or occasion I spend in Hell whether in the presence of Dread Lord or not!"

The Daemon overlord considered this for several long minutes while everyone hung on his decision. Out of sight of everyone a battered looking Balrog called Galbor came sauntering back into the picture. Something about the deal bothered Paul but he couldn't decide what it was and asked Dirk to repeat the request which he did word for word. *'If he has ninety percent he would be almost my equal but with just enough difference for my self to reign supreme; even so he doesn't really want for much and I could quite easily kill him with that ten percent difference but if I have his soul I would be quite the untouchable. Uncle Galbor would have to wait an eternity before he could challenge me again. Part of his soul, he said a part.'*

At length the Demonic veined one spoke. "Ye say ye offer half your soul, very well, I accept if thee volunteer the best of your being..."

Dirk smirked to himself in reply. "I will **not** *volunteer* my good side but I will trade it in exchange..., ...*Let's do this shit then*! I offer you the purest and holiest half of my soul in exchange for granting me the power I had before I last left the Inn of my mistress, in addition to ninety percent of the power of any current and future Dread Lord, for any time or occasion I spend in Hell, whether in the presence of a Dread Lord or not."

"...Done...!" Paul agreed and greedily shook Dirk's hand through the bars of the cage before turning to face his uncles foreboding presence. "Aah Uncle Galbor, guess what I have just come into the possession of? No, let me give a clue..., ...It's Dirk's soul..."

"What do you mean; his soul!" Galbor bristled, "Dirk please tell me you have not done any stupid deals with this one..."

Grot was still trying to figure out the deal in his head and how Dirk's wish could possibly help them when Boris beamed a bright smile of comprehension. "Oh I get it; yes, yes, very, very clever that, very clever indeed; why my old granny used to say; 'it's only those thicker than you that think you're thick at all..."

"Boris me old sunshine... Why don't ya go visiting your 'dear old granny' while we're here? I'm sure we're in the right place by the sound of her…" Grot couldn't help himself.

"Grot, you're a silly old thing! Granny would hit you with a clog if she heard you talking disrespectful around her…, …besides she isn't dead!"

The Dwarf was about to protest when Dirk piped up, "I like the analogy Boris, nice one…"

"**Silence Hunted!**" Paul shot back forcing the bars constraining Dirk to shrink uncomfortably close. Then again turned back to his late arrived uncle proclaiming: "Dirk and I have just struck a deal by which he gains a fraction of the strength of my own controlling powers in exchange for half of his soul; his good side to be precise, which means I simply have to end his life to gain the whole of his soul…, …Now can ye guess dear uncle, what it is I intend to do next?"

"Kill me?" Asked Dirk in Galbor's stead, leaning his elbow upon the Dread Lord's shoulder conspiratorially. Dirk's confinement was nowhere to be seen. Everyone did a double take to check all the same.

Dread Lord was momentarily shocked. "Why yes but how did ye remove…, …No matter Dirk Heinemblud, ye cannot do me lasting harm with ye limited powers, besides which; even if *ye* could kill me, ye would only harm ye self in doing so. I have won this round whether ye like it or not but I must rest now, so ye shall all forgive me if I bid ye all adieu!"

"Check again Dickhead…" Dirk chided, "You did a deal for my purest, holiest part all right but all ya helped me do was get rid of a stubborn, psychotic do goody nut job, lodger…, …Kalamere get out here."

The ghostly apparition of a wounded Kalamere, complete with missing skull and hip section, came sulkily into view…

"Why have ye abandoned me to this fate? Hath mine powers not helped keep thee alive these past years and in life afore that; had I not forced thy own hand into survival when thou would otherwise have froze? Did I not help thee with thy magical abilities; nay impart the courage for thee to ascend the bell tower in Devil's Gap?" Kalamere seemed truly crestfallen.

"That was you?" Dirk reasoned: "Then ya really are a psycho bitch! I wondered why I began running into battles instead of away from them and yeah it did strike me a bit odd that I got good at magic but as for ya being the one responsible for that silliness in 'the Gap' well, all I can say is good bloody riddance ya nutter and may I never be so heroic again…"

"I don't understand," Dread Lord muttered. "I can't leave. What have ye done Heinemblud?"

"Done? Who…, …Sweet, little innocent me? What makes ya think *I've done **anything**…*? You're the one that made the deal. *You* asked for the good part, the purest part of my soul and I gave it ya; it's called Kalamere: A pain in the arse do goody type of psycho that has been leeching off my body for quite a while now. Ya can check the deal out and you'll see I have held up my end of the bargain; as, I can see from how easily I made those bars disappear, so have you." Dirk was gloating he knew but his risky dealing had made this smug moment seem all the sweeter and he was determined to enjoy his clever success.

"But how have yer given him Kalamere and why?" Grot asked.

Dirk grinned at his own ingenuity and walked over to stand with the Dwarf who had addressed him. "See Grot, Kalamere's a clever bastard and so he'd decided to sort of stitch or knit himself to my soul; his becoming meshed up with mine so much that even fate couldn't separate us; if there really is a nasty mother out there messing with our lives…"

Boris seemed confused by everything, "why though? I mean why give Kalamere to the Dread Lord…, …Doesn't he want to kill us all?"

"Yes Boris," Dirk soothed, "Paul here; the Dread Lord incarnate, wanted us dead because of Kalamere. As for why Kalamere wanted to kill us I do not have a friggin clue but he still stayed attached to my soul so as he could flee to the sanctuary my existence offered whenever danger threatened. At the same time he kept trying to get my body to do things I would sooner it didn't; like rescuing people and shit, *and* not letting it do enough of the other shit I wished it would, like running away or wanking…, …So Dread Lord he's all yours, which is funny because you said your fate was to enjoin battle with Kalamere from which it was unclear who would survive. Well let me give you an update; if his doom will be sealed with your own then ya might wanna follow what I'm gonna say next…"

Dirk went to stand with Galbor casually slipping a friendly arm around the horrendous Demon's waist. "It has come to my attention my baldy mentor that Dread Lord is not to be trusted. Moreover, the arsehole wants me dead, so I have a little 'deal' I'd like to offer you, yourself…"

Galbor snorted down at the cheeky chap beside him. "What could you possibly offer me Dirk Heinemblud?"

"Well I was thinking how about a deal along these lines: You resurrect poor Boris here and transport me and my friends back to Eyrthe within a hundred feet of Boris's vicinity and in return I'll kill or rather make it possible to destroy the Dread Lord known as Paul!"

"You'll what?" Grot, Dread Lord and Qoua questioned in unison...

"...Agreed...!" Galbor leered, greedily awaiting further news of Dirk's plan despite his intended target being stood by also.

"Ye think I'll be put aside by such as ye Hunted?" Dread Lord boomed in annoyance. "How dare ye discuss my intended destruction in my presence? Have ye no wits? Do ye think I'll stand here and let ye continue?"

"I don't really care what ya do or think; try leaving Dickhead..." Dirk answered and Paul did indeed repeat his attempts to teleport to no avail.

"How have ye..."

"I just got what I wished for..., ...Bye, bye." Dirk taunted and within the blink of an eye the Daemon Lord and Kalamere snapped out of existence to be replaced by a rather rough looking human of around forty years of age.

"I think you'll find that's Dread Lord's former mortal self; Paul..., ...Who Galbor, if I've learned anything in my time here, ya might wanna kill." Dirk suggested. "That is if ya really do wanna become the next Dread Lord."

An unholy dark corona spread around Galbor in response and the Balrog sent a rash of molten rock into the trembling figure of Paul, incinerating him where he stood.

Galbor let off a satisfied sigh... "Aah, I love it when a plan comes together. Clever student Dirk, now where we're we?"

"You were about to transport us back to Eyrthe I believe..." Qoua quested.

"Yeah that's right, we wish to be transported back to Devil's—no, wait, we already have our bodies!" Grot said narrowly avoiding a mistaken wish.

"We want to be transported back to earth, without detriment to any of us..." Grot edged in taking control.

"What all of you?" Galbor asked unreasonably.

"Yes of course, all of us. What bloody use otherwise?" Grot hissed. "We want Boris brought back to life where he is and us transported by his side..."

"I am sorry but that is simply not possible, I could get you fairly near but little more I am afraid." Galbor countered.

"How near, I mean how near is near to the bugger, for Keldor's sake?" Grot asked ignorant to the fact that the Halfling was in fact quite spectrally present.

"Has he not told you? He was due to be eaten, so he crammed himself full of poisonous herbs so he might give his digestively destined Half-Orc an upset stomach for his troubles." The Daemon leaned his elbow forward on a wickedly bent knee, and cupped his chin in his open palm. "Funny thing is though, the little fellow only succeeded in killing himself his only Eyrthely sin, which sent him here, and now the general is waiting for the bloating to go down before he eats Boris's actual corpse. Strange the things people hide from one another, is it not?"

"So you'll raise Boris from the dead and transport us to his vicinity? Qoua asked.

"Of course... It's the least I could do. Yes Boris?" Galbor asked of Boris who was tugging at the hem of his robe.

"Can you please tell me something? What happened?" The Halfling asked innocently, "I mean I know you're offering to help us and all, but aren't you supposed to be the bad guy? I mean, I met up with Kalamere and he told me all about you and how he had tried to save Dirk's soul but he was doomed and-"

Grot quietened Boris by placing his hand across the Halfling's mouth. "He *is* the enemy Boris. But it was Kalamere that wanted Dirk dead, not Galbor..."

Boris seemed surprised, "But!"

Galbor interrupted, "I still want him dead little one... But just not today..."

Dirk's knees wobbled and he felt faint again at the thought of his life being in danger; still he was glad to have his old self back. Qoua looked shiftily at the Daemon and Boris scratched his head in confusion.

"Look this is silly, I know you're a Demon and I've no doubt your all vengeful and all, but isn't it a pain in the bollocks hunting down an elusive bugger like Dirk?" The Dwarf remonstrated.

Galbor shrugged from shoulder to bottom lip, "I enjoy the chase to be honest..."

"Yes, but, Keldor's name be done... He's a miserable fart and his magic is pretty naff. So he hardly poses any significant threat does he? I mean surely there's something he can do about the... Err, old priest cap." Grot circled a finger over his own head to indicate his point.

Galbor appeared outwardly calm but the grizzly edge to his voice said otherwise. "You think *this*... Bothers me? You do not think it could be the persistent *boils* or the *crabs* and *herpes* too, hmmm? Never wandered how a true Daemon prince goes on when he is lecturing his minions for picking their noses only to suddenly suffer a bout of diahorrea and phlegm... No? I'm *surprised*..."

"I've suffered it almost every day thanks to Grot's cooking!" Dirk suddenly shouted a fair bit louder than was called for.

The Dwarf retaliated, "My cooking? What about yours? At least what I cook comes out. It doesn't block your innards up for a week like most of your stuff; the bear stew aside! And why the bollocks are you picking on me anyway? I'm doing my best to save your arse, here. Though I don't know why I bother you selfish shit! You were better off catatonic; at least yer gob didn't get you into any more trouble."

"And do not forget, he made a very good decoy when dealing with the Dragon..." Qoua added with a cheeky grin which showed of her single two teeth: A pair of pointed retractable fangs.

"...Qoua! You look different..." Dirk remarked, his senses were rapidly returning to him in no particular order and he noticed she was looking remarkably less lizard-like than previously.

Qoua's hand reflexively rose to touch her own face as Grot once again spoke out. "Look! All I'm saying is; I mean sure if that were me and I'd be pissed, believe me I'd be more pissed than a Giant drinking elderberry wine but! There must be something a powerful bugger like you yourself can do about it…"

"Yes there is. I can ask the person responsible to undo it, or another of greater power than the caster!" Galbor seethed, he hated being honest.

Grot sighed with huge relief. "Good, good! Then that's simple, Dirk can remove it… I mean, if he'd have only known…"

"…Known? Known? Of course he has *known* all along. The first two times I caught up with him, he knew. I even let him go the first time, because he promised he would be round the next morn to undo his nasty work. Could you guess Dwarf, if he turned up that following morn…?"

"I w-what…? So I probably had a bit to drink…, …oh no, that's it – I remember that first time. It was the morning after. I had been boasting about it in a little grotty tavern on the shitty side of town and some bird asked me to jump her…" Dirk raised his head to check they were all listening, which they indeed were, including the blushing Boris.

"So erm, oh yes! SO, she turned out to be the mayor's wife, although I had had a few beers but you'd have swore she was more like his daughter; anyways, I was pumping her, when the old man turns up and says 'out.' Then he puts a dagger to me nuts and says if I wasn't out of town by morning, he'd remove them. What could I do? I mean… You know…"

"See…!" Grot repatriated, his arms wrapping around Dirk and Galbor and bringing the two together, "He would have removed the curse if not for an angry husband. He was just a victim of circumstances himself."

"So what off the second time; after I had freed you from the clutches of those Chimera?" Galbor tested.

"Oh the second time…" Dirk lingered.

"Come on, yes… Tell me your great excuse for abandoning me that time!" Galbor pressed.

"Whoa! Hold on there let's not jump to conclusions here…" The Dwarf said standing between the two, "Tell him about this *second time*…"

"The second time…" Dirk repeated, "…I couldn't be arsed!"

Galbor leapt at him and wrapped his fingers desperately around Dirk's throat, his skin's super cold touch merely chaffing Dirk's neck muscles, leaving three cold wheal marks upon his skin, before Grot managed to prise the two apart. "You see what I mean about you and your big gob?"

Grot shoved Dirk towards Qoua and a little gingerly led away Galbor, so he might calm down a little. "Look, I know Dirk is a tit, but you know it makes far more sense for you to be off threatening other demons, rather than chasing him down. So what about it then? I get him to heal you or whatever and you agree to stop hunting him down like some animal?"

"That is all I ever have wanted." Galbor protested. "Wise Dwarf, get him to help me and I promise you shall receive no further torment from I…"

"*Hold on a mo!*" Dirk was remembering quite a bit more '*shit*' than he had ever done. His head was positively thrumming. "Look here! At the moment; I can't even remember the name, of a لإخﻢعﻷכשؤؤﻷﻊﻊﻷﻊakc ﻞﺹ, oh right, erm I guess I do." He giggled. "…*In fact!* I remember the words and motions… I bet I could cast it if I wanted… Grot! I think I can remember what I did with your ring *too!* Your mother's ring I mean… I ate it! It was when I was feeling a bit moody, because you'd –Oof!"

He was interrupted by a strike in the gut from the Dwarf. "You lying bastard! You swore *blind* back then *and* since, that those *Elves* had nicked it. And to think I battered one of the bleeders half to death…"

"Yeah, but you never liked him anyway did you? I was *just* getting you to give him the kicking you *know* he deserved…" Dirk gloated.

Grot purpled with rage, digging bit-back nails sharply into his palm… "But you bloody weren't were you? You were telling me a load of bollocks to protect your own wise fhrrrmmmmmmmmmmmmmm!" Just shh! Don't you say another friggin' thing you son of a zombie's offspring. Just take back your curse on Galbor and that's it. Go on arsehole… Do it…!'"

Grot spent two long minutes tapping his toe and watching Dirk looking very busy at doing nothing in particular. During which time, no-one dared speak. "Well…?"

"Well you told me not to speak… I've gotta speak to remove the curse…"

Grot paid no heed to Dirk's pedantic logic and the wizard, after standing sulking for a few seconds more, decided to participate. He touched Galbor's bald crown, then his genitals and stomach, before brushing his hand up and down Galbor's own arms several times over. All the while, murmuring a chant. The whole procession took the better part of an hour, at the end of which Dirk issued the command "Şůœ##Ůξ-Ψάέ..."

Both Dirk and Galbor were quite aware that nothing barring the final command was all that was needed, but Dirk was in too obtuse a mood as to let them all get away with such a short ceremony. Besides, given Grot's mood; the Dwarf would probably kill him were he to discover that the torture he had endured during his spell in Galbor's tower could have been ended with such a singular command. The fore-mentioned Daemon for his part, found it quite amusing that the Dwarf who professed to his being Dirk's friend could so easily be duped by the wily wizardly cadet.

"Why thank you master wizard..." Galbor bowed in an over-expressive gesture. "So tell me... Do you have some request? Some virtuous ideal or perhaps something other I can help you with? Surely there is something that my best student could wish for?"

"...I'm your what?" Dirk choked on the words.

"*Well? Is* there something you desire?" Galbor quizzed.

"Your name..."

"Ha ha-ha, trust you to think of asking for that Dirk?" He leaned in close and whispered, "*My name is Balrog...*"

"That's not your name, it's your nature."

"No Dirk!" Galbor cut him short, "I was my species first. My name *is* what **I** am. I only tell you because by tomorrow in Eyrthe time, everyone will know it."

"Oh is it your birthday?" Boris, who had been listening closely, smiled widely.

"Tomorrow will be all of my birthdays in one, little one; tomorrow, I will become The Dread Lord, Lord of the Daemonic realms and the first thing I am going to do is to march my minions into heaven." Galbor explained.

"But you can't!" Boris cried, "You will not be able to pass beyond the gates. None of the damned can, unless given express permission. I know because Kalamere told me so..."

"And who, little man... Gives permission to the damned...?" Galbor prickled. "Who decides who can enter the gates of Heaven?"

"The Gods…" Boris admitted uncertainly.

"…Or the Keeper of the Gates…" Qoua and Grot chorused.

"Well then we'll just go and warn the keeper." Boris resolved.

Qoua shook her head and Dirk mouthed a few expletives so it was left to Grot to explain to the Halfling. *"Boris,* we have got a one shot deal to get out of here and Galbor is the one offering it, obviously because he wants us out of the way. Now I admit I didn't know the slimy sod was planning this, but let's face it, even if we stayed here to warn someone what could we do?"

Boris stamped his foot and pouted, "Oh Grot! Don't be a silly-peg! We could go and warn the Keeper of the Gates!"

"Boris! ***HE is the keeper of the bloody gates of heaven!"*** Grot shouted. He bit back the strong urge to inflict bodily harm. "Let's go!"

"You are ready heroes of the prophecy?" Galbor asked, rankling Dirk who felt as if he knew too little of events directly concerning himself.

"Ya know, I'm kinda getting pissed off at hearing about this prophecy…" Dirk moaned.

"Yes I know Dirk Heinemblud but at least things have worked out well for everyone…, …for my self especially…" Galbor concluded. "Know that I could keep you here if I chose too but I see that your powers here in hell are as much a match for my own and I really do have the pressing matter of a holy war to attend to, so I will say simply this: It isn't over yet between you and I…"

XIX) **Back To Life, Back To Reality**

Ixie, Dixie and Trixie, or Dirk, Grot and Qoua as were their real names, came tumbling into existence roughly toe stamping distance of a rather large Orcish grunt who had been placed on guard, which invariably meant he was pretending to be awake by learning to sleep on his feet; *which,* as I mentioned they came back to reality in foot stomping distance of...

Well as Dirk got to work on the stamping part and Grot made a fuss of tying up the befuddled behemoth, Qoua did the quick Job of slitting it from ear to ear. They made a good team in a crap way, each of them intent on proving that their own methods were the best, but thanks to their muddled efforts, the companions managed to pick their way through the periphery of the massive army camp they had been transported to without setting of any alarms of any sort and incapacitating several sleeping and one wake guard in the process.

Dirk and Qoua huddled in some bushes that could only be described as thinning if baldness could be described as a state of not having a load of hair. Dirk plucked an extinction threatened leaf from the bush and cringed as it shook about in overdrive but amazingly none of the silhouetted creatures in the camp appeared to notice the rustling bush.

"What are you doing at all?" Qoua asked Dirk in the hoarsest possible whisper, to which he replied by waving the leaf and sticking it in his mouth to chew on. The look he gave her was fantastic! As if suggesting she were the one reacting irrationally.

Grot skittered rat-like across the pools of light that pocked the campsite between them and the tent the Dwarf had just been investigating. His feet skidded home as he too crept into the refuge of what was perhaps; the only anorexic plant in the world.

"Well?" Qoua mouthed.

Grot shook his head in the negative. "I don't get it... He's the boss. We –**well, *I*,** have searched all the big tents and I tell yer; **that** one is *easily* the biggest, but he aint there!" Grot panted through the half-breathed words.

"That's because you don't think right old chump!" Dirk whispered rather more harshly than the others and chomped down hard on a rosy red apple he had surreptitiously procured from a supply barrel.

"Don't look at me like that; I'm frigging starving! I feel like I haven't had a bite to eat in centuries; which I haven't so there!" Dirk crunched into the apple, cringing at the chomping sound his chewing produced.

The Dwarf swatted at the apple, while Qoua jammed her palm into Dirk's open mouth and almost screamed out herself as his starving teeth made contact with her flesh.

"Stop it Dirk!" Grot admonished quietly, "Or I swear, I *will* whack you..."

"Well make it stop raining then and get me some dry bread from by that campfire..." Dirk had a point; the night was truly dank and miserable.

"I p-how, listen yer ignorant tit, we're all starving but we aren't both crying about it like you remember what Galbor said about, erm, what's he called..." Grot tried to think of the fellow's name. "Yer know, that other Daemon that erm, did, something..."

Qoua looked at Grot in confusion: "I think you may be referring to the-the, oh, I can't think of his name; the-hold on, how many Daemons where there now? I remember Dirk had a friend there..."

"Oh yeah called mistress, Dirk think about your time with, bastard, who was we talking about?" Grot ventured.

"My Mistress," Dirk said, "what are ya talking about?"

"That's her, yes, your mistress!" Qoua excitedly whispered.

Dirk shrugged and bit on a piece of fallen bark which he quickly spat out again before attempting to reach for the fallen apple. Grot swatted at Dirk's roving hand with his heavy boot in warning... "Leave the bleeding apple alone Dirk! Now what are you on about him having a mistress, cuz I'll warn ya he's got several; haven't yer!"

Dirk had a mouthful of leaves and grass but still replied, "Grot I have not a friggin clue what ya talking about..." He objected spitting half chewed vegetable mass as he quietly retorted, "all I know is we're supposed to be rescuing Boris and I am for some reason starving..., ...Now can we friggin well rescue Boris before Galbor gets here?"

Qoua spoke in shocked realisation as she stared back at the chomping wizard: "Dirk, your voice…, …it's different…"

"Yes and he's what I always thought he was; a big girl!" Grot hissed.

"What dya mean a girl!" Dirk shot back, "I'm more of a man than you'll ever be… How many woman have you had Stunty?"

"No Dirk!" Qoua intervened in the mounting argument, "he merely means you are a woman!"

"Ya bloody cheeky bitch!" Dirk almost shouted, "I do hope ya know that's an insult to a Human male?"

"No…" Qoua responded with splayed hands, "You *ARE* a *woman!*"

Dirk looked down in defiance running his hands over his robes, feeling at his arms, knees, breast and neck; he did a double take and again felt at his breasts. "My breasts…" Dirk mused hoarsely, "*my breasts! Shit, I've got breasts!*" He said, his voice rising. "Shit Grot, I'm a woman!" He almost screamed, "**I'm**…"

Grot thumped the wizard hard on the side of his jaw, displacing the lower section momentarily and causing Dirk to pass out. "I get it Qoua; we're forgetting shit, someone sent us here from Hell, where we got involved in something and then they sent us here; for some reason I keep thinking of the name Saul, maybe this Saul guy sent us here…"

"I remember a mistress and my own God Khan; I feel something strange, like: Grot! I killed my god…, …I know I did, for I feel divorced from him and the prophecy foretold that I would travel to the nether planes to do battle with him…, …It must have come true Grot; I am my own God's…"

Qoua broke down in tears unable to continue less she begin to whale. Grot put a consoling arm around her and, while pinching Dirk's nose with his free hand, did his best to soothe the inconsolable princess. She wept silently for fifteen minutes or more when Dirk began spluttering as he came to… "What!"

Grot clapped his hand over Dirk's mouth, "Ssh, we're near the enemy camp, ya got slugged by a wandering guard but we took him down," Grot lied better when he whispered it seemed for Dirk sat up in reply and looked about the camp as if seeing it for the first time. "Have they got any food in them barrels ya reckon? I dunno about *you* guys but I'm positively starving as a bastard!"

"Shush!" The Dwarf fumed in semi-silence though happy at Dirk's seeming forgetfulness. "There aint no time for food, we gotta get Boris and get outta here okay? Right it's time for an assault somehow…"

"Right, well if it's time to fight, I'm off getting some cover." Dirk said and ran over and dived into the nearest tent, raising alarming looks of consternation upon the faces of his two still bush-bound friends.

Qoua looked to Grot for incentive and he jabbed a finger towards the tent, "Go and get him back, quietly, and try not to wake anyone," Grot enthused, "I'll try and get a little further in to the centre of those tents over there near the small campfire…"

The Lizardman followed the line of his thumb and she sighted a tight grouping of blackened tent-halls, around which troops could be seen milling to and fro. She nodded. "I'll join you two clicks west of them, by the carts…"

Both then went their separate ways in as stealthily a manner as they could muster. Qoua slipped between the tents opening flaps with barely more than a shiver. Inside, smashed boxes and crates littered the floor and rotten fruit spilled out from their wounded sides. The debris inside offered very little in the way of shelter however and Dirk was nowhere to be seen. She slipped quietly out the rear, via a finger-nail gouged exit and continued her search of the next tent by entering in a similar fashion.

Grot made it across a forty foot expanse of clear ground without a single cry of alert and into a pit of deep shadow, where his footsteps slowed to a creep. Around him the sleeping troops' varying bulks, swam with the varying colours of their bodies' multiple heat patterns and the Dwarf picked his tread with practised care.

This was no spry Elf however, but a Dwarf. And even one so well trained as Grot would, with his hobnailed boots on, not feel the soldiers sleeping fingers until he had transferred his full weight onto them. By that time, the crack of bone and the scream of the shocked-awake soldier had already informed him of his error anyhow.

Grot cursed his boots and then blessed them and sang their praises as; a few quick kicks to several nearby heads, immediately quelled the noisy rousing fracas of those waking around him.

Grot quickly looked about for the least defended escape route, but as he wheeled off in his chosen direction, a strong arm caught his own and wheeled him around to face the Dwarf clutching him. "Don't go…!"

"What?" Grot guiltily thought of sparking the Dwarf clean out, but several more jumped up behind him and then several more behind them.

"Yeah, don't run! Why should we? We're sick of running…" Another brave Dwarf strode forward and nudged one of the sleeping Orcs gathered around Grot, with his boot.

The Orc shook its bulbous head in annoyance and disbelief as it rose, shaking its nearby companion as it did so. Grot's brain was in psycho gear number five and his fingers itched to grab some weapon but he resisted, while he awaited the outcome of the conflict.

Another, rather rotund Dwarf moved to the front of the miniature rabble as he spoke. "Well *I* say we *don't* take *crap* from these shits no more… They nicked our *beds* last night and the same again tonight, in the morning they'll be into our *breakfast*…! *I say*; it's time to *stop* the kicking and running tactics and *start* standing up for our selves!" The Dwarf huffed up his chest to a cheer of tiresome applause and signalled his arms at Grot hoping to elicit the Orc kicking Dwarf into doing something.

Grot shook his head to indicate he had no intention of doing *anything* and watched as a huge Black Orc, that stood a full foot above the others of his kin who had arrived and wore a particularly nasty scar across where half of his face should have been; looked down at the tubby little Dwarf who stood around a half of his height and thumped it hard in its generous abdomen. The Dwarf fell to his knees and the second orator shot to his friend's side, punching the Orc in the knee at full tilt.

The brute collapsed, but his knee caught the fat one with a nasty gash to the head and a full scale riot broke out between the newly arisen ranks of Dwarves' and Black Orc.

'*Piss to this*!' Grot thought and headed off towards the tent area he had earlier indicated. Nobody stood in his way and he was off from the area and heading, hopefully unseen, towards the busy thoroughfare, which turned out to be a mess hall type area, with soldiers' tucking into their thick, chunky broth with gusto.

Further back someone shouted for the guard commander to come and take charge of the battling squaddies he had left behind, but Grot's eyes were hunger-fastened onto the huge lumps of meat in the stew as one man scooped up a spoonful and greedily ate the broth. Grot had been in a few armies himself and had never seen the common man given so hearty a rationing of beef, nor a gruel so savoury smelling. Course there was not another Dwarf in sight, just many Orcs; mostly of the black hued variety and Grot deduced this must be the cause of the other Dwarves belligerence.

His stomach rumbled fiercely as if it had also seen the food and now demanded some and he dashed into the nearby catering tent without caring who saw him enter. Inside, four long simple wooden tables were flanked by equally long, splinter inducing benches that looked as though they had been cut down that same day, from the way sap continuously wept from their cleft trunks. Soldiers; mostly Orcs, formed a sort of orderly queue towards a massive solid tree stump, upon which had been placed several large vats of the said broth.

Grot looked about for a bowl and saw several scattered across the floor where somebody had knocked the stack and not bothered to rectify it. Two soldiers; a Ratman and a Halfling both rushed jokingly over to the spot and retrieved a bowl. Grot followed suit before pouncing back to his place in the line. He stood there queuing for a good minute or so and nobody questioned him, nor even gave him a second glance, and Grot deduced that it was probably a rag tag army of mercenaries, or to be exact, Mercy-hunters.

Bands such as theirs would often offer any captured quarry his or her life in exchange for a five year service, after which they would be free to leave. The arrangement suited those that chose to join and those that chose otherwise were shown zero mercy. They were a vicious lawless bunch of small prize armies and even managed to outdo the fearsome reputations of their sea bound cousins; the Pirates.

The queue lessened and Grot found himself two steps of being served by a particularly thick looking Gnoll. Grot was surprised by the racial variety that ran throughout the camp and deduced that they must have a very strong leader in deed to keep the unruly lot in line. Of course if *'the leader'* were to die… Grot thought back to the rowdy Dwarves and their hated racial enemy the Black Orcs and started to formulate a plan as a huge Cyclops came stomping through the rank and line and snatched up a whole vat of the stew and carried it to a rapidly emptying table.

Shouts and moans of *'Greedy Bastard*!' rang out from the rank and file, but nobody actually dared challenge the rumbling one eyed giant. Grot wondered if this brute was the leader of the rag tag army and after pausing to have his own bowl filled, while resisting the desire to punch his server, the determined Dwarf made straight for the abandoned bench opposite the Cyclops. "How do numb nuts..." Grot greeted his intended lunch partner, and sloshed down his bowl as he took up a position opposite the mammoth humanoid...

***

Qoua sneaked a quick peek inside yet another tent on her hunt for Dirk and found it too to be devoid of any signs of life. Letting the leather tent flap fall closed, she reconsidered her surrounding arena and loped off in the shadowed outer edge of the tented outer ring, making for a large round big top, something flitted across her sight and she briefly wondered if she had been spotted already but no sign came and she continued to plot her route...

***

Dirk slung open yet another random tent flap and walked in to come face to face with a particularly ugly Gnome whose large bulbous nose dominated his face. "Excuse me? I'm looking for my pal... He's a fat little Halfling called Boris; you haven't seen him have you?"

The Gnome shook his head, a look like that of a startled goose crossed the nostril faced fellows watery eyes... Dirk followed the Gnomes darting eyes but saw nothing and was about to leave the tent when a silhouetted movement caught his eye coming from the large tents sleeping area. The figure that rose behind a silk curtain had the shadowed ears of an Elf and Dirk was struck with the notion that he should somehow remember the Gnome. The chap looked scared stiff for some reason that Dirk could not fathom as the apparition behind the curtain stretched out its arms in a languid motion. Recollection whacked at Dirk with all the subtlety of a size twelve kick up the arse. He did know the shaking Gnome and he also knew the Elf rising behind the silk screen.

Issuing a silent appraisal to Grot's many 'Toughening-up' sessions, Dirk delivered a quick whack to the Gnome's obvious nasal target and fair erupted from the tent as his fleeing form took flight... Followed by an alerted Elven foe called Adin...

***

Qoua stealthily approached the large dome shaped tent and came across two loutish looking Hobgoblin guards asleep outside the tent's entrance. She slipped into the tent silently, keeping her eyes locked upon the sleeping guards as she did so. The light inside washed over her and she immediately pulled the flaps closed as a shaft of light pierced out across the tents darkened silhouette. When she turned, Qoua found herself staring back at a small commune of Halflings. The Halflings raged in both sex and age, though they were predominantly male and mostly over the age of twenty, though one or two babies could be heard in the throes of their baleful attention seeking cries. She wondered if Boris was here and was just about to ask when a rather grey and wrinkled Halfling stepped to the front of the huddled rabble and broke the silence as he addressed Qoua.

"Please eat me!" The elder Halfling begged, "Please, we have so few of our young ones left and us older males' aint so bad… Sure I may not look much but I'm sure you'll find my meat not too tough, in fact it's probably like cured ham, plus my arthritic hands prevent me being any real use as a cook…" The old man attested and looked around at those gathered behind him, who returned agreeing nods.

"I am sure if you were to try me you'd find me most palatable. You could perhaps roast me a little over a nice open fire; I'd recommend using Beachwood for the fuel with a few sprigs of Fennel stuffed in my arse. If you cooked me for about an hour and twenty two minutes, it'd be just long enough to crackle my skin so it's nice and crispy –not unlike Pork Scratching in fact, but not so long as to ruin the tender parts beneath!" The Halfling paused to rub his stomach and lick his lips as the rest of the Halfling horde made a positive hum of savoury appreciation that made Qoua wonder whether they were cannibals.

"Add a few roots from a tuber stewed for twenty minutes in a cauldron of water in which you would boil my head firstly for stock, several boiled sweet potatoes and a few nice garnishes of spring-grass or cabbage and well…" Wiping saliva from his mouth, the old Halfling brought his pitch to a close. "You would have a feast fit for Haggryd himself!"

"Who is Haggryd?" Qoua quizzed. The stupid statement caused a small furore amongst the gathered midgets, who began a veritable deluge of garbled information almost as one, completely unintelligible unit.

One of the guards sleeping outside the Halfling tent; a fairly good natured Orc with a wicked sense of humour, called Jishg, heard the noise from inside the tent and decided to investigate. Initially he was about to wake his sleeping companion, but the fellow had no love for *anyone*, let alone Halflings. So Jishg left his sleeping companion-at-arms and ventured into the tent alone.

As the Orcs head popped through the flap Qoua's tail whipped out and struck the thing around the throat, yanking it to the ground in front of her face down where her Glistening clawed toes made short work of cleaving a channel along the decimated Orc's spine. The Halflings' began cheering and jeering and generally mumbling their way through a rising hum of appreciation until the elder stepped forth again and quietened the others with a crack of his walking stick. "I apologise for the others; are you here to liberate us from our disdainful oppressors? Are we to embark upon some quest for salvation like Magonk and his Untrustworthy Disciples? Are we saved madam? Are we...?"

Qoua looked at the assembled mass of frightened, desperate people and re-evaluated events; she now assumed this tent to be little more than a food pen, the fact of which should not have bothered her in the least. Her people had been cannibals in the past and some were even in the present day; so seeing a living, walking, talking race being kept in this way should not have bothered her...

But it did. She remembered her little gabby friend Boris was being held for consumption and wondered briefly if they were two late, this place at least held no sign of him. She looked about again but although they were mostly juvenile to old age males, most were made of sterner and far less porky stuff than Boris, being somewhat taller and much skinnier than her stunted, plump pal.

"Where are all your children? I see only three here!" She questioned.

"Why, the Great Haggryd ate them, or at least his men claim; to be honest I don't think he cares, but it aint him; its his sneaky commander I'm betting. Haggryd might be nicknamed '*Animal*?', but I doubt even he would want to eat babies." The grey elder moaned.

"And the beast shall rebel against her nature, her fangs; though few, shall hunger for the flesh of the fearful one him self... And she shall strive forth to defeat the animal within..." One of the 'passages' of the prophecy flashed into the mind of Qoua, and she wondered if this was the occasion...

Slowly, her tail unwrapped from the throat of the expired Orc's warm-blooded corpse as she glowered at the apparent leader of the Halflings. "*They eat your yearlings and you let them...?*" The disgust in her voice was richly evident as her deepening scowl zeroed in on the Grey one.

"Well yes…" The elder Halfling moaned with a slight tremble in his voice, "If the great Haggryd commands it then we must-"

The old Halfling never got to finish his declaration as Qoua struck out with her tail again pulling the old man's feet from beneath him and knocking the wind from his sails. "You need a new leader… One who is strong and not bent to the will of this Haggryd, is their one amongst you who dare lead a rebellion against this tyranny?" She looked about for any signs of a volunteer but found none forth coming. She was surprised; these here looked to be in far better physical shape than Boris, yet he was unique in his bravery it seemed.

"You make me sick!" She gasped, "Where are the brave amongst you? The ones of you who are willing to lend their lives to the saviour of their others? Where are your kings and Queens: Your generals? Tell me you will not sit back and watch without defence as your race is made ready for extinction by consumption?"

One of the 'bravest' of those males pushed forward a little, "Please miss, don't kill me for saying it; but we Halflings are a peaceful race… We have no need for kings and queens or generals for that fact, we simply wish to live and be left alone. What can we do if others don't wish to do the same? Should we stand and fight against Goblins and Orcs? Ogres and such make meals of us, we understand but it doesn't mean that we should begin attacking our consumers does it? Besides we would only fail; Halfling's aren't meant to fight, our talent lies in the pleasure of life; cooking, farming, exploring new avenues of experience…, …I don't mean to offend mind…"

"Well, we could join with the dirty 'Scrumpers'!" Another Halfling shouted a little riled, though he neglected to make his presence known.

"Who-" Qoua began.

"The Scrumpers are the ones who agreed to join the army, they cook for them! They're…" Words escaped the fuming red faced Halfling.

"They cook *you*…" Qoua mouthed in an almost silent whisper.

"They're traitorous b-b-b… D… I'm sorry, but they're Big Fat Pigs, that's all there is to it!" Another nearer female shouted and the others stared at the red headed verbal exponent in wide mouthed astonishment at her name calling statement.

"Then why do you not rise against them? Fight for your lives and that of your kin?" Qoua's words were this time directed at the female who had just spoken.

"But I'm a mere maiden, what could I do? I just wish to find me a husband and live a happy life…" Her smiling reply was delivered more coyly towards an admirer in the crowd of males, more than to Qoua herself. She was about to make another response when a growling collage of curses issued from beyond, interrupted briefly by a girlish scream, followed closely by a guttural roar from the darkness out yonder. Qoua ran out to investigate, closely followed by a rabble of inquisitive Halflings.

***

The Cyclops thumped the half-trunk table, splintering its length and upsetting the contents of Grots bowl in the process, but the famished Dwarf stealthily managed to save most of his mead as he fell back in a saving dive onto the floor. Rising to his feet without the use of his arms, the Dwarf greedily gobbled up his broth's scolding remnants and belched loudly in appreciation. *This damn broth was good!* Climbing up onto the bench that ran along both sides of the table, the Dwarf dipped his bowl into the Cyclops's stolen cauldron and it re-emerged almost full, the Dwarf cursing a torrent of abuse as he did so at the scolding heat penetrating his hand.

Settling the bowl down on the table and cursing some more, the Dwarf burned his good hand too by hastily fishing out chunks of fleshy meat from the hot seasoned stew. All the while the Cyclops huge single ocular device was affixed to Grot's motions as he went about his blatant abusive thievery.

Half way through his stolen fourth course, the Dwarf decided it was time to instigate a little conversation. "Fo tuell muh," he mumbled through half chewed rations, "Are yer the eyeball who's in charge around here?"

The eye of the Cyclops wrinkled as a crease of laughter rippled along its torso and exploded from its throat. "In charge me? Me not think? Stupid Dwiff: Eat stolen man stew. No speak!"

"Man stew?" Grot wondered, "Did yer steal it from humans? It's absolutely gorgeous…" The Dwarf paused to chomp down a large lump of meaty gristle, "I would never have thought humans could make something so good…"

The Cyclops took a massive sip from the steaming cauldron and shook its head as it wiped the foamy brown liquid from his mouth. "Not made stew, stupid Dwiff. *In* stew…, …Stupid Human, stupid Dwiff all in stew. Some snake too. Is good, yes: Stupid Dwiff? Eat stew. No speak."

Grot coughed on a ball of half swallowed beef, and almost went purple before the Cyclops whacked him on the back, sending the offending article spewing across the mess hall in a trail of blood and spit.

"Stupid Dwiff eat Dwiff knuckle bone?" The Cyclops ventured laying his large wooden baton upon the table. He regarded the Dwarf with a belittling one eyed look before hoisting up the cauldron and greedily tipping back the little cooled contents down his throat.

Grot snatched up the discarded baton and whacked himself 'quite' hard in the forehead. ***"Yer hungry Dwarven dickhead you…!"*** He roared at the club in his hands, whacking himself some more: ***"You've just been eating yourself, yer kin! You're all eating me: Aargh!"***

The Dwarf sang a rapid and constant stream of half human, half Dwarven curses as he brought the club smashing down hard on the base of the cauldron, causing the makeshift bowl to smash through the teeth of the Cyclops in its possession. The Dwarf twisted away and pirouetted around on the table, bringing the wooden instrument down hard on the back of the Cyclops neck, paralyzing him and breaking the club in two in the process.

Grot snatched up his bowl and tossed its boiling contents at the nearest figure of a bugbear, who scampered away whimpering, having taken the brunt of the broth directly in the face. Grot did not bother to pursue the bugbear however as his plan had been to get at its sword, that lay discarded on the bench, next to where it had been sat.

Snatching up the weapon, Grot weighed up his options as he clambered onto the table. The tent was by now almost three quarters full; save the table he and the Cyclops had occupied and he had spotted at least another six similar mess tents in the nearby vicinity: Now if they too were filled to their maximum capacity or thereabouts, that would make for odds of roughly two hundred and thirty to one.

"…Time to even up the odds then!" Grot harrumphed and raced down the length of the table, swiping the crude blade side to side in a pendulous axe chopping motion. Most of the tents inhabitants had now figured out that the murderous Dwarf before them seemed fully bent to a killing spree and half had sprinted outside to safety. Most stood and waited to see if this was a private vendetta however, rather than a full on slaughter and thus Grot managed to scythe the heads and various limbs from a full table length of feasting onlookers, before they eventually took retaliatory action as a single, decisive unit.

***

Outside of the tent, Dirk's fully alert mind was moving at a far greater pace than his jellied legs as he dived for cover in a mess of abandoned gruel, barrels and hacked up flesh picked bone. "Ouch!" He could not help saying as a vicious discarded rib jabbed into his own. He lay as still as he could in his hiding spot for several moments and then cursed as he remembered the power of an Elves night-vision. He looked behind him at the tent flap and beyond as his own 'borrowed' eye saw the things around him in a whole host of altered states such as heat, magical essence, and aura; none of which enabled him to sight the known to be lurking Elf.

Dirk sighed in relief after five minutes and grabbed up a few rotten pears from the pile at which he huddled, as he munched on them, the various sickening smells aroused his stomachs interest despite the stench and he grabbed up a half full bowl of stew which contained only a little bit of vomit. He was about to devour the contents when a gentle, almost delicate tap on his shoulder brought about knowledge of the Elves position. He turned exhaustively to Adin, who slapped him hard across the face twice; "Welcome back from the dead my bitchy nemesis!"

***

Haggryd struck down hard with his sword, but he momentarily let his attention slip towards that of the trussed up, tubby little Halfling and his strike took out a slave and a lantern by accident. Haggryd was miffed and his opponent; Corag knew it, and lowered his own sword immediately in supplication. A Goblin slave or two were expendable but Lanterns of a good Quality were very hard to come by... Corag dismissed the remaining quartet of sparring opponents and sat down on a large sack of grain.

"Just cook the little bastard already yes?" Haggryd instructed his Halfling cook who was busily striking up a fire, over which his fellow Halfling Boris, was to be spit-roasted.

"My fire will not light! That's a bad sign for those that follow

Coulin..., ...Bad, bad sign!" It shouted back; its last living statement.

Haggryd tore the Halfling's head from its standing torso and took a crunching bite from the skull in his palms. "Fair enough cook!" He bellowed, "I'll eat him raw then!"

Haggryd wasted no time in snapping the stick to which the Halfling was tied and unravelling the troublesome ropes, while Corag excused himself and stepped outside of the tent in which Haggryd had set up his residence. As he emerged from the tent, sweating in the nightly air from his exertions at swordplay, Corag heard a few screams and muffled shouts, followed by a colourful tirade issuing forth from the mess area and jogged over to investigate, clutching up his much-bloodied mace as he did so.

Inside the tent, Haggryd picked up the limp Halflings body and folded the tubby fellow's legs up behind his ears, like an impromptu sandwich. "I eat like this maybe..., ...but maybe poison not gone; poison spoil taste!"

A goblin slave shook his shoulders and trembled, unsure if his master was talking to him: "Would master like me to try, maybe?" He said at length but Haggryd merely cuffed his ear painfully and laughed.

Haggryd considered telling the Goblin attendant that he was impervious to most known poisons then thought better of it as he would only have to kill the speaking Goblin who did have a point, after all; it was his job to check everything for poison. "No, I think not..." He said at length, "any poison within him will surely have died by now; I'll risk it on this occasion."

He was about to take a large satisfied bite, when Boris came screaming back to life, quite literally..., ...The freshly reincarnated Halfling came dreamily about with a floating sensation, only to discover that the ugly Human holding him aloft was about to take a chunk out of his midriff. "*NO!*" he screamed in a long feminine wail and jabbed his thumbs painfully into the eyes of his lunch date to be.

The startled commander dropped him and Boris wasted no time in bolting out of the tent as fast as his stumpy fat legs could carry him, closely followed by the infuriated and somewhat surprised Haggryd whose lunch had most definitely not been ordered on the go.

***

'*Thirty three down and Keldor knows how many to go!*' Grot

thought as he sliced his way through the tented wall and out into a throb of would be warriors. The band of Goblins nearest to him charged on sight, led by a scarred Black Orc. Grot rolled to his knees and came up cutting, denying the Orc in question the chance to digest his previously consumed dinner, before dealing several savage blows to the leaderless Goblins so-called attacking him also.

No sooner had he dealt with the last of those was Grot quickly surrounded by the troop of Black Orc's with which he had tangled earlier, some still bore the bruises and held themselves with ill restraint as their half jawed leader came forward.

"I'll takes it myself Stunty!" He growled and other members of the rag tag army pressed in to get a better look. Half-face stalked around the Dwarf with two gleaming daggers held in each sweating palm and its first slash caught the Dwarf off guard stabbing into his arm and forcing Grot to lean hard on his latest borrowed weapon, bending it in the process. The wily warrior was at a disadvantage now but he quickly executed a new strategy.

"...Oy! Yer great, low down, dirty bastard Gobbo! This body's new you stupid shit!!!" The Orc seemed puzzled at the unexpected verbal onslaught and was himself, unprepared for the Dwarf's responding head-butt. It connected perfectly; sending the clutched daggers spraying out from the Orc's splayed fingers as it crashed to the ground.

Grot expected no honour from these Orcs though, and indeed he got none but as they moved in for the kill with assorted weapons pointing, several ranks fell mysteriously to the ground one after the back-turned other, amidst wails and painful cries of alert. The cries coming too late to warn the assembled Orcs as the Dwarven contingent from earlier began cutting their way through the calves and hamstrings of their Goblin kin comrades.

"No more shit!" the antagonist from before cheered over to Grot waving his hammer aloft, before his soft belly succumbed to the cleft of an unwelcome Orcish blade.

All around him, a small riot-cum-rebellion was spilling out, entangling an ever expanding web as those on the fringes began to get involved in the infectious melee, many fighting simply for the sake of it.

Pausing briefly to pick up the hammer of his fallen Dwarven saviour, Grot smacked the Orc responsible firmly into hell, before taking a hasty, yet relatively undisrupted route back towards his proposed meeting area.

***

Qoua burst out of the tent and into the darkened night too quickly for her night vision to settle and she was set upon by the remaining black Orc guard, who took her to the ground with a timely swipe of his stone club.

The big Orc fell upon her dazed form and started bashing her thick skull repeatedly with left and rights. The Halflings gathered about started to cry but none came to her rescue, while across the tented way a human was dragged along the ground and into the light by Adin, the mysterious Elf, favoured by Haggryd himself: Speaking of which; Haggryd came storming out continuing his annoyed bestial bellows as he chased a Halfling across the light spill and straight towards the assembled Halfling collectives' position...

Haggryd the 'Animal' would have caught the panting Halfling too, were it not for the Dwarf who suddenly stepped from the shadows to block his path: A hammer dripping with gore, hanging loosely by his side.

"You, Halfling: Stop!" Most of the Halflings' shouted at their fleeing cousin as they filed back into the sanctuary of their cattle-pen home. But Boris continued running without pause and the ten or so Halflings still stood outside could not believe what their tubby kin did next.

Rushing up to Qoua's enormous aggressor, Boris shouted at him to stop his delivered beating; which the Orc momentarily did, then even went so far as to ask the eternal question 'why?' of Boris.

"Because my Granny always said; bullies should be taught a lesson by those not being bullied!" The Halfling quoted, "And I am not being bullied!"

With that, Boris kicked a cloud of dust up that choked both he and Qoua as well as the Orc restraining her, and he made a determined dive for the Orc's throat, toppling him from Qoua's prone, dazed and dusted form and rolling about several feet to either side. The Black Orc was not injured by the wimpy fat Halfling, but the surprise of actually being attacked by one, reminded the Orc of the company he was currently keeping and so, throwing Boris to the side, the Orc leapt to his feet and half ran, scrambling for cover. The Halflings' loved it and swamped their newfound leader in a deluge of emotional hugs and kisses.

***

Adin looked over to where the Halflings were celebrating and then turned his attention back to Dirk who he now held by the scruff of his collar in a small pool of lantern light. "Okay, I will make this quick as possible, as every time I get you, our resourceful discussions tend to lead to your inexplicable escape and my agonised suffering as I search the world for your whereabouts once more..." He paused again to slap at the face of the human whom he held in such vile contempt.

"I used to play the flute you know...? I *used* to be able to utilise a form of hypnosis that required a great deal of dexterity and do it with such panache that my victims would kill themselves without them even knowing quite why..." The Elf sneered, leaning in close and withdrawing a sleek looking dagger, which dripped with some undoubtedly venomous black sticky substance.

"So why can't ya? I can't see what your crappy flute skills have got to do with me...?" Dirk said stalling for time. It was an obvious ruse, but it had worked more than once in the past against the proud and egotistical Elf. "Besides which my mate Boris reckons you already did ya dagger trick back in the 'Gap'..."

"Why? Because of you! That's why! After our meeting in Galbor's tower my right side was left crippled. Then when we met in the town of Devils Gap, we chanced upon those two friends of yours do you remember?" The Elf felt fully chagrined at having to explain things, but he wished his elusive target to know the full brunt of his hatred before he died.

"My friends: I don't recall any 'friends', I do remember those two blokes who I had lost all our kit to at poker... That was after you must have hypnotized me... I'm a bit confused..." Dirk tested.

"That is because of the hypnosis; oh never mind. Listen you stalling buffoon; those two goons followed us outside and mugged me for my 'magical' hypnotic dagger: Badly breaking my other hand in the process; this hand!" He proclaimed, lifting the dagger as he did so.

"Yes but what's that gotta do with me?" Dirk objected. The Elf was startled and lowered his arm slightly.

"Do not act ignorant, you know why I am after you, and you know that I cannot... Oh, Dirk! Look it's as simple as this, you owed a debt. One you refused to pay, and so I come along to collect with interest. You know how it works; we've had this discussion countless times..."

Dirk protested, "Yes but I paid Kizgarowe; We; I, don't him a penny."

"I do not care! You worked for him too Mr. Oh so Righteous… and look at what *you* did to me: After promising we would break the system together you left me alone to rot in prison for two years… Some 'nicest Human being I have ever met' person *you* turned out to be! Then when I eventually escaped and tracked you down, you promised to bring back the good old days only to leave me to hang for *your own* misdemeanours." The Elf riled, waving the poisoned weapon dangerously about.

"In *Hubadad*, you promised to pay off our debts to the sheik only to leave me to his assassins, who I incidentally joined up with and learned from. They taught me to find the route of my evil, the cause of most of my pain and you know what Dirk? It is you!" The Dark Elf ranted; his hot breath washing over Dirk as the deadly dagger moved to and fro in his face.

"In Felbric's tavern you left me to that Dwarf over there and then in the tower you pushed me over the edge onto that prohibitively painful lightning mosaic where, I only survived thanks to skewering my right arm on the chandelier and in the Gap you abandoned me to the ministrations of those two 'Grippers' only to get to grips with some common underage floozy…"

Dirk looked a little embarrassed; "You must hate me, eh?"

"Hate you Dirk…?" The Elf struck up a most sarcastic tone; "why ever would you say such a thing? I hope my words have not struck an ill chord?" Adin refuted, tossing the venomous dagger up into the air and catching it by its blade mere inches from Dirk's throat. "I would *hate* a little thing like yourself being the reason I no longer even own the rights to *my own soul* to upset you; *or* for the numerous *beatings* and incarcerations served to *me* in *your stead* to somehow *bother you*…" The Elf bitched as he dabbed at his feverish brow. He felt a little queasy and his stomach cavity rumbled though not from hunger. "Whatever… Would give… The impression that… I… Hate… You…?"

Dirk considered his response and decided upon honesty, "Because as well as all that shit ya just mentioned and the bits ya didn't, you've also just caught yourself with that poisonous looking dagger you're waving about!" With which reply Dirk pushed the quivering Elf to one side, taking care to steer clear of the poisoned blade…

***

"…Move Grunt!" Haggryd ordered of the obstinate Dwarf blocking him, his beard and scalp bore scalds and burns in patches making for an unusual and rather unforgettable appearance. "Hold on…, …I know you! I killed you before; at the tunnel leading from Devil's Gap!"

"Yeah and now I'm gonna return the favour…" Grot threatened viciously smiting the unarmed Orc chief in the process. He delivered several deadly blows before the still living Haggryd rose up and threw the Dwarf some small distance against a nearby small tent, which collapsed upon impact, sending its occupants into struggling confusion. The Dwarf quickly recovered his wits but could not do likewise with the hammer.

Rising unsteadily to her feet, Qoua lurched forward several steps uneasily, before relenting to the concerned Halflings' pleas not to stand. Boris ran forward undeterred however. In fact, the fat fellow was brimming with confidence thanks to being cheered on by his newly rescued kin.

Dirk went and picked up the poison dagger by the handle as the Elf lost consciousness, presumably passing to his death. He toiled with the idea of throwing it at Grot's opponent across the way as the Dwarf and Haggryd got to grips with each other atop the collapsed tent, wrestling and rapidly exchanging jaw-numbing blows without much obvious effect either way.

Dirk closed one eye and aimed, he knew it was a big risk. He might very well hit his mate, but, he concluded it was a risk *he* thought worth taking. "Dirk NO! Wait, give me the dagger." Boris appealed rushing to the Humans position.

"Fair enough…" Dirk replied, gingerly handing over the weapon.

Boris took the dagger and ran to the melee betwixt the two combatants, "Hey pig face come and take me on if you want to eat me, you big ugly slug! Or are you scared your dinner might be too tough for you?"

Haggryd, momentarily having the better of Grot, utilised the strength of his frame to shove the Dwarf reeling into one of the local campfires and barged into Boris, striking him to the ground before he could respond, and sending the venomous blade spinning off to the side.

The daggers glistening arc alerted both the Dwarf and Half-Orc to its dangerous possibilities and they both dashed for the fearsome weapon. Scampering on all fours, the Animal Haggryd made it first and whirled on the approaching Dwarf, who made a rapid turnabout as the Orc chieftain chased him in the other direction.

Boris tried to roll back over but as porky as he was, this proved no mean feat. Qoua was still feeling too queasy to move and the Dwarfs dashing and darting was the only thing keeping him from fatal contact with the dagger. Everything rested on Dirk.

Dirk ran for cover.

Grot's gaze shot with rage and knowing disbelief at his cowardly mate, causing him to re-evaluate his own fleeing status. Rounding several kegs, the Dwarf toppled them and rounded on his pursuer, who narrowly avoided nicking himself with the blade as he dodged the fallen barrels contents.

Grot reached out with both hands and grappled his larger heavier opponent to the ground, their arms locked together as the blade flashed from one to the other, without piercing the skin of either. The rolling battle led to the interlocked warriors clutching at the dagger with both hands as the Dwarf struggled to keep the Half-Orc from rising to his feet and thus gaining the advantage and vice-versa.

Meanwhile, the camp in general was erupting into flames as the small riot started by Grot earlier; escalated to an all out revolution: One that the rebels were winning. Everything remained on a knife edge. It just needed something to tip the balance one way or the other...

A Halfling maiden made the difference. Jerking to his knees, Haggryd ripped himself and the Dwarf upwards, thanks to his Ogres strength, but the Dwarves determined grasp on the blade resulted in it again spinning off; only this time it fell into the shadows. Neither rival contested the dangerous blade a second time, nor did they give it a further thought as they battled fist to fist, nose to nose. The maiden did though, she crept into the darkness alone and though frightened was of a resolute mindset.

She scanned about in the shadows, which while deep enough to hide a blackened blade, were not quite dark enough to enable her night-vision, so she scrabbled about with blindly groping fingers with little thought to her own safety. It took only twenty seconds or so to discover the article and even less time to creep up behind the two static combatants as she poised to deliver the lethal blow to the great Haggryd the Animal's exposed back.

Haggryd span around catching the girl by her wrist and forcing her to drop the blade, while holding Grot aloft in the air with his other hand. "You stupid Halfling woman, did you think you could catch me off-guard? Many better than you have tried before and failed. I would break this flimsy wrist if not for spoiling your meat. Bend down and pick the dagger up, you want to cut me, yes: To poison me? Well, bend down and pick it up…"

Boris had just about managed to stand and when he did, he was holding the referred to dagger. "I hold the weapon now Mr. So why don't you let the beautiful red headed maiden go…?" Boris complimented.

Haggryd shook the girls wrist sorely and threw her backwards simultaneously dropping the choking Dwarf to the floor and advanced the few feet to Boris. "You wish to poison me now do you? Well go on," the Orc leader said, tearing open his flaxen shirt: "Cut me!"

Boris shook his head as he spoke, "Oh I had something far more painful in mind but Granny always said never pass a passing chance so here goes…" With which Boris stabbed the leader through his careless heart. Haggryd's hands sought blindly for the blade in his chest but his eyes were instantly wide and vacant. With a final wheeze, the fearsome leader's reputation began its descent into history.

"Well done Boris, well done! Your Granny is a wise sounding woman yer know; I know I've said that before but this time I mean it!" Grot said and he did, "You're a brave bugger yer are. Bravest Halfling I ever did see no doubt about it, and I've met a few!" Grot's chest heaved with pride as he massaged his throat speaking on: "Know that you'll always be welcome in the Halls of Keldor if I'm there! Maybe yer should stick to daggers instead of messing about with slings eh?" At which Boris smiled back numbly, his expression not even changing when the red headed maiden planted a more than grateful kiss, right on his motionless lips.

Dirk came strolling back into view as the Halfling mob helped Qoua to stand steady thanks to a smelly concoction of herbs waved under her resisting nasal tracts. Grot guarded their position in case of any infringement but none came as those nearby Orcs who had witnessed their Captains demise, declared unto themselves titles and rank. Each immediately wanted what the other had self given and within moments of Haggryd's death, the remaining collection of mercenaries had also fallen to fighting amongst them selves.

The companions, helped by the troop of wonderstruck Halflings, were whisked away from the battle torn encampment, through a series of roofless caverns filled with a copious canopy of vegetation and on through an artificial collection of tunnels leading out into a forested area, which they reached by nightfall that evening. No interest was shown as they left; nor pursuers gave chase and so the journey; though hasty, was relatively calm.

Grot decided against stopping out in the wild, especially so near to the well travelled tunnel network and so they forged on for several hours with only two snack breaks in between. As they came to the forests edge one of the middle aged Halfling's began hopping about joyously from foot to foot. "Caernthorn, it's Caernthorn, we're nearly at the Human capital!" Grot cracked his way through the remaining clutching bracken and came out onto a freshly ploughed field; just one of those belonging to the surrounding farmsteads that bedecked the thirty mile approach to Caernthorn proper. Here, the said Halfling who was a knowledgeable chap known as Dave Sizzler thanks to his expertise with a flame grilled barbecue; diverted them to the outlying house of some old friend. The friend turned out to be a helpful and amiable farmer, who; after hearing of how they had overcome the bandit army, allowed them to stay in an empty barn for the night free of charge. He cooked them all up a roast pig supper too, or rather his home maker wife did and they all ate, laughed and shared in tall tales aplenty as was understandable in the company of so many happy Halflings.

In the morning, the Halflings helped the farmer in gathering up his ripe harvest of fruit and healthy crop of corn while in the barn, the companions were helped to bathe; their clothes cleaned and mended. The farmer and his wife had been adventurers in their youth and if some of the previous nights tales were to be believed, quite used to malicious looking monsters. For Qoua's part, she found this to be true as the farmers wife; a tall, strong woman despite her fifty plus years, took the slightly reptilian woman to her own bed chambers to help her bathe and dress in privacy… Qoua undressed to wash and was shocked into silence.

The farmer's wife groomed her for some forty or fifty minutes as the princess lay in stunned silence, she was used to this, being groomed by one or more attendants; she would have been talkative normally, relaxed around those of her own kind, or slaves of another but she had only now realized her body was different. She was almost human in looks and proportions; or seemed herself to be without ever actually seeing one naked. Her legs we're still long and slender yet now ended with toe-webbed five digit feet, she had nails; sharp black ones but they were not her usual claws. Her abdomen; especially the lower part was most definitely different; her chest too was less muscular and rather more pronounced and her scales were so pale that they almost seamlessly interlinked.

Yet even so she was not so human to fit in completely; she still had her tail for a start; though it was several feet shorter than it had been where a blade of some sort had cleaved it apart though she could not remember why or how. As Qoua aroused from her stupor she asked her helper why she did not appear afraid, to which the woman replied she'd seen far scarier things than Qoua out on the farm late at night.

Later when sitting by the interior hearth Qoua asked Grot and Dirk if they had noticed anything different about her and both replied in the confused affirmative, not being able to explain what it was. She assumed them to be teasing her and after several attempts to make a serious discussion of it she gave up and joined in the teasing about Dirk's own new body. Dirk was offended by every word and when some Halfling child joined in by innocently asking why Dirk wanted to be a man, he stormed off in a huff and the conversation died before ever getting down to discover why the twin transformations had taken place: In fact it was thrice, for even the Dwarf's previously age blemished skin held a more youthful appeal than before.

By the evening the crops were in and they all were invited to a hoe down by the gracious farmer and his wife. As well as several of their neighbouring relatives who had taken part in the harvest. The event turned out to be a great relief to most though it brought a tear to Grot's eye as he remembered the last night he and Dirk had spent in similar circumstance. The Halflings cheer more than made up for Grot's solemnity and they danced, played and sang like it was their last night on Eyrthe. Clarissa; the red haired Halfling turned events sombre for a while when she announced to all, her intention to depart the realm in order to seek out a land where Halfling's could live together. Boris who had been caught snuggling her several times was taken aback by her declaration, and though he continued to dance for some time, his heart was elsewhere.

Dirk was dancing festively around the fire, occasionally linking arms with a drably dressed Qoua or some other maiden as they danced a local jig neither of them knew in the slightest. They made an odd looking couple to the watching Dwarf, who played his hand at cards, having lost again, not that he was overly concerned: In fact he was already beginning to enjoy the experience for what it was, when Boris ambled over.

"Phew! Those Halfling girls can really move can't they?" He whooped with emotion and meant it. Boris was completely puffed out.

"Yeah, they're something all right. I think it comes from accepting freedom. They realise what it means..." The Dwarf rejoiced, gracefully dabbing the tears from his eyes.

"What do you mean? Accepting it?" Boris asked.

"Well as I see it Boris me old chum, any fool can go around waging war, and it takes a fool to accept slavery and domination: So you tend to get a load of idiots with mouths the size of Dragons arses and brains as big as a Squirrels nuts heading the different authorities, while the people in general, mill about in poverty waiting for an authoritative kick up the arse. Are yer still with me?"

The Halfling nodded clueless to the Dwarves meaning. "Well, I am sure that's easy to understand, please go on..."

Grot shook his head and smiled a genuine smile of affection for the Halfling, "You're a good one Boris, you just turned up at the wrong time that's all..."

"You really liked Zen didn't you?"

"I did me fat little chump, I did. But that was then and this is now. No, what I was saying before, about people. Its not exact I know, but the point is; is that it takes a brave man or woman to accept freedom. Freedom means you're responsible for everything you do... Freedom means answering to your own conscience. Take that Clarissa lass of yours..., ...She'll make a good leader if she's brave enough to accept the responsibility."

"Yes she will," the Halfling spoke with a saddened voice then as he aired his own rash decision, "and she'll need a good counsellor if she's to negotiate successful deals with the other races. Knowing who to trust or what is right; following what your instincts tell you, like Granny said: 'If you can't trust yourself who can you trust?' That's what freedom is, isn't it, sharing and coexisting: Helping others to be the best they can."

The Dwarves voice cracked as he spoke. "That's right Boris... You gonna say goodbye to the odd couple?" He gestured in the direction of Dirk and Qoua before being overcome with emotion.

The Halfling nodded and placing his hand gently upon the Dwarves shoulder as he rose to his feet. "Sure I will Grot; and I'm sorry to leave and everything but right now," he sobbed too, "right now, I wanna dance…"

The Halfling waved to his female counterpart as he wiped a tear stained Snurch trail along his arm and regretfully forced his hand from Grot's shoulder… "Oh I noticed you're weapon-less now too so I thought, well… My Granny always said; 'there's a time for quitting and a time for just giving up.' I always thought she babbled a lot my Granny but I guess she just meant that there came a time when you just had to accept when you were bad at something no matter how hard you practised and well, I was never any good with it at all so you may as well have it…" Boris ran over to Clarissa and swept her off her feet and into the whirling dance. Left behind with the Dwarf; Boris's 'trusty' slingshot and the large leather pouch he'd used to hold stones in.

xx) **A Gathering Darkness**

The Halfling contingent left late the next morning, Boris came to say his final farewells though they had already done so over far too many beverages the night previous but when he came to Dirk, the cad was nowhere to be seen. So Boris and the others departed leaving behind a wailing Grot who Qoua left to the farmer's wife the task of attempting to console. Qoua sought out Dirk while the farmer in turn sought out some better fitting clothing in which to disguise Qoua against those less tolerant than they.

Dirk was discovered sprawled naked, face-up, across the straw deck in one of the cattle shed quarters; 'his' tits were scratched and matted with straw and his legs were splayed akimbo. Gloriously exposing the world to Dirk's inner sanctum of womanhood; a few spot traces of blood marking his inner thighs…

Qoua fell aback against the nearby post of the pen in which Dirk lay; her mind suddenly assaulted by a mixture of emotion as she grasped at the concept of Dirk's possible rape and began reliving her own. The smooth textured scales on her back ripped and bled as pressed against the roughly hewn beam on which she leant; the former princess sank to her alien bottom. Hate, rage, disgust and regret bashed at her conscience with equal recourse as she huddled up first then broke out against imaginary assailants. Sobbing and begging like a child for her invisible tormentors to stop…

Slender arms wrapped protectively around Qoua's own and Dirk, freshly awakened pressed her head against his ample bosom in pity for the sobbing creature and stayed there some half hour more as she slowly came to terms with herself once more. "I'm sorry," she managed at length.

His hands brushed at the delicate flesh of her back. "You've hurt yourself, look, ya really gotta take care of yourself a bit more; stop being so stuck up and macho all the time…, …Believe me, I know; as Grot would say; 'buggers that walk around with sticks up their arses go to pieces when all the shit comes tumbling out!' He reckons that's why Dwarves aren't afraid to cry in public places but if ya ask me, I reckon it's just cause Dwarves generally are loud and annoying anyways…, …Not that you're annoying me: I just meant, damn, I'm sorry… Do you mind if I leave you it's just that…"

"Please don't leave Dirk, not yet!" Qoua pleaded, embracing him firmer and burying her head in his cleavage.

"Yeah, all right but ya really do look awful sexy in that tight, little, farmer's wife outfit…, …I'm sorry I'm not normally into big chicks! Well, not big; tall and…, …Muscular. No, I mean, well I don't mean to sound like a dyke but ya know; you are one sexy looking princess!"

"Ha!" Qoua spat, "I am no sweet princess I assure you!"

"That aint what I meant; I'm just saying that as much as I like holding you it's giving me a hard on-well actually, a wide-on I suppose. Must be morning still, cause I always get horny in a morning so I guess it's just me; are you crying again?"

"Dirk you've been raped!" The princess declared in an astonished whisper she barely dared breathe.

Have I?" Dirk looked indifferent. "Maybe I guess; there is a fair bit of blood, is that normal?"

Qoua shook her head, "I am unsure…, …I know that it is normal to bleed when another takes your honour but how much is beyond me…"

Dirk giggled; the mounting frenzy in his nipples and groin momentarily put to one side. "Oh ya don't need to cry for me; I've not lost any honour or whatever; if I *was* raped I know at least some of those that did it but I'd sort of asked them too when I was pissed up to the eyeballs. It was those two farmhands in their twenties or thirties; I remember one of them kept on grabbing my arse while I was dancing and well, me being me; I'd forgotten I was a woman so I went of to the house to get some peace: I thought he was queer, ya know; odd. Well to cut a long story short they must have took that as a come on and followed me in; so we all got to laughing about the misunderstanding and noticed a bottle of the farmer's hooch in the kitchen. So we gobbled that down and a few more bottles of whatever and then played strip poker and well I'm not sure why we ended up here in the horse stables but I suppose ya could say I was flirting with them a fair bit…"

Qoua took a few moments to respond, wondering whether to air her own shameful experience but felt trapped by the explanation: '*How could you let yourself be raped…*' she thought in an almost alien voice. "But why Dirk, why let someone take your honour so easily?"

"I dunno really; I was frisky," said Dirk, "and if that was a matter of honour, I guess I don't have any…, …Besides that little red headed Halfling was getting me going. Man is Boris in for a treat with her! Not that I envy him or anything, I'm just saying that when she danced everything moved…"

"So you still find females attractive despite being…"

"…Despite being a woman?" Dirk responded, "Yeah I suppose I kinda do…, …I mean, well that's what I've been trying to tell ya, sitting here like this; seeing down your top; *you* resting *your head* against *these*…"

"Oh I am sorry!" Qoua declared and lifted her head, brushing away the stubborn straw remnants and delicately caressing Dirk's swollen breasts. "I did not mean to cause you any discomfort; are they very sore?"

Dirk's rejoinder was passionate and he leant forward, planting his lips fully on Qoua's own, gently squashing back the ruby red fullness of her own then parting them slightly as he pulled smoothly back, trailing his bottom lip over the upper of her own.

Qoua felt very confused amid a torrent of emotions, though the one that stood out was desire. For the first time in her life, Qoua kissed another; it was messy and she head butted him gently too in her botched practice but Dirk merely laughed and snogged her passionately, her slim, forked tongue sending waves of responding pleasure crashing through his torso where Qoua's still lingering hands continued their gently mounting caress, sending the already horny Heinemblud into a lusty response.

"You are one horny bitch," Dirk said with less grace than a buffalo. "Ya make me so wet…"

Qoua laughed at that. "Dirk silly, you are dry as a bone…"

"I don't mean; well, look, feel here…" Dirk said guiding her hand.

Qoua's fingers, whose delicate sensations she was still coming to terms with, touched the slightly parted folds of Dirk's forested mound. Tracing a touch receptive digit or two across his clitoris and down towards his very moist hole. Dirk's erogenous zones were fair exploding and he resumed the art of kiss teaching as he began fingering himself with Qoua's unresisting hand…, …After several minutes Dirk let go and Qoua continued the action with a natural affinity, sending him into rapturous moans and Dirk reacted by pushing his own hand down towards her barely there pubic patch; rubbing, padding and probing her pussy if not with

486

affinity, then definitely a practised art... Qoua moaned and groaned anew but now it was in passion and she lay back upon the hay as Dirk traced his hot, slavering tongue over each and every inch of her speedily undressed body, slightly ripping the borrowed blouse in their impulsive haste. After a good hour or so Dirk paused at her clitoris, delivering deft flicks and strokes from his tongue...

Dirk sucked at her Clitoris a little too roughly to be completely pleasurable but the long appreciative licks he delivered to her glistening holes more than made up for it. She almost felt as if her insides were about to explode outwards when Dirk relaxed his ministrations and lay back in a similar pose to the one he had adopted in sleep.

"My turn please..., ...You've gotta lick my pussy; it's so wet I'm dripping all over..."

Qoua hesitated a moment in spite of her racing mind but as Dirk's blonde vagina came into view while he attempted to straddle her face, Qoua caught sight of the blood still seeping from his 'wet' vagina and forcefully though not violently, pushed him aside. "Dirk you are not 'wet'; at least not simply wet alone..., ...I think it is time you and I had a womanly chat!"

***

Violence came too easily to the Dwarf; he knew that and he swore he would have to be more tolerant as he thumped the farmhand in the back of the head. "Did I tell yer to nail that there, did I?" He asked of the stunned worker. "No..., ...I told yer to nail it to the upper cross section; widthways."

Grot was helping out on the farm while waiting for the farmer to return with some suitably apt clothing for the former princess. He wondered for the fiftieth time were the other two had got too but as Dirk never helped with manual labour it was only really Qoua and her height he was missing. He looked up at the slanted beam and wondered how the hell they would get the roof righted as Dirk and Qoua appeared from a building across the field. They looked like two fugitives as they came skulking across the newly planted field as well they might.

"Work dodging bastards!" Grot moaned then turned to the startled workers assembling the new cattle house: "Not you lot: Them! Mind you we can get this bloody cross section done *properly* now..., ...I can't believe none of you sods own a bleeding ladder for Keldor's sake..."

Qoua dutifully got to work upon her Dwarf-instructed arrival and even Dirk pitched in throwing up thatches of straw to use as roofing. He broke the nail on his forefinger while doing so and found that it stung like crazy.

"Pain may be in the mind but that shit stings like a bastard." Dirk moaned out loud. "I broke a nail."

"Aw poor bugger…" the Dwarf said taking the piss. "Can the little woman not handle being involved in a little *man's* work….?"

"A woman can damn well handle whatever she wants!" Dirk blurted, at which retort the whole gathered work force fell about laughing. Dirk looked amongst them and spotted the faces of his-her possible abusers from the previous eve and briefly thought of asking them right here and now what had happened but a knowing wink and a cheeky smile from the more handsome of the two got Dirk thinking he may not be so innocent in the matter as he had suggested to Qoua and besides they both looked to be fairly honest, open men; perhaps open enough to discuss in detail what occurred. He looked about and most of them too were making some sort of leering, knowing gestures. *'Have I shagged them all? Is that why I'm bleeding so heavily: I know what Qoua said but her race might be different to ours and besides they're all looking at me like they've seen me naked…, …Which they probably have or worse or…'*

Dirk shouted over to Qoua. "Do men always look at women like that? I mean there's only the Dwiff that aint perving and he's probably gay!"

"I think you'll find Grot is merely being respectful while these others are not. His sexuality is another matter entirely…" Qoua replied.

"Oy bitch queens do yer mind *not* discussing my sexuality; unlike golden locks here I don't have a one track mind when it comes down to it…" Grot berated, "besides which I know where Dirk's been so I wouldn't wanna go there if yer paid me!"

"Hey ya cheeky bastard, what are ya trying to say? I doubt ya can call me a slapper after just a few nights as a woman…" Dirk doubted looking around him, "…and even if I was I wouldn't shag you anyways…, …Now shut up because I am in a right foul mood and I warn ya, if this is how ya monthly cycle makes me feel; I can be a right nasty bitch! I'd bite ya dick off for just mentioning the word 'slap' in passing okay? And don't any of ya smiling dickheads over there go smirching my honour either or I'll have ya by the balls…, …grrrrr: Men!"

Dirk used this as an opportunity to stomp off, ruining a half dozen straw tiles as he did so and headed out along the village lane barefoot, tossing his tied back pony tail defiantly as he did.

"Dirk is highly unstable at the moment attempting to come to terms with him being a woman," Qoua shouted to Grot after Dirk had left. "He's very diplomatic, erm, no, apathetic, no; easily injured in a mental sense by your words. Would it be okay if I borrow one of these large, workers head adornments and follow him?"

Grot nodded his approval and Qoua, having finished the high cross beam section at least went off to join up with the wandering Dirk.

Forty minutes later Qoua caught up with Dirk at the entrance to a field packed full of neck high, sweet smelling wild flowers; he was talking to a group of local youths. Dirk stood with periodically swaying hips, in the flimsy cotton summer dress he had been loaned, eyeing up a voluptuous looking female teen while her two male friends stood leering after Dirk's sensuous curves in return. Any conversation they may have been having, Qoua surmised was merely incidental to the blatant flirting that was taking place. She quickened her pace and walked over, standing in their midst.

"…Oh hello Qoua…" Dirk greeted the odd newcomer, "this is my friend Qoua from far to the east; these are erm shit, well I'm a bit shit with names but anyway they're from round here; they were just telling me how that field is full of Nymphseed crop. Young lovers go there every year to erm, make out with each other, ya know like; snog, get it on and shit man…"

"I see," Qoua ascertained, "The smell is most…, …Intoxicating!"

Dirk smiled in a randy manner: "That's why they call it Nymphseed, the seeds are roasted and shit to make an aphrodisiac but just the smell is…"

"…Too intoxicating!" The princess declared and grabbing Dirk's dainty hand in her larger own, turned to walk away. She froze though, for there coming along the lane was a small division of knights. "We simply must go and sample these flowers and try out this snog you mentioned…" and she pulled him, much to the fantasising youths' alarm off into the field.

"But Aisha…, …We sit on this wall and snog, we don't go in the field…" The youngest fellow shouted after them.

"You aren't allowed to go in the field itself: If farmer Maun saw you he'd go ballistic…" the second young lad warned.

"Aside that," the brazen young girl began to her friends: "The flowers scent they say would drive you wild with; well actually they don't tell us what with but it sounds a bit naughty. Should we go in after them or what? I wanna see if they really do snog or if they're just avoiding those soldiers over there for some reason…" The three of them looked at each other all minds on a similar path; similar I say because men are men and boys are boys and the suggestion of a snog had led their minds down its own well ploughed path of sexual frustration. The two nodded agreement and headed into the field hoping that their mutual girl friend was thinking the same way.

Qoua dragged Dirk along for a hundred feet or so, stooping as she did and Dirk too was left wondering if his sex-clouded mind had mistaken her intention or if she were simply attempting to avoid the soldiers for some reason; Qoua obviously hadn't realised or didn't want to acknowledge to her self, that at first glance she looked human and quite sexy with it; albeit in the manner of a towering, muscular Dyke meets Adonis with breasts.

They crashed down as the marching armies footsteps came into earshot and Dirk giggled then thrashed about a little; "let's play with each other, I'm bored and horny as hell, come on ya big bitch; screw me!"

A ripple of laughter to their left made known the presence of the teenagers and Qoua shot out a hand and pulled the owner in possession of the arm into her and Dirk's presence. It was the girl and she let out a little scream to which they all heard a questioning shout rise from one of the passing soldiers. The girl stood up in the tall field, her head barely visible amongst the grass but the questing soldier spotted her.

"Right about yer self are ya miss?" The soldier enquired as his troop continued to roll by.

"I dunno, that'd depend on whether these are gonna snog or not?" The teenage girl replied. Qoua looked at her through dopey eyelids and imagined licking her in the same manner Dirk had done to her earlier. The thought provoked a further response that ran from her ass to her crack and back again and she snogged Dirk with the urgency the situation dictated.

"All right then young miss!" The soldier raised his hand in farewell.

The girl looked down on the two women whose bodies were

entwined in convulsing rhythm as they plucked eagerly at the fastenings on each others vestments: Qoua gave up trying to pull Dirk's dress down and merely lifted it and rubbed eagerly at his pubic mound.

"I chucked that towel! I've stopped bleeding look! Ya can lick my pussy now can't ya?" Dirk said in rather puerile prose.

Both Qoua and the girl (and two still hidden boys) did indeed look and to Qoua's complete surprise the bleeding had indeed stopped. "That makes no sense unless…"

"Unless what?" Dirk demanded.

Qoua shrugged and nuzzled his hairless, flat abdomen. "Unless you were still a virgin when we…"

The girl, who was no more than seventeen years of age, couldn't resist her urges any longer and crouched onto her knees: Licking away like a hungry lapdog at Dirk's pussy-pudding and gravy.

Qoua in turn, bit ever so gently on the girl's plump round ass, tearing her dress in two with her nails to reach the aromatic smell of her nubile mound, which she kept completely shaven. Lying on her back, Qoua shifted the girl's prostrate into place and began delivering calculated flickers of her tongue over the youngster's vital areas.

The revealed action proved too much for the lads themselves to resist; not that they wanted to and they too jumped into the small mix of luscious ladies. Within seconds of pulling a large ten inch penis from his reluctant pants the first lad had blown his load. The resulting mess flew out over them all, covering patches of them in its sticky white liquid. The second male, though his penis were half the size of his mate, found he could control his urges a little better and with a clamour of 'yes please' from the frantic ladies he proceeded to embed his small penis in each one in turn.

All three were practical virgins with limited sexual experience; though in Dirk's case this only extended as far as him being a woman, and so proved that control and stamina are the two most important factors when it comes to pleasing a woman as the lad lasted well over an hour and a half making each of the females come several times before exploding his overly healthy sperm count out over the others. Big dick, as the other youth was referred to several times, having recovered his erection thanks to an appropriately 'wank' blow job from Dirk again tried shagging first Qoua, then his girl friend, then Dirk, each one refused though, unable to comfortably accommodate his penis and so all gave him a collective sympathy blowjob. Dirk was inspired, he felt like he had done this before; '*it must be natural or I must be...*' he assumed then stopped, distracted again by the sweet smell of desire.

Some time later and the girl introduced herself as Bethany while Dirk was receiving a pounding by the smaller of the lads. "But I thought I heard one of your friends call you Aisha earlier..." Qoua mumbled over sucks and lavishing licks of the big ones cock. The girl laughed, licking and fingering Qoua's personal haven as she replied, "Aisha is your friends name..."

"Oh I need sex..." Big dick spoke: "Proper sex and all; surely one of you can fit me in now you're all wetter than water!"

"Try me..." Dirk dared and looked in awe at the three inch thick mammoth meat coming eagerly at him. "I wish I'd been that big in my former life..."

The farm boy laughed. "I bet you were a filthy dog of a man..."

Dirk didn't know whether to be offended or affronted by the jibe but he didn't have an opinion either way after big dick thrust the first several inches inside his swollen vulva. "Woah boy!" he opted to cry instead but the boy wasn't for woah-ing any time soon and began ramming away like a thoroughbred, forcing his thick shaft inside the moistened slit inch by pain stabbing inch. Dirk loved it; it was pain and pleasure and for some reason he found he got off on both in equal measure.

"...Oh yeah...!" Dirk cried out as the lad shipped eight inches inside and pumped away at Dirk's bent double person. "Deeper man, give it me friggin well all. Oh yes, come on baby; that hurts so much..."

Dirk felt in absolute ecstasy and this was compounded by the sudden arrival of the two girls who began nibbling at his delicate bits in unison. "Oh come on baby!" Dirk cried out, "one more..."

Big dick pounded him with his full length once, twice, then was gone, disappeared, his penis withdrawn painfully quick which only served to excite Dirk more, sending him into sexual orgasm.

"Oh wow!" Dirk cried out to anyone who cared to listen, "If that what sex feels like for women, I'm friggin well glad I am one."

***

"So what did that girl mean about not being a woman...?" One of the workers was asking Grot; it was lunch time.

"Nah ya big daft prick...!" Another replied; "she said she'd only been one for a few nights but she definitely felt all woman to me last night I'll tell ya for nothing!"

"Yeah well she probably weren't so experienced eh? Bet she only lost her cherry a few nights ago..." another rejoined.

"Well I dunno but for me she knew exactly what she were doing and if we were wondering when exactly she lost her virginity, I'd say years ago probably..., ...Yer should have seen the way she licked at me plums and shaft," the second man again spoke up, "why ya would have to pay good money in Caernthorn for one with her technique. It was like she knew exactly what a man wanted tracing her tongue around my..."

"Listen here!" Grot said smacking the heads of the three chatters together and kid punching the one who had last spoke. "That is my mate you're discussing now stop it, h-she has got enough problems already..."

"What like? She aint got the pox has she?" One of the men said, rubbing at his head and holding his crotch in defence as he asked.

"Well I guess with Dirk any pox would be the least of his worries, so yeah probably and I say he's got problems 'cause he has, okay?" Grot was getting frustrated by the small talk; all these people seemed to talk about was farming and sex. "What about Caernthorn: Have we missed the carnival?"

"Hold on a minute, why did you just talk about Dirk, when we were talking about Aisha?" A fourth speaker joined in.

"Who the bloody hell is Aisha?" Grot raged. "I thought you were on about my mate Dirk being a floozy, not some other bint..."

"So who's Dirk then?" A confused listener asked.

"Dirk is the name of my mate; the one who yer probably all bedded last night no doubt." Their faces showed no signal of recognition, "Keldor's beard..., ...The one who we were talking about a minute ago. The horny bitch that danced half naked last night and then turned up before in a dress so see through she might well have been wearing a glass overcoat..."

One of the workers saw the light and mentioned as much; "that's who we're on about: Aisha; her name's Aisha and she gives a good blow job!"

"I know!" Another agreed and several others nodded too.

Grot purpled with embarrassment and rage and he thumped the fellow with a cleanly delivered uppercut. "His name is bloody well Dirk; I should know, I've know the troublesome bastard too many years and I do not want to hear another word about his bleeding sexual expertise!"

One of the farm hands with a bump on his head backed off a little before he again attempted his original line of questioning: "So why do ya keep calling her; this Dirk or whatever, that is; why you keep saying 'he'?"

"Hey everyone, look up there," shouted one of the younger workers who had been lay back day dreaming. "Isn't that a Dragon?"

The others all followed his gaze and saw a mighty looking brown winged thing swoop down, clutch up some struggling humanoid from a field and peel away into the sky. From this distance it could as easily have been a Wyvern they were seeing but either way, the creature didn't look too friendly as it dropped the Human it was clutching from roughly three hundred feet up and began swooping down again towards the same area of grassy field.

The Dragon was by no means the largest of its kind and may well have been a whelp but considering most people had never seen one it still had enough about it to instil fear in the locals. With a wingspan measuring some eighty or so feet across and a length of maybe one hundred and twenty foot from head to tail, the brown was by no means tiny in comparison to those it now terrified below. Its scales were lumpy in places like calluses but softer seeming in others and it had no forearms at all just two wide, strong looking hind legs ending in serrated talons and its head was given over mostly to the set of the things huge prominent jaw; lined with nasty pointed teeth.

Everyone began running towards their houses or hiding in hay bails in screaming panic but Grot merely swore to him self about selfish bastard wizards always having to make life difficult and began running towards the distant field, avoiding the milling fracas as he forged on. He was some twenty minutes running time from the sighted Dragon's position however and he dearly hoped the small procession of knights that had passed by moments before, had also noticed the Dragon and were in a fighting mood.

***

Dirk lay moaning in ecstasy while Qoua and the teenage girl made short work of licking up his copious gushing quim but the other boy, who had been stood behind the Dragon plucked 'Big Dick', started making a silly 'ooh' sound over and over. The others paid him no attention, intent on their sexual endeavours and moments later his strange sound finished abruptly as he too was snatched from the ground by the returning Dragon and tossed without ceremony some hundred feet away as the great brown beast wheeled and turned, sighting its next target.

The procession of knights and their accompanying soldiery had indeed noticed the Dragon and were charging back towards the lower field containing the lovers. The knights on horseback were first to make it into the field's boundaries and the Dragon swept past Dirk and the others and headed in the direction of the danger posed by the approaching knights. As it passed over them in a shallow swan dive the beast released its bowels and covered most of the men and their mounts in a stinking brown veneer of shit, forcing them to fall or jump here and their and generally bring the rescuing charge to a momentary standstill. Four of the knights had already abandoned their steeds however and were forging towards the middle, searching for the missing lovers when the Dragon struck again. This time its unleashed talons were utilised to knock the wind from two of the men, while a third dashing knight was snatched up in its mighty maw and devoured whole; armour and all.

The fourth however dived for cover upon the Dragon's approach and landed next to the three ignorant girls, still continuing their depraved orgy. The knight thought to warn them, then looked again with misty eyed lust at the three fornicating lovers and ripped away his lower armour, eagerly pulling out his engorged penis and thrusting it into the nearest hole, which happened to be Qoua's pussy. She squealed and smiled; looking back at the invasive newcomer only to see his head get ripped from his body as the returning Dragon made a botch of plucking the man from his rocking perch. Qoua was instantly shocked from the erotic trance but Dirk's roaming fingers and the intoxicating smell made her forget all about the Dragon.

Qoua lay back down all the better to be sent a quiver as Dirk and their teen companion delivered some frisky strokes of their own to her most erogenous areas. The Dragon circled above. The soldiers had began firing their bows and these things hurt, or at least prickled like a needle but when you are being plugged full of needles the prickling becomes so much more.

The Dragon decided it needed to either snatch up its prize or call upon one of its local cousins for back up; she was a red and two or three times bigger than he. What's more, she had fiery breath which would have made short work of his target and the associated sexual enthusiasts. Then again as it thought of her fiery breath it was reminded of its own recently callused hide and decided against interrupting her again with little need. He decided to go for it and swooping down amidst a hail of arrows, the brown Dragon opened up its talons in reflexive readiness as it zeroed in on its target. Ten feet from impact and a fire arrow impacted against one of the Dragons large blisters upon his wing and his instinctive flinch sent him crashing into the field besides the three fornicators who only now stood up in unity and gawped in amazement at the Eyrthe shaking Dragon's appearance.

The young girl fainted, the proximity of the dragon too much for her already racing heart to take and Qoua and Dirk were left holding hands, looking at the terrifying creature as it flapped about in abject agony; one of its wings bent at an odd angle beneath its own mighty mass. Qoua initially thought to help the poor creature out but Dirk's squeezing hand reminded her of him and his safety. She looked at him and saw that he had a large bloody weal traced across his shoulder.

"Dirk, you're hurt..." Qoua whispered, "I shall see to it."

Qoua began kissing his injured shoulder and Dirk was in agony heaven. He pulled Qoua down next to the heaving Dragon and they renewed their nuptials in earnest as the military approach sounded.

The Dragon heard the Knights approach too and with a roar of pain he shifted his neck about and snatched up the young teen in his teeth, gobbling her whole then changed his own shape and physical appearance to that of a Human; matching his just consumed meal.

"It's disappeared!" One of the knights shouted as the Dragons huge frame did indeed appear to vanish, his transformation into Human form as sudden as a thought. The detail of the features took several seconds more to match to the girls and he could do nothing about his broken 'arm' but his untimely break and confounded predicament was soon forgotten as he looked down at the two engrossed girls. He had expected to find a woman and a man, not because they were having sex but rather more importantly because that is what he had been instructed to look for not six hours ago by Y'shael but here was two women before him. He briefly wondered which to kill as the sound of the soldiers closed in and decided he would have to take both: The thought of taking both took another meaning in his mind and as he breathed deeply of the surrounding Nymphseed aroma his loins began longing for sex. He bent down to nuzzle on the buttocks of Dirk..., ...The soldiers would be here any second, the brown Dragon knew but he simply couldn't help himself and within moments he was licking and probing away at Dirk's double entry while the female wizard went down on Qoua.

Two soldiers came crashing through the field and had any of them been standing they would surely have been cut down by the scything blades they swung at the plant-life. The two looked down at the threesome and forgot all about the Dragon as they too succumbed to the sweet smelling flowers temptations.

***

Grot arrived at the scene a wheezing wreck, his feet had carried him to within fifty feet of the Nymphseed field but now he retched for all he was worth; the previous night's ale pouring out from his mouth and nose in black and yellow streaks. He felt terrible and sat down knowing full well that his friends needed rescuing but feeling thoroughly beyond the task. He was thankful for his youthful body, for his old one would have took over an hour but Grot had managed it in fifteen minutes. His ankles, calves and hamstrings burned in equal contention as he puked some more and stood somewhat painfully to take in the situation... A great deal of moaning and groaning issued out from the fields whose depths contained several dozen heaving bodies, on the verges a small platoon were washing themselves in a nearby watering hole and around the fields perimeter a host of squires and such bustled about occasionally calling out the names of someone or other.

"Nymphseed..." The Dwarf fathomed upon scenting the potent herb and he staggered back down to his knees, lifting his divested sick in his hands and rubbing it into his face before staggering back to his feet and plodding towards the field.

Grot punched a squire on the head in passing and nicked the fellows sword which he used to hack a path through the field, wrapping his torn shirt sleeve around his nose and mouth. He had been chopping a random path for some several minutes when Grot came across the first revellers and he hastily backed away before the soldiers grabbed him too. Five minutes and many more passed orgies later and the Dwarf alighted upon Dirk and Qoua. They were in the company of ten or so soldiers in various states of undress plus an unknown girl of a youthful age. Grot waded in with punches and kicks and in one reluctant bloke's case a sword held to the chopper; pulling his two friends and the young girl from the tangle of limbs and dragging them, snogging and groping one another all the while, to the fields outer edge where he tossed the sword back to the previously thumped squire.

The gathered squires, comprised almost completely of the male variety; looked upon the nibbling, finger stroking antics of the newly arrived naked females with hopeful leers and gestures but Grot shot them back a growl and a look that said; 'go on, try it...'

"They'll stop and realise what's got into them in a moment; then they'll feel like right proper bastards you'll see..., ...I lost a fine party of Dwarves to this stuff years back; they were all too busy bumming each other to care about anything else." Grot shouted out, then seeing some of the disproving faces he added: "See someone so intoxicated will just keep going on and on; shagging away without even pausing to eat. Course I never knew back then how to avoid becoming a sucker myself but even so, they were Dwarves and there's no way on Eyrthe I was going to run in and try to pull them out..., ...I was only a nipper back then and quite handsome too in a cutesy kind of way: I wouldn't have stood a chance!"

"So how long are they likely to stay like that?" One of the younger assembled squires asked. "Hours, days, what...?"

"Dunno really, depends on the constitution of the person involved; could be minutes; could be days..." Grot sighed.

"Well will they remember what they've done and can we join in?" A braver, randy foot soldier inquired.

"Yeah, let's have some; I aint seem my wife for over a year now..."

"No it's too dangerous..." Grot admonished.

"It's okay I don't mind a little danger; we're soldiers aint we?" Another man laughed.

Grot whirled on one man who had dropped his trousers behind Grot's back and was receiving a wonderful course of double headed oral. "Don't go forcing yourselves on them: They'll remember what they've done..."

"I aint forcing nobody..." The soldier denied and was right.

Grot wondered not for the first time what Dirk would do if the situation were reversed then discounted the notion out of hand. His friend would most certainly go with the flow, if not be the first to join in himself. He had to move them but where; not only did they fondle and stroke the exposed extremities of each other and anyone within touching distance, nor was their the small matter of the disappeared Dragon to contend with or the errant young girl whose father would surely be unpleased to discover her antics but worst of all, each of the three were completely naked and this led to three cold, hard facts amongst the sex starved soldiery. Primary concern were the said soldiers who were all ready closing rank and file around the small orgy and randomly joining in at the sight of so much debauchery. Secondly, he could hardly walk them through the farmer's communes while they frisked each other constantly and thirdly Qoua was obviously not human, not from this distance and so graphically exposed. The only reason the soldiers hadn't paused to consider this fact was due to their proximity to the wildflower and the intoxicating scent the Nymphseed gave off. Grot struggled to think of a solution; '*what would Dirk do again; oh right…*' he thought.

"Wait up; I've got a solution…" Grot called out to the engaging soldiers. "These other two are too inexperienced, ya need a proper slut… A girl that's been around the block if ya ask me…" A statement to which the stripping soldiers readily agreed and so he pushed Dirk onto his back and bade the first of the rapidly thickening cue to plug away…

Grot then yanked the younger girl to one side and put her in the temporary care of two young lads aged about twelve and shoved Qoua off to the side, who he began dressing in the doffed soldiers gear as she attempted to undress him in return. Dirk meanwhile, took on two and three soldiers at a time as their impetuous libido took hold, lending Grot the required time and distraction with which to re-disguise the rampant Lizard woman. Grot then tied a small piece of rope around Qoua's waist, slipping the rest around a tree trunk and tying a deft knot beyond her reach.

As the Dwarf finished tying the knot he came back around to the front of the tree and noticed two things happening at once; several of the larger men had pushed Grot's two young charge-hands to one side and, after mounting the girl on the back of a nearby hay cart, began taking her several at once. At the same time he noticed Qoua or rather more likely the male mounting her had managed to pull Qoua's borrowed pants down and was busily screwing her, much to the former princess's delight.

Grot ran towards the hay cart containing the young girl but as he passed Dirk he realised that his friend was receiving a large amount of abuse from the men too; who were plugging every orifice with their swollen members; at least one hole containing two of their cocks. As much as Dirk was seemingly enjoying it, he realised the sex starved men would most probably kill his friend in their endeavours. His conscience pulled at the Dwarf; who to save first. Qoua only had one man on her but was tied up and therefore was at that ones and any other soldier's mercy. Dirk needed help before he had a heart attack or lasting physical damage and the young girl simply didn't belong in this mess to begin with. Then farmer Maun turned up...

The farmer was none too pleased at the damage done to his crop and went off to find an officer to argue with; he was directed over to the hay cart where a man acknowledging himself as an officer was about to take his turn with the young girl. The farmer recognised the young girl and waded past the half dozen troops having intercourse with her and started screaming at her in the manner expected of a family relative. Many a declaration of 'wait till thee father hears o this young un' were spurted but the girl simply attempted to seduce the farmer in reply.

Grot used the decoy as a decision maker and ran over to the soldier humping Qoua and booted him in his loosely hanging genitals from behind. The dropped-trouser warrior staggered back holding his balls and fell over his own feet as the Dwarf ran off to save Dirk from the remaining twenty or so of his abusers. As he neared Dirk's position he could hear the farmer shouting at the girl still and admonishing her for not recognising her own uncle. Grot knew tact and diplomacy would be no use so close to the fields and so he dived at the huddle above Dirk feet first, taking out several of them with his impromptu flying kick and landed atop his friend.

Grot winded Dirk who had already been struggling for breath and attempted to get off his friend quickly but before he could stand, a barrage of kicks from those still upright, rained down upon him and the trapped wizard.

Qoua came too with sudden dread, it took her a moment or five to get her bearings and realise where she was and why she was tied up with her pants down but then her conscience came rushing back at her and she screamed out like a Banshee...

The shrill screaming coming from Qoua made everyone stop and take notice as several knights; now clean of shit thanks to the nearby irrigation supply of water, came rushing over screaming at their men to dress themselves and stop their actions. Farmer Maun was in no army however and he delivered a stinging backhand slap to the face of the girl still attempting to pull down his pants screaming "Stop it, Bethany; it's me Uncle Maun!"

The Dragon looked at the impudent Human that had just slapped him with shock and dismay; he had no idea what he was doing here and how or why this man was attacking him but he was definitely in some human settlement and amongst a fair few of them.

"Insolent beast, who do you think you are striking?" The Dragon growled in a voice far two guttural to belong to any female of the Human variety, let alone a young girl. The farmer looked down at his niece in shock and awe as she flipped to her feet and shoved him effortlessly back of the hay cart; the farmer flew some sixty feet or so where he landed with a loud crack, snapping his neck like a twig. The Dragon and everyone else's sight alighted on Qoua and he suddenly remembered why he was here. In the blink of an eye he had changed to his true form; flattening the hay cart and squeezing the life from those of his sexual assailants beneath his weighty mass. The captain who had been about to go next before becoming involved in an argument with the farmer stood pissing his pants in fear mere inches from the Dragon's massive jaw and the brown creature chomped him in two before launching its great bulk towards the tied up snack that was Qoua.

Grot unheeded, thanks to most of the men cowering in Dragon fear, chased back across to Qoua as the Dragon's thundering footsteps rivalled his own. The mighty agitator noticed the Dwarf's speedy response and leapt up, spreading its wings to glide and promptly crashed back down with a thump, having obviously forgotten about its previously broken bone. Grot made it to the tree ahead of the skidding Dragon and yanked on the rope while ushering Qoua around the other side of the trunk. Qoua toe-tapped around the other side just as the Dragon's slide came to a halt, thumping into the opposite side of the tree and shaking the rosewood to its core. Grot worked his muscles, taking the strain of the rope, while Qoua slipped out, hastily pulling up her downed drawers.

A number of dismounted knights ran over too and they utilised their various blades with amazing vigour stabbing at the stunned Dragon which could only operate its Jaw in defence for some unknown reason; a great sword lodged half way down its spine the cause of paralysis. Its snapping attack took out several of them in one sweep of its mouth but the Dragon couldn't reach behind it. By the time Grot and Qoua had found a weapon with which to help the ordeal was over, one knight standing proudly atop its twitching head and neck; his blade buried hilt deep in its uppermost eyeball.

Those gathered cheered loudly and as most of the others wits came to they joined in also; a hero was born that day called Simon; he was a simple man with an easygoing outlook on life; never asking of anything beyond ones capabilities and commanding his troops and followers with an unassuming air. Many would come to serve under him as word of his Dragon slaying deed came to be known, the soldiers that came to serve him even inventing a childish game with which to while away the bored intervals between warring and not, called Simple Simon Says. Simon however, like many others before him would one day find his boasts had reached the wrong ears entirely and exactly three years to the day from his historic slaying of this brown Dragon, a bronze would turn up and lay waste to him, his men, and his castle; such is the circle of life.

In the aftermath of the slaying, commanders took control of the situation; ordering rescue missions for the men still trapped in the field proved no easy feat and while they were distracted and Simon took applause, Grot and Qoua searched around for Dirk. They found him in the gulley that ran along each field; having sex with two errant soldiers and wasted no time in pummelling them and snatching Dirk up; each holding a fidgeting arm.

They headed for the next field; half full of hay ready for harvesting and out through several more. Climbing over hedges and walking through barns while fighting off yapping dogs and the occasional charging bull. They put several minutes distance between themselves and the remnants of the small army and stopped against a lone oak to gather their wits and strength. Dirk nibbled on Qoua's restraining fingers as she spoke: "Do you have any idea where we are? I am hopelessly lost my self…"

"Not a bloody clue…" The Dwarf announced with a grumbling shake of the head. "We're in a bleeding rat's nest of farmland, which means I'm as lost as yer self. Give me tunnels; a tight jungle or forest or even a creaking crevasse over this shit any day… Keldor keep us safe; I'm not too good with open spaces; a bit agoraphobic yer could say and shit at finding stuff."

"I understand-please stop it Dirk-I am also a little similar, I do not hold well with wide spaces. Why do you think the Dragon came for me; oh and thank you for not mentioning my aroused state, it wasn't my self acting out of conscious though I do admit to holding a strange attraction to this struggling Nymph-Dirk stop it!" Qoua slapped at Dirk's hands as he cupped one of her breasts and bit down upon it.

"Qoua ya just gotta learn how to handle the wanker when his mind goes; here let me have a do!" Grot said standing and coming between Dirk and Qoua. Dirk reached up, cupping Grot's groin and moving his head upwards which was great as the Dwarves fist came smashing downwards knocking him senseless.

A passing farmer saw the act and called out to Grot, berating him for hitting a woman: "Wha dya tink yar doin ittin awn a girly…" To which Qoua responded in protest: "Why what's wrong with hitting a woman?"

The farmer seemed flustered to be so challenged by a girl and reverted his attention to the Dwarf asking; "owdyu liken er to be ittin ya sel?"

Qoua responded again before the Dwarf could speak, painfully punching him several times in the arm. The farmer seemed either baffled or satisfied by her assault and fairly flustered still, continued on his way.

Grot too was a little flustered by her assault. "What the bollocks are yer hitting me for; yer should be hitting that backward bastard for not being able to speak properly! That reminds me: Didn't yer used to speak funny?"

"I was simply diverting his attention…" Qoua said in defence of her actions, "besides, women should be able to hit men and vice versa; though it is often a pity for some of those males that cannot defend themselves I agree…, …As for my speech; I remember it changing but I cannot say how or when other than it was in the presence of a higher being…"

"Or lower being…, …My bet is it happened in Hell: We've hardly had a chance to discuss it have we: maybe if we do we may remember things from our time there?" Grot bargained.

"You are correct to speak so Grot but I think now is not the time," she said rising and pointing back down the nearby lane to where the insulted farmer had gained the attention of a few scouring soldiers.

Grot nodded and jumped to his aching feet, throwing Dirk across his back he nodded to the nearby hedge and they headed away as fast as they could in the opposite direction to the soldiers.

It was going on for early evening when the two; who found them
selves travelling towards Caernthorn happened upon a dilapidated building
whose associated farmland was overgrown with assorted weeds and
shrubbery. They made camp there, the Dwarf intermittently punching Dirk
when his touching and groping went too far and talked long into the night.
They discussed every little glimpse of fractured memory from their time
there but discovered little more detail for all their efforts. Their attention
then turned to other things rather more practical like where to find a
disguise other than the liveried gear she wore now, or what to do about
Dirk being a woman; it wasn't merely his current state that bothered them
but his whole being a woman and they knew as much as Dirk was currently
revelling in the sexual side of his state at least, he too would be seething on
the inside.

Qoua stopped Grot's latest punch as Dirk reached out and touched
her arm upon resuming consciousness. Dirk spoke very hoarsely;
unsurprising given the amount of man meat consumed and cried out every
time he moved. He did thank Grot, for being an understanding prude and
for stopping him going to first, second or any other base with his Dwarven
pal. He cried out all night and though he snapped when questioned about
his feelings, Dirk denied feeling any sense of shame or sentiment about his
ordeal.

They all new he was lying but Dirk was happier for saying it and the
others were glad to see him simply coping. Grot wondered why he never
cried; sure he had sniffled a few times when his life had been in danger or
Grot had beaten him a little too hard but he had never known Dirk to cry
for the sake of crying and it bothered him that his friend was building up
too much pent up pain and anger.

Qoua for her part, having been raped and viewing her sexual ordeal
in a similar light, saw Dirk's denial as a way of coping and slightly envied
him it. The truth was her rape had been far more unpleasant and totally
enforced against her will but that bothered her too as her previous nights
pleasures had also been against her will. That night she had been drinking
this alcohol the Human's seemed to love and so had Dirk, so maybe that
was to blame in a similar way that the Nymphseed had affected them,
maybe she was blameless in all of her sexual encounters; maybe but she
herself couldn't help thinking otherwise and her erroneous guilt gnawed at
her soul. She really did envy Dirk his simple denial and yet, even now as
she examined him she felt a stirring of passion. "Could it be that I have
fallen in love with you so readily?" Qoua thought she thought.

"What?" Grot asked, unsure if he had heard correctly.

"I…" Qoua had to think quickly, "I have grown an attachment to you both; a love for you already." She said realising she must have spoken aloud. Qoua felt desperate and felt her cheeks flush with blood in response. How much, she wondered, of what she had been 'thinking' had she unwittingly uttered aloud.

The Dwarf saved her, whether intentionally or otherwise she didn't care. "Why do yer think that Dragon was trying to kill yer Qoua?"

"I am unsure…," Qoua conceded, "I asked you the same thing back by the great tree…, …Maybe it is to do with the Prophecy I follow; it tells of a change occurring within my soul; it did not mention a change without but perhaps these are related as may well be Dirk's own mortal coil…"

"So tell us about this bloody prophecy of yours; it had me in it didn't it; I remember you saying back at the hanging tree in the 'Gap'. So just tell us about that," Dirk argued, "for instance does it have anything to do with Dragon's and sex changes and if so, who, when, why, where and how do we change friggin well back?"

"I am sorry," Qoua said truthfully, "but it is forbidden to discuss it upon pain of a pre-destined death; I myself and others; particularly my priest Fh'l-Qoua, have discussed it in length but for our efforts we are destined to die in a wholly unpleasant manner and I simply could not bring myself to deliver either of you into the same fate."

"Bloody Prophecies…" Dirk moaned and *he* meant it too.

Grot wandered off to collect firewood for even though they were a mere five miles from the town their bodies were hurting and it was long after midnight. Dirk grumbled ever so much about being uncomfortable and Qoua volunteered to give him a massage, secretly longing to lick, kiss and fondle him; she limited herself to his touch and Grot made short work of building a small cheery fire in the shelter of the only remaining roof section of their refuge. Dirk didn't mention the sexual experience they had shared and she decided to let the issue rest for now; reluctant to discuss things in the Dwarves presence, besides which their experience was unique and personal matter. Qoua snuggled Dirk for warmth and was snoozing within minutes.

"She fancies you…" Grot said quietly as the transformed L'iezsh'mat drifted off to sleep.

"I think she's a lesbian ya know…" Dirk whispered back to Grot when he was sure their companion was fully asleep, "Me and her had sex last night for hours on end. She was a proper goer, lady sex is friggin amazing man, listen up, I'll fill you in…"

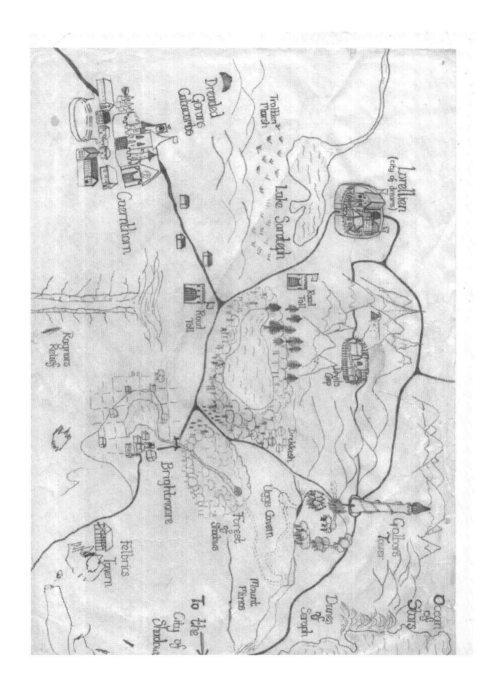

XXI) **Epilogue**

It was a beautiful day in the sprawling metropolis of Caernthorn, both in and around its city quarters the sun charged down relentlessly against the brickwork of the vast multi-story network of homes and business. Small lizards and their rodent foes ignored their constant hunting and scavenging in order to seek refuge in the dangerously dark recesses of the sewer that cobwebbed beneath the city surface.

Only in the kingdom sized public park could birds be heard to sing; yet the chaffinch, common house martin, odd barn owl, and of course the ever present sparrow ceased in their foraging and sought refuge within the human homes, whether they were nested there or not. The humans themselves were out in their droves. Today was the first day of a general holiday extending over two weeks and occasionally beyond: 'Champions day' in Caernthorn; the source of dreams for many a refugee.

Caernthorn's sewers were said to run through silver pipes and mainstays such was the cities reported wealth and its streets were said to be decked out with nuggets of gold such was the reputed fortune of the citizen and its inhabitants: Of course this was a myth borne of an exaggerated truth; the royal palace had an inner courtyard whose stone cobbles were mingled with that of a golden ingot every third step. The ruler of the kingdom; though it was often referred to as an empire, was a certain King Leo Van-Magnus Vitoria the twenty fourth who was; as the name suggests, the twenty fourth in a successful lineage of much loved kings. Some large portion, if not the capitals entire populace, even thought the current king would be well served to expand upon the kingdoms borders, and thus bring others under their beneficial rule.

The king would have none of it however thanks to some unknown reason; for he too was afflicted with the same ultra benign countenance of every other of his ancestors before him. And so the plotters failed such was his close advisors personal loyalties and any attempts at assassination; no matter how provocative, would always be deterred by his Royal guard whose undying admiration would prompt them into near suicidal action in order to defend their treasured ruler. Even so; the sewers were rumoured to be full of carnal beasts and dangerous villains but even these phantoms of the populace it seemed, had enough respect not to disturb the King's peace on Champions day: Leo, as he liked to be addressed was quite busy today. The first champions day was honoured in the very first year of the first of his line; one Leopold Van-Magnus Jin.

Today, Leo would be required to go out about the city dishing out medals for bravery, awards for special contributions to society and so forth: Of more important note: King Leo *was* rich and the sewers did indeed run with the occasional nugget of silver and fashionable piping; gold and sometimes the odd sapphire too would be found lying about the city streets. What's more, when Leo found himself to be particularly overawed by the brave and hardy, Leo would often shower them with fabulous gifts, tidy sums of money or in many cases a job; not only for them but their entire family too.

Therefore it was not too hard to see the reasons why many tales, even the wild fabrications of children; should not be taken too lightly when they involve Caernthorn. It was rightfully a magnet for those that wished to seek their fortune, so too was it a place of relative harmony despite the manifest seedier element, for it was a society within which one truly would be blessed for being of an enlightened mind and a purity of heart.

Funny then that this should be the place Dirk and Grot were headed, Qoua in tow. But then, as with every thing shiny; if you scratch it up a little it starts to look flawed. The 'rumours' about the state of the sewers were if anything under-reported, for its depths positively seethed with both creatures and wicked men; far more deadly than the odd looking contagious rats that dwelt there.

Above ground too there were problems; a slum quarter of dubious incriminations went largely un-policed and an aggressively expanding belt of a shanty town swamped about the city walls: Bringing an abundance of disreputable elements galore as well as the usual increase in opportunistic crime. In fact, were it not for the generosity of the king and kingdom's inhabitants, this alien swell would probably strangle any rising economy but the king; or more accurately his grandfather; was a very wise man.

As the un-housed populace began to expand around the town, the veteran ruler had made certain proposals to the more organised elements of the socially unacceptable outlaws'. Certain rules of engagement were introduced that formed the acceptable boundaries of thuggery that would be tolerated before all out war on crime became a priority. In addition, the king would regularly make payments to certain 'houses' in exchange for certain privileges. These privileges revolved around several areas both private and governmental, not least of which was a standing tribute to the assassins' guild to protect against the king's health and that of his family and co-workers. It was a chaotic state of affairs but the important thing is the process worked. To say any more would be treasonous.

That stated, even these seedy elements too were working to a far laxer pace than usual on this gloriously placid day. Nothing dared disturb the tranquillity. Pickpockets took their time picking out possible marks. Foot-pads or brute-thieves would only take down one or two unsuspecting revellers and even the burglars only attempted the wealthiest homes on this day.

The sun beat down hard against Grot's exposed arms. He wore a practical sleeveless scale-mail shirt of decent quality and a pair of plain brown flaxen chaffs. His upper arms; stung from the suns rays, where blistering the scabs covering the tattoos he had had etched into both biceps.

The two runic Dwarven characters that he had added to his blossoming account; a story that already ran the length of his shoulders and some way down his back, represented his trial by torture in the tower and his return from Hell. It was the seventh time he had been reincarnated to be exact, and he felt he would not be adding another.

When the Daemon Galbor had re-birthed them, he and his associates had suddenly felt in fine form, fresh as a newborn's fart. This led Grot to thinking: Why had whoever responsible for their revival been so helpful? Where now where the familiar pains he had endured...? The answer Grot knew was that these bodies were not their own. Their original corpses' were contained within the stomachs and bowels of a certain fragmented army, though Grot omitted to inform the others about his gruesome discovery.

Their new bodily vessels were far from exact replicas of their original forms... Qoua for example had a more human look to her physical features and had been inexplicably blessed with an ability to speak perfectly.

Grot himself could move like he did when he was a mere forty years of age; a thousandth of his current status. The tattoos were in place all-right, but the dodgy pain in the joints had miraculously disappeared, along with most of his recent scars; such as those inflicted by Galbor himself: Yet all the while an oppressive feeling of death hung over him.

Dirk too seemed a little better looking; healthier in a way beyond grasp. His cheeks had lost their hollowed look and in the few weeks since their arrival he had even managed to put on a pound or two in weight, but his mind seemed more fragmented and unsure by the day: Just as Grot felt his life being sapped from him, so Dirk seemed to clutch at life more desperately than ever. Maybe it was simply him being a woman and learning to cope with men like him self had been or maybe a whole more besides. Either way Dirk had been the least talkative of all when it came to their shared incidents.

All in all their current bodies had been given to them by a Daemon or foul God of that Grot was sure; the most untrustworthy creature one could happen across possibly and Grot felt with surety that any further demise would become absolute. He wasn't sure how or why he felt this way but he imagined that these quick healing replicas would somehow be incapable of recalling them to life should the worst happen.

Qoua sat to Grots side; she was covered head to toe in a plain brown robe such as the silent monks wore, though with her newfound oral ability the temptation to speech was great. She huddled further back into the creeping shadows of the small café veranda at which they sat looking out onto the packed square a dozen or more feet below. There, frantic punters dashed up and down around the cordoned racing arena, frantic to get the best tips and place the canniest bets at premium odds, while bookies drove for them to do the opposite. Pickpockets; what few could be bothered working stole mostly the tickets from big betting punters on a deal with the gathered bookies, replacing their authentic betting slip with an illegible fake.

All around this betting perimeter a high wall rose up some fifteen or more feet in the air, where at its top, buildings, café's, shop's and even a funeral parlour had set up residence at its very crest. Each of these shops and so forth were built directly onto the thousands of granite slabs that made up the steeply rising curvature of this great arena, and shoppers, traders and visitor alike all crammed together upon its perilous stands.

The centre of the massive stadium was named the 'Heroes Parade' and its multi-use pitch was divided by rings of magic for the now: These were glowing faintly at the moment but in full use during competition they would shine with brilliant colours. Around the pitch glowing lines of white magic repelled any attempt to cross them, and so people such as those involved in the 'Spear Chucking' event could gladly go about their business while the greased up wrestlers safely grappled some short way up the field.

Many various events were hosted here over the two week holiday period, but by far the greatest of all spectacles and therefore the most entertaining, was the Wyvern races: To whose sport the entire centre circle of the obscenely sized arena was dedicated…

Rising fully three hundred feet in the air, a huge spiralling corkscrew like construction flowed from end to end in dizzying contemplation. It was made of four separate tracks that ran in close parallel to the others, but its magical nature meant the number of tracks could easily be divided or multiplied, according to the whims of the Wyvern Racing Association.

Each of its wide twisting raceways was the path along which the riders had to drive their thoroughbred Wyverns, bumping, flapping and biting to the finish. The tracks' merged often and at each intersection contestants were free to swap lanes as the rising and dipping, magical strip along which they raced would often throw up a sudden shortcut, or just as rapidly extend a lane previously thought shortened.

Many a tousle took place between both riders and mounts alike and it was not unheard of for a race to finish without a winner. In fact it happened so often that bookies even offered odds on it happening each race.

The rules of Wyvern Racing were simple enough; no weapons, no magic or magical devices were allowed and both rider and mount had to cross the finish line at the same time in order to complete the race. The non magic ruling worked perfectly thanks to the powerful anti magic flux given off by the rings of light operating around the stadium and their own tracks and lanes. The non-weapon rule however, did not encompass aggressive self armour adornments such as spikes and their ilk and so the races had become an altogether more deadly affair than past endeavours.

Qoua considered their environs to be similar to the passages of an ant hill and twice as claustrophobic; a home from home for her then. The untrustworthiness of those strangers around her, mingled with the beguiling charm of the money-mad locals, made for an uneasy sense of false security to which she had always been accustomed to amongst her own people. In general she felt that the other humanoid races *were* far more amicable than her own people but nonetheless they each held their own agenda.

They had decided upon her disguise before parting company with Boris, and it was due to his ingenuity that she had reinvented herself in this fashion. Although she could now talk very well, he had instructed her to speak very little and only give her advice when asked, the essential ingredient to her disguise was that she retains an aloof and mysterious air. She could handle that side of it. She too had her own agenda and to remain aloof suited her aims perfectly. They had briefly discussed their 'deaths' but she had more than a suspicion that each of them were hiding something. She knew for sure that she herself was being secretive. The Dwarf seemed haunted by some discovery and Dirk's erratic behaviour masked an unearthly scar upon his throat. Thinking of Dirk's deteriorating mental health she briefly doubted the integrity of the prophecy but as she considered its predicted outcome she dismissed the doubt. She had undergone the foretold changes to her physical and social state and those that fate had set aside for Dirk and her, also seemed to be blossoming into reality.

Qoua and Grot shared the realisation that another fatality would send them all hell-wards and she wondered if Dirk too shared in the knowledge; such was his quenchless thirst for living. In the few weeks they had been in the town he had already whored around no less than seventeen times, sometimes with more than one woman, many times with men. She felt a curious pang of jealousy whenever she thought of such things and it was growing harder than ever to contain those feelings. She knew Grot had knowledge of her and Dirk's tryst though he had only let it slip once while arguing drunkenly. Yet he did not seem to mind or at least was unaware that Dirk would regularly make love to her also. How the Dwarf had come about his knowledge she was unsure but she doubted he knew of how deeply her and Dirk were involved. Either way there would be no chance of either of them having a child by the other for the foreseeable future. Dirk might very well fall pregnant any time however given the amount of men he had been dating: For her own part she had avoided taking part in intercourse with men sown to the fact that she so hated and despised the thought of men in general. Her feelings were deeply rooted within her soul by her previous faith and culture and expanded upon thanks to her mortifyingly regretful sexual encounters. As the sun beat down upon a sweating fat Halfling, crossing the busy thoroughfare she thought back to Boris briefly and wondered how he too was coping in his newly decided upon role, but her reverie was infringed upon as Dirk made his presence felt.

Dirk popped his head over a nearby wall which he had no business climbing. He had ditched the wizardly look all together and instead opted for a charming little not-so-common whore number. A small barmaid type lace blouse with deep plunging neckline was cut short to expose the midriff and his lower half was held in check by a long flowing skirt that seemed to hug his swaying bum for warmth as he moved. His long golden tresses were held back in a pony tail and his already attractive facial features were further enhanced by a minimal combination: Lip gloss; which today was the colour violet, a barely rouge powder for the cheeks and a deep purple eye-shadow to add an air of charming mystery…

"Yo Dickhead," Dirk said meaning Grot, "give us one of Boris's diamonds…, …After all, the bugger must have got them because of me! I was blasting a wall of the bastards when we must have died remember." Grot seemed irreverent. "Come on pal; I'm gonna back a cert this time I promise! Old Harper Green told me the WRA are gonna ban this bloke because of his gear but they can't 'til the race is pissed off and done with, so the others are gonna let him win…, …Come on its Dark Foreboding in lane three, she looks a deadly bastard all right, what dya say?"

"I say no…, …Now piss off!" Grot replied dryly.

"Besides, you've spent enough of them already; we don't wanna flood the market…" The Dwarf added nudging Dirk's clinging fingers with his still hobnail booted toe. The wily woman was right though, Boris's secret gift had been most welcome, especially after Dirk had admitted to losing all but a handful of their own booty; not that what had remained had held much value either. When Grot had made a point of stating that Boris's ammo pouch probably held far more rocks of value than their own, then proceeded to empty said bag out, their eyeballs and those of the patrons of the Inn at which they'd been visiting, positively popped out on stalks…, …Every 'stone' had been a diamond and even the smallest was worth a months worth of expensive lodgings for all three of them.

They had made it. Not only in time, but with long enough to spare for them to settle in to single room lodgings above the taproom of an Inn appropriately named the Grotty Inn, where they could spend their ill-fated gains a few at a time without bringing overdue attention to themselves. Dirk kept harping on about wanting to move to a finer establishment such as the Crossway hotel they had heard tell of. Each time Dirk requested them to spend any great deal of wealth; Grot would be quick to remind him about the misplaced gems Dirk had so-called secreted within his oversized boots. Boot's in which he were now standing tiptoe, as he clutched at the walls high embrace.

"Grot…? About that hot tip we or should I say; I got before… Was it number forty two in the four thirty or the number thirty four flying later in the five o'clock…?" Dirk rallied his wits and tried another angle, "what I'm saying here is we gotta edge our bets, that's what all the gamblers keep telling me and they should know cuz they gamble…, …A lot! So really this latest tip is like a godsend from Keldor, even Gordon said…"

"Don't go bringing Keldor into this and I don't care about any buggering one of your men friends be they gamblers or not, especially not from one calling himself Gordon: How many of these gamblers are rich buggers eh? Edging bets, what's edgy about it is their theories hang from the bollocks of an angel…"

Dirk looked at Grot crossly, it was taking effort to hold on here and the Dwarf was not making it any easier with his refusal to hand over hard currency. "Well if this bet's hanging by some angel's bollocks it must have a chance right?"

"Wrong," said the grouchy Dwarf, "Angels don't have bollocks!"

"Well ya just said-ah! I get it; ya being a smart arse again…"

"Oh come on Grot please; tell him Qoua. He's being a bastard with me and you'd stop him if ya cared for me but no; ya just sit there quiet all the bloody time! Oh Grot matey, come on with a name like that it can't lose…"

"What was it called again?" Grot innocently asked.

Dirk visibly brightened: "Dark Foreboding, why…?"

"Because," Grot drawled, "I get a sense of *dark foreboding* every time you tell me you've got a dead cert ya senseless bitch…" and he pushed down harder on Dirk's fingers.

A grumpy steward approached shouting at him to get down…

"Suck on me tits!" Dirk shouted back and the elderly steward came over attempting to grab at his ankle (in which he was successful) but Dirk strained against his stretching embrace. "Get ya friggin' foot of my hand ya hairy stump!" He shouted up at Grot, who did as he was told just as the steward below gave a forceful yank that caused one hand to come loosen its holding, Dirk thought back to a similar predicament in the tower and in his distraction, the elderly steward shouted and tugged again, forcing Dirk's grip to fail him and cross gendered companion fell atop the staggering chap; who had seen up Dirk's skirt in his attempt to dislodge the hooligan: The sight of his freshly shaven haven too much for the old mans heart to take as the steward collapsed beneath him.

Dirk looked about quickly and realising that several other wardens were running over did the first natural thing that came into his head. He fled, pushing through a throng of people and slapping down two gold guinea on 'Dark Foreboding' to win at the first bookmakers he came across, then as two more steward sped towards him in earnest, he evaded their advance by diving over an apple cart; rolling up onto his feet on the other side, apple in hand and vaulted up and over a nearby high wall.

Dirk never thought to check things out first; both in a theoretical sense and when it came to leaping over the edge of things, sometimes rightfully figuring that if he did he'd probably be too scared to take the leap of faith that so often led to his downfall. As it did now; him coming to land atop a panting, clawing Wyvern; perched in stall number three. Its skin looked like treacle it was so dark and Dirk looked about with a slight sense of regret for its dislodged intended rider who lay splattered some hundred feet below.

"Oh, erm... Sorry!" Dirk whispered down to the dead jockey.

A bell rang out and sirens sounded as the 3-2-1 countdown began and Dirk craned his neck up to see a spiralling racetrack above him: winding upwards in almost implausible spaghetti twists which begin thrumming with a myriad of magical fluorescence.

Thankfully his thighs had gone through rigorous daily workouts these last few weeks and he clutched his legs tightly about the Wyvern's saddle as if it were a well blessed lover. "Dirk Hang On..." He heard Grot shout and turned to look at the café veranda on which his friends could be seen standing; besides several thuggish brutes from the WRA. Dirk gulped as the signal flare ignited and the starting gates flew open and suddenly he was pulling away at high velocity without a clue what to do...

C'est La Fin pour les duration. Esta Finito benito. La Ghorn! Ueli Guelli. Saionara. Hasta Luega. Dasvidanya. Until the next time mon ami, adieu or "Brakk'akk gneg" as Grot would say: (Don't break your axe.)

XXII) **AUTHOR BIO**

Lee Gresty was a troubled kid from a broken home. Born the youngest of 4 in the rugby town of ST.Helens to an impoverished but wonderful single mother... They owned a dog that the family would fight over the rights to 'hog'. Those initial years were complex, hurtful & rarely joyous as he tried to figure why his biological father would abandon him. He decided if he was to be a bastard; he would be a right bastard...

From early on he had an interest in the arts but his early attempts to break into acting and writing left him feeling down and he turned to a life of crime as an act of rebellion. In his youth he epitomised many things wrong with human beings: A thug, a petty criminal and a bigot of the worst kind. When he was 14 a life changing event taught him to re-examine his ideals and started him on the path to enlightenment.

As an adult, Lee became a father quite young and revelled in the role even after his marriage broke down. He dedicated the next 20 years of his life to being the best father and friend he could be and lives today in much the same way. He has visited many countries throughout the world and attributes this as much as the event at 14 to why he is now tolerant to all race, colours and creeds.

He champions the rights of all to live a life of happiness (perverts, paedos and politicians excluded) and lives by the motto he devised when 17: "Treat others as you WISH they would treat you."

He now lives with his family of 7 and his dog Guinness and spends most of his time writing, playing games and wishing for a better world for all.

CONTACT INFO

cheezypees@yahoo.com

SNAIL MAIL.

33 THE PEWFIST,

WESTHOUGHTON,

BOLTON,

BL5 2EN

62385621R00290

Made in the USA
Lexington, KY
06 April 2017